Foreword

This novel has over eight hundred pages which you are now considering reading.
The foreword has five which you are now considering skipping.
Come on.

After finishing *Keepers of Terra*, I found myself at something of a crossroads. I knew I wanted to keep on writing and I had a basic roadmap for what I wanted to do with the *Saga of the Days After* universe.

I knew Mira al-Sayid would be part of it and I knew Thomas Müller wouldn't. I knew I wanted to write a standalone book set in the same universe telling a completely different story with a very different cast of characters. But, other than that, I didn't really have that much to work with other than the worldbuilding I had spent over ten years daydreaming into existence. I didn't really know where to go and that kept me feeling out shadows in the dark for quite some time.

The key pieces of the puzzle were two minor side characters from *KoT*: Laur Pop and Silvia Murărescu.

I had needed a 'Laur Pop' to fulfill a very specific role in *KoT* and I had always wanted to try my hand at the 'magnificent bastard' trope. It wasn't be the first time I've come-up with a character on-the-spot simply because I wanted to riff off something I had read or seen somewhere else. Yet, writing Laur in those few short scenes he was part of in the first book felt... *different*. He was incredibly easy to write and not just because he was a Romanian from Bucharest born in the '90s. There was something a bit more to him which I couldn't really put my finger on.

The answer came to me in a moment of procrastination while I listened to a Joe Rogan podcast in which the guest was struggling to explain the philosophy of Carl Jung (and, no, it wasn't Jordan Peterson; though I've noticed him struggle with the same task as well). In that moment, I had an epiphany.

Laur Pop was an expression of *my own* Jungian 'darkside'. That was why I had found him to be so easy to write. For lack of a better term: I *knew* the guy. I was simply writing a man who stood in the dark mirror of my own self and I knew then that I wanted to look into that dark mirror through the pages of my next novel.

Yet, there was a problem. Laur was a bit too heavy of a character on his own. Everyone likes a good burger (*yeah, I said it*), but eating grilled minced meat by itself is gross. Every savory patty needs a good bun to hold it, as well as some lettuce, maybe an onion or two, some people like a slice of tomato, and there are endless cheeses, sauces, relish and other such pairings, to not even mention the side of french fries!

I needed a foil. I needed a yang to his ying. I needed a tails to his heads. I needed someone who could cut through the heavy richness of Laur Pop with a balanced dose of sharp freshness, else the story of *Many Names of Cain* would very quickly devolve into something that would be, to put it mildly, beyond the realm of publishable decency.

Silvia was the natural choice, simply due to her proximity to Laur. I had already written her as a more or less background character in *KoT* and I knew that there was a very promising seed left planted inside her. What I discovered (when I actually started writing) was that Silvia simply refused to be just a palatable foil to Laur's psychosis. As the story progressed, I figured out that her story was just as compelling as his and she became (through the literal strength of character) his equal from a storytelling perspective. This is why the story of *MNoC* is told the way it is; through the alternation of Silvia and Laur's points of view (with a few other characters taking center stage from time to time). She is also the reason why I had to break *MNoC* into two separate books. By the time I had finished writting the last pages, I came to discover that I had ended-up writing a novel almost as big as the first four *Harry Potter* books combined.

Once I had Silvia and Laur, I knew that their dynamic would grow to become the engine of the story and my own interest was well and truly sparked by what was going on between them. Yet, it wasn't enough to start writing. I needed something more. I needed a place, I needed a quest, and I needed some chaos.

I knew Mira would be part of the story, so I knew that there would be plenty of chaos.

I had also intentionally left over a breadcrumb in the form of a questline from the first novel, which I knew could very easily provide the necessary plot development needed for a standalone novel. But I also knew it wasn't enough. I didn't really want to write a detective novel and that's what *MNoC* would've become if I would've decided to just tell a story about Laur Pop and his band of colourful characters looking for missing children in a galaxy far, far away, even if I knew that there would be more to it than appeared at first glance.

I had always wanted to write a book about the Romanian Revolution of 1989, of all things. Given that, by this point, I knew that my two main characters would be Romanian, it seemed like a great opportunity to do just that! I needed some intrigue and I knew that I had in my own backyard a political mystery on par with the JFK assasination in terms of scale and depth. I also wanted to stay true to the origin of the *Saga of the Days After* universe, which started out as a worldbuilding exercise I would tinker with in my dorm room back in university, when I was studying history in the Netherlands. Suffice to say, I only picked out a few droplets of intrigue out of the bucket of drama that was the revolution of '89 and it was more than enough political intrigue to fuel *MNoC* a hundred times over.

It was around this time that I realized I needed the Hajduks in their entirety.

I knew at this point that the fundamental synopsis of *MNoC* was that Laur Pop would drag his personal legion, the Hajduks, with him on some fever dream of a mission in the Pisces Galaxy. But, I had a choice in regards to which Hajduks he would bring along with him. My initial instinct was to restrict the number of Earth-born characters to a reliable Romanian handful. However, upon the well deserved elevation of Silvia to the rank of main character, the story's need for a foil for Laur was now compounded and Mira just didn't have the time to help out, since she was would be out doing her own thing for most of the novel. Hence, the inclusion of the complete line-up of Balkan Hajduks into the narrative.

Without the inclusion of the Balkan Hajduks, *MNoC* would've rather quickly devolved into 'Romanians in Space', which would've likely been a somewhat comical, yet fundamentally empty about story strong female characters, angry dick jokes, and homecooked stew, since that is what the core values of Romanian culture essentially boil down to. It would've been hilarious, but it also would also be quite unremarkable. I have always believed that the true beauty of the culture I was raised in resides not in its essence, but in its context. Most Romanians would disagree. That's fine.

One final problem remained:

'Where are they going?'

I knew that the place they were going to was called 'Shangri', but that was about it. I had assembled all the actors. I knew what would play out. I even had the outline of a script written down. But, I didn't have a stage.

What does Shangri look like? Who lives there? What language(s) do they speak? Do they have social media? How do they move around? How does Shangri *feel* like? I had dedicated most of my worldbuilding to Terra and I had a vague idea of how a few other places in the Milky Way Galaxy looked and felt like... but *Shangri*? All I had was a name and blank pages.

Whilst struggling with my little worldbuilding puzzle, I took a spontaneous trip to London and all the pieces finally fell into place.

Shangri was not a planet, it was a 'City'! It was one massive supermegalopolis built into the crust of a incomprehensively colossal solar panel wrapped around a dying star. The rich lived on the inner Brightside and the poor lived on the outer Darkside. It was a merchant hub that had grown wealthy as it drained the surrounding galaxy of its resources and ferried trade for neighbouring empires across the stars. It was ruled by a monarchy with a peculiar line of succession. It had been built upon the ruins of a conquered homeland of a people that now toiled in the silent darkness of the world their invaders had built millennia ago. Most of the 'City' was an arid wasteland, as people crowded those few urban centres where job opportunities lay. Certain technologies were banned since their spread might disturb the peace the ruling House of Gisevius had worked so hard to keep. There was a citywide network of organized crime run by bear people led by an albino grizzly bearman. An ancient race of warrior-nomad wolfmen comprised the city's police force. Troglodytes dwelled at the edges of derelict shantytowns, feeding on those miserable souls fortunate enough to be less destitute than them. An oppressive pangalactic empire of a trillion stars had set-up shop in one of the city's districts, hoping to sway it into joining the fold, as a place that felt eternal began to crave change.

I now knew how Shangri looked like and the stage was set for Silvia Murărescu to follow Laur Pop and their motley crew of Balkan Hajduks, as his squirming mind brought them to the City of Shangri on a secret mission under the guise of a diplomatic posting. Mira al-Sayid would join them for reasons known only to her and in the silent darkness around the shackled star of Shangri-La, someone else would be watching.

There's also a pivot into organized crime in the middle act of the novel, which happened quite naturally, since Laur is an actual *intelligent* sociopath. I often found myself filling in the gaps of his personality and worldview by drawing inspiration from other, more established, fictional antiheroes. As an additional hint, I gradually came to realise that I was writing a story about immigration and I fully embraced that revelation.

One more thing...

There's a talking cat that drinks human blood and says the n-word. Readers of *KoT* will likely be thrilled/horrified by the inclusion of Mira's bigoted feline companion in the narrative. For those of you who are not familiar with Lorgar Erebus Aurelian, he has *very* strong opinions concerning certain minorities and he rolls out ethnic slurs (with a *very* hard 'r') with little-to-no provocation, context or reasoning. The current political climate would suggest that I distance myself from his remarks and his choice of language. Yet, I am of the opinion that my readers are intelligent enough to see Lorgar for what he really is.

If you're wondering why I'm taking the risk of signing a second contract with Lorgar as a featured character, all I can say is this: I know how to write stories that *I* like. If other people also like my stories, well than makes me very happy! But, I do not know how to write stories that other people say are great, but which I myself find to be boring. I started writing to entertain myself and I intend to stand by that core principle throughout this entire literally journey and if I can also bring value to other people, then that's just a bonus.

I made *MNoC*'s cover art myself with *Midjourney* and *Powerpoint*. If you've managed to get this far, I think we can both agree that it turned out pretty well, didn't it?

I'm now planning ebooks for both *MNoC* and *KoT*, so stay connected to Black Lighter Originals' social media for updates on those projects.

Lastly, if you like the book, please help out with a 5-star rating on *Amazon* and drop your own comments!

Enjoy!

Contents

FOREWORD	3
PROLOGUE	8
CHAPTER I:	14
CHAPTER II	32
CHAPTER III	48
CHAPTER IV	72
CHAPTER V	86
CHAPTER VI	104
CHAPTER VII:	129
CHAPTER VIII:	164
CHAPTER IX	187
CHAPTER X	230
CHAPTER XI	284
CHAPTER XII	316
INTERLUDE	351

Prologue

Balloons are deflated
Guess they look lifeless like me
We miss you on your side of the bed
Still got your things here
And they stare at me like souvenirs
Don't wanna let you out my head

That wretched song has been playing throughout Milady's house without end for almost an entire week now, ever since she came back from the Little Lady. I, Lorgar Erebus Aurelian, find my days tormented by the nonexistent melody of that god-awful song.

She hasn't been the same. Usually Milady is strict and uptight (a far cry from the Omma and her household, or the Little Lady and hers), yet now I, Lorgar Erebus Aurelian, find myself missing her usual restrictions. She doesn't even feed me properly. I, Lorgar Erebus Aurelian, survive off the scraps of her meals and sometimes, when I, Lorgar Erebus Aurelian, am fortunate enough for her to be reminded by her headvoice of my existence, she even grants me meals. Yet, I, Lorgar Erebus Aurelian see that they are with granted with little care for variety. It was minced meat four days ago. Then it was beef cubes, with some beef stock poured on top (cold, mind you!). Then, for two days (*two days in a row!*) it was – *once more!!!* – minced meat!

I, Lorgar Erebus Aurelian, find myself longing for the Omma's household. There I always receive all the attentions expected by me at adequate times and in fair fashion. It's not like here, where I, Lorgar Erebus Aurelian, sometimes gaze upon the birds of the sky and am reduced by hunger to daydreaming of the juices within their bones.

Milady should have just left me there.

I languished at the Omma's household there after Milady threw me out of the car after we had that detour so she could check-up on those friends of hers almost a month ago. Those filthy bastards by the lake put their dirty hands on me, locked me in a cage and had me locked up in a bright-lit room for an entire night before I was brought to the Omma's household where, despite the clearly tense atmosphere, I was looked after and nourished for three blissful weeks, until Milady returned from the Little Lady and brought me here, to her territory on this queer island of hers.

I must confess that I initially enjoyed Milady's decision to bring me here. Ryadh is a lovely place, yet so crowded! All the rightful attention gets rather overwhelming once you've had your full. For the first week, I enjoyed the freedom granted by Milady. I had walks around Milady's territory and inspected my own pockets of ownership. I battled the native birds and was even challenged by one of these wretched hawks. He left a scar on my forehead, yet escaped before I could finish him (which I clearly would have, had he not shown himself to be more craven than raven).

I enjoyed Milady's distress at the sight of my wound, for it made me feel loved.

That was all the attention I received, after all.

Milady has not left the island since our arrival. Quite frankly, she almost never leaves the house. Whenever she does, all she does is stare down at the marina below, yet she always returns to her house in a rage when the sun begins to set. Her schedule is distressingly chaotic. She used to make her way to the chambers beneath her house, where she will fight the humans with the strange temperature that are to be found down there. I once made the mistake of sipping their blood from the floor after she was done with them and can still taste their acidic gore in the back of my throat when I think of them. She fought them often in the first week, but then she grew tired of them.

Nowadays, she rarely ventures there.

Mostly, she will sit in one of the house's chambers or on some terrace, where she will simply stare off into the distance as she smokes cigarettes and blasts music through the entire house. You can hear her song even on the outskirts of her territory. I should know. I've tried getting away from the damned ruckus one time too many! Over time, I have begrudgingly become accustomed to it.

As is typical of Milady, just when some semblance of a rhythm befell her, she began stirring the pot of disharmony.

Two men came to the house.

I recognized neither of them. One came in a box and the other came in the shuttle in whose trunk lay said box. Milady greeted the man in the shuttle, whom I realized she had summoned a few days before, when the music had stopped suddenly during the afternoon.

I jumped up into of those accursed dragon trees when I saw the shuttle approach and observed their exchange.

'Miss Mira al-Sayid, I presume?'

Milady had nodded. 'Mister Theobald Gaudin?'

'*Fiobield* is how you'd sai it, miss. My friends call me *Bield*, which you are more than welcome to do!'

He was one of those Hyperborean humans. A very talkative people they were. They all seemed to have that strange sing-song voice some humans had. *Wippity- wopity-machielni-macopi*...

Though, he was rather short and scrawny for a Hyperborean. Most of them were quite large, many were even larger than Milady's people.

'Your package is in the back. I've got one of those movers set-up on the box, so you won't have to bother with it. Where do you want it to go?' he asked in his sing-song voice.

Milady responded, 'There's a room facing the ocean on one of the lower levels,' she instructed.

'Very well, the mover will take it there? Is the road clear?'

Milady nodded.

'Good! You're going to want to inspect him.' With those words, the Hyperborean man opened up a small latch on the front of the box, revealing the man that stood unmoving within. 'Male. Forty-

Seven years old – well, by your Terran count, at least. His name is... lemme check that...' He fumbled through his Hyperborean clothes and pulled out a notepad. '... Ketalin Elarfials Durq.'

'Where's he from?' Milady asked, as she looked through the latch at the man within.

'Avallon, as most human ones are – well... at least the ones I deal in! You insisted on a human one, I believe?'

Milady nodded.

'Excellent. I was just making sure. It's hard to get an actual imperial and the Alliance prefers it that their own deviants get dealt with via the instruments of the state. So, it's mostly Avalloni, with a few others thrown in the mix when the market gets flooded by some new shipment.'

'Flooded?' Milady inquired.

'Oh, yes, miss! Every so often they find a new world with unseeded humans – such as your own people – and the first thing they do is weed out all the undesirables. If it's the Urheimat doing the discovering, they just get processed instantly by the system and it's hard to smuggle any of them out. But, if it's anyone else, they either sell or pass them on to us and, if they don't, we just grease a few cogs here and there and we get them anyways. The bulk of them, at least.'

'I see.' Milady's eyes wandered for a moment. 'Yes!' she seemed to softly remember. 'Your payment!?'

'I sent the invoice over yesterday and the payment came through instantly. I believe there was a mistake on your end. You seem to have forgotten the deposit you paid when you made the order! Thus, the sum received was larger than what was invoiced, so I attempted to send what was on top back to your account, yet your payment processor denied my attempt.'

'There was no mistake. I understand that you are a man of principle that only delivers quality. I am certain the sum was well earned.' Milady even attempted a disheartened smile out of the corner of her mouth.

'Well... thank you very much! But it's a lot of money!'

'Money isn't a problem.'

'I've heard.' The Hyperborean glanced at Milady's house. 'You can keep the mover then! I've got plenty and I know people like being private about the whole process. Well... people *like you*, at least.'

Milady nodded. 'Thank you, Mister Gaudin!'

She made to leave, but the Hyperborean interjected rudely. '*Uhm*! My apologies, Miss al-Sayid! There is one more thing I must ask of you!'

'What might that be?'

'The market is heavily regulated and the law requires that both you and I are aware of the package's transgressions.'

Milady didn't really seem to care. 'I am aware.'

'With all due respect, despite the fact that I know that you are aware, the law requires that I make sure that you are!' The man raised the notebook in his hand towards Milady who, in a very uncharacteristic manner, hesitated for a moment, before reaching out and taking the notebook from his hand. She turned the screen to face her and pressed down on some symbol upon it.

From where I was situated, I could not see what Milady was looking at, yet I could hear some noises. It seemed to be a recording of human children playing one of their insufferable chasing games. I couldn't tell if it was one child or several, yet all I could hear was that high-pitched screaming and the wailing stupid human girls make when they're tickled. Milady stared silently at the screen as the girl squealed in some alien language. After a while, the noises changed and the girl went from screaming to mumbling, likely having had her voice grow hoarse.

Milady's face never changed, yet she slowly passed the screen back to the Hyperborean man once the noises completely ceased.

'Excellent!' he said, before seemingly remembering something else. 'D'you like *Star Wars*, Miss al-Sayid?' he asked.

Milady was as clueless as I was. '*What?*'

'Star Wars? Darth Vader? Luke Skywalker? All of that?' he replied, as made his way to his shuttle. From within, he pulled out a roll of cloth wrapped around what appeared to be a selection of shiny sticks.

With one swift motion, the man unfurled the fabric, revealing it to be a kind of display case. The displayed objects appearing to be metal and ceramic rods, the largest of which seemed to be roughly the same size as my tail, though far less gorgeous.

'These are Vanir replicas. Limited Edition. You see here?' he pointed towards something written on the cloth. '*Terran Star Wars Edition*!' he read out the words. 'Darth Vader Red!' he pointed towards the uppermost rod. 'Luke Skywalker Blue!' he pointed towards the one opposite the Darth Vader one. 'I also have Luke Skywalker Green. Darth Maul Double Red. Ashoka Tano Dual White. Qui Gon –'

'No!' Milady interrupted him. 'I'm not a Star Wars fan!' She smiled curtly. 'Thank you!'

'Oh! I see!' the Hyperborean man furled the cloth once more. He placed it back in his shuttle, before pulling out a –

Sword!

I was startled and so was Milady, visibly reaching towards her own side weapon.

The Hyperborean man was unfazed, however. '*Lord of the Rings*?' the man asked, causing both myself and Milady to freeze.

'What?' Milady asked after shaking her head.

'*Anduril*! Flame of the West! Reforged from the Shards of Narsil! Aragorn's Sword from the *Lord of the Rings* movies!'

Milady released the hilt of her own blade before glaring at the Hyperborean merchant.

'It's custom made by a company in Andromeda that specializes in such merchandise. It has the same appearance as the original, though it is made from adamantite and it also has a few special features.' He swung the sword in a very odd manner, causing it to –

Catch flame!

This time, only I flinched, for Milady had apparently understood the merchant's intent. 'No. It's fine!' she said.

'I see! A bit to exaggerated. I understand!' he pulled out a scabbard, pressed a button on the sword's hilt, causing the flames to dissipate, and sheathed the blade, before placing it back in his vehicle and pulling out –

A hammer?

'Ghal Maraz? *The* Warhammer?' he asked.

Milady shook her head.

Then he pulled out another hammer and a shield.

'Mjolnir? Captain America's Shield?' he gestured with each item as he presented them.

Milady shook her head once more.

He then pulled out another sword, this one far more rugged-looking.

'Frostmourne? *World of Warcraft*?'

Milady shook her head once more and was clearly losing her patience.

The man was undeterred, instead now pulling out another sword. 'A Hatori Hanzo sword? Kill Bill? Volumes I *and* II?' he proposed.

'I already have one.'

'Very well!' The merchant finally seemed to relent. He placed the last sword back in his shuttle, then paused. He reached out one more time and pulled out a small box. 'Those I would've sold you, if you would have wanted them. However, *this* I can offer as a gift!'

He opened the box's case towards Milady, revealing a rather small and bizarre... *handgun*?

'A phaser! From *Star Trek*?' The merchant didn't even wait for a response. 'In real combat it's not so good, I know! They are very easily neutralized. But, they *can* muster up lethal force if they are active. They also have a 'set to stun' function' – which you can activate with this little button, right here! You can also use it to watch movies, play music, set alarms and reminders, and it also tells the time. It's approved by Terran regulation, since it cannot be used to broadcast and cannot receive external information. You charge it with the adapter located at the bottom of the case.'

He extended the gift towards Milady. 'Free of charge!'

Milady begrudgingly accepted the gift and the man finally left.

She took the boxed man to a chamber beneath the house. It is a pleasant room, carved into the cliffside, with one wall overlooking the marina below. She placed a single table and a chamber before the great windows that opened to the outside, whilst leaving the box in the room's center.

She then proceeded to cook the most wonderfully-smelling steak I have ever whiffed in my entire life, though she did pair it with fucking potatoes and that disgusting green rubber humans seem to fancy, as well as some rotten milk sauce. She brought this dinner to the room with the man in the box, together with a glass of red vinegar and a coat hanger bearing a bathrobe. After laying out a lavish dinner table facing the outside sea, she approached the man's box and opened it.

The man inside had cables and wires sticking out of his holes. She began by removing the two wires wedged within his tear ducts. Then she pulled out the two cables going through his nostrils, then the cable going through his mouth, then the wire that travelled up his peeing pipe towards who-knows-where. Then the cable going into his poophole and, finally, she removed the two wires that reached into his ears. She then flipped the box and the man fell naked to the floor.

I wanted to give the man a good sniff, but Milady picked me up and brought me with her.

She brought me over to the room where she keeps all the sharp things which are not stored inside her kitchen. After placing me on the only couch she knows I find adequate in that particular room, she turned on the music on full blast. A song rang out, yet it was not to Milady's favour and she quickly changed it to another song for which she did not seem to be in the mood for. It took a few more songs for her to find just the right one.

I can't get enough,
Told you I just want it all!
I can't get enough,
You ain't been doin' enough!

With the song blasting through the room, she began to walk in a way which caused me great and personal offense, for she seemed to be mimicking the movements of some clumsy cat. As the song went on, she gradually began to dance the way a clumsy cat with an ear infection might. Her movements were strange, as she seemed to combine her dancing with the selection of certain objects. First a club of some sorts, then several knives of many shapes and sizes, then a small axe, then a long stick...

You're startin' off fresh, man,
You feel out of pocket!
You fucked that girl you met at that party!

Her eyes opened a little bit too wide for a moment. She seemed to falter slightly, as something had somehow taken her away from her rhythm. I saw her close her eyes and resume her movements.

I still wanna be with you, trust me!
I know that's insane.
I'd rather fuck on you than fuck on lames!
I did some shit in **Berlin** –

Out of nowhere and with no warning, Milady stopped the music and slapped her hand down upon the table she had been placing her selection of blunt and sharp instruments on. The slap startled me and I jumped out from my place on the couch, but before I could inquire as the meaning of her gesture, Milady was already out of the room. Her movements were quite energetic and I became curious, so I jumped off the couch and sneakily followed her and I quickly figured out where she was going.

The room with the boxed man.

Who was no longer boxed. He was now clothed in the bathrobe provided by Milady and I could see that he had begun to enjoy the meal she had prepared for him.

He was in the process of turning his head towards the sound made by Milady's entrance when she put a bullet in his head and one in his back in quick succession.

The gunshots startled me, yet I did not flinch, for I knew that the boxed man's demise meant that I would be entitled to the leftovers of his last meal. However, I did wait for Milady to leave the room, which was what she did almost instantly after killing the boxed man. I saw her walk purposefully down the corridor, likely on her way to fetch one of the humans with the weird temperature to clean up the mess. Right as she turned the corner I trotted towards the table and my steak. Just as I prepared to jump onto the table, something caught my eye.

Blood! Real human blood!

I neared the dark puddle slowly, catching sight of my own reflection within. I seized the opportunity immediately, for I had never tasted the blood of a human before! As my whiskers touched the liquid, I felt it's warmth and the feeling sent shivers down my spine. I could barely control myself as I leaned in to lick...

... and I found it to be awfully tart and very metallic...

Disappointed, I jumped onto the table and began devouring Milady's gorgeously rare sirloin steak, being very careful to eat around the white rotten milk sauce.

Chapter I:

Shards of a Broken Crown

'So, we're going to Shangri...' Nick's voice pierced the somewhat tense silence.

'You're jumping to conclusions. As always...' Silvia had thought of the reply for long before the words had even left his mouth.

Silvia knew that Nick was jumping to a very reasonable conclusion, yet she did not enjoy suppositions, no matter how pertinent. She particularly disliked having said suppositions being spoken out loud, regardless of how secure their surroundings.

The two Hajduks shared an office in the Citadel of Bâlea, high in the Carpathian Mountains. Nick's seat stood facing northwards, towards the green lands of Transylvania, whilst Silvia's faced south, towards the indoor lake that stood at the heart of their Legion's headquarters. Between them stood the timbers of a great oak, the salvaged remnants of what had been the door of a palace in the old Romanian capital of Bucharest, now serving as their shared desk.

Nick looked up annoyed, barely concealing an irritated smirk. He glanced sideways towards Silvia's half of their desk. *'We're going to Shangri!'* he repeated.

His comrade shot back with an equally annoyed glare, though no words left her lips.

'Come on... it's just me and you in here!' he pointed out.

Which was an atypical situation...

They both enjoyed the company of their respective soldiers. Their office was larger than that of the other Centurions (though they were the only two which actually shared the same chamber), and was frequently full of the sounds of conversation and movement, as the two went about their day receiving their respective legionnaire's reports, giving orders, collecting intelligence and doing anything else General Laur Pop thought necessary to ensure the smooth operation of his Hajduk Legion.

Today was different, as most of the Hajduks had gathered on the edge of the Lake of Bâlea located at the heart of their Citadel. It was a rare occasion all on itself for the entirety of their outfit to have gathered in a single place, as the Hajduks were a multinational Avenger Legion, one of only a dozen such units that still existed on Terra. Over thirty years before, virtually every Terran Legion had been multinational, with only a handful of exceptions. In the aftermath of the Terran population boom, most had been intentionally split up into smaller units, meant to serve as recognizable and relatable paragons of Terran martial prowess to the rest of their kin. The Hajduks themselves had fractured on several occasions and the remaining national contingents rarely found themselves all in one place, with such locations being almost entirely limited to their Citadel of Bâlea or their capital ship, the *Doina*.

The Serbs, Shqiptari, Bulgars, Croats, Bosniaks, Macedonians and Slovenes were frequently away, usually overseeing matters back in their respective nations. It was only the Romanians and the Kalo that claimed a near-continuous presence within their Citadel and, in the last two years, even they had mostly been away from Bâlea, as Pop had moved some of the Legion to Jerusalem to better oversee Project Kralizec. Now, given what was likely about to happen, the entirety of the Hajduks had been summoned to their stronghold in the Carpathian Mountains.

Silvia and Nick had stayed in their office, after giving leave to their men to greet their recently returned comrades in the Great Hall that encompassed the Lake of Bâlea. The sound of backslapping, laughter, greetings, boasts and exaggerated storytelling rose up to their window from the legionnaires gathered below. It had become custom for the Hajduk Centurions to only join such reunions after they had all gathered in Laur Pop's meeting room and had been briefed by their General as to why they had been summoned.

'Why do you think he's gathered us?' Nick continued.

Silvia was certain she knew exactly why they had been summoned.

It was plain and obvious. One only had to look down upon the lake below and see that there were not only the twenty-five hundred Hajduks that gathered that day. Over three thousand legionnaires from the Druzhina, Cossack, Cataphract, Jannissary and Betyár legions could be seen among their former comrades, as these five outfits had been splintered from the Hajduks by Laur Pop in the years after the Legion's formation, over thirty years before. Their respective Centurions had initially been promoted to the rank of Legate, only to later be promoted to the rank of General, thus becoming Pop's equals in rank. Upon their promotion, each new General had formed their own Avenger Legion. Mikhail had taken the Russians and formed the Druzhina. Dmitry had taken the Ukrainians and formed the Cossacks. Elena and Emre had taken the Greeks and the Hajduk's Turkish contingent and formed the Cataphracts, only for Emre to break away naught but five years later and establish the Janissaries. Lastly, Árpád had left with the Magyar to form the Betyár, less than a year before.

In order to promote a Legate to the rank of General, Pop needed permission from the rest of the Terran High Command, as well as at least one other General in attendance at the formal promotion ceremony. On this day, he had gathered five Generals at Bâlea and there was only one Legate among the Hajduks.

Rumen Lakhana.

Thus, it was quite obvious as to why Pop had gathered them.

'The Bulgars are getting their own Legion and Rumen will be their General,' she informed Nick.

'*Pfff*... Do I have the face of a fool?' Nick scoffed, as he usually did.

'A little...' Silvia didn't look up from the faces below.

'Obviously that's why he called *them* here. I mean what are *we* gonna do *next*?'

'Train the new recruits.' Silvia's eyes wandered to the overwhelmed and fresh faces trying their best to fit in with their new comrades. Laur had commenced a new recruitment drive after the Ratden

Closure. In the last three months, over six hundred new Hajduks had been inducted into the Legion's ranks.

The influx had not been performed so as to make-up for some horrendous number of casualties, since they had only lost elven men at Ratden, which was a paltry, albeit painful, number by itself.

No. Such was always Pop's way whenever he was getting ready to sunder his Legion. Rumen's promotion to Legate had come more than a year before, in similar fashion to Árpád 's promotion naught but two years before that, as Rumen became Legate the day Árpád become a General. It had come with a renewed focus on Bulgar recruitment, as the Betyár's formation had been preceded by an influx of Magyar recruits.

It was all quite clear, really.

Pop was about to sunder the Hajduks once more and he would be promoting a new Centurion to the rank of Legate.

Though who that Centurion might be was something of a mystery, even to her. Silvia had been quite surprised by how varied the current recruitment drive had been. One hundred Romanians, one hundred Serbs, one hundred additional Bulgars, one hundred Bosniaks, one hundred Croats, one hundred Shqiptari, fifty Macedonians, fifty Slovenes and about a dozen Kalo. No one had received any true favouritism during the current allocation, hence no clear candidate for legate had emerged.

Her old friend frowned at her. 'Are you gonna sit here and eat shit and pull my dick all day? Or are you gonna take things seriously?' he asked, before his eyes returned to the horizon to the west.

'No. At one point he's going to summon us.' Silvia turned her gaze towards her long-time friend. 'Once Gigi gets here, of course!'

'Let him have his little fucking symbolism. Bojana just flew in. He'll be here soon' Nick predicted.

Silvia knew that, despite his casual manner, her fellow Centurion's eyes and ears were always open. Though he always acted as if he didn't have a single care in the world, she knew that he had been restlessly scanning the horizon, awaiting the arrival of his Shqiptar friend.

Of all of Laur Pop's centurions, Gjergj Çorbaci ('Gigi', to his friends and peers) was by far the most unruly. A former mafioso who distinguished himself during the End Times, rising to the position of leadership of the entirety of what remained of the Albanian people by the time of the War of Vengeance, he had been one of Laur Pop's first lieutenants when the Hajduks were first formed in the aftermath of the Battle of Prague. Though fiercely loyal to Pop, the Hajduks, Terra and the Alliance, Gigi was notoriously independent and strong-willed. Silvia knew that he likely would have been the first one to splinter away from the Hajduks (if given the choice), were it not for the fact that his contingent had a habit of always taking heavy casualties, which had always resulted in the Shqiptari never managing to reach the numbers needed to break away. Even at Ratden, of the eleven casualties they had taken, eight had been Gigi's men. Despite this trend of high attrition, the Albanians had managed to become the fourth largest contingent within the present-day Hajduks, only narrowly behind Bojana's Serbs and way behind Rumen's Bulgars or Silvia's own Romanians.

Rumen Lakhana was quite beloved among all of the Hajduks, regardless of nationality. He had met Pop during Ragnarök in Hungary, as the two military officers had led the remnants of their peoples across the Pannonian plain, towards the rumoured and relative safety of Western Europe. In the aftermath of Doomsday, Pop and Rumen had been nigh inseparable, as the Bulgar had taken to heart the duty of keeping the diverse cultures and personalities of the Hajduks at peace.

Once upon a time, the Russian and Ukrainian contingents had been the primary danger poised to their Legion's unity. Once they had departed, it had been the Greeks and the Turks that had taken upon themselves to sow a rift within Laur Pop's Legion. Once Elena and Emre had left to form their own legion and, upon earning the right to divide themselves once more after the Ayve War, Árpád Kocsis and his Magyars had progressively become the main headache Pop, Rumen and the rest of the Hajduk leadership had been forced to deal with. In the end, thanks to some heavy-handed manoeuvring by Pop and Rumen, he had been granted permission by the High Command to get rid of Árpád and allow him to start his own Legion.

Nowadays, it was the Serbs and Albanians who were the two bodies between which friction could be felt within the Hajduks.

It wasn't something loud. Quite frankly, an outsider would likely never be able to notice it. Yet, no Hajduk turmoil ever was. It was more of a vibe, really. A slowly simmering tension building up in the background of not-so-casual conversations and ever-fewer encounters. A dark glance here and a fake laugh there; never something truly egregious. One could argue that it wasn't even palpable. Árpád had actually been the most conspicuous of them all and the most he ever did was criticize fellow Centurions in a (somewhat subjectively) *excessive* manner.

As the most battle-hardened of Laur Pop's Centurions, Gigi should have been the one most revered by his fellow Hajduks. He was nevertheless still respected and well liked. Yet, he was often forced to share the spotlight with some of his younger peers. He never complained openly, yet a noticeable shift had taken place in his demeanour in recent times. He had become quiet and absent, often delegating the task of meeting with his peers to those underneath him of lesser rank. It had been Laur Pop himself that had first pointed out this tendency to Silvia, as the peculiar behaviour had begun in the months following Rumen's promotion. Pop believed that Gigi had felt looked over and had taken to sulking in frustration.

This theory had seemingly been confirmed on Ratden, when a relentless Gigi had led the charge into countless ambushes in the tunnels that led into the mountains surrounding the elven stronghold, as opposed to simply waiting for reinforcement from his fellow Hajduks. Gigi's brashness could've been explained by his vendetta against their enemy and by his desire to finally rid the universe of those that had taken so much from him, yet many Hajduks whispered that it was his desire to remind everyone exactly how valiant he and his warriors were. Gigi himself had never really put forward an explanation for his actions. When Bojana had called into question his actions in the aftermath of the Ratden Closure, he hadn't even bothered to provide an answer, merely turning his back to his colleague without uttering a single word.

Nick was an exception to this self-imposed isolation. Silvia remembered how Nick used to worship Gigi back when they were children, with a palpable admiration carrying over into adulthood. They might have been of the same rank now, yet one could still mistake Nick for a nephew dotting at the feet of his favourite uncle. This had endeared him in the Shqiptar's eyes, as Gigi had quickly taken Nick under his wing when he and Silvia had joined the Hajduks and their close relationship had persisted to this very day. It had been Nick who had put forth the idea that everything Gigi seemed to be doing was simply his way of voicing his dissatisfaction with the manner in which promotions were taking place.

Gigi was still cordial with Silvia, perhaps more so than with the other Centurions. She had always wagered that his friendly attitude towards her might have something to do with her close friendship with Nick. Gigi still liked Rumen too, but, then again, everyone liked Rumen. He also seemed to still be on good terms with the others, particularly Lejla, the leader of the Bosniak contingent. The only true exception was Bojana, whom he frequently treated coldly and sometimes openly ignored.

'There he is!' Nick got up from his seat as he nodded towards a distant black dot in the sky to the west, now swiftly, yet also casually, rushing towards them.

Who else could it be? His contingent got here exactly one hour ago.

'Well, I guess he got his symbolism across...' she muttered.

'General Pop requests your presence in the Council Chamber!' Îngeraș's voice rang out in Silvia's head. She needed not turn to Nick to know that his cybernetic assistant, Aghiuță, had likely relayed the same message, as he was already checking his uniform in the office mirror they shared.

Silvia also got up from the desk, yet all se did was just glance towards the mirror for some aesthetic confirmation, having made sure that her outfit was pristine before they had even set foot in their office several hours before. The two proceeded to make their way towards their meeting with the rest of the Hajduk leadership. Their office was connected by a causeway to the central tower which housed Pop's own residence, as well as the Hajduk Council Chamber itself.

'My money's on Gigi getting promoted to Legate after Rumen gets made General, then *El Patron*'s gonna tell us we're all getting shipped over to Shangri!' Nick put forth his wager, using one of Laur Pop's many nicknames.

'There are more Serbs than there are Shqiptari. Plus, Bojana is popular among the High Command and the Allies,' Silvia explained.

'I'll take that bet!' Nick smiled before leaning in slightly. 'I take it you're not comfortable betting that we *won't* be going to Shangri?'

'It's not in the power of anyone here to decide whether or not we will go to Shangri. Not even *his*!' She nodded towards the tower above them, as they climbed up the steps towards Pop's abode.

'If El Patron wants to go to Shangri, he'll figure out some way to go to Shangri,' Nick pointed out.

'Maybe he *doesn't want* to go to Shangri?'

'Silvia, sounds to me like *you* don't want to go to Shangri!'

Nick was right. She didn't.

She knew what they might find there. She knew what they might have to do there. She knew what kind of dangers they might have to contend with there.

And she wanted none of it.

She wanted to stay here on Terra and just *chill* for a while. Unlike almost every other Avenger Legion, the Hajduks had been in a near-continuous series of operations for their entire existence. When she and Nick had joined the Hajduks, it had been right after the Senoyu War. In the almost three decades that had since passed, they had found themselves embroiled in a never-ending string of reconnaissance, sabotage and assault missions, countless security details, prisoner interrogations and intelligence gathering operations, as well the fevered hunt for their people's sworn enemy, a galaxy-wide war and the task of assuring the secrecy of Terra's greatest endeavour: Project Kralizec.

She needed a break.

They *all* needed a break.

She still remembered what she had felt on Ratden, after the last elf gave his final breath. It was as the Esho had finished drilling into the shattered mountain and pulled out the bodies of two Terrans, one low elf and forty dark elves from inside the enemy Genitrix Chamber, that she had felt it stir inside of her.

The feeling had at first made her dizzy, then her eyes had swelled and she had wept and she had not been the only one! All around her, Terrans, low elves and trolls shed tears of... of...

She couldn't even describe the feeling!

Relief? *Joy*? *Exhaustion*? She still struggled to comprehend the feelings of that early morning on that dark dead world.

It had been a stunned Nick, her childhood friend and partner-in-crime that had somehow found her letting loose tears before the early rays of a foreign sunrise. He knew how she felt, for their paths had been the same. It had been as they hugged that she had heard it.

The wail of a banshee.

The image of Mira al-Sayid hugging the lifeless corpse of Thomas Müller still haunted her. The wails still rang in her ears, though she only heard them when she was alone and in complete silence. The boy's body had been broken beyond hope. Though the weight of the collapsing rubble was enough to guarantee a swift death, it had been the hot lava that had seeped towards the body and boiled his nervous system within his skull that had brought the young Terran's body to a point completely beyond recovery. She had rushed to Mira's side just as the young Arabian had shoved a compassionate Sorbo Falk away from what remained of her friend. She had initially fought Silvia as well and she had struggled to hold on to the thrashing Mira as she raged and wailed her grief. It took all of Silvia's strength to hold on to her until her struggling had turned to soft trembling and heartbroken sobbing.

And still, even then, she had felt relief.

Relief that it was all finally over. Relief that the young German Captain would be the last Terran life claimed by their dreaded *Enemy*. Relief that no more would anyone else born of their world ever suffer as she had. To lose her parents. To lose everything. To see the world she had been born into, full joy and hope and wonder, be torn apart by the hated *dushman* that had shattered their world all those years ago. Relief that their hunt was over and that the Enemy finally lay completely annihilated. Relief that perhaps, now, they could finally return towards life and build for themselves a world in peace and away from the horrors of what might lay in the darkness between the sky and the stars.

And then she had seen *him*.

Over forty-five years before, she had seen him open the door of the Vault in which she, Nick and the rest of the children had been stashed away in beneath Prague. He had spoken in English, then in Romanian, then he had tried to utter the same sentence in German, French and even Serbo-Croatian.

'We have won!' he had said, the light of a hope Silvia could not remember seeing before in the eyes of another now shining bright in his eyes! The Battle of Prague was over. The Enemy had been defeated. Doomsday had passed. They lived. The light of a wondrous sun could be seen in the distance, as some of the children squealed in joy at their hero's words. They had rushed towards the outside, finally free from the captivity that had been the safety of the vault, running right past the blood-soaked rags that hung to the body of Laur Pop.

She still had nightmares about the sounds they had heard and the thunder they had felt in that vault on Doomsday. The light had went out just as the fighting had begun. For seven straight hours the battle had raged in the streets of the ruined city above them, as four hundred terrified children trembled in the hot darkness. Theirs was one of many 'Vaults', as they were called, though in reality they were little more than makeshift tunnels hastily dug into the sides of Prague's existing subway system. Theirs had been the Malostranská Vault, named after the nearby station, and it had been one of over fifty such hideouts spread out across the besieged city.

Only eight Vaults had survived the battle. Most had collapsed under the pummelling bombardments above. Many had been opened by combatants fleeing the elves, only to be forced to turn and meet the foe once more in one last stand, as they beheld the cold eyes of their enemy before them, and the terrified eyes of hundreds of small children behind them. Some Vaults had simply run out of oxygen, revealing bundles of small, stiff rags inside them when the victors had opened their doors.

One Vault had been found empty. A hundred-and-one children had been spirited away from within by their foe from the Staroměstská Vault. The surviving Terrans had found the bodies of seventy-eight children piled up near the subway entrance above, yet the remaining twenty-three were gone without a trace. The children had been stolen by the elves in the waning hours of Doomsday and they had not been the only ones.

Estimates suggested that over eighteen hundred Terran children had been stolen by the Enemy over the course of Ragnarök. One thousand four hundred and eighty-seven had been recovered by the Warhost of Terra during the War of Vengeance, yet many remained unaccounted for. The Terrans had learned in horror the fate of these children.

The elves had sold them to the Urheimat of Humanity, their new Enemy from across the stars.

The children they had discarded had been the sickly, the malnourished and the ones traumatized beyond sanity. The 'healthy' ones, as it were, were shipped across the cosmic void, towards a new home somewhere in the distant galactic North within the Domain of the Urheimat: the *Sprachbund*. That vast galactic empire craved new human genetic material as a man in a desert craved water, for so it was that within the gigantic mass of humanity that dwelt within its borders, inbreeding ran rampant. Since the Urheimat banned all genetic editing and rejuvenation, what had resulted was a population which behaved more like a crop than as a people. One virulent blight could wipe out entire harvests in that bloated realm of humanity.

This problem requested a solution and the solution employed was the continuous acquisition of new genetic 'stock' from *unseeded* human populations which retained some degree of genetic variety, yet also unadulterated 'purity'. This had been the case for Old Earth humans, yet not modern-day Terrans, whose genetic code had been heavily modified beyond any degree that could be deemed acceptable by the Urheimat's purity police. Such was the case that the Humans of Terra could rest assured that the Urheimat presented no current interest in the 'acquisition' of their children. However, the Terrans had never forgotten those three hundred children stolen by the elves and acquired by the Urheimat, the dust of Old Earth still clinging to their frightened little bodies.

Well, two hundred ninety-eight, to be precise.

For that had been what they had learned at Ratden. That had been the number written down within the notebook Laur Pop had emerged holding among the rubble of their revenge.

The 'Ratden Log', as it had come to be known.

Pop had located the log in the office of the late Elafas Perem Goujnar, the dark elf that had managed to infiltrate Terra and slaughter an entire family before being slain by Thomas Müller and Mira al-Sayid. Goujnar had become the last spymaster of the Svart and, by the time of their eradication, was essentially the only spy the dark elves had at their disposal. As such, for thirty-five years he had played a cat-and-mouse game with the Republican Alliance, with Laur Pop playing the role of the predator and the dark elf that of the prey.

When Silvia had seen Pop's blank stare and his stiff fingers on the notebook in his hand, she had dreaded what might come. She knew that they would almost certainly not find the break they all so desperately craved.

However, something strange had happened.

Pop had seemingly attempted to relinquish the log.

He had looked over it, of course, likely submitting all the essential details to memory, but then he had just walked up to Tomasz Ashaver and placed it on the Hierarch's chest, before collapsing into his old companion's arms and weeping openly, the first time Silvia had seen such an outburst from her

General. She had overheard Ashaver telling Pop that he would 'have to bear it, at least for a little longer...'

That exchange had given Silvia some sliver of hope.

Maybe he's let it go. Maybe he realises that he's done everything he could to make up for every single mistake he's made. Maybe he'll finally move on. Maybe he'll finally let us all move on...

And such had been the case so far.

Pop had confided in his Centurions as to what the Ratden Log contained, yet he had not pursued things further. The notebook was still in his possession over three months after the Ratden Closure, yet Pop had made no move to act upon the information contained within. He had even said that he had no interest in taking up any more of 'Tomasz Ashaver's homework, no matter the subject matter...'

Let's hope things stay that way.

'Ten bucks! One-to-one odds!' Nick spoke just as they reached the door to Pop's office.

'What?' Silvia had yet to successfully recollect her thoughts before entering the Council Chamber.

'Ten dollars that we're going to Shangri!' Nick insisted.

'... *Fine*! Deal!' They shook hands on it before opening the oak doors before them.

The Hajduk leadership shared a round table that had gradually become less and less crowded over the years. Five of those that used to sit at the table now stood near the window to the far side of the room.

Mikhail had always been a handsome bastard and nothing had changed in the time Silvia had last seen him. The General of the Druzhina stood resplendent in his blue and red uniform whilst gazing out the large window that ran across half of the circular wall of the Hajduk Council Chamber. He turned and gave Silvia and Nick a suave smile as they came in. Next to Mikhail, and also gazing out the window, stood Dmitry, now General of the Cossack Legion. She was a gorgeous woman with a gentle frame and a penchant for revealing clothing, particularly those of the golden ultramarine variety. She mirrored Mikhail's movements as she turned to gracefully smile at the new arrivals. Silvia liked them both a great deal, though she had never served alongside either of them, as the Druzhina and the Cossacks had split from the Hajduks years before she and Nick had joined the Legion.

Though she had been fortunate enough to serve alongside Elena and Emre. The two Generals had been sharing a couch and a coffee table, likely engaging in some debate or another, as the two were by far the most talkative individuals to have ever worn the insignia of the Hajduks. *What the hell, they make Nick look like an introvert!* The two immediately stopped their conversation upon seeing their old colleagues. Elena virtually ran across the room to shower them both in hugs and kisses, while Emre presented them with hearty handshakes and more kissing.

Rumen had been sitting across from his two former comrades on an armchair he always favoured when his presence at the round table was not deemed necessary. Similarly to the two Aegean Generals, he was also one of the more social and light-hearted in the Hajduks leadership, both past and present. The Bulgar stood in stark contrast to his former Magyar comrade, Árpád , who lingered near one of the chamber's walls, observing the various heraldry and battle honours the Legion had claimed over the years. Silvia noted that he had been studying the *Battle Honour of Ratden*, the most recent addition to the Hajduk trophy case. Knowing Árpád , he was probably bitter about missing the chance to take part in the Ratden Closure by so little, as the Betyár had split from the Hajduks only mere months before the event had taken place.

Silvia, Nick and Árpád exchanged only curt nods in greeting. Árpád had become overly critical of all his fellow Hajduks in the years leading up to his departure from the Legion, though his remarks had always had a tendency to be directed at either Nick, for being too silly, or towards Silvia, for being too cautious. Again, such comments never truly crossed the line of constructive criticism, yet they were a bit... *undermining*, which was something both Centurions had found irritating, to say the least. It had been after one such remark addressed towards Silvia that Pop had told her that he couldn't 'wait to get rid of him, already!' and that he didn't realize 'he would be one of those assholes who grew cuntier with rank!'

These had been one of the rare honest words of genuine care the man who stood at the head of the round table had ever said to her.

Laur Pop was a friendly man, at least superficially. Seeing him now, surrounded by so many of the older Hajduks, Silvia was once more reminded of how she had seen this man when she had been younger. She still remembered him as he had been at Prague. That heroic protector that had kept the monsters at bay in the red darkness of the Hour of Twilight, up until the moment when the light of their old sun had broken through to pierce the night at Dawnbreak. She remembered walking past him, as she and the rest of the children rushed outside to glimpse the ruins of Old Earth and behold the dawn of Terra. She remembered looking up at him in fear and hope, grateful for his mere presence.

She remembered how much she had yearned to join the Hajduks. Nick had been there alongside her the entire journey, of course, as they had fought their way towards the gaze of the great Laur Pop, though she and her old friend had never truly believed it to be possible that they might one day become Hajduks. She still remembered how she had felt when Pop had placed the insignia of the Hajduks on her breast in the waning days of the Senoyu War.

She had been so happy.

It was a bittersweet memory now. In her time with the Hajduks she had been blessed with the company of heroes. Men and women of ability and drive she sometimes saw as truly superhuman. She had been fortunate to have made many friends, though she had also been cursed to lose so many of them.

As one of the Hajduks, she had earned the freedom to do so much and see so much more.

And some of what she had seen had been too much...

A truly wicked man he was.

Yet, a great man also, he somehow still was.

She had seen Laur Pop do truly unspeakable things and heard him contemplate much worse. He was manipulative to a point beyond machiavellianism and paranoid beyond sensible reason. His cruelty, if witnessed, could make one wonder if he understood what 'mercy' even was. Beneath it all lay a deep bitterness of which he never truly spoke, yet was likely the most tangible thing about him. It lay upon his eyes, that tired sadness of those who had lost something only they knew they had ever had. Many of those to have fought their way through the End Times bore the pangs of loss, yet for Pop, it was so much more than that. Silvia had always thought that he looked like a man who could not get rid of some rancid taste in his mouth.

'Twisted' was the word she saw chiselled in his soul by his own hand, for he was not, for all his faults, truly evil. His condition was something far more tragic. He was a good man at heart. Silvia sometimes saw glimpses of a dormant kindness inside of him and he clearly knew what being 'good' entailed, for he often emulated the characteristics of someone with a keen sense of justice, in a way in which only one that was truly unscrupulous ever could.

If one could take every single Terran General and quiz them on what 'being a good person' meant, Laur Pop would almost certainly be the only one to ace the test. His competition wasn't exactly challenging, since the Terran High Command was a motley crew of psychopaths, sociopaths, narcissists, demagogues, authoritarians and other dwellers of the dark triad of human emotion. Yet, Laur still managed to be the most disturbing of the bunch, despite being the one most aware of his own faults.

He epitomized both the best and the worst of Terran society. He was cunning, brutal and cruel, yet he was also effective, relentless and thoughtful. He was the monster that kept at bay the terrors of the darkness. He was the beast that pursued the creatures of shadow into the deepest night. He was not only the one who gazed into the abyss, but the one who tormented it.

It was he who had sealed, in the cold blood of treachery, the unity of their people. It was he who kept forever his watch upon Terra's battlements. It was he who was the nameless terror their people's enemies dreaded, yet could never grasp.

And he knew it all too well.

Silvia knew that he had wrought upon himself a life of constant dread and restlessness. Even here, in his own halls, surrounded by his closest companions – men and women who would die for him before he could even make the request. He sat there, charming and composed, yet full of suspicion and drowning in the bubbling waters of his continuous psychosis. It was even here, atop the house he had built, that he sat consumed by angst, ungrateful for the company of those who saw him for what he was and loved him nonetheless.

'You're late!' It was Carlos, the Macedonian Centurion, who had spoken. He, together with Lejla of the Bosniaks, had been sitting at their seats, which lay to Rumen's right and right opposite Pop.

'Oh, yeah? *You* were late last night!' Nick replied swiftly.

'Oh, yeah? What was I late for?' Carlos, already smiling, played along.

Nick pulled his seat back. 'You were late for sucking my dick!' He slouched down loudly, never breaking eye contact with his fellow Centurion. 'You always come suck my dick at midnight, last night you were four minutes late and I missed you, baby boo!'

Carlos tried to answer, but accidentally chuckled.

'Yeah! I missed hearing *that*! I missed that *hawk!tuah!* and that *gawk!gawk!*' Nick proceeded to make vulgar choking sounds, to the embarrassment of many and the amusement of a few more. 'You know I don't sleep well if you don't tuck me into bed at night!' At this point, chuckling began to spread thorough the room. Nick continued, 'Were you sucking someone else's dick last night, baby boo?'

This time Carlos managed to answer, 'No!'

Before he could say anything, Nick was already following up. 'Good! Cuz you know I'm jealous and it would break my heart if you did –'

'Oh, shut up, Nick! You're like a broken record!' Bojana had a remarkably deep voice for a grizzled warlord, let alone a woman. She was, however, elegant in her movements and light in her steps, as she often gave the impression of a growling white cloud.

She had walked into the Council Chamber followed by Iosip and Bor, the leaders of the Croat and Slovene contingents. Their appearance was met with more exchanges of greetings and banter, as they took their seats. Silvia saw Laur's gaze twitch towards the last empty seat.

Its owner appeared almost two minutes later.

Gigi was the oldest person in the room and, indeed, one of the oldest in the entire citadel. At the age of ninety-five, he was a full seventeen years older than Laur, Rumen and Bor, all of which were seventy-eight years of age. Despite this, to an outside observer, he would have appeared to have been the youngest.

Most Terrans opted for an outside appearance of around thirty-years of age. Some, such as Rumen and Bor, opted for an older appearance, closer to forty, usually due to the fact that this had been the age when they had first employed the now commonplace genetic templates that had ceased their aging. Silvia herself, despite being in her late fifties, looked closer to twenty-five years of age, also due to the fact that this had been when she had first employed a genetic template. Laur, a man whom she had met when he had been thirty-three and she had been seven, looked barely a day over thirty-five.

Gigi looked like he was barely twenty and, sometimes, he had an attitude to match. Whilst the other Hajduks, despite their appearance, clearly possessed the behaviour and mannerisms of the old men and women they really were, Gigi had somehow managed to retain (and even cultivate) an increasingly youthful demeanour. To be more precise, the ninety-five year old often behaved much like the rebellious bad-boy teenager he had once been in the days of Old Earth, complete with a black Nike Tech fleece, large white sneakers and a tattoo of the Shqiptari double-headed eagle strewn across the entirety of the front of his throat.

He recalled Pop once telling her that Gigi's evolution (or 'devolution', as he sometimes referred to it) made him wonder whether or not the genetic templates really did prevent dementia in Terrans. Immediately after the comment had been made, Nick had walked into the room and proudly announced his acquisition of the last original Charizard Pokémon card in existence on Terra. At that precise instant, Pop's phone (the General didn't trust cybernetic operators) had begun to ring, revealing the caller to be none other than Tomasz Ashaver himself, who had called him to share his excitement over the result of some football game from over half a century before. After informing him that the Italian National Team would fail to qualify for two of the next five world cups and hanging up the phone. Pop had confided in Silvia that 'we can abandon all hope, as everyone else seemed to have abandoned all reason...'

'Traffic on the autobahn, Gigi?' Rumen inquired, as Gigi took his seat next to Bojana.

'No, I just couldn't bring myself to come see you go!' The room's air swelled with sombre melancholy for a few moments, until Gigi started pouring himself a glass of red wine from a nearby pitcher. He turned slightly towards his commanding officer. 'The good stuff?' he asked, nodding towards the wine.

Pop, now sporting one of his tired smirks, nodded. 'Italian.'

'Nice!' Gigi replied, placing the pitcher back on its coaster. 'Well,' he continued, 'can you give the news so that we can toast?'

Pop let out a long sigh, before turning to look at the rest of the table. He tilted his head towards one of the other wine pitchers spread around the table. 'The rest of you should also fill up your glasses.'

Expectant smiles could be seen tickling the corners of sealed lips all around the room as Rumen, Nick, Mikhail, Elena and Dmitry refilled their glasses and the rest of the Hajduks, old and new, poured themselves new glasses. Once they had all finished, Pop leaned back in his seat, as he always did before he was about to speak at length.

'Rumen, I haven't prepared a speech. Plus, I can tell by looking around the room that there's no real need to be long-winded about this.' He tilted his head towards the five Generals behind him. '*They* know for sure. *You* know for sure. Everyone else seems to be pretty damn sure. So, without further ado...' He paused slightly, as his eyes became downcast and thoughtful for a moment. He then got up from his seat and walked towards a nearby cabinet, from which he pulled a single file, within which were likely several sheets of white paper and black ink. He walked over to Rumen's seat and placed the file in front of him with an audible *thump!*

'The High Command has agreed that you have earned the rank of General –'

Pop was interrupted by the sound of eight happy Hajduks banging on the table in joyful agreement. Rumen stood immobile, the only change in his demeanour being a smile he couldn't contain from spreading cheek-to-cheek as he beheld the file before him.

'Shut up, you lot! You're just happy to get rid of me!' He shouted over the loud cheering. His now former legionnaires obeyed the freshly minted General's orders.

Oh, no, we're not! We'll sorely miss you, you loveable bastard!

Pop sat down once more in his seat and continued. 'Together with Generals Krasnov, Vinnychenko, Paraskevopoulou, Bey and Kocsis, I am pleased to formally grant you the rank of *General* and all that comes with it! You are to receive a fiefdom from the High Command,' he turned slightly towards the Generals behind him, 'which, I understand, is to contain the territory of the Nation of Bulgaria, the Black Sea, a territory located on the eastern bank of the Volga River –'

' – *Hah*! Volga-Bulgaria, eh?' Nick interrupted to share a giggle with Rumen.

'Yes, Nick, that was the idea...' Pop commented, before going back to his enumeration. '... a territory east of the Volga River, Northwestern Australia, Southern Paraguay, the Anzhu Islands, Chatham Zealandia...' Pop paused for the most imperceptible of moments. '... and *Macedonia*.'

Oh? Didn't expect this one.

Pop turned to face Carlos. 'Carlos, you're going too! You and your contingent will join the Bulgars under *General* Lakhana.'

The Macedonian's eyes widened in a look of utter and complete surprise.

'Come on, Carlos!' Rumen quipped. 'I'm not that bad of a boss! Plus, you won't have to suck Nick's dick at midnight anymore!'

Laughter erupted around the room, piercing the startled silence left by Pop's announcement. As surprise gave way to applause, Silvia glanced towards the five Generals, seeking something which Dmitry provided with a subtle nod. *They knew about this...*

Once silence had returned to the room, Pop continued. 'One of your duties – as you already know – is to oversee the repopulation of those regions in your fiefdom that are under-populated. You are to erect a Legion Citadel within the territory of the Nation of Bulgaria and *only* on the territory of Bulgaria!'

Rumen nodded.

'Good!' Laur smiled a rare honest smile. 'Have you decided upon a name for your Avenger Legion?'

'The *Konniks*!' Rumen immediately responded, only to be met by a few knowing chuckles.

'Another *Age of Empires* legion?' Bor asked.

'Another *Age of Empires* legion!' Rumen confirmed.

'Excellent!' Laur himself was stifling a smile. 'There are four hundred and thirty-seven Hajduks of Bulgar nationality, yourself included, as well as the eighty-nine Macedonians of Carlos' contingent. Within the file in front of you is a transfer agreement – signed by me, stipulating the transfer of all of them to your newly founded legion.'

He continued, 'You will also receive your own capital ship, which I understand was finished yesterday. Have you decided upon a name?'

'The *Proshka*,' Rumen replied, this time in an uncharacteristically sombre tone.

The Forgiveness.

Pop's face changed slightly, then immediately returned to a look of almost completely genuine happiness for his old friend's achievement. 'Well, let's not keep Gigi thirsty!' Pop got up from his seat, wine glass held high.

'To General Lakhana and the Konniks!' he pronounced.

'*To General Lakhana and the Konniks!*' they all echoed.

And then... an expectant silence.

Which they all knew they all felt.

Pop sat down in his chair and his gaze shifted towards the empty space before him.

Here we go...

Pop reached forward across the table and let his glass rest on the table. The sound echoed across the expectant room.

'With the exception of Bor, Silvia and Nick, you are all being promoted to Legate.'

Silvia blinked.

She wasn't the only one.

The silence was deafening now. Only the sound of fifteen hearts beating expectantly could be felt atop the Tower of Laur Pop over the Citadel of Bâlea.

What the fuck? Silvia's eyes betrayed her.

She glanced quickly towards Gigi, seeing no reaction; then to Bojana, seeing her eyes open wide; then to Iosip, who had raised an eyebrow; then to Carlos, Bor and Lejla, all of whom seemed stunned. Lastly, she shared a slightly longer glance with Nick, whose brow was furrowed in confusion.

'I would congratulate you all, were it not for the fact that you all look like I just called *all your mothers whores*!' Pop's voice was mocking, yet also honest. 'I mean, I can understand why Bor, Silvia and Nick would be upset since they're kinda being left out, but what's up with the rest of you?' he asked, annoyed, as usual.

It was Iosip who answered, after a short moment in which he had likely gotten his thoughts in order. 'Well, it's a bit unexpected, Laur!'

'It's also *good* news,' Bojana continued. 'Good news never comes cheap,' she pointed out.

Particularly around here...

'I guess what we're trying to get at here is... *what's the catch?*' Iosip gave voice to everyone's thoughts.

Pop leaned back so far in his chair that his head now stood flat against the wooden boards behind him. 'As you all very well know, we are currently enjoying times of almost complete peace. After Ratden, there are no more Svart to worry about. The last Senoyu left Andromeda over twenty-five years ago. The Aesir are completely integrated into the Alliance. We have effective treaties and partnerships in place with virtually every known neighbour of the Republican Alliance and its member states. The Urheimat is being kept at bay – at least for the time being – and all the spawn we know off have been contained or eradicated. For the first time in over fifty years, we are not at war. Furthermore, for the first time in our entire history, no conflict rages on Terra itself!'

'But it will not always be so,' he continued. 'War will come again. I think you can all see the countless scenarios that make that statement an inevitability. What we can do in the meantime is prepare.' He took in a big breath, putting together his words as candidly as he could. 'There are now one hundred and fourteen Terran Generals, each one in command of more than a million men. Or, to be accurate, they *should* be commanding one million, since no one is at full strength. Everyone is building, training and consolidating, with the help of the repopulation programs, which are having their desired effect, as more and more reach fighting age with each passing year. These new cohorts will need new Generals to lead them and new Avenger Legions to guide them.'

'You're building a pipeline!' Bojana realized.

'He's not the only one!' It was Mikhail who spoke. 'With your promotion to Colonel – or Legates, as you're called around here – there will be over one thousand five hundred Colonels. Each one is a potential General. Like Laur said, with each passing year, we'll have more and more soldiers and we need to assure a steady supply of leaders. You are now all part of that pool.'

'It is not just the regular Army that needs you,' Laur stepped in once more. 'We are to recruit an additional thousand men over the coming months.'

'*What?*' several voices, including Nick's, rang out.

Laur squirmed in his seat, now visibly annoyed. 'Jesus *fucking* Christ!' he muttered. 'It's a *break*, you fucking *morons!*' He tapped his armrests with his wrists before leaning on his table. 'You are each to appoint new Centurions. After the next influx of recruits, there will be three thousand total Hajduks. There should be thirty centurions total, each in command of one hundred men, as well as the four new legates. With the exception of Bor, Silvia and Nick, that leaves twenty-seven open positions.'

He turned to his left. 'Gigi, you get seven!'

Gigi nodded softly.

'Bojana, you get seven!'

The Serb looked down and swallowed in acknowledgement.

'Iosip, you get four, plus two Slovenes, which will join Bor under your command!'

The Croat did not move an inch.

'Lejla, you get three.'

The Bosniak nodded.

'Silvia and I will select the remaining Centurions together. There will be some national overlap, but I'm not expecting that to be an issue.' Pop didn't wait for Silvia to nod and leaned back in his seat once more. 'You are all to establish cohesive units, with a good mix of veterans and recruits in each respective unit, and then you are to commence training exercises.'

'Over what time horizon?' Iosip asked.

'Indefinitely.' Laur spoke as if he was stating the obvious to a bunch of ungrateful morons.

I can't believe it... It's finally happening. We're getting a break!

Laur was quiet for a moment, once more staring off into the distance of the empty space in front of him. After a few tense seconds, he let out a breath of constricted air.

'How many of you placed bets that we are going to Shangri?'

He was greeted by an awkward silence, followed by even more awkward shuffling as some of the Hajduks squirmed uncomfortably in their seats.

'*Ahem, hmnnnph...*' Nick let out some of his characteristic onomatopoeia before raising his hand. He was followed by a hesitant Lejla and a puzzled Bor. Silvia subtly lifted a finger.

Pop's eyes drifted towards Gigi, who, after a quick smile and short pause, said, 'I abstained from placing a bet, but my guys tell me that the odds were five-to-one!'

'Oh, but for fuck's sake! I took three-to-one with Lejla!' Carlos announced, clearly annoyed.

'Shut up! I've been going around offering two-to-one like a gentleman!' Nick protested, before looking at Silvia and winking.

You offered me one-to-one after you saw I only leaned slightly towards not going... asshole...

'Well, then you three will likely end up having to pay up! We are, most likely, *not* going to Shangri.'

Silence, once more, filled the room. This time, it was somewhat surreal.

I don't believe it...

'Are...' Bojana moved in tentatively '... are you *sure* about that?'

Snorts of stifled laughter and poorly-feigned amusement came from the five old Generals behind Pop, as well as the new General now sitting directly across from him.

He answered quickly. *Too quickly.* 'As you all very well know, unlike most other Legions, we have been on active duty from the moment of our inception. Whether it be hunting dushman, overseeing reconstruction, counterintelligence and even active warfare. After Diwali Day (when you all know what happened) and the elimination of the last dushman on Ratden, we have officially exhausted every single mandate we have ever received from the High Command, the Warchief and the Council of Hierarchs. We have no outstanding duties left and it is my belief that we should keep things like that for as long as we can!'

He always answers quickly when he's trying to convince himself that he believes in what he's saying...

'To address the obvious elephant in the room, I believe that you all took the discovery of the Ratden Log to mean that we would likely be embarking upon a new mission, in conjunction with existing Allied interests in the City of Shangri? *Hmmm*? Or was it just Nick who jumped to that conclusion?'

The table answered by being silent.

Pop continued, 'Well, I will remind you that *Operation Changeling* is Hierarch Tomasz Ashaver's mandate, not mine!'

That didn't stop you from making us do Ashaver's job on a dozen other occasions. We're basically honorary Old Guards by this point! What's stopping you this time?

Pop's eyes became unfocused and his lips began to move slightly, which Silvia knew meant that he was preparing a half-lie; all facts and no truth. 'We are the best Terran Avenger Legion specialized in covert operations. *I* know it. *You* know it.' He pointed to the men and women behind him. 'They know it! And so does the entirety of High Command. But...'

Something happened.

Something Silvia had never seen before.

Laur Pop hands began to shake as he lifted one palm to his forehead and pushed his hair back across his scalp. She noticed that he had begun to break a very light sweat, which was atypical, to say the least, for a man that was usually cold as ice.

Is... is he about to tell the truth? Even if it'll mean showing... weakness?

'We would be the best possible team for Shangri... Of that I am certain! Of all the Legions, we have the most knowledge of the subject matter, we have the perfect skill set and we would be righteous in our cause. However...' Pop's blinked a few times.

It was another gesture Silvia recognized. *He's about to state the obvious...*

'I have always feared that I might be pushing you all *just a bit too hard.*' He paused, seemingly just about to start his next sentence–

Yet was interrupted by a chorus of thunderous laughter from across the room. Even the more sombre Hajduks in attendance, like Gigi, Iosip and Bor, burst into fits of merry chuckles now. *Well, there's an understatement... just 'a bit'?*

Pop allowed himself to join them with a smile before continuing. 'It doesn't *have to be* us! There's going to be a meeting on Tristan da Cunha the day after tomorrow. Tomasz returned from his trip to Menegroth two weeks ago, as you all know. The formal reason for his visit was to recover Mira al-Sayid and bring her back home. However, in truth, he went there to speak with Daw al-Fajr concerning the end of the current Shangri diplomatic mission.'

Maybe he gave a shit about Mira too, you know?

'He also met, in secret, with Quentyn Andromander, who was returning to Nargothrond from a trip to Pandora, where he conferred with Vorclav Uhrlacker in regards to the soon-to-be vacant position of *Ambassador of the Republican Alliance to the City of Shangri*, as well as the discovery of the Ratden Log and its implications for Operation Changeling.' Laur's eyes wandered, as he likely saw the document flash before his eyes.

'The elves are a good choice for Shangri. They have history there, after all. However, we killed every high elf which would have had any influence in Shangri a long time ago. The low elves finished their last diplomatic rotation less than a year ago, under Arlena Beifong. Uhrlacker is concerned that a primal ef presence in Shangri, particularly given the task at hand, would draw too much heat to the Alliance. Plus, it's not like their standing in Shangri is any better than that of the high elves. So, that rules out the elves as a whole.'

'Jimmel is the current ambassador and his term ends in three weeks, so that rules out the goblins. The Hyperboreans, Aesir and Vanir admit, by their own accord, that they don't have anyone up to the task, as they're far more interested in reconstruction at this time, than any potential involvement in the Pisces Galaxy. The trolls are too few and Falk has made it clear that he can't spare enough men for such a mission. They'd also attract too much attention, as would the demani, whose presence would be seen as being too... *provocative*, given the situation on the ground.'

"The orcs, though masters of warcraft, possess no skill in tradecraft and, as such, are out of the question. The remani and the ursai are... well... they're *too* well connected to the local population. Furthermore, the Peacekeeper of Shangri, Otto Gisevius, had made it quite clear that their *unaccompanied* presence would be a gigantic blow to our diplomatic efforts, given certain historical realities... Nevertheless, it's been agreed that whomever will be going *will* be accompanied by a small number of remani, so as to help gather intelligence and better understand the local population. This will not an entirely new practice, as remani have accompanied Republican delegations before in the over forty years since we began formal diplomatic relations.'

Going off-topic now? You've thought about this. I know you have! Silvia glanced around the room. *It's clear for all of us to see...*

'So, that leaves us Terrans to pick a General and an Avenger Legion to replace Jimmel and his goblins once their term is over. The High Command initially shortlisted three legions: the Jinyiwei, the Sayeret and the Hajduks. Together with Tomasz, we are to decide exactly which of us are to go to Shangri, under the pretence of completing the diplomatic rotation with the goblins. That's what the meeting tomorrow is for.'

Pop exhaled. 'And... it will be Feng and his Jinyiwei who will go. Neither Ruben, nor I, wish to go. We're just going to the meeting to make things formal. I...' Pop's eyes fixated on a nearby wine jug. 'I have neglected this Legion's needs for far too long. I actually worry often that I've pushed you to your breaking point. Quite frankly, I often wondered how hard I could push you all until you snapped! However, when I did push you, I only did so when I was certain you could take it.'

'Now, as the years have gone by and the threats diminished and our excellence was needed less and less, I still pushed you because...' Pop scratched his head and let loose an exhausted breath of air through smiling lips as he raised his eyebrows and tilted his head. '... because I'm a control freak who constantly wants to take matters into his own hands, because: if you want something done right, you'd better do it yourself!'

You would have been an idiot not to know that, but hearing you say out loud is truly startling! What's going on with you?

'And, with the assistance of everyone in this room, I've managed to make a career out of doing just that and I plan to keep on doing that! But!' Pop raised a single finger from his armrest. 'But, we have a saying in Romanian. I'm certain some of you might have heard it before:'

'*You can only take the pitcher to the well so many times...*'

'At one point, the pitcher breaks and I don't want that to happen when we are most needed!' Pop smiled a strange, bittersweet smile. 'So... no Shangri!... Maybe next year!'

He looked over a room in shock and Silvia could understand why.

This wasn't really like him.

Everyone present had only seen one Laur Pop in their lives. The maniacal, obsessive and relentless juggernaut that only seemed to be comfortable whilst taking on the most difficult of tasks. He took breaks, yes, but they were minuscule. Silvia thought of them as 'fake breaks', since he was always secretly working on something. When he did take an actual break, he only did so when he was utterly and completely exhausted, as he had after Kralizec's conclusion, when he had collapsed in his bed in Jerusalem and not woken up for three whole days.

Not that anyone would have noticed, for he had left everyone else exhausted also. The only reason Silvia knew of Pop's collapse into slumber was because she and Nick had lived in the same house as Pop for the mission's duration.

Because that's what Pop thrived on. He would work himself and those around him into complete exhaustion and then completely shut off for a few days, which he would normally spend sleeping. If he didn't go about things like that, he had nightmares.

Literal nightmares.

Silvia didn't know what they were about, since Pop never spoke of them, but she knew he had them and she knew they went away when he completely exhausted himself.

How's he going to handle taking things easy?

He'll probably turn the induction of the new recruits into torture!

Pop slapped his armrests. 'Well, enough of that! You all get the picture! We're going on a break and we should start things out with a party! We do have something to celebrate after all!' He pointed with his palms towards Rumen as he got up.

'Have you decided upon a Legion song, Rumen?'

'Fuck! Here we go!' Rumen began massaging his forehead in embarrassment.

Elena spoke up from her seat on the couch. 'Whatever you pick, Rumen, it will not be better than *Zorba the Greek*!' The Cataphracts had one of the best Avenger Legion songs of all the Hajduk descendants.

'*Her Gece* is clearly the better song! No discussion!' Emre shot back at his wife.

What followed was quite typical. Silvia had heard the discussions many times before. She knew every Legate had a song prepared for when they would become Generals with their own Legions and they would no longer hear Goran Bregovic's *Kalashnikov* so often. She knew Rumen's ideas were all very corny and, thus, the subject of much ridicule.

It was good that the conversations that followed had been rehearsed many times before, as she knew every single one of them was shocked. She could feel it. She knew they all felt it. Normally, one of them would have pointed it out and they would have addressed things as a group, for that was the way of the Hajduks.

However, somehow, it had been too much.

Strangely enough, she couldn't tell if Pop's decisions had caused relief or revolt among them. She eventually realised that everyone likely felt the way she did: confused. Pop's presented reasoning was so out-of-character that it was shocking. As day gave way to night, the Hajduks and their former comrades did what they always did on such occasions: they got ridiculously drunk, as old warriors always do, so as to numb away the horrors they had been through together.

Today, the drinking was different. Everyone seemed to be drinking simply so that they could fall asleep and wake up the next day. Hopefully, once they did that, they would be able to have a moment to themselves to understand exactly what the hell was going on. Silvia was quite certain of that, simply due to the fact that no one really brought up what had been discussed during their meeting.

It was only when dawn broke that she found a moment alone with Nick as they both stumbled towards their respective bedchambers.

'Ai ain't givin' da mani yet!' Nick blurted out as they reached their rooms.

'*Huh?*' she replied, not understanding what he was talking about.

'Da *money* fe' da bet!' he tried again.

'*Wat?*' she asked again.

He switched to Romanian. '*Stick my dick in it*! Those ten bucks for the bet we made about Shangri!'

She followed suit. 'Ah, yes?'

'You mark my words! Once he'll have a moment of peace and realise that he's going to have to endure that moment of peace for who-knows how long, he'll find something for us to do!' He managed to open the door to his room and stumbled in before pausing in the doorway. 'If it's *not* Shangri, I'll give you the money!'

'Good! Goodnight, Nick!'

'*Ciao!*' He shut the door and Silvia heard the sound of one hundred and eighty kilograms of pure muscle, honeybone and intoxicated tissue collapse onto what was hopefully a bed; or at least a couch, hopefully.

She stared at the door for a moment, gaining a moment of clarity.

'*Shit!*' she blurted out towards Nick's closed door.

He's right...

Chapter II

I think now only of the Passing of Spring

Laur woke up in a bad mood.

The day was well into the late afternoon as he got up from his bed and made himself his morning cappuccino. He didn't have a hangover, but he did seem to be experiencing some kind of hangxiety.

He couldn't really figure out why he was in such a bad mood on this particular day.

He also didn't plan on figuring out why, since he had planned to enjoy himself today! It would be a short day, since he would have to rest before flying out to Tristan da Cunha the next day.

Why the fuck did he have to build his Citadel literally in the middle of fucking nowhere? I know he thinks he's Superman, but what's with the fucking 'Fortress of Solitude' bullshit?

'He' was Tomasz Ashaver and he could have built his Citadel wherever he felt like. It had been his prerogative and the decision had been made back in the days when Ashaver used to frequently place himself in various forms of self-imposed exile. Whether it be making himself ambassador to some far-off neighbour of the Alliance or by choosing to spend his time on the Vigilant, Pandora or Moria, helping with the construction of the Solar colonies, or simply going off the grid on some island in the South Atlantic, Ashaver had gone through a phase when he had decided to stay as far as possible from the centres of Terran power.

Laur didn't have anything to prepare, since he never really needed to prepare for anything anymore. All he had to do was go down to Ashaver's island and tell him what he already knew.

He had done enough and needed a break. He needed to bring his Legion back up to full strength and finally achieve the complete integration of his men. For forty-five years he had led a rag-tag warband of former bloodsworn enemies, which he had moulded into the most elite covert operations unit in the entire Republican Alliance.

Yeah, sure, in a fair fight, the Hajduks would easily be outmatched by most of the other Terran Avenger Legions, let alone some of the more martially formidable units in the Alliance, such as the

Orcish High Guard, the Aesir Einherjar or Ashaver's own Old Guard, but the Hajduks never really got involved in fair fights.

They fought dirty and that's what Laur wanted them to do. That's what the Republican Alliance *needed* them to be.

Most Terran Avenger Legions were little more than glorified bodyguards or crudely formidable shock troops. The Hajduks were different. In an arsenal of hammers, swords, spears, axes, rifles and machine guns, his men were daggers. While others flourished in the heat of battle, the Hajduks dwelt in the cold shadows of the ambush, the skirmish and the infiltration.

In almost half a century he had turned them into one of the most elite covert units, not just on Terra, but in the entire galactic cluster, on par with the remani of the Black Knight Pride or the Hunter Clades of the Primal Elves. What had once been the shards of a dozen shattered armies, he had welded together into a dark scalpel with which he had slashed, crippled and annihilated the Alliance's enemies, be they foreign or domestic.

Yet, he knew the welding points of his instrument could still crack.

He saw exactly where his blade might break and how. He had also seen where the blades of others might break.

He hadn't let Mikhail leave because he wanted to get rid of him. If anything, he missed him! He was an honourable and moral man of true virtue. He had his faults, yes, like any man, yet he was one of only a few human beings left on Terra that were both great *and* decent. But, he had let him go because he had to make sure that cuntflap Yulia and her fucking Spetsnaz wouldn't stir the Russians into some new irredentist shitstorm. Why that psycho had been made General, he had no idea! War hero or not, she was a fucking loose cannon and everyone knew it! She had only risen to the rank of General because everyone above her had gotten themselves killed and the domineering bitch just wouldn't die! Mikhail and his Druzhina would keep her in check, never allowing her to work the Russ into a frenzy.

He had went a step further and allowed Dmitry to leave and start the Cossacks. Dmitry had been an arrogant bastard as a man and now he was an arrogant bitch as a woman, but he was calculating and that made him trustworthy. With Dmitry further biting into Yulia's recruitment pool, he knew *that* whole bullshit would stay stable in perpetuity. He also believed, at the time, that he couldn't keep Mikhail and Dmitry together for too long. It was weird when they were both men and they kept their distance from one another. However, when Dmitry became a woman and they started fucking... *fuck that, there was enough drama already to go around!*

Case in point had been Elena and Emre.

Those two had also ended up getting married, but not before almost coming to blows on several occasions. Elena had also managed to convince the High Command that the Greeks deserved an Avenger Legion and he had been pressured into letting her go, despite the fact that she only had eighty Greeks when she left the Hajduks. He made Emre leave with her, since the Ayve War was starting and he knew that if they were busy fighting someone else, they'd keep the peace with each other.

They got married a year later, the weird cunts.

The Árpád situation had been inevitable, in retrospect. Laur had fucked up and made him Legate, because... well, he had earned it! The Magyars had never truly grasped the finer points of subterfuge and espionage which Laur had cultivated within the Hajduk; which was in no way an issue, since a good blade with a sharp edge needed a strong fuller to bear the strain of heavy blows. Together with Gigi and Rumen, Árpád had commanded the more martially gifted segment of the Hajduks and that had been fine with Laur. But then he had started acting like a cunt. Initially, it seemed to be simple misogyny, as he seemed to single out Silvia, Bojana and Lejla. He then thought it was some leftover nationalism, since he really seemed to give Silvia and Bojana a particularly hard time. A few tense standoffs with Nick had made him suspect a hefty dose of racism. In the end, the realization had come to him out of nowhere:

Árpád didn't get it. He didn't get what the Hajduks were.

His brother, Attila, had been convicted of Terran homicide just before the Senoyu War and the shame of being related to one of only twenty Terran murderers convicted after the *Last Fitna* had stifled impulses that had inevitably lingered beneath the surface. Time heals all wounds, including shame, and it took about forty years for Árpád to show his true colours: those of a cunt.

But, he was remarkably competent, fiercely loyal and surprisingly brilliant... at times. Laur had used a great degree of leverage to get him promoted but, in the end, Terra gained a capable General and the Hajduks were relieved of a headache.

Rumen Lakhana had to go and he just hated it.

He liked Rumen a lot. He was by all accounts, including Laur's, a good guy. He kept the peace among the Hajduks and he did so sincerely. He didn't *want* to see conflict within the ranks because he legitimately *loved* all of them! Laur saw most of the Hajduk leadership as his friends. Rumen saw them as family and he, as a caring uncle, never hesitated to ensure that his nephews and nieces got along harmoniously. In truth, Laur had at one point realised that it was unfair to keep Rumen pinned-down underneath him. He had long ago outgrown the rank of Legate, let alone Centurion. He and his Konniks would serve Terra well and Laur would honestly miss him.

Carlos also needed guidance and Pop knew that Rumen was one of the best sources of quality mentorship available.

He acknowledged this to himself, as he had many times before, while having his last supper with all of them together that evening. He looked at all six of them now. Mikhail, Dmitry, Elena, Emre, Árpád and, now, Rumen.

How he missed them! They had their faults, yes, but to look at them all now... he saw them for what they were, each and every one of them.

Beautiful. Imperfect. People.

May they prosper! They deserve it, after putting up with me for so long and after everything they'd been through!

His eyes drifted towards what he was left with.

This fucking lot...

Gigi was great, but he was so impenetrable. Of all the Hajduks, he was the only one whom Laur had never really figured out.

By all accounts he was the most loyal, dedicated and selfless of them all. At least that's what his actions always suggested.

Yet, his words were so few that their absence made Laur uneasy. He was always uneasy around people he hadn't figured out yet. Gigi had remained an enigma for almost fifty years. In that time, Laur hadn't really found anything wrong with him, though there had been some changes in his behaviour recently. He had become even more insular and distant, not just towards his Hajduk General, but to the Hajduks in general. Nowadays, he didn't even bother to ask for permission to return to his beloved Shqipëria. Laur usually found out via email.

Bojana was also great. In a way, she was the greatest. Dignified, tactically brilliant, cautious, yet never hesitant. The only problem with her was the fact that, before the End Times, she had been an escort. Her Serbs had administered several beatings to those unwise enough to bring it up over the years, yet the stigma had stuck and he knew whispers still haunted the corners of Bâlea Citadel. In all frankness, this particular issue was the one Laur hated having to navigate the most, since her past life was never reflected in who she was now. *It wasn't like she goes around throwing slices of pussy at hapless bystanders.* On the contrary, she was one of the least promiscuous of the Hajduks, on par with Silvia, who was downright saintly in that regard. Also, concerning Silvia, who happened to be the most attractive of the lot, Laur had never observed Bojana trying to outdo her in any way, seemingly never feeling truly threatened by her, or Lejla for that matter, as a woman. Nevertheless, she still had to deal with shit, usually from Gigi, who seemed to frequently dismiss her as both an officer and a person.

Iosip was a cannibal, but that was virtually the only issue with him. *I mean, there's the blatant psychopathy too, but that's stable and under control.* He got along great with the others, was likely one of the most intelligent men in the Legion and was rigorous in such a way that did not impede the constant emergence of swift and impactful results from his endeavours. Laur did find him to be a little creepy at times, with his Hannibal Lecter charm and his love of classical music, but he couldn't the deny that, of all the leaders of the larger non-Romanian contingents of the Hajduks, he was the one least likely to stir up any kind of trouble. He was trustworthy, likeable and dependable, though Laur never ate any bite of food he offered. *Just in case.*

Of the leaders of the smaller contingents, the least problematic was Bor. Bor was, well, *boring*. By Avenger Legion standards, Bor was perfectly mediocre. He wasn't the best at anything, but he wasn't bad at anything either. His tactical and strategic thinking were so orthodox, Laur found him to be quite dull as a military man. Usually, Laur would've found relief in knowing that he had at least one officer he could rely on to be dispassionately consistent. Yet, said consistency came at the cost of him being incredibly predictable and completely average. Strangely enough, Bor wasn't even a particularly great spy, which was peculiar, since being unremarkable was a highly desirable trait in the field of espionage. Nevertheless, Bor somehow managed to be *too* nondescript, to the point where he often attracted attention even from non-Terrans, who found him to be so stereotypically Terran, that they began to suspect that he might be some enemy infiltrator.

Lejla was not boring at all, though Laur frequently wished she were. She was the *Doina*'s pilot and her Bosniaks acted as the de facto garrison of the Legion's capital ship. She was, by all accounts, an incredible officer. She was well liked, both by those under her command and by her fellow officers, though she did frequently align herself closely with Gigi, in stark contrast to the supremely neutral Silvia, Bor, Iosip or the chaotically troublesome duo of Nick and Carlos. The issue with her wasn't her fraternization with her fellow Muslim Hajduk, but the fact that, of all of them, she was the only one who showed symptoms of post-traumatic stress.

Every Terran oldtimer had harrowing amounts of trauma they had to control, suppress, ignore or otherwise deal with. Those that struggled were often relegated to the lower ranks. Lejla's neurosis had never crossed over into a full-fledged psychotic episode in the forty-five years he had known her, yet she always seemed to be right on the very edge of a breakdown. It was most obvious in battle, when she would go almost fully berserk, striking down her enemies with rivers of tears streaming from her eyes and maniacal laughter rushing from her wide-open smile. Laur often worried that, one day, she might fully snap, yet he hadn't been able to deny her leadership skills. Her fellow Bosniaks followed her and only her and they did so with a fanatical devotion that matched her own maniacal tendencies.

Carlos had been, by far, the most troublesome of the Hajduk leaders. First of all, he was young. He was actually one of the youngest Terran oldtimers, being only fifty-seven. His first military engagement had been the Battle of Prague itself, as a twelve year old child soldier, one of many that had been forced by necessity to take up arms during those dark days. His irritating antics would've kept him firmly in the soldier ranks, were it not for his exceptional understanding of advanced technology, which had ultimately led to his consecration as the leader of the Macedonian Hajduks. He had clashed frequently with Elena, even as a lowly legionnaire, when the two had shared the same outfit. Nowadays, he had dedicated himself to the continuous irritation of every single member of the Hajduk leadership, with the exception of Nick, who saw in him a kindred spirit.

Because Nick was a wild soul. The Hajduks had never hesitated to take in Gypsies within their ranks, yet Laur had found that they had perchance for getting themselves killed rather quickly. For a long time, he suspected that their lack of formal military training was the root cause of their mishaps, coupled with some lingering racism within the Hajduk ranks. All that changed when Nick became Laur's twenty-first Gypsy – or *Kalo*, as they were now known – Centurion in just as many years, a position he had risen to simply because no one else wanted the job, since, by that point, the position was considered to be cursed.

However, Nick had managed to survive, in no small part, thanks to the continuous efforts of Silvia, which was always there to (sometimes *literally*) scoop him out of trouble. Moreover, Nick had become incredibly popular among the Hajduks, whom he frequently entertained with his good-humoured antics. Even his fellow officers liked him and he remained one of only two Centurions he had ever had which had stayed on consistently good terms with almost every single one of his colleagues. Laur liked Nick a great deal, in no small part due to his colourful personality, but also on account of the fact that, despite his chaotic nature, he was an outright tactical genius and a dependable one at that.

If Nick was a roaring wildfire, Silvia was a quiet mountain. The duo had joined the Hajduks during the closing days of the Senoyu War, after distinguishing themselves on numerous occasions within the regular army. He had initially recruited them on account of their martial prowess, their combat experience (which was substantial for those of their generation) and their proven understanding of covert operations. However, over time he had come to realise that he had scored a jackpot by recruiting them. If Nick was consistently spectacular, Silvia was spectacularly consistent.

She had risen through the Hajduk ranks at a much slower rate than Nick. Laur would have promoted her to Centurion after just a few years of seeing her in action, yet had felt compelled to continuously delay her advancement. He had worried that her promotion to a leadership position would be met with opposition on account of her age, nationality and even her gender. Most of the Romanian Hajduks were oldtimers who might have had an issue taking orders from a youngling. The other Centurions might have seen her rapid rise as some kind of Romanian favouritism. Lastly, the girl was gorgeous and effortless in her elegance. He worried what people might think if they saw him favour her over other, less comely, potential candidates.

About three years before, when old Tony Tapalagă had died in the Ayve War, he had been presented with the dilemma of choosing a new Romanian Centurion. He knew Silvia deserved promotion more than any other, yet he was torn between being purely meritocratic and being politically conscious. The issue had been resolved when Nick and the other officers, together with some of the more senior Romanians, had come to him and insisted that he choose her as the new Romanian Centurion.

In a Legion as rife with intrigue, chaos and volatile characters as the Hajduks, Silvia was a much needed locus of calm, constructive energy. Despite commanding the largest contingent, the other Centurions never hesitated to place even more men under her command, something which they almost never did among themselves (*without at least bickering a little first...*) In her years with the Hajduks, she had managed to establish herself as a keeper of the peace, and Laur suspected that she would often clear up dissent in the ranks before it even reached his ears. She was conservative tactically, never truly resorting to any bombastic manoeuvre or strategy, yet she was not dogmatic, as she constantly innovated, much more so than the other Centurions, who had a habit of always falling back on the established strategies they felt most comfortable with. She had also cultivated excellent relations with other Legions, the High Command, their Allies, and even the Romanian population, all of which allowed her to be used in a diplomatic capacity, something with which the others, bar perhaps Iosip, often struggled with.

If we would have gone to Shangri, she would have been invaluable!

Laur blinked, remembering his surroundings and the context.

He looked around the table he was sitting at, up in his council chamber atop the Carpathian Mountains.

Mikhail, Dmitry, Elena, Emre, Árpád and now Rumen. The old Hajduks, his companions from the days of the War of Vengeance. He had kept them safe from the enemy and from each other. It had been difficult at times, but he had pulled it off. In the end, he had let them go and now their destiny was no longer his responsibility. He had left them with everything they had needed to become distinguished Generals in their own right. A fine work he had done with them!

It can still all got to shit with one mishap.

He turned to look at the powder keg he now had beneath him.

He had managed to keep the peace through thick and thin. At times, he had even thought that maybe it was over. Maybe his efforts had paid off and perhaps the demons of the past were finally all dead. But, then he would see sparks; little embers rolling around in the wind. He caught most of them quickly, but a few he was always unable to reach.

He had been lucky.

He did not like being lucky. He wanted to be sure and now he had a chance to (finally) be sure. He would take the free time they had all earned and fix them!

A year. Two. Three? As long as there would be time available, he would keep the Hajduks on Terra and restructure things. One by one, he would make all of them Generals, until it was only he who was left.

Well...

His eyes found Silvia. She was seated next to Árpád and the two seemed to be engaged in some delightful small talk.

Always making sure everything is alright, even if it comes at the cost of her dignity.

Laur hoped she would make it.

He hoped that once it was just the two of them left in the Hajduks – or whatever Legion they became – he could finally rest. With Silvia in charge, he knew they would be in good hands. God knows, they deserved her and she would deserve it.

She would deserve to be rid of him.

But, first, there was much work to be done and he needed to be ready for it. So, once dessert was served, he excused himself and went to his apartment upstairs.

His rooms were soundproof, as had been his desire. It had been a decision he had come to regret.

Growing up in Bucharest, in an apartment block overlooking a busy boulevard, he had become accustomed to falling asleep no matter how much noise came from the street or from the neighbours.

Then, when the Fimbulwinter had come, he had slept in cities under siege, refugee camps, military bases and sometimes even in moving car seats. When the War of Vengeance began, he had boarded packed spaceships, most of which were frequently damaged, overpopulated, old or just plain noisy. It hadn't gotten any better whenever he had made planetfall, for often it had been to wage war and war is *loud*.

It had only been when he had finished building the Citadel of Bâlea that he had realised that he couldn't fall asleep in the deathly silence of a soundproof room atop lonely mountains.

He had intentionally left the windows open in the Council Chamber and now he opened the windows of his bedroom, letting in the chill alpine air and the sounds of merriment still coming from downstairs.

Content with the volume, he checked his nightstand for his loaded pistol, then he checked the space behind his pillow for his other loaded pistol, and then he collapsed into his bed. His last waking thoughts were of Tomasz Ashaver, who had probably just learned that Manchester City had won the treble all those years ago. *He's not going to stop talking about Cruyff and Guardiola...*

He felt himself twitch and, sure enough, as he always did, he fell asleep soon after.

He started drifting or, actually, he started walking.

He walked through a ruined city, reclaimed by the wetlands upon which it had been built. What had once been buildings were now boulders. Dark green shafts topped with brown revealed themselves to be reeds littering the broken bog he now crossed. Lumps of sharp brown bushes had once been cars. He passed a canal at the bottom of which had once been a subway line. There were bugs and there were many of them and their song was loud and oppressive.

Somewhere, a sweet voice was singing in Romanian.

'Hard as the stone!'

It grew darker as he neared his destination. His feet left strange imprints on the ground he passed over. Ripples, they were, spreading all around him, bending not just the dirty water, but also the clay mud, the rocks and even the many oaks and willow trees he passed.

'Swift as the arrow!'

The buzzing of countless mosquitoes met the skittering of roaches in an apex of cacophony, pressing into him from all around. He felt goosebumps spread across his body, yet had no reason to fear the creatures of the bog for they did not touch him.

'Hard as the iron!'

His ripples became smaller and smaller as he neared his destination. A great wall stood before him, behind which he knew there was a large pond which he walked towards. He could hear the sound of a child singing somewhere behind it.

'Swift as the steel!'

When he passed the ruins of the broken wall, his heart began pounding. The ripples disappeared. As he walked on the swamp grass, it didn't bend beneath his feet. The night was complete now, only a crescent moon lay above and a million stars. The bog began to tremble.

He passed the wall.

He saw... *it*.

No!

'She'!

His heart was pounding. The buzzing had turned to screeching. The bog shook all around him. She moved slightly. He saw her cheek now. Pure white and wet with tears.

Silence.

His heart stopped beating. The screeching stopped. The bog stood still.

She turned her face and he saw her eyes and her eyes were white and they grew big and they grew bigger and so did her mouth as she *screamed* and her mouth and eyes grew bigger than her face and bigger than her and everything was white –

Laur woke up.

His bedroom was chilly, as it always was in the dead of night, yet he was drenched in sweat.

He breathed in.

Fuck...

They were more frequent now.

Since Ratden, these specific nightmares had been happening at least once a week. Between Diwali Day and Ratden, it had happened three nights in a row and before that, they had happened maybe three or four times per year and only when he had been on Terra. They had started directly after the War of Vengeance and they were always the same.

The bog. The noise. The song. *Her.*

He turned and got into a comfortable sleeping position. After trying out a few poses, he let loose a sigh.

Well, who am I kidding? No more sleep for tonight...

He got up from his bed, put on a bathrobe and made his way towards his office, where he found his tobacco box. As he sat down, he lit up a cigarette and tried to relax. He spent a good ten seconds there, trying to clear his head, before he turned on his desk lamp and reached towards one of the hidden safes he kept scattered around his office. After opening it, he pulled out the stasis box within and placed it on his desk.

He opened it and stared at it for a moment.

It was incredibly nondescript. A simple, plain notebook bound in that smooth brown fungus leather the elves loved so much. Within were seventy-two individual sheets of elf papyrus, with its distinctive smooth look and rough touch. Blue Svart script littered each and every page, albeit in varying ways. Once, the notebook had been very well ordered and structured, with each of the almost eighteen hundred entries being well organized and properly detailed.

That's the original owner, Ifriq Laudiano. Just some scribe working for his masters.

Laudiano's handwriting was neat, orderly and also elegant. Laur was often reminded of Japanese kanji calligraphy when he saw Svart script expressed by a low elven hand, on account of its beauty and its discrete functionality. Every stroke and every bend in each letter had purpose and meaning. From just a few words, one could already understand so much of what needed to be communicated by the suave blue markings, even if one didn't understand the Svart language.

This was a log. It was meant to track *things*. The one that had compiled it seemed to have been completely unaware of the fact that what he was keeping track of was not a collection of *things*, but a group of *people*. The log kept track of *what* was *collected* from *where*. How much *it* weighed. Distinctive markings. Male or female variety. Age. Percentage of body fat.

This was the 'State of Collection' section. The following section, 'State of Inspection', featured information concerning the quality of the *item's* development, as well as 'gene quadrant', which was how the elves referred to specific clusters of the human genome. 'Cartal' was the word for Chinese. 'Ulasti' was the word for Ethiopians and other East Africans. 'Baliantotian' was Northern European. If a child had a Moroccan mother and a Dutch father, they were 'Itik Gobol', if they had an Italian father and a Dutch mother, they were 'Gobol Salim'.

Laur had learned the gene quadrants well. He had even been surprised to discover that the Basques had their own quadrant, 'Filtrieli'. This was hardly surprising given that there were over ten thousand gene quadrants for the human species, of which only slightly over half were present on Old Earth before the End Times. Nowadays, the number ran closer to two thousand.

The quadrant system had been invented by the Humans of the Urheimat, in their attempt at defining what it meant to be 'human'. It was primarily used to map the genetic health of a specific population. If too few gene quadrants were represented among a population, over time, with successive generations, inbreeding would begin to run rampant, as well as the myriad diseases that came with it. This was a major problem in the Urheimat, whose strict genetic purity laws resulted in the complete homogenization of its population, with virtually all Urheimat citizens belonging to around ten quadrants.

The way the Urheimat counteracted this widespread inbreeding was by introducing fresh genetic stock to its population, with 'unseeded humans' (i.e. humans that emerged naturally on isolated worlds) being the preferred source of this genetic variety. Such had been the case with the humans of Old Earth, whose children had been stolen by the elven invaders to be sold to the Urheimat's gene merchants, to be placed in foster families and to become assimilated.

Up until the discovery of the Ratden Log, no one could have truly known with accuracy how many such children had been taken. It had been written by Ifriq Laudiano on orders from Anteo Perem Svart in the days of the War of Vengeance. Then, it had been taken from the Nargothrond archives by those that would later become the dark elves, just as the Allied forces had arrived in the Nargothrond system, as the first of the fleeing Svart departed their doomed capital to live out the rest of their existence on the run.

It had come into the possession of Cantor Perem Abrasax during this time. The elf would become one of the two co-leaders of the dark elves, together with Elafas Perem Goujnar, his only surviving cousin. While Elafas had led the dark elves' espionage activities, Cantor had focused much more on the diplomatic aspirations of their people. Laur knew that Cantor had petitioned the Tribes of Elvandom and even the Urheimat for assistance and had even attempted to obtain asylum for his people in Shangri, Avalon and who knew how many other worlds, only to be rejected time and time again.

It had been from Allied sympathizers in Shangri that Laur had first learned of the existence of the Ratden Log. Cantor had attempted to blackmail the Peacekeeper by threatening to divulge to the Republican Alliance that the stolen children of Terra had passed through Shangri on their way to the Urheimat. Unbeknownst to Cantor, the Peacekeeper had been the one to inform the Orcs of Vigilant of the possible atrocities committed by the Svart within their fief in the Milky Way Galaxy, thus spurring them into action and leading to Terra's salvation during the Hour of Twilight, as the orcs had arrived to save the embattled humans from complete annihilation.

Masterful he is.

The Peacekeeper had managed to keep Shangri independent for thousands-upon-thousands of years. At first, it had been easy, since Shangri had been located far outside the Urheimat's reach. However, as the Great Leviathan had pushed ever onwards across the borders of its domain, it had come to border the City of Shangri itself. Yet, the Peacekeeper had managed to navigate both the hungering embrace of its voracious neighbour and the pressures of Shangri's tumultuous internal politics. The City still stood free, wedged between the Republican Alliance and the Urheimat.

Playing both sides. As Shangri has always done.

The Peacekeeper claimed no knowledge of the children's current whereabouts, yet the Laur had always suspected that there might still be someone in Shangri who did. The Ratden Log had revealed to him who that someone might have been.

'Paragon Shipping'.

His eyes drifted to the right side of the page in front of him, where he saw the name of the Paragon Shipping executive that had signed the customs papers allowing the Svart ships of *Rylol*, *Gojer* and *Pentaper* access into the Port of Shangri, where they had transferred their 'cargo' to the possession of the Shangri branch of the Urheimat's Trading Company.

Quint of Carth-Fountainhead – Inspections Officer First Class.
Whoever goes to Shangri should find him first.

Laur let out an angry breath of air as he sat back in his seat, making it squeak slightly. His ears twitched as he realised that, up until his chair had made that small noise, he had been sitting in complete silence. The party downstairs must have finished and all was quiet. It had likely been quiet for some time now.

He looked outside, seeing the black of the star-crossed Terran night sky turn to the dark blue of morning. He looked for his watch, an old black Breitling Cosmonaute gifted to him by Mikhail, and checked to see that it was early morning, naught but an hour from the moment when he would be departing for the meeting on Tristan da Cunha. There he would deliver the Ratden Log to whoever would take up the position of Ambassador of the Republican Alliance to the Free City of Shangri.

Is Feng up for the task?

Laur closed his eyes, telling himself not to have such thoughts.

He had done enough. It didn't matter that Feng might be too rigid for what had to be done to –

No!!! Stop!

His men needed him! He had neglected them for too long! He had pushed them for too long. Silvia, Nick, Gigi, Bojana, Iosip, Bor and Lejla were just the survivors. Everyone else was dead and they had died because of *his* failures, *his* neglect, *his* plans and, yes, even *his* intention. Every other Legion had taken a break. Every other Legion had taken the time needed to assure its unity, if it meant division through sundering. The Marines, the Jaegers, *hell*, even the Ghazis!

Every other commander that had found themselves in his situation had taken the time needed to set their house in order. While the Ghazis had taken the time they had needed to reorganize themselves *and* Arabia, the Hajduks were away hunting across the stars. When the Khevsurs turned back towards Terra and settled millennia old quarrels and qualms across the Caucasus Mountains, the Hajduks had delegated the task to lesser men. While the Akali finally turned to healing themselves and their sister legions, the Hajduks had exhausted themselves in a frenzy of obsession and intrigue.

Ruben? Ruben and his Sayeret? Ruben had splintered the Ashkenazis into the Maccabians of America, rebuilt Jerusalem, turned his men into the premier security force on Terra and overseen the security of Kralizec. The Hajduks had merely been a back-up, yet they had still given more than would have been thought possible. Ruben... Ruben would have been worthy of Shangri! Just that he was too smart and too well adjusted to embark on such an endeavour.

Feng? Feng and the Jinyiwei? A brilliant Legion they had become and likely the most versatile. Tried in battle? Yes; upon the battlefields of the Milky Way, Andromeda and Triangulum, the latter of which being such a resounding testament to their valour that it had earned Feng the rank of Marshal of Terra. Experienced in the subtle art of subterfuge, espionage and cloak-and-dagger diplomacy? Of course... but *why*? Would it be in their interest to go to Shangri?

Feng was patient. He had a clear head and he protected the sanctity of that clear head. He had combed the entirety of Old China for men and women of exceptional ability, even by Terran standards and he had safeguarded them! With Feng, gone were the days of massive disregard for Han casualties. The Jinyiwei were cautious in the extreme.

Is that a good thing? Wouldn't Shangri require more brashness than anything Feng could muster-up?

Laur angrily got up from his desk and began pacing in anger. From time to time, he would leer at the notebook on his desk. *If only I hadn't been right about your existence, contents and purpose, I might have been spared of this bullshit!*

Tomasz Ashaver and his damned Superman island be damned! It was so far away, he could fly around the world *in the other direction* and get there at the same time if he left now and took the short way.

So, that's what he did. He got fully dressed, packed a suitcase with every single item pertaining to the *Stolen* children of Old Earth, including the Ratden Log, and went on his balcony to where his car was parked and took off.

He drove fast as he flew northwards, reaching speeds of almost eight thousand kilometres per hour at times, as he fought to make the journey just difficult enough for him to be forced to focus entirely upon it. He didn't want to think about the alternatives. He didn't want to think about what was going through his mind. He wanted to get to Ashaver as fast as he could, whilst still arriving at the agreed upon time, and he did just that. He approached the islands of Saint Helena from the south, after having flown past the Southern Polar Shield, just five minutes shy of the agreed upon time.

Ashaver and his Old Guard didn't refer to their Citadel by the name of Tristan da Cunha. Instead, they called their fortress 'Angbad', a bastardization of the name of the fictional fortress of 'Angband', the home of Tolkien's dark lord: Morgoroth. Much like how one might imagine, Angbad was a dark place, at least on the outside. The sinister towers of the fortress jutting from the dark blue ocean were just what one might expect from the abode of the undead. A mix of smooth dark grey stone and dark spikes marked the Citadel of the Old Guard, shaped as one single monolithic construct.

Thirteen concentric platforms made up the levels of Angband, the smallest of which extended a full kilometre into the sky. Ashaver had insisted that the central tower possess blades of sharp steel running along its edges, with eight long shafts protruding past the pinnacle, forcing a resemblance to the towers of Barad-dûr or Isengard.

He sure loves his Lord of the Rings, that's for sure...

Laur knew it was all a facade, as the citadel was quite homely on the inside. The dour outside demeanour was merely a way of keeping up appearances. Inside, the Old Guard tended vast underground gardens. They brewed their own beers, wines, soft liquers and hard liquors. They also made their own cheeses, hams and jams. Many a chamber of Angbad had been taken over by some artsy Old Guard with an affinity towards painting, sculpting or even pottery. The sounds of those musically inclined Old Guards met the constant sounds of gladiatorial combat taking place in the Pit of Tristan, once the caldera of the island's volcano.

Ashaver himself was a man of many hobbies. Pop often found himself annoyed by his old friend's frivolousness, as he jumped from one strange passion to another. Right now, Ashaver was (hopefully) nearing the end of three-year long love affair with football which, thankfully, would some come to an end on account of the Apocalypse that had taken place almost half-a-century before. He told himself that he would indulge Ashaver as best as he could once he started ranting about Manchester City and Pep Guardiola.

It's all I have to do. It's all I'm here for. Once I do that, maybe I could start watching some sports myself. Or films. I never saw Breaking Bad. I can do that!

Laur knew Angbad's hangar well and as he parked his shuttle, his eyes were drawn to the other vessels within. There were plenty of Old Guard vehicles, as one might expect. There were also three other Terran vehicles.

Ruben, Shoshanna and Feng.

Then there was another shuttle. A shuttle that was not Terran.

Braca.

Uh-oh...

The orc was Ashaver's best friend and that alone explained his presence here. *Tomasz must have asked him to advise on the selection process. He was once Ambassador to Shangri, after all.*

Laur's relationship with Cingeto Braca had always been strained, primarily due to the orc's character and Laur's actions. They had never clashed openly, yet Braca had always regarded him with suspicion, dismissal and, occasionally, cold hostility. Laur himself had never really figured out why the orc disliked him so much, yet he was quite certain that it had something to do with certain strategic choices Laur had made over the years.

His participation in the Rivendell Massacre.

Poisoning the water supply of Eriador...

Sending political adversaries to the front lines to curb dissent...

Public executions in Nargothrond after the formal signing of the instruments of surrender...

The Last Fitna...

Espionage on the Vigilant itself... Which came in handy during the Bloodbrother Crisis...

The list went on-and-on.

Laur's repertoire of tactics was full of actions that were thoroughly un-orcish in both their barbarism and their callousness. He was not the only Terran to regard war crimes as viable military stratagems, yet Braca and the other orcs had always seemed to single him out. Their dislike of him had been subdued by his actions during the Bloodbrother Crisis, when the mind-controlled orcs of the Vigilant and the Ersatz had attacked Luna and laid siege to Terra itself. Laur had led the defence of Luna and had managed to fend off the attack thanks to his knowledge of the Vigilant's weaknesses. Knowledge he had attained after decades of covertly gathering intelligence on the orcs, which had, up until that point, been Terra's most stalwart allies.

What the hell would he have to contribute? Everything pertaining to Shangri and what needs to be done is by no means his specialty. Tomasz must be feeling guilty about Ratden. He's staying close to Braca, hoping he can wipe the blood of his hands by clutching at the orc's white robes.

'Hello, Laur!' Sam Metzen greeted him as he got out of his car. The American was one of a handful of Old Guards that could be seen in the hangar.

No Alex Demetrian, however. Good. 'Hello, Sam! All good?' Laur actually liked Sam. He was a bit of a cunt, but at least he had maintained his sanity, which was something admirable for an Old Guard.

'Yeah, just got back from Mexico!' Sam smiled as he shook Laur's hand.

'Ah! Nice! Vacation?'

'What? No. I was visiting Esmeralda.'

Oh, shit.

'You know? Marco's widow!'

Of course I know. Fuck. I fucked up there! 'Oh, yes! I see... How is she? How's Esteban?' Esteban was Marco's son.

'Well, she's as you'd expect. Esteban's a little better, though it clearly got to him. The other kids are... well... you know...'

'I see...' *They don't really care that their father died a hero. Good for them. It'll build character. Marco always spoiled them.* 'Well, it's just the way things are!'

'Yeah... Yeah...' Sam rubbed his nose a little and seemed to stifle something. His voice shook a little as he spoke. 'Well! You're a little late so... best be on your way! They're all probably in his office.'

'Yes! Yes, they likely are by now!' *I'm not going to justify being late to you! You all tell Tomasz everything! I wish my guys were like you. They always feel compelled to cherry-pick the news I get and I hate having to go digging!*

He bid his goodbyes to Sam, as well as some of the other nearby Old Guards and made his way to Ashaver's office, which lay on one of the middle levels. He reached an elevator and sat within, admiring one of the greenhouses it overlooked. He paused to inspect the livestock within.

Black Angus cattle and... mangalița pigs... someone's really got time on their hands around here!

I should raise some sheep. I always thought them to be quite annoying but I always liked the cheese... I could use the fleeces to decorate Bâlea...

Laur's farming plans were interrupted as the elevator stopped unexpectedly. He checked the floor they were on.

Third floor. The office is on the eighth.

Instinctively, his hand drifted towards his concealed weapon, a Beretta model pistol. He had two other pistols on him, one hidden, one not, as well as six blades and two explosives. He didn't like being unprepared and wouldn't be caught unawares even somewhere as safe as Angbad.

He took a deep breath as the doors opened.

Well... that didn't take long.

Cingeto Braca was massive. Orcs stood at around two and a quarter meters tall, though orcish leaders were instructed to grow around an inch in height for every rank gained. Thus, Braca stood at around two and a half meters tall, given that he was essentially one of the highest ranking orcs of his clan. Like all orcs, he was a gigantic mass of hard muscle, bone and sinew. He had a friendly, yet serious face, with great big bushy eyebrows that almost obstructed his forehead when he stood at full height, towering over the average Terran. His bright hazel eyes stood nestled by the heavy brows and bulging lower eyelids typical of his race, though Braca's eyes were particularly piercing, with his eyes seemingly being somewhat larger than that of his kin.

Laur noted how the orc's skin was currently a dark green, meaning that he had likely been somewhere with a lot of greenery. Given that it was still morning, it could only mean that he had spent the night in one of the Old Guard's greenhouses. A quick glance at the orc's gigantic hands revealed several containers nestled within a picnic basket he held in his left hand.

'Laur.' The orc's voice was deep and oddly melodic for one of his race. Laur had always felt that the orcs carried an accent that was a mix of Persian and Russian when they spoke in English, though Cingeto's odd musicality added an extra... *Mediterranean* twist to his words.

'Cingeto!' he responded, nodding his head. *I'll shake his hand after he extends it.*

Sure enough, Cingeto put forth one of his gargantuan hands, meeting Laur's in a firm handshake.

The orc walked past him towards the back of the elevator and began surveying the livestock below. Silently.

Well... making it awkward now, are we? No need for that. I'm dealing with enough bullshit as it is! He glanced at the picnic basket. 'You're testing out the local produce?'

He saw Braca glance towards the basket. After a few, typically orcish, awkward moments, he spoke. 'Yes.'

With that, he reached towards the basket with his right hand and pulled out a jar of... *are those Maraschino cherries?*

Demetrian...must be Alex Demetrian...

'I see Alex's harvest is in,' Laur observed.

'Several of his harvests came in. Alex is quite proud of them! I find them enjoyable as they are now, yet I understand that it is customary to serve them with mixed alcohols or sweet deserts.' The orc reached into the basket once more, placing the jar of preserved cherries back inside and moving closer to Laur, revealing the basket's other contents.

That's... that's ice-cream... a cheesecake... a bottle of... tequila... orange juice... that's probably grenadine –

'I never liked you.'

The orc's voice wasn't menacing. Braca's voice never really was. Yet, it was firm and it carried with it an assurance that made it clear that he spoke from the heart. Braca did not like to hurt people. He didn't even like threatening people. His words never sought to put down, only to uplift or, at least, to keep level.

The orc once more took a step towards the Terran General, coming less than two feet away from his face, as looked down upon him.

Laur didn't feel threatened. No one would dare harm a Terran on Terra. Let alone a Terran General in a Terran Citadel. Let alone Laur Pop in Angbad.

Moreover, of all people, it wouldn't be Cingeto Braca who would commit such an act.

Thus, Laur felt more intrigued than threatened. He was shocked, yes, though his curiosity swiftly overpowered his surprise.

Braca continued. 'I never liked you because you were the worst and the fact that you were also one of the best never gave me much comfort. While everyone else around you was like a tree sprouting leaves in a forest wreathed by wildfire, you were always like a vine, clinging at the trunks of those stronger than you, never truly able to stand on your own and hold upon yourself the weight of others. I never liked you because you tainted your brothers and sisters with the darkness of your own twisted ways and your own troubled mind. I never liked you because you found no rest until you could see only threats in the wills of others.'

The elevator let out a soft *ping!* As they reached the eighth floor.

'I never liked you because you always had a talent for bringing out the worst in those around you to suit your own needs, hiding behind your gift of seeing that which lies within the shadows long before there was anything within the dark to see!'

The elevator doors opened and Braca moved in slightly closer, to the point where Laur could feel the heat of his words upon his cheeks.

'But most of all, I don't like you because you made me *hate*. You made me *hate* you and I *hate* you because, in your own abhorrent ways, you were always able to do exactly that which *I* never could and you forced me to accept that. You forced me to accept the fact that I could never protect anyone the way you can and, without men like you, there would always be threats that could not be face!'

Braca drew back. 'Because the only way you can see the threats is by *being* someone like *you!*' He moved slowly towards the elevator doors, taking great care to not disturb the contents of his basket. ' And I would never wish such a thing upon my vilest foe!"

'Why now?'

The orc paused midstride upon hearing Laur's words, before coming to a complete halt and turning his head slightly.

'Why do you tell me this now?' Laur repeated.

Braca turned and looked him dead in the eye. 'It is not right to see something that causes harm in another and to let it be so without offering aid, just because it suits your own purposes. I understand that you are finally taking the time needed to rest and recreate. In that time, you can become a better person, but only if you accept your own nature. I do not know who you are. I know only that which I can see and I have done what is just and told you what I see. Now, as you enter a period of what can be reflection, I am doing for you that which, perhaps, you might have done for yourself, eventually.'

The orcs brow furrowed as he picked the words. 'I am not *giving* you something! I am *taking* something from you! From now on, you can never say that no one told you what you are. Someone has. From his moment onwards, you cannot say you never had the truth before you! What you will do with the truth is in your power alone. There are no more elves for you to blame for who you have become and behind whose actions you may hide your own wickedness! Though you may never escape them, you may no longer claim to be their victim. From now on, you will be forced to take responsibility for your choices and accept the outcomes as your own.'

'You will have to, for it shall be *you* who will have to live with *yourself*! In the silence that you will now face, you will now have no other choice than to decide who it is that you now wish to be!' He paused and the silence hung between them for some time.

'Come, Laur Pop, our presence is expected!'

Laur followed him silently all the way to Ashaver's office.

Braca knocked quaintly at the door and waited for Tomasz Ashaver's voice to allow him in. Inside, their host got up from his seat, arms stretched outwards to his sides, a look of joy upon his face. Across from him sat two men and one woman.

Ruben Zaslani, General of the Sayeret, and the closest thing to a true peer to him. It had been with him that Laur had first laid forth the outline for what needed to happen in Shangri.

Xi Feng, General of the Jinyiwei, and former Warchief of Terra. A man of extreme reliability, intelligence and discipline. It would be he who would have to go to Shangri and do what had to be done.

Shoshanna Adler, General of the Marines and current Warchief of Terra. A woman made of steel and silver, for which he cared for more than he had ever allowed himself to admit. Shosho, they called her. A woman who, in the last year, had done more for the wellbeing of their people than Laur could ever had expected of a mere mortal.

Shosho smiled at him from her seat across from Ashaver. He saw something in her eyes that had always been there and that made him look away.

'Ah!!! Cingeto! Laur! I was just telling them about that AC Milan team that lost to fucking Liverpool in Ista–'

'I have decided that I will be going to Shangri!' The words flew out of Laur's mouth and settled like snow upon the room before him.

Shosho froze.

Ashaver attempted to straighten up and take on a more dignified posture, yet succeeded only in knocking back his office chair. Startling almost everyone in the room except Laur, who had seen the chair begin its fall.

Braca slowly took out the jar of cherries and placed it on a nearby table.

Ruben's expression, usually as immobile as a cliff face, slowly gave way to a smile, as the Israeli General closed his eyes.

As Braca placed the jar upon the table, it let out the softest of *clinks!* and, yet, they all heard it.

Including Feng, who let out the most unexpected of chuckles, as he let loose a breath of relief.

They all turned to look at him, as the Han General laughed nervously and pushed his hair back.

He saw them staring at him and let out another breath of air before speaking.

'Well, what can I say? It's probably the first time he's ever walked into a room and given me good news!'

Chapter III

Encore une Fois

'And what did Feng have to say about it?' Silvia asked, about twenty seconds after Nick had asked the very same question.

Pop, who was sitting with his hands clasped before him, gave her a somewhat irritated look before leaning back, gripping the armrests of his seat, as he lay there, puffing his chest. He had already answered Nick by telling him that Feng had been relieved that, for once, he had not been the bearer of bad news. His face made it quite clear that he was very much irritated that Silvia was making him reformulate his answer.

Pop let out a loud exhale before rephrasing his previous answer, 'He said that he was only going to do it because no one else would or would!' Pop tapped his fingers on his armrests, his look blank as he, once more, seemed to recall Feng's words. 'He said he looks forward to a much needed and well deserved break for himself and his men. He also said that he had never really understood why I had been so adamant about *not* going to Shangri.'

Silvia couldn't help herself. 'Feng is a wise man.' *None of us really understood. We just all hoped you'd go through with it. Now you've done what you love so much to do: you take from us that which you miraculously offered mere moments before.*

Nick must have felt the gathering storm, as he decided to change course. 'So, how are we gonna do it?'

Pop glanced towards him, before returning his gaze to Silvia's. After a few more tense moments, he leaned forward and seemed to gather his thoughts. 'We move forward with the new recruitment drive, as planned. We have an entire pipeline of new recruits, as well as the ones from the last influx. We also need the new centurions to have time to adjust to their new roles and some of them, together with a large number of veteran Hajduks, will be staying on Terra to help assimilate the new blood coming in.'

'Bor will stay behind with all the Slovenes and assume command of the Hajduks that will remain on Terra. Bojana, Gigi, Lejla and Iosip will take one hundred of their veterans each and join us..'

'Lejla will dock the *Doina* in the Shangri Harbour and guard both the ship and our diplomatic pier. Gigi will take over the barracks we operate in the Shangri Military District and fulfil the joint military exercise commitments we've made to the Shangri Colonial Constabulary. Bojana will take up residence in the Estate in Belagravia and take over command of the Chamber of Commerce and Iosip will take the Sanjak Manor in Borbakhan, where he will assume the role of *Emissary of Terra to the City of Shangri*.'

'We three will take the Alliance Embassy in Convent Square.' He turned to Silvia. 'You are to handpick one hundred and ninety men. You know the skills that will be required, so you'll know who to bring.'

Silvia nodded. *Of course. You want me to pick the most Hajduk of the Hajduks.*

Pop turned to Nick. 'You are to bring ten men, but you'll also take direct command of ninety of Silvia's men.'

Of course he will. That's how we always work. She didn't even have to look at Nick to confirm. The Romanians and the Kalo were the most porous of the Hajduks, with their command structures often merging and their units frequently interweaving over the years.

Their General once more leaned back in his seat and started looking around the room. The three of them found themselves in the Council Chamber of Bâlea and the day was late in the afternoon. Pop had returned from Tristan merely a quarter of an hour before and had immediately summoned the Hajduk leadership present within the Citadel to his chambers. In practice, this amounted to Silvia and Nick, since everyone else had departed for their home Nations. Silvia had known that Nick had won the bet the moment she had seen their General's distant eyes stare blankly towards her as he had gotten out of his shuttle, the gears of scheming, plotting and planning already turning within him.

'Are we going alone?' *Like we have so often?*

'Not entirely. We'll be bringing Technowolf and Basenji along, though they will primarily be working as liaisons to the local populace.' Pop paused and scratched his temples.

'Tech *and* Basenji?' *He's uncertain and it's clear why.* 'Two remani?' she asked.

Nick scoffed.

Pop's brow furrowed. 'You have a problem with remani, Silvia?'

Don't try this shit with me! 'Oh, I don't. But the remani on Shangri will.' *Having only Terrans and remani make up the delegation is going to raise eyebrows.* 'The Single Star Pride? They're the main remani group, right? The Single Star Pride who've been acting as enforcers for the Peacekeeper for what? Three *thousand* years? The Single Star Pride who pushed for *neutrality* in the War of Vengeance?'

Pop's cheeks twisted as he readied a reply.

No, fuck you! 'And that's just the main group! There are – what? – a handful of other minor prides? All of which see the Black Knight Pride as pariahs? And that's just the remani! There are *tens of millions* of Libra ursai on Shangri, all of which hate *our* Libra ursai –'

' – They don't even call themselves 'Libra' anymore...' Nick added.

'To not even mention Senoyu remnants, Aesir exiles, Fili bast, orcish rhonin, the high elf asylum seekers, the low elf migrants and all the other minorities who either hate, fear or wish to have nothing to do with the Black Knight remani, Terrans or the Republican Alliance?'

'You forgot the murine of Nimkalabeth...' Pop pointed out, his mouth twisted in an annoyed snarl.

Pipe-dreams now? 'How could I forget that our primary sympathizers in the City of Shangri are ratmen with no money?

'They are the second largest minority after the humans?!' Pop's tone and expression were those of an ignorant child answering a simple question. 'Potentially the largest, if our intelligence is correct.'

He is boiling, however. 'The largest minority without political influence, economic power or social standing in Shangri!' Silvia could feel her temples beating to the rhythm of her furious heart. *How dare he give us hope and then throw us into the shit?* She smiled bitterly and continued, 'I hear they also have pigeons in Shangri, are they also one of our key –'

'I SAID WE ARE GOING GODDAMMIT!' Pop shot up from his seat and banged his fist on the table. *And now he has burst.*

He starred Silvia down for a moment, before glancing at Nick, who looked away. His furious stare turned to meet Silvia's. He opened his mouth for a moment, then breathed in, his teeth showing and the corner of his mouth twisting.

Say it! Say it! Make me feel guilty! Do it! It's so easy, you can't help yourself...

'It could've been *you* in some container on some dock in Shangri!'

Of course. Of course you'd say that! You manipulative bastard!

Pop tilted his head towards Nick. 'It could've been *him* too!'

Their General glared at them for a few more seconds before returning to his seat. He spent a few moments composing himself before returning to his orders.

'Can I bring Drogon?' Nick's serious voice asked comically.

Silvia couldn't help but smile. *The dear oaf... trying to defuse the situation. He knows the answer is -*

'*No*! You are not to bring Drogon!' Pop's rage had flashed into an old trauma, before turning into annoyance.

It worked: I'm smiling and he's just his usual irritated self. The confrontation is over

'Nor any other wyvern or drakonid of any kind!' Pop's eyes ventured towards one of the empty seats at the Hajduk's table. 'And Bojana can't bring her rook...' Pop seemed to be thinking of something he couldn't remember.

Silvia knew exactly what that something was.

'*Perce.*' *That's the bird's name: Perce.*

Pop's eyes met Silvia's. He began to look for something once more, though this time not within his own memory, but within Silvia's eyes. Once more, she knew what that something was. *I am not going to move a single muscle on my face! I don't want you to think that*

I am agreeing to this!

But, I'll do as you bid. That's what the Hajduks will need right now.

'Yes. Perce!' Pop's shoulders relaxed, seemingly content with her acknowledgement of his command. 'No wyverns! No rooks! No nothing! *No beasts of any nature*! No tanks either! Other than the twenty on the *Doina*. We are also not allowed to bring shuttles on Shangri, due to their stupid traffic regulations, so you'll have to speak with Zaza and bring three hundred automobiles, at least forty of which must be twelve-person vans. Electric engines, with a combustion engines as a back-up. We need them armoured and full of hidden compartments.'

'Arsenal?' Silvia asked.

'I leave that to you and the others. But bear in mind that we are not allowed firearms of any size or nature, since the City enforces very strict gun laws which we don't want to break. Carrying blades is also prohibited, but the Shangri police does not check anyone with a diplomatic passport. Also, the embassy will never be checked: their judges cannot issue warrants for diplomatic locations. But the other locations could be checked if shit pops off!'

'Of course!' Silvia paused as she considered what other information was essential.

'A week.' Pop answered before she could even ask the question.

'More than enough.' *There is something else, however.* 'You will tell the others?' *Because that I won't fucking do. At least be a real man and stand behind this shit!*

'I will send messengers summoning them within the hour. We'll have a commander's meeting tomorrow evening and a general assembly in four days time.' Pop got up from his seat and made his way to the stairs that led to his private chambers. 'You're dismissed.'

Silvia and Nick got up from their seats and had almost reached the door when Pop slammed the door to the stairway behind him.

Nick leaned close and spoke softly. 'You owe me ten dollars.'

'The money is in your bottom drawer, next to your Pokémon card collection.'

Nick paused as he was closing the door to the chamber behind them. 'You knew?'

'You made a convincing argument.' *And I hate you for it!*

'Huh, I did?' Nick seemed confused.

Silvia remembered that her colleague sometimes forgot things when he drank too much. 'Yes, after Rumen's promotion party.'

Recollection seemed to slowly dawn on him. 'Ah... I hate it when I'm right!'

'Me too...'

Over the next day, the Hajduk leadership begrudgingly converged upon Bâlea. Gambling debts were settled, as the disappointed losers paid their debts to the equally upset winners.

Bor had initially been pleased to be left out, yet upon realising that the task of inducting over fifteen hundred new Hajduks would fall upon him, he quickly realised that he would be spending the next year wishing that he was on active deployment.

Iosip took the news in stride, confessing that he had been disappointed to learn that Pop had changed his mind, yet ultimately pointing out that Shangri was not the worst deployment the Hajduks had been on.

Lejla received the news with stoicism and the Hajduk messenger that had brought the news to Gigi had discovered the Shqiptari Hajduks already mustering for deployment. Their commander had apparently decided to prepare for a mobilization even before Pop had overturned his own decision. *Gigi's age shows in his wisdom.*

Bojana was, as always, the most vocal critic of her General's plan, resulting in Pop having to call her personally and argue with her over the phone, which was something neither of them enjoyed. Nevertheless, she attended the leadership meeting at Bâlea and her Serbs joined her after a symbolic five days, in solidarity with their commander's protests.

Like she always did, Silvia set about putting her General's plans in motion. Each Avenger Legion was supposed to be self-reliant, independent, and, thus, capable of operating for long periods of time away from the bountiful resources of the greater Terran military or those of their Allies. The Hajduks were one of the few Legions who took things a bit further, as their constituent national contingents had a great degree of autonomy. Many of the Hajduks leadership were accustomed to operating far away from the watchful gaze of their General. Truth be told, the only assets they formally shared were their name, their Avenger Legion Crest, their motto, their song, the *Doina*, the Bâlea Citadel and Laur Pop himself. Going even more steps further, the contingents had chosen to delegate specific activities needed for the proper function of their Legion to specific units.

The Bosniaks crewed, piloted and guarded the *Doina*, on account of their leader's penchant for intergalactic spaceflight. They also maintained the Hajduk's tanks and artillery, primarily due to some Old Earth joke that Laur Pop had taken too far and Lejla had gone along with.

The Serbs acted as cavalrymen, scouts and beastmasters, and were the primary caretakers of the Hajduk's bestiary and stables, mainly due to Bojana's love of wildlife.

The Slovenes handled the administrative issues, the Croats took care of medical (*and technological*, now that Carlos was gone) issues, the Shqiptari managed the arsenal and the Romanians... oversaw logistics (among other things), which meant that Silvia was responsible for packing everyone's luggage and making sure no one forgot anything.

With Lejla, she readied the *Doina* for their departure, making sure that the ship was well supplied and well armed and together they selected the vehicles required for their tenure on Shangri. With Gigi, she selected the arsenal that would be required. Then, together with a task force of some of those Hajduks particularly skilled in smuggling, tradecraft and contraband, she set about stashing enough guns, blades, munitions, armour and explosives to run a decent insurgency for a few years. She also hid seventeen thousand Chihuahua-class nuclear warheads throughout the *Doina* and within the engine blocks of several vehicles.

She convened with Iosip and filled the *Doina's* hangars with enough food and drink to feed ten thousand Hajduks for ten years. Terrans were picky eaters as it were and the Hajduks were famous among the Avenger Legions for the high expectations they had when it came to rations. They were also famous for their love of alcohol, tobacco, as well as an assortment of other psychoactive substances. Silvia knew 'Hajduk mathematics' (as they were jokingly called):

Six hundred men for three hundred sixty days (plus forty days for travel and other unexpected delays), that's three hundred thousand litres of hard alcohol (plus a million litres of soda, fruit juice and sparkling water), two hundred thousand packs of Terran tobacco cigarettes (plus two tons of rolling tobacco and four cubic meters of rolling paper), seven tons of cocaine and two whole storage containers filled with an assortment of other substances. She also made sure to pack enough pervitin to make a tree want to get up and go for a run and enough opium to put the sun to sleep.

She had also followed Pop's instructions and had stashed several hundred metric tons of contraband throughout the Doina. A hundred psychoactive stimulants, uppers, downers and everything in between, as well as a broad selection of psychedelic substances now lay buried in secret chambers within their ship's walls. Many were of Terran origin; some were procured from their allies; all were illegal within the City of Shangri. These substances, together with a whole host of luxury goods and precious materials, were to be used as bribes. Other Republican Ambassadors had used this tactic to curry favour among the city's elite before, yet Laur Pop was clearly planning on taking things to a whole new level.

This as much she could tell, as she watched her men hide their most dangerous asset within the bowels of one of their vehicles, disguising it as the engine block of a Mercedes S-class.

They called it a 'Hogwarts'.

'It's done,' Cosmin told her. 'No scanner will be able to find it as long as it's turned off.'

'It has both the matrix and the generator?' she asked, just to make sure.

Cosmin smiled a worried smile. 'What's a gun without a bullet and bullet with a gun?'

I don't know, but I know that it's all highly illegal in Shangri…

With less than a few hours to go before their departure, Silvia found herself in the Council Chamber together with Pop. The last of the General's belongings lay packed inside a small Terran military briefcase on the table before him. The bulk of his luggage was now inside a shipping container the size of a small shuttle, already loaded onto the *Doina*, as the great ship lay docked within the great hangar within the mountain beneath them.

'Four cubic meters per man?' he asked.

'Yes. Plus another two for centurions, legates and yourself,' she replied.

'Discretionary space, not mandatory equipment and materials?'

There he goes again with the double – no! – triple checking, at this point.

'Yes! The four and, respectively, *six* cubic meters are for discretionary items, not for mandatory ones. Those are all separate and leaves us with three thousand cubic meters of storage as a back-up.' *In case we come back with more than we left with… which wouldn't be a first.*

'Good! Are all the men ready to board?'

'Lejla finished boarding yesterday evening. Iosip and his men finished boarding four hours ago. Gigi and his men are doing their final checks. Bojana is still loading and so are Radu, Cosmin and Ela, who are overseeing the last of the loading. The rest of my men are already onboard.' *Nick is chillin' with Gigi, but that's fine since I've packed all his things and got them on-board this morning with my things.*

'Good!' Pop paused. He hadn't been looking at her, as he had been selecting the last of the documents he would be taking with him. He stopped to look up at her.

Maybe to ask me if I've said my goodbyes to the kids at the orphanage?

'Technowolf and Basenji have arrived?' *Of course not, that would be too human.*

'An hour and a half ago. They already boarded.'

'Good!' Just as Pop finished his selection, they heard the sound of Bosniak music ring out from outside, followed by several load roars. 'Lejla is firing up the ship, I see.'

Silvia smiled slightly. 'Yes.'

'Great!' Pop packed the documents tightly together, then reached out into one of his safes and pulled out one final document.

A ledger. A log, to be precise.

I'm already beginning to dread that thing.

He placed the Ratden Log, together with the rest of his most valuable files, inside his briefcase.

'Silvia,' he began. 'You've done great!'

I always do.

'And I want you to know one thing before we embark on this… endeavour.'

Oh?

'I know you didn't want to go to Shangri. I know that you still think going is a bad idea. I also know that you think it's a bad idea to endlessly postpone our well deserved break; not out of concern for *your* own survival or well being, but for that of our men. I also know you disapproved of the manner in which the decision was made.'

I disapprove of the way <u>you</u> made the decision.

'I want you to know that, in part, I agree.'

Oh… would ya look at that! She hadn't expected that.

'I also want you to know that –'

' – That shuttle is unscheduled.' *The sky should be clear. Any shuttle would be unscheduled.*

She saw Pop look her in the eye for a second, before turning his eyes towards what she had seen.

A shuttle had flown in from the south, descending upon the Bâlea Citadel. Silvia recognized it as a Terran shuttle. As it neared, she recognized it as a black Mercedes Upsilon, a carrier shuttle, typically used to carry a mix of people and cargo, just like the shuttles they were just now loading into the *Doina*.

'Îngeraș, whose is that?' she asked her operator, just as the shuttle neared the landing bay located just outside the Council Chamber balcony.

'Who is that?' Pop asked her, just as he got up and made his way to the balcony doors.

Îngeraș told Silvia who it was, though she couldn't believe it. She paused right in the balcony door as Pop made his way towards the shuttle now expertly parked at the end of a long causeway that led to Pop's personal landing bay. The General also stopped, just as the shuttle's door opened.

Captain Mira al-Sayid was dressed all in black. She bore no weaponry upon her person, bar only a look of stone-faced determination as she got out of her shuttle. The wind picked up suddenly, lifting up the long black cloak the young Arab Captain had brought with her to the cold peaks of the Carpathians, and revealing a black Terran uniform beneath, with no insignia bar her captaincy lines. It was a shipsuit of the type Terrans typically wore when aboard their spaceships. Silvia and Pop themselves were dressed in similar gear.

Oh, no...

Mira walked across the causeway towards the Romanian General, though her gaze remained fixated upon the Council Chambers behind him. Sure enough, she walked right past the dark shape of Laur Pop, who turned his gaze to follow her and his expression betrayed several emotions.

Anger. Curiosity. Worry. Dread.

Silvia had just enough time to take note of her General's reaction before Mira was upon her.

The young Captain had always been striking. Silvia had first laid eyes upon her when she had been naught but less than an hour old. A small thing she had been, wrapped in warm Keshik blankets and covered in her mother's blood. It had been in the cold wastes before the Antarctic Shield that they had first met. Silvia remembered now the events of Hellsbreach and she recalled the image of Manda Khan carrying the infant across the ice towards her and her fellow Hajduks. It was a scene burned into her mind, melded with the weeping of Daw al-Fajr, who had arrived to spirit away the child, only to return her to her father's family in Mecca less than a week later.

Mira had always possessed a remarkable beauty, even as a small child. Silvia knew that the girl had never altered her aesthetics and had grown into the woman nature had intended her to be. She had long, thick and jet black hair, which she kept perfectly straightened at all times. Her face was mostly her mother's, which was to say that it was beautiful, though one might quickly lose sight of it upon seeing her eyes.

Dark and stormy almond eyes. *Her father's eyes.*

Eyes which were now starring right at her.

'Hello, Silvia!' she said, her tone serious, yet also somewhat cheerful. Silvia could also feel a deep sadness beneath her words or, perhaps, she was merely hearing the echoes of the young girl's wails on Ratden, as she clutched the shattered remains of her friend.

The German boy, Thomas Muller, her charge during Kralizec.

'Hello, Mira!' she responded, as she moved out of the doorway and allowed their guest entrance into the Council Chamber of the Hajduks.

They didn't touch.

The last time they had touched, Silvia had grabbed her as she had wept and lashed out at those around her who had sought to comfort her at the birth of her grief.

The memory was interrupted by Laur Pop, who barged inside right past her.

'What are you doing here?' he asked, his voice colder than the wailing winds outside.

Mira walked across the room, her pace slowing as she seemed to make a show of admiring the chamber's decorations.

'I heard you're going to Shangri,' she answered, her voice firm, yet also playful and... somewhat lost.

Silvia felt the icy glare of her General now upon her.

Don't look at me! I didn't tell her.

Pop turned back towards their guest. 'Where'd you hear that idea?'

'From people.'

Silvia saw something worrying. Pop had become completely immobile. *That's not good. He doesn't like it when you fuck with him and when you fuck with him and he completely freezes... he's about to do something drastic...*

'Could you be a bit more specific?'

Pop's appointment as Ambassador had yet to be formally declared. The Hajduk preparations had taken place in utmost secrecy and the details of their next mission were known to only but a few members of the Terran leadership. *And the Hajduks' families. Most of them would have been told.*

Why are you asking her? It could've been any number of people, many of which you have absolutely no authority over.

'No,' Mira replied.

'*Pfah...*'

Ok... here we go.

'Do you plan on sitting there all fucking interesting and mysterious all fucking day? Or are you going to stop acting like a child and speak like an adult?'

'You never paid the debt.' Mira was still studying the room. She had spoken the words just as she was inspecting the seal of the Druzhina, gifted to the Hajduks by Mikhail when he had left to start his own Legion, all those years ago.

'Oh, yeah?' How the hell did I come to have a fucking debt to you?' he asked, as he sat in his chair at the head of the table. 'Please, enlighten me!'

'Guilt.'

Mira's answer resulted in Silvia seeing something that could only be described as magical. It was as if the young Arabian girl were a witch and she had just now cast a spell upon him.

Laur Pop was never truly disturbed by others. How could he be? It would truly be out of character for a man so insular in nature. Even his selfishness was immune to the opinions of others, in a way only accessible to a true narcissist, for only a true narcissist could ever be completely free from the curse of his own image in the minds of others. Even when receiving the most damning of news or enduring the harshest of criticisms, she had never seen Laur Pop... *flinch*, for lack of a better word.

And, yet, he did so now.

'Is that enough?' Mira asked, still studying the other gifts and trophies the Hajduks had collected over the course of their existence.

Pop responded quickly. *Too quickly.* 'I'm guilty of a lot, girl. So much so that I'll probably never get to pay every single debt.'

'I don't think so!' She spun around and finally met his gaze. 'I know you blame yourself for it! It was so long ago and yet it still weighs on you.' Mira smirked. 'Don't worry, you haven't given it away. It's just a deduction. You confessed to feeling responsible for it when it happened, so it definitely bothered you at the time. I also know you're obsessive and you never really let things go. So, of course it's still there, eating at you, after all the years...'

'What the fuck are you on about, Mira?'

'Mira?' not 'girl' anymore? Holy shit, he's rattled!

'I'm talking about my birthday.' Mira didn't pause. 'I'm talking about Hellsbreach.' Instead, she now moved closer to Pop, slowly nearing the Hajduk round table.

'You got tunnel vision!' she announced softly. 'You knew my mother was inside the Shield and, when you rushed the gates, all you saw was the carnage within. You ran inside with your men and set about securing the entire citadel. You yourself made your way towards the command room where you found my mother dead on the floor and Daw crying next to her.'

Pop had fully tensed up now, as he stood completely motionless, his fists balled shut as his eyes rushed and avoided Mira's.

Silvia herself was struggling not to tremble, as she remembered the cold Antarctic wind, the blood-spattered muddy snows before the Shield's gates and the dark catacombs of death they had found within.

'You knew she was dead. You saw the burn marks in her eyes and you knew from Daw's tears that she was gone and you phoned it in and then you sat there! You sat there while they sent the news a galaxy away, to my father, who walked to his death to join his wife and his unborn daughter.'

Silvia was nauseous now. Her face itched, yet she dared not raise her hand for fear that one might see her shake. She felt the guilt also. She had also rushed in without thinking. The outskirts were to be secured by others: the Almogavars, the Galloglaich, the Keshik and elements of the Terran Home Army. The Hajduks had just charged into the beleaguered fortress, the first among a dozen Legions that had arrived to repel the Urheimat's infiltrators.

Indeed, if only one of them had found the presence of mind to look around, they would have noticed the lone Terran shuttle from which a red line of motherly blood made its way towards the fortress gates they now charged.

'Thirty-three minutes. Wasn't that the number? It took thirty-three minutes from the moment you landed in Antarctica, until you told Lejla that my mother was dead and so was I?'

Pop remained silent.

'Thirty-three minutes after that, after my father received word that my mother and I were dead, he was dead as well.'

Mira was now sitting right next to Nick's empty seat at the Hajduk table. Without turning her eyes from the Romanian General, who still did not meet her gaze, she asked, 'Silvia?'

Silvia snapped out of the memory. 'Yes, Mira?'

'How long until the *Doina* leaves?' Once more, Mira's eyes never left Pop's downcast expression.

Oh, shit... she's timed perfectly, hasn't she?

Silvia checked her watch. 'Thirty-three minutes.' She struggled hard to keep her face from moving.

Pop finally met Mira's gaze. 'Does Tomasz know you're here?'

Mira blinked for the slightest of moments and Silvia felt her own heart sink as she understood what had happened.

Poor girl thought for a second that he meant another Tomasz... a 'Thomas', actually...

'Yes,' she answered coldly.

'And he approves?' Pop continued.

'He hasn't crashed down from the sky in a cloud of black smoke yet, now hasn't he?' Silvia couldn't help but take a quick glance out the window upon hearing Mira's words.

'Not yet he hasn't.' Pop looked towards his briefcase for one moment, before quickly glancing back as Mira, just as her eyes also took note of his briefcase.

'Silvia?' her General asked.

'Yes?' she answered, just as Pop turned his face slightly towards her.

'Have Captain al-Sayid be written down on the flight log as my personal secretary.' He turned his face back towards hers. 'I am allowed, under our diplomatic agreement with the Shangri state, to bring along up to ten diplomatic attachés.'

Mira smiled slightly. 'I didn't even have to say it.' It was a mocking smile.

'*Huh?*' Pop huffed back at her.

'I didn't even say I wanted to come.' *She didn't actually.*

'Oh, Jesus fucking Christ, Mira! Do I look like I was born yesterday?' he answered angrily, getting up from his seat. 'But – listen to me – do you know *why* we are going to Shangri?'

'Because *you* can't help it?'

Mira's deadpan delivery finally broke through Silvia's composure and she had to quickly wrestle a smile away from her lips. She quickly glanced towards Pop, hoping he hadn't seen the rupturing of her facade. Instead, she saw something else.

Laur Pop was smirking.

It's a fake smile, but there is some truth behind the forced corners of his mouth

'That's only part of the answer. Do you know the official answer to that question?'

She smiled cordially as answered. 'We are completing our yearly diplomatic rotation and we are arriving to take over from Hierarch Kimmie Jimmel.' *Perfect. She couldn't help but sound mockingly formal, but that's alright.*

'Correct. Do you know why it will be *we* who will be going to Shangri?'

Mira's pokerface returned with a vengeance. Only her eyes moved, as she turned only them to face the briefcase next to him. 'I know it's in that briefcase somewhere.' *Excellent. Vague, yet also precise. Never reveal too much. That's how we do things around here.*

'Correct.' Pop grabbed the briefcase and began walking towards the exit. 'Have your shuttle loaded onto the *Doina*. We leave soon but, then again,' he turned around briefly as he walked, 'you already knew that!'

No, wait! There's more! 'Why do you want to come to Shangri?' Silvia asked. *Why don't you care why she wants to come? Why didn't you ask?*

'Oh... yeah... *why do you* want to come to Shangri?' Pop asked, just as he was opening the door.

'I need something to do. Shangri's by far the most interesting thing going on.'

True... and the second part is, unfortunately, also true.

'You think you know enough about the status of Republican operations in the Local Cluster to be able to make that statement?'

'Yes. I also reckoned you would need some help.'

'Huh?' Pop asked. Mira's comment had seemingly interrupted his thought process as he had likely been pondering how efficient their counterintelligence apparatus was.

Of course Mira know these things, she's everyone's favourite niece! A princess such as her always knows what goes on at court!

'I am the only person on this entire mountain that has actually been to Shangri before.' She raised her eyes, looking not just at Pop but also at her. 'Reckon it might help to have someone who knows the lay of the land along for the ride.'

'Well, you're right. It would.' Pop decided that he wasn't done with his security audit, however. 'How long have you known about it?'

'I found out after Ratden that there's a mission planned for Shangri. I learned the specifics about two weeks ago.'

'Oh, yeah? Why didn't you talk to Feng about it?' *Since, two weeks ago, this was Feng's operation.*

'Feng doesn't feel guilty.'

Snaaap! She's still got that umphhh!!!

Pop stood motionless for one second, before summoning enough fake charm to smile and say, 'True!' Still smiling and his eyes still on his new personal secretary, he spoke to Silvia. 'Get her settled! She's your responsibility!' And then he left.

The sound of the shutting door stirred Silvia more than Pop's command. 'Are you sure about this, Mira?'

Mira changed. She saw her slump her shoulders slightly and look across the room one last time.

Why? What's pushed you, girl? What happened to you? Something is gone from within you and you seem to be in pain still! What wound inside of you there is now that has taken so much from you? You now seek to join men damned by their devotion to a paranoid madman into the dark flames of what might come?

Did you love him that much?

'Yes!' she answered, her voice empty, yet also resolute.

Silvia nodded slowly. 'Good... Good! Let's go! Did you bring everything you'll need?' she nodded towards Mira's shuttle.

'Yes.'

'Good! Well, have the shuttle park itself within the *Doina* and come with me! The ship's about to leave!'

'Sure... it's not like it can leave without us!' Mira smiled mischievously at her own little wit, as well as her disdain of authority, and her disrespect of other people's time.

Oh, Christ, I forgot how you were like, Mira! Looks like some things never change no matter how much you go through.

'Sure, they won't.' Silvia smiled. 'But I don't want to spend ten days in the Greyspace with six hundred irritated Hajduks and neither do you, so let's go.'

Mira chuckled. 'Still the "Grumpy Legion" are we?'

'Still led by the "Grinch" too!' Silvia smiled sorrowfully.

They shared a friendly chuckle as they got going.

They took off just as the sun set far to the west of the Carpathian Mountains. It would be the last the time the Hajduks would experience natural sunlight for quite some time, as they would enter the Grayspace just after passing Luna's orbit. They would spend almost an entire week in the Greyspace before emerging in the Triangulum Galaxy docking on the world of Thule, where they would bid their farewells to Republican Space, before crossing over into the Realm of Shangri.

The Realm of Shangri lay within what the people of Old Earth had once referred to as the Pisces Dwarf Galaxy. Far smaller than the Milky Way, Andromeda and even Triangulum, Pisces was a tiny galaxy of around three hundred thousand stars, less than half which had any actual planets orbiting them. Of these, the vast majority were little more than uninhabitable lumps of barren rock which the Shangri government had never bothered to terraform. Instead, they had become a collection of mining, research and manufacturing facilities and way-stations. Little more could be said of those inhabitable planets that existed within Pisces, for those worlds had been given over to agriculture. In the eyes of the ruling class of Shangri, there was no need to invest in the development of these worlds, for all that mattered was Shangri itself.

Long ago, colonists arrived from within the ancient Old Realm of Mankind and crossed through Pisces on their way to the more vibrant and numerous worlds of Andromeda and Triangulum. In time, the need for a waypoint on the road to these galaxies lead to the emergence of a permanent settlement on the world of Shangri-La, then only a planet orbiting a red giant star, such as Terra's own sun. When the Old Realm was sundered by the War at the Gates of Heaven, refugees fleeing the conflict reached out towards the fringes of the Old Realm and Shangri blossomed into a gigantic metropolis and a beacon of civilization, shinning the light of commerce throughout the entire Local Cluster.

Such was the might of Shangri, that when the world's sun had threatened to destroy it during its waning years, its inhabitants were able to safely transition the raging dying star into a friendlier living white dwarf, which still powered the great metropolis to this day. What had once been the world of Shangri-La had evolved into a giant superstructure called Shangri, which now encompassed what had once been their red sun.

The *City* of Shangri, as it was now known, was actually a collection of colossal habitats that had been erected around the white dwarf they now encompassed. What had once been the actual planet of Shangri-La was now merely little more than the structure upon which sat the most affluent and powerful of the City's Districts.

It had been right at the beginning of their journey, while they were still within the Milky Way, that Laur Pop had gathered the Hajduk leadership in his quarters aboard the *Doina*. Technowolf, Basenji, as well as Mira, had also been present.

'As you all know, the Embassy at Convert Square, as well as the Sanjak Manor and the Belagravia Estate are located within Shangri, on the Brightside, meaning the side of the old planet that faces inwards and is lit by the white dwarf star to whom the Shangrians refer to as La, "the old man".'

'Yeah, about that,' Nick interrupted. 'How are they called in English?'

'What?' a confused Pop asked.

'Shangri? Shangrians? *Shangresians*? *Shangrese*? I've heard all sorts of versions.'

Pop blinked a few times as he stared into the empty space before him. 'Well... I call them "Shangrians", but I've heard other terms too.' The General's brow furrowed as he realized something. 'It doesn't matter! The primary language spoken in Shangri is Shangrianese and you'll just use that when speaking with the locals.'

He was about to go on, but Nick interrupted once more. 'What about the other languages?'

'What about 'em?'

Here we go.

'Do we have to learn all of them?'

'I would prefer it if you did. We are on a diplomatic mission after all. The point is to make friends. So, you speak whatever needs to be spoken! *Except among each other!* We stick to our languages for our internal communication!'

'Ah, you hear that Mira?' Nick turned around, finding Mira seated in between Gigi and Basenji. 'You gotta speak, like, four extra languages!'

'Six...' Bojana commented.

'Oh, *oops*! I forgot! Serbian, Croatian and Bosnian are "completely" different languages.'

'No, I don't!'

'Well, tough shit, Mira!' Pop intervened. 'Nick's right, we need you properly integrated, so you gotta learn the languages.'

'That I've already done!'

'You have?' Nick looked stunned. 'Me and the lads... we've been talking shit about you in front of *you*, ever since you got here!'

'I noticed.' Mira raised her eyebrows as she let loose an amused little smile. 'Though I don't need to know that much gypsy language to know that you're singing something about "your Arab girl", "your Indian girl", "your Creole girl", "you broke my heart"... "*ratatata*"!'

Mira paused for the laughter to die out. 'But I will be speaking English to you all!'

'And why is that?' Bojana asked.

'Because you all speak among your own groups in your own languages, but when others are present you all switch to English! If I spoke to all of you in your languages, it would look suspicious since I would be the only one to do so!'

'Fair point,' Bojana concurred. 'But why would that be suspicious? We're not hiding the fact that you're not a Hajduk!'

'You are not, but my understanding is that our stay in Shangri will be marked by events of a more... *covert* nature?' The blank stares around the room confirmed Mira's assessment. 'Wouldn't it be best if we kept behaviours that would attract any extra attention to a minimum?'

'Well, well, well!' Nick's voice sang out in surprise. 'I didn't know they knew that much about subterfuge in the Ghazis!'

'Oh, you'd be surprised!' Mira quipped back.

'I wouldn't.' It was Pop who spoke. His words were echoed by some of the older Hajduks. He continued, 'She's right. We'll set our standard language to English within the embassy. You will instruct the men to set English and Shangrianese to 'interelligible' within their translators modules. All logs and reports are to be filled in English, with Shangrianese highlighted when necessary. When we do *really* need the privacy, we switch back to our languages!'

'Done!' they all confirmed.

Pop continued. 'We are all to split our time between our diplomatic endeavour in Shangri and the search for the Stolen. What that means in practice is that each of you is to go about performing those activities expected of you, whilst also investigating the Stolen's fate and eventual whereabouts.'

'Gigi, you act as military attaché.'

'Bojana, you act as commercial attaché.'

'Iosip, you will take up your duties as Emissary of Terra.'

'Lejla, you stay with the ship!'

'Silvia, Nick and myself will stay at the Convent Garden Embassy and handle communication with the Peacekeeper and the rest of his inner circle. Together with Tech and Basenji, we will cultivate our relationships and partnerships with the various factions within Shangri. It is about these factions that I wish to speak with you today, though I expect all of you, as well as your men to become familiarized with all of them!'

They all nodded. 'Good.'

Thus he began, 'First, there are the humans of Shangri, who make up the largest group, though they are by no means the majority. They do, however, make up a majority of the *upper* classes of Shangri society! The highest echelons of power, such as the Peacekeeper and his family, are descended from the original human colonists that first settled the original planet. However, the largest group is comprised of descendants of the refugees that fled the War at the Gates of Heaven. Unseeded humans from the Pisces Galaxy are also present, yet they make up an insignificant and marginalized minority. There are also the numerous descendants of the many merchants, explorers, exiles and fugitives that have sought refuge in Shangri over the millennia. Shangri is, essentially, a caste-based society, with intermingling between the bloodlines being minimal. Thus, these groups have maintained their distinct identities over the many years following their arrival in Shangri. Ideologically, the humans are split between those advocating for continued independence, those that wish to join the Urheimat and those that wish to join the Republican Alliance... *in that order*. From what we can tell, less than ten percent of the human population supports joining the Republican Alliance, so do not expect a great many friends in the ranks of our fellow humans!'

Garden variety humans.

'The murine make up the second-largest racial group. Their origins are mired in obscurity, though it is believed by the Hyperboreans, the Vanir and the Aesir that it is *they* who are the original inhabitants of the Pisces Galaxy! Though this is difficult to say for sure, given that no written records of their presence have survived. It is only through the oral traditions of their people that we can piece together their origins as an early interplanetary civilization that developed independently within Pisces before the arrival of humans from the Old Realm, and even *before* the emergence of the native Pisces humans. By all accounts, they are the ones who view our Alliance most favourably. However, they are also the most disenfranchised, as they primarily make up the working caste of Shangri.'

Ratmen with no money.

'Mira, you're the only one here that's been to Shangri before. You're also the only one here to have ever seen a murine before! Thus, I think this is an excellent opportunity for you to earn your keep! You will act as the main point of contact between the murine and the Embassy. Your position shall be informal though, since the Shangri government forbids us from cultivating formal relationships with the various racial groups. Basenji will be assisting you, if needed.'

Mira nodded.

The largest group of sympathizers gets Mira? Looks like he's switched from hostility towards her presence to downright dependency! What would he have done without her? Have Basenji, a wolfman who doesn't speak, converse with chitterling ratmen?

Sounds like someone is feeling guilty indeed...

'The Fili bast were originally inhabitants of the world of Fili, before it was annexed by the Urheimat. They are essentially a people of refugees, though they have become established citizens of the City of Shangri. They are a fractured and independently-minded people, with some favouring the Alliance and what it stands for. However, the vast majority are fervent supporters of independence and consider us a threat to their way of life. Of all the inhabitants of Shangri, the Fili bast are the most liberal in their views of race, with many bast either living or working in multiracial environments.

Thus, they have no centralized community of their own, with their members spread out across the various factions of Shangri.'

Catmen who don't like other catmen.

'One such faction are the Ursai Cooperatives, a blanket term for the network of interconnected businesses controlled by the Libra Ursai of Shangri. Now, to my understanding, these ursai are rather different from the Libra Ursai of Barlog, their estranged brethren who are now our brothers-in-arms! From what our friends in Barlog and Nargothrond tell us, the rift between the two groups emerged as a result of a difference in their views on debt and, more particularly, the practices of a now defunct financial institution: the Libra Bank.'

'When they arrived in Shangri after the annexation of their homeworld, the ursai brought with them both their tradition of communal lending and a large influx of capital. They quickly obtained a banking licence and began providing loans to the established humans of Shangrians. However, in time, a rift emerged. The Ursai of Barlog has always regarded imposing interest upon a debt as unethical, as you all very well know. The Ursai of Shangri, however, came to have no issue with requesting interest on loans. This difference in opinion led to the two groups eventually splintering, with the Ursai of Shangri becoming the sole owners of Libra Bank and the ursai of (what would become) Barlog, departing for the Milky Way. However, over time, the bank devolved into outright usury, and the Shangri government revoked their license.'

'Nevertheless, by all accounts this has not stopped the Ursai of Shangri from keeping their traditions alive. As such, the Ursai Cooperatives, though covered by a veneer of legitimate business practices, are actually little more than a front for the far-reaching criminal enterprise that is contemporary Shangrian ursai society.'

The Bear Mafia.

'Loansharking is simply their most well known-service, as they long-ago branched out into smuggling, racketeering, prostitution and gambling. They essentially hold a loose monopoly over all criminal activities within the City of Shangri and are lead by an informal Chairman, much like the Ursai of Barlog, names Gamal Bittercastle, though I understand that he is primarily referred to as "Big White".'

'Because he's big and white?'

'He's a fucking polar bear that walks upright, Nick! What do you think?'

'Just making sure.'

'Big White has also been, covertly, a close collaborator of ours in the city and, quite, frankly, he is probably our most powerful ally outside of the Royal Palace, despite the fact that the ursai themselves are predominantly lukewarm to the idea of rejoining their long-lost brethren. The Cooperatives maintain strong relationships with our friends in Andromeda, Triangulum, as well as the elves of the Milky Way. Thus, having a formal relationship with the ursai falls well within the limits of acceptable diplomatic behaviour. Thus, I'll handle the relationship with the ursai.'

You don't like ursai... They always seem to freak you out...

This will be interesting...

'The remani present on Shangri primarily belong to the Single Star Pride. They are...' Pop glanced at the two remani present, Technowolf and Basenji, before moving on '... *not like* the Black Knight remani we know so well.'

'They're also white?' Nick joked.

'No. They're actually predominantly black and red.' Technowolf finally spoke. He was sitting on one of Pop's many armchairs with a glass of cranberry juice sitting half-empty in front of him. He leaned forward and took the glass in his hands. 'They were once wanderers, such as we once were, though they're objective was always to find some corner of the universe to settle in. While we of the Black Knight (eventually) came to view the Milky Way as our own, due to the necessity of our presence, the Single Star came to join with the Humans of Shangri since that had always been their wish: to find a worthy master.' Technowolf took a sip of his juice.

'Which they found in the Peacekeeper?' Bojana asked.

'Which they found in the of the current Peacekeeper, more than three thousand years ago! Over time, they have become his fiercest supporters and most loyal subjects! Shangri has a police force and an army in the form of the Constabulary and the *Colonial* Constabulary, both of which are predominantly made up of remani. Yet their true protectors and enforcers are the remani of the *Royal* Constabulary: a kind of Secret Service... *or a Gestapo...*' Technowolf placed the glass back on the table. '... (Depending on how you look at it, really)... which is *dominated* by remani.'

Silvia was reminded of how peculiar he was for a remani. Glancing towards the ever-silent Basenji sitting in one of the corners of the room, she was reminded of how peculiar *these two* were in particular. Basenji never spoke, though he most definitely could. Technowolf was... well... he was odd. What with his love of music, particularly techno (hence his namesake) and his struggles with alcoholism, he was *incredibly* strange. remani were reclusive by nature – or at least the remani of the Black Knight were. These two were by far the most outgoing and sociable of their entire population, yet one of them didn't even speak. *I wonder how strange these Shangri remani are.*

'They are... very different from us.' Apparently Technowolf was pondering the same question. 'We of the Black Knight are fastidious. We're secretive. But we are also light-hearted and... we celebrate freedom and free will! Those of the Single Star are far more rigid and far more restrictive. They are much more militaristic.' Technowolf scratched one of his ears. 'How should I say this? When I arrived on Old Earth, there existed these people called the *Prussians*. Later on, they became completely assimilated by the Germans.'

'You arrived on Old Earth in the 12th century?' Nick asked as he smiled, for he knew the answer to his own question.

'*What*? No! The other Prussians! Frederick's Prussians!'

'He knows!' Gigi intervened, 'He's just fucking with you. Please continue!' *Huh, it seems Gigi's finally decided to get his game face on.*

She glanced at Pop, who had also noticed the exchange. *Maybe now you can calm down about Gigi turning senile.*

'The Prussians were Germans, yes, much like how the Austrians were Germans – well... they're all Germans now, I suppose. However, the Prussians were...'

'They were an army with a country, not a country with an army.' The old cliché was spoken by Iosip, who had remained silent up until that point.

'Exactly! Now, the Austrians had a certain *joie du vivre*, a joy of life which made them quite different from the Prussians – and from the other Germans, by that matter. They saw war as a means to an end, not an end goal. Well...' Technowolf snout twisted into an old snarl.'... most of them, at least.'

'Hear! Hear!' A few of the older Hajduks muttered. The reference was lost on Silvia, however.

'You can still see it today, with the Rittebruder taking up that old Prussian identity and the Landsknecht being more representative of old Bavaria and Austria.'

'And the Black Knight are like the Austrians, while the Single Star are more like Prussians!' Mira had spoken little and only when spoken to, since she had left the council chamber on Earth the day before. Her tone was strange, as she didn't seem to be asking a question. Rather, she seemed to be moving the conversation forward, even if it meant stating the obvious. *Did something bother you just now, girl?*

'Yes. They're a rigid, dour lot. Always more obsessed with rules and regulation and how things *must* be and what *work* must be done. They're not like *us*!' Technowolf gestured towards himself and Basenji. 'And I recommend you remember that! When interacting with them, bear in mind that they're *very* different from us!'

Our remani are wolves and these are hounds... interesting...

'What do they think of us?' Bojana asked.

'Of you? Unseeded humans from a place called Terra? They think of you whatever the Peacekeeper and Shangri's elite think of you!'

'What? That we're misguided savages looking for trouble?' Bojana attempted to understand.

'That you're upstart savages that will get in trouble if you threaten Shangri, which they see themselves as the protectors of!'

'Huh... I see the Prussians have at least a few things in common with the Austrians.' Bojana finished her remark with a smile.

Technowolf smiled back. 'We have *a lot* in common, nevertheless! We share the same language, the same religion, the same origin... many of our customs are the same! But the ways in-between the stars have led us down different paths.'

'What do they think of *you*?' Gigi pressed.

Technowolf was silent for a moment and then he snorted. 'That we're meddling hippies and hypocrites.' He let his words linger upon a room of faces either concerned, confused or just amused. 'When they settled in the City of Shangri, our forefathers were quite vocal in their criticism of their decision. They viewed it as amoral to abandon our nomadic way of life and our neutrality, in service to a member of the very species that saw us as little more than talking monkeys! They took the Single Star's pragmatism in joining forces with the Humans of Shangri as a kind of betrayal. They saw their decision to plant their banner into the ground as the mark of warmongers and extremists. We of the Black Knight wasn't the only Pride to criticise them, though we have become the only such Pride to do virtually the same thing over three thousand years later. Hence, they see us as hypocrites.'

'And they control the police?' Gigi asked.

'They *are* the police.' Technowolf emphasized.

Gigi sat quietly for a few moments. 'You said we're not going to be under too much scrutiny,' he said to Pop.

'I did and we won't.'

'Huh, sounds to me like the people in power don't really like us much over there.'

'They don't like us much, but they understand the *necessity* of us. There have been over twenty Republican ambassadors to Shangri since we began diplomatic relations with them. With each year, our standing in the city has improved and the Peacekeeper understands that choosing between us and the Urheimat had become inevitable. The population itself is divided and the Peacekeeper has always desired to keep his options open. Doing so requires that he maintain excellent diplomatic relations with both us and the Urheimat.'

'Did the Peacekeeper inform these Single Star remani to stay off our ass while we go around his city looking for people to kidnap, interrogate and eventually kill?'

'Not yet. But that's not your problem.'

'Sounds to me a lot like it is.'

'For the time being, your problem is another one.'

'*Uh-oh.*'

'Yup! Your problem is that you're going to be right in the middle of all those remani and their human colleagues in the military, teaching them Republican warcraft while they fill you in on all they know about the Urheimat's military strategy and tactics!' Pop eyed Gigi intensely. 'You are the only one out of all of us, bar Lejla on the *Doina*, who will be allowed to openly bear arms, even if you will be restricted to the military district. Furthermore, of all of us here, your tasks are the most straightforward: make friends with their military, teach them all you know about killing imperials and learn how to kill imperials better from them!'

'I won't be taking part in our *special* activities?' Gigi seemed a little surprised.

'Oh, you will! I'm quite certain that by the end of our stay, all of us would have shed a little blood in a new galaxy. But that will come along the way, as we piece things together!'

Pop, who had been leaning on the back of his own seat while standing up behind it, began tapping on said seat's headrest. 'The City of Shangri is the most densely populated solar system in the whole Local Cluster, with a total population bordering on almost a trillion. The humans, the murine, the ursai, the remani and the bast make up the majority of the known population, but there are other groups.'

'Orcs, elves, goblins, trolls, demani, kobolds, taori... hell, there are even a few mandrakes that have taken up residence within the city, as well as an unknown number of troglodytes that dwell within the poorer areas of the city, far from the easy reach of the Peacekeeper's Constabulary. Every branch of the Tree of Man blossoms within the City of Shangri. You might think that such multiculturalism might incur some inherent sympathy for our own multicultural endeavour, yet you would be mistaken!'

'While the non-humans abhor the Urheimat (for good reason) they do not automatically see us as natural allies, for they greatly value their independence. The humans themselves are split, with many openly supporting an annexation by the Urheimat. Furthermore, the imperials have a head start.'

'We have an embassy and a few disparate holdings scattered throughout the city. The Urheimat has *an entire district* on *each* side of Shangri!' Pop flicked a button on his desk, bringing up a blue holographic projection of an outer section of the City of Shangri. He flicked another button and a district within the section turned red. Within the middle of this region of the city, a giant red edifice rose up into the dark sky.

'This is the Darkside Urheimat District, located around the Urheimat Pier. It is the larger of the two areas of Urheimat control and the one where the imperials are seeing the largest gains in control. They have their own laws, their own semi-autonomous government, and they even have their own police force. It is, by far, the more difficult of the two Urheimat districts to surveil, though we know that they frequently clash with the Ursai Cooperatives in turf wars, as they're constantly encroaching upon the bearmen's territories and markets.'

'How are they handling it?' Nick asked.

Jesus, Nick! Have you read none of the reports?

'The bearmen? They're slowly being pushed back! Though they have so far succeeded in containing the imperial presence to this district... *more or less* This containment comes with a lot of opportunities for intelligence gathering and most of what we know about what goes on within comes from Big White, in exchange for... *tokens* of our appreciation!'

Pop flicked another button on his screen, revealing an inner section of the City and a red-coloured area, much smaller and directly opposite the previous one, facing the city's inner sun.

'There is the Brightside Urheimat District, located relatively close to Shangri-La, the Old World of Shangri, which is where Convent Garden, Sanjak and Belagravia are located. One of our principal tasks will be to take over the task of coordinating our intelligence gathering operations in this area, together with the other Republican Embassies. Given that we' unlike Jimmel's *goblins*, are *humans*, we will be taking on a much larger operational role than our predecessors, for obvious reasons...'

Laur's eyes fell downwards, as he remembered something important. 'I wish to point out that what we are now looking at is likely going to be the primary focus of our *other mission* on Shangri, which I expect all of you to become very well acquainted with this area in particular.'

They all nodded.

Bojana spoke. 'And what's the first step in *that* direction?'

Pop returned to his desk buttons, replacing the map of the Urheimat Brightside with the visage of a human man with ginger hair.

'Quint of Carth-Fountainhead – Inspections Officer First Class. His name was in the Ratden Log. We checked with Jimmel the moment we found out about him and he, in turn, looked him up in Shangri. He's middle management in the Paragon Shipping Company, which is a business specialized in the sale of 'goods' from the Local Cluster to the Urheimat. He lives in the Urheimat district on the Brightside with his wife and four children.'

'And how do we start with him?' Bojana continued.

'I haven't figured that part out yet. It's one of several things we'll have to figure out together in the coming days, while we make our way to Shangri.'

Pop finally sat down. 'We need to become experts in Shangri!' he said, giving Nick a self-explanatory glare. 'We downloaded every single piece of intelligence we have on the city before leaving Terra. I expect all of you to become intimately familiar with the city and its people by accessing said information! We will work together on piecing together a plan and, once we arrive in Shangri, we'll set the plan in motion!'

He had let them go about their business after that.

They followed his orders diligently, as they always did. Silvia spent the next day rigorously studying the history of Shangri and its people. She learned the transportation network by heart and knew the geography so well that she started dreaming about individual alleyways in neighbourhoods she would likely never visit. She learned the customs of the city, as well as its various races. She learned to distinguish between (and how to replicate) the many accents and dialects of Shangri and she even began studying the different customs and fashions of the different classes.

The Hajduks had long become familiarized with working independently of one another, so the idea of spending more than a year spread out over different locations was not a troubling one in itself. Furthermore, this was not their first diplomatic assignment, as Pop had previously served as Terran Ambassador to Pandora, Nargothrond and Menegroth. It had been on Pandora where the Hajduks had discovered their love of wild beasts, hence Nick's pet wyvern and Bojana's pet rook. Even Pop had joined in the native's pastimes, as he had developed a keen interest in big game hunting. On Nargothrond, they had essentially acted as a kind of foreign secret police, as most of their time had been dedicated to tracking down potential Svart sympathizers. Their assignment on Menegroth had basically been one big ruse, as the Hajduks had spent a majority of the time collecting information on the surviving Svart. All of these assignments should have recommended them for a task on Shangri, yet something else was at work here that made Silvia restless.

What was truly troubling about the whole operation was how complex their objectives were. Officially, they were simply operating in a diplomatic capacity. Thus, they had to foster good relationships with the Shangri government, cultivate commercial relations with Shangri's many merchant companies, improve and maintain the Republican Alliance's image amongst the general populace, and formally nurture a military alliance with the city's armed forces. However, in reality they would have to actively work against the interest of many of Shangri's elite.

The Republican Alliance wanted Shangri to come into its folds and there was a great degree of hope that a breakthrough was near. The previous ambassadors had worked tirelessly over countless hours of gruelling negotiations with the Peacekeeper, his inner circle and the city's many factions, with the single-minded purpose of bringing Shangri closer to the Alliance and away from the Urheimat and its formal sphere of control: the 'Sprachbund'.

Yet, their opponents were many.

Apart from the Urheimat itself, which actively worked to undermine their efforts, they also had to contend with the Shangri human elite. They were aided by the fact that most of these elites saw assimilation by the Urheimat as a catastrophic blow to their power. Yet, many saw the Republican Alliance as an equally dangerous prospect and, thus, the spirit of independence was strong.

Beneath this already difficult balancing act was layered another task, one which was profound of importance to the Terrans themselves: the search for the *Stolen*.

They had long known that the *Stolen* had passed through Shangri on their way to the Sprachbund. Yet, the Ratden Log had allowed them to pick up a tangible lead. Up until its emergence, the Terrans had never had a way of knowing where to start, as the Peacekeeper had never divulged who it was that had been involved in the children's passage into the realms of the Sprachbund. Furthermore, he had never allowed anyone the authority needed to openly investigate his citizens, let alone prosecute them. Such things would have been 'instigation' and 'persecution' and were a red line set by the Peacekeeper, who would likely not take kindly to the tactics the Hajduks planned to employ within the shadows beneath his authority.

Silvia knew what they would do first. They would find this Quint of Carth-Fountainhead and interrogate him using who-knows-what kind of horrific selection of tricks the Hajduks had picked up along their many dark and murderous hunts for their enemies. They would follow his trail to the imperials and, from that point onwards, who knows what they would have to do?

But, whatever that may be, it would have to be silent. It would have to be something that could not be attributed to the Alliance, for to do so would court war on a scale unimaginable.

All of this because he just can't let something go...

The Hajduks were tired. They were tired on Terra before Pop's decision and they were tired on Terra after Pop's decision. Now they were tired on the *Doina*, as it traversed through the Greyspace on its way to Shangri. There was no true rest waiting for them on Shangri, for they all knew of the work that would have to be done. The Hajduk leadership spent most of the time aboard among themselves, planning the upcoming operations, since it would be the last time in quite a long while when they would be all gathered together, in a room where they would know for sure that no one was listening in on them.

As the hour of their arrival grew near, Silvia found herself in a rare moment of temporary peace among the last few moments before their exit from the Greyspace. They would emerge right on the borders of the City of Shangri and approach the city whilst in realspace, with the *Doina* eventually docking on their pier in the Shangri Harbour.

Silvia never liked how the Greyspace looked.

The older Terrans, the ones who had fought on Doomsday – oldtimers, as those born after Doomsday called them – described it as looking like a television screen with static. The amount of static was dictated by the amount of traffic passing through the Greyspace. In a relatively untraveled area, such as that near the Southern Milky Way, the Greyspace looked primarily black, only crisscrossed by the occasional white piercing lines of what looked like shooting stars, as these were the marks of intergalactic travel. In an area of the Greyspace that saw a lot of intergalactic spaceflight, such as the area near Shangri, the Greyspace was a crowded mix of black and ever-shifting white.

The Greyspace always gave her an eerie feeling, in a way in which the star-filled view of their own universe never made her experience. Silvia had always been claustrophobic, a condition she shared with most of her generation. Their childhood had been marred by continuous feelings of constraint and imprisonment. The Vaults under Prague were little more than the pinnacle of a (then) short life spent stashed away within moving vehicles, bomb shelters and small derelict rooms. Starships felt oddly similar, no matter how modern, spacious or luxurious they looked, and the *Doina* sometimes felt no different to one large, yet still cramped, train wagon.

It would be a relief to gaze upon distant stars once more, knowing one of them would be their own Sun and, with such a sight in mind, she made her way to the Doina's observation deck, located on top of the ship, at the end of a passageway leading up from the control room. Inside, she was surprised to find many more other constrained souls within.

Nick was even more claustrophobic than she was, so seeing him there didn't surprise her. He was joined by Technowolf and Basenji, as well as by a pensive Mira.

Silvia hadn't seen much of her since boarding the ship. She came to the daily leadership meetings, though she usually stayed quiet, silently sharing a couch with Basenji for most of the time. Outside such moments, she had virtually spent the entire journey in her room. Silvia had invited her to the *Doina*'s canteen for several lunches and dinners on a few occasions, yet Mira had always answered that she wanted to spend some time alone. From what Silvia could tell, these moments were broken only by the occasional sparring sessions she shared with Basenji, who was the only person Mira accepted within her chamber.

Poor soul. At least she has someone she can let in. That's good.

The group greeted her warmly and some friendly conversation was attempted. 'Well, Mira, how long has it been since you've been to Shangri?' Nick asked at one point, as he looked off into the cluttered Greyspace.

'Seven years,' Mira responded.

'You came here with Daw, right?'

'Yup! Her first state visit to the City; she had me take a leave of absence from the Host and join her.' Mira paused for a moment, as her head tilted slightly, her mind seemingly remembering something. 'You already knew that,' she told him.

'I did.' he agreed. 'How is it?'

'The city? Haven't you been reading the *novels* Pop has been sending us?' Mira asked, a long of tired annoyance descending across her face. *She's beginning to fit right in.*

'I did.' Nick smiled as he turned to her. 'But *how* is it? How's it like? What's the vibe?'

Mira slowly smiled back. Her eyes became downcast as she gathered the memories needed to answer Nick's question. 'It's... chaotic at best and *psychotic* at worst!'

'Oh... you should've mentioned that in the meetings!'

'It wouldn't have been worth it.'

'Well, fair point. Still, go on, don't be shy!' Nick got up and came closer to her, before sitting down on one of the seats spread out the observation deck, right behind one of the radar modules. 'Better late than never!'

Mira's smile had faded and was replaced by a smirk. 'There's <u>a lot</u> of people.'

'I expected that from the largest urban centre in the Local Cluster.'

'It's the density that you should really worry about!' Mira drew in a breath of air. 'How many people live in Brașov?'

'About... I think there's about fifty thousand at any given time.'

'And in the whole of Romania? Including the Kalo lands in the south?

'Around eight hundred thousand.'

Accurate...

'I think that's about right. I trust you've been to Menegroth?'

'I have.'

'How many there?'

'I think they're bordering on three billion nowadays?'

'Across the whole world, yes.' Mira glanced at the empty darkness outside. 'Imagine three billion people crammed into an area the size of Romania.'

'Hmphhh... I've been to Moria. I doubt it's worse than that!'

'Oh, it's worse! <u>A lot</u> worse.' Mira's eyes wandered and she ventured forth an honest smile as she reminisced on her last visit. 'Daw and I stayed within the Royal Palace, as guests of the Peacekeeper. When she would finish her duties, we would walk around the nearby parks. We would even sometimes go out and eat at the nearby restaurants. We would sometimes even visit the local shops and browse their wares. It was fun. But we always felt crowded.'

'One night, we decided to disguise ourselves as commoners and venture outside Belagravia and into the city proper, where only the Shangrians themselves live.' Mira rubbed her nose, as if it had remembered something. 'Belagravia, Sanjak, Convent Square... those are the rich neighbourhoods, where the upper classes live and even there you often feel cramped!'

'Most people in Shangri are not upper class. They're middle class... at best and, unlike the rich people in Convent Garden, they can't afford the luxury of space.' Mira sat back in her seat and exhaled. 'I've never seen so many people in my entire life. I never realised how much I valued my personal space until I rode the Shangri tube.'

'Tube?' Nick seemed a little confused.

'Public transport. Underground metro system.'

'Ah! I understand!'

'No... No, you don't. There's just *sooo* many people... sometimes it's hard to breathe! There's... an *anxiety* that grips you there! This continuous feeling of impending doom! I wouldn't call it a permanent state of fear, but it is... *unnerving.*'

Nick scratched his head. Mira was a hardened combat veteran. He and Silvia had gotten to know her during the Ayve War in the Triangulum Galaxy when the Hajduks had found themselves fighting alongside Mira's former legion, the Ghazis, against the Aesir. Silvia and Nick had feared that she might have become some spoilt brat, given her lineage, her upbringing and her status, yet they had been pleasantly surprised to discover that she was remarkably down-to-earth, humble and, most importantly, resilient.

Whether it be under artillery bombardment, within muddy trenches, against ice cold winds or scorching suns, they had seen the young Arab weather hardship with stoicism. Yes, of course, Mira was strong-willed, demanding and sensitive in her own way, yet she was never superficial. If she said that Shangri was so crowded it made her uncomfortable, her words definitely deserved credence.

Nick turned in his seat towards the two remani. 'You two have never been to Shangri before, right?'

'Nope!' Technowolf answered, stilling a burp. Silvia noticed the non-alcoholic ginger ale in his hand. 'We're too young! Our first duties were on Old Earth and we haven't wandered far in that time.'

'Aren't you like two hundred years old?' Nick asked.

'Two hundred seventy *and* born in Old Earth orbit!' He gestured towards his fellow remani. 'Basenji here is seventy-six and he never even left the solar system until the War of Vengeance!'

This stirred Silvia's curiosity, as she remembered that she actually did have a question on the topic. 'But Black Knight remani did pass through Shangri during the End Times? When you were gathering support for us?'

'They did.' Technowolf took another sip of his ginger ale. 'Brindle, Chewbacca and Jack-off Jackal; those are the names you know them by!'

'And what did they have to say about the City of Shangri?'

'Well, Jack-off and Chewbacca passed away during the War of Vengeance. They never really had time to share their impressions. Brindle...' Technowolf stared at his drink and raised his eyebrows. '... Brindle said it was very *crowded*...' Technowolf chuckled a little as he took a swig of his drink. 'So, we have confirmation!'

'I understand.' Nick turned back towards Mira. 'Anything else?'

'You constantly have this strange feeling that you shouldn't be there!' Mira looked around at the gathered Terrans and remani. 'In a *fundamental* sense! It doesn't feel like... a *world*! It doesn't feel like a *planet*. It feels very... *unnatural*. The sunlight is strange. The horizon... its shape just feels... *off*. It doesn't feel like an *environment*. It feels more like a *habitat*. There's no wind. Only drafts and odd currents of air when the ventilation system turns on. When it rains, it doesn't *feel* like rain. It doesn't *taste* like rain.'

'It's not water?' Silvia was intrigued.

'Oh, no, it's water! Just that... it's too... *uniform*? It doesn't have the *randomness* of normal rain. It falls down to the ground in such an ordered way, it almost feels as if the rain is just... *doing its job*!?'

'You're saying it doesn't feel natural,' Technowolf concluded.

'Yes and no! I am quite certain that if you studied the rain, you would find that, at a physical level, it's virtually identical to natural rain. Just like how the artificial gravity feels indistinguishable from normal gravity or how the grass in their parks looks like regular grass. But... there's an anxiety it causes, which you don't truly feel in a natural world.' Mira let her words linger before continuing with her most striking impression.

'What is truly unnatural is the sunlight, particularly in those areas that face towards the dwarf star. Its light is strange enough on the Darkside, yet on the Brightside it's –'

Mira's words were cut off as their eyes were suddenly drawn towards the observation deck's windows, which were suddenly lit up by a million distant stars.

The *Doina* had finally exited Greyspace.

Silvia had little time to feel the comfort of this strange new arrangement of stars, for her eyes, and the eyes of everyone else present on the deck, were immediately drawn to what lay right before them.

They must have been as far from it as Luna was from Terra and, yet, there was no doubt that Shangri was well and truly immense. Silvia wasn't even sure if it was a thousand or a million times larger than the Earth, nor could she remember from her research at that moment. All across its surface, one could see countless lights, with lines both red and white criss-crossing its surface. Silvia came closer to the window to see that there were massive... *clouds(?)* that obscured sections of the City the size of Terran continents.

The surface was not smooth and Silvia quickly realised what all the round bulbs that littered the surface were.

Planets. Those are planets and moons! Bound to the structure! She glanced towards the largest such bulge, which she knew was roughly as large as the world of Mars in their Solar System. *That must be the Darkside of Shangri-La itself, the old heart of the City of Shangri.* She looked towards the darker areas. Some were either obscured by the great smog clouds and artificial weather fronts for which Shangri was famous for. Others were dark, due to underpopulation and abandonment. Some were simply the barren roofs of the great factories that lay beneath, likely teeming with the light of machinery or the fires of mankind.

She had studied maps of Shangri and could not claim to be truly taken by surprise by the world's appearance since she had seen the world's image projected in front of her many times before. Yet, now that the city lay before her, she couldn't help but gaze in awe at its gigantic scale laid out tangibly before her.

'*Majestic.*'

Silvia knew the word had come from Nick, though she did not look away from the sight before her.

Neither did she turn towards Mira upon hearing her reply.

'I guess you could say that...'

Chapter IV

Enter the Shangri Man

Laur had never thought he would see a Dyson Sphere in his lifetime.

In the days of his youth, when Terra was Earth and his people had believed themselves alone, there were theories as to whether such constructs were possible. A Dyson Sphere had been a hypothetical concept put forth, that proposed that it was possible to wrap entire stars in one giant sphere, with the goal of harvesting all of its energy for use by an advanced civilization.

After the End Times, Terrans had quickly discovered that the idea of harvesting a star's entire energy was in no way something hypothetical. The elves employed rings that surrounded their suns harvested fractions of their energy. They had never progressed to complete spherical encasements, for there simply was no need for such a thing. Stars were gigantic fonts of energy and a civilization would be hard-pressed to put all of it to use, particularly when there were much cheaper and more efficient means of harvesting a heavenly body's energy than putting it inside a giant box.

The orcish worldships could charge up their batteries to complete saturation in a matter of months by drawing sunlight from a single feeble star. It was neither advisable, nor was it ever really necessary, but they could do it nonetheless. Within the Andromeda Galaxy, the ancestors of the demani had impregnated many of their stars with their elder magics, giving birth to the fabled Dark Stars that transferred energy directly across their ancient web energy wherever said energy was needed. The Senoyu had snuffed out and harvested many of Andromeda's stars, yet many still remained and they were more than enough to power the demani's newly liberated realm. In Triangulum, the Aesir and Vanir had built many such spheres around their stars in their distant past, yet they had found that such structures were vulnerable to the dangers of all-out war on a grand scale. They could be used as gigantic bombs, tearing apart entire systems in truly titanic displays of cosmic power. Some had even been detonated within the Greyspace, leading to vast sections of the pocket dimension becoming dangerous to traverse.

The only true Dyson Sphere that existed within the Local Cluster was the City of Shangri, capturing within its embrace the world's dying star *La*, which was almost the size of Terra's moon, Luna. Such a star nevertheless produced far less energy than the Urheimat's gigantic engines of solar might, yet even the sprawling City of Shangri found little need for all the energy their harvesting sheets produced, with many Districts lying abandoned or underdeveloped.

Much of the energy used went towards maintaining the City's gravity, which was artificial, with the Shangri 'lattice' (the core component of the massive construct) acting as a conductor for the great gravity generators on which the city depended to keep itself together. Wisps of a strange white-blue light escaped the superstructure through gigantic vents the size of small moons, while hot red light was emitted from large crystalline constructs coated in red rock which extended upwards hundreds of thousands of miles into the dark void surrounding the city. One of their main purposes was to expel excess heat, which was something Shangri had to do to prevent the giant structure from overheating and falling apart. These great towers, as thick as Terra itself, extended forward towards the outer void at regular intervals, giving the City of Shangri the appearance of a giant sea urchin. These were the great Piers of Shangri and they also acted as docking and power station for visiting starships.

The *Doina* made its way to one of these great towers and, upon coming up right next to it, began to move forward and descend towards the City's surface. This particular tower was one of the three Diplomatic Piers, where all of the many states that maintained relations with Shangri received a certain section of the Pier from the Shangri government to use as their own docking station. Initially, the Republican Alliance had received one of the highest section of their Diplomatic Pier (which would actually be regarded as one of the *lowest* section, since it lay farthest away from the City itself. However, due to recent developments in the Andromeda and Triangulum Galaxy, the Republican Alliance had grown into the second-most powerful of all of Shangri's neighbours, after the Urheimat of Humanity itself.

Hence, the Alliance now controlled the section of the Pier closest to the surface, whilst states such those of the Avallon, Erebor and Liliput, lay further away from the City's surface. This seemed impressive, up until one realised that the Urheimat of Humanity, controlled an *entire* Diplomatic Pier, whilst the Others Unaligned also shared the third Diplomatic Pier among themselves. This would be one of the many instances of the Shangri showing their true colours, as the Piers, though formally granted as gifts to all the partners of Shangri (whom the Peacekeeper insisted were all equal), were actually granted to those states whom the House of Gisevius either feared or wished to flatter.

Lejla and the rest of the piloting team had little problem identifying their destination, as it lay right next to another Republican Alliance docking area and this one was occupied by the *Azorian*, Kimmie Jimmel's ship. The *Azorian* had been constructed on Moria during the days of the War of Vengeance, after the goblins had recovered the wreckage of a ruined Svart military vessel. The shipwreck provided the goblins almost everything they needed to reverse-engineer the design and their ingenuity filled the gaps in their knowledge. The *Azorian* had once been merely a prototype, yet Kimmie Jimmel had warmed to the vatgrown abomination and had made it his flagship.

For that was what the *Azorian* was: the result of the first goblin attempt at breeding one of the black *Unialki*, the great living ships that bore the elves across the cosmos in their bowels. The goblin ship was not as sleek and elegant as the elven-raised unialki, yet it was charming, in its own way. The goblins had not figured out how to stimulate the *Azorian* in such a way as to have it secrete the gels that would merge into the traditional black carapace of a unialki warship, yet they had figured out that they could simply cover the ship with artificial ceramic plates. The result looked very much like the offspring of a shark and an armadillo, in the sense that it was shaped like a predator, yet its demeanor was quite comical overall.

The *Doina* was actually of an orcish design or, at least, the Terran *interpretation* of an orcish design. It was not alive, at least not in the way the *Azorian* was. Yet, this did not stop the *Azorian*'s mind from hailing it as a fellow Republican vessel and its chirruping greeting noises were broadcast across the Hajduk ship by an excited Lejla, who had always found the behaviour of such ships to be absolutely joyful. The *Azorian*'s greeting was followed by a call from the vessel's goblin captain, which welcomed them all to the City of Shangri.

Laur had arrived upon the observation deck just as they began their descent towards the City. He now gazed upon the *Azorian* and noted the long line of vehicles currently boarding it. They had messaged Jimmel with news of their impending arrival naught but a few hours before and the goblins seemed to be well underway in their departure. Laur picked out a phone from his pocket and called the goblin captain.

'Hello, Captain Ontario?' he spoke into the device's microphone.

'Hello, General Pop! I trust you had a pleasant journey?' Ontario replied.

'We did!' *Not really, but it was ok.* 'I see you're already getting ready to depart?'

'Yes, sir. Mr. Jimmel wants us on our way and out of yours in no time!'

'Huh... is it that bad around here?'

'On the contrary, sir! The City's quite charming, albeit a bit chaotic at times! I'm certain you'll come to be quite fond of it as time goes by! I know I have!'

'Glad to hear it, Ontario!' Laur glanced towards the space between the docking *Doina* and the docked *Azorian*, where a large number of people were gathered. From their appearance, he could tell that they were government and military officials among their number, though the vast majority of the great crowd that had gathered appeared to be simple civilians.

'I see we have a welcoming party.'

'Eh, no, sir! I'm afraid you don't. I believe that what you're seeing is our *Goodvye* party,' Ontario responded.

'Oh... I see...' *Jesus Christ... Jimmel's messages said relations were at an all time high; now I see crowds gathering to celebrate their departure.* Pop came closer to the window to inspect the crowd. *That's at least twenty thousand people. What the hell happened?* 'I don't recall the other ambassadors mentioning this in their reports.'

'Well, it hasn't happened before, sir.'

What? They hate Kimmie Jimmel... in particular?! What kind of people are these?

Ontario offered additional clarification. 'I've actually asked some of the other captains on the Pier if they've ever seen something like this before, sir. Apparently, it is tradition in Shangri to wish guests that have conducted themselves honourably and gained popularity within the city a good journey home! It is not uncommon for such visitors to attract crowds on the day of their departure.'

'Ah... I see now.' *Pfewww... now that makes sense. Of course they loved Jimmel. Everyone loves Jimmel.*

'Of course, sir! I understand that you will be splitting up now into four convoys, with each convoy taking over a separate location?'

'I confirm.'

'Excellent. I've designated four of my lieutenants as guides. They will take each of your convoys to its respective destination. You'll find them together with the leader of the local welcoming committee right outside your ship. I know you could've found your own way to your posts, but I thought it best if you had someone along to assure you that you were on the right path! Once you reach your destinations, our colleagues will guide you through the transition process.'

'That's much appreciated!' *And only natural.* 'Thank you, Ontario!'

'Excellent, sir! Now, sir, with your permission, I have preparations I need to make for our departure.'

'Of course! Best of luck, captain! And enjoy your journey back home!'

'Thank you, sir! Enjoy your stay on Shangri!' With that, Ontario ended the call, leaving Laur to stare at his phone for a moment. *I wish my centurions – and legates, now – were so civil and polite.*

Laur joined his Hajduks as they gathered in the *Doina*'s main loading bay. Most were already in their vehicles, ready to ride out into the city. He saw his commanders gathered together near the *Doina*'s massive doors, which still lay shut.

'Welcome to Shangri, comrades!'

'Everybody get your passports ready!' Gigi joked.

Laur had no patience for comedy now. He turned towards one of Lejla's men, perched up in one of the loading bay's observation platforms. 'Open the gates!'

As the man nodded and began to follow his order, Pop turned back to his men, knowing that it would be a while until they would all be gathered in one place again. 'The goblins have arranged for guides to lead us to our posts.'

'What? Do they think we don't know how maps work?' an offended Bojana immediately interjected.

This is exactly what I'm talking about. 'It's a *courtesy*! Now, listen here for fuck's sake! All of you!'

For once, they were quiet. Laur gave them all a long look.

Iosip. Lejla. Bojana. Gigi.

I hope they don't get themselves killed while they're out of my sight...

Fuck... sometimes I wonder why they haven't killed each other while they were in my sight.

'Once you get to your destination, let me know! Once you're all settled in, let me know!' he began.

'Once you tuck yourselves into bed, *let him know*!' Nick continued.

Laur had had enough. 'Good! They will! But, are *you* gonna text me in the morning?'

Nick was visibly confused for a moment and so were Silvia and Nick. *They have no idea what's coming.* 'Why would I text you in the morning?' *Ok, maybe a bit of comedy works.*

'So that I can send you the picture I take every morning,' Laur said, as if the answer was obvious.

'What picture do you take every morning?' Nick asked.

'Every morning, when I wake up, I take a picture of my dick and I send it to everyone who texts me in the morning.' Laur didn't allow any reaction to break out yet, though he did see Gigi hide a smile. 'Do you know why I do that, Nick?' he asked, coming in closer to his young centurion.

'N-no?' *What else is he gonna say?*

'I do it so that they can see how big my dick is!' Laur said, his face dead serious.

Iosip snorted as he closed his eyes.

Gigi shook his head in disapproval.

Silvia, Bojana and Lejla, being the ladies that they were, simply smiled in embarrassment while they pretended to look away.

'I don't get it,' Nick confessed, causing the entire group to burst out laughing.

Laur rolled his eyes. 'Well, it's better to try and be funny and fail, than to try and be taken seriously and fail...' he said, before turning towards his Bosniak Legate. 'Lejla, take care of the *Doina*!'

She smiled faintly and nodded.

'Silvia, Nick, get in your vehicles and get ready to roll out. The rest of you, let's go!'

The *Doina*'s doors finished opening just as Laur finished speaking, revealing a ramp that led towards the Pier's platform, upon which waited four goblins flanking two humans. As they neared the small welcoming committee, one of the humans spoke.

'General Pop! Welcome to the City of Shangri!' his voice was noble, yet also somewhat pretentious.

He spoke in the High Tongue of Shangri, the language of the City's upper classes and a language Laur and his men had learned in preparation for their arrival. Laur caught himself just as he was about to extend his hand to shake his. *This is Shangri. He's highborn. They don't shake hands here. They don't touch one another in greeting here.*

'It's great to finally be here!' he said and smiled politely as Laur took note of the Shangri human now before him. He was pudgy and his skin was of a deep brown, though ethnically he reminded Laur of a pasty Englishman. His hair was thick and long, tied up in a topknot he kept covered by some type of fez. He wore elegant robes of the colour red, with shoes of what appeared to be some kind of white leather. He held his hands hidden beneath a fold in his robes, reminding Laur of Varys from *Game of Thrones* or some Ottoman court eunuch.

Laur nodded to the goblins and his gaze then lingered upon Vox's human companion. He wore something resembling a three-piece suit, coloured in a deep purple, with the exception of his shoes, which were of a mahogany brown colour. His face was much more friendly than that of his companion, yet he did not speak.

The pudgy one spoke, 'I am Vox of Loughlery-Castamere. His excellency Gisevius the Fourth, Protector of the Free City of Shangri, Warden of Pisces, Speaker of Tongues, Caretaker of La...'

Lord of the Seven Kingoms, Protector of the Realm, Khaleesi of the Great Grass Sea

'... Lord Patron of the Single Star and Keeper of the Peace, sends to you his warmest regards!'

Eh? Does he now?

'Much appreciated!' Laur glanced towards the procession that had gathered before the *Azorian*, as Jimmel's men continued loading their ship. A few of their number had turned to behold the new arrivals. Laur saw many humans and (what he assumed to be) remani among their number, though he did spot the occasional goblin, troll or elf now observing him and his Hajduks. Most of them seemed curious, some seemed sceptical and quite a large number seemed concerned.

'His Excellency insisted that I inform you that he is currently dealing with matters of the utmost importance and that he hopes you understand the situation,' Vox explained.

'No need to apologise! I understand his majesty is a busy man! His station naturally comes with responsibilities that stretch him thin.' *Just that I don't think that's the case.* 'I trust he is on top of things?' *Lie to me. Let me see how it looks like when you lie.*

Vox smiled a curt smile. He moved in slightly closer to him and Laur saw that he was a full foot taller than the pudgy Shangrian. The bureaucrat shifted his eyes upwards as if to signal that what he was about to say was meant only for his ears. 'General Pop, his Majesty has presided over the leadership of our city since before the Romans – those are your progenitors, I believe?'

'So the story goes.' *Well at least you bothered to do some research...*

'*Huh*, I see!' – since before the Romans were little more than hunched cavemen piecing together huts out of wet clay and dry grass. His father before him (may he rest in peace and may his memory never die!) watched over the City since times far before the first human of Earth had summoned up the wit needed to place one rock atop another! His great-grandfather (countless blessings may be upon him) was born in a time when the universe itself was young and men were as rare as fur on fish! To answer your question, yes, he is on top of things!'

Fuck off and go to my dick, you little faggot! 'Well, then I must apologise sincerely for my use of language! My intent was to be courteous! It brings me naught but distress to have it be that my first words spoken within your wondrous realm be ones that must lower the standing of my people under your gaze! I ask only that you understand that, for all intents and purposes, it *is* my first day here! It fills me with shame to have gotten off to such a rough start and it pains me to know that I cannot take that back. Yet, I can promise you that, as time will go by, I know with all certainty surmountable that words of friendship and veneration of your own tongues will spring forth from mine own in ways you may find graceful!' *There: fuck you! I know how to play games too!*

Vox nodded slowly. 'I'm very pleased to hear that, though I would recommend becoming accustomed with our traditions sooner, rather than later! You will find that when you do that, things go much more smoothly. Within Shangri we have an order to things! Without said order, everything crumbles to dust. I'm certain you understand?'

'I do, of course.' *I know that you're one of the upper classes and upper classes tend to always want to keep things the way they are, lest they find the world turned upside down.*

'I'm certain you do!' Vox finally acknowledged Laur's companions with a nod and a bow. 'I understand that Ambassador Jimmel has delegated these fine gentlemen as your escorts and I see that you have prepared to complete your arrival! Enjoy Shangri, general!'

What a welcome. 'I'm certain I will, *your grace*!' *Bite! Please bite!*

Vox was about to leave, yet he turned around stunned. 'I beg *your* pardon?'

He bit. 'I must beg *yours*, once more! Did I say something wrong?' Laur feigned ignorance.

'*General Pop, I am not of the Royal House!*'

Laur opened his eyes wide in mock shock and raised his shoulders to highlight his 'confusion'.

'General Pop, "your grace" is only used when addressing members of the royalty!'

'I see,' *I know.* 'How does one address a person of your station?'

Vox seemed on the verge of apoplexy. 'You may call me "sir", if you so wish.'

'I do!' Laur waited for Vox to make to depart once more. '*Sir?*' he asked.

Vox stopped once more and looked upon Laur once more, irritation in his eyes.

'If I may ask since... well... as you just saw earlier, I am not familiar with local custom... How does one refer to a foreign ambassador?'

Vox stood motionless. Laur had to raise an eyebrow to force it out of him.

'*Your Excellency.*'

'Ah! I see! I just wanted to be certain that I understood the proper order of things! We'll be one our way! Thank you for your kind words. We can handle ourselves from here!' *Chubby motherfucker, don't you have liposuction or Ozempic or some shit around here? Fat fuck...*

As Vox began walking to a nearby limousine, Laur turned to the assembled goblins and greeted them. After exchanging a few quick pleasantries, he introduced each goblin lieutenant to their respective Hajduk. By the time Laur had finished saying his goodbyes and shaking hands with Gigi,

Iosip and Bojana, Vox had reached his limousine, and Laur caught his first real glimpse of a Single Star remani.

His coat was brown, as Technowolf had said it would usually be, and Laur was reminded of the brown of a German Shepherd's coat. The resemblance to dogs continued, as Laur fully understood why the Single Star were like domestic dogs, while the Black Knight were more akin to wolves.

It was during *Fuga*, which was how Romanians referred to their westward exodus during Ragnarök, that he had first caught glimpse of a remani in the Little Carpathians of western Slovakia. Ninety thousand soldiers, mainly remnants of the Romanian and Bulgarian military, made up the rearguard of the last great refugee column heading west. As a million wretched souls, the last remnants of their peoples, pushed onwards towards the rumoured safety of the west, Pop had found himself looking out the window of his jeep towards a nearby forest. He hadn't eaten in days, the water he had been drinking came from a muddy river they had crossed the day before and he hadn't slept in two days. Thus, when he had seen the wolfman trekking ominously along the treeline, with a rifle slung across his back and his canine face downcast, likely pondering the next phase of the defence of the Humans of Earth, he had assumed that he was simply (and finally) going completely mad. He would later find out that said remani had been Basenji, who was now next to Mira in the car she had brought over from Terra.

At the Battle of Prague, he had first seen remani up close. One of them he had later found out had already been christened by Ashaver as "Van Helsing". Laur had seen the same Hugh Jackman movie Ashaver had seen and, indeed, this remani looked exactly like the titular werewolf. A gigantic mass of muscle covered in dark fur. A wolf's head with tall and tufted ears rising above a sharp jaw full of menacing fangs. Only his hands and feet revealed that this man was no canine, but a type of giant intelligent lemur, his people one of many of their race that wandered the stars. Nevertheless, the similarity to werewolves had stuck, as most Black Knight remani had wild, wolflike appearances and coats that were reminiscent of those of the beasts that had roamed Earth's wilderness. On that same day he had first seen Technowolf and another called Lassie, a rare warrior female of their race. She and Van Helsing had died in Prague, their bodies recovered by Technowolf, who had survived, and were later cast into the fires of Terra's sun.

These Single Star remani were definitely much more doglike. The remani that opened Vox's door could've simply looked like a wolfman with a fawn coat, if it weren't for the droopy ears and his snout, which was shorter and slightly thicker than that of the Black Knight remani. Laur did note that they also had a penchant for mimicking the fashion choices of the humans they found themselves amongst, as this particular remani also wore a dark blue suit, similar to that of Vox's companion.

... who had not followed him to the limousine.

'We weren't expecting the Alliance to send someone like you!' the words were not spoken in the High Speech of Shangri, but in the English of Terra. Laur turned to face the second Shangri human he would ever meet in his life. He saw a friendly face bearing very bright, curious eyes. Unlike Vox, who reminded him of a Westerner with a good tan, this one looked very much like an actual Mediterranean European, bar his eyes, which were a bright blue and his hair, which was quite fair. Laur looked down to see a hand extended towards him.

'Well, nice to meet you too!' he reached out and shook his hand. *This one knows our ways. He is also willing to go along with them.*

The Shangri man was unfazed, seemingly more interested in something else. 'We've grown quite fond of Kimmie Jimmel during his time spent here. He will be sorely missed and we look forward to his eventual return; perhaps in a more informal capacity.'

'I hope you will find me equally endearing!' *You're certainly not making it easy though.*

'Oh, make no mistake, *I* do,' he said, sparing a quick look and a cheeky smile in the direction of Vox's limousine, which had not yet departed. 'You are definitely an intriguing character,' he turned to look Laur in the eyes. 'Though not as intriguing as the message your presence here sends.'

The Shangri man gestured towards the Hajduk convoy which was about to depart from within the *Doina*'s landing bay. 'Come! I do not wish to preoccupy you for too long! You have much to do and I know your time is precious!' he said, patting Laur on the back as he gestured towards his convoy.

Laur went with it and they began to walk slowly towards the Terran vehicles.

'The Urheimat knows of your appointment already.'

What???

'Oh! Don't be so concerned! It's all quite simple really! Kimmie Jimmel received word of your appointment, then he proceeded to grant us knowledge of your impending arrival. Such knowledge must be shared and it was unavoidable that it reached the ears of the Imperial Ambassador on Shangri.'

'I see.' *I see your government is full of leaks and snitches.*

'The Imperial Embassy has already sent us a formal letter concerning their opinion on the matter.'

'And what might that be?' Laur asked.

The Shangri man stopped. They found themselves midway between Vox's vehicle and the first Hajduk car and he turned to face Laur, whilst lowering his voice to speak discreetly. 'That you are a war criminal.'

'Oh, they left out "race traitor", "trucebreaker" and "apostate"?'

'Of course they didn't, but, then again, every now and then they'll use those words to refer to us as well. Quite frankly, it was those denouncements made that pertained solely to *your* character that we found most intriguing.'

The Shangri man resumed their walk before continuing. 'Your presence here is seen as a provocation both by the Urheimat and by those of Shangri's citizens that find it distasteful to receive someone with your reputation as a dignitary. I would have assumed such aspects would have been considered prior to your appointment.'

'You assumed correctly.' *It's actually all my fault, really!*

But you don't need to know that...

'It comforts me little to know as such. I also assume that the reason behind your appointment has to do with matters beyond those discussed and agreed beforehand.'

Laur remained silent pondering his next words. Fortunately, the Shangri man seemed to not be interested in whether or not his assumptions were correct.

'I will remind you that the Peace of Shangri is kept not just by tradition and custom, but also by trust in our institutions and by the respect of our laws.'

By this point they had reached the Mercedes Maybach that would serve as Laur's primary means of transportation within the City. He turned towards his host and spoke. 'I can promise you that we are aware of our quality as *guests* in your house and that we shall grant you all due respect and consideration! But, please understand that we are as bound to our own traditions as you are bound to yours, and that we are *civilized* men and, thus, we are obliged to honour our commitments, no matter how challenging they may be!'

His partner in conversation smiled slightly, 'The City of Shangri is a vast realm and in such havens of mankind, one may find every shade of the soul there is to be and that might come to be! If you come about those tints of darkness which haunt your dreams, it would be best that you either shine our light upon them or that you bury them in a darkness beyond the eyes of men! But, never forget that there exists nothing in *between* and nothing *beyond*! If what will come about in the night slips from your hands into our day, you will find that we will see your *shade* as one and the same!'

'I understand.' *A bit poetic, but given how public this place is, it's necessary poetry.*

'Good!' The Shangri man reached out and opened Laur's car door, bidding him enter. 'Best of luck, Laur Pop!'

'Thank you!'

He extended his hand and Laur shook it once more before getting into his car, which swiftly took off as the Shangri man made his way to his own vehicle.

Flying was illegal within the City of Shangri. It was apparently a measure that had been put in place long before to put a halt to the horrendous traffic jams that had long plagued the City. Transportation within Shangri was facilitated by leylines, which were essentially massive temporal accelerators. One would enter a portal hole at one end of Shangri and emerge on the opposite side of the city in a matter of minutes. Nevertheless, few journeys required a complete traversal of the city and the Hajduks journey was no different. One by one, the four Hajduk convoys were split up, as Gigi departed for the Military district and Bojana for the Commercial District of Belagravia. Within twenty minutes of their departure from the *Doina*, the Hajduks emerged in the Diplomatic District and beheld the sun of Shangri for the first time.

It was not something truly spectacular.

Its light was just like that of Terra's sun and, quite frankly, like that of any other sun. What *was* peculiar was the fact that Shangri's sun, La, did not move. It just stood there, right in the very middle of the sky, completely motionless, as if it were a lamp that hung from some invisible ceiling and shone over the wondrous Brightside of Shangri.

They had emerged right within the Diplomatic District and Laur was shocked by how familiar the area felt. *It looks like fucking Kensington!* The impression came primarily from the architecture, which was very European and very evocative of a colonial metropole. The buildings and the avenues and even the trees were much larger, but overall, there was a sense of heritage and authority about the place.

The British had an empire for what? Three hundred years? These motherfuckers have been running a galaxy for over three hundred thousand years! The place is actually remarkably mundane if you really think about it! Those were the numbers Laur tried to wrap his head around as Iosip's column split towards the location of the Terran Embassy: the Sanjak Manor. There, he would relieve Colonel Diop of the Terran Army of his duties and take up the position of Emissary of Terra.

He observed Shangri from his car window. The city was obviously incredibly advanced, with technology that truly boggled the mind and, yet, it was all so... *normal*? 'Comprehensible' was a better term and Laur had seen comprehensible galactic empires before. The Svart, with their timelessly perfect technology. The Senoyu and the magic they sought to transform and shackle, once more, into a discernible technology. The Aesir and the Vanir, which had destroyed each other for millennia, their conflict never allowing them to reach truly grand levels of advancement beyond the Bifrost and a couple of other things.

Yet, the City of Shangri outclassed all of them in its... *reservation* towards unrestrained technological advancement. Sure, the city was known to have grown far beyond its capacity to efficiently sustain a population that was prosperous in its entirety. Yet, it had never sought to combat demographic challenges through further scientific innovation.

Laur looked towards the mass of pavement and took note of the Shangri themselves. He saw mostly humans, a few bast, even fewer ursai and a smattering of a few other races, mainly elves, as well as kobolds, which he stared at a little, since he had never seen a kobold before. He had spent the last week becoming familiarized with Shangri culture and he could tell from their clothing and mannerisms that those he gazed upon now were all upper class.

Everyone in this district was well dressed, though as they neared their destination, it became harder and harder to observe individual citizens, as their numbers seemed to grow at an exponential rate the closer they got to the embassy. Soon, they encountered a police barricade, which was swiftly removed as the remani constables that manned it identified the incoming vehicles as the diplomatic convoy they had been expecting. Soon after crossing the barricade, Laur swiftly realized why there had been the need for such an obstacle.

The streets were truly packed with people now, and the constables struggled to keep the road clear of jaywalkers. To his surprise, Laur noticed that many of those in the crowd were waving flags.

Republican Alliance flags and... the flag of Moria?

It was here that Laur also saw murine up-close for the first time in his life. They greatly resembled the remani, though they were less physically imposing. Their coats seemed to be predominantly a monochrome brown, though he did spot a few red, black and fawn ones among the crowd. Most of them lacked tails and they were missing the large canines and muzzles of the remani, though they did compensate with their large incisors. Laur noted their clothes, which were of far lower quality than those of the gathered humans.

He would have studied them longer, were it not for the fact that they had arrived at their destination.

It kinda looks like the old Musée d'Orsay, back in Paris.

The Embassy of the Republican Alliance at Convent Garden had initially been the residence of some wealthy Shangri businessman, only for his children to convert it to office space at one point in its history. It was a massive building and its style reminded Laur of an old Parisian palace. He knew that the building was rectangular in shape, with a large indoor area at its very centre, and right behind it was a ballroom beyond which lay a yard and a waterway that acted both as a security feature and an enjoyable luxury, as the area between the canal and the building could be used as a terrace. On its sides, the embassy shared walls with two other buildings of similar design. From what he had seen in the building's schematics, both of these buildings housed an assortment of Shangri hedge funds and think tanks. *And probably the Shangri Constabulary's counter-surveillance operation.*

Laur glanced across the building's front steps, where the goblins had erected a barrier, of sorts, made up of mobile fencing placed between the trees that lined the walkway before the Embassy. Beyond this barrier lay a large mass of people; most clearly civilians, though Laur could also see the unmistakable signs of-

Press teams... I haven't seen those in a long time and I'm as annoyed by them now as I was back then.

Most of the Hajduks remained parked outside the building, waiting for the eventual departure of their goblin predecessors and for space to free up underneath the great structure, within the underground parking lot. Laur's vehicle parked right in front of the main entrance, just as the goblins moved aside part of the barrier, allowing him to open his door and take his first step in Convent Garden

'General Pop!' one of the goblins greeted him.

'Commander Tlaloc!'

'We've almost finished packing our luggage. We expect to depart within the hour.'

'Excellent!' *Where's Jimmel?*

'Kimmie's inside. He said you should join him in the central hall.'

'He did now?'

'He said he wanted to pass the torch to you personally!'

Ah, meaning he wants to talk privately. Got it! 'Well, then I'll get to it! You remember Centurions Murărescu and Lăutaru?' he said, as Silvia and Nick approached, having exited their respective vehicles.

'I do, sir! I've also had the pleasure of remembering Technowolf, Basenji and Mira!' Tlaloc smiled in a particularly fond manner as he greeted them all as they approached.

'Hi, Courdaleine!' Mira smiled curtly as the goblin hugged her after saluting and shaking hands with the others.

Little princess now, isn't she? 'Excellent! Centurion Murărescu will handle the technical handover. I'll go see Kimmie and sort out the formal transfer. Commander Tlaloc, may you have an excellent journey home!'

'May you have an excellent stay in Shangri, sir!'

Laur walked through the embassy's great doorway and into the reception area. There were still some goblins about and they saluted, just as they proceeded to carry away the last of their luggage. Laur greeted them, then proceeded to walk by the main reception desk and through one of two large doors leading to the central atrium and the location of one of the wondrous sights he had seen in his life.

The tree was ancient, that much Laur could tell just by looking at it. He didn't have to know from the schematics that it was just over fifteen thousand years old. It had once been the mere sapling of a Shangri laurel tree, which reminded him of a mix between an oak and a willow, with leaves similar to those of a fig. Its trunk was creased, coarse and thick, as the tree seemed to coil its way upwards. The embassy building had five floors, with each level being at least four meters tall, whilst the ground floor itself was over ten meters tall. Yet, the tree itself twisted its way upwards, passing every level, its upper canopy embracing the great glass dome that caped the central hall's roof.

At its base stood a goblin or, rather, at its base *lay* a goblin.

Kimmie Jimmel had changed in the forty years Laur had known him. Once quite carefree and jovial, he had taken to a strange melancholy as times had gone by. *Ever since Hellsbreach... That's when it started. He's felt the guilt ever since.* Said guilt had only seemed to grow within him as time had passed by and more and more sorrows had piled themselves upon him.

The Goblins of Moria were not like the Humans of Terra. They had not weathered an apocalypse. They had not seen their world turn on them. They had not held their lifeless loved ones upon fields of death beneath skies of darkness. They had known war, yes, but it had always been a war *abroad* for them. A war fought in the hinterlands beyond their sight, against a future they could not comprehend. They had won, yet the price had always been small and, when victory comes cheap, every penny spent bears the weight of a thousand bars of gold.

Before Laur now lay one such man, who had won so much and lost so little, and yet upon whom the cost had still left a wound too deep to heal and too painful to neglect.

Once a gorgeous man, Jimmel had now grown gaunt and haughty. He still carried himself as a bearer of authority, yet the spring in his step was gone. He sat at the base of the tree and at his side stood a small pot in which he had only just now placed a tiny sapling, while before him lay an open cut he had apparently made upon one of the great tree's roots. His goblin hands lay covered in dirt, which he rubbed upon the slight wound he had wrought upon the ancient life before him.

Laur saw that they were alone. No goblin remained within the Great Hall and the upper levels of the floors above them also seemed to have been cleared. He did not speak, for he did not wish to disturb Jimmel, who seemed to be caught within a moment of reflection.

'Her time has nearly come!' Kimmie remarked.

Most goblins had voices Laur found to be annoying. Either too raspy or too squeaky and almost always with some peculiar accent that made certain words hard to understand. Yet, Jimmel's voice had always been soothing and friendly. Now, it carried with it the sense of loss that had germinated within him over the decades, as well as an odd... *disillusionment*?

Laur did not respond, instead choosing to walk slowly towards Jimmel and the tree.

The goblin continued, 'When Arlena passed guardianship of this place to me, she told me that the time would come soon, perhaps during my tenure here.' Jimmel finally turned to openly acknowledge him. 'It seems that it shall likely be you who will come to see her pass.'

Getting right into it now, are we? 'Hello, Kimmie!'

'Hello, Laur!' The goblin got up from the ground and picked up a cloth with which he proceeded to clean his hands. 'I've come to be quite fond of her and likely so will you!' He pointed towards the fourth floor. 'That's where your office is. From there you have a wonderful view of the canopy, though not the trunk. For that, the middle levels are best.' He tapped the roots beneath him. 'These go deep into the ground. You can see them, though you'll have to go to the basement for that!'

'Do you recommend it?'

'I do, actually. You should consider doing it as soon as you're all settled in, though I am certain that during your time here you'll find a time to do so.'

'Oh, I will!' Laur paused, mulling things over for a moment.

'The roots aren't the problem!' Jimmel turned back to look upon the laurel tree. 'The structure is strong and resilient. It's weathered things which beings such as you and I can't even comprehend, though we may sometimes lie to ourselves that we can fathom such passing of time! The soil is healthy. It should not go to waste! Once this tree will be no more, another may grow in its place and prosper.'

'Did you have any specific tree in mind?'

'Yes. I did, actually.' Kimmel glanced down at the ground and took a deep breath. 'I'd like to think that I didn't have the time to see it through myself. In actuality, I had a lot of time.' Silence followed as Kimmel's gaze wandered. 'In truth, I couldn't bring myself to do it.' His eyes shifted towards the old tree's ancient canopy, before falling down towards the base of its trunk. 'No tree such as this has ever grown on Moria, as I believe none has grown on Terra! Within its core lies a seed, roughly the size of a man's fist. It is hard as rock and virtually indestructible. As it has to be. It has to withstand fire!'

'These Shangri Laurel trees do not ever truly die! They do not ever truly breed either. They come from a world far off into the Urheimat's domain, a world now lost to the darkness of antiquity. A world of fire and of little moisture. These trees would grow on small islands nestled in fresh lakes surrounded by seas of grassland bordered by an abyss of rock and fire. Once in an age, the fire would burst forth in rage and hunger, burning to a crisp every blade of grass and carrying their sizzling cinders across the dry winds up until they reached the islands upon which these trees would languish.'

'The trees would burn, but they would remain. Within their ashes, upon the scorched earth, scattered all around the dead isles, they would leave behind rocks the size of a man's fist, from whence a new tree would rise again.'

'I know the story.'

'I had no doubt. You always seemed to know everything.'

'Not everything.'

'Oh?'

'What of the saplings?' Laur asked.

Kimmel smiled.

Laur continued. 'This tree was once a sapling with a father and a mother. That's three tree-rocks already on a little island and I'm certain they weren't the only ones. Wouldn't their island become crowded?'

'It did. Hence why it was brought here.' Kimmel turned back towards the tree. 'It is the nature of the young to crave their own little place in the world.'

'And this tree was fortunate enough to receive it.'

'It was, as its forefathers before it and as its *sapling* after it.' Kimmel smiled, looking at the little piece of the tree he had set aside for himself. 'Only the sapling that would spring forth from the tree-rock, that is. This little fellow will live for some time, yet he will one day wither away and join the nature of his new home!' Kimmie smiled melancholically. 'Some life is more fortunate than others!' he reminded himself.

'Speaking from experience, now?'

'Speaking from *lack* of experience.' Kimmel's smile faded. 'I'm happy it's you who came.'

Laur stood motionless. 'Are you, really?'

'Your hands are rough, yet they are steady!' Kimmel bent down and picked up the small container. 'I trust that you will have the time to do that which I could bring myself to carry out.'

Laur wanted to answer, yet he found himself struggling to pick the right words.

Kimmel noticed the pause. 'It wasn't a question, Laur. It was a statement. I know you will!'

The goblin moved closer and extended his hand, which Laur gripped in a gesture shared by both the goblins of Moria and the humans of Terra. 'Laur?' this time the goblin definitely asked.

He replied by raising his eyebrows ever so slightly.

'Be gentle! Do it softly!' he gently whispered.

'I will. I always do.'

'No, you don't!' The goblin stared at him sternly, as if he was already guilty of breaking his promise. Then, another sadness tugged at his eyes. 'Mira is here?'

I was expecting that question. 'Yes, though I still haven't figured out exactly why.'

'*I* have.'

Laur raised an eyebrow. *I mean I think I know why, but why are you so cocksure? All that you know is what you've heard through vague hints and concocted hearsay.*

'One of her reasons is to learn from you.'

Laur scoffed. *Now you really are smoking the oils, Kimmie...*

Jimmel's face never moved. 'She wants to know how you do it.'

'And what might that be?'

'How you live with a heavy heart.'

Laur froze for a moment. For some reason, he thought of Mira's mother, Sara. He thought of how sweet she was. How gentle. How kind. How light-hearted she was. Her memory now a ghost, it felt as though she had always been a creature of the morning haze, as joyful light danced between flecks of cool mist.

What cruelty of the world has taken Mira's face – Sara's face – and placed weight upon it...

It is not the same, Kimmie! The weight in my heart, I placed myself. Mira's heart has had a piece of it sliced off. It is a different pain...

'I see you, Laur!' Kimmie smiled gently, looking deep into his eyes. 'You think your burden's different,' he continued correctly.

I forgot how good he is...

Kimmie walked up to him and placed a hand on his shoulder. 'Focus on the task at hand! Mira has her own journey. You will see her look into you from time to time. Allow her to search for what she is looking for. Do not intervene, Laur! Let her find her own way across her suffering.'

'What if there isn't?' Laur asked. 'Is that not a cruelty all on its own?'

Kimmie's eyes drifted. 'I fear that for men like you and men like me, there just might not be a way through it. But, Mira is not like you or like me. Her eyes see things which ours can't. Let her watch, Laur! Let her see the way through it! She is better than us!'

'You *want* her to be better,' Laur mused.

'And so do you!' Kimmie once more stated Laur's feelings accurately. 'And the first thing that is necessary for her to actually *be* better, is for us to *believe* that she can be!'

I've missed you, Kimmie! When this is all over, we should see each other again. Your misery is different from mine, yet they both love company.

'Perhaps you could visit me on Moria? Once this is over? It's been over 10 years since you last visited!'

'11.'

'Again, too long, old friend! Too long... Especially for such short a trip... which reminds me, how was the journey here?'

'Long,' Laur smiled out of the corner of his mouth.

'I know!' Kimmie let go of his shoulder. 'I'm going home, Laur! The Embassy is yours! Best of luck!' he said, before picking up his doomed sapling and walking towards the door.

He was almost at the exit, when Laur just had to know.

'Is there no other way?' he asked, his eyes on the tree next to him.

Kimmie stopped in his tracks and turned slowly towards him. He smiled a pained smile and unleashed the truth upon him.

'You wouldn't be here if there was...'

Chapter V

The Yetzer Hara

Almost every Terran legionnaire did what was asked of them by their General.

Laur Pop rarely had to ask Silvia to do anything. At least not anymore, not for many years now. *At least not these little things...*

And the big ones? He knows his words are only ever met with at most hints of commentary, yet never rejection.

Kimmel had his own Legion, of sorts, under the guise of the DGS-PGD-1, the *Directorate of General Safety – Pan-Galactic Division One,* though it was an entity of a fundamentally different nature than the Hajduks. Whilst the later were a Terran Avenger Legion, an organization that had only just recently been little more than a glorified warband, the DGS-PGD-1 was a Hierarch Legion that had originally been a goblin government agency. As such, Kimmel's men functioned in a manner similar to an exceptionally well organized institution of the state, meaning that they were both rigorously bureaucratic and purposeful in their actions. As such, they had diligently prepared their departure.

It was not the first time the DGS-PGD-1 and the Hajduks had traded roles, though it was the first time the goblins had handed-over operations to the humans. Back in the days of the Senoyu War, Laur Pop had joined Djibril al-Sayid, Mira's father, amongst the worlds of the Andromeda Galaxy, where they had aided the demani in their uprising against the Senoyu. Silvia's first duty as a Hajduk had been to assist Kimmel's goblins in settling into their new roles, as the Terrans, suffering heavy casualties, withdrew from frontline duties and returned to their homeworld to recover.

'You've changed, Silvie!' Tlaloc had smiled as his car, pulled up behind him.

She hadn't responded, instead simply smiling and wishing the goblin a safe journey home. *I have, dear! In ways you cannot even imagine. I may look the same on the outside, but on the inside I feel so old. So tired. So exhausted.*

Used.

She had overseen the Hajduk takeover of the Convent Garden Embassy in its entirety. Weapons, drugs and tools of a million purposes had been swiftly stashed in a thousand corners. Cases, boxes and packs had littered every floor in every hallway, room and the foot of every cupboard and wardrobe. One by one, each item found its place and each Hajduk their post.

Two dozen of their number would always find themselves in the basement – or, rather, *basements*, since beneath the embassy could be found several floors and chambers. Most had been given over to parking spots for over fifty vehicles of varying specs and a myriad styles. All above the parking lot's ceiling, Silvia had smiled to see the gnarled roots of the great tree above lining the lights that shone upon the Hajduk car fleet. The goblins had told her that it was a homely sight, as it seemed to resemble the great den of some mother beast, cradling her litter of newborn metal pups.

Beneath the main parking lot and loading bay area were several other levels. Some housed power generators. Others were simple storage areas.

A few had purposes.

Some had a clear one, others less so.

Some had a nefarious one, others less so.

Another, Silvia wished they would use as much as possible.

One would hopefully never be needed.

Another would be a secret until the very end.

There were six entrances into the parking lot. Two were elevators, one of them a formal elevator, to be used by distinguished guests and gullible dignitaries, the other a 'service' elevator, to be used for provisioning and by those visitors whose presence required discretion, on account of their truly absolute importance and necessary presence. Two were stairways descending from the ground floor: one from the main lobby; one from the back rooms, where the security control room lay. Two more were ramps that led outside: one to the 'north', one to the 'south'. Both led into Wiltshire Boulevard, since that was their address: Covent Garden Ends, Wiltshire Boulevard, number 616.

There were three entrances into the building from the direction of the boulevard. Two smaller entrances lay to the side of a grand arched gate that opened up towards the grand lobby, which took up about a fifth of the building's surface area. To its sides lay several smaller chambers and corridors: reception areas, leisure areas, meeting rooms and dining rooms. Behind them, towards the building's rear and facing towards the canal, was the Embassy's banquet area, which the goblins had made much use of, apparently.

The Hajduks had swiftly transformed the great hall into an empty husk of a room, for it was too exposed: one could peer from across the canal and observe too much of their dealings inside. Back on the *Doina*, when they had reviewed the building's schematics, Pop had immediately ordered her to remove the banquet hall windows and replace them with panels of such strength, they could block tank fire, let alone the sight of unwanted observers. Until that moment would arrive, only a dozen Hajduk sentries would languish within, for that had been the watch regimen that they had put in place:

At least two dozen Hajduks in the basement at all times.

Fifteen in the front area of the ground floor at all times and a dozen more always on 'casual walks' on Wiltshire Boulevard and the surrounding area.

The dozen in the banquet hall, as well as a ten more in the garden between the canal and the Embassy.

Ten more in the central atrium of the Laurel tree, as well as a full ten to be always located near a window, keeping a close eye on the outside.

The control room on the ground floor would hold five men at all times, coordinating the whole security system Silvia and Pop had put in place.

Two hundred Hajduks would work in four shifts of ten hours each, with a five hour overlap, ensuing that, at all times, there were at least a hundred Hajduks on active duty protecting the building. *What from, I don't know yet. But we always have to be on our toes, don't we?*

And that's where she had been: on her toes.

It had been twelve hours since their arrival and barely now did she find the time to do her final task of the day: unpacking her own things.

She opened the door of her new apartment before glancing to her right towards Pop's door. Behind her lay Nick's apartment, which he would share with Technowolf. They would have their own individual offices, bedrooms and lavatories, yet they would share a living room. Silvia would do the same with Mira. Pop, on the other hand, would share his apartment with Basenji.

Their three apartments all faced towards Wiltshire Boulevard, and were spread out on two levels, with the upper quarters containing the bedrooms and lavatories, while the lower levels were comprised of a large area near the entrance which was usually meant to be used as a kind of reception area or perhaps a more traditional living room, whilst the relatively smaller offices would be located towards the backs of the apartment's first floor. Pop had immediately decided that 'this won't do' on account of the fact that he didn't like his offices to have windows, since someone might peer into the making of his many schemes.

To his merit, he had handled the unpacking himself, though he had clearly done it for the sake of his traditional reasoning: 'if you want something to be done right, you should do it yourself...' Silvia had assisted him in setting up this office, to some degree, together with occasional assistance from some passing Hajduk.

Two hours before, Pop had declared himself satisfied with the result and moved on to set-up his living room and bedroom. He had then dispatched Silvia to 'make sure everyone's on schedule!' And that's what she did.

She checked in with Nick, whose team was setting up the basement area. Then with one of her Optios, Micky Moldoveanu, who was busy setting up the 'tree room', as he called it. Then she checked in with Luca Constantinescu, who was busy securing the banquet hall. Then Veronica Tănase, who was setting up the control room. Then Nea Nicu, who was on the roof, making sure the terrace, the roof gardens and the lounges up there were properly secured. *Meaning that he's hiding bombs, machine guns and cameras up there.*

Finally, she had visited her other Optios, Andrei Carlingă, Mickey Spagă, Miruna Andreea, Stelian Sârmă and Gabi Găinaru, all of which were scattered across the building's six above-ground floors.

All of which had finalized their initial tasks and had now turned to more personal set-ups.

Now it's finally my turn.

She opened the door to her room and walked into her and Mira's living room. *Well, this a nice surprise!*

Mira hadn't just unpacked her own belongings, but Silvia's as well. She looked around the room to see how her roommate had chosen to decorate their mutual living quarters. *She has good taste.*

The room was around a hundred square meters in size, with a ceiling of just over one hundred meters, which was the norm for the Convent Garden Embassy, as most of the building's chambers had been office spaces before the Alliance had acquired the real estate over thirty years before. Such expansive chambers always ran the risk of feeling austere and disparate, on account of all the empty space emphasizing the absence of people. Indeed, for the past few hours, Silvia had observed many of her colleagues attempt to fill the spaces provided to them, so as to make their dwellings at least slightly welcoming and warm.

Mira had blasted through the challenge with remarkable ease, breaking up the room into several intermingling spaces, brought together by a tastefully eclectic assortment of styles.

There was a dining area broken out of a Tuscan villa, which bled into a warm circle of couches, armchairs, futons and pillows around a low coffee table facing a fireplace, next to which stood a reception area of sorts, full of wardrobes, tall tables and several benches covered in pillows and blankets, beyond which stood a single long couch next to another long table under which were numerous drawers filled to the brim with her and Silvia's belongings. Across the dining area stood another comfy couch before a large television screen, with another coffee table, while in the distance opposite the entrance, she could see the entrances to the single kitchen Mira had converted into a gastronomic laboratory.

She could see threads of peppers, onions and garlic around a large French stove, with copper pans resting on a dozen hangers, surrounded by rows upon rows of pantries, as well as a range of ovens, refrigerators, microgreen gardens, dry-agers. Silvia could just about peer into her future office as she walked towards one of the couches next to the long table and collapsed. Even as she sat down, she found herself unable to completely unwind. As she sat on the couch, she found herself leaning forwards expectantly, as if one of her Hajduks would somehow jump from behind a chair, informing her of some other matter than needed her attention.

Instead, it was a cat that jumped from behind a nearby coffee table.

Silvia had heard the animal's heartbeat as she had entered the room, as she had suspected she might from the moment Mira had boarded the *Doina*.

'Hello, Lorgar!' she greeted the black tomcat before her.

'Greetings, Lady Silvia! Thank God you finally came! I was overjoyed to hear from Milady that we would be sharing a room together! You cannot imagine how relieved I am to find our current lodgings to be such an improvement upon the absolute doghouse that was our accommodation for the last weeks!' Lorgar spoke, as he sat upon his furry little behind, eyes closing and rubbing against Silvia's open palm.

'You mean the *Doina*?' *What else could he mean?*

'Yes! I believe that was the name! An abhorrent place! With no windows! Horrific! Milady had me holed up in a room the size of a cupboard for two whole weeks!'

Of course she did.

She didn't want anyone to know she was bringing you along! She knew that she wouldn't be allowed to do, if anyone saw you while they were boarding the Doina. If anyone saw you, they would have made a big deal out of it! Now that we have reached our destination, she can just put everyone in front of the fulfilled fact of your presence!

Good thing Silvia had made sure that no one would check Mira's luggage, nor even ask her what she was bringing along. Good thing she had ordered every single Hajduk under her command to never disturb Mira within her quarters and to never enter her room, unless invited.

'I assume Mira hasn't fed you?'

The cat got up on all fours and started pacing, his eyes glancing maniacally towards hers. 'Lady Silvia, you are a true godsend! *Yes*! No, she hasn't! Please help!'

That's what I've been doing all day...

Lorgar's mouth began to tremble as he followed Silvia towards the kitchen. *Damn! She really went to work here!* Silvia had never seen a kitchen so well organized in her entire life. Even Lorgar's meals were neatly organized in his own designated stasis pantry, with clear dates and times written on his premade meals. She picked out today's dinner and found a large bowl with Lorgar's name on it. After enduring Lorgar's excited yapping, she filled his food bowl, as well as his water bowl and left the satisfied feline behind her, returning to the living room to the living room and that comfy couch Lorgar had found her on, where she once more collapsed and took a few tired breaths before getting back on her feet.

This time, it was her own needs that beckoned her to quickly rise from her rest. She walked over to one of nearby armchairs, next to which lay a large low-lying table that housed beneath it a series of drawers. She identified the one at the same level as the armchair's armrest, within easy reach of anyone resting on it, and opened it.

Silvia smiled as she observed its contents.

She actually put a lot of thought into this! She's organized everything better than I usually do myself.

A neatly stacked and carefully unpacked collection of slim needles and thick bolts of string, twine and simple fabric lay arranged before her. To one side she saw a set of scissors, sorted by size, while on another, she saw a collection of leathers, buckles, zippers and buttons. Silvia reached within and drew out her favourite set of needles. *I'll just get to work on a simple scarf.*

Grey. Wool. Narrow.

Stylish. Cozy. Elegant.

She pulled out some grey wool of an Aesir variety, then sat down upon the armchair next to her sewing station, as had been clearly prepared by Mira, and began work upon her new project.

She liked knitting because it was consuming and because it allowed her to consume herself in thought and she had the Fräulein to thank for that! The Fräulein had taught all the girls how to knit.

The Fräulein's real name was Erika Wurtshaft and she had been the headmistress of the orphanage in Graz where she and Nick had spent close to four years of their childhood in, pending their transfer to the burgeoning military academy that would train them to become soldiers. Nick had never gotten along with her, as he had been something of a rambunctious youth, a harbinger of the cantankerous man he would become. By age eleven, he had already assembled a gang of his fellow gypsies, a smattering of Romanians, as well as an assortment of other orphaned boys of a dozen nations. By age twelve, he had a small team of specialized thieves clearing out the odd unattended shipment of goods. By age thirteen, he had several drug growing operations littered around the Graz compound. By age fourteen, he was pimping out some of the older girls to the young cadets from the Graz military school.

But not Silvia.

Silvia had known Nick for almost as long as she could remember. They had huddled together under Prague when they had been naught but small children weathering out a storm they did not understand. She had seen something then which she believed, with some degree of certainty, that no one else had ever seen before or since:

A terrified Nick.

As terrified as she had also been, yet she had held it in. Not with any particular goal in mind, as showing her fear would've mattered little.

No...

It had been her instinct. Her nature. She was frequently afraid. She simply never showed fear. Nick feared very little. Somehow, even she sometimes believed that he feared nothing and no one. Yet, in their dark corner beneath the red darkness of Doomsday, she had felt him shiver. She had felt his hands cold. In the deep blackness of the trembling darkness, she had heard his eyelids seal shut and his temples tense and pound as a small boy felt true mortal terror for the first time.

They had been the closest of friends ever since. So much so, that Nick's wife Camelia had always felt uncomfortable knowing Nick spent so much of his time around her. She had been cold and distant and, at times, downright hostile. It hadn't help when Nick had insisted that Silvia be the godmother of six of his fourteen children. Silvia had been compelled to spend many an afternoon at the Lăutaru residence pretending to be at ease with the menacing glare of Nick's (then) wife.

They had divorced almost a year before. Camelia had quoted infidelity (which was true, but not directly involving Silvia), as well as spousal and offspring negligence (which was half-true, since Nick was a good husband and an even better father... *when* he was around the house). Silvia still visited her godchildren, for she had grown to love them, though now she was forced to endure Camelia's scowls alone, for Nick refused to see his (formerly) beloved wife, let alone visit their old and (now) broken home.

I can't forget to write to the children! Nick's and mine.

I'll write to them the day after tomorrow, when –

She had probably managed to get about thirty seconds of alone time before Mira showed up.

She emerged from her office dressed in casual wear. No uniform. No insignia. No nothing. Just a girl in jeans, boots, a white T-shirt and a black leather jacket.

'Hi!' Silvia said.

'Hey!' Mira responded, before making her way to the kitchen.

She closed the door after her, though Silvia could nevertheless hear the tell-tale sound of an espresso machine earning its keep. The loud sound of frothing milk startled her, as Mira seen to work piercing and gurgling air into a delicious frothy beverage.

Twice.

After a couple of minutes, she emerged carrying two coffee mugs and followed by her furry feline friend.

As Lorgar jumped upon a nearby window sill and immediately began doing volunteer sentry duty, Mira made her way towards Silvia.

'I love what you've done with the place!' Silvia smiled genuinely. *I actually really like the arrangement you've gone for! Consulting me would've been nice, but it's even nicer to have someone else –*

'Oh, really?' Mira smiled faintly. 'I took a few gambles, but I'm glad it came out well!'

'Well, it really did!' *What is wrong girl? Are you, please, just finally going to tell me now?*

She didn't say anything; she just made her way to a nearby armchair, onto which she simply sat down with her coffee mug in hand. She was quiet for some time. Silvia couldn't tell if it was seconds or minutes. Mira just gazed into the empty space before her. At one point she took a sip of her coffee and Silvia decided that it was perhaps best if she went back to her knitting. *She'll open up again... eventually –*

'Do you ever feel like you have nothing to live for, Silvia?'

Silvia nearly stabbed one of her fingers with a needle.

The words rattled Silvia.

They rattled her both for how sudden they were and how true they were. A part of her lurched towards the later reaction and smothered it swiftly. *This is not the time for that! She's in distress! That was clear before and it's clear now. She's not talking about you, she is talking about herself. Get a grip and come up with an answer that's good for her!*

Ther was no need to, as Mira was the next to speak. 'You're always busy. It's the first time I've seen you do something just for yourself, unless you're making that scarf for some fellow Hajduk who gets chilly around the neck!'

It's for you, what the – are you really talking about me that much?

'I almost always just see you running around, in a blur, either making sure something is going well, or that someone is well, or just checking that all is well.' Mira chuckled faintly and fleetingly, before smiling as she made eye contact with Silvia. 'It's either that or you're motionless; which is when I see your eyes just look around from face-to-face and from thing to thing, always looking for the next thing to take care of or the next situation and how it can be handled. Even at parties I see you working!'

Enough Mira! Is this how living together is going to be? You're just gonna attack me in my own living room? 'Where is this coming from?'

'I'm simply wondering what your actual goal is?' Mira's gaze went back to the empty space before her. Her lips went for the coffee mug she absently raised towards her mouth. 'I was just wondering what you live for?'

What in the... this fucking little spoilt bitch – God-bless her father and her mother! This is no way to handle grief you entitled upstart cuntflap of child! 'Well, what do you live for, Mira?' *Your anger is her anger. Silvia, you are better than this! This is her lashing out. It's not about you, it's about her!*

'Other people, *mostly*...' she looked up when she reached that last word.

Why are you saying that with that accusatory look on your face? 'For yourself too? No?'

Mira paused for a while and leaned back into the tired embrace of her armchair. 'I guess... though I do feel that somewhere down the line I've lost sight of what that means. Somehow, it's now all just reeds of people just obscuring my sight towards *myself*. Some of the reeds, I've never even met! Some of them are burned.'

The boy

'Now, I mostly think about what the reeds live for.'

Awww... you're saying I'm a reed you care for?

Are you fucking with me now? 'Mira... I've known you since you were a little baby –'

'– No, you didn't! You *saw* a little baby! You didn't *get to know* a little baby. The first time we *met* was in the Bifrost.'

The War in Triangulum, yes...

Within the parallel dimension of the Bifrost...

Mira had been a Ghazi then; not legionless, as she was now. They had served together as the Ghazis and the Hajduks, together with Kimmie's goblins, Quentyn Andromander's high elves and the Vanir themselves, battling the Aesir across the webway's many lanes and junction citadels. Mira had been valiant then. Silvia had been reminded much of her father, with whom she had once shared a battlefield. Yet, it was the warmth of her mother, one which Silvia herself had never felt, yet heard so much about, that she had experienced most strongly alongside her.

The two had become quick friends, their relationship enduring through the conflict's end and leading up until the dark day of Ratden. They had never been truly close friends, yet they had kept in touch for most of that time, even working alongside one another during–

Don't think about that! Not here!

'You were a lot more agreeable back then!' Silvia remarked.

'Times were different back then.'

Indeed they were. 'Mira...' *breathe gentle* 'what is this about? I can tell you upset.'

Lightning passed across her friend's eyes.

'You coming along... the sulking... the hiding... The inconsistency... what's happened?'

Mira was quiet for a long time. This time it definitely felt like hours. She took a sip of her mug and then seemed to find the words.

'I'm trying to find a purpose...'

To torment me?

'... I'm... trying to remember who I was.'

A breakthrough...

But why did you try and break me first?

Mira got up from her set and walked towards the window where Lorgar lay supervising a perimeter. It was still day outside, though the sunset (or, rather, the sun*cover*) was approaching. 'It's... less crowded here.'

There are so many people outside, I get anxiety just by looking out the window...

Though I know it to be true, I can't believe that there are parts of the city that feel... worse?

'Back home... everyone is away,' Mira explained. 'I wanted to stay in Menegroth a while longer, but, when Tomasz came to pick me up, I didn't argue. I knew it would be good for me. So, I went back home and sat in my house and tried to feel good about things again.'

Mira scoffed. 'It didn't work. It also didn't help that everyone else had scattered and those few that remained thought it best if they just left me by myself until I figured things out. About a week in, I genuinely considered going back to the Ghazis... but I didn't want them to see me like this! Another week went buy and I thought about listening to Tomasz and going to live with him on Angbad for a while. Cingeto was also visiting. It would've been fun, he said.'

Mira paused and Silvia moved slightly, attempting to catch a glimpse of her face.

'But the thought of Cingeto, Tomasz and everyone else on that island working overtime just to make me feel better about myself... even if it came from the heart... *that*! *That,* I knew, wouldn't be good for me.' Mira finally turned around revealing something Silvia had not seen in quite some time: Mira's mischievous face. 'And I wasn't going to live with my grandmother, I can tell you that!'

'So it came down to us or Uma?' *Your actual aunt... five-times removed or something?*

'Uma pester me with a million questions without end! It would have driven me nuts! I would be burning the countryside out of sheer frustration within a few weeks.'

'So... so you came to Laur Pop?' Silvia chuckled as she finished her sentence and Mira followed suit. *I'm not sure if you're lying or you're truly serious about going for one hell of an overcorrection!* 'He only has two settings: interrogation or manipulation! But, you already knew that! And since you don't want to be interrogated, I take it you look forward to making you do his bidding? Sounds dreadfully out of character, Mira!'

'Is that what he does to you, Silvia? Interrogate or manipulate?'

What the fuck is it with you and the biting of the hand that is trying to help? 'No... not anymore, at least. Mostly he informs me of his decisions and he sometimes asks me how I plan to go about manifesting his decisions.'

'That's just what any commanding officer does. What does *he* do that's different?'

Silvia tensed up in her seat. She didn't like this. She didn't like this one bit. She was more comfortable being accused of depression and nihilism. *Alright... time to make stand. I am technically her superior officer. Princess or not. Friend or not. There must be some level of distance here.* 'You'll see.'

It should be any second now...

Two quick knocks were instantly followed by the door to their living room immediately swinging wide open.

'Ohhh... I like it!' Nick announced, as he surveyed Mira's design choices. He turned towards the both of them, yet his eyes quickly observed the third resident of their apartment. 'Hello, Lorgar!'

'*Sweet Hitler*! It's the caravan nigger!' Lorgar yelled, jumping from his place on the window sill underneath a nearby coffee table. 'Milady! Hide the things! ALL OF THE THINGS!' he roared, before hissing at Nick, as her fellow Centurion walked casually and giggled his way towards the coffee table.

'I missed ya! You little cunt! Lemme pet ya!' he said, as he bent down towards the furious feline, only narrowing evading a swipe from the cat's paw. Silvia saw the eggshell white of Lorgar's claws emerge and retreat within a fraction of a second.

'Still a hairy turd, I see!' he exclaimed to himself as he rose to face the two women. 'Am I interrupting some type of roommate administrative session?'

'I guess you could say that.' Mira responded, as Silvia nodded slowly.

'I see. Sorry about that! Me and Tech are barely halfway there!'

No surprise there...

Nick made his way towards the window previously occupied by Lorgar and proceeded to look towards Wiltshire Boulevard. '*They*, however, are right on time!' he said, as he looked towards the entrance to the embassy garage and Silvia took his words as confirmation that a vehicle was just now entering the building.

Radu and Cosmin are always on time. It was why she had personally recommended them to be promoted to Centurion.

Understanding the meaning of their arrival, Silvia got up from her seat, just as she heard the sound of the Pop's door unlocking in the corridor outside.

'I take it that's supposed to mean something?' Mira asked, her eyes followed Silvia's movements.

'It means we have work to do!' Nick answered, just as the image of their General passed through the hallway before their doorway.

Mira's eyes opened slightly. 'That quickly?'

'We like to hit the ground running!' Nick responded, as he followed Silvia through the door. She didn't even turn to see him open the door his apartment and shout inside. 'Tech! Come! We'll finish tomorrow!'

'*We*? Who is this 'we'? I've done all the work!' the remani shouted from the inside. He exited his apartment just as, Mira exited theirs and Basenji walked out of Laur's office.

Not that Silvia had turned to acknowledge them. Her thoughts were too focused on what had to be done in the basement. In the special room she had prepared for this exact purpose.

It was actually a room within a room. The outer room was an interrogator's room, complete with various monitoring and recording devices. It was separated from the inner room by one-way glass, which allowed for those outside to peer within. This outer room was furnished in a dark grey, while the inner chamber was almost entirely black, bar the occasional lighter crease upon its rough stone floor. The inner chamber was roughly thirty square yards, while the other room was over three hundred square meters in size, though it did feel incredibly cramped, on account of all the... *equipment* the Hajduks had brought with them. Their... *tools of interrogation.*

Not that Pop actually enjoyed using those... *No... He uses them only as a last resort. He has... other things he tries first.*

It was this outer room which Pop, Silvia, Nick, Technowolf, Basenji and Mira entered, finding Ela and several other Hajduks inside, just as Radu and Cosmin dragged a struggling human with a black bag on his head and large earphones around his ears, into the inner room, before unceremoniously shoving him on the floor. As they took the bag off his face, the air mask of his nose and the gag out of his mouth, he gasped for air and immediately began shouting.

'YOU THINK THIS IS HOW THINGS WORK HERE? YOU FUCKING ANIMALS!' He was speaking Shangrianese. 'We have RULES HERE! LAWS! PERSON RIGHTS and RESPECT FOR THE PERSONAL CONDITION!'

'It's him?' Pop asked, as he observed the struggling Shangri human, as Radu and Cosmin began taking of his restraints, as well as his clothing.

'Yes,' Silvia replied and flicked a nearby screen. A Shangri ID card showing a man with ginger hair appeared onscreen. 'Quint of Carth-Fountainhead. Inspections Officer First Class.'

'Good!' her General replied quietly, as he checked his watch. It was an old Terran relic, a black Breitling Cosmonaute 1965, with a custom black adamantite chain link bracelet. He gestured towards a specific time and Silvia nodded.

With that, he left the outer room, re-entered the hallway they had arrived from and purposefully made his way towards the inner room. He entered just as Radu and Cosmin had finished undressing their victim and after, once more, shoved him towards the floor, causing the man to graze his elbows across the rough stone and drawing blood.

Nick also walked out of the observation room, though he left the door open so he could eavesdrop.

Pop stood in the doorway as the man looked up at him, fully naked apart from a pair of red underwear.

'That's a lucky colour where we come from!' their General quipped, waving a finger at his captive's crotch.

Quint was apoplectic, pausing, mouth wide-open for a few seconds. '*I beg your pardon?*' he managed.

'The underwear!' Pop pointed towards his crotch as he circled the room, walking towards a nearby table upon which he began leaning. He was sitting right in front of Silvia, Nick and the rest as he relaxed his shoulders and his shirt creased. 'Where we come from, you wear red underwear on New Year's Eve for good luck in the year to come!' He reached into one of his pockets and pulled out a pack of cigarettes and his black Zippo lighter. 'Do you know what New Year's Eve is?'

Quaint didn't respond, as he sat on the floor, perplexed.

'Do you have a New Year's Eve here?'

'*You're demented!*' the Shangrian managed, before one of his elbows buckled slightly.

'Now, that's no way to speak to a foreign dignitary! You're supposed to refer to me as 'your excellency'!'

'You can go to hell for all I care! The devil can call you what he may!'

'Oh! I see you're a real wordsmith, now aren't you?'

'I am a citizen of the City of Shangri and in the City we have words you might not have in whatever hut you come from! Words like 'justice'! Words like 'accountability'! Words like 'decency'!'

'Oh, no! We have those words in my hut as well! It was actually about those words that I wanted to talk to you today! It's why I had you brought over!'

'Oh, but fuck off! I am under no obligation to speak to you, nor to any other criminal!'

'Of course you aren't! You see, we know about your mind encryption – fascinating bit of technology, might I add – and we know we can't *take* the information we *need* from you by force! So, that leaves us with two options:' Pop reached out towards his left, where Silvia had made sure an ashtray was placed. He pulled said ashtray slightly closer before continuing.

'Option number one is that you tell us the code to unlock your mind encryption on your own accord or – option number two – you sit here in this room until we both figure out a way to make option number one happen!' he said, discarding his cigarette's ash in the tray.

'You threaten *torture*? Huh? Is that it?' Quint asked, as Pop shrugged his shoulders. 'I am an officer of his Majesty's Port Authority! I belong to the House of Quint-Fountainhead! A *noble* house! We trace our history back into the days of the Old Realm! We hold a seat in the Camaril, guaranteeing our valour within the eyes of this City that was ancient when your people not yet knew how to scribble letters unto rocks! Do as you may *Lore* Pop – '

'– *Laur*! My name is–'

'Your bloodline is naught but *muck*! *Muck and whores*!'

Pop was quiet for a few moments. Silvia couldn't see his eyes, though she could tell that his cold eyes were likely looking straight into his victim's. *Or, rather, right through his victims.*

In the end, he spoke, and Silvia was genuinely impressed by how much superficial charm he was capable of summoning. 'I see you've studied Terran history! From whereabouts came such an interest in our little blue marble –'

'I have studied your character and know a son of a whore and loose filth when I see one!'

'I see our two cultures have much in common! You see, I'm Romanian and, *in Romania*, we also enjoy insulting the character of one's mother –'

'I do not care from what lavatory you claim heritage!'

'You sure seem to like to interrupt other people, now don't you?'

Quint was silent.

'Are you buying time?' Pop asked.

'*What*?' Quint squinted.

'Are you buying time to think? Is that why you keep interrupting?' Pop leaned forward. 'You see, you haven't asked me why you were brought here! I know *I* haven't told you. I know the gentlemen that picked you up from your front door didn't tell you. It would seem, *to me*, to be a reasonable thing to wonder out loud!? Perhaps, now that you have been acquainted with a more talkative captor – meaning *myself* – you may have been interested enough to ask as to the reason for your captivity!?'

'I am not interested in your reasoning. You behave like an animal. You have the reasoning of an animal! And the reasoning of *feral beasts* does not concern me.'

'Even if the reasoning of said animal allowed for a way to resolve this... *kerfuffle*, in an expedient manner?'

'I am not giving you the keys to my mind, fuck off! YOU HEAR ME? FUCK OFF!!!'

'You're a very diligent customs officer. You seem to be quite familiar with who I am – you knew my name, albeit if even you've butchered the pronunciation –'

'Are you mocking me now?'

'No more than you butchered the letters 'A' and 'U' to the point where you made them sound like 'O'!'

Quint looked up, his face still perplexed, though now also... slightly rattled. 'You are a garbage person! You do not deserve my attention! Nor my words. I will speak to you no longer!'

'Oh, that's perfectly fine! I will continue, nevertheless.' Laur stood up from his seat, ashed his cigarette, and began pacing.

'If you know my name, it means you know that I am the new Ambassador of the Republican Alliance at Convent Garden! You also must also know that I am Terran and – because you are a diligent customs officer – you are most likely aware of the... *history* of the relationship between Terra and Shangri? *Hmmm*? Perhaps you might be aware of some... *accusations* made by Terra against the great City of Shangri? Accusations involving, chiefly, the conduct of and shipping practices of the Shangri Port Authority and its Harbormasters? You might be aware of the fact that we have... called into question the business dealings of some of the various shipping companies based in your city, as well? Such as your own 'Paragon Shipping Company'?

Pop began to walk towards a nearby stool. 'I trust you know why we've done so.' He grabbed the stool and began walking back towards Quint. 'Can you confirm?'

Quint was looking to the side, his face one of rage and feigned ignorance.

'I see,' Pop muttered as he lay the stool down a yard away from where Quint lay, still sitting on the floor, his backside and one elbow propped up beneath him. 'You must understand that this topic is of extreme importance to us. It *always* has been!' Pop leaned forward on his little chair, his elbows resting on his thighs, as his hands stood clasped before him. 'Do you know what I'm known for? You know my name and I'm assuming you know a little something about me?'

Quint stood motionless. Only his eyes moved, as he pretended to study the ceiling.

'On Terra, they call it *The Last Fitna*. The Last Kinslaying. The Final Purge of Earth!' Pop's eyes seemed to glaze over and he raised the cigarette between his loose fingers his lips, as he pretended to remember something. 'In the hour of our victory, as everyone else jollied and celebrated, I was somewhere in some dark, ominous cave writing down names on slabs of rock. *The Writ of the Damned*, some would call these slabs. I sat there, like some wretched ghoul, after having endured the Apocalypse and after I had brought dark terror upon worlds of hopeful bliss like some harbinger of shadow, and I decided that there hadn't been *enough* blood spilled! As if I wanted it do drip from the carnage above me into my own filthy lair!'

'So I started plotting and, within the year, on the anniversary of our great triumph, Forty-seven thousand six hundred and seventeen of my kinsmen lay dead. Slain by their brothers and sisters. All felled in one fell swoop!' Pop leaned back on his little stool.

'The number could've been much higher! No one ever talks about that! No one ever talks about how much I struggled with every single name... How each and every one of them was my brother and my sister! How there were men on that list whom I *admired deeply*! People I wish there were more of in this world! Ever single letter of their names was its own little shard of our past, which would be shattered into dust for all eternity!'

'No! Everyone just remembers that I was the one to write down names to begin with and little more. Everyone forgets how many came to me with their *own* suggestions and recommendations.' Pop smirked. 'Probably because most of the people who came to put forward the names of others immediately had their own names written down!'

'It was all about civility, you see!' Pop leaned forward once more and began to gesture with his hands. 'It wasn't the dissenting voices that had to go, you see. *No*! On the contrary, we would *need* dissidents in our society! Without them, we would stagnate! We would develop the very weakness which we were striving to exploit in our enemies! *No*!'

He began pointing somewhere in the air. 'It was the dissidents which we *wouldn't be able to reason with*! It was *they* that had to go! It was the ones who might hurt us *as a whole*, in the pursuit of their own ambitions and beliefs, that we had to get rid of! That's why I came up with another list, though this one had only one thing written on it!'

He gestured in the air, as if he was writing on some piece of paper before him.

'*Thou shall not kill... your own kind...*'

'*After. One. Last. Kinslaying!*'

He leaned in suddenly, now pointing at Quint, whose eyes turned to glare at the finger shoved in his face.

'*If* you do kill one of our own, we can't kill you! *If* you are one of our own! If you aren't one of our own, then we *have to* kill you! But, we can't have *you* killing one of our own, because that's just the same as killing one of our own, only with extra steps!'

'*No*! If you're a Terran that has killed another Terran, we put you in prison instead! With no fancy upgrades by the way! *Nooo*! We just leave you there; the way Mother Nature intended you to live! Naked and in the dark!'

Pop made a face like a child tasting something sour. 'Every now and then, there's a robot that comes and force-feeds you and sucks the shit and the piss our of you, but – other than that – it's all very natural!'

'You grow old. You fall ill. There's another robot that makes sure you don't die too quickly from sickness and another that makes sure you can't kill yourself because – *remember!* – we can't have you killing yourself now, can't we? You'd be killing *yourself* and *you* are a Terran and we can't have you killing a Terran, now can't we?'

Pop waved an imaginary fly away from his face. 'It's a grim fate! It has to be! It has to be so that people *stay civil*! Because, if people stay civil, then they can *talk* to one another! And talking fixes everything! That's why I'm here with you!'

He pointed at his captive. 'I think we can sort this out right here, right now. Like civil men! Are you a civil man, Quint?'

Quint had returned to gazing around the room, ignoring Pop.

'I think you are!' Pop sat back and puffed his cigarette. 'I think you find this shocking! Us kidnapping you like this! Dragging you here, to this dungeon. Stripping you naked. Leaving you on the floor like that! *Heh...*' Pop feigned a laugh. '... having me in here giving you lessons on the basics of civil discourse!' He paused, puffing on his cigarette. 'It's all true, by the way! I wouldn't have you here if I thought you weren't a civil man! A man of reason! A man of... of... of *noble stock*! If I would've thought of you as some animal – wild *or* domesticated – I would've just had you brought down here and we would've just gone to town on you!'

'But I'm not doing that, because that's something we have to do to *animals*! Not to civilized people! Not to people who believe in dialogue! Not to people who... who understand the value of other cultures! Not to people who... who understand the *value* of other *people*.'

Pop leaned forward in his stool swiftly, almost rising from it, as his bottom now barely touched the seat beneath him. '*You*! *Quint*! You strike me as someone who understands the *value* of *people* very well!'

Quint did respond to the compliment or to the implication.

'What was your gross margin?' Pop leaned in. 'I mean I know the cost of goods sold: Twenty five thousand imperial trade credits, I believe? That's how much you paid the Svart? You probably paid the equivalent of a thousand trade credit as expenses: storage, maintenance, quality management, that sort of thing. I know you didn't pay a shipping tax for it, since you never filled a tax return on it! So it must have been just the flat one per cent Shangri income tax. You borrow money from a Shangri bank at 6% interest. So the rest must have been just pure profits. How much was it, exactly?'

Quint refused to acknowledge anything.

Pop leaned in even closer. His voice sank, dropping much lower than before. 'I know you didn't hurt them. You're a professional. You take care of your cargo! I'm just... picking up the trail, you see! I'm trying to figure out who is next one on the chain. I'm trying to figure out–'

Pop was interrupted by the sound of the dungeon door swinging open, as one of his Hajduks held it. Another one of his men could be seen dragging another man inside. This one also had a bag over his head, as well as large headphones covering his ears.

Pop stood back suddenly, his look one of surprise. 'You're early!'

'Sir, you said you'd finish quickly! It's been five minutes! It's this one's turn!' the man holding the door, Marcu, replied.

'Yes... I did.' Pop replied, turning slowly to look at Quint. 'I got a bit carried away by our conversation!' He got up and pretended to brush some imaginary lint from his pants. 'Is he the last one?'

'Yes, sir! It's just the gentleman here and *this* one we just brought in now and that's it for today!'

'Ah, I see!' Pop raised his eyebrow. 'Very well, bring him in! We'll take care of him quickly!' He turned towards Quint, now sprawled on the floor wide-eyed. 'My apologies for this! We're still trying to get into a rhythm and sometimes timeslots get overbooked,' he said, as Marcu leaned back, allowing Bogdan to drag the hooded man into the room.

Once inside, Bogdan shoved him onto the floor.

Very roughly.

Quint looked on, his wide eyes rushing between those of his new cellmate and those of his interrogator.

'Oh, this won't be long! This other guy is just a deckhand! Not a gentleman, *such as yourself*! With him, we'll just skip a few courtesies and get straight to the point. We won't be long now, don't worry!'

Bogdan was ripping the man's clothes off.

Violently.

Unlike Cosmin had done with Quint, Bogdan left this man almost completely naked, bar only a broken shirt that now hung from his shoulders, his chest exposed. Also unlike Cosmin, Bogdan punctuated his undressing frequently with kicks and punches that left the man bruised, swelling and, rather quickly, *bleeding*. Finally, Bogdan tore the bag from his head, causing the headphones to drop onto the floor and rattle as they hurdled across the coarse tiles.

Pop addressed the new arrival. 'Mr. Barabas Castan. My name is Laur Pop, this is my colleague, Bogdan!' he gestured towards the Hajduk, who confirmed his identity with a backhanded slap that broke Barabas' lip and bloodied his teeth. And this is your colleague, Quint of Carth-Fountainhead...' Pop's paused for a moment, before turning to face Quint.

'Do you recognize him, by the way?' he asked, his look one of feigned curiosity.

Quint's eyes rushed between Barabas' and Pop's.

'Ah! It must be a big company!' he turned back towards the new arrivals, just as Bogdan began unbuckling his belt and pulling out his cock.

'I'll skip the courtesies, Mr. Ephialtes. We know you're an Urheimat collaborator. We know you sold them Terran children. We know you were part of the operation. We know you have mental encryption and we need the code because we don't trust you not to lie to us. So, Bogdan here is going to go to work until you give us the code! We know you're ex-military and we respect your decision to withhold information! Bogdan, go ahead... though you clearly weren't waiting on my permission...'

Barabas began screaming.

It took a couple of minutes for the screaming to die down and for Bogdan to finish. Tech turned away about thirty minutes in, joining Basenji as they both starred at the wall behind them, arms crossed. Ela had an excuse; she was busy monitoring the scanners collecting data on what was happening inside the inner chamber. Mira's jaw dropped slightly, before she swallowed nervously and looked from Silvia, to Bogdan and Barabas, then to Pop and, finally, to a horrified Quint. Silvia saw everything, yet she focused most intently on the squirming inspections officer, since she wanted to see what Laur was looking for.

With a hoarse breath, Barabas began to whisper, as Bogdan was still moving. 'Seven... Eight... Five...'

'What was that?' Pop asked, sitting up from the table he had been leaning on.

Barabas gasped for breath. 'Seven, eight, five, five, one, five!'

'Ah! Ok! Excellent!' Pop began walking to a nearby wall and pulled out a wire jutting out from it. 'Good thing you use the decimal system too!' He dragged the wire over to Barabas' watery eyes and placed the tip right into his left eye duct.

'Silvia?' he asked loudly, startling Quint.

'Yes?' Silvia flicked a button on the screen before her, activating the speakers. 'Yes?'

'Is the code correct?'

'Yes!'

'Good! Well!' Pop straightened and announced. 'Excellent work, Mr. Castan! Bogdan here'll take you to our medical saloon and we'll get to work transcribing your memory.' Pop turned to leave. 'Oh!' He pretended to remember something. 'We'll be sure to wipe your memory of the last day clean! So, don't worry! You won't have to deal with this! It'll be like a dream or, well, a *nightmare!*'

'... Anyway –'

'Four, Four, Eight...'

All eyes, as well as Pop's body, swing towards Quint, who continued. 'Seven. Six. Nine.'

Pop walked slowly towards his quarry, wire in hand and squatted before the terrified Shangrian. He placed the tip of the thin wire right into his Quint's left eye duct and pushed slowly, as his victim stood completely still.

'Silvia?' he asked loudly, startling Quint.

'Yes?' Silvia was already checking their mindreading systems.

'Is the code correct?'

Her eyes darted from one indicator to the next, right as a pop-up window emerged on the screen before her with the results.

'*Yes!*'

Well... that was easy!

Relatively...

Pop let go of the wire, yet he did not pull it out, causing it to drop down on Quint's face, with part of it resting on the Shangri's lower lip, as his mouth stood slightly open, drawing in heavy breaths. Silvia could see that, despite the ambient temperature that had been preset, he was sweating profusely, with globs of salty liquid already congealing upon his forehead, their glint caught by the dim lamps mounted upon the ceiling merely hours before. One of the drops had formed right above his right eyebrow, near the top of his nose and was just about to tumble down towards his cheek.

After pulling up his pants, Bogdan picked up a trembling Barabas and cradled him in his arms like a wounded child, Pop stood up and slowly started to walk backwards as he spoke to Quint. 'I knew you were a *gentle* man!'

That was Silvia's cue.

As Pop took his tenth step away from his quarry, she pressed and held down one of the buttons on the control panel before her.

A faint humming could be felt, rather than heard, as the stasis field activated. Quint froze, quite literally, in time, as his body was caught in stasis. The bead of sweat, which had just commenced its descent, stopped midway and hung to the side of his nose like some shiny wart.

Bogdan, still cradling Barabas, knocked on the door and Marcu immediately swung it open. Pop did not linger any more than he had to, as he swiftly moved towards the ashtray he had left on the table, squishing the bud into the ceramic bottom, before proceeding to exit his dungeon.

Silvia turned to a nearby Hajduk a squad leader, Optio Casandra Drăgănescu, and instructed: 'Let's try to have a mental summary by tomorrow evening but, for today, I think it's enough just to finish scanning!'

Casandra nodded in complete agreement and proceeded to prepare an extraction device for quick use. They would use Quint's encryption code to access and then copy his memories onto a physical server. They would first comb it using a Hyperborean software they had obtained from their allies in Triangulum, but then someone would have to sift through the individual highlighted memories in order to piece together a coherent narrative. That someone would likely be Ela, with Casandra likely assisting her. But, they would do it tomorrow.

They're tired too... It's been a long day...

Silvia turned towards the door of the observation room and walked swiftly outside, knowing she would find her General right around the corner. Pop was just walking up to Nick when Silvia arrived in the doorway.

'Tomorrow evening?' he asked Silvia.

'Yes.'

'Good, I'm busy with the prince tomorrow. We'll look over it in the evening!'

'I'll set up a meeting after dinner!'

'During dinner. We'll eat in my office!'

'Understood.' *That you don't care about other people's dinner plans.*

Nick intervened. 'When do we take care of him?'

Pop turned slightly towards the location of their frozen prisoner. 'As soon as possible. Compost him... and use him on the tree! The leaves are a bit dry!'

'Good. I'll chop him up with some of the guys. It'll be quick!' Nick turned towards Technowolf, who was just now exiting the observation room. 'I'll finish unpacking tomorrow.'

'Well you'd better!' the remani replied.

'You haven't unpacked yet?' Pop asked Nick.

'Nah, I've been inspecting all day!' her fellow Centurion replied, in a completely relaxed manner, as he stopped leaning on a nearby wall and swaggered towards the dungeon's door.

'Oh,' Pop raised an eyebrow. 'Well, did you find anything interesting during the inspection?' he asked.

'Yeah, that Mira's a real interior decorator!'

'What now?' Pop was intrigued.

Mira had followed Technowolf out of the observation room. Silvia spared her a quick glanced. *She's hiding her shock well, but I know it's there! She's seen her fare share of the horrific, yet the Ghazis have a way of doing things that was gruesome, as opposed to the Hajduk's sinister. The way we do things... can be hard to swallow.*

Which is good... it means we still have enough of a moral conscious to see it for the evil it is...

'She set up their living room!' Nick pointed towards the two roommates with his thumb. 'Absolutely *gorgeous*, feels like a proper home now!'

'Ahem?' Silvia scoffed softly, raising an eyebrow.

Nick turned to face her playfully, though she could tell that he was a bit rattled too.

Nick never liked seeing things like that. It's why he always waits outside and just listens.

'Look, you can turn your office into Dr. Melfi's therapy room – as you always do!' he said to Silvia. 'I'm just saying its gonna be nice to hang out in your living room and not have it be like in a psychologist's office – regardless of how much good taste you put into it!'

'Understood!' she said curtly as she smirked.

Tech interjected. 'While ours is going to look like a shithole...'

'I said I'll do it tomorrow!' Nick insisted.

'Hey!' Pop softly interrupted him. The General locked eyes with his Centurion. 'Get it done tonight and tomorrow you can all chill in Mira's living room all day while I meet with Prince Joffrey!'

'Joffrey?' Nick raised an eyebrow. '*Game of Thrones* Joffrey?'

'No, Geoffrey Rush –'

'– the guy from *The King's Speech?*' Nick interrupted.

'No, the one from a *Game of Thrones*.' Pop explained.

'... Geoffrey Rush wasn't in *Game of Thrones*...'

'Jesus fucking Christ, Nick! You know what I mean...' Pop looked on frustrated.

'I know.' Nick shrugged his shoulder. 'I just didn't know the prince was a cunt. Thought I missed a line on a memo or something.'

'Well, you didn't. By all accounts, he's a nice guy. But, I'll find out tomorrow.'

Of course you assume that the Prince is a cunt. You always assume the worst in people.

'Anyway.' Pop made to leave. 'Good start!' he informed his men and began walking towards his room.

Silvia began making a mental checklist of everything she had to do before going to bed, yet she was interrupted by the return of Bogdan and Barabas.

Barabas was now wearing a comfy bathrobe and a pair of sneakers that had been set aside for him in a nearby room. His wounds had begun to heal, despite the healing suppressant he had taken before being dragged into the room by Bogdan. The later was at his side, only slightly uncomfortable, as he always was.

It's why they're here and not in their room. They're making sure we're ok... which means they're ok. That's good.

'All good?' Bogdan asked.

'Yes,' Casandra replied, as she walked out the observation room struggling with the two giant suitcases she was handling.

'Lemme help you with that!' Bogdan insisted, grabbing one out of her arms.

'Thanks!' she replied, as the two made their way towards Marcu, who was still diligently guarding the dungeon room.

'Do we know for sure that the code is valid?' Barabas asked his fellow Hajduks.

Nick turned towards Silvia, who nodded towards both of them. 'Yeah...' Nick's brow furrowed as he stifled a smile. 'Why? You wanna go for round two?'

'No! I still have unpacking to do!' his fellow Hajduk replied. 'I'll help with the composting!'

'Oh, but for the love of God please shower!' Nick blurted out. 'It'll take an hour for Casandra to finish scanning him.'

'Sure, sure! I agree! Well...' he turned to Silvia and Mira. '... I'll see you guys tomorrow! You gonna get some sleep?' he asked Silvia.

'In about two hours...' *Three, if things take longer than expected, which they frequently do.*

'Great! That's eight hours of sleep!'

Silvia smirked. Barabas likely knew how early she liked getting up and was just trying to suggest that she get some extra sleep after such a long day.

'I'll see you tomorrow!' Barabas told them as he smiled. He then turned and began walking towards the quarters he would share with his husband and fellow Hajduk, Bogdan Ponta, during their time in Shangri. As he passed his partner, he spoke. 'I'll see you later!'

Bogdan nodded subtly.

'Bet the Ghazis don't do that, eh?' Nick commented, his eyes fixed upon Mira's.

Good! He's making sure she's alright too...

'No... No, they don't...'

They have decency...

Chapter VI

Come join the Murder

Now this is a palace!

Laur had seen palaces before. The Palace of Parliament that had once stood in Bucharest had been massive, so he had always had high standards for such things, but the palace of his birthplace had been a massive tasteless thing of dirty marble, rusty pipes, cracked wood and cold light. The palaces of the Svart had been true works of beauty and many matched and a few even surpassed the Palace of Parliament of Old Bucharest in size. Yet, they had all felt quite small, particularly within the grand scheme of galactic superstructures. The orcish worldship Vigilant had ruined all concepts of scale for Laur when he had first walked upon it. It was the size of France and was essentially a large disc floating through space and all across its surface it lay covered in... *buildings!?*

Always found it weird how a spaceship could have buildings on it.

Heh, technically we're on a spaceship right now!

A spaceship so large it swallowed up planets and moons, as it cornered a wounded star.

The entire Palace compound was basically the size of Europe. The inner palace, where the Peacekeeper and his close family lived, was essentially the size of Switzerland, the inner half of which was set aside solely for the family itself, with the outer circle being comprised of what were Royal Offices as well as the barracks of the Royal Shangri Constabulary and, thus, the home of the single Single Star remani. The remani edifice alone covered an area the size of Greater London, while the Royal Offices covered areas comparable to entire cities of Old Earth, all the while being connected to the royal compound itself and it was within one such office that Laur now found himself.

Near one such office. I hope... I do not feel like walking all day.

He had left the embassy naught but an hour before and had travelled via the Shangri leylines directly to the edge of the Inner Palace, having left his convoy in one of the reception bays of this massive construction he now traversed on foot. Protocol dictated that he leave his Hajduks behind and he was now accompanied only by Basenji, as they both walked behind their guide.

Who was tense, for some reason. *Never seen you tense while beyond a hair's breadth away from death before. What's going on?*

As they passed one particular intersection of two massive corridors, their presence was acknowledged by the four figures watching over said intersection. The four remani royal guards stood at attention within the four corners of the junction and they all saluted, before glaring at them as they crossed their little pack's territory.

Though they seem to glare at Basenji more than me or this butler...

Oh...

Basenji was also a remani, though he was a Black Knight remani, not a Single Star. They had known his presence would cause some... *hostility* during their visit, yet Laur had decided that his attendance would be invaluable. Basenji's presence was necessary because, first of all, Laur still didn't really feel... like a...

Like *a space... guy*?

Sure, he had his own spaceship, he had been to seven separate galaxies at this point, he had met dozens of new races of humanoids and he had access to stasis fields and flying cars and power armour and a million new and advanced... *space guy* technologies.

He would never admit it openly, but he always felt uncomfortable doing *alien* things, given that he was, at the end of the day, just *some guy* from Romania. He told himself that everyone was just some guy from *wherever* doing *whatever, whenever*; and it usually worked. Just that, every now and then, when he had to do something like meet the Crown Prince of an alien civilization whose history went back three thousand years in time, and who lived in a place which spanned the size of an entire country, protected by an ancient race of wolf people...

It was best to bring along an actual alien *space guy* in situations such as these!

And I get to bring along a member of the one race these dog people bear animosity towards...

The remani all stayed civil and Laur himself managed to contain his irritation with their long journey from parking lot to princely office. As they finally turned one last intersection and walked down another corridor, they stood before two massive blue doors, flanked by four more remani in their full regalia as household guards. Their guide, whose name Laur had already forgotten and to which he now mentally referred to 'the Butler' stopped before the entrance, then turned to face them.

'Before you enter, I wish to be assured that you are aware of the proper etiquette that must be employed when meeting the Crown Prince!' he informed them, in that annoying British accent the upper classes of this world seemed to gravitate towards.

We already know the fucking rules. 'Oh, is that so?' he played along.

'Yes, I'm sorry to say that it *has* to be so!' and with that, he jumped right into it:

'The current Crown Prince is quite liberal in his demeanour and conduct, yet you are still expected to refer to him as 'Your Grace' and to only initiate physical contact upon his direction and to not –'

'– stick our thumbs up our assets and nibble on what we find.' Laur did not pause, despite the Butler's reaction. 'Sir, this discussion's necessity is somewhat insulting!' he continued. 'We know how to be polite and civil. Such things are universal. Now, please, without further ado?'

The Butler stopped his flustering in the nick of time.

Right before he was about to say something that would trigger a diplomatic incident...

He then smiled curtly and spoke. 'The Crown Prince is a very considerate man. Dare I say far more considerate than any Crown Prince we've had before. He took the time to read up on you, *your Excellency*, and he has even asked us all to become familiar with the great *deeds* of Laur Pop. Such reading has produced many reactions among his retainers. You must understand that many among his retinue have advised against him ever being in the same room as you!'

I think I know which side of that argument you're on.

'You are a war criminal. You are also a sociopath. Your reputation paints you as being fundamentally antisocial, conniving and vulgar and I will instruct you only this:'

'Do not think that anyone here would behold your aptitude for violence – that is both cruel and crude – and see something worthy of respect, reverence or fear. Only repulsion and rejection.'

He let the silence sit between them for a few moments. Laur noted how the four remani before them, as well as the one that stood right next to him, were all glaring right at him. Before he could make the next move, the Butler turned and began walking towards the blue doors.

'Then why am I here?' *I can't help it. I have to fuck with him.*

'I beg your pardon, your Excellency?' the Butler paused, his hand midway towards a massive gold door handle.

'If I'm such a small and horrible man, what use am I to a man such as *him*?' he nodded towards the doors, emphasizing his question.

'You are a foreign dignitary, *your Excellency*!' the Butler began reaching for the door, once more.

'There are a thousand foreign dignitaries that enter this city every month. They don't all get to see the Crown Prince. What makes me different?'

'Your Excellency, such matters should be discussed with the Crown Prince, not with one such as myself!'

'Oh! I see. Well, I know *why* anyway!'

The Butler turned towards Pop and he felt an air of annoyance coming from him, as his hand dropped from the doorknob. 'And what reason might that be?'

'Such matters should be discussed only with the Crown Prince!' *Suck my dick, you stinky ass-picker.*

As the Butler glared, Pop raised his hand to flamboyantly gesture towards two doors that should be opened.

The Butler turned in as civil a manner as he could muster and finally opened the two blue doors.

The Crown Prince's office was remarkably small. Laur quickly realized that his own office was likely slightly larger and certainly far less well illuminated. It was built as a semicircle, with the flat edge opening up towards one large window that covered the entirety of one side of the spacious, yet cozy, chamber. The ceiling was domed and stood covered in many small openings through which sunlight passed gracefully, bathing the office in a warm, welcoming glow.

The room lay decorated in shades of blue and gold, with the floor being of a dark aquamarine, crisscrossed with small streams of gold, and at its centre stood a great desk of blue stone and golden wood. Right next to this desk stood a remani and this one was fierce.

The Single Star remani were far more intimidating than Laur had expected. He had gone with the assumption that, since they were more doglike, they would somehow appear to be less ferocious, but that had not necessarily been the case. They seemed more... *mindless* than the Black Knight remani he was used too.

Must be the eyes. Basenji, Technowolf and their lot all have those inquisitive eyes, in the style of a predator, albeit a very pensive one. These ones have cold, dead eyes, like those of a guard dog eyeing an intruder...

Their coats were also quite ridiculous and, again, far more doglike than the midnight darkness of the Black Knight remani which was only occasionally peppered by some white spot or another, such as Technowolf's white chest, abdomen and groin. These Shangri remani reminded Laur of German Shepherds, Bernese Mountain Dogs, Belgian Malinois and (*very* rarely) Labrador Retrievers. It was only this domestic look of theirs that chipped away at their intimidation factor. Laur was quite grateful for this reassuring attribute of their otherwise unusual appearance.

But the remani that stood before him now, looked like a *real* werewolf.

Basenji was jet black, like a black wolf, yet his coat was quite short, giving him more of a jackal-like appearance. This remani was jet black and his coat was long and thick, with giant tufts of fur jutting out from his collar, as he eyed the new arrivals with a cold intensity. He stood fully erect, with his hands clasped behind his back, since on his chest he bore the tabard of the Crown Prince's royal household proudly and would not have it defaced.

The Crown Prince, on the other hand, was just some guy.

'Ah, *Lord* Pop!' the Prince got up from his seat and extended a friendly hand.

Oh yeah... I'm technically a 'lord' for some people here.

'Your grace!' Pop closed the distance in a brisk walk and shook the Prince's hand. *It's friendly.*

'This is Gonzo!' the Prince gestured towards the massive black remani, who nodded politely towards Pop, whilst continuing to gaze straight ahead. 'You'll have to excuse him. He has taken an Oath of Silent Service, much like your friend over there. *Basenji*, I believe?!'

Laur realized that Basenji had remained near the doors, even as the Butler had shut them closed behind him. He turned to see Basenji also nod while looking straight ahead. *What the...?*

'They have their own sign language, you know?' the Crown Prince remarked.

Yeah, I know.

Though he did not suggest as much, Gonzo did react to his Crown Prince's words. He relaxed his arms, drawing them from his back and allowing them to sit relaxed to his sides, even swaying them back and forth slightly for a few moments. Then, he raised his left hand, palm upwards to the right of his navel, before drawing an imaginary line across his midriff.

That's a welcoming greeting. Hopefully that'll make some of this strange cultural tension go away...

Basenji also relaxed and put his own left hand forward, palm facing towards his own navel and pulled it inward in one smooth motion.

He's expressing gratitude at being welcomed.

'Seems everything is going well!' the Crown Prince remarked.

'Seems so.' *Let's see that this whole thing goes well!*

'Please, take a seat!' the Crown Prince gestured towards the seat right opposite his.

Laur swiftly accepted the invite, though Basenji did not. The remani made his way towards one of the nearby decorations adorning the Prince's walls, while Gonzo moved slightly in the opposite direction and seemed to pretend to look out the window.

Laur glanced towards the Prince's eyes to see that they were also studying the two remani and likely also wondering how this strange display of mutual dismissal would play out.

'Welcome...' the Prince outstretched his arms in an embracing gesture, as he sat back in his seat. '...to our Great City of Shangri.' He was a handsome guy, as all humans seemed to be nowadays. His aesthetics were pleasing to the eye: a square jaw, an elegant and thick stubble, as well as bright blue eyes that studied Laur intently. He had a gentle olive skin and a friendly disposition about him. He did not seem arrogant, neither did he seem in any way disingenuous. 'I trust you had a pleasant journey?' his host continued.

Passable. 'It was long, yet enjoyable. Moreover, it was quite useful, your grace.' *Take the bait!*

'Oh, how so, Lord Pop?' the Crown Prince humoured him.

'We had time to become accustomed with... well, your customs!' Quite the statesman we are today, Laur... Come on! You can do better...

'Oh! As we have with yours, *General* Pop!' he leaned forward in his seat and smiled. 'I must confess, Lord Pop, that, though my appearance is that of my actual age, I am only twenty-nine years old, in your years. My life has been marked by certain events, as has been everyone else's, for that matter! You see, I was only a small child during *the Crimson Trek Across the Stars*, the *War of Vengeance*, the *Bloodbrother Crisis*, *Hellsbreach*... I was, I must confess, *enthralled* with such tales! '*Enamoured*' one might say.'

'Oh,' was all Laur could say, as the Crown Prince seemed to behold him not as a person, but as some representation of something.

'Your children have – *fairytales*? Yes? Is that the word?' the Prince continued.

That is the actual word in English... Yes? You took the time to learn words in our language?

'No!' the Crown Prince raised a finger as he seemed to remember something. '*Basme?*'

Oh, boy...

'That is the word in *your* language: Romanian? Is it not?'

Oh boy... 'Correct, your grace!' *He's going to want a lot from me...*

'Excellent! Well, you see, for me growing up, Terra was a fairytale, a *basm*! It was this strange and savage world the Svart Elves had found and had attempted to exterminate, so as to preserve their dominion over this strange new realm they had arrived in. Yet, guided by the remani of the Black Star, your world endured. With the arrival of the Orcs of the Vigilant, you triumphed! Together with the Trolls of Kalimaste and the Goblins of Moria, you brought vengeance across the stars in letters of red fury. One of your own, a man named Tomasz Ashaver, raised from the dead – not once, but twice! – with the aid of a proud house of Primal Elves, produced an Avatar of Sentience: a girl who would take the name Daw al-Fajr! This girl would be raised by the famed Djibril al Sayid and the great Sarasvati Singh and would grow into a weapon of liberation of the Low Elf serfs, helping tear off the yoke of their oppressors. Cingeto Braca would duel the Chairman of the exiled kin of our own Libra ursai and earn the neutrality of his proud race of warrior craftsmen. At the Battle of Bahr Aldhabh, your Republican Alliance would triumph over their foe and crush them into a rout!'

The Crown Prince seemed to wander off, which Laur welcomed.

That's a lot of memories kid. A lot of other stuff happened between those words. A lot of stuff that doesn't sound so epic, so glamorous and so endearing.

'As I matured, just as I grew out of the innocence of my own youth, it would appear that you followed in step by foregoing your own!'

Is he using the sandwich method on me?

'The Rape of Rivendell, when trolls and humans began tormenting innocent civilians. A field of bodies at the Bahr Aldhabh, as far as the eye could see! Some claim that one could walk for a week in a straight line and not reach the carnage's end! Atrocities beyond comprehension, as you made your way to Nargothrond. Were it not for the hasty act of Quentyn Andromander, his entire world would've burned in the fires of your revenge! Your own people, *purged* during one last night of kinslaying on your own grieving world. In Andromeda, you supported a pan-galactic insurgency whose principal tools were terrorism and racial cleansing. Now, word has reached us of the most recent massacre in your history; of a place called 'the Rat's Den'?'

'Ratden.'

'Ah, yes, Ratden! Pardon me!' he leaned back. 'By your own accord, you slaughtered thousands of innocents. Young boys and girls that weren't even alive when Nargothrond yielded. What danger did they pose to the Republican Alliance, General Pop?'

'Most those events you just mentioned now, were happening at the same time as the ones you spoke of before.'

The Prince's eyes narrowed into the most hostile expression he had yet portrayed throughout their short discussion. 'Your point being?'

'We were – no, *are* – *both* of those things! We are the ones who did all of those fairytale things and we are also the ones who did all of those horrific things. We had to be.'

'I understand,' the Prince acknowledged solemnly.

No, you don't.

His host continued, 'Many do not, however! Every time the Republican Alliance decides to send over a *Terran* Ambassador, it causes quite a stir! Yet, never something as intense as what your arrival has triggered. I would imagine that your Warchief, your Marshal of Terra and your Allied High Council would have foreseen such a reaction?'

'They did.'

'And still they chose to send you.'

Ok... there's just a bit too much context here for me to comfortably drop, so I'm just going to deflect here... 'That was the decision, yes!'

'I see!' the Crown Prince, who had been leaning forwards in his seat, leaned back in his seat. 'General Pop, we stand here in the City of Shangri at the crossroads of two great powers. I must confess to you that, while many of my countrymen refuse to give word to such thoughts, I must make clear my belief that *yours* is the far lesser of two evils! With the Urheimat, we face the certain and complete eradication of our identity, our freedoms and of our way of life. That fate, dare I say it, is a fate far worse than whatever danger the jingoism of the Republican Alliance might trigger.'

'Your perceive my presence here as a danger?'

'I *perceive* that you didn't dare to deny the jingoism behind your government's decisions, only the danger posed by their implementation!'

Fair point.

'It is my hope that the City of Shangri will join your Alliance and, in the long run, hopefully others may also be swayed to the cause, in the face of the evil of the Urheimat. Yet, we find ourselves in the present and steps must be taken towards this future I believe we both desire! I had only hoped that your Alliance would treat this commitment with all its due diligence and never falter into negligence!'

You're saying that they sent me here by mistake, now?

'So, General Pop. How do you wish to proceed?'

Laur took a deep breath. *Finally, an easy topic!* 'My men under Legate Gjergj Çorbaci will continue our longstanding commitment to the expertise sharing agreement we have between our states. Legate Bojana Novak will continue to foster trade relations between the City of Shangri and the members of the Alliance. Legate Iosip Hodočasnik will continue with the active reconciliation of former opponents of the Alliance, together with the other ambassadors of our individual member states. I will personally focus on fostering the relationship between the City of Shangri and our Republican Alliance as a whole.'

'How do you intend to go about it?'

'It is my belief that we have been neglectful in our approach towards your hearts and your minds. I've spent some great deal of time looking over our reports on what goes on within the City of Shangri. I must confess that I have come to think that not enough has been made to improve our relationship with *the actual people* of Shangri. Insofar, we have dedicated the bulk of our resources towards improving the relationship we had with the peaks of your mountain and have neglected all that lay beneath!'

Before he could continue, the Crown Prince intervened. 'Ambassador Jimmel was a dearly beloved man by the people. Sometimes I even wondered if he had become more popular than most Shangri politicians.'

'A trend I wish to continue,' Laur stepped in.

'Did you have anything specific in mind?' the Prince pushed back, once more.

Getting technical with the questions now, are we? 'Well, we will be organizing a Dawnbreak Gala event at the Convent Garden Embassy, on the anniversary of our salvation and the passing of the End Times, to which I wish to now formally invite *your father* to attend!' *Good that I can get that out of the way.*

The Crown Prince's face did not give away any confirmation of attendance. 'Marvellous,' he simply replied, as if he expected more examples.

Okay... 'Well, that and other events, activities such as community outreach, intercultural exchanges and trade deals.'

'These are all excellent courses of action. Yet, they are also the normal course of business for any embassy and *any* ambassador. Why waste the talents of one such as yourself with such tasks? Was there truly no one else more suited to the task?'

Fuck it.

Laur leaned forward, for the first time during the conversation. 'I have steady hands, your Grace, and these are perilous waters. I appreciate your light-heartedness – *sincerely*! It genuinely makes me feel welcome! *However*, I think we can both agree that things are not as *static* as they might seem now. There are many things at play within the cosmos and we here in this room within your house upon your world are merely flecks of dust inside a hollow rock. Things have changed much within *your* lifetime; though, trust me, not as much as within *mine*!'

Ok, now let's weave the truth with the lie a little. 'I am not here because the Alliance is being negligent or provocative! On the contrary, I am here because the Alliance is taking the *utmost* care! I am here not because of my reputation, but despite it. I am here because *here* I can do what I can do best!'

'And what is that, General Pop?'

Laur took a deep breath as he studied the eyes of the man before him. 'Look for weaknesses.'

'Lord Pop...' the Crown Prince sighed, leaning back, dejected. '... our weakness lies bare before you and its name is *geography*! Ironic that what was once our greatest strength is –'

'– *No!* Not *your* weaknesses! The weaknesses in the Urheimat's hold upon you!' Laur also leaned back into his seat, satisfied that he had seized control of the conversation. 'You see, your Grace, right now, you find yourselves, whether you like it or not, caught in a tug of war you never wished to be a part of. Up until this point, we have focused primarily upon having the stronger pull. I am here to understand why the other side's pull is so strong.'

'Why do you think it has such a strong pull?'

'I don't know yet.' *Guilt, maybe?* 'Though I do intend to find out.'

The Crown Prince gazed at him, slowly nodding, as wry smile perched itself in the corner of his mouth. 'And what will you do when you find a weakness? Will you reach out and loosen your opponent's grip?'

Laur smiled now broadly. 'If no one is looking, yes!'

The Crown Prince chuckled, as he studied the man before him. Finally, he let out a loose breath, before admitting something to himself.. 'I don't believe I have introduced myself.'

'Crown Prince Turan Gisevius!' Laur smiled and tilted his head.

'Indeed...' he nodded. 'You can call me 'Turan'!'

'You can call *me* whatever you want... *Turan*!'

The two men looked at each other and gave themselves one final measure, mirrored by their remani companions, which also studied one another, without the intrusiveness of eye contact.

'Well, *Laur*,' Turan's eyes revealed an inner assessment of the situation. 'I will confer with my father concerning his attendance, though I wouldn't get my hopes up if I was you! He hasn't appeared openly outside the Royal Palace in a *very* long time and I do not expect him to change that policy any time soon, even if it were to honour a guest as esteemed as yourself!'

I expected that... though I don't like it! 'I'm certain we can address any concern that might prevent his attendance!'

'I'm certain you can! I'm also certain you cannot *challenge tradition* in Shangri without expecting to be *challenged* from time to time!' The Crown Prince smiled warmly. 'I expect this to be the first of many meetings we will have together, Laur! I expect that this shall remain a topic of contention for *another day*!'

Gonzo turned slightly towards them upon hearing the last sentence.

My time's up! 'If they're all as productive as this one, Turan, I believe we might soon find ourselves in a scenario where we only meet to enjoy each other's company!' he said, rising from his seat. *Shit! Is this ok? Is there protocol here? Should I only get up after he gets up.*

The Crown Prince nodded gracefully as he also rose from his seat and shook Laur's hand. 'I share in your optimism, Laur! Please! Do not let your mission here distract you from enjoying our beloved city! I think you'll find many sights in Shangri to be of your liking!'

'I trust the same, Turan!' he bowed his head as gracefully as he could, before turning his back towards the Crown Prince, as he gestured for Basenji to join him.

'Laur!'

Aw, shit, did I fuck the protocol up again? 'Yes?' he said, as he turned around instantly.

The Crown Prince's look was now far more stern, yet still somewhat friendly. 'Do not ever forget that this is *our* city. Not *yours*! You'll find that things will come along far more smoothly if you bear that in mind *at all times*!'

Laur slowly nodded, before admitting, 'I had no intention of finding out how things would come along if I didn't... *your Grace*!'

Laur spent the ride back to the Embassy digesting the man he had just met.

Shangri had something of a peculiar approach to succession (or so it appeared to Laur, at least). There had never been such a system in the entire history of Old Earth. How could there have been? The people of Old Earth rarely got to live to be a hundred years old! Within the City of Shangri and, indeed, throughout the entire cosmos, that number seemed almost infantile in its irrelevance. The average Vigilant orc was five hundred years old. The average elf lived to be thousands of years old, with a rare few even claiming birth during the days of the Old Realm, possibly aeons in the past. There were entities within the cosmos for which a human century resembled little more than a fleeting second within the context of their actual lifetime. So, if one ever became a king among the stars, one could reasonably expect to sit upon his throne for quite some time, up until eventually the day would come when he would lie within his tomb and another would rise to claim the bloody seat the old monarch had left behind.

Succession is a fickle thing. Here and everywhere. It always is.

Instead of the oldest born becoming heir, the tradition of the House of Gisevius was to have the second youngest child of the reigning Peacekeeper become heir. The reasoning was that it would be best that, if times ever changed so drastically that the old ruler died in the shifting of powers, it would be ideal if the new ruler would be someone born and raised during those times of turmoil that lead to the old ruler's fall.

It would be too dangerous to have the youngest becoming heir. For that would mean that such a situation may arise that the *Crown Prince* ascended the throne as an infant and either rule ineffectively or appoint a regent to rule in his stead. Thus, the youngest only received the title of the *Prince-in-Waiting*.

Every few decades, once the current Prince-in-Waiting had produced two children of his own, the Peacekeeper's wife would give birth to a new child and the Prince-in-Waiting would receive the title of Crown Prince. The previous Crown Prince would join the ranks of the many former Crown Princes and still carry the rank of 'Prince', though their importance within the functions of state would deteriorate with each new generational permutation. When the reigning Peacekeeper did die, the current Crown Prince ascended the throne, with the new Peacekeeper's children becoming the new Crown Prince and Prince-in-Waiting, while the old Princes would see their power deteriorate further, as they, in turn, became 'Elders' and the old Prince-in-Waiting would become the first of the new Princes.

Thus, the House of Gisevius consisted of dozens of Princes and thousands of Elders of three generations, each one the former heir of a galactic kingdom and once seen as the future of their people. *Now cast aside with little to no actual power, bar only their relationship to their father, or brother, or even just a nephew. Every so often, he throws each one some bone or another: a sinecure, a title, even actual responsibilities. The real power he only shares with the Crown Prince, the Camaril and the Senate.*

The Senate (also known as the House of Commons) and the Camaril (also known as the House of Lords), together comprised the Shangri Parliament and were thus a much more familiar concept to Laur's mind. It was a two-chamber parliamentary system! They had something of the like back in Old Romania, though Laur found the Shangri system to be more reminiscent of the Old UK. Seats in the Camaril were obtained by inheritance, yet the Senate had actual free and open elections, though they were spread out, so as to prevent sudden changes in the political spectrum arrayed within the Senate Chamber.

Within their parliament they debated policy, regulation and morality *at nauseam*, as the real power continued to be held by the Peacekeeper.

Who remained almost perpetually removed from public life, devoting his time primarily towards running his government via his extended family and the highest members of the Camaril. He did sporadically consort with the occasional senator, yet in reality he spent most of his time raising his children and grandchildren. The Peacekeeper rarely emerged from his palace, having only had six public appearances in the last hundred years: one each upon the conclusion of the Wars in the Milky Way, Andromeda and Triangulum Galaxies, and three times upon the ascension of a new Crown Prince.

Always before the Senate from behind the lectern of the Senate Chamber...

Laur's pondering was cut short.

Flashing red and blue light startled him as he caught the glints of colour coming from the outside. He tensed up, then quickly relaxed himself. He drew a pistol hidden within the armrest of his Mercedes, in whose rear seat he was travelling in, and placed it under his cloak. He noticed Basenji, in the seat to his left, do the same. The flashing lights grew more pronounced and were quickly matched by the ringing of a siren.

Their police uses the same tricks our own cops used back in the day!

Just that there wasn't supposed to be any police.

They had been escorted by members of the Royal Guards on their way to the leyline node located near the Crown Prince's quarters. The remani had left them less than a minute before, just as the Hajduk convoy had entered the leyline.

This was not of the Royal Guards' purple cars.

What swiftly overtook them was a regular white Royal Constabulary car.

'Radu?' he asked his centurion, sitting in the front passenger seat.

'I don't know,' he replied and Laur didn't even have to check to see that he had also reached for his sidearm.

'The dog boys are telling me to stop, sir!' the driver, one of his Hajduks legionnaires, a man called Filip, noted in a calm, yet serious manner.

This wasn't in the itinerary. *What the fuck is going on?* 'Well, let's do that and see what happens!'

Laur did a quick recap. Their convoy had five Hajduk vehicles, each with four men. That meant twenty legionnaires, plus the twenty Shangri Royal Guards that had escorted them. If need be, they could quickly be hailed to return and they could make it to their position in less than two minutes and assist them. *If they're actually on our side.*

As they came to a standstill, a second constabulary vehicle pulled up right next to them.

He scanned their surroundings. They had just exited the Shangri leyline, now finding themselves in between two major intersections in the middle of a tunnel that led beneath one of Convent Square's many parks. It was well lit... albeit a bit too quiet. Laur quickly realized that this wasn't normal.

So... traffic happens to come to a standstill right as we're driving through a fucking tunnel with no witnesses?

Laur began to ready himself for a fight, just as the police car's passenger door swung open and a large figure got out.

Oh, shit... one of these bear motherfuckers...

It was a brown ursai, though not a particularly large one. He had heard that the Ursai of Shangri were supposed to be slightly smaller than their Milky Way brethren, yet that did not take away from how terrifying he had always found them to be. *Particularly these brown ones who look like fucking grizzly bears.*

The ursai had always made him feel uneasy.

It wasn't the fact that they were three meter tall bear people that unnerved him, but their whole vibe.

While the remani were likely more ferocious than the ursai in appearance, they all tended to have very well balanced and calm personalities. Indeed, once you got around their tendency to sit perfectly still and quiet in the corners of badly lit rooms, you quickly got used to the fact that they were... well... werewolf-looking *people* with weird quirks.

The ursai were different.

Their temperament was... *off*. Always intense. Always focused. Always looking at you with a bit too much... *intent*. Their movements were expansive and would have come off as threatening even if they had been made by small cats.

When it was a half-a-ton bearman that was gesturing at you like an Italian grandmother, you had a tendency to get a little uneasy.

Sure enough, this particular ursai waved towards Laur's car and gestured towards the driver's window.

'Sir?' Filip asked.

'Let it play out, whatever it is. We're all here. If something happens, we're good,' he instructed.

Filip nodded and paused only slightly before lowering the bulletproof window between himself and the hulking bearman. 'Hello, good officer! Might I ask why you've stopped us today?'

The bearman leaned onto the car door with his gargantuan arms as he pushed his lower back out and faced Filip at the same level.

'Yes, you can!' he seemed to growl, though his tone was deadpan, somehow.

Then there was silence.

Too much silence.

Laur's hand moved slightly, as he adjusted his grip and his aim, right at the fucking giant bearman's head.

He knew that Basenji, Radu and likely every other Hajduk in the two cars in front and the two behind was probably doing more or less the same. He glanced towards the two constabulary cars. Both had tinted windows his eyes could not piece. *But they can't hold more than four bear people each.*

His rapid thinking was interrupted by something he had once been told was the sound of ursai *giggling*.

'That was a lil' joke for ya! No need to tense up!' the ursai turned his glare towards Laur. 'Mr. Pop?'

'Depends who's asking.'

The ursai, his hand resting on the car door, gestured towards his chest. 'Anwar Brownhen! Pleased to make your acquaintance!'

'The pleasure is all mine!' *Something is here.* 'Not *constable* Anwar Brownhen?'

The ursai flashed what passed for a smile among his kind. 'No, sir! I don't even drink!' he said once more in that deadpan tone.

Is he joking? Most constables here are remani. That must be a jab at the remani...

Oh... the remani have a drinking problem here too?

Oh... now that's interesting...

Maybe it's just because the police drinks a lot here too...

Anwar cleared his throat. 'No, I'm just hitching a ride provided graciously by our friends in the Convent Square Precinct,' he explained.

'Oh?' *I'm not sure if this is good or bad.*

'Yes, sir! I'm here to pass on an invitation.' Anwar continued. 'It's from *someone big*.'

That's saying something coming from you, but I think I get your meaning. 'I'm glad to hear. I like receiving invitations.'

'He's just forty minutes from here!' He turned to Filip. 'Just follow us!' With that he lifted his massive paws from the car door and the jeep wobbled slightly.

'Now?!' Radu asked.

Anwar paused and placed his gigantic palms on his knees, once more returning to eye level. 'D'you got anywhere to be?' He didn't wait for an answer, as he turned towards Laur once more. 'Someone wants to see you as soon as possible. *Now* is when it's possible! Or do you have someone else to meet?'

You know that there's no one else to meet today. You know a lot. This 'someone big' runs a pretty good operation.

'We can push a few meetings. We could make some time.'

'Good!' he turned back to Filip. 'It'll be zigzag! We want to make sure no one's following. Keep up!'

With that he made his way back to the police car and sped off ahead of their column.

'Sir?' Radu asked.

'Tell our guys to follow him. I'm guessing the second car will trail us. Call Silvia and let her know we're taking a trip to Arkham, which should take around three hours. Have our location be transmitted every second with our status!'

Laur knew Radu would be frowning. He also knew that he would soon raise his eyebrows and say, 'Sure thing, boss!'

The ride took almost an hour, as they crossed boulevards and alleyways, traversing neighbourhoods and sometimes even doubling back. They ultimately came upon a region of parkland marked only by the occasional country club. Their destination eventually became clear as they reached a lone compound. Laur didn't even need to understand Shangri script, for he knew where they were before he saw the plaque upon the entrance to the institution they were now approaching.

Peaceful Harmony Home for the Mentally Challenged.

Financed by His Majesty's Mental Health Improvement Fund.

The compound was split between two constituent parts. One was a large circular containment wall, akin to that of a prison, crisscrossed by guard towers and security turrets, with one large gatehouse and a parking lot out front next to the main gate. The other was a vast sprawling network of small houses and large buildings that could be seen in the distance through the gate's portcullis.

The Shangri police vehicles stopped in two designated areas, leaving five free parking spots in between, which the Terrans took as their own. Laur saw their guide get out of his seat and walk towards their vehicle.

'Radu, Basenji, you two come with me!' he said, as he got out of the car and walked towards Anwar.

'He's out back! They'll let you in when they see you. They won't ask for papers or ID,' the ursai instructed.

'Excellent!' Laur agreed, as he began walking next to Anwar towards the gatehouse.

Let's try to learn something.

'I'm guessing you work for the company?' he asked the bearman, as they walked towards the gatehouse.

'You're a good guesser. I'm the CEO.'

'Oh... not a partner?'

'Big doesn't have partners. Not anymore, at least.'

'I've heard. Bit of a corporate raider, I've heard he is!'

'That's what they call a shareholder who didn't want to get bought out *first*! But, you already knew that! Just as how you knew who I was when I told you my name!' The hulking bear glanced towards him and held his gaze for too long, as his race always had the habit of doing.

'Am I that transparent?' Laur tried to quip.

'No. But you *are* comfortable, even when things don't go the way you expected them. You didn't know you were gonna have a detour today. Yet, you didn't ask too many questions when you found out.'

'That might just mean I'm a trusting guy.'

'Trusting guys don't have your reputation.' Anwar pointed out, as they reached the guard post next to the portcullis. 'One guest,' he informed the human guard.

What? 'What?'

Anwar turned slowly towards him, his big, black and only vaguely soulless eyes peering into him. 'The conversation will be private.'

Fuck that. 'I would very much appreciate it if said privacy included my partners, seeing as they will be privy to what will be discussed regardless!'

The bearman blinked, before slowly leaning in.

Laur felt his hot breath upon the goosebumps of his open throat as the bearman lowered his voice. '*We don't have to kill you here!*'

Laur's fingers twitched as his hand opened up to feel the air between itself and his hidden pistol. Out of the corner of his eye, he spotted Radu's body posture change, knowing that his countryman had overheard the ursai's words.

Anwar continued. 'And about *that*...' he brought forward his hand, his massive paw open and facing up. 'You're gonna have to hand *that* over, just as you're gonna have to hand over the one in your jacket, the one tucked into your belt, the blade on your back, the dirk in your right boot and the switchblade in your left sleeve. To not even mention the bomb, that recording device attached to the bottom of your watch and the wire wrapped around your right wrist.'

How... the fuck kind of eyes does he... scanners?! Scanners when we were stopped. That's how he knows!

The ursai provided additional details. 'They'll be here, with your crew, waiting for you when you get back.'

'Assuming I will get back.'

'You will. Like I said: if we wanted you dead, we don't have to do it here.' Anwar grinned a fearsome sight. 'We can't have weapons inside a place like that,' he said, tilting his head towards the distant buildings. 'We can't have the loonies get their hands on knives and broomsticks! So, hand them over!'

'You expect me to walk into an insane asylum unarmed and alone?'

The ursai's face did not move. Had he been human or any other race, Pop might have been able to discern what may be going behind those black eyes. Yet, his was a strange race. One which Laur had never truly figured out. 'I heard you were there when our kinsman fought your orc paladin. I heard you were there when the Ursai of Barlog made an oath and you were there when they kept it. I make an oath to you now: no harm shall come to you by our design inside the walls of this place!'

'I *was* there.' *I still feel the ice upon the wind landing on my eyes.* 'Yet, you are not the Libra Ursai of Barlog! You are the Libra Ursai of Shangri!'

'You do not trust me.'

'We've only just met...'

'You're not a very trusting man.'

'Did my reputation give it away?'

'Did you trust the Ursai of Barlog to keep their oath?'

No... He's got me there.

The ursai let the silence sit for a while, before slowly moving his open paw closer towards Laur's chest. He stopped when he was naught but a child hand's breadth away.

'I don't have a blade on my back,' Laur announced.

'Then you need to work on your body posture.'

'I do.' *Fuck it.* 'Radu?'

'Yes, sir?'

'Come here! Don't shoot him!' he added.

Anwar withdrew his hand and leaned back, observing what came next.

One by one, Laur removed his weapons, including the one on his back, and passed them to his Centurion. Once finished, he turned towards the human guard and presented his empty hands, as well as his empty holsters, sheaths and scabbards.

The human guard nodded and pressed a nearby control module, causing the portcullis to rise. Anwar gestured towards the entrance.

'You're not coming with?' Laur asked.

'No. Like I said. It will be a private meeting,' Anwar reiterated.

'And he has no partners. Only employees,' Laur teased.

Just as the portcullis began lowering behind him, Laur saw a glimpse of something fly across the ursai's black eyes.

'*Correct.*' *I can hear it in the voice too.* 'Clementine Ward. It's the one with the orange windows.' Anwar instructed through the iron bars.

They have clementines here? Well, I guess that's nice.

The whole place was nice. Soothing colours. Calming architecture. Water fountains. They even had a garden and, judging by the chaotic rows of vegetables, he assumed that its caretakers must have been the patients.

One of which, a wild-haired human with even wilder eyes, came-up out of nowhere from behind some shrubbery. He was remarkably tall for a Shangrian, though he did appear to be quite skinny. Laur immediately concluded that, even though he could likely neutralize the man in the blink of an eye, it might be best to attempt the peaceful resolution of any conflict first.

The human's voice was erratic, yet oddly polite. 'Sir! Sorry, sir! Sir, please, sir!'

Laur stopped in his tracks and stood up straight as he eyed the madman. 'Yes, sir?' he replied.

'Begging your pardon, sir! Could I, by any chance, bite your ear off, sir? LEFT! *Left* ear, if you would be so kind!'

Laur's reply was prompt. 'Oh, but of course! However...' he leaned in slightly towards the raving lunatic next to him. '... I'm just now on my way to meet a friend!'

'Yes!' For some reason unknown to anyone (especially him) the madman felt compelled to approve.

'He's a very good friend!'

'As all friends should be!'

Well said. 'He has something very important to tell me!'

'He means to tell you where the children are sleeping?'

What the fucking... 'I don't know! But, I'm going to need my *ear* to find out!'

The madman did not respond, as he seemed to be integrating the information. 'You have a spare!' he realized.

'I'm a bit deaf in that one,' *I actually did use to be a bit deaf in that one.* 'Thus, would you be so kind as to bite my ear off when I get back from him? It will only be naught but a moment! He's right there near the orange house.'

'Oh! Certainly, sir! It's no issue at all!' the madmen suddenly saw the wisdom of Laur's words and waved him on his way.

He soon reached the clementine building and he walked inside to discover it to have a large central courtyard, with four walkways leading to it from opposite directions, converging into a central fountain, carved into the image of marble bear cub pissing into the crystal clear waters.

Heh... kinda like a little ursai Manaken Piss...

... it's actually kinda cute-

'*Ah*! Mr. Pop!' a deep, rumbling voice called out from behind him and Laur turned towards it.

Oh, shit he's biiig!!!

A truly gigantic polar bear walked with alarming speed towards him, as he raised one massive paw the size of two fire hydrants put together, up in the air and towards Laur's frozen frame.

He was much bigger than Anwar and thoroughly enormous. He was easily the biggest ursai he had ever seen in his life. Hell... he was the tallest *man* he had ever seen in his life. He was wearing a large white shirt (*no, it's not one of those looney straight-jackets, but it sure looks like one!*), loose pants like a hippie and sandals like a German tourist. His gait was broad and he closed the distance between them disturbingly quickly, as he lowered his hand to greet him.

Handshake!?!?!? Laur lifted his hand and the ursai gripped it within his colossal palm. *Yup... just like in Barlog... and he is so ridiculously strong! WHAT the ACTUAL FUCK!!!*

'Welcome to Shangri!' He sounded quite friendly, in all honesty.

Don't sound rattled. 'Hello, Mr. White!'

'Ah, no need for that! My friends call me Gamal! Please! There's a nice place for a chat right over here!' The bearman gestured towards a nearby square garden table, flanked by benches on either side, at the end of one of the walkways. He then began going on about architecture, though Laur couldn't properly listen, as he fought with himself, forcing himself to become accustomed with the gargantuan polar bear mob boss next to him, giving him a quick rundown of the facilities provided by the mental institution he resided in.

As they walked through the arched hallway and emerged on the other side, he saw that their destination was the largest of nine tables spread out throughout the garden, of which only two were currently occupied: one by a blonde human woman clutching what appeared to be a large plush toy (*is that a wombat?*), the other by a South Asian looking human having a very hushed conversation with the empty space before him.

'Good trip?' Big White asked as he sat down upon his bench, which could have easily accommodated four decently built Terran men.

He seems almost cramped! 'Excellent, actually!'

'Good to hear! I've never been off-world, myself!'

'Oh, is that so? How come?'

'*Bah!*' the ursai waved away the issue. 'Never had the time!'

'I see. Well, from what I can tell, there's plenty in Shangri to keep you entertained!'

'Oh, yes, indeed there is!'

'So...' Laur hadn't exactly planned this far. He usually liked to get ready before those things. *Not be fucking ambushed...*

'*So...*' Apparently his counterpart was clearly used to others coming to him prepared, even when he had them sporadically summoned to him.

Laur decided to be courteous and break the silence. 'I take it you're a guest of the government?'

Roaring.

Laur had never understood the expression but, now, hearing the terrifying sound coming from the ursai's throat through his jaws, he finally got it:

Roaring with laughter.

He was also not the only one to be taken aback by Big White's laughter, as the blonde woman began tearing up. As her face began to contort, she put a hand to her eyes to stop the sobbing.

'*Calina*! Calina, no!' the ursai gestured towards her. 'It's a joke! We're laughing! He's a funny man!' He outstretched a calming paw in her direction, even though she was over ten yards away. 'Funny man!' he continued. '*Ifchevron!*' he addressed the South Asian schizoid. 'You hear that? He's a funny guy!'

Ifchevron turned, shook his head, then nodded.

'Yeah! Yeah!' Big White continued. 'Tell Nicander! Tell him he's a funny guy!' the ursai gestured towards the empty space the human had been having a conversation with just moments before.

Ifchevron nodded and turned back towards his imaginary conversation partner, likely whispering praise of Laur's humour.

'Oh, Mr. Pop!' the ursai whipped snot from his nose and tears from his eyes. 'You're a funny guy, Mr. Pop! I like you!'

'I'm glad!' *What the actual fuck have I gotten myself into? What am I working with here?*

'Oh... '*guest of the government*'...' the ursai chuckled some more.

It wasn't even that funny.

'Yes, Mr. Pop, I'm currently enjoying His Majesty's hospitality...' he giggled some more. '*Uhhh...* yes!' he gently slapped the table and began studying Laur.

Who did not enjoyed being studied. 'May I ask how the current housing arrangement came to be?'

More roaring.

Jesus Christ, I was being serious. I almost shit myself this time.

'Oh, Mr. Pop, *you're gonna kill me*!' the ursai paused to stop himself from choking. 'There was a...' he stopped to grunt and clear the snot from his throat, '... there were some murders...'

'Oh...' *No surprise there.*

'I'm told they were quite gruesome.'

'Oh, my...'

'Yes! I was involved, *apparently*.'

'Good Heavens!'

'Yes, yes... not that I would know, of course!' ursai pointed to his head. 'I had a motorcycle accident when I was a child.'

'Oh, no!' Pop's throat feigned emotion, yet his face didn't bother to follow suit.

'Yes, yes! The doctors fixed it. There's no trace on my brain, but such things can leave marks no scan can detect!'

'I've heard!'

'Yes, yes! Only very few psychiatrists can even diagnose such disorders!'

'Only the best!' Laur confirmed, knowing he was consensually being lied to.

'I found one! A psychiatrist, that is!'

How surprising!

The ursai put his palm on his chest. 'He's a good friend of mine!'

Marvellous.

'He testified that, even though I clearly have memories of the event, their existence proves nothing, since the forensic analysis team could not scientifically prove that such memories were not just figments of my own imagination!'

'Fascinating.' *And creative, as perjury usually is.*

'Normally, the scanners would've been able to discern if such memories were real or fabricated – *but* given the head injury –'

'– from the motorcycle accident?' Laur wanted to show that he was following.

'Precisely! Who knows what's been going on in there!' he said, pointing at his thick skull. 'The good judge – *bless his heart*! – took kindness to my affliction and had me sent here, instead of prison!'

'How fortunate!' *I'm guessing the judge's family lived and all his kids got new shoes...*

'Yes, yes! Very! So...' the ursai stopped to chuckle. '... that's how I came to be a guest (*snort!*)... a guest of the government!'

'Well, it's lovely place!'

'Yes! That it *actually* is! I have a garden, do you like bok choy?'

'I beg your pardon?' *You see, I know he didn't just say 'bok choy', like the fucking vegetable...*

'*Bak*! *Choi*!' he emphasized. 'It's a vegetable! From your homeworld!'

Oh, shit, he really did say 'bok choy'... 'Ah, yes! It's a type of cabbage, isn't it?' *Asian lettuce or something.*

'Yes, yes! Very tasty. I enjoy it very much! The seeds were a gift from Mr. Wei!'

Ah, ok... 'Mr. Wei, yes! He was Terran Ambassador eight years ago!' *He left the fucking bok choy seeds he gifted to the mafia bear out of his reports...*

'I loved Mr. Wei!' the ursai confessed.

'He is a lovely man, yes!' *Also a whoremonger and an angry drunk, but, whatever, nobody's perfect.*

'Mr. Wei came to me, right after he met the Crown Prince!'

'I'm glad I could measure up to the high standards he set.'

'I didn't have to send anyone to fetch him,' Big White said.

And the air changed for a moment. He stopped smiling, laughing, ranting, giggling, choking, pointing or roaring. The massive polar bear just glared at him with the empty eyes of his race. They were so disproportionately small in comparison to his head and so sharp, like two black pinpricks scraping the surface of Laur's own two eyes, seeking to cast aside the two little shields guarding his secrets.

He is right, in his own way, of course.

I must throw him a bone and see if gnawing it placates him. 'What did you know of Mr. Wei before he came to visit?' he asked his host.

Big White leaned back slightly.

I caught him unawares with that one... Goo!, now I can push... 'Please be frank, Mr. White!' *A bit forceful, but should be enough... without crossing any lines... hopefully...*

The ursai let loose a small breath of air, akin to a snort, before recollecting. 'He came from a place called 'Honkong' on your world. His men called themselves the *Boxers*. He was.... well... we knew that he would be partial to some of the finer things in life which we here in Shangri cultivate... and *distil*.'

Whores must sprout on this world like blades of grass after a shining spring rain. Wei probably felt like it was Disneyland and you knew he would take a liking to you if you were Mickey Mouse... or... what was the name of that bear from Jungle Book? It was the nickname of that ursai from Barlog... the one with the... never mind... 'What of his military record? I'm certain you would've found it to be of interest.'

'A war hero! Very interesting indeed! But I'm told that's the norm where you come from!'

'It is,' Laur confirmed and he was pleased to see the ursai raise a brow slightly.

'... I recall him telling me of how he marched across his country taking back his land from elves! *That* and how he used to beat some of his men to death when he was drunk!'

Yup, that's him alright. 'Did he mention why he doesn't do that anymore?'

'Yes... yes he did.' Big White crossed his arms and leaned back. 'Because, one night, *you* killed thousands of your own people and now you lock-up anyone who ever do it again, no matter the reason.'

'It wasn't *just* me,' Laur said and waited.

'My apologies, it wasn't *just* you. It was you and everyone else that did the killing that night.'

'But you mentioned me first.'

'I did. I hear it was your greatest achievement.'

Unfortunately, I often think the same. 'What else do you know about me?'

'I know that you just finished hunting the last of your enemies into extinction. But, other than that most recent achievement, I know you're a man of great many deeds, Mr. Pop, *I wouldn't know where to start!*'

'But you *did* start with those two. Do you notice what both have in common?'

'Your success?'

'That and the fact that they're both dirty things!' Laur leaned forward. 'If I were to ask you what you had heard of Tomasz Ashaver, Djibril-al Sayid, Sarasvati Singh, Shoshana Adler, Pedro Valverde or Tobias Gründer, you would have had other things to say about their achievements. Completely different words could be used to describe them. Heroic. Savage. Magnificent. Resilient. Debonair. Pragmatic. Those would be words one might use to describe them, yet not me.'

'I know. Which brings me to the one question I couldn't stop thinking about: *Why you?*' the ursai leaned forward. 'What do *you* get from coming *here*?'

Am I some sort of riddle for these people? Am I featured in the daily gazette or something? 'It could have been any single one of us... It was just *I* who had the spare time!' *A lie. A truly wretched lie. But also true; in a way. It'll suffice.* 'You also had another question: the one about my initial choice for our first encounter. My reasoning was that, if I would have come to visit you as early as I now have, there was a chance that someone might see me do so and word might get out! And when word gets out, the next question will be: but why would Laur Pop be doing meeting with Big White so early on in his assignment? What could be so important for us to discuss that I would meet with you right after I met the Crown Prince of Shangri himself!'

'And what *are* we discussing, Mr. Pop?'

'Something *dirty*.'

'And what might that be?'

There you go... taking the bait. 'There is an endpoint in my enemy's victory which coincides with *your* own demise, Mr. White! If the Urheimat closes the hand in which it holds this City and brings you into their dominion, what will become of *you* and your people?'

'There's no need for me to answer, Mr. Pop. That has always been the reality on which our relationship with the Republican Alliance has been built.'

'Yes, it was. But, now, the fingers are moving and what we have built together needs to run its course.'

'*Have* the fingers moved?'

'Slowly.'

'And you quickly came *here*? You could be crushed too, you know?'

'The fingers will not have time to crush anything.' Laur stared blankly into the ursai's eyes, knowing that he must have great care with what he was about to say. 'I'm here to make sure they feel the heat and pull their fingers back!'

The ursai started smiling, albeit Laur couldn't be exactly sure if it was mocking or sincere. 'Is that what you are, Mr. Pop? *The heat?*'

'Part of it. There are others. I'm told that you might be one such man.'

'You're told correctly.'

Hopefully, not hot-headed. 'There are certain adversaries of yours who've encroached on your territory. I understand that some of them are... *sympathizers* of the Urheimat?'

'Sympathizers?' he snorted. 'Well, they're a lot more than *that*!'

'Precisely.'

'Huh... and what would you propose that we do with these adversaries of mine?'

'Burn them.'

'Do you think that'll raise the temperature enough?'

'It's a beginning.'

'Ah... I see. *A beginning.*' The ursai eyed him for a moment, before turning to look off into the distance. Then, without any warning, he swiftly leaned forwards into the table and came mere inches from Laur's face, who struggled not to flinch.

'*That's not enough truth, Mr. Pop!*'

'Sorry?' Laur struggled to sound nonplussed.

'What you say is all true, yet it is not enough. There is something else! There is more reason behind your actions. It's why I wanted to see you. I wanted to see what else is there to the story of your arrival.' The bearman's eyes narrowed and his voice grew soft. 'Any Terran warlord could've come to lend their muscle to us in the hopes of currying our favour. Why is it *you* who came?'

Very well. It's come to this. He asks for more truth, then so be it. I will give him more truth and see him satisfied.

'Do you have kids, Mr. White?'

The bearman immediately pulled back. 'I have a few cubs with some baby mamas. What of it?'

'I never had any children. Quite frankly, I would have very much liked to have children before the doom of my world, though I know in my heart that they wouldn't have survived what was about to come and, well, after Doomsday's passing... I never really wanted to have children just so that the universe might once more take them away... But, the mind is a strange thing and I find myself seeing others as my own children, like some strange uncle who never married for some pathetic reason or another.' Laur paused, blending his feelings into that which was needed to get just the right information across. 'And the universe still reached forward and pulled those children I saw as my own away from me.'

He met the ursai's gaze, since now the coast was clear and he could speak frankly. 'The Svart stole thousands of Terra's children during the End Times and passed them through a series of hands to the Urheimat, from whence I know I can never wrest them back. The Svart are now all finally dead and, soon, the last of the Senoyu shall pass from this world – that I can promise you! Yet, there are still fingerprints which remain unaccounted for...'

'And the hands to whom these fingerprints belong?'

'Are to burn also.'

'Heh...' the ursai glared at him for a few long moments, before looking off into the distance. 'Do you like fights, Mr. Pop?'

Well... I guess he's changing the subject... I hope. 'I beg your pardon?'

The ursai turned back to face him. 'Mixed-martial arts? Hand-to-hand combat?'

'... you...' Laur turned around to check for witnesses... or maybe even cameras, albeit he would have been furious to have had their conversation up to that point be eavesdropped upon. He turned back to the great white polar bear with more muscle in his chest than he had in his whole body. 'You want to do it here?'

The ursai's eyes narrowed for a moment before his jaws parted ways to once more roar with laughter, causing great distress in his fellow patients. 'Mr. Pop! You crack me up! No! There's an event in a couple of days time! The *Mixed-Weight Exposition: One-shot Contender's Edition*. It's organized by some friends of mine! I have a special derogation to attend. Would you be interested in attending as my honoured guest?'

Sometimes this surreal reality hits a bit too suddenly for my liking. 'Mr. White, though I am charmed, would you not agree that such a public presentation of our relationship be unwise? For the aforementioned reasons?'

'Are you saying that if people would see us together, they would think less of you?'

Oh, come on... don't do this shit... 'On the contrary, I'm more concerned about what damage my image could do to yours! You're a man seeking peace, at least publicly. Wouldn't your association with a figure such as myself tarnish that perception?'

'A fair point! But, there would be more perception than that at play!' The ursai froze and once more locked gazes with Laur. 'I've had many such meetings with your Ambassadors over the years,' he said, gesturing towards the two of them and the table they shared. 'Always in the dark or, at least, *out of sight*! You and your predecessors have always offered much and you have, to your merit, always delivered. However, you've always cut short of two things: public association with the Libra Ursai of Shangri and active lethal support of our operations.' He raised two fingers to emphasize his point. 'Given that it would appear from your words that you are about to provide the second, I must insist that you also provide the first!'

'We can grant you one finger *now* and promise our entire arms at *a later date*.'

'Well put, but you have to understand that you do not *own* me and I do not *depend* on you! If anything, I'm risking a great deal by doing business with you.'

'A gamble you took which we've always honoured.'

'Indeed, though, I'll say this again, you *do not own me* and you do not get to decide my destiny, nor the destiny of my organization!'

Such an ursai thing to say.

Big White went on. 'When have you ever skirted away from publicly associating yourselves with our distant kin in the Milky Way? Never, that's when! You wanted the whole wide world to know that you had a new ally you were proud of! What makes *them* better than *we* here in Shangri?'

He makes a valid point. 'Circumstance.'

The ursai slowly leaned back so far, Laur thought he might roll over.

I'd best continue. 'You are correct, however, that we do not own you, nor do we wish to! No one has ever joined the Republican Alliance because they were forced by its members to do so. Quite frankly, our peoples have only ever come together due to the actions of others. You judge that our support must become visible. I trust your judgement! I will attend – *but*! There is something else that you should know about me, Mr. White!'

'I'm all ears, Mr. Pop!'

'I don't like waste and I would hate it if all that we have invested into our relationship would go to waste!'

'Are you threatening me now?'

I expected him to say that. Good. 'I am doing many things, Mr. White. Threatening you never crossed my mind, yet I will assure you that I do see *you* and I do see your *power*. I see your threat. I see your choices. I might even see your intent. I will have you know that if I had any doubts about it, you would have never even seen me waste my time by showing my face, let alone hear me threaten you!'

'Hmmm... you are a determined man aren't you, Mr. Pop?'

'Isn't that what we always offered, Mr. White? Determination?'

'You Terrans, at least, certainly always did. I'm pleased to see you also offer consistency!' The ursai tapped his hands on the table, startling Laur. 'A gift, Mr. Pop! I have a gift for you!'

The ursai got up from his seat, making the ground tremble as he stood and gestured for Laur to follow him. He led him through the nearby hedges, making the Terran nervous, as he saw an eventual behind every corner. The tension only lasted a few minutes, until they arrived in a clearing, of sorts, within which rose a great cage of cold steel and clear glass.

Roughly thirty by forty meters, with an arched roof resembling that of a church, it rose up around twenty meters into sky. Inside, Laur's eyes saw dense vegetation surrounding a small artificial stream which began in one corner and ended at the other, the sound of crisp water punctuated by the songs of those few birds that were perched on top of the great structure, outside the reach of anything within.

A botanical garden? Or a zoo?

Wait... there are a lot of ledges and branches...

A volary! Like, for birds!

His suspicion was confirmed, as inside the cage was likely one of the strangest creatures he had ever seen.

It was not the creature itself, which was actually rather mundane, but its surroundings, that drew Laur's attention. The volary was populated with trees and other such vegetation, such as low-lying shrubs, violet flowers, tall grasses and the occasional vibrant moss, yet its occupant lay perched, not upon a brown branch amongst green foliage, but within a dark burrow of its own making, surrounded by a thick, white web that funnelled towards the red eyes of its occupant.

It looked like a raven and, when Laur drew near and Big White began opening the cage doors, the creature revealed itself to likely be a creature of such a shape, as it crawled out of its den and began flying in swift jumps from one branch to another. It was much larger than the crows and ravens Laur remembered from the days of Old Earth, with long black wings possessing of a charming grace that could cover the breadth of Laur's height with ease. Its claws were true talons and were of the darkest shade, though they paled in comparison to the bird's plumage, which was of the most consuming darkness. So black they were, Laur thought they would have drawn too much attention at night, let alone during the day. Its beak was of the same shadow as its feet, yet the eyes were so much more. Within a sea of ruby crimson, one could see dots of true oblivion which pulsed excitedly as it observed Laur and his host.

Big White walked over to what must have been a door and began unlocking it. '*Camio*, they are called, in the old tongue of Shangri. They're quite rare nowadays, or so I am told!' he explained, as he opened the door and bid Laur join him inside.

'I'm assuming the pigeons drove them off?' Laur quipped, as he reluctantly joined his host inside.

'The pigeons are the main staple of their diet, though not their favourite! *No*, they're rare because they hunt each other. The perverse black bastards actually prefer the meat of their own kind!'

That sounded oddly racist, for some reason.

'They used to be prized as guardians in the homes of the aristocracy, yet they fell out of fashion since the nobles got tired of fighting over whose bird killed the other!' the ursai said, as he bid the bird fly to him.

The creature swung down from its most recent roost, straight towards the two figures below. At first, Laur had assumed that the creature would honour Big White with its presence, but the bird had something else in mind, as it flew right around the ursai, before it landed on a branch right next to Laur.

'Oh, would you look at that! He likes you! Come! Raise your arm!' Big White insisted, just as the camio landed on the green grass of the volary before them.

Laur eyed the creature for a moment, as it, in turn, trotted around before his feet, trying to catch a good look at him. It seemed oddly intelligent, akin to some jittery sheepdog, just waiting for a new task to complete. He also noted that the bird kept its distance from the ursai, occasionally eyeing him with suspicion.

Oh, what the hell...

Laur raised his hand forward, as he had seen many a Ghazi, Keshik and Pandoran do to welcome their pet hawks. The creature quickly tilted its head, judged the distance, then jumped to his forearm, bringing its eyes level with his. Very inquisitive they were and Laur was pleased to see them acknowledge him, as the bird blinked and moved its beak towards his breast, where it began inspect his chest. For a moment, he worried that this might be the world's strangest assassination attempt.

Wouldn't that be a thing? To die stabbed in the chest by an emo chicken.

But the creature merely pecked at one of his buttons, before shifting its focus underneath one its wings. It began pecking one armpit and Laur realised that this must have been how birds scratched their itches. His mouth moved slightly as he felt the urge to smile.

'There you go, Mr. Pop! One of the best presents I've ever delivered!' the ursai announced. 'Now, remember, these things are carnivorous, so keep him heavy on the protein: pigeons, rats, maybe even the occasional cat!'

Good thing there's no cats at the embassy. 'Does it also eat giant spiders? Laur glanced towards the webbed burrow from whence the bird had descended.'

The ursai looked towards the white hollow, before quickly turning back towards Laur. 'He *is* the spider!' he explained.

Now, Laur was a bit intrigued. 'Huh?' he said, looking towards the shadowy webbing.

'Camios are avian arachnids. They emerged on Shangri-La a long time ago as one of the indigenous species. They looked nothing like this one. They used to be small and all they did was hunt one another; until only the biggest remained! By that point, they were one of the apex predators of their world. Now, they're little more than pets, with the aggression being bred out of them long ago.'

The bird gave a strange little *chirrup!!!*

'... my apologies!' the ursai corrected himself. 'There's still some aggression in them, despite the breeding! Yet, they are clever little things!'

'I... Thank you!' Laur mumbled. He genuinely was grateful.

He liked this thing.

'Good! Well... that's about it from me! I'll lead you to the gate! I don't want you bumping into Olmo!'

'Who's Olmo?

'Just some crazy guy who bites people's ears off around here...' the ursai casually replied.

They did not encounter Olmo on their walk to the entrance. The ursai spent most of the time talking about the various vegetables he had been planting, as they passed his allotment (which was actually much more tidy than the others). Laur feigned interest, though, in truth, he had little care for the ursai's gardening technique, due primarily to the fact that it was nevertheless quite lacklustre. He was far more interested in this awesome little flying cannibal bird spider thing on his forearm, which would occasionally caw when Big White would exaggerate the size of some melon or another.

'Wait!' the bearman had announced at one point, before stopping to pull out a white bag from one of his huge pockets. 'The bok choy is just ripe!'

No, it isn't yet. Laur saw the giant bearman bend over and pull out some Chinese cabbage from the ground. They looked like cucumbers in his massive paws. 'Oh, but there's no need!' Laur insisted.

'D'you like tomatoes?' Big White asked, looking at him with eyes that seemed to ask whether he liked being or not.

Laur's eyes glanced to a nearby vine. *Who gave him tomatoes? Also, they're not ripe yet either...* 'Those are lovely, but they're not ripe either!'

'*Either*? Are you saying this bok choy isn't ripe?' Big White asked, his tone suddenly becoming quite menacing.

Oh, shit! 'I'm no gardener, but...' For the first time in the conversation, Laur genuinely stumbled. *I really hope this motherfucker is just acting a fool and that he's not a genuine madman.*

The ursai met his gaze, then looked at the tiny chunks of bok choy in his hand. 'Ah, well...' the ursai placed the bok choy in his bag, then moved over to another plant; one which Laur couldn't identify. 'This is *flintfinger*, it's kind of like a potato that grows on a bush and I *know* this one's ripe!' He reached into the bush and pulled out several purple plantain-looking tubers and began filling up his bag. Once he was finished, he passed the bulging sack to Laur.

Who decided to humour the giant. 'Thank you! I'm most grateful!'

'You're welcome, now let's get you out of here, else you might catch schizophrenia!'

'I hear it's quite contagious.'

'Nah, it's not that bad!' the ursai said, giving Laur a slap on the back that realigned some of his vertebrae.

When they reached the vicinity of the gate, the ursai drew closer to one of the nearby hedges. 'This is where I'll leave you. In here it's private, but out there might be a different story.'

'So people might find out that we've met?' *I thought you ran a tight ship.*

'They won't, but there's no need to put my boys to work pointlessly.'

'I see... Mr. White?' Laur asked.

'Yes?'

'Where should we begin?'

The ursai paused and once more studied Laur with his dead eyes. 'I see you Terrans are all alike. Pragmatic bunch, aren't you? Despite all the pretty words and that image of restraint you all cultivate.'

*A fair assessment... though I *hope* he's right, more than I *know* he's right.* 'We do value our word and we are pragmatic. Yet, this is a thing of *balance*! You have granted me many gifts!' he shook the bag in his hand, as he nodded towards the camio on his arm. 'I wish to return the favour and, thus, commence our cycle of prosperous growth!'

'I see...' the ursai appeared to be pondering something, though the little black eyes never left Laur's.

'*Power*,' he simply said, before looking up towards Shangri's captive sun. 'The sun powers everything in this city and much more! The price of energy was long-ago capped, yet a surplus persists until this day, though the government still forces the populace to pay for energy consumption.'

Yes, I read that in the reports...

Oh... You mean to-

'Seems a bit unfair, now doesn't it?' the bearman asked.

'If only there were ways for the population to safely and cheaply *access* the surplus...' Laur quipped.

'At least those in the populace willing to pay a one-off fee, as well as recurring maintenance costs...' the ursai pointed out.

'Costs that would still be much cheaper than if they bought power from the grid...'

'Someone would have to distribute, as well as install such systems. Though someone else would either have to manufacture or import the necessary materials.'

'Has someone ever done so?' Laur asked.

'Many have and a few still try, though procurement has always been an issue.'

'The Port Authority?'

'First and foremost, though the Department of Energy makes weeding out such devices one of its main directives. That is, until recently, when we in the Libra Corporation secured a power maintenance contract, for coverage of certain areas.'

'A legitimate business, I assume?'

'One of our cleanest, though the main benefit has been the fact that we have limited jurisdiction over our areas, meaning that we get to decide *what* gets inspected and *when*.'

'Congratulations!' Laur's eyes narrowed. 'Have you considered manufacturing?'

'Impossible. The process would attract too much attention and the press and the dog boys would be all over us in a heartbeat.'

'So, it *must* be imports?'

'For the time being.'

'I see... Have your people deliver the necessary blueprints – of *both* the power grid *and* of the necessary devices – and we'll get to it!'

The ursai nodded. 'You are a generous man, Mr. Pop! I like–'

'– Four Shangri spheres per astrowatt taken from the grid. We'll calculate an estimated number for each day based on the number of known sales. Payment may also be made in Asgardian Guilders or Imperial Trade Credits.'

The ursai was deathly quiet for a moment. 'What need have you of credits, Ambassador? Don't you have access to the wealth of three entire galaxies?'

'I do. And now we will have access to part of the wealth of a fourth! In untraceable format, which we can use to finance future operations, which we will be ramping up in the following period of time, if our collaboration continues to evolve favourably.'

'I see... working with you will be a gift that will keep on giving?'

'That's the idea.'

'Very well,' the ursai extended his great paw. '*Deal*!'

Laur shook his hand and worried that he might get his arm torn off.

The raised eyebrows of the Hajduks waiting for him by the asylum's gate were nothing compared to the look Nick gave him when the giant spider raven jumped from the backseat of Laur's car after the General got out.

'Heard you had a little detour!' The Gypsy giggled and smiled at the creature that had just now jumped onto his General's arm. 'What's that?' he asked.

'It's a gift.'

Nick gave him a somewhat irritated look.

'It's called a *Camio*, apparently.'

'What now?' Nick asked, as Silvia appeared next to him, a perplexed look on her face.

Laur continued. 'Big White also sent us some unripe bok choy and some banana potatoes!' which he passed to Nick.

Silvia pressed her lips together as she regarded his new pet. 'Would you like me to find him a perch? And a water bowl?'

'Yes. Maybe some raw chicken too... and see if we can't set up a pigeon trap on the roof!'

'Does he have a name?' she asked.

'Yes... His name is...' Laur raised the bird slightly, causing it to lock eyes with him. '... *Spideraven*!'

'You're getting better with the names...' Nick said sarcastically, his mouth turned into a scowl of anti-climatic contempt. '... *sir!*' he added, after Laur gave him a dirty look.

Chapter VII:

Usually you're screaming about us

Silvia woke up late the next day.

Not *late* late. Just later than what she would have preferred.

Shangri ran on a perfect 24 hour cycle, with roughly 10 hours of clear sunlight, 10 hours of night, and two hours each set aside for what counted as dawn and dusk. The massive 'sail' (as Silvia thought of it) that covered those sections of inner Shangri that were meant to be experiencing dusk, had a large translucent section that dimmed the light as it passed, creating some kind of strange hazy light that passed as either the light of dawn or the darkening of dusk. She had to admit that the light itself wasn't the issue, as it mimicked twilight rather well.

Her problem was with the sun, which never moved.

That was what was fucking with her, she had come to believe. Why else would she be having issues sleeping the exactly 8 hours she usually slept every night?

How the devil do people get used to that?

The natives likely didn't find it strange, but newcomers must have found it disturbing. This was her fifth morning in the City of Shangri, and it was already beginning to get to her. At first, she had thought of it as some quaint oddity. After all, she had spent over two decades of her life living on many a strange foreign world. In Andromeda, the Hajduks had spent months on a world which did not spin as it circled its sun, causing one side to be permanently scorched, and the other permanently frozen. What little life there was lived on a narrow belt of a hundred kilometres covered in dense woodland. *That* she had found strange, at first, but she eventually got used to the ever-sunset of that world's horizon.

This thing in Shangri was somehow far more disturbing than that.

The fact that it's <u>pretending</u> to be natural. That must be it!

It's the most artificial environment one could imagine, yet it pretends to be natural in a way a spaceship, or a world incompatible with human life, does not.

From her vantage point in her living room, holding a freshly brewed cup of coffee, she bent forwards slightly towards her windowsill, to better observe the street below.

She hadn't pulled back the curtains. Quite frankly, she would likely never draw them during her entire time in Shangri. They were made of a special fiber woven in a very particular fashion, which allowed them to block light coming out of the apartment, yet the light coming in, although they did distort it slightly. From the outside, all one could see was white curtains, while from the inside, one could observe the entirety of Wiltshire Boulevard without being spotted.

They were also bulletproof, which Silvia really liked.

I am not getting sniped ever again.

Though she bore no scar from the event, she still felt pain in her lower back from the time she had been shot in the back by a Senoyu sniper. The bolt had shattered her pelvis and turned everything between her taint and her spine into a bloody tangled mess of flesh, blood, metal and fabric.

Good thing I was only carrying a third of my eggs in me...

She had been lucky, naught but only a month before their departure to Andromeda, the Terran High Command had instated a new policy requiring Terran women to never carry over a third of their ovules inside them at any given time. At least a third would always be stored on Terra and, as a Terran woman, Silvia had the right to decide how her eggs would be used. She had labelled her eggs to be *Off-limits, with the exception of Urgent Repopulation*. Yes, of course, if there was ever a need for new mass-produced citizens, spawned from the random mixing of female and male Terran seed-stocks (which was something that would likely occur in a scenario where she was very much likely *very* dead) she was fine with having her genes being passed on.

But she was not comfortable with her eggs being used to spawn Terran sunriser children in some vat, to be then shipped off to Gardener family and raised among dozens of brothers and sisters, the same age as them, but with no true blood tie to them.

Silvia had lived for seven years in an orphanage.

Two orphanages, actually. First the one in Graz, which had been all right, and then the one in Brașov, which she had truly felt safe and at home. It had been a clean orphanage, surrounded by adults that cared for her, brothers and sisters with no blood tie to her that had loved her and whom she loved. An orphanage in a green forest in Romania with lots of food and clean water and places for children to play.

But, it was still an orphanage.

I wouldn't want my children to live like that:

Alone.

No, her eggs would remain in the vaults, at her discretion.

She glanced towards the stairs to her bedroom. A third of her eggs were located in a medical chest in her room, which she had firmly secured to one of the walls with construction bolts. The last third was split between stashes at Bâlea Citadel, her home in Brașov, her doomsday vault on one of the Spines of Terra, as well as one small stash she had left with Andrada and Valentin, who ran the Brașov orphanage.

She carried no eggs inside of her and she had paused her cycle.

It was a decision many Terran women took, by virtue of the fact that they were usually somewhere where there would be violence and sometimes that violence was of a sexual nature. A rape was horrifying enough on its own. Becoming pregnant due to a rape was nauseating. Not only due to the reasons known to women all across the universe, yet also due to Terran Law.

A Terran woman wouldn't be able to kill the child, for any fertilized egg would technically be a *Terran* fertilized egg. A choice would be given: carry the baby herself and raise the child as her own or have it removed and placed in a special Gardner family, which would raise a child oblivious of its heritage and the nature of its conception.

As if a Terran woman would be captured, raped, impregnated and somehow escaped...

A well meaning law for horrific moments, yet somehow still moronic in its naiveté...

Silvia did not plan on ever making such choices. The box upstairs had a self-destruct that triggered if the wrong access code was input one too many times. She was also in artificial menopause, which she could exit if she forced herself through either meditation, medication or a combination of the two. If she ever decided to have a child, she had all the resources available at her disposal to do just that.

I'm pushing sixty and still a virgin... why the hell am I so obsessed with birth control?

What time is it? she asked Îngeraș.

Only to be met by silence.

Oh, yeah. I'm offline... Some other bullshit I'm gonna have to get used to... AI operators were illegal on Shangri, she kept having to remind herself, after getting used to having one around, particularly in semi-civilian settings such as the one she now found herself in.

She checked her watch.

6:03.

Pop was going to be awake in (hopefully) 57 minutes. The morning meeting with him was at eight. She had until then to do her morning rounds. In about twelve minutes, there was going to be a knock at her door. Radu, Cosmin and Ela (hopefully Nick as well) would have their morning meeting with her for about ten minutes, which meant that she would also have time for –

Knock! Knock!

Silvia was startled by the noise. She turned to stare at her door as she walked towards it, making sure to avoid walking right in front of the windows. *I like and I trust these curtains, but you can never be too careful...*

'Yes?' she asked, gripping the pistol in the concealed carry holster behind her belt buckle.

'*Cosmin*!' Cosmin's voice replied.

What the fuck? What's happened?

Her thought was interrupted by more knocking.

'*Yes*! Now!' she informed her visitor, as she reached the door and opened it wide.

Cosmin was not wearing a jacket, which meant that something had interrupted his morning routine.

'Yes?' she asked.

Cosmin's eyebrows went up as he thought of a response. 'Well...' he started '... I think it's better if you come and see!'

He didn't truly seem to be worried... whatever it was that had happened clearly wasn't truly dangerous... He did seem a little... *surprised*? *startled*? Maybe *perplexed*?

She closed the door behind her and the two began walking towards the stairway that descended to the main chamber, where the great tree resided.

'Well? Could I, at least, get some colour on the situation?' she asked, still worried, but now also slightly annoyed.

'A van pulled up to the parking lot entrance. The driver gave the correct code for 'morning delivery' and said that they had been called by Mira to execute services due as per an invoice she had issued on the Embassy's name. Inside, we confirmed that the van had twenty occupants, including the driver – '

'You let them in?' Silvia stopped in her tracks.

'*Radu* let them in. Apparently, Mira gave last night's watch a heads-up.'

She began walking rapidly towards the central staircase overlooking the main lobby. *They can't be so –*

'Nah, Silvia! It's fine! We scanned them. Frisked them. They're ok! We brought them to the tree to keep an eye on them 'till I got you.'

'And what services are they – '

Silvia couldn't finish the question, as she had just arrived at the stairway and glanced down towards the ground floor.

Rats.

Around a dozen of them. All over the ground floor. Some of them appeared to be hunched over, as if skittering across the floor. Silvia squinted towards the one right beneath her, observing it crawl up towards one of the nearby tables, pick up one of the vases she had selected as decorations and –

'*Cleaning Services,*' Cosmin informed her, just as the rat began vigorously brushing the vase.

Silvia was startled, perplexed... and furious. 'How long?' she asked, eyes still scanning the shapes below.

'Twelve hours, they said. Apparently Mira contracted them as full-time housekeepers.'

'Have them finish cleaning the lobby and then put them in the parking lot reception room until 18:00. Pay them their severance (if Mira promised them something like that) and have them on their way!'

She didn't wait for Cosmin's reply as she stormed back towards her apartment.

The one she shared with Mira.

She walked right up to the door to Mira's room, unlocked it and barged inside, to the sound of a jumping cat attempting to flee.

'*Lady Silvia!*' Lorgar stopped scampering across the floor upon realizing who she was. 'Lady Silvia! This is most unexpected!'

Silvia had no time for him, as she walked purposefully towards Mira's bed.

'Wake up!' she demanded.

'Has something happened?' Mira asked, as she stifled a yawn.

'*Has something...* there are *rats* in the lobby!'

Lorgar's ears shot up and his eyes widened as he stood at attention.

Mira began rubbing her eyes. 'I'm pretty sure that's a racial slur!'

'I don't care if it's a racial slur! There are *people* in the lobby! Unscheduled and unexpected!'

Mira reached towards her watch, flung aimlessly on her nightstand the night before. 'They're nine minutes early!'

'What?'

'It's 6:06, I told them to come at 6:15 so I could meet them!' Mira said, as she got up and began looking for her pants and a shirt.

'Mira, have you gone mad? They're outsiders!'

'And they're going to clean to place. Did I get the wrong impression?'

'Mira, you can't bring outsiders unannounced!'

'I announced their arrival last night.'

'You gave them a code and told the night shift that a delivery was coming in! You didn't say ratmen were going to come and stay in the building for twelve hours!'

'I actually did.'

'What?'

'Mișu Moloz, Joey van der Merwe and Nucu Paulică were on duty last night. I told them that cleaners would be coming.' Mira began putting on shoes. '... though I did do that at two in the morning, when you were already asleep. Hence why you're probably so surprised right now.'

'Mira, be that as it may, I don't care! We can't have outsiders skittering around here during the day! We have shit to do! *Clandestine* shit! Which they might see!' Silvia's eyes widened. 'What if they steal?'

'If they can steal anything from us, they deserve to keep it and we deserve to have it stolen,' she said, just as she finished dressing and walking towards the door, Lorgar right behind. 'NO!' she commanded her pet. 'You stay here today!' Turning back to Silvia, she continued, 'They're only going to clean public areas, private quarters are off-limits and, more importantly, *on-demand* and *extra*!'

'So is that how you thought this would work? We're all going to have to keep twenty ratmen under observation at all times?'

'I think that's something doable.'

'Mira, we don't *need* housekeepers!'

'We don't. But, we do need friends!' Mira paused as she neared the staircase. 'Have you ever read *Dune*?'

What the fucking... '... I saw the movie!?'

'Do you remember a character called the Shadout Mapes?'

'Mira! What the fuck?! Stop being so fucking cryptic and childish! This is serious!'

'We can rewatch the movie later. Right now, let's just – '

'– Mira! The Atreides fucking *died*!'

'Oh, so you do remember!'

'Mira, we're Hajduks!'

'I know. I just didn't know that Hajduks had a penchant for science fiction. Just the Sopranos and Martin Sco–'

'– *What* did you *do* in the Ghazis?' Silvia started angrily, not truly concerned with her fellow Avenger Legionnaires' pastimes.

'What do you mean?'

'*To chill*, Mira! To chill!?' *Or did you never chill? Is that why you're stressing everybody out!?*

'Well, we cooked and ate together and... and we read books... played sports...? Why do you –'

'Because here in the Hajduks all we fucking do all day is drink, watch movies, do drugs, play board games and listen to fucked-up music, Mira! So, yes, I know about fucking Shadout Mapes and the fucking Crysknife or whatever the fuck!!! I've seen the Denis Villeneuve movies at least a dozen times and I've watched the David Lynch version whilst under the influence of every single drug known to man! My question fucking stands, for the name of God! *What the fuck are you doing bringing outsiders here?*'

'*Desert power!*' Mira announced dramatically, though she was stifling a small smile.

'*Woman*, this is not Arrakis! *Those* are not fremen! We have robots that clean! *We* can fucking clean! Why, in-my-dick, do we need rat people here?'

'Listen to me! We need them here so that they can have a way in. A way to reach us.'

'A way for who-*my-dick*-to reach us?'

'I don't know yet!' she replied, appearing to be perfectly at peace with the insanity of her statement.

'Mira...' Silvia pinched her forehead. *Laur is going to think you're a problem, because of this and – you know what? – I'm going to be agreeing with him!*

'Silvia, listen to me! There are billions of ratmen in Shangri. Countless billions. The data we have is from the Shangri Census Bureau and we all agree that it's likely a flawed source. The number is likely higher than what we can fathom. Now, who leads these billions of ratmen?'

'No one, Mira... they're billions of ratmen at the bottom of society, held in the position they were born into by a system that's been running smoothly for millions of years! They are not unified, because they are the lowest class – or they're the lowest class because they are not unified! I don't know...'

'I would agree with you, were it not for the fact that they are *people* and there are *many* of them. They're not brainwashed. They're not lobotomized. They are not drugged and they are not unaware of their station and, because they are *people*, they cannot be all the same! There must be at least some small number of them whom the others look to for leadership.'

'Yes, Mira, and there's probably one great horned rat who leads a council of thirteen white rats who meet under a black ruined fortress where they hide from the surface dwellers...' *you fucking problem-child...*

Mira frowned. '*Warhammer Fantasy?*' she asked surprised.

Silvia confessed, 'It was in the farsight reports... I had to read it... Plus that Nick and some of the Shqiptari play the tabletop game, *whatever*... these aren't *skaven*, Mira!'

'Then they are *not* our enemy and they *can* be our friends!'

'Mira, I know, but – '

'– But we will never know that, if we do not communicate with them and contact their leadership!'

'You said you were going to speak to the Neighbourhood Councils and to the leaders of their community that are legitimate: doctors, scientists, lawyers, journalists – '

'– I've spoken to them and they're all Uncle Toms!'

'What the fuck is an... you've spoken to *all of them*?'

'I've spoken with enough to make an impression!'

'And your impression is that the leader of a race of ratmen is likely a sanitation worker?'

Mira chuckled.

Silvia almost smiled at her own joke and at Mira's reaction, but her rage kept any facial movement in check.

'Perhaps. But, I do know that whoever those leaders may be, there should be a way for them to reach us. *Quietly. Certainly. Consistently.*'

'So you brought them here to spy on us until they trust us enough to contact us?'

'Precisely!'

This is downright demented, yet I do see here how she reached her conclusion. 'Mira... this is stupid...'

'It'll work.'

'That's a supposition and it's something that's too risky to gamble on!'

'Maybe it is, but, while we're at it, let's go say 'hello'!'

She walked right past Silvia, leaving her fuming. *It doesn't matter. Nothing I do or say will match up to what he's going to do when he hears of this...*

I'm going to have to cover up for you, Mira. I'm going to be paying your bill!

'Hello, Mrs. Cri!' Mira greeted one of the rats. *One of the female ones, apparently.* To Silvia's shock, despite the ratwoman already beginning to bow, Mira stopped her mid-curtsy and grabbed her hands. *Jesus Christ, they look like very skinny human hands with long fingerbones!*

Her nails were very well kept and clean, however.

'Miss Mira! Hello!' the ratwoman had a remarkably soft voice for a creature so...

Fuck it! I'll say it: vile! She looks like a rat and it's vile. She's also overweight! I think...

'We'll be here for a while, Mrs. Mira, my apologies! The carpets are not good. We need to pick the lint.'

Lint? What the fuck is she...

Oh, wait, there is a little lint; she's right...

'That's fine! You can take your time, the lobby opens at ten.'

'*Oh*, Miss Mira!' The ratwoman's eyes moved... in a very humanlike fashion. Silvia picked up on the emotion. It was... a kind of *horror*? She could tell that it was something exaggerated, but not in a mocking way. The ratwoman seemed shocked. 'Mrs. Mira! We do not have time until then for everything!'

Ratwoman! It's clean! I had everything we brought over from Terra cleaned before we left and I've had this entire fucking building swept at the atomic level. That lint is just what has settled since the last drone cleaning yesterday!

Mrs. Cri began gesticulating towards the great tree that dominated the lobby. 'The tree drops dirt and the insects make a mess! It makes *dust*, Miss Mira! We also have to manicure the tree –'

'That's fine, Mrs. Cri. There'll be plenty of time. You've met Silvia?' Mira asked.

'No!' the ratwoman began bowing to Silvia and, unlike Mira, she didn't interrupt the gesture.

'Greetings, Mrs. Cri!' she tried to be polite.

'Greetings, Miss Silvia! I am sorry for the mess!' she said, gesturing to two of the other rats (which, on closer inspection, also appeared to be female), who were currently sweeping underneath a table they had moved slightly out of place. 'We'll finish by ten!'

Silence. *What the fuck kind of fucking situation of shit have you dragged us into, Mira?*

'Oh, come on Silvia, they're doing a good job!'

The three women turned towards the voice.

Radu, who had been observing the exchange alongside three other Hajduks, continued speaking as he had begun: in Romanian, not English or some Shangri language. 'They wanted to polish the parking lot floor! Let's let them clean here at least!'

'*Let's?*' *Have you lost your mind too?*

Radu raised his hands. 'Under our supervision, of course!'

She glanced quickly around the lobby, spotting around twenty Hajduks spread out across the ground floor and the upper floors, including Radu and Cosmin. Though she could tell many shared her concern, most seemed to be vaguely amused, with a few of the older Romanians appearing to be... *sympathetic*, but not towards her...

Being pushed into a corner here now ain't I, you fucking shits?

'*Let's!*' this was also said in Romanian, though the speaker was not.

As Technowolf appeared from on top of the staircase, Silvia didn't even have time to react, as Mrs. Cri reacted first. She seemed to squeak slightly, just as she seemed to grow smaller. Her shoulders slouched slightly and her look became pinned firmly on the ground before her. Silvia saw the other ratwomen follow suit.

'No! No! No!' Technowolf spoke softly and in standard Shangrianese. 'No worries! I like what you've done in so little time! You have a good team here!' he said, lifting an open palm in a soothing, welcoming manner.

The rat woman nodded slightly and bent her head forward slightly more.

Technowolf, visibly uncomfortable, began walking towards Mrs. Cri. 'I am Technowolf, but my friends sometimes call me Tech! You are?'

The rat woman's response was instant, robotic, clear and well worn. 'Cri Barok Tinuvash Cri Pli Cri.'

'Ah, I see! And how do your friends call you?'

'Cri,' the ratwoman squeaked sheepishly.

'*Mrs.* Cri,' Mira elaborated.

'Very well, Mrs. Cri! Thank you for coming on such short notice! I can already see that you are doing a diligent job cleaning and, as you can see, this place needs it!' Technowolf attempted the most friendly remani smile possible, showing little-to-no teeth.

Motherfucker! Were you in on this?

'I believe we have a meeting to attend soon?' he said to Silvia and Mira, his eyes far more stern than those he had graced the ratwoman with.

Silvia glared back. 'Yes. Yes we do!'

She nodded to Radu, Cosmin and the rest and joined Technowolf and Mira as they walked up the stairs back towards their quarters.

Just as they were out of earshot, Technowolf spoke. 'We cannot alienate potential allies. If you would've kicked them out, they would've told their kin that the new Allied emissaries are all a bunch of racist cunts. That information would then spread throughout the city like wildfire!'

'Would you rather have us be completely exposed?'

'No. But this hardly counts as a real security breach.' He turned towards Mira. 'Your doing?'

'Yes,' she replied.

Oh, so you just swooped in for the rescue? You weren't in on it?

'We'll discuss this in the meeting today. For better or for worse, we're stuck with them now.'

'I'm going to bed,' Mira announced.

'It's twelve past six!' Silvia blurted out in indignation.

'And the meeting is at nine. I'll make it,' she responded, right as they entered their room. Mira walked purposefully towards her private chambers, leaving Silvia alone in the middle of their living room.

Is this what she's been doing at night? She comes in late two nights in a row and now she's coming up with bullshit cockamamie schemes involving ratwomen maids?

'I assume she called it in, else they would not have been allowed inside?' Technowolf asked her.

Silvia turned towards the remani who was leaning into the doorframe whilst still staying outside her living room.

'*God*, Tech! You can come in!' remani *and their weird politeness.*

'She is a Captain,' Technowolf continued as he entered. 'Even if she isn't a Hajduk, she's perfectly in the right.'

'She did not ask for permission and neither did she consult with anyone else!'

'No. She didn't, but, then again, I thought being proactive was a quality to admire in an officer.' Technowolf began inspecting a nearby tea jar, opening the lid and sniffing its contents.

'It is. But this is reckless.... And, dare-I-say, *stupid*!'

'Hindsight will be 20-20 on this one! Maybe months from now it'll be just some funny stupid thing we tried. Maybe it'll be one of the best decisions we'll ever make here!'

Silvia walked towards the long table near the entrance. 'Do you seriously think he's going to allow this?' she asked, turning towards the remani and leaning on the table with her behind.

'Laur?' Technowolf made a strange snorting noise. 'Laur gave Mira the job of liaising with the murine because he had no idea how to approach them! I noticed he always delegates the tasks he cannot handle to those he deems best suited. I suspect that he will be irritated by Mira's lateral thinking, but he will allow her plan to move forward nonetheless...'

'Is that so?' Silvia asked, thinking about what Pop had delegated *her* to do over the years.

'It is very much so!' Tech smirked. 'The Hajduks have been my charge since times before your legion's birth, yet I have spared the time needed to accompany other Avenger Legions in the years since Earth's death and Terra's birth. You have always been a Hajduk and I can tell that sometimes you forget that not all Generals are alike and neither are their Legions! Laur might seem controlling to you, given that you know him so well. Yet, I will have you know that he often confounds his peers with the degree of independence which he confers upon those under his command, *if* he judges them worthy of said independence, that is!' Tech paused.

'And if he judges them to be unworthy, he makes them disappear,' Silvia finished the thought.

'If he judges them unworthy, he does not even grant them the chance to be independent.' Tech stretched his neck and grunted as his vertebrae cracked. 'I don't like tension in the morning! Mornings set the tone for the whole day... I'm gonna go take a dust bath! I'll see you at the meeting!'

As Tech began to walk towards his room, he paused. 'They can't find the things we don't want them to find, can't they?'

He turned towards her as she exhaled in frustration before admitting, '*No*... not with us watching them...'

Tech stared at her, a subtle smile curling in the corner of his mouth.

He didn't have to say anything. Silvia uncrossed her arms and let them fall to her sides as she stopped leaning on her desk. 'They probably couldn't find anything if they had an entire day to sweep the place,' she confessed.

Tech raised his bushy eyebrows and tilted his head sideways.

Silvia exhaled in instigated annoyance. 'I won't harass them,' she promised.

He nodded and finally left.

She spent the next couple of hours compulsively knitting a small vest for Lorgar.

Silvia was the first in Pop's office after the General himself, as well as Basenji, who sat on a couch the General had placed up against the wall directly opposite his desk. His new pet, Spideraven, sat perched upon a makeshift roost that had once been a coat hanger. Upon seeing Silvia, the bird immediately took flight and landed on Pop's desk, right in front of her usual seat. Understanding the bird's expectation, she reached into one of her coat pockets and pulled out a small slab of salted pork, causing the creature to caw in excitement. As she extended her open palm, Spideraven gingerly picked up his morning treat and flew over to one of the room's corners.

Silvia's eyes widened slightly as she realized that Pop's new pet had built a web right under the ceiling in one of the room's corners. She also noticed three small chunks of wrapped webbing spread out across the creature's domain. *Those must be the other morning snacks I've been giving him.*

Just as she began inspecting the bird's webbing, Nick and Technowolf entered the room, followed by Ela, Radu, Cosmin, as well as a still sleepy Mira, who walked in with a cup of coffee in hand.

'Well, what's happened?' Pop's voice asked.

Silvia did not flinch, though she did take note of the clear irritation in his voice.

'Mira hired rat cleaning ladies and Silvia's a racist!' Nick announced, without missing a beat, as he made his way to his usual seat opposite Pop and next to Silvia. The three new centurions took up their respective seats to their General's left, on a couch they all shared, as Technowolf made his way behind Pop's desk where he sat down in an armchair he favoured.

Laur's eyes narrowed. 'What?' he asked Mira.

'I hired rat cleaning ladies,' she confirmed, as she collapsed onto her usual seat on the couch next to Basenji.

'... and Silvia's a racist. Yes, I heard that part! I was hoping for a bit more colour on the situation.'

'I haven't been able to reach the murine leadership, so I'm facilitating a way for their leadership to reach *us*!' Mira explained.

Pop's eyes flashed. Silvia had seen it before. It was like watching a slot machine spin. One could only hope that it would land on a favourable set of cryptic symbols.

There's rage. There's self-control. There's amazement. There's some neutral thinking. There's a revelation? Is... is that?

'Did it work?' Pop asked.

Acceptance?

'Not yet, though they did an excellent job of cleaning the lobby,' Mira pointed out.

'Did they find the guns?' Laur asked casually.

'I don't think so,' Mira replied, suggesting that she didn't really care if they did. Though she did look towards Cosmin and Radu.

'No,' Radu replied. 'They're actually quite discrete and respectful. They just cleaned. They didn't even open cupboards or drawers or anything.'

'Where are they now?' Pop asked.

'Still in the lobby. They're spraying the tree with some kind of polish. It's making the leaves shiny and... and *vibrant*,' Radu noted, surprise evident on his eyes.

'Is that good for the tree?'

'I... suppose so... *I'll check*!'

'Good! Please do! Does it look good?' their General asked.

'Yeah, to be honest.' Radu admitted.

'Good...' Laur scowled to himself. 'They are forbidden from entering personal quarters, as well as the basement levels!' He turned towards Silvia. 'My quarters are off-limits. That includes this room.' Pop stopped and Silvia could see him gathering his thoughts. 'How'd you find them?' the General asked, raising his eyes towards Mira.

'I found an add on their internet.'

Silvia breathed in, readying herself for an outburst, as Pop's eyes glazed over and he began blinking in utter perplexion. He quickly put his hand to his eyes and began rubbing them.

'Sponsored add? *Personalized*?' he asked. Silvia could tell that he didn't really care what type of commercial Mira had come across.

'Forum post,' she explained. 'They're cheaper than drone systems. They're also slower.' Mira breathed in. 'There's also a prejudice against them on account of the fact that... well... they're rat people! But, apparently, they're germaphobes, which confers upon them a certain compulsion to clean! There's a forum where people give them reviews. Mrs. Cri's Cleaning Company is the highest rated agency certified to work in Convent Garden!'

'Not entirely surprising,' Technowolf chipped in.

What? They're rat people for fuck's sake. You mean to tell me that they're cleaner than a robot?

'Yeah, I suspected as such...' Pop finished rubbing his eyes. 'They live in cramped, overpopulated urban centres. It's quite common for creatures living in such environments to become obsessed with cleanliness and grooming and that sort of thing...'

'So, you're not paying for their expertise, you're paying for their pathology?' Nick surmised.

'Essentially, yes,' Tech confirmed.

'Well... at least we come out cheaper...' Pop concluded 'No need to run maintenance on drones –'

'Their rates are half the costs associated with drones,' Mira interrupted.

Pop did not like to be interrupted. 'Yes, that's very nice–'

'– I offered them twice their usual rates and requested their exclusivity. I also negotiated an extra 50% bonus scheme to incentivise speed and efficiency.' Mira announced.

Jesus Christ, Mira... fuck it to the devil... he does not like waste!

'Well... you have from where...' Pop mused, referencing Mira's vast inherited wealth.

'Oh, I'm not paying for it!'

Shit.

Now Pop finally seemed to grow annoyed. 'Mira, you may be a Captain, but you are not a Hajduk! Accessing Legion funds as a non-member –'

'– I didn't use Legion funds!'

'You didn't?' Laur's brow furrowed, the lines of his forehead growing dark and tense.

'No! I used the ADC-SPV.'

Pop's face turned to stone, though Silvia could tell that his mind was racing.

Nick must've seen it too. 'You used *what*?' he asked.

Either that or he didn't read the Internal Memo explaining what the ADC-SPV was.

'The *Allied Diplomatic Corps Special Purpose Vehicle*! The one set up for running the Embassy!' Mira replied, somewhat surprised by Nick's ignorance.

The room was silent for a few moments, the tension only broken by Pop's new avian pet, which dropped the piece of salted pork Silvia had gifted it and jumped to the floor, attempting to pick it up. Its beak made a clicking sound as it struggled to pick up the greasy slab of meat.

Then Technowolf, Nick, Radu, Cosmin and Ela burst into laughter. Basenji struggled to stifle a chuckle. Even Pop himself seemed to stifle a smile.

Silvia made no such attempt. *This woman is crazy, mourning be damned!*

'You used Allied taxpayer's money to hire cleaning ladies?' Pop smiled.

'What else was I supposed to use?'

'Jesus Christ, Mira...' Pop began rubbing his eyes again. 'Look...' the General exhaled loudly. 'This isn't ok but, I'll allow it! Quite frankly, I think it's a good idea. *But*!' Pop rushed to finish his point, interrupting all the eyebrows being raised around his office. 'But! Despite the fact that I really like personal initiative and spontaneous improvisation –

You don't... you just like to reap the benefits of our autonomy...

'– the way you went about it is not okay! I take it you did not consult with anyone?' he asked, addressing the question to Mira, but turning to face Silvia.

Silvia remained silent.

'Nick?'

'No,' Nick replied.

'Radu? Cosmin? Ela?'

The three new Centurions shook their heads.

'Tech? Basenji?'

'She did not,' Technowolf replied.

Silvia spotted it just as Pop looked towards Basenji. The remani was silent, but he somehow managed to be... loud, in his silence. No shaking of the head. No shaking of any finger. No hand movement of any kind. He just stared at Pop.

She told you, Basenji?

As if to respond to Silvia's question, the tip of Basenji's tail rose slightly from where it lay resting on the couch and shook slightly in a manner that (she had learned) was confirmatory.

Pop smirked his annoyed smirk. 'Did you grant her permission?'

The tail stood still for a moment and then wagged twice.

'He did not forbid it,' Mira explained.

Pop smiled sarcastically. 'Very clever, Mira!' As a member of the Legendary League, Basenji technically held the rank of Colonel and, thus, outranked everyone in the room except Technowolf, who held the same rank, and Pop himself, who was a General. Informing Basenji of her decision to employ murine cleaners in order to encourage a potential line of communication for underground elements of their race meant that Mira had, in fact, been diligent in her planning.

Silvia fought back a smile. Despite finding the whole plan to be rather kooky, she couldn't help but find Mira's course of action being remarkably... *clever*.

That's why she didn't give a shit about my opinion: she knew Basenji's consent meant my own orders were ultimately null.

Pop leaned back in his seat. 'Mira, what's on today's agenda?' he asked, looking up at the ceiling.

'I would assume that the topics cover things like Big White, the mixed martial arts tournam–'

Pop interrupted. 'Why are we friends with Big White?'

'Well, we *want* to be friends with him because he runs the Shangri underworld and we want to have the Shangri underworld on our side because –'

'What will the Shangri underworld help us with?'

Mira blinked, appearing to lose Pop's exact meaning. 'The *Stolen*? Hearts and minds? The –'

'How exactly are we going to go about doing that?'

'Well, insofar, we've kidnapped, interrogated and murdered a Shangri customs official, we've smuggled weapons, drugs and other contraband into the City, we've bribed offiicials informaly with said contraband. We have weapons of mass destruction spread out over five locations... I assume I don't have to go on?'

'A fair assumption and a fair assessment! I'm glad you're up to speed on everything! Does any of that seem safe?' Pop asked.

'No.'

'You've noticed that we Hajduks have a way of doing things that is quite... atypical?'

'If you're referring to the fact that you're more of a cloak-and-dagger type of outfit, as opposed to the Ghazi's sword-and-shield, I can guarantee that I am constantly reminded of the difference...'

'Well, you see, that's not a good thing! Ideally, when running a cloak-and-dagger operation, it's best if people can't label it as such! But, that's beside the point... Mira, we here do all sorts of batshit and despicable shit! I'm sure you've heard?'

'I have and I've also seen.'

'Good! Now, we're no strangers here to creative thinking. To be honest, plans like yours fit right into our playbook. But, what has allowed us to be so prolific at what we do here is *trust*. Without that trust, it all goes to shit pretty quick! So, here's the deal:'

'You either trust *us* enough to communicate when you're about to try your hand at doing some cloak-and-dagger type shit, or we don't trust *you* to leave the embassy!'

Mira didn't flinch and all humour fled Laur Pop's chambers.

'You report to Silvia directly from now on! *Basenji*, Tech, Nick and everyone else, including myself, will be completely out-of-the-loop. I'm fine with any initiative and plan you come up with, as long as you inform Silvia of it before taking steps towards its enactment. If Silvia tells us that you've been going rogue, you'll be forbidden from leaving the embassy's premises. Am I being clear?'

'Very.'

'I'm glad! Silvia?'

'Yes?'

'She's not a child!' Laur castigated her.

Out of nowhere.

As he does, from time to time.

Though the message is particularly peculiar this time.

Laur explained himself, pointing towards Mira. '*She* has a way of seeing things that is quite different from ours! I would actually encourage you to learn from her, but do not confuse whatever it is that she's up to with insanity or stupidity! Be understanding, but do not tolerate outright insubordination! I know you like her! We *all* like her! However, our mission here is too complex for us to have to factor in any additional wildcards!'

Pop began tapping his fingertips on his desk. 'We're spread out thin and our tasks are many,' he said to all of them. 'We're all going to have to learn to work independently. Everyone's plate is going to be full. We cannot communicate freely with Gigi, Bojana, Josip and Lejla. They have their objectives and we have hours. We're wearing a lot of hats here and there's a lot to juggle. We're *all* going to have to show autonomy here! What Mira did today was brash and, dare-I-say, *insolent*. *However*, those types of decisions are going to have to become commonplace due to the nature of our mission. We're going to be doing a lot of outside-the-box thinking and, sometimes, what's outside the box looks insane. Everything will be on the table. However...' he turned to look at Silvia, then he glared towards Mira '... when given the opportunity, the *right* hand must know what the *left* is doing! Am I being clear?'

After Silvia nodded swiftly and Mira slowly, Pop turned his gaze to each person in the room and, one-by-one, they all nodded.

'Excellent!' He leaned forward onto his desk. 'Big White's tournament is tomorrow night. It's in an arena. There will be close to a hundred thousand attendants. That means there's going to be bookkeeping. That means there's going to be drugdealing. That means there's going to be prostitution. All of it will be facilitated by Big White's organization!'

'I want us to catalogue everything! I want surveillance in place and I want wiretaps in the entire arena so that we collect as much information as possible on the Libra Syndicate. Any ideas on how we're going to do that?'

They spent the next hour brainstorming ways of performing mass surveillance. When they were finished, they all left Pop's office, as they always did, without even needing their General to inform them that he wanted to spend the rest of the day scheming by himself.

'You wanna catch brunch?' Mira asked, as they heard Tech close the General's door behind them.

Silvia was taken aback. *What exactly would this brunch be about, Mira?*

'You know... a meal between breakfast and lunch. A *br-unch*!' Mira explained.

'I know what *brunch* is, Mira...'

Nick's voice rang out from behind him. 'So do I! Let's go!' For such a big man, he was remarkably stealthy. Silvia realized that he had likely been trailing them since the meeting's conclusion. 'There's an ice cream place around the corner! I had a scone there yesterday,' he explained.

'*Gorvada?*' Mira asked.

'Yeah! You've been?'

'Yes.' And the look on her face suggested that she hadn't been impressed. 'There's an actual brunch place off Wiltshire down on Sanctaphrax. I think it's called *Sanctaphrax 88*. I was thinking maybe about going there.'

'The one with the pancakes?' Nick asked.

'Yes, the one with the *American* pancakes.'

Silvia looked at her in confusion. *This is Shangri, Mira. There aren't any Americans here.*

Mira spotted the look. 'They're thick pancakes. Not thin, like French crepes. They're not... *clatite?*' she struggled for the word.

'It's pronounced clătite, but sure. You've been? Any good?' Nick asked.

'No, I haven't been.'

'Then why not get some ice cream from Gordava?' Nick insisted.

You're pretty opposed to gambling, for a person who plays dice games at least an hour every day, Nick...

'Because I *know* that the ice cream there tastes like soap! I *don't know* if the pancakes at Sanctaphrax 88 taste like soap.'

'Fair point, I guess...' he mumbled. Silvia didn't have to turn to know that Nick's brow was furrowing behind her. 'Mira, what kinda soap do you use?' her fellow Centurion asked.

An excellent one. She put a dispenser in the living room bathroom. Smells like hibiscus and maracuja. Your hands feel like clean cotton sheets after you use it.

'Well, soap that tastes like the ice cream at Gordava, I guess!?' Mira pulled out her phone. 'I'll ask Basenji and Tech if they want to come too.'

Tech was busy with Pop, yet Basenji was happy to join.

Sanctaphrax 88 was a roadside terrace, as was the style typical of the Convent Garden neighbourhood. Silvia noted how the venue was almost at full capacity, with only a few disparate tables being free. The occupants were primarily humans, though she did spot an ursai couple, a group of remani women, as well as a few elves and goblins. The three Terrans and their remani companion choose a corner table off to the side of the boulevard and used their phones to browse the menu.

'Mira, what's *kals*?' Nick immediately asked.

'Salted goat cheese,' she replied.

'Ah... salted goat cheese and honey?' Nick raised his eyebrows. 'Didn't know they had goats in Shangri...'

'It's not an actual goat,' Silvia replied, as she slowly scrolled through the menu.

'Huh? Then why'd you say it's *goat* cheese?'

'The animal is kinda like a goat, but it's actually not a goat.'

'Oh... what is it?'

'Some kind of pygmy donkey with horns like a ram. The cheese itself kinda tastes like goat's cheese.'

'Ah... I see.' Nick went back to studying the menu. 'Are the honey bees *actual* bees?'

'Yes,' Mira answered. 'But, if you look at the honey in that dish, it's chamomile honey!'

'I see... why is that relevant?'

'It's relevant because the food combinations *these people* have make no goddamn sense!' she said, seemingly referring to the entire Shangri population.

Silvia actually agreed. 'I'm assuming red oak syrup is maple syrup?' she asked.

'Yup, and they pair it with chicken bratwurst and cultured yoghurt,' Mira scowled in disgust as she read the ingredients.

'Smoked boneless rabbit ribs with shrimp syrup reduction and fried sorghum crumbs?' Nick read out, as he raised an eyebrow. He looked towards Mira for feedback.

'That one looks interesting, but it's a bit on the heavier side for a morning meal.' she assessed.

'Hmmm... good thing it's not morning then!' Nick declared, as he flicked an icon on his screen and then placed his phone in his inside jacket pocket. He leaned back and turned towards Silvia, 'What you gettin'?'

'I can't say I'm a fan of any of the mixes, but I do like goat's cheese and I do like plain honey. I'll ask that they use plain honey instead of chamomile.'

Mira looked up from her phone. 'Yeah, something like that.'

'You like goat's cheese too?' Nick asked and Silvia smiled.

I wonder if she knows.

'I do, but I was thinking about getting the regular pancakes with peanut butter chicken, just that with creamed spinach, instead of tomato sauce.' Mira seemed to pick up on the question's background. 'What do you mean, do I like goat's cheese *too*?'

'Eh... nothing.' Nick kept silent for less than a second. 'Your father liked goat's cheese! In Andromeda, when he found out about how they had goat's cheese, he went nuts for it! He had a whole refrigerator packed with the stuff on the *Nasredim*.' He pointed towards Silvia with his thumb. 'That's why *this one* likes goat's cheese. She never had any until your father found out.'

Silvia became worried as she saw a pinch of sadness cross Mira's eyes. *Nick, stop, don't hurt her, you clumsy oaf! I know you mean well, but there's no need to ruin brunch...*

'He did?' Mira asked.

'Yeah, he gave her like four kilograms. Made us wait in the loading bay until he had one of his boys... *Azhek Ahriman!*'

'*Afzal al Rahmani*,' Mira corrected him.

'Exactly! He had him bring over like a whole box!'

Mira smiled. 'Was it any good?' she asked Silvia.

Before Silvia could answer, Nick jumped in. 'Oh, it was great! We had it with the rye bread, remember?' he explained, tapping Silvia on the shoulder with the back of his hand

'*He* had most of it... But it was great!' Silvia detailed.

Mira was silent for a moment and Silvia felt Nick begin to question his choice of topic.

'Well, I'll go for the peanut butter chicken!' Mira announced, dissipating the moment. She turned towards Basenji, seated next to her, who pointed with his thumb towards something on his phone. 'Blueberry jam?' she asked.

Basenji nodded and Silvia saw the tip of his tail rise up over the table and quickly wag before descending.

'With smoked soy sauce?' Mira asked sceptically.

Basenji shook his head, as he began typing instructions.

'Well, pancakes *are* a dessert dish, after all...' Mira said, making her selection and putting her phone in her jacket's outside pocket.

'Maybe don't do that,' Nick said, as Basenji and Silvia finished writing their instructions to the kitchen staff.

'Do what?' Mira asked.

'Outside pockets are a bit exposed! Inside's best!' Nick instructed, as Basenji put his phone down on the table. '*That's* even worse! Anyone can take it from there!'

Basenji picked up his phone and put it inside one of his inner coat pockets.

Mira did no such thing. 'You do know that the petty theft rate in this part of Shangri is virtually non-existent?' she asked.

'I do. But I also know that not all crime is reported or even noticed! I also know that *virtually* does not mean *completely*! I also know that there's a first time for everything and I also know that not everyone *has* something worth stealing!'

Mira smiled and seemed to relent...

Rather quickly... that's atypical.

'You know Nick,' the young Captain began. 'Sometimes I forget that you're a Hajduk,' she said, moving her phone from one pocket to another.

'Is it my roguish good looks?' Nick asked.

Silvia snorted. *You're a handsome man, Nick, but you dress like a teenager. It makes you look like someone put a child in the body of an adult.*

Mira also chuckled. 'No, those seem to be the norm!'

What now? Silvia caught Mira's eyes swiftly dart towards her before quickly pivoting back to Nick.

'You are all so high strung all the time!' Mira explained. 'Except you, that is!'

Nick leaned back in his seat and crossed his arms. 'What do you mean 'high strung'?'

'You're all on edge all the time. Even in moments when there's no real reason for you to be!'

Oh, no, you won't! 'Well, we weren't worried that unexpected visitors might drop by one morning to swipe the floors, until you put us in front of the fulfilled fact!' Silvia explained.

'I meant before that,' Mira quipped back.

Silvia glared.

'She's right, you know!' Nick remarked.

Silvia looked around. 'Of course she's right! And now she should be able to see why everyone's so worried all the time,' *There's a lot of people here. There always are a lot of people here in this City.* Anyone could overhear their conversation. She would have to be discrete and speak in riddles. *We could've had this conversation back at the embassy in privacy.*

'You do know we can't control the universe?' Mira said.

Our previous assignment is over, Mira. There's no need to philosophise anymore –

... wait...

You're thinking about the boy, aren't you?

Mira continued, 'Sooner or later, things always slip out of control...'

She would have continued, but Nick started giggling.

Both women turned towards him. Silvia noted how a slight smile also crept into the corner of Basenji's snout.

'What's so funny?' Silvia asked.

'She's talking like Ashaver!'

Jesus, Nick! Not here in public! That's literally the type of intelligence a spy would die to hear...

Mira's brow furrowed as she seemed to squirm slightly in her seat.

Nick raised a reassuring hand towards her. 'No! Mira! No! I love it!' he turned towards Silvia. 'This is why I was so excited to have her in the meetings!' Turning back towards their Arabian friend, he continued. 'You ever seen them talk?'

Mira pursed her lips. 'I have...'

'I love it! It's like seeing Mr. Rogers speak with Batman!' Nick detailed.

Mira smiled and Basenji's eyes widened. Even Silvia managed a slight smile. *Sometimes it's like seeing Captain America speak with the Tony Soprano, but sure, it is kinda like that too...*

Nick managed to break through his (clearly hilarious) intrusive thoughts to manage:

'*If we believe there's even a one percent chance that someone is our enemy we have to take it as an absolute certainty... and prepare!*' he said, imitating Batman's voice and Laur Pop's typical look of superiority. '*It can sometimes be easier to forgive our enemies than our friends!*' he continued, now using a mild-mannered tone and an expression of mock surprise at the wisdom of his own words.

Laughter finally broke in sincere certainty at their table.

'*It can be hardest of all to forgive people we love!*' Nick continued, meeting Mira's chuckles and Silvia's snorts.

'You're saying I sound like that?' Mira asked, once she managed to catch her breath.

'You sound like that just enough to make every interaction you have with *him* be *amazing* to follow! Like, this morning: we walk in, Pop realizes something's up (probably because *this one* looked like she'd seen cows shitting in the lobby), we're all freaking out because we know that he might lose his shit and call us morons and fucking idiots by the end of it (I was already thinking he was going to have you wear an ankle bracelet!!!)... and then you start going on about budgeting and checking accounts... you know... like it's just Tuesday and you're dealing with some menial shit!'

Mira's eyes became distant as she seemed to be contemplating something. 'You do know that he's different, from any other General, I mean?'

'Oh, we've noticed!' Nick also noticed the food arriving. He leaned back to allow the human waiter bearing their orders to place their meals before them. 'Are you referring to anything in particular?' he asked, picking up one of the fork-like utensil that had been waiting for them on the table.

Mira waited for the human to leave (which was something Silvia liked seeing) and then continued, as she began cutting a piece of her pancakes. 'It's not just that he's different. You Hajduks are different too!' she said, before pausing to try out the peanut butter chicken. Her expression had initially been one of reserved curiosity. After a few chews, it became one of contempt. 'Most Legions treat their Generals like a king – I mean, well, the Ghazis are different! Khalid insists that he's simply the first amongst equals, but that's not the case *here*!' She began gesticulating with her fork, as if using it to communicate was a better use for it than wasting its abilities on the disappointing food before her.

'You know you're all famous for your loyalty to him, though I have noticed (in my short time spent on this little detachment) that you seem to balance your devotion with a heavy dose of... *disrespect*?' Mira blurted the words out. 'I mean, don't get me wrong, I see where both those things come from, yet I find it surprising how you're all so open about it! I'm even more surprised by how he tolerates it! Again, don't get me wrong, I know all Generals are more lenient towards their legionnaires than to the Regular Army, but... the fact that you guys have so many nicknames for him...' Mira's words trailed off, just as she lifted her eyes from her plate towards her fellow brunch party attendants.

It took Silvia a second to understand why, though the way she figured it out was unsurprising to her: she looked at Mira's almost untouched plate of stacked pancakes and then she glanced at her own plate, as well as Nick's, which were basically clean. Finally, she looked towards Basenji, who had only eaten one of five pancakes stacked before him.

Silvia and Nick were Yin: orphaned Terrans whose parents had died during the End Times. Their early childhood had been spent during the harsh famines of the Fimbulwinter and Ragnarök. Their meals had grown more consistent during the early days of the Crimson Trek among the Stars, when the orcs of the Vigilant had shared in their bountiful food stocks with the starving humans and trolls, while their elders brought savage vengeance upon the worlds of the Svart. Yet, it had only been during the later stages of the War of Vengeance that they had known true abundance.

When the genetic templates had been incorporated into their genome, the first outcome experienced had been a ravenous hunger for sustenance, which had lead to near continuous gorging on food which still marked the eating habits of most Terran Yin. Only the sunrisers, those born after the War of Vengeance, who had benefited from both times of plenty and the implementation of the Hyperborean genetic template in their late adolescence, such as Mira herself, were spared the development of the instinct to quickly consume any sustenance available, no matter the speed, quantity or even the food's quality.

'Well,' Mira began. 'I guess that's another thing that's different from the Ghazis...'

There are barely any Yin in the Ghazis. The Yin are all in the Jund, most of the sunrisers are in the Ill Ghazis. They're almost all oldtimers and Djibril al-Sayid never let his men go hungry.

Nick stifled a gag, as he almost choked whilst stifling a laugh.

At least I chew my food a little.

He managed to speak. 'It's not that bad! Yes, *El Patron* is a little overbearing and, yes, they don't call us the *Grumpy Legion* for no reason. But, as opposed to some of the other emo edgelords out there (like the Jaegers, the Sayaret or the fucking Seals), we don't like to pretend that our seriousness means we're special. We're a fun lot when Pop isn't being a dick and, yeah, when we go to work its pretty fucked up but, hey, we're Terrans and we have reputation to maintain! About the shit-talking: the general rule around here is that you can eat as much shit as you want as long your breath doesn't stink!'

Nick waved a hand, dismissing some notion that he had been addressing in his own head. 'I wouldn't worry about it. Mira, we love you! Fuck these fucking Romanians and their bullshit! They're good people under the surface! You'll find that they grow on you and, if you ever get tired of their shit, we can ask for a detachment to the Shqiptari. They're equally grumpy, but more bohemian. Plus, I reckon their taste in gastronomy might be more to your liking! But, that's besides the point. Even here, you'll fit right in! After all, Pop only recruits orphans into the Hajduks or, as he would say it, 'the motherless and the fatherless'! As the most famous Terran orphan, it's only natural that *you* spend a semester or two on detachment with us!'

Jesus Christ, Nick... Silvia instantly looked towards Mira and saw her smiling. *Thank the Lord...*

'You're a Terran Avenger Legion, Nick. That's not saying much!'

'It says enough,' Nick smirked.

Silvia felt the movement just as Mira tensed up, Basenji's hand dropped near his hip and Nick's arms flexed slightly, noticing the Arabian attaché's change in mood. *Someone's approaching us. Right behind Nick. Doesn't appear to be armed.*

'Good morning!' said the human that appeared between Nick and Mira's seats. He was quite tall for a Shangrese, though Silvia suspected that a lot of his height was made up of his upright posture.

He had dark flowing hair, parted neatly down the middle, with straight waves of thick strands coming up close to his shoulders. *Giurgiu hair, as Laur calls it.* His eyes were green, though his sclera was not clean, instead showing a slight yellow tinge, with small bloodshots emanating from the edges of his sight. His clothes were plain, almost priestly, bar only a purple vest he wore upon the backdrop of grey robes, which flowed out towards very loose goose-stepping pants that tightened around his calves and tucked into plain brown sneakers. He wasn't armed, at least not openly. Silvia's eyes darted back towards his face, just to confirm the clenching dread in her chest. *Yes... yes... shit-*

'I see you're enjoying a lovely meal on a lovely day!' Jenner noted, his voice outwardly friendly.

The four stared at him with a various mix of expressions. Nick and Silvia maintained blank expressions, though she did wonder if Nick recognized him from the reports. Basenji leaned back and studied him. Mira's expression was also blank, though she did allow one raised eyebrow, hinting at her being intrigued by his appearance.

'Wary of strangers I see! Like good little children!' he continued.

'We know who you are,' Nick broke the silence.

Thank fuck for that!

'The recognition is mutual, Mr. Lăutaru!' Jenner's eyes shifted to Silvia, 'Mrs. Murărescu! Am I pronouncing that right?'

Silvia did not respond. She let the silence sit. Intentionally. *Part of whatever he's doing involves us feeling uncomfortable. The feeling (and the intention) can be mutual...*

'I see! I've heard that some Terran women are not allowed to speak to foreign men! I was not aware that Romanians were one such people! Very well, I will respect your customs!'

'We can speak to whomever we wish,' Mira announced, her face not blank anymore, yet only subtly hostile. Silvia saw her grip her fork in a slightly more menacing grip.

'Ah! The fabled Mira al-Sayid, daughter of the famed Djibril al-Sayid and the illustrious Sarasvati Singh! I hope you find our city as charming as you did when you were last here!'

This time Mira gave him the silent treatment.

Silvia took the opportunity to check their surroundings. *Is this idiot here alone?*

No. Can't be. There must be witnesses nearby. Witnesses he would've brought along for his own safety...

Jenner's eyes remained fixed on Mira's, before subtly moving towards Basenji's subdued expression of silent alertness.

'He never speaks, so don't even bother,' Nick informed him.

'I wasn't going to,' Jenner replied. 'So, given that you are by far the most talkative, Mr. Lăutaru –'

'– my friends call me Nick,' Nick interrupted him.

'Ah, very well, Nick. Given that–'

'– I said my *friends* call me Nick!' he interrupted.

'Well, are we not friends?'

'I don't know, you tell me!'

'I do not understand where this hostility is coming from! I saw four distinguished guests from the Republican Alliance and I took the chance to come over and inquire as to your wellbeing! I wish nothing more than to improve relations.'

'*Saw?*' Nick asked.

'Yes, saw. I saw –'

'You were just walking by and happened to see us?'

'Well, *yes*!' Jenner seemed confused.

'You come here often?' Nick followed through.

'As often as is needed.'

'Ah! And what brings you around this neck of the woods on this lovely day?' The Centurion leaned forward, one elbow on the table before him.

'Mr. Lăutaru,' Jenner began. Nick nodded and the Shangrian continued, 'Shangri is a free city; its citizens can come and go wherever they please, whenever they please.'

'That's very nice.' Nick leaned back and scratched his beard. 'So you were just walking by on personal business (maybe some meeting or another) and you just happened to bump into us?'

Jenner nodded graciously.

Liar.

'Then you thought you'd just come over and say 'hello'?'

'But, of course!'

'Huh! I see...' Nick turned to his companions. 'He was just walking by and saw us and thought he'ed say hello,' he said, before turning back to their unwelcome tableside attendant. 'Right?'

'But, yes, of course!'

Nick leaned forward. 'Well, then grab a seat! Sit down! Tell us how the weather's like!'

NICK! What the shit are you doing, in my dick?

Jenner was as taken aback as Silvia, though his surprise was also expressed verbally. 'Oh, I wouldn't mean to intrude!'

'No worry! You already have! Might as well tell us a tale! Grab a chair!' Nick's tone was a mix of menacing and friendly.

'Very well...' Jenner hesitantly relented.

'Over there! Grab a chair!' Nick whistled towards the three human occupants of a four person table, causing them to turn. 'Pardon! Is that seat taken?'

The humans seemed startled.

Nick took that as a 'no'. 'See! Take that one!' he urged. 'Thank you!' he said, not waiting for the three to confirm the vacancy. 'Cheers!'

Jenner slowly turned towards his fellow Shangrian humans. 'May I?'

They nodded, seemingly realizing who Jenner was.

'Mr. Jenner, right?' Nick asked, just as he pulled up the chair and sat down.

'You said you knew who I was,' Jenner smiled at his own clever observation.

'Watch it, buddy!' Nick threatened, though he complemented the harshness of his words with a playful smile. 'My face may be pretty, but my dick is ugly!'

Oh, boy...

'There's no need for such language, Mr. Lăutaru!' Jenner responded after a moment of silence.

'Yeah, you're right! That one was for free.' Nick agreed, now the epitome of innocence. He didn't apologise though. 'So, tell us a story!'

'I beg your pardon?' Jenner seemed perplexed and irritated now.

'Tell us a story! You're a journalist, I hear. What have you been journaling about? You working on a story?'

'Several, actually!'

'Ah, sitting with your arse on two boats! We'll take one!' *Nick, that expression doesn't translate well.*

'Well, they're quite confidential. I don't discuss what I'm working on whilst I'm still in the investigative process,' Jenner explained.

'I see!'

'If you wish, you could read some of my editorials, to get a taste of my viewpoints... and my journalistic focus.'

Oh, we have.

'I don't read much.'

True.

'Well, then tell us a lie!' Nick urged.

'Sorry?'

'A lie! A non-truth. A fable. A fabrication or a fabulation. Bullshit? A shit!' Today was, apparently, the day Nick had decided to show-off his vast and sophisticated thesaurus.

'Mr. Lăutaru, I know you don't have journalists where you come from.'

'We don't! You know a lot about where we from!' Nick noted.

'Thank you! If I may explain the tenets of freedom of speech –'

'That won't be necessary,' Nick cut him off. 'Unless if that explanation is the lie I requested earlier.'

'It is not. It's the truth!' Jenner didn't understand anything now.

'Ah, well, don't bother. We have freedom of speech on Terra.'

'How can you have free speech, if you do not have journalists?' Jenner asked, clearly preparing some diatribe about the merits of a free press.

'Well, like I said, we have free speech,' Nick said... and that seemed to be his whole point.

'But, no journalists?' Jenner asked.

'Yes.'

'Do you not find those two things to be contradictory.'

'No,' Nick quipped.

'If I may ask how you arrived upon such a conclusion?'

'It's not my conclusion, so your question doesn't have an answer.'

'So it's simply something you were told.'

'No, rather it's something I observed.'

'Ah, and what exactly have you observed?'

'If you really have free speech and an educated population made up of intelligent individuals, you don't need journalists.'

Jenner let loose an arrogant laugh of certain superiority. 'How exactly does that work, Mr. Lăutaru?'

'You only need journalists when people don't have the freedom to openly say what they're thinking or when they don't have the mental faculty or the knowledge needed to express their own thoughts; at least not without being ridiculed by their peers or punished by their superiors! A 'voice for the voiceless', as it were! Seems to me that journalists depend on the absence of freedom of speech to make a living!'

'Very poignant, Mr. Lăutaru. I'll be certain to make a point of that in my next article!'

'Glad to help! So, no stories from you? Real or otherwise?' Nick began rummaging around in his jacket.

'I feel as if none of my stories would pique your interest.'

'You seem trustworthy, so I'll go with your intuition on that.' He fished out a toothpick from inside his pockets.

'Perhaps you might tell *me* a story!' Jenner urged.

'Well, those pancakes are giving me heartburn!' Nick observed, pointing towards his empty plate, as he began to pick his teeth.

'I thought Terran genetic meddling made one immune to such mortal inconveniences.'

Uh-oh, he's getting political.

Nick turned to their brunch guest. 'Yeah. It does. Might just be you then!'

'You're a very pugnacious individual, Mr. Lăutaru! Dare-I-say, you're not very sociable.'

'Oh, I'm very sociable, in the right company.' Nick absent-mindedly picked at some potentially imaginary leftover between his canine and a molar. 'But ambiguity kills ne,' he remarked, pulling out the toothpick, to reveal that, indeed, he did have a bit of lamb caught between his teeth. 'Why are you here? You can't tell us a truth; you can't tell us a lie. We don't have any stories for you,' he turned to his brunch companions, questioning them, 'Do we?'

Basenji shook his head. Mira and Silvia both raised their shoulders and responded with subtle looks of disgust and dismissal.

Nick continued. 'So, if we have nothing to share, what are we gonna do?'

Jenner stared at Nick for a moment, his lips slowly moving in between bouts of irritation. His eyes never left the Kalo Centurion's, though one could tell that his mind was elsewhere. 'Why are you here?' he almost hissed the words.

'We heard the pancakes slapped!' Nick replied instantly. 'Turns out they're mid, at best!' he said, continuing to gesticulate towards their plates with his toothpick.

'I'm sorry to hear, but that's not what I was referring to.' Jenner leaned forward and Silvia knew he was crossing into Nick's discomfort zone. 'Why are *you* Hajduks doing here in Shangri?'

'Diplomatic things,' the Hajduk replied.

'Diplomatic *things*,' Jenner repeated as he nodded the words. 'Diplomatic things that required the talents of Laur Pop?'

'You know, I've asked myself that very same question.'

Careful Nick! I think I know where you're going with this, but careful!

'Up until meeting you just now, I didn't really have an answer,' her fellow Centurion explained.

Good... sort of good, at least.

'Is that a threat?'

Yes, you idiot, it's a threat!

'Do you feel threatened?' Nick asked curiously.

'No. We –'

Jenner would have continued, but Nick cut him off. 'Then I suppose it's not. You shouldn't make so many presumptions!'

His counterparty faked a courteous smile, 'But, of course! So, why *you*? Why the Hajduks? Why Laur Pop?'

'I see where this is going.'

You do and now you're going to derail the conversation... Good!

'You're religious, aren't you? You believe in God and destiny and that sort of thing?'

Jenner smiled, this time almost genuinely. 'I believe that things happen for a reason.'

'Like I said, you're a man of faith and fate! If you walk by a tree and an apple falls into your hand, do you ask the tree as to its reasoning for dropping the apple at the exact moment your hand was beneath it?'

'I don't understand the question.'

'Ah, well, now you *are* telling me a lie! Don't worry, I'll answer for you:'

'*You wouldn't*. You'd consider yourself fortunate. You'd think that the reason why the apple dropped was simply because of fortuitous chance! It was meant to happen! You *deserved* an apple! You've walked by a thousand apple tree a thousand times before. It was bound to happen one time!'

'Are you saying Laur Pop is a poisoned apple?'

'I am saying that you like oranges and you think the forest should respect your tastes!' Nick replied. 'Why do you think there's a reason? Why do you think it matters who comes or goes anywhere for whatever reason?' he continued.

'It matters because their reasons might infringe upon the lives of others.'

'They might. They might not. Again, you wouldn't be here if you approved. Why do you disapprove?'

'I neither approve, nor do I disapprove. I am simply trying to understand.'

'We already established that you wouldn't be here if you approved.'

'Did we?'

'We did. That's what the metaphor about the apple was about.'

'Why would I disapprove?'

'I don't know. I don't like making presumptions and you don't like telling truths or lies. So I guess we're at an impasse, unless if you'd be willing to break your principles.'

Jenner smirked. 'Then, I agree with you!'

'Good,' Nick turned to Silvia. 'See?! *Common ground*. Diplomatic things!'

'You haven't told me that Laur Pop came here for no reason whatsoever,' Jenner continued his prodding.

'I didn't, though I did imply that *you* might be the reason!'

'Am I?'

'Possibly.'

'And what is it about me that requires the explicit presence of Laur Pop?'

'I dunno; you'd have to ask him.'

'Are you offering to set up a meeting with him?'

'No,' Nick replied curtly, still picking his teeth and cheeking his toothpick for some uncovered treasure hidden next to his gums.

'Oh? Why not?'

'He likes being told the truth, but he loves it when people lie to him. Since you can't do either, he wouldn't really be that interested.'

'Is that why you're here? Only because you have an interest?'

'In having a conversation, yes.'

'And do I not strike you as someone who can facilitate one such conversation?'

'No.'

'I'm sorry to hear that.'

'I'm sorry to notice it.'

'I'm sorry to see that you aren't wearing your wedding ring.'

Nick's left hand froze and the toothpick's tip stood locked in place, ready to pierce soft flesh.

'It is a tradition, amongst your people, is it not? Those locked in holy matrimony to wear upon their hands the symbol of their bond? You wore one on Pandora, when you spent a night of drunken revelry with a crew of Shangrian sailors. You wore it when you met the Shangrian Ambassador to the Vanir. You even wore it during your infiltration of the Senoyu on Andromeda, even though you knew it might mean your death if the enemy recognised the trinket for what it was: a mark of your true identity.'

Ohhh, shit... This wanker actually did his homework.

'The absence of your wedding ring must be a symbol of the absence of *another*! If I may ask, is she gone from the space of our time? Or merely from your own life?'

Silvia did not glance towards Nick, but she did notice the stillness overcome him. *Nick, don't you fucking dare. Do not lay a finger on him. His time shall come, but now we are in the open.*

'She wanted to take the kids. I told her to take the house which I had built for us. She just takes *care* of the kids that way. Like she did before, just that I don't sleep over anymore.'

'*Hmmm*,' Jenner muttered, his eyes somewhere in the distance of Nick's thoughts. 'I'm sorry to hear. Seems to me a shame to lose one's home.'

Nick eyed Jenner with now openly murderous intent. 'Seems we do have some common views,' he conceded.

'On the contrary, Mr. Lăutaru, I believe we have very little in common.' Jenner seemed to retreat both physically and mentally from the coals he had so callously stoked. 'You see, I know a lot about you, your colleagues, your general, your world, your history and your many deeds. I know enough to say that you know a lot about me as well. I will answer your questions now as comprehensively as possible and, make no mistake, your presence here bothers me far more than my intrusion upon your little brunch could ever bother you!'

Jenner leaned back and spared Silvia, Mira and Basenji a sickened look, before returning to face Nick's glare. 'For over forty years we've entertained your presence here in our beloved city. When the

Terran Embassy opened in Sanjak thirteen years ago, I was the first to picket outside the gates in protest at the barbarism we had allowed into our midst. Whenever your Alliance appointed a Terran, a Kalimasti, or any other war criminal as Ambassador, I collected millions upon millions of signatures from concerned citizens fearing for the safety of our children and our lives, and brought them to the gates of the Royal Palace itself. When the Alliance supported terrorists in Andromeda, I interviewed thousands of survivors of the gruesome conflict you insidiously supported, bringing their stories to the attention of all of Shangri's citizens, as I did with the elves that fled the genocide of their people before, and the Aesir that still hold to their independence after you brought carnage to yet another galaxy.'

'In that time, your presence here has only steadily grown, permitted by the Peacekeepers leniency and the support of the ignorant, misguided, the degenerate, the vagrant and the vermin that gnaw at the foundation of our society. But, never in that time have your leaders truly and openly shown their contempt for our values as they did with the appointment of Laur Pop as Ambassador. A monster among monsters. A beast among the beastly. A man whose list of sins is so long, the devil himself would never reach its end! A butcher existing solely due to some ancient act of valour entitling him to not even the smallest fraction of the abominable acts he has performed for little more than his own twisted vision.'

'I take it that the Urheimat never sent someone so revolting?'

Nick... tread very lightly!

'Indeed they have not,' Jenner smiled slightly as he glared towards the Hajduk.

'Hmmm...' Nick smirked. He played with his toothpick for a moment. 'Was that a truth or a lie?'

'Nothing but the truth.'

Nick chuckled. 'Earlier you said you would not say either.' The Hajduk moved suddenly.

Jenner flinched.

Nick finished readjusting his position on his chair and smiled. 'You're not very consistent now, aren't you?' He was not interested in the response. 'You told me something and you called it a truth, now I will tell you something and you can call it whatever you wish.'

'No one here is going to change their minds! I'm not going to believe that you're just some saint, looking out for the moral high ground of your people and you're not going to ever believe that we're simply here to make friends and not enemies! Your followers aren't going to be swayed either way by any report you may bring them concerning your first impressions of the new Terran diplomatic staff, no matter how much you swear by your own open-mindedness and no matter how much we can contain our contempt for petty little tyrants-in-waiting such as yourself!'

Nick smiled and leaned in closer. 'You *smell*! That's the thing about *all-natural* human bodies: they have an odour about them... a *musk*, if you will! It's a very specific smell, you see, though it does have a spectrum. At one end is comfort, at the other is discomfort, and I can tell, right now, no matter how much you may have scrubbed yourself this morning and no matter how hard you try to hide your stench in the millions of odours that waft through the closed air of your lovely city, that *you*...' he paused for effect.

'... *are fighting the urge to run away*...'

'I am not afraid of you!' Jenner replied defiantly.

'Self-suggestion is an effective strategy in such scenarios and I commend your use of it! Though I might also add that it's only rational to not be afraid of me... *here*! There are so many people around us right now who would be more than willing to rush to your aid! There's even a friend of yours over there...' Nick nodded towards a lone man wandering nearby, whom Silvia had also taken note of.

'... there's that car over there...' Which had parked just one minute before Jenner arrived.

'... those two guys on that balcony over there....' who had emerged right as their unwelcome guest had sat down...

'...there's a lot of people here!'

'... and if there weren't?' Jenner asked.

Nick smirked. 'If there weren't, I would lean in real close...' which he did, '... and I would whisper into that recorder in your robes, that everything's gonna to be just fine!' Nick smiled and raised his eyes from the subtle bulge on Jenner's upper chest towards the Shangrian's eyes.

'But, then again, that could be either a truth or a lie; you'll never know and you wouldn't really care! If anything, you'd want me to do something *Terran* right now, wouldn't you? You'd love it if the world saw that you were right all along and we were nothing but bloodthirsty savages unable and unwilling to engage in civil discourse, wouldn't you?'

'Well...' Jenner began, '... *are you?*'

'Does it matter?'

'Yes,' Jenner said quickly, as if he had been trying to stay ahead of the conversation for once.

Nick smiled. 'Is there any universe out there where I answer your question with a *yes?*'

'I don't know.'

'Well, neither do I.' Nick cleared his throat. 'Well...' he stood up straight in chair '... good talk!' He slapped Jenner on the shoulder with enough force to make him stumble in his seat, yet nowhere near enough to cause any actual damage. 'Thanks for the welcome! You're a busy man, we appreciate your time! Don't let us hold you any longer! Go! On your way! This city needs people like you! *Voice for the voiceless* and all that!'

Jenner stood motionless for a moment, before forcing a smile, adjusting his robes and getting up. 'Pleasure to meet you!' he said with fake gratitude.

'If you say so! Bubye! Good day!' Nick waved in his face.

'I do not believe this is the last time –' Jenner began.

'– I said "*Good day*"!' Nick menacingly reminded him, never raising his tone.

Jenner smiled, nodded, then reluctantly shooed off.

'Charming fellow!' Nick concluded sarcastically once he thought him out of earshot.

Silvia waited a few extra seconds, until she was certain Jenner was out of earshot, 'We need to get back to the Embassy!'

'No, we don't; Mira isn't finished!' he gestured towards Mira's almost pristine pile of pancakes with his toothpick.

'Yes, I am,' she said, eyes locked on Jenner's back as he was joined by the wandering man.

'No, you're not!' Nick noted, eyeing her pancakes. 'Go! Eat! Take your time! We wouldn't want him to think he get to us and ruined our brunch!'

Fair point.

'Nick, these pancakes are *horrific*! I'm done,' Mira assured him.

'They don't look that bad to me; hand them over!' Nick picked up his empty plate and handed it to her, extending his open left hand to receive his second serving of Shangri pancakes.

Mira blinked a few times agreeing to the swap.

After Nick finished her plate, as well as the three pancakes left over from Basenji, they paid the bill, argued about the size of the tip, and then walked back to the embassy and straight to Laur Pop's office, finding their General with his pet raven, watching the bird type on a keyboard with his beak.

'Are you certain it was Glandarius Jenner?'

Why does he even bother to ask?

'Yep,' Nick replied.

Pop instantly turned to Mira, 'You asked Silvia out to make sure that it's all good between you?'

'Yup,' she replied.

Motherfuckers, I am right here.

'And you have no reason to believe that your activities drew him to you? On the very first day you four had brunch in the neighbourhood?' Pop followed-up.

'Nope,' she replied, finding little need to dwell on the matter.

'Do you suspect anything?'

'Many things, yet none to explain the coincidence.'

'A coincidence it is not,' Pop replied before turning to look blankly ahead, before raising his eyes to fixate on Nick's. 'You aggravated him?'

'Yes,' the three Terrans replied, as Basenji hid a smile with his open palm.

Pop nodded. 'Did you cross any lines?'

'Many, yes. But not anything major.'

'Good...' Pop's words trailed off, just as Technowolf entered, followed by Radu, Cosmin and Ela. 'Glandarius Jenner approached them while they were having brunch. He acted friendly. Nick kept him at a distance and then told him to fuck off. Silvia will give you all the details later!' Pop turned back to the four brunchgoers. 'Did he prod at anything in particular?'

'He asked if he could meet you,' Silvia responded.

'Did he now?' he asked, before turning to look at Nick. 'And your reply was?'

'That you wouldn't be interested.'

'*Huh...*' Pop leaned back in his seat. 'Maybe I might have been...' he trailed off, as he gazed off into the distance and digested the news.

'He knew things,' Silvia continued, as Pop raised his eyebrows, eyes still staring blankly ahead, bidding her continue. 'Gossip from Senoyu sailors. Reports from Shangri Ambassadors to Allied states. Senoyu Intelligence.'

'How did you piece all of that together?' Pop was now focused on Silvia.

'He noticed I wasn't wearing my wedding ring,' Nick replied.

'Oh...' Pop slowly mouthed. 'You wore it with the sailors, the ambassadors and in Andromeda?'

'Always,' Nick replied, his eyes now also blank. Silvia sensed his inner temperature rise slowly, as he reminisced on what his wife had taken in the divorce.

'I see... and he mentioned these things because...?'

Silence. Atypical silence. Laur Pop's office was usually ablaze with chatter during such times. This time, things were somewhat different. Silvia knew that Nick's fellow Hajduks and the two remani were allowing him to answer the question for himself, with his own words.

Mira, however, did not know the Hajduk's customs that well. 'He needed a comeback. Nick had beaten him into a corner. He needed something to regain his footing, so he responded with a personal attack to get to him.'

Pop's eyes flickered between those of the four brunchgoers. 'Did it work?'

'He did get to me, but I didn't say anything. So, no, it didn't!' Nick answered truthfully.

'So, that wasn't when you told him to fuck off?' the General asked.

'No. I told him to fuck off after he talked shit about you!'

Pop smiled. Genuinely. A rare sight. 'You did now?'

The Centurion chuckled and nodded.

'Nick, if you'd tell everyone who talked shit about me to fuck off, it'd be just you, me and you left!' Pop responded.

'Nah... just you and Silvia, boss!'

'I see!' Pop allowed himself to smile once more before asking. 'Well, what was it this time? Monster? Devil-worshipper? Beast of the night?'

'All of the above, though not in that order...' Nick struggled to remember the exact words. '*A butcher existing solely due to some ancient act of valour entitling him to not even the smallest fraction of the abominable acts he has performed for little more than his own twisted vision.*'

'Oh...' Pop had begun to wander mentally in the middle of Nick's sentence. 'I see he's a student of history...'

He paused and Silvia took the moment to try to understand what exactly was happening. *Why is he so calm? This is serious! This is a direct threat to-*

'This is only the beginning!' their General announced. 'Things like this will become commonplace.' Pop leaned on one of his armrests to gaze outside towards the buildings across Wiltshire Boulevard. 'They are watching us. Not just the Constabulary, but also Jenner's reporters. No doubt they're feeding the Urheimat every bit of intelligence that comes their way. On top of that, we've got the ursai likely keeping an eye on us, to not even mention...' Pop seemed to struggle a little, which was strange, since the General always had the right word for every occasion. '...*Civil society*, as a whole,' he said, after finally remembering a concept he had long forgotten. He smiled and turned back towards them. 'To not even mention the rats we've welcome into our house!'

He didn't follow it up with a scolding of Mira and her decision-making process. Instead he exhaled. 'Good job today! Keep up the good work, but remember that this is *nothing*! It'll only get worse!'

With that they left his office, though Silvia never left the conversation.

It bothered her. Something was different now and it was barely now that she began to feel it. It wasn't the complexity. It wasn't all the hats they had to wear. It wasn't the juggling. It wasn't the odds. Something else was amidst and she found it difficult to put her finger on it. The fumbling around for understanding led to her fidgeting through the darkness of ambiguity, as she struggled to make sense of what was happening.

Pop was acting weird.

On the one hand, it was understandable. A new galaxy. A new civilization. New challenges. Old enemies. Very tight rules of engagement. Several complicated objectives interplaying with one another.

Mira...

Mira was the difference. It was something about her. Pop never challenged her. Not *really*, at least. Silvia knew how Pop challenged his subordinates, even those as subordinate to him as Silvia herself.

Was it because of her heritage?

Mira was the splitting image of her mother, bar only her father's nose and his temperament. Pop had always acted strange around Sarasvati Singh and her death had often seemed to Silvia to have been the only one that ever really got to him.

Was it because she was a woman?

In a matter of weeks, Mira had shown more independence than Silvia, Bojana or Lejla had in decades of service.

Yet, it would have been so out of character for Laur Pop to lose his composure over a young girl with full lips, long green eyes and dark luscious hair. Many had tried and Laur had never even bothered to grant them a second glance, often delegating to Silvia the task of banishing them.

Could Mira be the exception?

She was so... different after all; so unlike anything Silvia had ever seen before or since. Perhaps Laur might see in her something from long ago, or from far into the future; perhaps an alignment of traits never seen before...

Perhaps they were entering a new age. An age of change. An age after Diwali Day, when Heaven, Hell and Here and Now bled openly into each other and things that had not been before *were* now.

An age in which something stirred within the howling gales of Laur Pop's heart, as the shadows bubbled with the searing flames of...

...of something.

And that concerned *her*. It concerned her that it was happening now. It was happening now in the time when they needed Laur Pop to be as much the master of manipulation and the king of cunning that he always was. They had followed him to the edge of darkness, riding the shifting times of changes before and they had emerged triumphant time and time again, though always due the cold, calculating and oftentimes cruel nature of his mind.

We came here at his discretion, though we could have enjoyed the respite we have craved for so long, and we did so both begrudgingly and loyally because we trusted him to be... him. Seeing him change would be... strange, yes, but it would not necessarily be a bad thing.

But, this... this is wrong. It feels wrong and danger wafts all around us as he plays with his little bird.

'The rat women left!' Nick said.

What? Oh, yeah... 'Yes... four hours ago.'

Nick and Technowolf had come to join Silvia and Mira in their living room after the housekeepers had left. They had been catching up on reports and relaxing in relative silence ever since.

'I know. You watched over them like a fucking hawk the whole time. I thought you'd be able to unwind now that they're gone!'

Shit. I've been sitting here scowling for hours, haven't I? Silvia put down her sewing kit in frustration. 'It's not them – I mean, well... it's them too!'

Nick leaned back in the armchair he had claimed as his own and threw the screen he had been looking over onto the couch next to him, startling Lorgar, who had been lying deep in slumber on said couch. Technowolf's ears twitched and Mira looked up from the Shangri mystery novel she had been reading all afternoon. 'Well. What is it?' her colleague asked.

'This mission is different. It's... complicated.'

'We're the Hajduks, Silly! All our missions are custom-made clusterfucks.'

'I know, but this one's too clustered! Perhaps a better word might be *cluttered*...'

Nick looked around 'Oh... you've got like a hundred square meters here, Silly! You saying you want me and Tech to fuck off back to our place?' Nick asked, knowing the answer.

'No... that's not what I meant.' *And you know it!*

'Eh... I know...' Nick rubbed his cheek. 'I think of it as a vacation.'

'Of course you do.'

'Yeah, and I could recommend you do the same!' he gestured towards the windows. 'We've got about four or five hours of real work to do every day and after that, we can do whatever the fuck we want *wherever* we want. And, in all frankness and sincerity, it's actually recommended that we do whatever the fuck we want, because, that way, it doesn't look like we're up to something!'

'And every time we leave this place we are exposed and, every time we are exposed, the chance that something escapes our control increases.'

'Silvia, that's literally how life works! What? We're supposed to lock ourselves in the house and never go out because something might happen?'

'No, because, like you said, that would be suspicious!'

Nick exhaled and turned towards Mira and Tech. 'You see what I've been dealing with for forty years?' he said, before turning back to her. 'If the point is to look at ease, why not actually be at ease, *Centurion* Murărescu?'

'No need to use that tone with me, Nick! We're supposed to be at ease, like you said.'

'Then what's with the brooding?'

'Jesus fucking Christ, Nick...' Silvia sat back in her office chair in frustration as she rubbed her temples. 'Are you certain you weren't seen?' she asked.

'What?' Nick asked.

'When you met with the ursai?'

'Oh... when I gave them the monkeys?'

Silvia nodded.

'*Monkeys?*' Technowolf asked.

'The power stealers. The thing Big White asked for and which Laur promised to deliver,' Nick explained.

Tech shrugged, smiled and nodded his understanding.

Nick turned back to Silvia, 'No, I was not seen! Neither was Romulus, Famous, Rukeli, Marius or Gabi Gâlcă, with whom I delivered the shipment. Zaza said he wasn't seen when he took the shipment from our space viking friends to the *Doina*, but given that we seem to be performing an audit now, Silvia, maybe I should call him over so you could make sure!'

'There's no need.' *Zaza is a good man; Lejla's most trusted lieutenant and one of the new Centurions. If he said he wasn't followed, I believe him.*

'This Jenner guy,' Nick continued. 'Have you read up on him?' Nick frowned at himself. 'Now what the fuck am I saying!? *Of course you have*!'

Silvia had indeed.

'Well? Haven't you noticed what this man and his company do for a living? They stalk political enemies of the Urheimat and they dig up trash on them to sway public opinion! Of course they're watching us! They saw us four go for lunch. They called their boss over. He decided to fuck with us to illicit a reaction, like any other shit-stirring journalist with no dignity or a backbone would, and we didn't give him one! End of subject!'

'It's not end of subject, Nick!' Silvia countered. 'We will have to be like this every day! Every time we go out, for one reason or another, we're going to have to behave as if we are being watched. We will *always* have to be careful!'

'We can sweep the neighbourhood for his people and weed them out...' Nick frowned. 'You think we *can't* be careful? We've been careful before!'

'Never with as many objectives and side-quests as we do now!'

'Jesus fucking Christ... Silvia, you're beginning to sound like *him*!' There was no need to explain who 'him' was. 'Are you saying that *you* want to handle the next shipment? It's tomorrow at three in the morning! I asked Ela to have Casandra or Regis do it, but now that you're so felling so diligent, maybe you'd like to wake up at 2 in the morning, drive around in circles for thirty minutes, before meeting up with the Bear Mafia in the parking lot of some fucking Judge Dredd housing project!'

Silvia leered at him. 'If you weren't so fucking lazy, I'd argue that you *want* me or Casandra or Regis to do it because you know you're not up to it and *you know* that you'll fuck it up eventually!'

'*Woman*! What the fuck has gotten into you?' Nick asked, still friendly, but now also clearly irritated.

Silvia placed a hand on her temple. 'Nick... it's not you...'

'Of course it isn't fucking me! I'm glad we agree, even though a few seconds ago you couldn't decide if I'm the weak link or just a lazy fuck!'

'It's the nature of what we're supposed to be doing here...'

'Which nature?' Nick asked annoyed.

'*Exactly*!' Silvia replied sternly. 'It's too fucking much that we have to keep track off and now it's fine! But you have to agree that this can go off the rails in the blink of an eye!'

'Yeah... it always can and it usually does...' Nick shrugged at himself for openly admitting his own worries. 'We'll handle it when it does!'

'It's not the handling that worries me! It's all the fucking hats we have to wear! On the one hand, we're here in a diplomatic capacity, but we're also looking for the Stolen, and we're also now helping the fucking bear mafia steal power. All the while we're supposed to be model citizens but, also, we are also supposed to undermine the Urheimat, as well as who-knows-what other quest pops-up along the way!' Silvia had been tilting her head to highlight each individual hat. She gestured towards Mira. 'Now we're playing white saviour for ratmen and she's also got some spirit quest she's on!'

Mira frowned. 'A *what* quest?'

'Spirit quest,' Nick repeated. 'It's how we call whatever you're doing when you're not here and not working.'

'How do you know I'm not working?' Mira asked, a frown clear on her face now.

Silvia snorted, 'We're the Hajduks, Mira, we keep tabs on everyone, including each other! We know you're up and about doing fuck knows what and it's fine!' *If it's part of your healing process go through with it.*

'Hey!' Nick interjected, waving a finger at Silvia. 'Why *don't* you give a fuck about what she's doing? She could be up and about and getting us fucked! Why isn't she a liability?'

'Because, whatever she's doing (as long as it doesn't involve any more unexpected visitors) isn't something that can come back to us!'

'Huh!' Nick mused. 'I call bullshit! I think you let her off the hook, because El Patron lets her off the hook!'

Silvia felt her cheeks blush as a hot flash sent her reeling. *Fuck. You. Nick.*

Her old friend turned to Silvia, 'No disrespect, Mira, but if it were anyone else doing what you're doing, with the midnight excursions, the misappropriation of funds and all the Type A personality shit, El Patron would have you in a straight jacket in the basement watching Netflix and eating lunch through a straw!'

'I'm honoured to have the freedom to watch Netflix with my hands free to eat dinner with a fork...' Mira noted.

'He's right, you know?' Technowolf finally spoke.

'Wonderful!... How am I right, Tech?' Nick asked.

'You're right about most of what you just said, but the key point that sticks in my mind is that part where you compared your current assignments – those *hats*, Silvia was referring to – as a *vacation*.' Tech took a sip of his cranberry juice, which he always kept in a nearby glass packed full of ice cubes. 'I spent over a century on Earth undercover and no one ever caught wind of who I was. The best advice I could give to someone pretending to be someone that they're not is to behave like an actual – well, a *regular* – *civilian*! Do what you tried to do today: go have lunch with your friends at an overpriced bistro!'

Now Silvia was reignited. 'Tech, none of us have ever been regular civilians!'

Nick snorted, 'Ironically, me and you were actually the only ones here who ever were regular and civilian, Silly!'

'Do you remember being a regular civilian, Nick?' she asked.

'No,' Nick chuckled. 'But it's still a funny thought!'

Silvia turned back to Tech. 'When the Elders asked that you go down to Old Earth and live among us humans, what were your orders?'

Tech took a deep breath and a sip of his juice. 'That we observe and learn from you. Keep an eye on your development, yet ***never*** intervene!'

'My point exactly! You did not come to Old Earth to meddle in our affairs! You didn't come to Old Earth openly, pretending to be benign, when in fact you went around hunting child traffickers or boosting organized crime!'

'We did, eventually...' Tech mused.

'And by the time you intervened, you were as much creatures of Old Earth as our forefathers! You knew the lay of the land, for fuck's sake!'

'Approaching this assignment as a regular civilian would allow you to acquire that very same feeling of brotherhood we acquired during our time spent among your forefathers.'

'My point is that you had time and you were well rested. You waited for too long, yes. I think that much we can all agree on! You didn't come to Old Earth *on a whim*!' Silvia muttered, though she regretted her words soon after.

'A *whim*?' Tech asked, shrugging. '*Laur Pop's whim*?' he deduced correctly.

The silence of the room greeted his question.

He took another sip of his drink, before leaning back in his seat, pondering things that were and melding them with things that had been. Tech's face grew distant and his eyes grew loose, as he peered deep into the mirror of the past. 'For years we fought a war in the shadows on Old Earth,' he said, starring towards Silvia's direction, albeit not really looking at her. Thoughts of days long past and of a world that no longer was, yet still endured, seemed to flow across the remani.

'At first death seemed to only ever follow in the wake of our involvement. It took some time for the death to find itself all around. Most of the time, we were fighting alone. Then, we started working together with the humans of your world. They were the ones we were trying to help, after all!' Tech got up from his seat and made his way towards the window and glanced out towards the street below. The farm golden glow of the night lights caught upon his fur as Silvia could see him sigh.

'At first we were killing only elves, but very soon it was humans also and by the end, the hands that held the knives began to blur into one bloody back-and-forth as Old Earth crumbled all around us. Many heroes of your race arose during those days, only to fall, with a few even rising yet again from within the grave itself. It was for the innocents and the helpless of your world for which we broke our vows and took up arms, yet I must say that there have always been among your kind a certain character of man alongside which one could fight on against any foe! No matter how hopeless the battle might have seemed.'

'As our efforts failed and the night grew darker and time and time again, I saw champions arise from among your kind, revealing themselves for the heroes they were, all in defence of their world, only to be felled by the hand of our enemy as they tore your world apart! By the end, we had abandoned any attempt at subterfuge and joined the fight openly, believing that maybe by bringing our full strength to bear, we might be able to halt the atrocity unfolding before our very eyes or at least delay it, until aid arrived.'

'We clenched the odd victory here and there and we were not outmatched. Yet, we were outnumbered. A hundred of our number died during those days. A paltry number when compared to the billions lost by your people, though each and every one was family. Each and every one was my kinsman! When the red darkness came and Doomsday befell us, we gathered in the dark corners of your broken homes and we said our goodbyes. Our women, our children, our elders, they had all left years before, spirited away to a safe place from whence they might once more wander the stars in search of a new home; fleeing, as always, the ignorant, the insane and the downright *evil* of civilization.'

'Those of us that stayed behind swore vows of service to your people. Not in the presence of any human of Old Earth, but among ourselves. As we released each other, from one bittersweet embrace to another, we departed for those places where we would plant our feet in the ground and face your doom as it were our own.'

'Basenji fought in Delhi, where he would join the Pandavas for the battle that was to come, while I travelled to Prague, where I would join the shattered armies of the doomed nations of half a continent, as the night grew darkest and the enemy moved in for the final blow.'

'It was there that I first met Laur Pop. In the mud of a besieged city as the walls were being torn apart.'

'Prague's beacon still held and the shield shone faintly as the enemy came like a tide and brought butchery and brutal end to all that lay before them. Artillery fire and missiles pummelled the beacon, but the shield held. It was in that darkest hour of twisted twilight that the flame of humanity's valour burned bright. The defenders fell back towards the west bank as the eastern city fell into obliteration and across the Charles Bridge there tumbled one last man fleeing the ruination behind him.'

'When I stood between that man and his pursuer, I did not knowing what he was, who he had been, or who might become. I did so precisely because I knew not who he was, only that he *still* was! As I battled the elven juggernaut in his wake, the man reached the western shore. I did not see what he did among the terrified mass of doomed defenders, though I did remember the fear in their eyes as I beheld them upon the battle's eve.'

'The elf wounded me. I managed to kill him, but he managed to strike me with his blade across my throat and I fell into the muddy bottom of what had once been the Vltava River. By the time I reached the western shore, I beheld a sight that made me think that the elf's blade might have drained all the blood from my body and my mind, for what I saw was a sight too valiant for such a dark place!'

'Rank upon rank. As many men and women as there were left in that dreadful place.' Technowolf let out a long sigh and then he smirked. 'You were naught but children back then! Mira hadn't even been conceived yet! I sometimes look on in horror at the callousness with which your elders suggest that your lives have been easier than theirs. You remember the Fimbulwinter?'

He turned to look at Silvia and Nick. 'You remember the dark days when brother slew brother and the whole world erupted into a great cacophony of conflict and violence, as hundreds of millions perished in what some were calling World War III?'

She did. She did not need to look at Nick to confirm that he did also.

'At first it was easy to tell who would fight whom. Russian fought Ukrainian. Turk fought Greek and Kurd. Serb fought Albanian and Bosnian and Croat. Some peoples fought among themselves, but not in your corner of the world! Not at first, at least. When the infighting began, it mixed with the wars you fought among yourselves, as Romanian helped Ukrainian fight Ukrainian, only to end up fighting Serb and the list goes ever onwards. By the time Ragnarök had come along, alliances and frontlines had changed naught once, not twice, but usually thrice in most places, with a few sides having swapped almost a dozen times in a couple of places!'

'Some held firm to their original allies, yet they were few and far between. Not even during the Revelation itself did the infighting stop! If anything, it grew more fierce in some places, as the traitors fought the betrayed! Even on the eve of Doomsday itself, after every traitor had been slain, when the night grew coldest and darkest, the peoples of Old Earth still found time to slay one another.'

Technowolf's eyes dropped, as he seemed to narrow down on one particular instance of belated fratricide. 'The first time I had ever been in Prague had been for a peace conference in my youth. My first mission, it was. How fitting, I thought, that my last mission would be in Prague. I arrived on Doomsday itself after the Storming of Prague, when the shattered armies had left Moravia and rushed to Prague under the cover of darkness slaughtering the Czech army that had sought to cordon off the city from the mass of refugees that had been allowed entrance into their country. I remember the hung bodies of Czech soldiers adorning the city's steetcorners and the greater stench of bloodshed and decay that hung in the air.'

'I did not have time to look over how the defenders were organizing, for the Enemy was immediately upon us. In my mind, I confess that I forced myself to not think of what was going on behind me. I did not want to consider that even in that moment, in the dying light of your people, that the blood of kinsmen would still wet the blades of kin.'

'Later, I would learn that they had not fought each other, though they also had not gone out of their way to work together...'

'The walls of Castle Prague held, as the dushman entered the city and fought your people street-by-street. Yet, the defenders of the shattered world were no match for the elves, which quickly pushed them back into this small pocket on the Western bank of the riverbed, where maybe fifty thousand survivors now stood ready before me. Among them was not a single one who had not been wronged in some way by another who now stood next to them. Yet they now all stood together as one and faced the same extinction *together*!'

'One man at their head! The man I had saved on that bridge and the highest ranking military man left among them, though that was not why they stood behind him! Not due to some obligation or some vow – *No*!'

'They stood behind him for it was he who was their leader now, at the end of their hope, when all those that had come before him had faltered, fallen or fled. There he stood, his cold face gazing into the abyss unblinking, his very essence urging them on to do that which would prove the nature of their souls, as they raged against the dying of the light, one last time!'

'Tens of thousands were slain, though they took *dozens* of the enemy with them. A heroic number given what they faced. Nevertheless, by the Dawnbreak came and the battle was won, naught but twenty-two thousand remained.'

'The original Hajduks!' The shattered *armies* were now the Shattered Army of Prague! Soon, it became known as Battle Group Prague, then the Prague Warband, before it became the Hajduk Legion after *the Last Fitna.*'

Nick suddenly felt the need to issue a reminder. 'When Pop killed everyone who might have been a problem...'

'Yes... when Laur Pop killed everyone who might have been a problem.'

'What's your point, Tech? What's the purpose of this history lesson?' Nick asked.

'The point is to remind you that Laur Pop has always been a man with more to him than what one might see at first glance! You think his decision to come here to be a reckless one! *A whim.* That there might have been others better suited for the task at hand! That perhaps the Hajduks were forced to come here, not by necessity, but by the needs of Laur Pop. I am here to remind you of something else. Something you all know very well, yet something you never speak of.'

Don't.

'Of all those that would rise to become Generals of Terra and members of the High Council, Laur Pop is the most *unexpected* one. He is no great warrior. Quite frankly, he's quite a mediocre combatant and I'm being generous. He is not the saviour of his people, the risen avatar of the kings of antiquity, come to aid his nation during their hour of need. He is not even – dare I say it in your presence – a *good* man! Every member of the Terran High Command has the blood of many races on their hands, yet even they behold the blood on his hands as being particularly... *thick.*'

Silvia snapped. 'What's your point?' Technowolf was beginning to get on her nerves. Another reminder of Pop's propensity for brutality was not what was needed.

'My point is that Laur Pop has risen to the occasion time and time again. That's what earned him his station. That's why he was the one to come here...'

Now Nick snorted. 'Every single man above the rank of Lieutenant has risen to the occasion time and time again, as well as most of those beneath it. That's not what makes Pop different!'

Technowolf starred down the two centurions, before finally smiling and stifling a laugh. 'Then what does?'

Nick breathed in and raised his eyebrows, likely looking for the answer to Technowolf's question. He seemed to find it, though he refused to say it out loud.

'Because he's a psychopath,' Silvia said it.

Mira chuckled loudly, and the three turned towards her.

'Well, technically, he's a sociopath,' she pointed out.

Hopefully. That would mean he has at least some empathy somewhere in him.

Chapter VIII:

No Anaesthesia for Synaesthesia

He had the Prague dream that night.

It began as it always did: he was rushing through the mass of refugees near Olsany Park, dragging a little brown-haired Romanian girl by her hand. He had found her hiding under a broken overpass on the outskirts of the city, as he led the survivors of the rearguard across the Bohemian plains towards the relative safety of Prague. Of his own Bucharest men, only a mere hundred still lived. Had it not been for Mikhail and the remnants of Russia's Army Group Centre, the enemy would've overwhelmed them. The Russian was with him now, as was Rumen.

Mikhail was trying to figure out who was in command. Rumen had come looking for his family, whom he had sent together with the first wave into the city. Laur was in the city only because of the little girl he had hidden in the trunk of his jeep and which he now pulled through the mass of starving refugees gorging themselves on the city's meagre food stockpiles. One of the Czech soldiers was dangling from a rope slung across a sturdy tree branch. He always remembered thinking he had seen the man twitch as he finally reached the subway station.

Flora.

He pushed through the huddled masses towards the checkpoint.

'Full! Full!' the Slovak guard was shouting towards them.

Laur got the message and picked up the little girl, shoving his way towards the side of the subway entrance and into the tram stop that stood across from it. He remembered checking the tram's engine, making sure it was one of the combustion ones. He circled the parked tram and looked inside, seeing it packed full of crates and children, all stacked up on top of each other, like terrified chickens in some hellish coop.

He found the Czech operator and remembered thanking God, for his eyes were those of an addict beginning to suffer withdrawal.

'*Friend*! *Bratr*! BRATR!' he shouted in what little Czech he knew.

'Full! Full!' the man said dejectedly and glanced towards the little girl. He pointed up the road. '*Jiřiho*! Next Station! Metro!'

He remembered his exact thoughts. *Nah, man, I got you!* He moved in close, and put his hand in his pocket looking for it; looking for the last of it.

He pulled it out. The package was the size of a used bar of soap. He held it in the palm of his hand, keeping it in place with his thumb as he reached towards the man to shake his hand.

The man had seen Laur pick something out of his pocket and quickly shook his hand, taking the little bag of pills into his own palm.

'Ok! Give! Driver cabin!'

There we go, you poor son of a bitch!

He tried to give the little girl to the driver, but she silently held on to him. Her grip was like a voice.

'Hai! Hai ca e bine cu domnu'!' he urged her in Romanian.

'Nu! Nu! Mi-e frică!'

Good. Fear is actually good now. At least you still have some hope, little one. The rest of us have none left and now we know no fear, though we wished we still did.

Forgive me!

He jerked her out of his embrace and grabbed one of her little wrists and pulled. She broke one of his pockets; her grip had been so strong. He could still feel his collar strangling him as she grabbed the top of his shirt, holding on to dear life as she began to scream and cry.

He shoved her into the driver's seat and shut the door behind her. The driver himself was forcing the last door of his tram shut, such was the mass of small bodies inside.

'*Jit*! Jit, bratr!' he urged the driver, who nodded and rushed towards the cabin's door.

Laur didn't wait. He knew the tram would leave. He didn't know if it would ever reach some semblance of safety. He didn't want to think about it.

He found Mikhail and Rumen arguing with a Ukrainian captain, though he never recalled their conversation in his dreams.

He always dreamt of their faces moving, before everything grew darker.

They ceased their arguing when they saw the shadow on the horizon.

A great void of darkness moved across the sky. They all knew what it was. High above the clouds, an Enemy lightshunner moved to blot out the sun.

They had heard rumours of such things emerging during Armageddon and Mikhail had told them that the Enemy had used one at Uralvagonzavod, but Laur himself had never seen one up until then. As the shadow neared ever closer, it left utter darkness beneath it, peppered only by the thousand fires of the Apocalypse, as the countryside burned with red flame.

The day was Doomsday and it was Earth's last.

The Hour of Twilight had come.

Prayers and screaming began to rise like a crescendo as they all stood still, knowing with grim certainty what fate had come to claim them.

Mikhail turned towards them and extended his hand. 'Gentlemen! It's been a pleasure!'

Laur grabbed his hand without thinking, yearning to feel a human touch, knowing he would likely never feel such a thing again. He sought out Mikhail's eyes and the two men acknowledged each other.

Then Mikhail's eyes had shifted and he froze. His jaw dropped slightly as he attempted to say something. His hand grew limp and Laur slowly released it as he turned towards his gaze.

'*Vŭrkolak...*' Rumen managed to mutter in awe.

The word was the same in Romanian: *Vârcolac*.

A werewolf.

Before the genetic augmentations, Laur had been six foot two inches tall. Even now, at his current six foot eight, Technowolf was taller than him at six foot eleven. But back during the End Times, on the eve of the Battle of Prague, the remani had appeared as a giant werewolf towering over them, draped in his panoply of war.

In his right hand he held his gigantic helm, bearing the typical Valkyrie wings favoured by the remani of the Black Knight, while in his left he held a colossal warhammer, with a shaft easily as long as he was. At one end, a long dark blade the width of a child's hand jutted out, while at the other, the shaft forked as it bore two hammerheads extending a hand's breadth from each side. One had a short blade coming out of its head, while the other was flat, like a blacksmith's hammer.

His armour was black and simple in its design. Laur could still remember realizing that it was the cleanest object he had seen in years, as everything had seemed to be filthy and covered in dirt, grime and grease during the End Times. He remembered glancing towards Technowolf's shoulders and observing the giant round shield slung over his back, when the giant wolfman turned his head towards the mortals before him.

His eyes were alien. How else could one describe the eyes of a man upon the face of a beast? They seemed sad, yet also determined. Laur remembered feeling the terror inside of him rise, just as the giant's jaws moved slowly.

'They come!' the beastman said, in perfect English, before slowly turning towards the nearing darkness.

He began walking towards the coming Apocalypse, lifting his helm upon his great head, as the crowds of terrified humans parted before him. In his wake followed two more of his race, one bearing something resembling a rifle, the other a bearded axe and a greatsword the length of a small car.

The battle was lost before it began.

The Prague beacon denied the elves their aerial superiority and held back their artillery, yet the defenders on the ground were no match for their assailants. Their numbers mattered little, for even if they outnumbered the elves a hundred to one, every elf slain left a thousand human corpses scattered across its warpath. There were no soldiers in Prague, as there were no civilians, bar only the children stashed away beneath the broken ground. The shattered armies were in truth shattered peoples, and the elves crushed their broken shards into dust as they made their way across the beleaguered city.

There did occur a few little victories, but a grand triumph was never truly an option. The remnants of the American military left stranded in Europe after the Yellowstone explosion had been the last to arrive in Prague and had been the first to perish, as a people without a homeland threw their aircraft, their tanks and the last of their infantry against the foe while, across the Atlantic, their kinsmen fought the desperate Battle of the Guyanas in the jungles of the Northern Amazon. They bought just enough time for the shattered armies of Prague to withdraw across the Vltava River.

By this time, over a hundred thousand had died across Eastern Prague and Laur ran for his life to make sure he would not join them.

Yet.

He reached the Charles Bridge, just as the last defenders abandoned their outpost at the bridge's eastern head. He saw Serb soldiers rush across the river, just as he caught sight of the western shores, which glittered with artillery fire both incoming and outgoing.

A lone Svart had leaped from one of the nearby buildings into the middle of the bridge, at first cutting off the fleeing soldier's escape and then their heads. Laur jumped behind the wreckage of a barricade, attempting to hide from the elf, yet he knew that there was no real hope. He pulled out his pistol and breathed in.

'I'm sorry,' he whispered to the cold fires of the Apocalypse.

He didn't have time to face his destiny, as the elf shot a plasma round towards his position, causing him to be propelled across the bridge, only narrowly surviving being impaled on the spikes of one of the barricades.

He always dreamed of the feeling that had come upon him as he saw the elf rush towards him. He had dropped his pistol and he could only stare right at the Svart as it pummelled towards him and he felt the wind touch his face.

And then a great dark mass of metal, hide and fury had come down crashing from the sky before him.

Technowolf battled the elven juggernaut and Laur didn't even bother to help. He had no rifle and no pistol and he was not going to use his knife to help. At best, he would just die quickly. At worst, he would get in the way and get the benevolent werewolf killed too.

He ran across the bridge, not looking back, shouting 'human' in a dozen languages as he reached the western bridgehead, praying the defenders would hear him and not mistake him for the Enemy.

There were no defenders.

He didn't want to be a hero. He had no epic last stand in mind. When he saw the scattered men and women of the shattered armies rush around the bridgehead like headless chickens, he had not rallied them like some rooster seeking to gather some flock of wayward hens. He had simply asked what he had asked a hundred soldiers a hundred times over the last few years, ever since the Bucharest Quake:

'How's in charge?' he had shouted to nearby a Turkish infantryman.

The man's eyes had been wide with terror and he had glanced towards Laur's chest, where his NATO insignia bearing the marking OF3/RO/DI lay identifying him as a Romanian Domestic Intelligence Major.

'You... *sir*,' the Turk had mumbled before falling to his knees and praying his last prayer.

Laur had looked around, seeing only fear and dead men. He did not *feel* empty inside; he *was* empty inside.

So he had felt no fear.

Hence, he was a dead man also.

He turned around to face the bridge and drew his knife, a long bayonet knife he had lifted of the corpse of some Hungarian militiaman in southern Slovakia. He had killed men with it. Perhaps he might shed some elf blood today, though in that moment he cared little. He hadn't grown attached to the knife for its utility. Rather, he had liked the way it felt in his hand.

He looked at it for a moment, feeling the hilt's coarse leather grind against his calloused hands. He held it loosely and began running his thumb across the steel guard's cold metal. Then he looked up towards the bridge and observed the collapse of a building on the far side. His journey had started almost a thousand miles away, across the river, in the ruins of his home, and had brought him here, at the end of mankind and the death of his world. Before him now he saw only the fires of doom and the black smoke of destruction as a city burned and the ground began to tremble.

He had done everything he could. Yet, he still felt dirty. He still felt guilty. He remembered *her*. He felt *her* nose move across his own and he saw the corner's of *her* lips curl upwards and then he saw the wet tears on *her* cheek. The warmth of flesh flashed across his waist where her legs had cradled him and his stomach sank.

There was nothing left to do but die.

Perhaps that might make the guilt go away.

The Svart had decided to be merciful, for once, and began advancing across the bridge. No shots were fired from either side. The elves moved in for the close kill and the humans had no more bullets left to fire. Laur breathed in as he put his left hand out and sought to feel the wind move through his fingers one last time.

His hand touched something hard.

His eyes darted to his left, where he saw a man. He had no mark of rank and no heraldry of country and yet there he stood, axe in hand, eyes shifting from the approaching Enemy to Laur's own. They nodded at each other. There was no need for introductions. They were about to die together. Their names mattered little. They already knew everything they needed to know about one another.

Then, the corner of Laur's eye caught movement behind him; *right* behind him actually. He turned slightly and saw another man come up, a long knife cradled in his hand. Another man moved into position next to him and then another. Then another. Another. Then a woman. Then another man. Then another woman. Then a man. More. More than he thought were left. He turned to face his enemy and saw a presence to his right and saw a man and to his right another! And another! And many more moving in behind.

No oaths were made. No horns were rung. No drum was beat and no speech was made. No prayers were uttered and no song was sung. The Hour of Twilight was nigh and the Enemy approached.

The fighting was meaningless. Despite being in the literal frontline, Laur survived by virtue of the Enemy's strength, which battered into him and flung him back into the men behind him. Hundreds fell as elven blades ripped through the last flesh of humanity. Here and there, a knife managed to slip through elven armour, yet human flesh was made bare all around. The human's greatest asset was the blood and gore of their own fallen, for it was so thick that it caused the elves to falter, as they struggled not to stumble over the broken bodies of their foe.

It was during one such slip that the elf before him had to drop his guard to stop himself from falling and Laur saw a thin line upon the armour of his neck, a place where the armour was weak and one lucky thrust from a strong wrist might break through to the soft skin beneath. He tried his luck and his knife sunk so deep into the Svart throat that his grip slipped and his hand slid over the guard and across the blade, cutting his palm open. He felt no pain, only frustration and he gripped the hilt once more and began jamming it back and forth, turning the elf's throat into a bloody mess.

Finally, he pulled out the blade and allowed the enemy to collapse, his eyes now catching the empty glare of another Enemy's helmet, which seemed to look right back at him. This one finished slaying the man before it and then disengaged, making straight for Laur, likely seeking vengeance for his comrade.

He had been lucky once. He knew lightning would not strike twice.

He stood up straight and waited.

He did not have to wait long, for the elf's blade did fall, yet Laur did not have time to see it.

The light was too bright for him.

It was not the searing light of technology, nor the soothing light of magic that pierced the skies, but the light of the sun!

Laur thought that he had died; that the elf had been swift beyond his understanding and had ended him in the literal blink of an eye. Then he heard it or, rather, he started hearing again.

The wails of the fallen. The shouts of the fighting. The thrusting of blades and even the occasional gunshot. At first they were deafening, but then they dimmed down, as the battle lines looked up towards the bright skies and began to glimpse the wreckage of the shattered lightshunners, now tumbling towards the ground. In between the searing shards of darkness, the keenest of eyes could glimpse white trails of vapour, as small black dots became blots of dark blue.

Laur's eyes recovered and he saw a shape near him. A Svart shape, turned with its back towards him, visor turned towards the heavens. A thin black line crossing the armour of his neck. This time Laur's grip was strong and his aim was true. He twisted only once, feeling the blade catch between two metal vertebrae and he pulled the blade down with all his weight and might, collapsing upon the falling Svart, as he felt the knife come out the other side of the elf's neck and chip the cobblestone beneath.

The battle turned, as the elves seemed to grow heavy in their movements. Laur saw one of his comrades stab a Svart in the neck, before drawing his pistol to shoot another elf in the face.

The bullet went through. It did not bounce back.

The elven shields were offline.

Many still died, but now every Terran took at least one elf with him. The Enemy attempted to rally, but then the dark blue dots began crashing into the ruined city and from within walked out giants clad in armour of bright gold and lapis lazuli.

The Orcs of Vigilant had come and not just to Prague, but to the Guyanas, to Jerusalem, and dozens of other fields of battle upon which the Humans of Terra still fought the Svart. Soon, the tears of tragedy gave way to the weeping of wonder, as the eucatastrophe unfolded and humanity pierced through the dark pinnacle of the End Times and beheld the dawn of a new age.

Laur did not dream about that part. He barely even remembered that part. The dream always cut to a door which he struggled to open. A metal door in a ruined tunnel beneath Prague. He shoved and he heaved and he pushed and then the door gave way and Laur stumbled into an empty room.

He then opened another door.

And another.

And another.

Dozens of doors.

Empty rooms.

Then he always woke up.

This time he woke up in the City of Shangri and he checked the time.

07:52.

Laur lay back in his bed and closed his eyes. He felt his heartbeat shake the mattress and his cold sweat sticking the bedsheets to his back. Sadness came over him and his mind seemed to ask him what he was waking up for. He diligently answered, as he always did.

MMA tournament today... Come on... It'll be fun. You always wanted to go to a UFC event when you were young! It'll be like that; just that with goblins, bear people and orcs. Maybe the ratmen know Kung Fu! Come on! Get up!

He stood up in his bed and walked towards the shower. His men knew how nightmare sweat smelled like. Back before the genetic enhancement, they would subconsciously know the meaning of the smell. Nowadays, they would consciously know exactly what it meant.

He couldn't have that. Particularly not now. Particularly not when it was happening so often.

He had to cheer up. He knew it would happen. It was hard, but he just had to get the day going and he would find something to obsess about or maybe even to enjoy. The emptiness would go away. He still thought that, maybe one day, it might go away.

This time I might be close! It's why I'm here.

It's why I am always here... still here...

He showered and got dressed. He tried to remember what he had worn the day before. He didn't want anyone figuring out that something was different today. He remembered that he had worn a hoodie bearing the emblem of the Hajduks the day before. *Casual. I've been wearing casual clothes for the morning meetings.* He checked his wardrobe and found a plain black T-shirt, decorated only with the symbol and name of the SRI, the old Romanian domestic intelligence service. The letters were golden and the font was that of the FBI, the American counterpart.

A funny shirt. It's casual... Come on! It's also kinda cool!

Yes, wear that with black jeans, a wide brown belt and those Timberland-looking boots. You'll look fresh and cool. You'll feel fresh and cool. It'll make it easier to start pretending to feel great and you can't start feeling great until you pretend to for a little while!

Mira's been doing funny shit. Silvia, Nick and everyone are worried I'll snap at her. I actually enjoy her shenanigans. They remind me of her mother. She used to make me smile. I'll act like Severus Snape in Harry Potter, but I won't punish her. It'll confuse the fuck out of everyone and I always like watching them freak out. I like Mira. She's like Sara. She looks carefree, but she's carrying the weight of the whole world on her shoulders. Poor thing is upset about the death of that Thomas Muller boy. She needs to get over it. Kimmie's probably right. He's good with empathy. She's here for help and I can help. I can provide guidance by day and, by night, she can piece things together alone. She needs to be strong again.

Silvia's a little racist. She's always apprehensive around new races. Gonna fuck with her a little! She needs to get over that shit. She's the future. We can't have her prejudice get in her way.

I wonder how Gigi's doing. I miss him and I miss Rumen already so much.

Mira was late for the morning meeting and Silvia looked like she hadn't slept.

'How are the mouse maids?' he asked her.

Nick snorted and answered for her. 'You could drop food on the floor and feed it to a baby, no problem.'

'Good.' Laur leaned back. *There might be other uses for them. Given how much we're paying them.* 'Do they do gardening?'

His men looked up. Basenji raised his ears and he could feel Tech's gaze into the side of his head.

Silvia answered, 'They have cleaned and pruned the tree quite nicely.'

'Good. Have them clean and prune the trees in front of the building too,' he instructed.

Silvia raised her eyebrows.

'And have them plant some rose bushes around the trees,' he continued. 'You like white roses, don't you Silvia?'

Silvia's face froze and she nodded slowly.

'Great! White roses and... Ela?'

'I like reds,' Ela responded.

'Excellent! White and red! They get to pick the layout! Just make sure they're nice and bushy. Keep the spines, obviously.'

'You're thinking about the Hogwarts, Laur?' Tech asked.

'Yes... though I do like roses,' he responded, gracing Tech with a playful side glance. 'Once they're done with the front, they can get to work on the back. Silvia, Ela and Mira can pick what we plant back there.' *This'll freak them out. It's also harmless. Also, I actually do like roses.* 'How *is* the Hogwarts?' he asked Ela.

'What do you mean?' Ela was surprised.

'Is it fully dormant?'

'Yes... why? Are we expecting trouble?'

'No more than usual.' Laur scratched his head. 'Thing is that I am not 100% certain that we are not being watched,' he turned to Silvia. 'And it's not the cleaning staff that worries me! I think that's how your brunch was crashed. I doubt Jenner was just in the neighbourhood by mere coincidence.'

'We've swiped the place clean,' Nick began. 'Before that, Kimmel's boys must've wiped the place clean a thousand times over.' The Centurion pointed towards the street with his thumb. 'It's from out there!' he said, before resting his gesticulating hand in his lap. His eyes rushed towards Spideraven and he raised his hand once more. 'Maybe it's your new friend over there!'

Spideraven took offense and cawed disapprovingly towards his accuser.

'Perhaps....' Laur acknowledged, his eyes wandering and his mind wondering. 'How are we for tonight's event?' he changed the topic. *Better take care of the matter at hand first.*

'Seven cars. Thirty-two of us overall. Cosmin will leave in advance to take care of prep with Sever, Adelaida and Gabi.'

'Gabi *Gâlmă*?' Laur asked

'No, no; Gabi *Gâlcă*,' Silvia specified.

She would have continued, yet Mira's chuckle interrupted her.

All turned towards the Arabian Captain covering her mouth as discreetly as was decent.

'What?' Laur asked.

'Nothing! I'm still getting used to Hajduk nicknames!' she managed to say with a straight face.

'Good!' Laur stared down at his desk, remembering something and forgetting something else. 'What was *his* name again?' he looked up. 'Ela?'

'Otto Benga,' Ela replied.

Laur nodded. Such a silly name for such a serious man. Regardless, that was the name put forth by Quint's mind. That was the name of the next link in the chain. That was the name of trade consultant that had arranged for the sale of the *Stolen* to the Urheimat. 'Any luck finding him?' he asked Radu and Cosmin.

'None, so far,' Radu replied.

Laur nodded slowly, before raising his eyebrows. 'Maybe we'll see him at the arena!'

The arena was not the largest venue of its like that Laur had seen in his life, yet it was nevertheless gigantic. What made if most impressive was that it was apparently not a multisport arena, instead having been built solely for the purpose of one-on-one combat sports. What made it feel even larger than it truly was, was the fact that the already large arena was surrounded by a multi-storey parking lot, which circled the round central structure. Meant to accommodate the vehicles needed by over one hundred thousand spectators, the parking section had its own transport system, separate from the four different subway stations that were scattered throughout the complex.

Laur also knew that there were dozens of bathrooms, food courts, stores and bars located throughout the building, nestled in the great circular walls that separated the arena from the parking garages. Yet, he did not get to see these facilities, as the Hajduk convoy drove down the central tunnel leading towards the arena's VIP section, whose parking lot was located underneath the complex, allowing for easy access to the front-row seats they had been gifted.

As they reach the reception area and got out of their cars, Laur recognized the leader of their welcoming committee.

'*Lord* Pop!' Anwar greeted.

'Hello, Anwar,' Laur replied, before narrowing his eyes and pretending to smile through a corner of his mouth. 'Calling me 'lord Pop', now?'

Anwar moved towards Laur at a casual pace which the Terran thought to be a bit too swift. *They're big and every step is huge.* As the ursai closed in on him, he began extending his hand in greeting. 'Glad you could make it!' he said, as Laur's hand was swallowed by the ursai's big friendly paw. Anwar moved in to speak for his ears alone, making the veins in Laur's neck begin to squirm. 'There's press here,' he just said.

'Ah, I see,' Laur had already presumed that the twenty people off to the side of the entrance to the arena, staring at them intently were not just observing his arrival out of curiosity.

'Boss is waiting. He wants you seated next to him before the matches start.'

'Does he now?' 'Waiting?'... 'Wants'? ... What kind of words are those? Pretty presumptuous this Big White... or it could just be his actual madness. 'No weapon checks this time?'

'No,' Anwar's snout twitched and he slowly leaned towards Laur. '*Too many witnesses here!*'

I'm not gonna lie, I like his sense of humour way more than his boss'. Laur and his Hajduks followed Anwar through the tunnel leading to the arena.

'So, how does this work?' Laur asked their host, his words for his ears alone.

Anwar turned slightly towards him. 'The seating? The fights?'

'You and *him*?' Laur knew the ursai caught his meaning. 'Nick tells me that you're the *one* two keep *his* hand on the pulse of the city!' Laur tilted his head theatrically. 'Which reminds me; thank you for *everything* from this last week!'

'Your men move fast. It was easy to meet their speed.'

Proud of his work ethic... Discrete... Maybe even loyal... 'I just want to know if you're the man I'll really be working with going forward!'

Anwar slowly turned to face him as they walked side by side, clearly thinking deeply about the question. 'You ask some very interesting questions, Mr. Pop! Could I ask you one myself?'

Attempts to seize control of the conversation... yet he does so politely. 'Please do!'

'If I was to ask your man, Nick, of *his* relationship to *you*, how would that make you feel?'

Laur's mouth almost twitched into a smile *Definitely understands loyalty.* 'I suppose I'd be a little miffed... *if* I found out!'

Anwar couldn't help but smirk as they reached the end of the tunnel. Two doors barred their way and the ursai leaned towards his ear. This time, the bearman made no effort to hide his hot breath on Laur's neck. '*Are you 'miffed' now, Mr. Pop?*'

Awww LAWD!

AWWW LAWWWD, I LIKE HIM!

Now Laur allowed himself a chuckle. 'No! Nick makes my life very easy!' *That's kind of a lie... but not really...*

'Well, then you know how *'it works'*?' Anwar grinned softly, with only a slight hint of contempt on his face, as he stood up straight and opened the doors of the arena.

They roars, yells, grunts, shouts, laughs and conversations of a hundred races and a hundred thousand races filled the tunnel in a thousand languages. They climbed up the steps to see the venue, packed to the brim by a deafening mass of mankind, and emerged right next to VIP box located around ten meters from the ring. Around a hundred seats where laid out before them on the platform Anwar led them towards, of which around twenty were vacant, with the rest being occupied by hulking ursai, vicious-looking remani, elven ladies of the night, bast cutthroats, human rogues and even one orcish rhonin, as well as several other dubious characters.

Those empty seats must be for us... nice... we can do some networking...

Laur's eyes jumped towards the front of the platform, where he saw his match.

Big White raised one of his aspen trunks to beckon him to come join him.

Anwar leaned into his ear and almost had to shout over the cacophony of noise. '*Everyone will find their seats! GO! FIRST FIGHT STARTS SOON!*'

Laur nodded and made his way towards his host, knowing that behind him followed his men, each one strapped with weapons. *If shit hits the fan and the witnesses don't matter anymore... I think we can make it to the cars?*

He shook hands with Big White before taking his seat next to him. As his behind made contact with the seat beneath him, something strange happened to his ears. *A dampener!* The roars of the arena subsided, as if someone had lowered the volume on the speakers from a deafening 100% to a more or less ambient 40%. *Nice! We can have a conversation in these things!* Laur realized that their two seats were almost completely isolated from the rest of the box, as to his left and to Big White's right, the railing gave way to the lower floors of the ringside seats.

When Big White spoke, it sounded as if it was just the two of them in their living room, about to watch a game together on the TV. 'How many men have you killed, Mr. Pop?'

No cameras here, eh? 'That's a bit direct, don't you think?' *Getting right into it now, are we?*

'I thought I'd skip the part where I ask you if you've ever killed a man.'

'How efficient.'

'It is.'

'... depends on your definition of it.' Laur glanced towards Big White, catching his eyes in a vice. *You ain't gonna push me around... and I think that if I push back just once, it might be enough to keep you away in perpetuity.* 'By my own hand? To be honest I've lost count. Hundreds... maybe thousands–'

'Have you ever killed a murine?'

'What? No!' *I just got here. It's been less than a week since I first saw one!*

'Ah... I see; you just got here!'

Son of a... 'And nothing I've seen makes me think that'll change anytime soon. Both by my own hand or –'

'Bast?'

Laur blinked.

'Have you killed any bast?'

'N-no...'

'Have you ever fought a bast?'

'No!!!'

'Have you ever seen a bast fight?'

'Not that I know of!'

'Ah... have you ever seen a murine fight?'

'No... I have not.'

Big White snorted, 'This fight is not for you!' he concluded dismissively, as he turned towards the tunnel leading towards the ring.

The bast was the first to emerge. He was bulky, for his race, though rather short. Laur was reminded of a fluffy winter lynx, on account of the man's coat, which was of blue silver, peppered by flecks of black. He likely stood as tall as Laur's upper abdomen and beneath the puffy fur of his race, Laur could tell than he was as yoked as a man with nothing to live for that had just discovered crossfit, or maybe just calisthenics. He wore loose boxers that hung loosely down to his knees and his very feline feet were wrapped in fabric, causing only the very tips of his feet and his trimmed claws to touch the ground. His hands were very human, which Laur found to be unnerving. remani hands were very apelike, but their dark colour and the absence of any hair made them seem otherworldly also. However, a bast's hand looked exactly like oddly proportioned human fingers extending from a very humanlike palm.

The uncanny valley continued with the catman's head, though not due to the resemblance to humanity, but rather, due to how feline it was! With the exception of the ears, which appeared to Laur as tufted high elf ears, his features were clearly those of a cat. A leopard, to be precise, though a slight resemblance to a lynx remained. He seemed fierce, though it was not the man's snarl that intimidated Laur.

His movements were troubling. Laur could tell that he was definitely enhanced, though likely within the accepted parameters of Shangrian law. His muscles were large and thick and his back was quite broad, though he was still a lithe creature. Laur suspected that Silvia, or any other Terran woman, might easily be physically stronger than him. However, Silvia did not move the way he was moving. His motions were so... *fluid* and balanced. Laur had seen it before, at least partly, in the gentle movements of the elves, yet this was much more and the realization hit him that this creature must be insanely swift, despite its current languid movements. Laur knew the bast could be fierce and they were renowned as good, fast fighters, yet all the reports and books he had read had not readied him for seeing such a man as he saw before him now.

As the feline fighter entered the ring, he began to casually stroll around its perimeter, saluting his supports with small and oddly dismissive gestures. *It's like if Julius Caesar was a cat.* 'He seems confident.'

'Bah! He should be. It's a nightmare to place fights for him...' Big White groaned.

'Introducing to you the light heavyweight champion of the City of Shangri, to all those in attendance or mere presence I present Ralderon Ka Gorribal Hashut!!! The Defending Champion! Undefeated in seventeen hundred and twenty seven bouts across his career!!!'

'It would appear that finding worthy contenders hasn't been a problem in the past!'

'He's eighty-eight years old. Been fighting since he was a little cub in his father's gym. In their youth, they all get a lot of contenders and they all *lose* a lot of fights! However, *he* never did and that used to draw people to him! Now, since he's dominated the division for so long, the younger up-and-comers have become old themselves and they're tired of losing to him!'

'I see. What are the rules of combat here?' Laur asked, just before the announcer began listing off a hopefully short sample of the bast champion's achievements and records.

He regretted his decision, as Big White ignored the loud announcer, only to rush right to Laur's neck and began shouting in his ear. *'No rounds, just one long fight – though in this case I expect it to be short. Blood cannot be drawn intentionally. No magic. No tricks. No tech. No weapons. If the opponent yields, goes unconscious or medically dies, the fight ends.'*

'What if they won't fight?' Laur asked.

'Don't be absurd, *bro*, they always fight!'

Laur did his best not to show his surprise. *'Bro'?!*

'The only way I can get people to fight him now is by offering them fucking obscene sums of money and not event that helps sometimes!'

'If they win? And if they lose, do they get –'

'*When* they lose!'

'*Oh*... and they've lost seventeen hundred and twenty-seven times?' Laur couldn't exactly figure out what kind of sums they were talking about.

'I make money off gambling on the fight!' Big White waved Laur's stupid idea away, his words meaning to be self-explanatory.

That doesn't make sense! 'You make money by just betting on him to win?' Laur asked, gesturing towards the bast pugilist still doing a pre-victory parade in the ring before them.

'I make money by loaning people to bet that he loses.'

'Huh...' *that still doesn't make any sense.* 'But if he's won so many times, why bet that this fight will be any different?'

'Because you can become rich beyond your wildest *dreams if it is different*!' The ursai replied, matter-of-factly, as if he was explaining something obvious to a child.

He was.

Wouldn't be the first time I saw a nation tumble as its citizen clutched desperately towards ways of getting rich quick...

'See all these people?' the ursai asked.

Laur did. It made him uncomfortable.

'Aye, well, you see, everyone's locked in place. Everyone in Shangri is trapped here, though no one is tying anybody down by the ankle!' the bearman explained, gesturing towards the crowds.

Getting philosophical now, are we?

'Everything in Shangri works like clockwork. The roads, the healthcare system, the court system (allegedly), everything! And do you know why that is, Mr. Pop?'

'I have my theories.'

'Me too! Mine are, also, *true*!'

Did you just take a shot at me?

'Everyone has to stay in their place and do their part and, if they do, they'll get rewarded for it! Within the measure of their station, that is! Everyone in this City is born and meant to live their lives trapped in some place, usually not really of their choosing, to live not really to their liking. They get things, yes, a great deal many things. Yet, they all know, deep down, that they'll always be trapped!'

'Then why doesn't anyone leave?'

'Because of what might happen if they stay. Look at him!' the ursai pointed to his champion. 'He was *nothing* growing-up! He was *meant* to be nothing! And look at him now. He feels like a god amongst men! He lives a life of such opulence and luxury, most of those here will never get to live one second of one day in the ecstasy he lives here, in this arena, today! The extravagance that is his life is something wholly beyond their comprehension.'

'Because he can fight?'

'Because he is *the best* at what he does! People like him escape, you see! They get through the cracks and they bite and claw their way to the top. Everyone else has their place and most of them will be stuck in that prison their entire lives. A prison we all maintain, together, as one people... like clockwork!'

As if to emphasize his point, the catman balled his fist and jumped into the air, just as the beat of his soundtrack dropped, causing the crowd to erupt in cheering as he landed in the middle of the ring.

The ursai wasn't done with his theories. 'Remani keep the peace, humans trade and administrate, and... they *maintain. His* people, don't do any one thing in particular, a by-product of their treacherous nature!'

That's probably why you've stagnated technologically... and there's some of that odd racism o his again... 'What do the ursai do in this system?' Laur quipped and immediately regretted it.

Big White's face twisted instantly to focus on his.

'Some of us provide.'

Before Big White could launch himself into some diatribe about the merits of organized crime, he was interrupted, not by the announcer, nor by any loud noise for that matter. Rather, his words were cut short by silence. It was only when the scattered silence turned to muttering did Laur spot the target of the crowd's ire.

This cinnamon murine was quite tall for his race, coming in at only a head shorter than Laur himself. He was not truly black, for his coat turned to a bluish grey across his belly, chest and neck, much like Technowolf's own contrasting streak of white on black. His face was non-descript and Laur would have been hard pressed to identify some remarkable feature or another. He walked slowly and tried to ignore the fact that, the entire way to the ring, naught but his own entourage of kinsmen, as well as the dubious looks of the onlookers gathered round, followed him.

No theme song...

No cheering.

No announce-

'*Introducing the contender: Cri Arron Shoem Skirta Salba Galbar!!!*' the announcer did his best to hype up the crowd to little effect.

Laur noted the absence of any murine in the seats around and across from him. 'Where do *his* people fit in?' he asked, pointing subtly with his finger towards the murine challenger.

'Everywhere and nowhere,' Big White muttered. 'If the murine ever woke up from their anxious slumber, they would rule this city, as they did in ages past, *allegedly*.'

'He doesn't seem anxious.'

'He doesn't. Likely because *this* is his role: to be a pit fighter! They all have their roles, you see. It's how they've survived for this long. They're obsessed with roles and the City likes that. Their jobs are roles. Their families are roles. Everything is a role and they all play their part. Yet, once you try to change their role, they recoil! They start to cower. They spread into the darkness like... well... I guess you know like what.'

Rats. 'Are they good fighters?'

'They're alright. Good with their hands, strong in the back and quick on their feet. Though they lack upper body strength and reach. Mentally they're not really resilient in a fight. Prone to scampering off back home to safety. Though they *are* very hard to read.'

Harder than you? Laur took a moment to study the ratman's lithe physique, before shifting his eyes to take in the ursai's massive girth. *'Upper body strength and reach'? Judging a fish on his ability to fly now, are we?*

'It'll be over soon; then we get to the interesting part!'

The fight commenced and was quite tame, at first. The two combatants began circling each other for some time, until their paths changed to those of a spiral. Then, rather swiftly, the distance closed as the bast came out swinging, nearly catching the murine on the chin. Laur was astounded by the speed of the punch... yet the swiftness of the ratman was not lost on him. The crowd did not forgive his skill at dodging punches either, as they booed him every time he evaded one of the catman's lightning jabs and thunder kicks, all the while maintaining an impressive distance from his pursuing opponent. After some time, the ratman sprung his trap as the feline champion was forced to overextend in a moment of brilliant footwork on the murine's part.

The ratman grabbed his opponent's wrist and pulled the fight immediately to the ground, where blood definitely spilled. Laur was surprised to see the catman rush to place his back on the floor and even managed to catch a few solid punches to his adversary's snout, much to the delight of the crowd. At first, the ratman seemed to be at an advantage, until his opponent, in a brilliant display of martial prowess, managed to turn the fight around and now the murine was on his back, taking a vicious pounding, as the catman used his nails as claws, and even drew blood across his opponents snout, all to the raucous roaring of the jubilant crowd.

Then the murine sprung another trap.

As the bast positioned his arm for another jab, the ratman grabbed an exposed elbow and pulled his opponent to him, catching his head between his shoulder, his neck and his other arm. Accepting the bast's punches to his ribs, he completely wrapped his legs around his opponent's waist.

Then he pulled and Laur felt the air rush out of his body, since he remembered an orc doing that to him in training once. It was a terrifying feeling, since you could flail all you wanted and it wouldn't matter: you'd still be having your neck choked. The ratman didn't need upper body strength, he just needed a strong grip and time, and it would appear that he had both.

The bast surely agreed as much, as he sought out the ratman's eyes and began gouging and still the murine did not relent. The catman began lifting his opponent off the ground and, after struggling for quite some time, miraculously broke free and Laur let loose a breath of relief. The catman had no time for such respite, for this was when the ratman truly unleashed himself, barraging his opponents with a flurry of punches, kicks, jabs, sucker punches and roundhouse kicks. He even tripped his opponent a few times, until he switched his focus entirely to the bast's neck and face and began pounding him.

The catman did his part and he did it well, but he never managed to regain any semblance of presence in the fight. On the contrary, from that moment onwards, the fight turned into a gruesome scene of one-sided violence, until, naught but a minute after getting up from the floor, the catman stumbled and his guard faltered. The ratman quick seized the opportunity, capturing him in a vicelike armbar and pinning him to the ground.

It took a while, but Laur eventually saw the bast go limp as he passed out.

And the room revealed its silence.

Then, he heard it. At first he couldn't place it. He couldn't even describe it properly. It was almost like a... *chittering*? At first it was soft and subtle, a frail little thing caught in the air. Then it began growing and Laur's ears told his eyes that the sound was coming from above and so he looked up and he saw them.

Dark shapes. In the upper sections of the arena, a black mass of a thousand forms was flickering excitedly, as the chittering grow to a thunderous cheer and the entire stadium shook as those in the lower, courtside, rich seats, began to shuffle somewhat in their seats.

Laur looked up and took it all in. He had seen it before in another galaxy as he stood side by side with Djibril al-Sayid. His eyes glazed over for a moment and a slight smile caught one corner of his mouth and pulled slightly. In that moment, the present returned to him and his eyes sought out one in particular. A set of eyes that had joined his Hajduks on this night of bloodsport.

Mira's gaze found his immediately.

Desert Power.

'It would appear that a number of people just became rich beyond their wildest dreams,' Laur commented, before turning to the astounded face of Big White next to him.

'At the expense of others...' he growled, fixated upon the battleworn murine in the arena below.

'I'm certain you'll recover.'

'You're not a gambling man?' the bearman spoke, after biting his lower lip.

'By necessity, not by choice.'

'All gamblers are....' the ursai scoffed. '... in their own minds, at least!'

'*Bah*...' the ursai let out a loud groan, which shook Laur's seat almost as much as the rumbling of murine cheering that began to subside. 'You don't ever bet on who wins and loses during war?'

'That's not really betting, now, isn't it?' *and neither is it sport...*

'Yes, it is! Don't you feel that heart pounding in your chest when you're about to either win or die? Maybe when a plan comes to fruition?'

'I do... I feel relieved after its passing.' *What's going on here, Mr. White? Are you trying to intimidate me again?*

'Who wouldn't? But, *then* you find yourself gambling *again*! *Always!*'

'Believe me, the relief is greatly diminished when you know you can't just stop gambling when you want to.'

'Why?'

'Because you can't just go home when you're in a war for survival. 'It's a necessity to gamble.'

'Ah... now we come full circle: it's a necessity, not a choice, to you?'

Fuck... he's good with the arguments. I'm gonna have to pull out the big guns. 'Have you ever lost something, Mr. White?'

'I just lost a lot of money just now...' he said, watching the murine champion make his way out of the arena, head held low.

'Something you could never win back?'

The ursai stopped moving for a moment and turned to face Laur slowly, his shoulder lowering, as he positioned himself for a clear look at his Terran guest. 'When you start out with nothing, you have nothing to lose. However, when someone takes that little something you dragged into your life with your balled fist...' the ursai flexed the fist in question, '... you don't really like losing things like *that!*'

'What do you think would happen to you if you lost everything?'

'I'd start over. I was poor before. I can find my way out again!'

'In Shangri?' he asked.

'If you can make it here, you can make it anywhere.'

So, it's fucking New York now? 'So, if the Urheimat came and took everything from you, you'd run away and start over?'

'The Urheimat will never take anything from me! I'd be dead before I'd let that happen!' The bear's tone was serious and Laur immediately began to wonder if all these witnesses really mattered to him.

'And if you failed?'

'Fail to die?'

'Yes.'

'Is that what happened to you?'

'... Yes.'

'Strange. You don't strike me as a failure, Mr. Pop. Things seemed to have turned out quite well for you!'

'It might appear as such and, in many ways, they have. But, believe me, my friend, (and this is something that I understand has never happened to you): certain things which you lose you can never win bac!. You can't win your peace of mind back once it's gone; you can't go back to a time before you lived in fear of what might descend upon you from the stars. You can't win back all those things and all of those people the universe takes from you. In time, those of lesser importance even begin to fade from your memory and sometimes you'll even struggle to remember how they looked like! You can't win back your dignity, after you've forsaken your honour. You can't win back someone's trust; they'll always know you for a liar and a cheater and word... *word goes around*!'

'I've never heard anyone describe you as a dishonest man!' The ursai studied Laur, trying to see if he was being insulted.

'I was just giving examples. Not everything has to be about me...' Something caught Laur's eye and overwhelmed his need to observe Big White's face for a reaction to the veiled threat.

'Introducing to you the middle heavyweight champion of the City of Shangri, to all those in attendance or mere presence I present Bellator!!! The Defending Champion!!!'

A remani emerged from the tunnel and Laur almost giggled for a second, until the man raised his head.

What had initially amused him was the fact that Bellator was a Dalmatian. *Where's Josip? The shit I'd say if he was here right now to see this shit... A white werewolf with spots of black on thick fur... get the fuck out of here! When I saw him on the roster, I thought it was a joke or that I was finally going mad but, no, here he is: the hundred-and-second Dalmatian!*

The white-and-black remani raised his gaze as he approached the ring and Laur's smile faded. *If I was Cruella de Ville, I'd switch to vegan fur if I saw him!* He had the eyes of a man who had seen true violence. True cruelty. He was different from the previous two combatants. He was different from any Shangrian Laur had seen up until that point, bar perhaps only Gonzo, the Crown Prince's man, yet he was simply fierce-*looking*.

This one *was* fierce, with no room for interpretation. His ears were cropped close to his head. His snout wasn't criss-crossed with scars; it *was* a scar, as the knotted mass of tissue resembled aged and weathered weather, not living flesh. His neck was thick and bulging, reminding Laur of a pitbull, as he took note of the man's broad chest and his huge arms. *So, I see Shangri does have some warriors in its ranks, not just cops and robbers!*

'I take it this won't be the first time you'll see a remani fight a human?' Big White asked.

'No,' Laur replied, thinking back to the Battles in the Bifrost and his time in Andromeda.

'Have you ever fought one yourself?'

Of that, Laur had no memory. 'No.'

'Ah... I have. It's a pretty clear cut fight. This one's ex-colonial constabulary. He's been fighting troglodytes bare-handed in tunnels slick with grease and shit for a living since he was a wee boy. Born off-world,' the ursai turned to Laur. 'Off-worlders are tough.'

'He's not from the City of Shangri?'

'No! He's from the province.'

Provincia... that is how we in Bucharest used to call the rest of Romania... 'I didn't know there were enough settlements in this galaxy outside of the City that could maintain a stable population, let alone stereotypes.'

'There aren't, but there are many of them, even if they're small. The largest ones usually have fewer people living in them than a small Shangri apartment buildings. But they're a hard group of people. Not to be pushed around. They're all either Colonial Constables drawn from the City Constabulary or children of Colonial Constables and, to be honest, I couldn't tell you which ones are tougher.'

'Introducing the contender: Felicity John Aspiration!'

What a name...

The man was queer of face and odd of gait. He was human and clearly so. His beard was short, as short as was possible for a stubble be called a beard and yet not provide something for an opponent to grab. His eyes were lost, yet also focused intently, the eyes of a fanatic. He had a calm, serene walk, as if he tumbled through life towards his certain destination. Behind him walked a silent ensemble of likeminded humans, bearing the hidden, yet blatant symbols of their true allegiance.

Laur tensed up, yet focused to relax himself. Of all the contenders he would see tonight, here was the only he knew for certain would do him harm if given the chance. He didn't have to look behind to know that his men had likely fallen silent, as they had also studied the roster and knew who had just know entered the ring

'And him?' Laur asked, as the remani's opponent entered the field.

'He's political.'

'Aren't we all?'

The ursai scoffed. 'Not like him we're not, particularly not me and you. No... he's a *symp*.'

What? 'Beg your pardon?' *Does he, like, pay for feet pictures of feet or something?*

'You've never heard the word? Symp? An imperial *sympathizer*.'

'Oh.'

'Uh-oh, indeed.'

'I didn't know this was an international tournament!' Laur feigned ignorance.

'It's not. He's homegrown, the fuck...' The ursai spat the words in clear disgust

'I see. And how does one become a symp in Shangri?'

'This one here's a reformed citizen! Twenty years ago, he was top shit around the fighting game. He was felling sons a' bitches left and right. But, he had a problem: he loved the liquor and he loved his woman. The woman was naturally upset by all the drinking he would get into after his fights and he loved her very much. So, one night after a fight, he comes home and his wife's fucking a big-dicked wolf motherfucker in his bed! Man lost his shit, killed the wolf and he killed his wolf-fucking wife, then plead guilty. I intervened on his fucking behalf, just to get his sentence commuted to five years!'

Five years for double-homicide? What kind of lax fucking legal system do they have here? 'How very charitable of you...'

'Two years in the can and he's a born-again fucking human supremacist. Believes that inhumans are the root of all evil, because his wife fucked one of them! Doesn't drink anymore, which makes him a *boring* son of a bitch! Plus, he's no longer signed to my talent management agency, unlike him!' Big White pointed towards the colonial constable.

Laur shrugged theatrically. 'Well, we have a saying were I'm from: *doing good is fucking of the mother*!'

'*Ha*!' the bearman exclaimed. 'Colourful place, this world of yours! Very creative language!'

'It's a Romanian expression, not a Terran one.'

'Regardless, the fight's starting and I have money on this one too!'

'Hopefully, you'll make a dent in your earlier losses.'

'Fat chance...'

The second fight was much longer and much more balanced than the first one. At least, it felt like that, on account of the bare brutality on display, as experience and savagery met talent and training. Laur had to immediately acknowledge that the human was clearly more gifted in the martial arts than the remani. He also seemed driven to dictate the fight, as he would force his opponent into styles of combat of his choosing, with the Dalmatian remani having to play a game of catch-up with him.

For a while, they sparred, as if they were boxers, since this seemed to be the human's preference. Bellator had to continuously rush towards him, closing the gap and constantly trying to grab a hold of him, without exposing himself too much and risking a knockout punch. Then, the human decided that he did want to wrestle, as the two connected into a vertical coil of combat, as the human constantly tried to trip his opponent and take the fight to the ground. Bellator, on the other hand, simply did his best to connect as many kicks and punches to his enemy's body.

Ultimately, the human succeeded in taking his opponent down with him, yet the damage was done. The human was not enhanced, meaning that his body was vulnerable as Laur's own body had been before the genetic templates. He was powerful, yes, far more so than Laur had ever been, likely more physically gifted than the greatest UFC fighter of Old Earth, and his form and technique was also superb, as one could clearly see Urheimat combat doctrines meet his inner talent in his style. Yet, the remani seemed to understand what fighting against such an opponent required, as time-and-time-again, Bellator would counter the human's refined technique with banal pragmatism, as he leveraged his understanding of true mortal combat with his opponents talent for violence.

In the end, as the human made a desperate attempt to gouge the remani's eyes out, Bellator simply pushed himself into his adversary's hand, sacrificing his own eye, but allowing to catch his opponent in an armbar. Ultimately, Laur saw the human's bones reach impossible angles, until, finally, it gave way.

Bellator jumped away from him just as the human's arm began to limp from his elbow and pummelled him with blows until, finally, the human collapsed, blood pouring from his nose.

It wasn't glorious and it reminded Laur of actual combat, as the fight's conclusion left many in the audience exhausted on account of how intense and close it had been. Indeed, Laur wondered if the fight could have ever been possibly correctly predicted or if it had always been a coin toss, to be determined by the most minute of decisions and even the faintest luck.

As the remani let go of the limp human, only to trip and fall himself, the announcer declared him the winner and Big White roared approvingly. 'Well, at least I won some of my money back!'

Really complex betting strategies you seem to have... 'Glad you did!' Laur felt the need to smoke a cigarette after what just happened. He pulled out his pack and pulled out a single cigarette.

Big White noticed, out of the corner of his eye. In a remarkably smooth gesture, he moved one hand towards his pack. Laur's reflexes kicked in and he immediately put the pack away, knocking into the ursai's poised fingers as he did so.

'Beg your pardon?' he asked, locking eyes with Big White, only just now realizing what he might be doing.

The ursai locked gazes with him for a moment and Laur felt his body tingle in worry. He was in no mood to start something here, so he decided to defuse the situation quickly. 'You can have one, Mr. White! Yet, I am going to need you to ask. *Now and always.*'

Big White stared at him with dead eyes for a few moments, his hand still outstretched. 'Could I please have a cigarette?'

'Of course you can!' Laur offered him the pack, opening it with one hand and knocking his ring finger into the bottom, causing a single cigarette to jut upwards. 'Will you be needing a lighter?'

'No, thank you!' the bearman said calmly, pulling out his own lighter and slowly sparking the cigarette. He blew out a puff of white smoke as he seemed to mull things over for a moment. 'You know, you're different from all the other Republicans I've seen over the years.'

'How so?'

'The other ones...' Big White looked around and Laur realized that the ursai did, indeed, consider this arena to be an exposed area with far too many onlookers. It made him feel safe, yet now he wondered what it was that he was about to say that required discretion. '... the other ones offered me a lot. They offered... *heavy* things.'

'You didn't believe them?'

'Oh, I believed them! Yet, I doubted they could deliver. That thing we talked about – with the *power*?'

You mean the power leeching devices we helped smuggle into the city in the time since we last spoke... Laur nodded.

'My associates tell me that your people moved quickly.'

And yours were a bit slow in paying... 'You thought we wouldn't move at all?'

'It was a possibility, though I was more concerned as to whether or not you would move... *purposefully*. Your people made quite an impression!'

'I'm sorry your impression of us wasn't held high by those that came before us.'

'Oh, you misunderstand me! My impression of you was very high since it was based *primarily* on those that came before you.' Big White moved his jaw, as he rubbed one of his upper canines with one of his lower ones. 'Everyone else that came before you was – how should I say it? – *honourable*. Yet, honourable men can often be... *lacking*, particularly in their understanding of things. *You...* you are...'

'I am a *man of honour*,' Laur interrupted. 'And you have much to learn yet before you can make statements such as that, Mr. White!' Laur bit into his cheek before refusing to lock eyes with the ursai. 'I understand that some things pertaining to my methods and my character might seem surprising to you, yet I would insist you refrain from comparing me to my predecessors, at least not until we've had the chance to know each other more.' This time it was Laur that leaned in, as he continued. 'Let me explain one or two things to you right now, so as to avoid any future errors in communication.'

'First things first: I am your *potential* friend. Whether you know that now is of no consequence. It will not change my actions. Your people had power in this city before my people learned to wipe their arses with something softer than coarse rocks. I will not dare to suggest to you that I am some miracle worker, come to deliver you race into prosperity, since it is my certain understanding that, if such deliverance would have been feasible in so little time, you would have achieved it yourself! However, I will inform you of abilities at my disposal (some of which you have become aware of) that may allow me to help you further your own objectives. Objectives which, to my understanding, are in alignment with our own. Is that, at least, clear?'

'It will be, once you tell me of all the other pieces of information you now seem so keen on sharing with me!'

'Do not ever speak with anything but reverence of my predecessors, my countrymen, my men and my friends, ever again!' Laur phrased it as a veiled threat, yet he kept his tone quiet. 'A day may come, Mr. White, when you may become my friend yet, right now, you are merely my prospective friend. You strike me as a man concerned with the value of things. Hence, I wouldn't be surprised if you have been wondering what the value of my friendship is.'

'I have,' Big White replied, his eyes appearing to be stern.

'Well, know only that if you were my friend and someone came up to me and told me that they thought of you as lacking, in any way, I would respond as I am responding now and bear in mind that my reaction is heavily tempered by the fact that *I do like* you, Mr, White, and I think that this might very well be the beginning of a beautiful friendship!'

Big White studied him for a moment, his black eyes ever-unblinking. He took a puff of his cigarette as he leaned back deep into his seat, his gaze still fixed on Laur, though his eyes did seem to wander at one point. 'I like you too, Mr. Pop! I like you a great deal... You're an interesting man. When I was coming up, I met many men that would chop a man's hand off for trying to take something from them without their permission. I've also met many men that would pull the tongue out of any man to speak ill of their friends. Yet, I can't say I've met many men that would do both. At least not any as composed as yourself...' The ursai seemed to ponder his next words.

Good... Good, if you really are doing that. I've got you right where I want you, no matter what you say, if I've really got you pondering something carefully!

The ursai slowly spoke, 'If I was the Peacekeeper of the City of Shangri, or a High Lord of your own Alliance, *you* would seem to be a very poor choice for an Ambassador, if I may say so.'

Laur allowed it, simply because he wanted to know where he was going with this.

'All the men and women that came before you were... *worthy* of the respect you so fiercely insist upon. Especially your fellow Terrans, who appeared to me as the dignitaries of an honourable warrior race. You, however, *stick out*! You seem to me to be... *of a different nature*. And that's what I worry about! That's what I don't understand! Why would the very same people that sent all of those dignitaries before you (all of which seemed to fit the part so well) send someone like you?'

'We've had this discussion before.' *And not just with you...*

'When you made that analogy with the heat?'

'So I recall.'

'If you're supposed to be the heat, why are you so *cold*?' the bearman pointed out, expertly.

Laur was surprised by his words, yet his eyes wandered to the ursai that had appeared on the pathway leading to the arena.

'Introducing the defending champion of the heavyweight division, Big Pussy Malanga!!!'

A cold wind swept over him. He saw it, in that moment:

The gates of the ursai citadel of Barlog. He saw it as that cold wind of that ice world blew over him and went into his bones like all those years ago. He remembered the gates begin to open. He remembered a lone ursai emerge from within. He remembered how he looked exactly like this ursai here in the arena now.

'What do you mean 'cold'?' he asked, to divert attention from his reaction to the heavyweight champion.

'You strike me as a man of cold calculation; of hard truths and plain action. You talk a lot, yes, yet it all seems to be towards some purpose in your head. To tell you the truth, Mr. Pop, I've made my fortunes by being able to tell exactly what the man next to me is thinking and I'd be damned if I can tell what's going on through that head of yours!' Big White leaned in, and he saw the hairs on his face move much the same way the ursai Chairman's face had moved on Barlog four decades before. 'That's what makes me nervous about you!'

Laur heard his words, yet he also heard the fluttering of flags behind him. The thousand banners of Terra and Kalimaste, as well as the standards of the Vigilant and a few even of Moria

Some, banners of the living. Many, banners of the dead.

He saw the light glint off orcish armour and the wall of armoured men that stood arrayed in front of tanks and the artillery behind them, as they stood assembled before the great fortress in the ice, and the lone ursai walked towards them in the cold sunset of his white world.

'You want to know what I want and you want to be certain of it?' he asked his host in the here and now.

'As much as any man can know anything for certain.'

He felt the ice crackle underneath his feet as he walked towards the two men that had already emerged to receive the lone ursai.

Fuck it! I might as well weave this fucking episode into the conversation. 'You scare me, do you know that?'

'W-what?' Big White let loose a strange smile.

'Have you ever been to war, Mr. White?' he asked.

'Not in the manner in which I think you are referring.'

Laur grunted. 'I fought your people once...' he said, as his memory appeared next to Djibril al-Sayid and Cingeto Braca.

Big White's face twitched slightly.

Tread fucking carefully here, Mr. White!

Though I myself should probably be a bit less provocative... 'Your race is a menace on the battlefield. Clad in power armour. Your daggers, the size of our swords; your swords, the size of our spears. Your helms, the size of a man's chestplate. Pauldrons the size of car wheels! And the fighting itself? Speed I couldn't even comprehend, at first. I remember looking at you and thinking: *"How the hell can they be so big and move that fast?"* Your strength... When I first saw one of your kinsmen swing a mace the size of a tree like it was a balloon, I must confess that my knees went a little weak. Stamina? I once saw one of your race take a tank shell to the chest and then sprint towards the tank and punch the fucking barrel!' he jabbed the air in front of him, to emphasize the image. 'He broke the fucking rotation mechanism!'

'But, to be honest with you, those not why you and your kind scare me and *those* are not even the most terrifying memories I have of your people!' Laur took a puff of his cigarette, as the gigantic bearman climbed into the ring before him and slowly raised his arms, as if to show that he could hold the world on his shoulders, like the titan Atlas of myth. 'It was your people's coldness that I always found to be so striking! It was... I remember looking at your people once, from a distance, observing them, studying them... and I remember thinking that they seemed to be a people that knew only of the colours black and white, yet not of grey.' Laur smiled. 'Very much like you now say of me, in some strange way...'

Seeing the orc made him stiffen up.

Dignified. Stoic. Head held high, yet also humble. He wore no jewelry, his body unadorned by any mark of valour or courage, whilst only on his forehead lay a single symbol whose meaning did not know. The orcish rhonin was large for one of his race burdened by shame and exile and his gait bore no difference from the slow walk of Cingeto Braca.

Laur saw him now, walking across the field of blue ice, as white powder twisted in the wind across the twilight of the golden rays of a distant sun. Before him stood the great ursai warrior, clad in armour forged in the heart of the world he now defended. The champion of Barlog raised his two great warhammers and rammed them together, unleashing a thunder that made Laur's bones shiver.

Cingeto drew his sword.

'We made a deal with them and I must confess that I didn't think they'd keep up their end of the bargain and, yet, they did. It was then that I realized what the coldness was!' Laur puffed on his cigarette for effect, yet, in truth, he was hiding. 'It was *seriousness*, Mr. White! It was that seriousness of a man who cares about something very much. A man devoted in his entire being to something he is... I cannot even use the word '*passionate*', because it is beneath that which I am trying to describe!'

'There's no need. I understand.'

Do you now? 'Good. Then understand this: I intend to make you into a High Lord of the Republican Alliance. Yet, first, I intend to make you a High Lord of the City of Shangri. And I say that *coldly*! In regards to the standing of this city, I can only say one thing: we have watched and we have waited; now, we must act! You might not understand why. You might not understand our exact motives. Yet, know this: our word is cold steel untainted by the passing of time! I promise you that now and I tell you this: you will never believe me until the moment you do! Until then, we are both acting on trust.'

Big White's gigantic head slowly nodded. 'What do you propose our next action together shall be?'

'I am not proposing anything right now. You are the one here who understands the situation. You know what needs to be done. So, you tell me...'

The ursai was silent for a moment, the cold wheels of his mind spinning methodically towards a thought he had (hopefully) contemplated before meeting with the Terran Ambassador. 'You did a good job bringing all those power-snatchers into the City so quickly on those allied ships of yours. If you could, perhaps, scale-up operations and consider assisting with other goods, we could have at our disposal all the funds we would need to push the Urheimat out of the streets and regain all the territory we used to hold before they arrived!'

Laur nodded. 'It is done! You will hear from my people!' Then he got up, shook the ursai's hand and left. 'I understand that you've received our invitation to the even we are hosting?'

'I'll get a derogation just for it!' The ursai frowned as he shook his hand and Laur sensed some irritation in him. 'You're not going to stay for the last fight?' Big White asked, just as Laur gestured for his Hajduks to follow him back to their vehicles.

'I already know how it ends,' he said, without turning back to see the orc knock out the ursai with his first punch. He didn't hear the thud, as the bearman fell to the floor, ushering in a moment of silence, followed by uproar and cheering. He didn't see the orc celebrate by going over to his corner and hugging his team.

Laur saw only the blood of the lone ursai Chairman dripping from Cingeto Braca's blade, as his body fell to the ground upon the ice of his homeworld of Barlog.

Chapter IX

A Bump in the Night

Silvia saw a flash of light and then she opened her eyes to behold darkness. She had been dreaming of goats eating cheese when something had snapped back into wakefulness.

What time is it?

She reached for her phone, only to find it to be closed, as if it had no power.

Shit...

Shivers went up her spine as it jerked into action. She drew her pistol from where it lay hidden between the mattress and the bedframe, as she rushed to pick up her night jacket from where it always lay neatly folded on a bedside table. She had a chance to check her mechanical watch, a golden Oyster Perpetual gifted to her by Elena after her promotion to Centurion, its thin hands just phosphorescent enough for her eyes to see that it was two in the morning. *Literally the best time to ambush us, as likely more than half of us are in REM sleep.*

She never turned the lights on, yet she did put her fingers close to her face and searched for it. *How did it feel like? How did light feel like? Oh, like that! Is it here? Is anything like it here?*

The darkness answered silently and Silvia put her hand away to pick up a dagger from one of her dresser. She sheathed it within her jacket, before quietly rushing out of her bedroom. Just as she reached the stairway that lead to the living room, she paused, only to hear a knock on wood. Then two more. *If it's not Mira, I might be fucked...*

'*Apples and Pears?*' she asked, just loud enough for her roommate to hear, if it really was *her* signalling her presence.

'*Stairs!*' Mira responded softly.

Thank Christ!

'Turn on the lamplight!' Mira instructed.

Silvia moved in the darkness towards the nearby lamplight, fuelled by short bursts of electricity, not by a continuous stream: a failsafe against EMP attacks, which this almost clearly was. She pressed the button, as she closed her eyes, preventing them from being blinded.

The warm rays cast a dim light over the room, yet it was just enough to allow Silvia to see Mira, scanning the room below whilst behind the barrel of a ridiculously oversized handgun. Mira, also in her nightclothes and wearing her Ghazi jacket, nodded that they would descend. The two Terrans quickly, yet diligently, checked their room for intruders. Just as they signalled to each other that their chambers had not been breached, Mira rushed towards a nearby cupboard and began loading up an AK-47. 'The scratching was Lorgar. He woke me up and I felt it immediately.'

'I felt nothing! I just woke up,' Silvia explained, as she pulled out a shotgun from behind a stack of umbrellas.

Mira moved in right next to her, as they stood to the sides of the door leading to the hallway beyond. She signalled that she would open and Silvia would clear.

Agreed. It's why I got the shotgun... Silvia placed herself directly in front of the door, as Mira bent on one knee and unlocked it. Before pulling the door handle in-words.

'*Leicester*?!' Technowolf's voice rang out from beyond the doorway.

'*Square*!' Silvia responded.

Technowolf quickly made the walk from the entrance of his living room to Silvia and Mira's. 'Felt it?'

'In a sense,' Silvia responded.

'It's probably ours,' he said, as he walked into their room and began peering through the long hallway to the stairway below.

'Nick?' Silvia asked.

'I didn't check. If he felt it, he'll wake up too,' Tech explained.

Well, that won't do. There had been no alarm sounded yet. 'I'll ring the soft mechanical alarm,' she said, just as the soft mechanical alarm began to ring.

There was another noise. A double-knock on wood. '*Dogs until death*!' a Romanian voice asked, from the darkness of the stairwell.

Cosmin. '*And beyond*!!' Silvia replied and Cosmin immediately rushed up the stairway, flanked by two other Hajduks. *Merdenea and Popeye*. 'All good?' she asked in Romanian, as Cosmin walked briskly towards her.

'Not really! The Hogwarts burst,' he explained, as entering the room.

Ohhh, shit. 'What do you mean 'it burst'?'

'*Burst*! Like when they get when you cancel them!' Cosmin explained, his face laid-back, yet also serious, as it always was. *Even in the heart of battle...*

'Was it turned on?' *It's Ela's watch!*

'Elia said it activated on its own, ran for about two minutes, then it burst.'

'The Shangrians must have detected and deactivated it,' Tech concluded.

'Who triggered it?' Silvia asked.

'Not us! Ela said it turned on, full-cycle, in the blink of an eye. It overloaded and the controls froze. The EMP knocked it out, as well as our tech. Inside's clear so far. We still have a few people that haven't reported, but there's no indication that there's been a breach.' Silvia didn't even have to ask for a report.

'Outside?'

'Outside's clear; *so far.*' Just as Cosmin spoke the words, the regular lights turned back on in the great hall below, and yellow light began to pierce the foliage of the great tree underneath its dome.

'Everyone report!' Radu's voice rang out through the building's intercom.

'How's the boss?' Cosmin asked.

Silvia, Tech and Mira exchange glances. *No one's checked.* She immediately turned around, walked straight towards a hidden compartment behind a painting and pulled out the spare key to Laur's office. As they were all about to return to the hallway, she heard the sound of something hard and... maybe *hollow?*... hit the floor, followed by the scratching sound from her dreams, just much louder.

Silvia immediately dropped the key and aimed her pistol at the sound of the noise, which happened to be the foot of the stairs leading up to their bedrooms, right behind one of the couches in front of the TV screen.

'Lorgar?' Mira's voice asked, a sense of hope and dread dancing through her voice.

From behind the couch Silvia was aiming at, a great bushy tail of black hair and orange specks sprang unexpectedly, yet quickly collapsed as the sound of scratching once more could be heard. Silva began lowering her firearm, yet, for a moment, regretted her decision to relax. She could now properly see the cat's shadow making its way on wobbly legs from behind the couch, illuminated by one of the recently activated lights. *Why is he so clumsy?*

The answer quickly become apparent as the cat turned a corner, glanced at first to Silvia, then towards the doorway, were Mira's wide eyes met his own.

'Milady, I feel dizzy,' he announced, his voice slippery and his eyes tired.

At that exact moment, Nick appeared in the doorway behind Mira, clearly having just woken up. 'Why the fuck does the cat have horns?'

Like ram's horns they were, though white as marble, with a subtle pink at their base, like those of youngling of some misbegotten race of demonic felines. They grew from right above the cat's brow and curved backwards and, eventually, outwards, circling his ears and arriving right beneath them, as they finally swirled inwards. It was hard to catch a clear look of them, as Lorgar's head was moving, ever so slowly, to his right, until the cat eventually lost balance and plummeted face first into the floorboards, causing a strange *thud*, as cat-horn met wood. The sound was followed by scratching as he struggled to regain his balance by using his paws, legs, and even his tail.

'Lorgar...' Mira began, slowly walking towards her cat. 'What woke you up?'

'Itching, Milady!' the cat began. 'Horrid and incessant itching... Milady, it still itches!' The cat lowered its head and began rubbing its forehead – or, rather, *attempting* – to scratch his forehead, since his horns kept getting in the way.

'I see!' Mira said, as she got down on one knee next to her beloved pet. 'Did you have a bad dream?'

'Actually, I was dreaming of a wonderful nap I once took in the gardens in Mecca!'

Cats dream of other times they slept well?

'I see... you didn't dream of goats or...'

'*Milady!*' the cat shot up. 'Have I actually sprouted horns, as the gypsy says?' he asked, his voice a blur of agitation.

Mira swallowed as she tried to smile, likely concerned with the feline's reaction upon learning the truth. '...*Yes*... Yes, you have!'

Lorgar's jaw dropped and began to move, yet at first no words came out. 'I mistook the tzigoiner's words for jests! Have I truly?'

He turned his wide-eyed gaze towards an equally wide-eyed Silvia, who nodded.

Lorgar turned back to Mira, stared at her, then swiftly darted from floor, to couch, to table, then up to the larger table in the middle of the room, then finally towards the floor again before the large mirror that his lady had tastefully placed on one section of empty wall. 'Milady?'

Mira had tried to catch him and she now stood, her hands before her, as her fingers caressed themselves in worry. 'Yes?'

'Milady…' the cat's words trailed off as it studied itself. 'MILADY, I LOOK FABULOUS!'

'*Jesus Christ…*' Nick muttered.

'I look… *fierce*!!! Like the harbinger of a thousand years of darkness and calamity!'

Mira fought back a chuckle while Silvia sighed. *If it's just Lorgar, that's fine, we can survive…*

'*Sil*! Key!' Nick beckoned and Silvia turned around, making straight for her General's office door. As her hand, clutching the spare key, began to rapidly descend towards the knob, the door flung open, revealing an empty office beyond.

'*Heads*!' Laur Pop's voice asked in Romanian.

'*And Tails*!' Silvia answered.

Her General's head peered from behind one of his doorframes. Upon seeing his men, Pop emerged fully through the doorway. Silvia could see him holster his pistol behind his back, as she moved out of the way. 'Well, come on, what's happened?' he asked, his eyes clearly going from concern to annoyance.

'Hogwarts' burst,' Cosmin informed him.

'Why'd you turn it on?' Pop asked, though he likely already knew the answer.

'We didn't! It turned on by itself, ran, then burst,' the Centurion continued.

'Anything else?' the General asked.

'No, sir! All seems to be clear…' Cosmin's words trailed off very subtly and Pop noticed.

'What?' Pop asked, growing visibly annoyed. He turned to each of them in turn, just as Lorgar wobbled out of his living room. The cat walked into the hallway, under the scrutiny of everyone present, as Pop's men readied themselves for an outburst. Sensing some upcoming moment of interest, Lorgar sat down on his feline behind (albeit not as gingerly as he normally would have) and began to inspect them all.

Silvia's eyes had darted between the freshly mutated feline and her recently arrived General, until Pop finally acknowledged her presence. 'Anything else? Other than *him*?'

'Not that we can tell. So far, everything seems clear.'

'Good…' Pop nodded to himself before beginning to clear his throat.

His men were silent as they waited for him to speak.

He didn't and, after an awkward silence, he pointed with his thumb to the office behind him. 'I'm just getting my voice ready for *that*!'

The phone on Laur Pop's desk started to ring and he began to slowly began to walk towards it. Silvia knew her General well and she knew his habits and mannerisms much better than she knew the man which presented them. Thus, she did not know what was going through his head, though she could tell that he was doing his best to fully wake-up.

He's getting ready for a performance.

Pop reached the side of his desk where his phone vibrated and rang insistently, took a deep breath, picked it up and placed it to his ear.

'Was it you?' he asked immediately.

The phone was set to private calling and Silvia could not make out the voice on the other end, though she could tell that there was a reply.

Pop continued, 'I see... No... No need... *No*... Communication and trust are the foundation of our relationship... Yes... Yes, of course... That goes without saying! ... Very well... Goodnight!' The call must have not taken more than thirty seconds before Laur hung up, tossed the phone onto his desk, causing a loud clattering noise as it knocked over glasses, screens and other stationery. He stared at his floor for a moment before turning towards his men.

'I take it that it's the matrix that's broken?' he asked calmly.

Cosmin replied, just as Radu and Ela came rushing into their General's office. 'I haven't –'

Ela interrupted him. 'Yes, it's completely collapsed!'

'Recoverable?'

She shook her head.

Damn...

'Very well, have the broken matrix detached, then make sure that it is completely dismantled and destroyed' Pop began staring at his carpet again. 'How loud was it?'

'Loud enough for any half-arsed sensor within a thousand kilometres of here to pick it up.' Ela replied.

'Some of the neighbours' alarms have triggered,' Radu informed them.

'*Stick* my dick in it...' Their General scratched his head.

It was all over the news the next day. A psionic event had occurred in the Convent Garden neighbourhood, likely originating somewhere in the vicinity (and probably from within) the Republican Embassy. The Shangri Security System had detected the disturbance around two minutes after its commencement and had proceeded to bombard the area with negation spells and EMP blasts. Publicly, the Alliance denied any involvement in the event, instead claiming that the bombardment had been unwarranted and that irreparable damage had been done to the building's infrastructure. Privately, Pop spent the next day on the phone apologising to a long line of Shangri officials and promising that such a thing would never happen again.

The mood in the Embassy turned grim, as Laur ordered that the Convent Garden Hajduks suspend all of their clandestine activities until the whole situation blew over. Their commitment to Big White was taken over by Gigi, Josip, Bojana and Lejla, who had scrambled to establish new smuggling routes for future Republican contraband. Nick was the only exception to this rule, as he had developed a budding friendship with Anwar, and it became his role to liaise with their contacts in the Cooperatives and coordinate their joint ventures with the other Hajduks.

Nevertheless, most of the Romanian and Kalo Hajduks hunkered down in their stronghold and they began to grow bored, anxious and restless. Silvia spent most of her days now checking in on her men and making sure that no one was going too crazy. Pop, Tech, Basenji, Nick and Mira, upon occasion still ventured outside, just to keep up appearances, with the Hajduks themselves only exiting the building to go on patrol or as messengers to the other Hajduks.

Essentially quarantined inside the Embassy, they did the most Hajduk thing that could be expected: they started day-drinking. Very soon, it became something of a challenge to find a single sober Hajduk within the two hundred of Pop's men garrisoned at the Convent Garden Embassy and when Hajduks drank gambling always followed, as was tradition at this point. The Hajduks never really ever stopped drinking, fornicating or engaging in games of chance with one another, yet Silvia had seen this scene before during their many years spent together and she knew what lay down the path for them.

Boredom was the worst drug that could infect her comrades and, when bored, the Hajduks had a tendency of becoming a menace to both themselves and those around them.

The Grumpy Legion.

Infighting never occurred; Silvia took great care of that and her men always appreciated her efforts. After all, they served in *the Lord Inquisitor*'s Legion and the architect of *the Last Fitna* did not need prove to them how willing he was to reassign some bellicose Hajduk to some suicide mission, just to remove 'a problem', as such men became in his eyes. Yet, their complaints were many, as men imprisoned within their own house had a tendency to question their condition.

'They've lost the trail,' Ela announced.

'Are we certain of this?' Silvia asked.

'They seem to be certain of it,' her fellow Centurion confirmed the worst.

They found themselves in Silvia's living room. Mira was away with Lorgar in Nick and Tech's room, doing God-knows-what to relieve their own boredom. It was three in afternoon and, like clockwork, Radu, Cosmin and Ela had arrived in Silvia's office to hold a 'sporadic meeting' which had now become a daily occurrence.

'How can you say that with such certainty?' Radu asked Ela.

'Tasha and Reli came by today at eleven to drop off paperwork. They said Bojana had no clue as to where Otto Benga has fled. Tasha said that Ljubi and Mario met with Armando and Iris in a dockyard cafe yesterday and they confirmed that the Colonial Constabulary informed the Shqiptari that the Port Authrity could guarantee that Otto Benga never left the City. Helikopter and Fuad were at Sanjak only yesterday and they confirmed that they've been watching his wife and kids and he hasn't made any contact with them.'

'Alright, so they know he's in the city and they know he's not where he usually is... so where the fuck is he?' Radu asked.

'That's what I'm saying, Radu: they have no fucking idea! He's somewhere in the city, hiding.'

'Yeah, but... what the fuck? Did he just snap out of existence?' he insisted.

'There are literally a trillion people in this place, Radu. If he wants, he could literally become like a needle in a haystack!' Ela explained.

'Then bring a magnet!' Radu instructed.

'Oh, yeah? What's the magnet in this analogy?'

Radu seemed to be caught slightly off-guard and Silvia smiled to herself. 'I dunno... me and Cosmin found that Quint the Cunt in a matter of hours and they've been looking for this fucking Otto Benga for weeks now. It's becoming–'

'Quint of Carth-Fountainhead had no idea you were coming for him! There have been Terran Ambassadors before and none of them snatched him from his house on the first day!' Ela cut in. 'Otto Benga *knew* when Quint went missing that someone was out to get him. He had time to make a run for it!' she reasoned.

'So what do we do now?' Cosmin had finally spoken, though not to his bickering colleagues, but to Silvia, who forced her satisfaction inwards, hiding it from her colleagues.

When Laur had instructed her to select Romanian Hajduks for promotion to Centurion, she had immediately proposed these three Hajduks that stood before her now.

Elia was a literal wizard when it came to technology, having long established herself as the preeminent expert on all things scientific and/or magical amongst the Hajduks. That alone did not warrant promotion, though her temperament did, as she was quite agreeable, especially for a Hajduk. Her men respected her, her fellow Centurions saw in her a dependable counterparty, Laur enjoyed her obedience and Silvia... Ela saw in Silvia an older, much wiser sister, despite the fact that Ela herself was twenty years Silvia's senior.

Radu and Cosmin were the best of friends, with a relationship that mirrored Nick and Silvia's. Radu was gregarious and quite comical at times and he was known to entertain his fellow Hajduks with long-winded stories about some absurdity or another. He had a lot of initiative, especially for a Hajduk, which made him useful since he could act independently. He was also quite nationalistic, though within reason, which meant that he had a habit of encouraging friendly competition among the various Hajduk national contingents.

In truth, Radu wouldn't have gotten very far were it not for his best friend, Cosmin, who was his exact opposite. He was quiet and serious, cared little for the differences between Romanians, Serbs, Shqiptari, or any other of their nationalities, and was always one to quickly squash any form of dissent in the ranks. Cosmin was also the more martially gifted of the two and exceptionally selfless when it came to risking his life to save others, even for a Terran Avenger Legionnaire.

Independently, each of them was an officer worthy of the Terran Avenger Legions. Together, they were quite formidable, though they all still looked up to Silvia, each in their own way. *They know they need me.*

That was one of the many lessons Laur Pop had taught her:

In any organization, there are those that are needed and the ones that work. Always be the one that is needed. Those that work can always be replaced.

'We hold tight,' Silvia replied. 'Do nothing. The Dawnbreak Gala is the day after tomorrow. We can focus our energies on that! After the event's conclusion, as per Pop's instruction, we go back to our initial approach, meaning that we will once again be allowed to go out for fresh air.'

'Good!' Radu said, as he got up. 'I've already done my part for that!'

'So have I,' Cosmin pointed out as he also got up.

Elia was quick to chip in, 'We still have some names that have yet to confirm their plus ones!'

'Fine! We'll run checks on them once they confirm!' Radu replied, before turning to Cosmin. 'You wanna play some *League*?'

'Yeah man, let's go play *League*! Ela, you wanna support?'

'Yup!'

'Great! Let's go!' Radu paused, before turning to Silvia. 'You wanna hang out too or...?'

'No, I still have errands left to run...' *Gotta go talk to Mira and see if she's handled catering.*

'You ok?' Ela asked, causing Radu and Cosmin to stop in their tracks and look to Silvia for an answer.

'What?' *the hell are you on about?*

'You've been trapped in here for two weeks!' Ela pointed out.

Silvia understood what she meant. She was the only one to have never left the Embassy for any reason, not even a walk, ever since Pop had them all lock down. Nick went out almost daily and he had even started bringing Mira along on his trips to Anwar and the ursai. Mira herself concocted a plethora of reasons to go out on her 'spirit quest'; reasons which Pop, for someone, had elected take at face value, despite clearly understanding them to be deceptive and vague. Radu, Cosmin and Ela had all been dispatched on missions from or with Pop. Only Silvia had truly been trapped in this urban fortress she had been charged with defending. Everyone else just came and went, just far less often than they did before.

'Yes, I'm alright!' *Oh shit! No! Gotta sound more convincing! They'll think I'm weak just because it is, actually, kinda getting to me a little!* 'I like it indoors and, to be honest with you, I look out the window and I see way more people per square meter outside than inside.' She had learned little tricks like that from Laur Pop. *Give them bits of different truths and have them piece together a truth of their own making.* 'It seems easier to get fresh air in here than out there!'

'That's true.'

Ela agrees.

'I still haven't gotten used to it...'

Radu confesses.

'None of us have.'

Cosmin muses.

Silvia remembered another one of Pop's tricks. *Make them talk about themselves. People like that. They'll pay attention to that!* 'There weren't crowds like this on Old Earth?'

Radu replied, 'There were, but not like this. I don't even understand why they do it! 99% of this place lies either abandoned or ignored. All the people just cuddle up into these few pockets.'

'Yeah, even here in Convent Garden, where it's relatively free, you sometimes get dizzy on the street!' Ela pointed out.

Good thing I don't go out then. 'Good to know. It's going to get crowded here at the party.'

'How many are there invited again?' Radu asked.

Silvia was slightly bothered by the fact that he didn't know the answer himself, as one of the organizers. 'Over one thousand...'

'My dick...' Radu whistled.

'We only have the worry about one or two,' Silvia sought to be serious, yet reassuring. 'My understanding is that RSVPs come in primarily on the day before the event, as well as in the intervening hours. We'll hold a meeting about the guestlist on the day of the event and we'll have another quick rundown right before the first guests are set to arrive.'

Her colleagues nodded, though she did notice that it took a while for Radu to nod.

Gotta remember to not undermine him with all the orders! Radu's a good man, but he is proud. I should make a joke... 'In the meantime, let's try to make sure no one starts playing Russian Roulette, no one starts a barbecue on the roof, no one...' Silvia smirked. '... you know what I mean...'

Ela snorted. 'We do...'

Balkan bullshit... 'It's just three more days! I think we can manage!' she said encouragingly.

'Heh! I lived through COVID. I'll live through this!' Radu quipped, before departing her office together with Cosmin and Ela.

Good energy at the end... I think that's not a situation I have to worry about... at least not if I keep an eye on it...

Now... where the fuck is Mira?

Spirit Quest? No, she's here! I saw her earlier when she said that... I forget what she said...

Ah! She's with Nick and Tech in their room! She took Lorgar with them too and I think Basenji's also there...

Silvia got up from her seat after finishing up some of Pop's reports, then made her way purposefully towards Nick and Tech's apartment. She reached the door thinking about what tasks were left for the day, and knocked once. She was met with no answer. She knocked again. Still no answer. *Strange... these are soundproof, though they're designed to respond to knocking... Tech must be away... It's only Nick in they're in there and he can be such an airhead at times...* She reached for the doorhandle and opened the door.

Take a line every night,
Guaranteed to blow your mind!

She was met with the thundering roar of guitar and bass as the music of Jon Bon Jovi erupted from within.

I see you out on the streets,
Calling for a wild time.

Nick and Tech's living room had a completely different aesthetic to the one she shared with Mira. Whilst theirs felt welcoming, yet also stylishly organized, theirs was much more cozy, and far more chaotically tasteful. While she and her roommate shared quarters that invested a great deal of effort in not appearing oppressively well structured, theirs was a mad, yet appealing, blend of the two men's wildly different personalities and interests, which somehow managed to come together in a clashing choice of designs.

So you sit home alone,
'Cause there's nothing left that you can do!

Both men enjoyed music and that had been the binding force of their shared accommodation. Whilst Silvia and Mira had furnished their room with harmonious little set-ups, like a dinning space where guests could also share stories together over snacks and desserts or a circle of sofas and armchairs surrounding a quaint little coffee table, where Silvia could sow, Lorgar could lounge and Mira could doze off while watching TV shows, Nick and Tech had transformed their living room into a recording studio.

There's only pictures hung in the shadows
Left there to look at you

There was a drum-set, where a shirtless Tech was beating away a 1980's drumbeat, as well as a mic stand where Nick was doing a remarkably authentic cover of the song they played together. Sitting-up at full height, Basenji held an electric guitar, which he seemed to be quite adept at playing

You know she likes the lights
At night on the neon Broadway signs

Mira spotted her surprised roommate and beckoned for her to come in and shut the door, just as she prepared her instrument for an epic bass solo.

She don't really mind.
It's only love she hoped to find
Oh, she's a little runaway
Daddy's girl learned fast
All those things she couldn't say
Ooh, she's a little runaway

One could hear nothing for a moment, as the music and Nick's singing reached a standstill for split second. Then Silvia heard it and turned to look to the sound of the newest symphony. Lorgar was sitting on the seat facing Technowolf's piano, one paw extended to a specific key, as he quickly tapped away, letting loose a continuous crescendo of a single sharp note.

Then Mira moved and slapped her bass expertly with one hand, causing a thunderous roar of energy to spread through the room.

And then again.

And again.

And again. Faster this time.

She then jumped into the rhythm of the song, carrying it forward, as Nick finished of the lyrics in a youthful haze of times gone by, yet still alive within the hearts of those that remained.

As the Convent Garden band was about to put down their instruments, the sound of a single piano king being repeatedly swatted rang out once more.

'Lorgar!' Mira began.

Lorgar ignored her.

'*Lorgar*! The song is–' she walked towards her cat, which refused to stop. Upon reaching him, she attempted to pick him up by the armpits, only for the feline to hiss angrily.

'Milady! *Milady*, no! The music! It courses through me! I feel it!' he wailed as Mira placed him on the ground and immobilized him, letting him have his little hissy fit. Silvia had grown quite used to this sight, as Mira would 'punish' Lorgar's excessive mischief by grabbing two of his paws in each of her own hands, while the feline would attempt to escape whilst on his back. These attempts were both playful and bloodthirsty, and Silvia never really knew which feelings crossed Lorgar's mind at such times.

Silvia turned, smiling, from this 'violent' little affair, just as Tech was passing her by. She realized he had been sweating, as his shitless chest glistened in the light as he almost bumped into her.

'Sorry, *ehhh*...' Tech mumbled. 'That was too intense for me! The vibes... the vibes were good!'

'You guys are getting pretty good!' Silvia observed.

'We've had a lot of time,' Tech commented. 'You're here with any change in policy?' he asked, looking to see if she had spoken with Pop.

'Catering arrangements, actually! With Mira! I thought *you* might have some idea regarding the lifting of the lockdown,' Silvia said truthfully.

'The official policy is still to wait for the Dawnbreak Gala, when our special guest will grant us an informal pardon.'

The Peacekeeper. 'Has he confirmed?'

'If you don't know anything, then neither do I!' Tech replied, a smile on his face, yet a pensive glint in his eye.

'Milady! Cease this intransigence!!!' Lorgar meowed particularly loudly.

'*Oh*!' Nick whistled from the seat he had taken, as he puffed his waterpipe. 'I thought you liked keeping your ass up in the air!'

As the comment flew from Nick's lips, Lorgar managed to break free of Mira's grip, and he darted across the floor, making straight for Nick, who managed to raise his hand just in time to stop Lorgar from going for a slice of his throat. As the cat bounced off Nick's fist, it flew in the air and landed on the floor next to Basenji and shouted. 'Shut up you fucking inbred gypsy bastard! Your breath spreads the tuberculosis! All you people have the fucking hepatitis!'

No one even was even able to respond at first, since everyone was fixated on Nick's hand. Lorgar had gashed the back of his hand, causing a thin sheet of flesh to be parted and blood began to appear. To wound scabbed over quickly, as only a single drop did not coalesce into the thin strip of scar tissue which would disappear within a few hours, as Nick's enhanced healing factor would make his body forget that he had ever received such negligible cut.

But Terran blood had still been split, as Nick himself looked at the drop lingering in the corner of the small mauling Lorgar had administered to him.

Nick can legally have him killed.

A man might be forgiven for such a slight injury yet, an animal, even one such as endearing as Lorgar, would never be pardoned for such an attack, even if he had been taunted. She glanced towards the culprit and saw Lorgar cower, clearly realising what he had done. He bent low to the ground, but also raised his ears and made his eyes bigger, as if to appear more adorable and harmless.

Nick eyed the cut and giggled.

Thank, God! Nick loves animals. Of course he would let it go! He wouldn't kill Mira's cat, what the dick...

He looked up at Mira. 'You should get him one of those dog muzzles!'

'And a straight jacket...' Mira commented, as she picked up her pet by the scruff of his neck. 'It appears that we have exhausted all of the civilized courses of action!' she said, as she walked to the nearest window. 'I think...' she said, opening the window, '... that...' she placed Lorgar on the window sill. '... someone needs to cool off!'

She shut the window closed, leaving Lorgar all alone, over ten meters from the ground. He stood on the precipice, gazing down towards the ground, which happened to be quite far from him.

Too far to jump. He looked to the adjacent window sills, noting that they were four meters away, yet they had dastardly decorations blocking any attempt for him to make the jump. Muttering under his breath, he turned to look through the window into the inside and tapped on the one-way, bulletproof and soundproof glass. He did so for quite some time, before turning to the ground for assistance. He spotted two of the Hajduks having a conversation near the entrance to the embassy.

The conversation was likely about him, since they were looking right at him. 'HELP ME!' he shouted towards them.

One of them puffed on his cigarette and replied. 'What have you done to deserve that, Lorgar?'

'Nothing! I merely defended my dignity against those interlopers that would have it tarnished!'

One of the Hajduks turned to the other and remarked, 'He probably called Nick a puked-out gypsy or something... Let 'em be for the time being! If anything, we'll talk to Silvia.'

The other replied. 'Enjoy the view, Lorgar!' before turning around to continue surveying the street for actual threats.

'Fuckin' half-breed mongrel swine...' he muttered, deciding to sit down upon the sill and ponder his next move. *Perhaps if I look really cute and neglected, Milady would take pity on my condition and come back to her senses!* So, he turned to face the window and put on his most Oscar-worthy poor-little-kitty-cat face. He even meowed pitifully a few times.

Something kicked him in the head.

Lorgar stumbled as he fell to the side, managing to regain his balance, just as one of his horns connected with the window sill and the other drifted over the nothingness that lay between him and the distant ground below. He scanned his surroundings quickly and realized he was alone. *Strange... must have been a strong gust of wind... Leaving me out here like this equates to animal cruelty.*

Another knock on the head caused him to hiss loudly as he narrowly avoided falling over the edge.

'SHOW YOURSELF, FIEND!' he shouted into the empty air around him. Lorgar eyed his surroundings, contemplating his next move, until a horrible thought occurred to him. *The skies... Could it be?* He looked towards the sky and was reminded of how strange the sun had become ever since they had spent that wretched month in that apartment with no windows.

Yet, he saw nothing.

Though he did remember that this building had multiple stories. He checked the window sills to his upper right, then to his upper left. Then he remembered that there was likely a window right above him, so he looked up, to see a large black triangle jutting out from the window sill above him. At its centre was yellowish-white circle, which was rapidly expanding.

Lorgar widened his pupils, attempting to better observe this strange phenomena, only to suddenly be blinded, as the white liquid reached its largest size, as well as terminal velocity. He panicked as he scuttled around, trying not to fall off the edge, yet ultimately failing, as he had to climb back up, his eyes stinging. Determined to not be caught blindsided, he scrubbed his eyes with his paw and forced his eyes open. They burned, yet he may yet live. He looked upon his now dirty paw and sniffed it. It smelt strange... almost like... like... there was a hint of...

POOP!!!

Lorgar gagged at the revelation of excrement and immediately threw up.

It's gotten all over my luscious horns as well...

Heaving from the sudden outburst, he leaned with one paw on the sill and began furiously tapping away with the other on the window. 'Milady! Milady, this is serious! LET ME IN!!! I AM UNDER ATTACK!' he shouted.

'*Caw-Caw!*' he heard from behind him.

He turned around swiftly, his eyes still burning and, upon seeing his assailant, he drew back, leaned low and began to meow as aggressively as he could. *A fucking shadow demon!*

It was a giant black bird with red eyes, akin to a crow. He looked at Lorgar expectantly and the cat drew his ears back and tried to intimidate the creature.

The camio tilted its head, pranced around for a moment, then opened up its wings, about to take flight.

Then, Spideraven jumped towards Lorgar, shoving him in the face and causing him to slide back towards the far edge of the window sill. Lorgar reacted by attempting to rush the creature, yet the camio dodged and Lorgar almost flew over the edge. He barely managed to grab the window sill with his two front paws, as he dangled of the edge and his claws made a screeching sound as they tried to dig into the stone.

Lorgar moved his back feet hopelessly, trying to grab a hold of something, but to no avail. Then a dark shape appeared before him and his opponent loomed over him. Spideraven used his talons to pin one paw to the ground and then pecked at his other paw, forcing the cat to pull it back and he now dangled by one arm from the edge of the window.

By the Übermensch! Is this how I die? Humiliated by some feather-negro?

Yet, this was not the day of Lorgar's last breath, for a saviour appeared in a flurry of white, knocking Spideraven back and away from Lorgar, who managed to crawl back up the window and regard the scene before him.

The camio squared off on the far side of the window sill, his red eyes irritated by the newcomer. Before him stood a splendid creature with a luscious fur of pearl and purest marble.

She resembled a feline form, yet she had membranes connecting her front paws to her back feet and Lorgar could tell that it was a *her* since she had raised her long puffy tail in order to intimidate the camio before her. The angelic creature made no sound, as it jumped towards Spideraven, causing him to flee.

It was then that she turned around and Lorgar was left stunned, poop on his face, as his jaw dropped.

She's... oh... oh, my... she's... she's the image of heavenly perfection!

They shared a painfully short moment, before she jumped high into the air, outstretched her limbs, and began gliding away from a heartbroken Lorgar.

'*Wait*! Wait! DON'T LEAVE ME!!!' he shouted. '*Don't leave me alone in this world...*' he whispered, as he looked around, not seeing this strange, loving white lightning that had rescued him from the apathy of an existence without her.

Spideraven used the momentary lapse into romantic desperation to knock Lorgar over the window sill.

His reflexes kicked in and he twisted in the air, managing to come face to face with the rapidly approaching ground.

Is this the day?

The day I finally feel alive!

Is it this day that I must perish?

Again, it was not, as something gripped the scruff of his neck in a vice and Lorgar found himself gliding across Wiltshire Boulevard. For a moment, he thought that he had perished, and that the Valkyries had come to bring him to real Valhalla (not that fake shit he had seen with Milady during their travels), where he would feast at the Allfather's table, until the day of true Ragnarök, when the superior would finally crush the inferior. It never occurred to Lorgar that the fact that the 'superior' had never succeeded in crushing the 'inferior' was proof of the equality of their strength.

It also didn't occur to him to prepare himself to land, as the pressure in his neck had left him limp like a kitten and, when it released, he was unable to prepare himself for a landing. He clumsily rolled on the ground, before 'gracefully' coming bolt upright, just as his horns bashed into a wooden surface. He had landed in the doorway of one of the houses opposite the Convent Garden Embassy. He looked around for both his saviour, and that wretched flying black gargoyle.

Fortunately, he saw the beauty before he saw the beast.

She was standing on a nearby window sill of her own, with one of her front paws pressing a button next to the window. Lorgar tried to catch her nonplussed blue eyes with that look of lovestruck fool that had just been hit in the head. She did bless him with a glance, though she immediately broke it, now looking off towards the sky above Wiltshire Boulevard. Lorgar followed her gaze, seeing dark wings circle above.

'What is it, Abiola?' a man's voice asked.

Lorgar turned towards the ledge of the love of his life, only to barely have time to see her bushy tail disappear behind a closing window. He stood there devastated, muttering a quaint little

'*No!*' before turning to look upon the door next to him. *Could they... Could they be connected? It might be the same apartment!* Lorgar turned towards the dark shape of the camio circling above, as it had drawn nearer.

Damn it!

He rammed into the door with his horns and all his might. Once. Twice. Three times. And again! No avail. It was likely one of those soundproof doors the humans here really liked. He turned around to see the camio dreadfully close, as it spiralled towards him. He went back to ramming his head into the door and he grew dizzy from the shock and the effort. Just as he was about to give up, he turned to see his nemesis hurtling towards him. As his heart pounded in his chest and his ears grew deaf, he turned around, mustered all his strength and prepared for one final headbutt. As he flexed his hind legs, he pushed with all his might and shoved himself with all his might...

... across the floorboards of one of the apartments opposite the Convent Garden Embassy.

He didn't hear Camio stop his descent, veer off and fly back to Laur Pop's open window. He didn't hear the door close slowly behind him, as a tall Shangri human, with a white cat in his arms, studied his unexpected guest with a confused look on his face.

The man looked towards his own pet, and asked. 'Abiola, who's your new friend?'

'I...' Lorgar began. '...am Lorgar. *Erebus*. AURELIAN!' he said, as he stood up and turned to face his saviours. 'And I...' he began, but then he noticed the looks on their faces. *Wide-eyed... Ohhh...* 'What? You've never seen a horned cat before?' he asked.

The human's lips pursed a little, as he seemed to tell himself that he hadn't gone mad. 'No...' he blurted out. 'Neither have I ever heard a cat speak before!'

'Yes, well... I am not just any cat! I... am *Lorgar Erebus Aurelian*!'

'And... where are you from, Lorgar Erebus Aurelian?' the man asked.

'Saskatchewan, Canada.'

'And... where is this world of Saskatchewan-Canada?'

'It's not a world! It's a place! Saskatchewan is a place in Canada!'

'So... you are from the world of Canada?' he surmised.

'NO! I am from the world of Terra!'

'Oh...' The man seemed to understand. 'You're from across the road, aren't you?'

'No! I am from Canada! Haven't I...' Lorgar understood his meaning. 'Yes, my temporary residence is Wiltshire Boulevard, number 616!' he confirmed.

'Across the road, isn't it?' he asked once more, pointing with one finger towards the outside.

'Yes, across the road!' Lorgar acknowledged.

They stared at each other for a moment.

'Well, would you like me to take you home?' the man asked.

Lorgar looked towards the sensuous beauty in his arms, 'Actually, perhaps you might treat a guest of your house to a warm meal and a bowl of water?'

The man was about to speak, but the doorbell rang. He looked concerned for a moment, though not at all surprised. 'I have a feeling I won't have the pleasure of hosting you for too long today, Lorgar!'

He opened the door to reveal Silvia and Mira.

Silvia took in the sight.

Lorgar seemed all right, though there was some dirty white goo on his smug little face.

The man was taller than her, which was peculiar. Most Shangri humans were a lot shorter than her, with only a few matching her height. This one was huge, almost a full head taller than her. Though of stocky build, he was by no means overweight. He actually seemed to be quite muscular, though he wore plain white clothes which did their best to hide the strapped body underneath. He looked friendly, with eyes that smiled as they greeted her.

'I'm assuming you're here for him!' he gestured with his elbow towards Lorgar. Silvia realized that the pillow she thought he had been holding was actually some kind of cat with a lot of loose furry skin underneath its arms. The creature looked quite beautiful and Silvia raised an eyebrow at the contrast between the man's size and his pet's cuteness.

'You assume correctly!' Mira answered.

He turned towards Lorgar, 'I suppose that warm meal and that bowl of water are for another time!' He seemed disappointed.

'Milady! Must we be so rude?! This gentleman has just saved me from the clutches of a black winged demon! Surely we could respond by sharing in our company for a few moments longer.'

Black winged demon?

Spideraven...

'You did?' Mira asked.

'It's the first time I hear of it!' he confessed, before looking at his cat. 'Must have been Abiola's work,' he spoke to them, yet the cat answered.

It meowed. A soft, gentle sound, unlike Lorgar's high-pitched ramblings.

'I was holding my own valiantly, yet it was in the midst of the combat that this creature revealed itself to assist me in my hour of need!' Lorgar explained. 'I must honour her!' he insisted.

Honour her? Oh. My. God. 'Lorgar!!!' both she and Mira exclaimed, though Mira also moved forward to catch her pet, walking right past the man. Silvia saw him smile in surprise out of the corner off his mouth.

'I'd ask for permission to come in, but it would appear that we have already claimed it!' she said to him, right as Mira began cornering Lorgar.

'Oh, don't worry, it's perfectly all right. Abiola sometimes runs off as well. I know the feeling,' he smiled. Silvia kinda liked the way she smiled and smiled back. 'I'm Ulfrik of Langley-Creekside, by the way!'

'Silvia Murărescu!' she introduced herself, extending her hand, which he shook in greeting. His hands were a lot bigger than hers, yet not freakishly big, like those of an ursai or an orc. 'My friend, and the *owner* of your unexpected visitor, is Mira al-Sayid.'

'Pleased to meet you!' Mira responded, as she got a hold of Lorgar and picked him up. 'Though I prefer the term *caretaker*! Especially in moments like this!' she wrestled with Lorgar for a moment. 'Thank you!'

'You're welcome! You're also welcome to stay!' Ulfrik began.

'We don't wish to intrude!' Silvia informed him.

'You wouldn't be!'

I feel as if that's true. 'Perhaps another time!' Silvia responded firmly.

'Milady! You are denying true love!' Lorgar began protesting.

Ulfrik smiled. 'Very well! I'm pleased to have made your acquaintance, Lorgar the Canadian!' Silvia found herself smiling back.

'As am I, Lord Ulfrik! Yet, you pale in comparison to the beauty your –' Mira clasped her ranting cat's jaw shut.

Abiola meowed again, causing Lorgar's eyes to widen.

'Well, if you ever change your mind, feel free to drop by!' Ulfrik informed the two women and nodded towards Lorgar. 'Abiola could use a friend!'

Silvia's hand jutted forward and caressed the little white cat in Ulfrik's arms. She surprised herself. She wasn't one for such gestures. *I should say something. It's awkward.* 'Is she all alone here?'

'Far more so than she used to be!' Ulfrik smiled, as he played with her nose. 'We recently moved back in together, due to work reasons. Before, she used to live at my parent's place!'

Abiola mewoed again.

Ulfrik smiled, scratching her forehead. 'She likes it here, though she does love to go exploring from time to time!'

'Adventurous little girl, isn't she?' Silvia thought the words were a bit weird. It was a bit out of character. She concluded that this was more than enough of the small talk that was warranted, 'We'll be on our way! Thank you!'

'Have a great day, Silvia! Mira!' Ulfrik said, though his eyes lingered only on Silvia's.

As the two women turned to leave, Silvia muttered 'You told him you're Canadian? Canada doesn't even exist anymore!'

'The Great White North endures in our hearts eternal! Fuck the Jewish-American usurpers and what they say!' Lorgar proclaimed through Mira's fingers.

Silvia tilted her head. *No surprise there!*

'Alright, that's enough, Lorgar!' Mira told her pet, as he lay cradled in her arms. 'Let's go home!'

Silvia gestured subtly, knowing that only her Hajduks would recognize the signal. She knew that, in that moment, around twenty fingers relaxed and released around twenty triggers.

The crisis had been averted.

'You put the cat on the window sill as punishment?' Pop asked them, in the meeting next morning.

'He said Nick had hepatitis,' Tech explained.

'What the...?' Pop shook his head. 'It doesn't fucking matter, now, does it? The cat has fucking horns, Tech! He got the horns because an *illegal* fucking Hogwarts burst and caused him to mutate! And *you* just put him there, on the window, for all to see?' he said, turning to Mira. He didn't raise his voice, yet Silvia knew he was being serious. 'He's a fucking talking cat, Tech! You want people to walk by the Embassy and have a talking horned cat tell them how it's being abused by its owners?'

Mira intervened on her behalf, 'It's not abuse, I always put Lorgar in time-out when–'

'– When he's a fucking racist piece of shit! I know!' Pop replied. 'But, here and now is not the time for kindergarten bullshit!' His eyes wandered for a moment.

'You let Spideraven out whenever he pleases and he's literally a flying omen of death and cobwebs!' Mira pointed out.

'Spideraven is an indigenous fucking species!' Pop countered.

'An indigenous *predatory* species,' Mira held firm.

Which was likely trying to predate her cat...

'He hunts pigeons, Mira, and he does so fucking inconspicuously and, even if he didn't, if someone walks by and sees a camio turning a fucking pigeon into a shawarma, no one would bat an eye!

You have a talking cat with horns and a hatred for ethnic fucking minorities, Mira! You can't just put it on the window sill facing the fucking boulevard and not expect bullshit like this to happen!'

Mira began, 'Lorgar even climbs up on the window by himself sometimes –'

'You've done this before?' Pop leaned back and rubbed his forehead. 'Jesus fucking Christ... Silvia, were you aware of this?'

Silvia stopped herself from being startled by his sudden pivot towards her. 'The cat doesn't like strangers; it wouldn't have asked passers-by for assistance; not if they weren't Hajduks.'

'And, yet, this time, a fucking *squirelcat* –'

'There we go with the naming conventions...' Nick interjected.

'Nick, shut the fuck up! Not now!' Pop turned back to berating Mira after silencing Nick. 'Mira, this is not how we do things here! This is fucking careless! The rat cleaning ladies where a boon and a good idea, I'll give you that, but this sort of thing is fucking moronic!' Pop leaned back, silent for a moment. 'How are the men?' he asked.

Silvia was a bit taken aback now. Despite the fact that five Centurions and one Captain were present in Laur's chamber, on top of Basenji and Tech, this was a question she knew was typically addressed to her. 'Coping,' she answered.

'Aren't we all...' Pop commented, as he rubbed his face. 'We need to completely lift the lockdown by the day of the gala.'

'*Heh*!' Nick exclaimed, before turning to Mira. 'Where you hit and where it breaks!'

'Nick, shut the fuck up!' Pop muttered, before raising his face to address his team. 'Go the Sanjak, Belagravia, the barracks, and the *Doina*; make arrangements with the others to begin active preparations for the event. It has to be fucking visible! Then, send word to the Republican Emissaries to begin final preparations as well. Have them send over confirmation lists, food, drinks, decorations, whatever... find something to do! No crime! No checking-up with the ursai! At least no more than the usual! No attempting to make contact with the murine! No harassment of imperials! No search for Otto Benga! No nothing! All legitimate! Do it gradually and make it appear as if we're simply waking up from a long nap.'

'Weren't we going to do that anyway?' Nick asked.

'Yes, we fucking were, just that now we have to be fucking *diligent* about it... We need to make this whole cat thing look like we're simply lifting our security precautions and that we feel safe again.' Pop frowned for a moment, 'Invite the neighbours too!'

'W-what?' she mumbled.

'Given that one of them was so kind as to come to the aid of one of our most treasured companions, it's only fitting that we answer our neighbour's grace with our hospitality! Send invites to the entire residential block, as well as one invite per business on the office floors. Cap it at one hundred; that should keep the numbers manageable. That way, yesterday's fucking little debacle – which, *thank fuck*, hasn't reached the press by some miracle – can simply be a cute little neighbourly encounter.'

'Understood!' Silvia acknowledged. 'I'll get right to it.'

'No, *you* won't! You and Mira are coming with me to the palace today! Get someone else to do it!'

'Did Tech piss on the rug or something?' Nick commented and Tech immediately and playfully shoved a knee into the back of his seat.

'Tech will be meeting up with our contacts at the Constabulary to help set up security for the event. The rest of you have your orders and I want Silvia with me because I've always taken at least one senior officer with me to the palace. I don't want to make it look like something has happened. Plus, you've been cooped up in here for fucking ages, you need some fresh air!' this last part he said to Silvia herself.

Did you just show concern for my well being?

Well, maybe Lorgar should have near-death experiences more often...

'I want *you*, Mira, to come along, because you need fucking babysitting and, apparently, we're in lack of a proper nanny!'

There we go... with the fucking paternalistic bullshit...

Laur had decided to visit the Palace in hopes of meeting with the Crown Prince to push for one final meeting with the Peacekeeper, in the hopes that Otto Gisevius himself might attend the Dawnbreak Gala. Soon enough, she and Mira found themselves somewhere in the Royal Inner Palace, waiting for Pop to exit his meeting with the Crown Prince.

One of the nearby remani guards suddenly spoke. 'Please rise!'

The sound startled both Silvia and Mira, who had been waiting impatiently on a bench observing the nearest of the Crown Prince's gardens. They exchanged a quick and worried look before slowly standing up, poised to take action if anything was to happen.

'The Royal Prince-in-Waiting Calia of the Royal House Gisevius approaches!' the royal guard that had bid them to rise informed them, just as a little girl gingerly turned a nearby corner.

Silvia freaked out for the moment, for she hadn't exactly prepared for this. She had no idea how to address the Prince-in-Waiting of the City of Shangri! *What the hell is going on? Does this just happen here? This palace is the size of Romania itself and it just happens that the Princess-in-Waiting just strolls by at the exact same time as we're here?*

Fortunately, the little girl handled her own protocol. 'Hello! You two are the Lady Silvia and the Princess Mira?' she asked innocently. She couldn't have been more than eight years of age and she had clever glint in her eye and a pure childish innocence to her voice.

Silvia smiled immediately, struggling to appear both honest and polite, 'Yes, your grace!'

'I'm Calia,' the little one informed her, then raised her hand towards her.

Silvia shared a quick glance with the nearby remani royal guards, when a woman came from around the same corner from whence the Shangri princess had arrived. She was a tall, stately woman, almost two heads taller than her, with pure white hair and grey eyes, clad in robes of red and silver, who seemed to watch over the little princess the way a mother eagle would watch over her own hatchinlings.

Just as she began observing this new arrival, she saw one guards lock eyes with her and subtly gesture towards the Princess-in-Waiting. She took the hint, extending her hand forward to meet Calia's own.

'I'm Silvia!' *Woman! What the fuck? She knows your name!*

'Come! Let us speak!' the little one said, pulling at Silvia's fingertips as she made her way to a nearby pathway leading through the garden. Silvia shuffled awkwardly after her and the little one turned towards Mira, bidding her join them. The three of them began walking down a cobbled walkway, as the giant woman trailed them. *There's something off about her, other than the size.*

'I've never met a Terran before,' the little girl remarked.

'We are a small people, your grace, few in number, particularly when compared with a people as numerous as yours!'

'You are few in number, yes, yet still your name is spoken often on worlds near and far from your own! A man came to visit my father, not so long ago. He came from a place in the Vale of Dreams so far away that it took a months for him to reach us and even in those worlds do men know of Terra and its people.'

'Your words are... uplifting, your grace. I only hope the words they speak of us are kind.'

'Why would they not be so? They know of a people, far off into the distant south, beyond which the stars sing the melody of childhood. They speak of a people of heroes and great warriors and they speak of a fate of struggle having been thrust upon them and of them accepting it with heavy hearts and sad smiles. Smiles such as yours, Lady Silvia!' the little girl stopped and Silvia's world trembled.

'I apologize, your grace, I did not seek to be disingenuous. I assure you that I find your presence lovely!' She glanced towards the giant woman walking in step with Mira behind them. *If shit hit the fan, can we take her? She's fucking huge and there's... there's something else about her I can't put my finger on...*

'As I do yours, Lady Silvia.' The little girl turned back towards the garden, as she gestured with her free hand. 'Here we have trees of maglauin. In the summer they make fruits of pale red. They make a nectar out of them akin to bee's honey. I love having it in my tea in the mornings! Tell me of your world! What colours are the fruits of Terra, Lady Silvia?'

'Many, princess, the colours are many. Red, orange, green and even black! We have orchards all across the world where we grow fruits you know as apples, oranges, peaches, pears, as well as berries!'

'I feel as though you like berries, most of all,' the little girl observed...

Correctly... 'Yes... In the mountains we grow strawberries... of a variety that is small and sweet, as well blueberries of a sharp taste that arrive in springs after the last frosts. One may also find blackberries and raspberries and, in the lands of North America, there grow huckleberries and a thousand others are grown across the world!

'I would like to see your world one day, Lady Silvia. You do make sound like a lovely place!'

It is... now.

The little girl seemed to be thinking of something that had just now sprung in her mind. 'What is a 'Centurion', Lady Silvia? I understand that is the title by which you are addressed on your world?'

'Not just on my world, your grace! I am a Centurion at all times and in all places. It is a... rank of military office.'

'And what does this rank entail?'

'That I am an officer of the Hajduk Legion. Had I been an officer of equal rank within the Regular Terran Army, or the Allied Host, and I would have held the rank of *Commandant* and commanded ten thousand men. As a Centurion, I command roughly a hundred Legionnaires and also I help guide the men of the units under my General's command, yet my duty, first and foremost, is to protect my General, as his bodyguard.'

'Your General is Laur Pop?' the little girl asked, awaiting confirmation for a fact she seemed to already know.

'Yes.'

'My brother tells me that Lord Pop looks like a man who isn't afraid of anything! I take that it is you whom he has to thank for that?'

It felt as if a grenade had just hit Silvia's head. The little girl had just given her the most elegantly elaborated compliment Silvia had heard in a very long time. She likely looked stunned for a moment before she composed herself. 'I assume he does, in part, your grace!'

'*Assume*? Why do you assume? Does he not tell this to you?' she asked, confused, as she began dancing from one polished garden rock to another.

After the most unexpected of highs, now came the steepest of lows, 'He does, your grace, in his way... Though, in truth, my General is a man that needs very little protection. I mostly assist in other ways.'

'What ways?'

'Whichever way I must, depending on the situation. Mostly I carry out his orders, I council him, I bring him information, though, at times, I do go into battle for him. Sometimes I even fulfil my duty as a bodyguard!'

'Hmmm...' Calia pondered, twisting her little lips into a serious analysis of the facts. 'On my world, you are a '*Lady*'!' she decreed.

Silvia smiled and let out a little laugh, 'On your world, I can be whatever you wish to call me, your grace! I am not a Lady on my world, yet I can be so here...' Silvia remembered something and gestured towards Mira. 'Just as much as Mira can be a 'Princess' here!'

'That is what I am told!' the little girl stopped and turned to face Mira, who stood at attention, a bit too rigidly.

Silvia noted the change in behaviour. Mira stood with her hands behind her back, her chest pushed forward, as if she were in a military war council before potential battle. *How odd...*

'Is your General also Laur Pop, Mira?'

'I... serve under him, as part of the Regular Army.'

'Where you hold the rank of Captain?' she clearly knew.

'Yes.'

'So you command how many men?'

'I... I was supposed to be commanding a thousand, though, upon asking to be part of this assignment, I was relinquished of my command.'

'But, were you not a *Ghazi* before this? Did you not hold the title of Captain of the Ghazis?'

If half the men under my command where as diligent as this little one...

'I... did... yes... I joined the Logistics Corps after I left the Ghazis, where I worked with the Hajduks.'

'And what did you do in the Logistics Corps with the Hajduks which you couldn't do with the Ghazis?'

Silvia's heart began to pound. *Mira!!! BE EXTREMELY CAREFUL!*

'We helped them hunt down the last of our people's enemies...' Mira glanced towards the big woman. '... the *Svart*.'

Pffffewwww... for a moment there... I thought you might have forgotten your cover story.

'I see. You see, everyone around here speaks often of Laur Pop and of his Hajduks, yet of *you* they speak often also and they have done so even before the arrival of Laur Pop.'

Mira remained silent, which drew Silvia's suspicion.

Calia continued, 'This isn't your first time in Shangri.'

'It is not.'

'It is not even your first time in this very garden, is it not?'

'I thought I recognized it,' Mira acknowledged, and Silvia's ears twitched as her heart began to hum in her chest.

What? The? Shit?

'I was not even born when you were last here. I didn't get to see you then and, later, when I heard of you, I was greatly disappointed to have not made your acquaintance!'

Once more, Mira remained silent.

'You came to my father's court with your sister, Daw.'

'I did.'

'You made quite an impression on him.'

'I'm glad, though I do not know when I had the honour.'

'My father is always watching what goes on in his home and you did stir up quite a fuss, from what I gather. My brother tells me that the palace couldn't stop talking about you for weeks on end.' The little girl looked up at Mira, unblinking, as she seemed to recall things. 'The Terran Princess. Orphaned daughter of a queen that gave her life to save her people and of a king who died of a broken heart. Sister to a goddess of elves. Raised on two worlds by two peoples that had fought each other naught but years before. My older brother told me that, the first time he caught a glimpse of your eyes, they seemed to find his, though he had thought himself hidden. He would tell us stories of how your eyes carried within a fire that burned through the darkness of the deepest night.'

Mira smirked. 'Sounds like your older brother is something of a poet.'

'He has his aspirations. Unfortunately, I cannot say that his way with words is his most fruitful foray, though I must say that I can now see that he can be quite astute in his remarks, at times..' The little girl blinked to herself, as she seemed to remember something. 'He also said that your Lord Pop is a horrifically theatrical man, albeit endearing... in his own way...'

Mira giggled as Silvia's jaw dropped slightly. She was about to say something to defend her General's honour, yet Mira beat her to it. 'I must say, your brother actually seems to be an excellent judge of character.'

Mira!!!

Calia smiled. 'I was paraphrasing. He was quite long-winded in his description.' She turned towards the big woman behind them, who subtly pointed to the sky with her thumb and twisted it swiftly, as if to gesture the movement of something. 'I will now lead you back to where we first met. I understand that Lord Pop will soon finish his visit to my brother.

'How clairvoyant of you,' Mira joked.

'I'm afraid it's not clairvoyance, as much as it is scheduling. I understand that scheduling is the exact reason why Lord Pop is here.' The little one seemed to squint for a moment. 'What exactly is it that you celebrate on this Dawnbreak event?'

'We celebrate the conclusion of the First Battle of Terra, your grace.'

'What happened during the First Battle of Terra?'

'The Worldship Vigilant arrived above Terra and saved us from annihilation, your grace,' Silvia explained.

'And what of this *Last Fanta*, event? Is it another holiday?' she asked, causing the blood in Silvia's veins to turn to ice.

'Last *Fitna*,' Mira corrected the Prince-in-Waiting of the City of Shangri with complete disregard for etiquette and immediately drawing critical looks from both Silvia and the big woman.

Mira shrugged.

Silvia collected herself. 'That was a separate event, your grace, though it did occur on the 11th Dawnbreak Anniversary.'

'My apologies, both for my ignorance... and my mispronunciation!' she said the last part to Mira, before turning back to Silvia. 'And what happened during the Last... *Fitna*?!' she turned slightly back towards Mira, who nodded.

Silvia struggled to find her words, as shame overwhelmed her. 'It... it, *uhm*... it was a purge, your grace... There were those of our people that would have had us side with the Urheimat against those that saved us in the Hour of Twilight. A decision was made that those people... were to be silenced.'

'You mean murdered?' Calia asked.

'*Your grace!!!*' the big woman finally spoke and her voice was thick and rich and full of flavour and fragrance. She also had an accent and Silvia immediately understood who she was.

Lord in Heaven! Of course! It was in the research...

'*Ooops*!' the princess pretended to take her seriously. 'I meant to say: *removed*.'

Silvia felt as if she were about to throw-up. 'Yes, your grace, a decision was made that they be... that they be *removed*. To assure our unity.'

'Huh... did it work?' she asked.

'It has... so far, your grace.'

'Nice! I'm very happy for you!' she said, as they neared the bench from whence she had recruited the two Terran women on her walk. 'But you don't celebrate the purge; you celebrate the victory over your aggressor?'

'Yes, your grace!'

'Because the victory came before the purge?'

'Yes, your grace!'

'And it's a yearly occurrence?'

'Yes, your grace, once every 360 days, ever since the end of the War of Vengeance!'

'Including on the day of the *Last Fitna*?'

'... yes...' Silvia said.

'So that's what those people who were purged were doing on that day? Were they celebrating?'

Silvia's mouth went dry, though she also felt her neck tense up, as if she were about to vomit. She didn't say anything. How could she say anything? It was indefensible. A revolting page in their history. There had been supposed benefits, yes, but-

Mira's voice rang out from behind her. 'Some of them were sleeping...'

MIRA!!!

Calia shrugged, 'Oh, well, I guess I understand why daddy isn't coming to your party!'

How couldn't you little one? How could...

Oh, no! What? 'I'm sorry to hear that, your grace.' Silvia swallowed. 'We worried that such would be his reply. I'm sorry to have come all this way to bother you and your family.'

'Don't worry, Lady Silvia! We've found your presence here to be quite charming! Yourself and Princess Mira, as well. Haven't we, Mel?' she turned to ask her guardian.

Mel nodded.

Then it happened. In that moment, next to the spineless Mandean roses and right across from a fountain of a pissing manticore, Silvia got an idea. 'We thank you for your hospitality, your grace! Perhaps, we might return the favour one day... Perhaps even during tomorrow's Gala!' the words came out and Silvia knew something was wrong. She felt it. She wasn't sure if it was her own mind realizing the stupidity of her words, of it was simply the reaction it triggered in the three girls around her.

Mira looked at her with a look that could be described as the perfect balance of pain and cringe, as she winced at the dead silence left in her word's wake.

Mel starred at her as if she were about to eat her whole.

Calia took a sharp, yet long, breath. 'Your invitation is most gracious, Lady Silvia!' she exhaled her words, as if this child of eight was Dame Maggie Smith and clearly more capable of navigating complex social interactions that Silvia, a woman who was allegedly older and wiser. 'Though, I am afraid I must decline!'

Silvia felt her heart sink as her skin crawled at her own clumsy attempt at intergalactic diplomacy.

'It is against custom for both the Crown Prince and the Prince-in-Waiting to be outside of the Palace grounds at the same time!' the Princess continued.

Huh? She glanced towards Mira to see that she had caught it as well.

'Unless, of course, if your Lord Pop is not as gracious as yourself and does not invite my brother to your Dawnbreak Gala.'

Silvia blinked a few times, as she processed the information. 'I... see no reason why he would not, if that is your father's – and your brother's – wish!'

'Oh, it's definitely my brother's! He is something of a *terrophile*. In truth, he's been positively dying to attend, ever since your Lord Pop mentioned the event during their first meeting.'

Oh... oh, thank God!

The whole thing from earlier was still cringe, but this makes it better!

She knew that Pop would be irritated that the Peacekeeper himself wouldn't be attending, yet she also knew that her General was nevertheless a pragmatist and he would take the second most important man in Shangri over the first on any day of the week, even if he would complain about it.

As they neared the entrance to the Crown Prince's office, Calia continued, 'Have you met my brother, Lady Silvia?' she asked.

'I'm afraid I haven't had the pleasure!'

'I assure you that the pleasure will be overwhelmingly his! He's always wanted to visit your homeworld, though father has insofar convinced him to delay his visit. I am certain that he is positively thrilled at the prospect of spending the evening in the midst of your people! To not even mentioned the chance of seeing Mira again!'

Again?

Mira caught it also. 'Hopefully this time I'll have the pleasure of seeing him back...'

Calia's face was motionless as her lips opened slightly and a mischievous whisper escaped them. 'Oh, you've seen him many times before, from what I hear!'

What? Silvia turned subtly towards her fellow Terran. *What is she talking about?*

Mira seemed to be as puzzled as she was.

Calia continued. 'Though his wife will be less pleased...'

Silvia almost choked on that one.

'*Your grace...!*' Mel hissed at her charge.

'*Ooopsie-daisy!*' Calia whistled, her voice clear and her mind clearly bereft of any regret.

They reached the place from whence the princess had co-opted them onto this most surreal of strolls and Calia bid them farewell, shaking hands with Mira and hugging Silvia.

Just as she and Mel were out of earshot, Mira shrugged before turning to Silvia. 'Well, you spazzed out for second there...'

'FUTU–' Silvia controlled herself and lowered her voice. 'That's beside the point now. *You know the Crown Prince?*'

'Apparently...'

'Mira, for fuck's sake, why didn't you tell anyone?'

'I couldn't tell something I didn't know I knew...'

'You do not recall meeting the fucking Crown Prince of Shangri? Where you high the whole time you were here last time?'

'Not the whole time, though I'm fairly certain I would've remembered meeting the Crown Prince, especially if he was anything like his sister!'

Just then, Laur Pop emerged furiously from the entrance leading to Crown Prince's office. His face was as furious as his stride, as he strode right past the two women, informing them. 'He's not coming!'

He means the Peacekeeper... Oh, shit, did he get angry and not invite the Prince? 'What about the Prince?'

'The Prince...' Pop began, before stopping in his tracks and turning suddenly to face his Centurion. 'The Prince said he would come in his father's stead...' Pop squinted. 'How do *you* know that?' he asked.

'Calia Gisevius,' Silvia replied.

Pop seemed stunned. 'First of all...' he looked around to make sure that they were, at least, *apparently* alone, '... it's *Prince-in-Waiting* Calia Gisevius and, second-of-all, what the fuck are you talking about?'

'She came over while we were waiting for you and...' Silvia struggled to find the words required to summarise, describe and explain the experience. '... she invited us for a walk through the gardens.'

'And she told you about the planned conclusion of the meeting we came here to have with her brother?' He looked up towards what must have been the location of her brother's office inside the massive edifice behind them.

'Yes, apparently,' Silvia confirmed.

Pop mulled things over for a moment. 'So...' He rubbed his head. '... *fucking theatre...*' he muttered in Romanian. 'Well...' he exhaled, seemingly at peace with things. 'Well, at least you two got some fresh air and you made a new friend!' He made to resume his way back towards the garage where the Hajduk convoy was waiting for them, but then he stopped and turned once more. 'Anything else?'

The two women stared at him for a moment and he immediately picked up a scent.

'What?' he asked.

'I... I invited her to the Gala, too...' Silvia began.

Pop stared at her, perplexed. 'You. Did. *What?*'

'It was after she told us that her father wasn't coming and before she told us that her brother would be. I thought–'

'*Fuck your thoughts*!' Pop snapped and scratched his head. 'What did she say?'

'She said she wouldn't come, be–'

'– Oh, but for fuck's sake, Silvia!' he interrupted as he slapped his thigh in annoyance.

'She said she wouldn't be coming because her brother wanted to come and it's not allowed for them both to leave the Palace!' she finished her report.

Pop exhaled angrily. He rubbed his eyes as he inputted the information. 'It's... it's fine! It's fucking fine! That was proactive of you!'

Oh? Oh. Thank you!

Say 'thank you' out loud, Silvia! 'Thank you!' she said.

'Next time...' he continued. 'Next time, try to think things over a bit longer before taking the initiative... but, that being said, despite the clear ignorance behind your line of thought, I commend you on your rationale, at least superficially! We needed someone from the royal family to attend. You thought she was as good as any at the time... it's fine! Don't do shit like that again and learn from this experience!

'It's ok!' he concluded, more for himself than for her. 'No damage was done. It's fine! The Crown Prince and his wife are coming. We need to get ready! We'll get back to the Embassy and set everything up and all of *this* that happened here, we can throw under the rug. *It's fine!* It's not great, but it's fine!'

This is the closest he's going to come to being forgiving, so I might as well smile and take it. It's a lot lighter than what I was expecting.

'Well, anything else I should know about?' Pop asked.

The two women shared a quick glance.

Pop saw it. '*What?*'

Mira nodded subtly and Silvia took a deep breath. 'Mira knows the Crown Prince, apparently!'

Now he seemed to be on the verge of complete discombobulation. '*What the...* you know the Crown Prince?' he asked Mira. '*When? Now?*' Pop realized that it must not have been during Mira's current stay in Shangri. 'With Daw?'

'Probably,' Mira answered.

'What the fuck do you mean 'probably'?' he asked, on the verge of apoplexy.

'I didn't know I met him,' Mira declared.

Pop threw his hands in the air. 'Oh, but *go to my dick!*' he turned angrily and made for the garage, muttering something about some '*Mark Twain fucking bullshit!*'

The next day, it was Silvia who was close to telling people to go to her dick.

'What, in-my-dick, do you mean: 'she's not here'?' she asked Bogdan Chiftea.

'She said she was going to go shower and get ready,' he replied referring to Mira.

'The first guests are coming in less than four hours and she's gone to shower?' she asked incredulously. They were in the kitchens, right next to a long row of humanoid robots busy preparing the dishes of the evening's feast. *What the fuck is that smell? It smells like fucking... everything?!* She angrily reached towards a stack of black papers with golden writing on them. 'These are the menus?' she asked, as she looked across the names on the list.

'Eh, no! She said they're... *taste maps?*' Bogdan answered.

'What the...' Silvia glanced towards the golden markings written on the paper. It was a map of the Terran regions of Rumelia, Romania, Ruthenia, Russia and Turkey, with the very edges of Siberia, Persia, Arabia, Israel, Maghreb Italia, Germany, Polska, Baltica and Scandinavia visible. Each region had the seal of its respective nations etched upon them, with different dishes written underneath, as well as a separate symbol for each individual dish. Silvia flipped Mira's menu around to see that each dish had a description and summary of key ingredients listed out on the back.

Mira was in charge of catering the event and she had assured Silvia that everything would be directly supervised by her. The Arabian Captain had spent a fortune (from Silvia's perspective), ordering ingredients from various merchants across the city. She had wanted a specific type of flour, a very particular type of tomato, three different varieties of oregano, as well as only a single variety of pomegranate molasses and hundred other irrelevant selections of foodstuffs... *and now she just left it to the robots?!*

'How long is this going to take?' she asked one of the robots.

'The first round of hors d'oeuvres will be made ready in three hours and forty-two minutes, Centurion Silvia!' the machine replied, as it etched different markings upon a plate. She saw that the markings matched the symbols Mira had chosen to represent... (Silvia glanced towards the map-menu, still in her hand)... *Saganaki?*

What the fuck is saganaki?

Feta cheese fried in... honey?! With black-and-white sesame seeds sprinkled on top?

What kind of degenerate bullshit... Oh... it's Greek?!

... It actually sounds nice to be honest -

– WHAT!?!?!? 'Three hours and forty-two minutes?' she asked the robot and Bogdan incredulously.

'Yes... she mentioned that she wanted the food to be ready in increments, so that it was always fresh and there was always new food coming in,' Bogdan explained.

Silvia stared at him.

'It honestly sounded like a good idea, Sil! That's how they used to do it in the old days!' the Terran oldtimer explained.

'I'm going to go get her,' she muttered. 'This is absurd!'

Silvia left the kitchen in a rage.

Everyone was up-and-about-and-in-a-hurry in the Convent Garden Embassy. Hajduks from Belagravia, the *Doina,* Sanjak and the Military District had already arrived to assist in the preparations. All of them men, for some reason, which was strange. The Hajduks had a 70/30 ratio, which was higher than most Terran Avenger Legions, thus making such overwhelming discrepancies noticeable.

She had already completed her third sweep of the building in just as many hours, making sure that everything was going smoothly. Security, entertainment, protocol, there were a thousand things that had to go smoothly and Silvia felt overwhelmed.

We're wearing too many hats again... We have to throw an amazing party and make sure we don't get sabotaged, infiltrated or otherwise attacked... and Mira's taking a shower...

She walked furiously towards her room, her boots making a loud thumping sound as she neared-

'SILVIA!' Pop shouted from his office, his door open.

Silvia stopped in front of her door. *Oh, fuck... what is it now?* She walked into Pop's office.

'Yes?'

'All good?' he asked.

She saw that he was alone, with only Spideraven keeping him company as he studied the guest list and the camio pecked the keys of the mechanical typewriter Pop kept in his office. 'Yes!' she answered, too quickly.

Pop raised his eyes. He seemed to study her for a moment and Silvia was a bit surprised to see his eyes move across her body for a few moments. 'What?' he asked.

'Well...' *fuck it!* 'It's Mira.'

Pop exhaled, though he did not seem to take her seriously. 'What has she done this time?' he asked.

'Bogdan Chiftea just told me that she left the kitchen to shower and prepare for the event and she left all the cooking and the plating to the robots after the food *she* ordered arrived and after–'

'So?' Pop asked.

Silvia blinked. 'W-what? She should be supervising–'

'You said Bogdan told you?' he asked.

'Yes!'

'So, Bogdan is in the kitchen with the robots?'

'Yes!'

'Well, then he can supervise them just fine! He used to be a cook himself!' Pop took a deep breath. 'At McDonalds...' he admitted to himself (though Silvia didn't get it) before continuing. 'Though, given we are talking about *cooking* and *Mira*, I'm quite certain she's planned everything out with the utmost tender, love and care!' he leaned back. 'Including her own *preparations*...' he muttered.

Silvia put on a fake smile. 'So, I'll just leave her to it and hope the kitchens don't catch fire –'

'They won't!' Pop interrupted her again. He took a deep breath and looked at his watch. 'How much time are *you* devoting to getting ready for the Gala?' he asked.

Silvia blinked in perplexion. 'I've been running around ever since I –'

Pop raised his hand and shrugged a forced smile. 'I know! *I know*!' he said softly. 'I mean...' he seemed to struggle awkwardly for a moment. 'What are you going to wear?' he asked.

Silvia stared at him. *Is he...?*

'Look...' he said. '*I'm* gonna wear a suit – a three-piece suit! – *not* my uniform! I'm gonna wear this watch!' he pointed towards his oldtimer watch, the Breitling Cosmonaute he had received in the aftermath of Doomsday. Many oldtimers, especially those that had held leadership positions during the End Times, had old Terran luxury watches as signs of their office. All of the Hajduk Generals, both current and former, as well as several centurions, wore Breitling Cosmonautes, a bit of jewellery left over from the World-that-Was, to mark their seniority and their prestige.

Like how they sometimes wear suits... and how they like dresses...

Pop continued. 'I have some dress shoes and I'm probably going to wear a bowtie! A dark blue one, to go with my suit!' Pop took a deep breath. 'You were going to wear your uniform, weren't you?'

Silvia took a deep breath. 'Well... the ceremonial uniform, yes...'

Pop exhaled.

'... with no weapons...'

Pop raised an eyebrow.

'... no *visible* weapons,' she explained.

He scratched his face and stared at his fingernails. 'I'm also going to shave...' he added, before looking up at her. 'I asked Hristache to come in and see me, since I want to discuss the poker game seating. He'll be in here for less than five minutes and then I'll tell him to pass the word around that I want everyone dressed to impress *and* in civilian clothes. I'm also going to order every female Hajduk to drop whatever it is that they're doing and retire to their chambers to get ready for tonight's festivities, as the *ladies* they are!

'... *if* they haven't done that already!' he added. 'The men will only get thirty minutes! I'll coordinate everything together with the male officers. Silvia!' he leaned in.

'Yes!' she responded in only a vaguely military manner.

'I am *ordering* you to go and make yourself as beautiful as you can be and I have only one instruction!' he raised one finger.

Silvia felt herself smile and she couldn't stop herself from giggling like a little girl as she answered. 'Yes?'

'Try not to be *too* stunning (which I know you *can* be) since we don't want anyone to be so stunned that they pass out! It would ruin the whole vibe!' He raised his eyebrows and smiled genuinely, as he tapped his desk. 'Am I understood?'

'Yes, *sir*!' she said, as she left his office and rushed to her room.

She always did what her General asked of her.

She made straight for her wardrobe and rolled back the two massive wardrobe doors behind which she kept her casual clothes and made straight for the rack where she kept the three dresses she owned.

The first was an orcish white, blue and gold kimono which she had always thought of as being incredibly elegant.

Too conservative...

The second was a demani muslin dress of dark red and fine yellow lines that she had bought in Andromeda for a very specific purpose which had never come to pass, yet had always lingered in its tomb within her.

Too slutty...

The last was a black Terran cocktail dress which she wore too virtually every Terran formal party she had ever been invited too.

Too boring...

'*Shit*!' she muttered.

Silvia left her room and barged into Mira's chambers, only to find her curling her hair on her bed, just as Lorgar jumped up startled from right next to her.

'What are you wearing?' she asked.

Mira looked at herself. She was wearing a black bathrobe. She smiled suddenly and looked up toward her roommate as she realized the meaning of her question. She then jumped out of bed and walked straight up to her own wardrobe.

'I thought you'd never ask!' she said, as she flung open the even larger space she employed to store her clothes, revealing racks upon racks of outfits. She turned around to study Silvia for a moment. 'Your profession is weaving, isn't it?'

'Yes. Mostly pants, shirts and scarves, though I've done dresses before... Do you need me to edit something?' she asked, studying Mira's collection. *This woman has impeccable taste... why doesn't she wear these more often? They're gorgeous!*

'We'll figure it out later!'

They spent the next hour trying out different outfits. They were both the same size, yet they couldn't make up their minds as to which dress looked better on who and in what style.

'Ok! This one looks great! Finally!' Silvia announced, as she stood resplendent in a flowing ruby red contraption of crimson fabric and dark obsidian.

'Maybe...' Mira mused, as she turned towards another section of her wardrobe. '... *if only it went... with the...*' she muttered, as she pulled out a box.

'With what?' Silvia asked, taking her eyes away from Mira's mirror.

'These!' Mira announced, as she pulled out a pair of high-heels from the box. Black, with red soles.

Silvia stared at the shoes.

Mira stared at her.

'Do... do you...?' she began.

'Not really...' she replied.

Silvia stared at her for a while longer, before she nodded. '*Ela!*'

The two made straight for the next room down the hall, which belonged to Ela and Casandra. It was the later who opened the door. 'DAMNNNNN!!!' she proclaimed, seeing Silvia's dress and Mira in her bathrobe. 'Centurion Murărescu! You look deadly!'

'Casandra,' Silvia began, 'do you know how to walk in those?' Silvia pointed towards the shoes in Mira's box.

Casandra sighed as she let go off the door. 'I was fourteen when the End Times started,' she confessed. 'That's too young for high-heels and I haven't really found the time to learn in the time since,' she said, before thinking things through for a moment. Silvia noticed that she was also wearing a bathrobe and that she had died her hair a luscious amber colour. 'ELA!' Casandra shouted towards her (technically) superior officer.

'*Da, da?*' Ela chirruped back as she peered from within the kitchen she shared with Casandra. Silvia noticed that she was dyeing her nails. 'Ohhh!' Silvia's newly minted fellow Centurion whistled, before coming straight towards them. '*Ohhh!*' she mused, seeing the box in Mira's hands. 'Christian Louboutin!' She picked out one of the shoes. 'Originals!' she declared after sniffing them. She checked the inside of the heel '... enlarged?' she asked Mira.

'Twice the original size,' Mira explained. 'In Menegroth...' she added.

Elia smirked. 'Shame... you could've had them edited on Terra, instead of having elves get their grubby little hands on them! Nevertheless, I have some Diors and a pair of Jimmy Choo's edited for myself, but *these* are *nice!*' she proclaimed

'Do you know how to walk in them?' Silvia asked.

'Do I know how to...' Ela began, before realizing that she was actually an eighty years old that had grown up and lived in a time when a woman on Earth could actually wear high heels without risking her life (too much). 'It... shouldn't be too difficult.'

Silvia's forehead crashed into Ela's coffee table a few minutes later.

'I don't understand...' Casandra muttered, as Silvia flipped herself onto her ass, angrily staring at the shoes on her feet. Casandra turned towards Mira. 'Why do you have high heels, if you don't know how to walk in them?'

'They were a family heirloom! I always take them with me, thinking that one day I'll have time to learn how to walk in them.'

'Aren't you like... twenty-nine years old?' Casandra asked.

Mira shrugged. 'I've been busy!'

A dejected Silvia sat bowlegged on the floor and removed her shoes, tossing them across the floor. 'This is fucking bullshit!'

'No!' Ela began. 'It's easy! Look!' Just like that, she picked up the shoes and casually slipped them onto her feet, before prancing around the room like a fucking antelope. 'See? It's easy once you get the hang of it!'

'I'm getting nervous just looking at her...' Casandra mumbled.

'Nah...' Mira muttered. 'Nah! I think I got it!' she walked towards Ela's own shoe boxes, and picked out a pair of neon green stilettos. 'These ones are a little weird...' (They were open-toed and had a slightly thicker hilt.)

'Those are the easiest!' Ela said. 'Try them out!'

Mira broke her ankle in about forty seconds. Lying flat on her back on the floor, she raised her leg towards the ceiling as her twisted foot dangled from her ankle, bent her knee, winced and flicked her leg in the air. An audible *crack!* rang out, as her ligaments pulled themselves back into position and her augmented healing almost immediately fixed the damage.

She then allowed her formerly broken foot to slump onto the floor. 'Three-piece olive green pantsuit... wide leg...' she announced. '... and a pair of Air Force Ones!' she concluded.

In the end, three hours later, Mira did wear her three piece olive green pantsuit and her Air Force Ones, while Silvia wore a long black cocktail dress with two long cuts along the sides, as well as two golden eagles made of sculpted whale horn adorning her shoulders. She had edited the dress, which was her own original Terran cocktail dress, adding the eagles and removing the fabric from her upper torso, right above her breasts.

As they walked amongst the mass of guests and Hajduks, Mira announced. 'How could anyone wear high heels and be comfortable?'

'I know, right? I mean, even if you can figure out how to walk in them, do they really make you look that good?' Silvia asked back.

'I take it you're the *maitre d*?' a deep woman's voice asked from behind them.

The two turned around to see Bojana in a gorgeous flowing robe of rich blue and golden jewellery, including a medusa's head belt buckle holding together her dress, which seemed to be both bursting at the seams in some places, whilst also being lasciviously loose in others. Silvia saw that the Serbian Legate was somehow almost five inches taller than her, which was strange, since all Terrans, both men and women, all shared the same height.

Her eyes drifted towards her feet, to find them perched graciously upon a pair of dark blue heels.

Well... I guess she didn't get Pop's memo to not look too stunning...

What's a 'maitre d'?

'I guess you could call it that...' Mira said.

'No, Mira, *you're* the *head chef*, and thank God for that, from what I hear!' Bojana replied. 'Silvia's the one in charge here!'

Ah, ok. So 'maitre d' means I'm in charge of the party! 'You want to file a complaint, Bojana?' she asked jokingly.

Bojana smiled a broad, happy smile, though Silvia did spot something hiding in the corner of her eyes. 'On the contrary, I'm here to offer my congratulations! This, I must say, quite an event you've put together!'

'Well, thank you!' Silvia replied, unsure as to whether or not Bojana was being nice or if she had secretly expected Silvia to be unable to manage such a task. *I've organized and executed military manoeuvres in active combat theatres featuring hundreds of thousands of troops, thousands of pieces of artillery, as well as aerial support, magical webs and negation fields... Putting together a party was remarkably difficult, yes, given the particularities, yet I'd argue I was more than qualified... plus, I had help!*

Bojana turned towards Mira. 'We haven't spoken since we got here. How are you?' she asked.

Silvia could tell that, this time and towards Mira, Bojana's words rang in complete accordance with her genuine feelings.

Mira's face was unmoving. 'Still getting used to how things work around here, but coping.'

'Yes...' Bojana nodded. 'It's a strange place... it reminds me of London a lot and Belagravia in particular reminds me of the countryside of southern England, though the weather is far more enjoyable!' Bojana lifted one of her eyebrows. 'The people are... *queer*, however, I'll give you that! Less cold than the English, but still arrogant as hell...' Bojana seemed to suddenly find the taste of her own saliva to have turned to the flavour of bitter snot.

'I wasn't talking about Shangri,' Mira replied. 'I was talking about the Hajduks,' she commented dryly.

Bojana's brow furrowed, yet a grin crept across her face as her eyes became inquisitive. 'How so? This isn't the first time around legionnaires, isn't it?'

She used to be a legionnaire, Bojana! She wasn't 'around' the Ghazis! She was one.

Mira smiled curtly. 'How would you refer to Silvia?'

Bojana shared a look with Silvia. 'What do you mean?' she asked.

'In the Ghazis, we would refer to each other as 'cousin', and the splinter legions all still use that word to refer to one another.

'... and here,' Bojana began, as her grin turned to full fruition. 'Here, we're all 'colleagues'...'

'Yeah... that's one thing I'm still not used to!' Mira admitted.

'Are you saying you find us to be less united than other Legions?' her Legate colleague asked.

'You *are* less united than other Legions, though not because you call each other *colleague* instead of *cousin*,' Mira replied.

'How so?' Silvia immediately interrogated.

'I don't know...' Mira replied, this time allowing genuine bewilderment to grace her face. 'Oddly enough, you *do* seem to be less united. You don't call each other words typically reserved for family members, yet you seem to be more of a family than any other legion I've ever seen!' Mira widened her eyes at her own thoughts. 'It's definitely dysfunctional and there's a lot of swearing...'

Now Silvia snorted. 'Look who's fucking talking...'

Mira rolled her eyes. 'I may be a potty mouth in the Ghazis, but here I sound fucking demure... what with all the 'in-my-dick', 'eat-my-dick', 'may-my-mother-die', 'fuck-your-mother's-dead-people'–'

'Ok, Mira, that's enough!' Bojana managed between giggles.

'No! I'm serious! And it's so fucking random! The other day, I was in Bogdan Chiftea's room, telling him what kind of cabbage I needed him to get for the *dolma* – or *sarmale*, which is how you call them – when Alex Berbec walked by and Bogdan, for no reason, said; '*Ayo*!!!'. And, when Alex turned around, he told him to 'eat his dick' – and he used a weird Romanian verb tense – *for no reason*! And then they laughed and they went about their day like nothing happened!'

Ohhh!!! That's nothing, Mira! That's just a running joke they've had for twenty years!

'Mira!' Bojana began. 'First of all, keep it quiet! We're in civilized company here!' she said, nodding towards the mass of dignitaries around them. 'Second of all, do not confuse the *Romanian* and, especially, the *Kalo* Hajduks with the Hajduks *as a whole*!' Bojana paused, as her eyes went blank and she turned to Silvia. 'Sorry, Silvia, but it's true!'

'I know...' Silvia acknowledged.

Bojana nodded through pursed lips before addressing Mira, once more. 'It's *pressure*, Mira, what you are feeling around you. Over *fifty years* of pressure! The swearing and...' she glances towards Silvia. '... and everything else, it's a way to blow off steam.'

'Every Legion has pressure,' Mira countered.

'Yes and every Legion has its own way of coping with that pressure! I will not defend the vulgarity and the degenerate behaviour you have undoubtedly witnessed, yet...' Bojana frowned, as she thought of something. Her generous lips spread into a smile while her eyebrows rose, as she thought of the best way to say what had to be said.

'In any relationship, even if there are fights and arguments, there is still hope, since it means that both people still believe in the relationship and that it's still worth fighting for! It is only if all communication stops, that you should begin to worry! Only *then*, is there no hope anymore and the relationship is over!'

God! I miss having her around and it's only been a month... Silvia couldn't help but feel disappointed in herself, as she realized that Sanjak Manor must be a much more peaceful place than the Convent Garden Embassy.

'Well,' Bojana took a deep breath, having said her piece. 'I have a contact which arrived around ten minutes ago, with which I wish to discuss some things. I'll introduce you all to him later on tonight! So, I'll leave you two to it!!' she cut off their conversation.

After a curt exchange of pleasantries, she turned around and left, leaving Silvia and Mira to look at her rolling shapes as she melded with the crowd and other glances, no-less flattering, yet far more lustful, followed the Serb Legate as she disappeared.

'I get the high-heels thing...' Mira concluded.

'Me too...' Silvia decided that she would dedicate around ten minutes each morning to learning to walk in those things. 'Let's go get Nick! He's probably assaulting the buffet and we need food left over for the guests!'

Mira glanced at her watch. 'The second round's gonna come in any second now.'

It had better, Mira. It had better.

They found Nick virtually glued to one of the buffet tables, next to Anwar and a mackerel tabby cat man.

'Mira!' he said, holding a meatball in his hand. 'These are fucking amazing! What the fuck are these?'

'Moroccan Keftas.'

'These are fucking amazing, they're better than fucking *ćevapi* or *mici*, Sil! They're tremendous!' he said to Silvia.

'Nick!' Silvia moved in closer. 'You're supposed to leave some for the guests!'

'Like *I'm* the problem!?' he gestured towards the two guests next to him. 'These two assholes are gulping down plates!'

'*Nick!!!*' Silvia glanced towards the two Shangrians. *Holly shit! The brown bear is fucking Anwar!*

'Oh, right! Where are my manners?' he turned to the two guests. 'You two remember Anwar?'

'Hello!' the giant bearman bellowed in a friendly manner.

'Mister Brownhen, yes! We remember you, of course! You work with Mr. Bittercastle!'

'I work *for* Mr. Bittercastle, Lady Silvia!' the bearman replied. He turned to Mira. 'Lady Mira, Nick tells me that you were the one in charge of the buffet?'

'Yes...!?'

'This is some of the best food I've had in my entire life!' Silvia saw that the hair around his snout was glistening with fats and sauces. In his hand he held a plate with a large slab of white cheese soaked in what appeared to be honey. 'I came here in advance to check things out for *my guy*, and I have to say that Nick's hospitality and your cooking is making my job very difficult!'

'Well, I'm glad I could be a hindrance!' Mira smiled graciously. 'Make sure to leave some room left over for later! I sneaked in some quiche later on in the evening!'

The bearman seemed to frown. 'I'm sorry, Lady Mira! What is '*quiche*'?'

'Eh...' Mira began. 'It's like a savoury pie with...' Mira's eyes narrowed. 'You don't know what 'quiche' is?'

Anwar seemed taken aback. 'No... it's why I was asking you!'

'Huh... strange...' Mira responded cryptically. She noticed the weird looks she was getting from all around. 'The, uhm...'

It's not like her to 'uhm' What the fuck is she...

Oh...

Nononononono!

'The Ursai of Barlog love quiche!' her Arabian colleague said.

Jesus Christ woman! They have beef with the Ursai of Barlog! Don't mention...

Huh? Silvia had initially wanted to sneak a quick look towards Anwar to see exactly how offended he was, only to find something else across his dark ursai eyes, which gave her pause.

Is... is he sad? Pensive? What the -

'You've been to Barlog?' he asked Mira.

'I lived there for a few months when I was young. My sister took me there when she was visiting.'

'I see...' he replied. The strange melancholy that had seemed to overwhelm him continued, as his eyes drifted and he took a deep breath and blurted out a question. 'How are –'

He stopped himself, blinked his eyes closed in annoyance at his own little lapse in judgement and turned to the catman. 'Where are my manners? This is Kroton Grenra Lonza. He's a friend of ours in the Colonial Constabulary. He's helping us out with the thing Nick's been seeing us for!'

'Pleased to meet you!' the bast greeted them and extended his hand, likely having picked-up on Terran customs from Anwar, who in turn had learned it from Nick.

After introducing herself to Kroton and, as the catman shook hands with Mira, Silvia continued to study Anwar. *Something... there is something there! Information, at least, and...*

... potentially something else... 'Mr. Brownhen, if I may, what was it that you wanted to ask?' Silvia ventured, suspecting that there was something to be found within the reply.

'It's... it's nothing, Lady Silvia! I... I had a curiosity that's all! Nothing for now!'

'Huh!' Nick scoffed. 'Clearly it wasn't nothing, *Annie*! Come on! Out with it! Whataya wanna know?'

'*Annie*'?

Anwar put his plate down on the table and Silvia saw him glance towards the main entrance. Once content that his boss hadn't arrived yet, he turned his gaze to Mira. 'What kind of people are they? Our kinsmen in Barlog?'

Mira's face became blank, yet Silvia knew her well enough to know that her mind was racing. *Good! Don't fuck this up! Whatever 'this' is!*

'Have you ever met a Libra Ursai of Barlog?' she asked him.

'No... I haven't. It is...' he turned to Kroton. '... *taboo*.'

The catman nodded in understanding. *He respects him. He is saying that he will keep this secret and Anwar trusts him to do so.*

Anwar continued. 'It is taboo to even speak of them or acknowledge their existence openly. To be honest, I didn't know that much about them until they showed up on the news with...' he looked at the three Terrans and spoke softly. '... with *your thing* in the Milky Way and then later in Andromeda and Triangulum.'

'I see...' Mira mused. 'What would you like to know?' she said.

'Are they...' the ursai frowned, seemingly changing his mind. 'How do *you* see them? Your people have been at war with them and now you're allies – *friends* even – you must know a great deal about them. You must *think* something of them! What... what do you think (or feel) when you hear of the Ursai of Barlog?'

Mira smiled. 'I think of the smell of cinnamon in the air on a cold morning.'

Anwar's eyes quivered for a fraction of a second.

Yes, Mira, go on!

'I think of the smell of toasty bread meeting the tartness of an overnight yeast, still cloning to the cold air! I think of the sun, coming through melting ice, in little rivers that make a friendly, sparkly sound as they rush towards a bustling public square. I think of patches of ice between cold springwater as the sound of crackling fires meets the rough-and-tumble of children playing in the snow. I think of deep singing trembling through the halls of rock carved into the mountains long ago, when the world was young. I think of evergreen moss and fir trees resting upon rolling hills underneath rays of smouldering stone and the feeling of a warm woollen cloak around me, as nearby a cave-sheep brays against the cold vapour of a hot cup of chocolate and a feeling of home.'

Silvia glanced towards Anwar, seeing his eyes to be dreamy.

The young Mira continued. 'A home that was not mine when I first set foot inside, but which quickly became one, on account of the warmth of the people within, who saw the world outside to be a cold place, but from where could come warm friends that must be treated to the warmth of their own hearths. I think of that feeling a child feels when he wakes up at a time of his choosing and walks in is pyjamas down the stairs to where his own inner world sits huddled around a freshly cooked meal.'

She smiled, both to herself and to Anwar. 'There is quiche and there is roasted lamb... and all the sauces are honey and berries and soy sauce... and there is a little corner for you, where you can listen in on everyone talking about...' she chuckled. '... mostly food, mostly other times they had seen each other, sometimes politics or some movie they saw or a book they read. Sometimes they talk about friends they have not seen in a long while and how...' now she faltered a bit, '... and how they *missed* them. How sometimes the world takes from you, bit-by-bit, and people go away... and how, when they go away, you should remember the times you were with them in places such as those... next to them, with a bowl of warm soup in your hands...'

'Moments that... never really go away...' she concluded.

It took a moment for Silvia to snap out of her nostalgia for the dream of an absent childhood Mira's words had carried her into. In truth, no one might have snapped out of it, were it not for the loud entrance of a gigantic albino bearman through the main entrance of the Convent Garden Embassy.

Anwar's eyes darted towards the new arrival and he seemed to stand up straight as he slowly shook his head, as if to cast off the flakes of Mira's spell. He put his hand forth and grabbed one of Mira's hands in one of his massive paws and Silvia saw him give her a good squeeze. The tips of the young Terrans fingers curled over the bottom of the ursai's paws, as they also squeezed back.

He rumbled softly. 'I hope that we are also *that*! In our own way; one which you will not leave this City without feeling for yourself – if you have not felt it already! *That*, I promise you! But, now, I must go!' he let go of her hand and turned to Kroton. 'Come! He's gonna want to introduce you to their General Pop himself!'

Kroton nodded.

'I hope to see you all again, Lady Mira, Lady Silvia!' he tilted his head towards both women, before nodding towards Nick, and the two Shangrians made towards their boss, a look of anticipation and a whisper of embarrassment upon his brown face.

'Did you spend Christmas in Barlog?' Nick asked, once they were out of earshot.

Mira rubbed her nose. 'Every day is Christmas there!'

Silvia saw that some of her make-up had caked around her eyes.

Before she could say anything, Mira looked at her watch and said, 'I need to go make sure they didn't overcook the *bürek* !' she immediately excused herself and then made straight for the kitchen.

'I ain't gonna lie to you, Sil, that was fucking beautiful!' Nick said to her, a look of contemplating still on his face, as he bit into another meatball. 'Made me feel all warm inside!'

'It did...' *It really did... poor thing... she was thinking about the boy, Thomas, towards the end of it*. She sighed, just as she saw Nick reach towards a small vegetarian sarma wrapped in sauerkraut leaves. '*You* need to stop gorging here like an idiot and start mingling!'

'Mingling?' Nick asked, just as two human women emerged next to them and began trying some of the food on offer at the buffet.

'Yes, be sociable!' Silvia instructed as Nick took clear notice of the two women.

'How could I not be with *situations* such as these in the vicinity!' he said loudly, switching to English. 'Wella and Pravana, right?'

Silvia glanced towards the women. *Yeah, that's right! They work at the Vanir Embassy. Category I Staff Clearance, the highest we give out for non-republican staff...*

Silvia gave Nick a quick side-eye. *Fuck your mother, Nick! You read the guestlist just so that you could check out which potential curvettes where coming over?*

She quickly returned her gaze to the two women. They were both human and on was almost two heads shorter than a Terran. Silvia quickly identified her as the *real* 'situation', Wella, who was athletic, full-breasted, narrow-hipped and clear-skinned, with full lips, bright blue eyes, long lashes and, most importantly, *blonde* hair, very much like Silvia's own golden locks.

She's Nick's type... which is weird. It always was weird. It's still weird, but at least I'm used to it now. His ex-wife had been a Romanian woman who looked exactly like that, with the only notable difference being that she also hazel eyes, unlike Silvia's own bright blue eyes. All the women he had cheated on his ex-wife also fit that mould, in one way or another, even Joey, his fellow Hajduk, who despite having a slightly narrower face with sharper features, as well as smaller breasts, was also a naturally blond woman with long eyelashes and full lips.

Silvia turned towards the other one, Pravana, who was quite a different kind of situation.

She was taller than Wella, with a lithe frame and darker features, captured by a wide chest and skin the colour of thick vanilla ice-cream. Thick brown locks were held together in stylish ponytail that flared towards her back, while her upper lip was not as full as the one beneath it. Her eyes were dark amber and the light played mischievously in the space between her thick eyebrows and her luscious lashes, while her jawline seemed remarkably robust and sharp for a non-Terran woman. Unlike Wella, who was wearing a dress of beige and gold, she was wearing a sultry cocktail dress of deep ultramarine and red accessories. Silvia's gaze slowly followed the curve of her slightly open mouth, all the way to her eyes, which were locked on hers.

'Come on! Didn't they have you learn English over there at Borbakhan Way?' Nick asked, referring to the location of the Vanir Embassy. Silvia knew that he was speaking to Wella in particular.

'Yes, they do!' Wella blurted out. 'You must be Centurion Nicolae Lăutaru!'

Silvia's eyes went straight towards the blonde Shangri woman and she saw the look in her eyes and heard the stutter in her voice. *Well, good job, Nick! I guess you're not going to bed alone tonight...*

'Guilty as charged! I see you've done your research! What do you think of the party?' Nick went on.

'It's quite lovely, actually! The food looks tasty!' Wella answered.

'And it's not the only thing that looks tasty!' Nick commented, his eyes never leaving hers. 'Are you being careful?'

Wella was quiet for a moment, visibly confused. 'Why? Are we in danger?' she giggled nervously, sparing a quick glance towards Silvia.

'Oh, no! This is Silvia!' he said, gesturing towards his oldest friend. 'Don't worry about her! She likes girls too!'

Nick... Silvia's eyes rushed from Wella's towards Pravana's.

Who held her gaze...

Yum.

'Anyway, I'm Nick! Didn't they tell you over there at the Vanir Embassy that Terrans are dangerous?'

Wella giggled nervously. 'You don't look that dangerous!' she replied.

Silvia granted Pravana another heavy look, which she reciprocated very generously.

'Looks can be deceiving, baby girl! I'm all savagery behind this thin veneer of gentlemanly poise!' Nick explained.

'Oh, really?' she replied.

'Oh, yeah! I grunt and I rut and I do it a lot! You like hogs? Boars I mean?' he asked.

Wella smiled. 'I...' she chuckled. 'I work at the Vanir Embassy. What do you think?'

'I think they don't serve pork at the cafeteria over there!' Nick glanced towards the table beside them, stacked high with food and squinted. He sniffed the air for a moment and shrugged. '... and neither do we...'

He turned to Silvia. 'This is what happens when we put an Arab in charge of catering!'

Indeed. I didn't notice that...

Nick turned back towards the two guests. 'So, if you wanna have a taste of the forbidden meat, you're gonna have to work hard for it.'

'Oh, yeah?' Wella replied.

'Oh, yeah!' Nick responded.

'What if I don't want a taste of the forbidden meat?' (She clearly did.)

'D'you got a boyfriend?' Nick immediately asked.

'Y-yes?!' she replied.

'Do you cheat?' he asked

'No!' she replied sheepishly.

Nick gave her a look.

'... *Yeah*?!' she confessed.

'You see, I knew you were a pretty little liar the moment I saw you! Both of you! Lie to me a lil' more! I like being lied to!' he instructed them both.

Silvia couldn't help it anymore and chuckled. 'Christ, Nick! Let her be!'

'You girls like cocaine?' Nick asked, unfazed.

'Yes!' this time it was Pravana who answered. Immediately.

Nick pointed towards the dark-haired minx. 'I see you don't like doing as you're told! And *I* like that!' Nick turned to Silvia and opened his palm. 'I think we should go over to the fourth bathroom on the left of the second floor in the East wing!' he turned back towards the two guests. 'We'll show you some of our friends; maybe you can show us some of your girlfriends! We're good hosts! You can make yourselves feel like home!' He turned towards Wella. '... you can put your feet up and everything...'

'Weren't you supposed to be dangerous?' Pravana asked them both with her eyes.

'Why are you being so judgemental? Is it because I'm a Terran? Didn't your mother teach you that it's not nice to be racist?' Nick said, pointing at himself in mock surprise.

'You said earlier that you were dangerous!' Wella pointed out.

'Well, maybe I'm pretty *big* liar myself!' he admitted. He turned to Silvia. 'Come! Let's go!'

'You go on!' she informed him, noticing Pravana's look of disappointment. 'I'll powder my nose later once our duties for the evening are completed...' *Which is what you will do after you're done tweaking with these two in the bathroom where I had Gabi Gâlmă hide the cocaine which I had to figure out how to smuggle and hide here!*

Nick scoffed. 'That's Silvia for you!' she informed the two. 'Very responsible! I'll see you in the second half?' he asked his colleague.

'You need to see me a few times in the first half too!' she muttered through a smirk.

'Yes, yes! Will do!' he confirmed. 'Are you responsible?' he asked Wella as he invited her to take him by the arm.

'I'm very responsible!' she replied, holding his arm as Pravana took a hold of his other arm, right after giving Silvia an inviting look.

Nick went on. 'Well, you be sure to keep *me* out of trouble!'

'That's funny, because you seem like *you're* the trouble!' Wella played back.

'Oh, what an astute little thing you are! Did you ever hear the story of Little Red Riding Hood and...' he began, as he took them both away.

Silvia watched the three leave. She did agree that the dark-haired one was kinda cute.

The party did, indeed, have two phases: the formal event and then the informal party afterwards. After the dignitaries and the bureaucrats and the civilians would leave, the Hajduks and their friends from the other Republican embassies would stay on further into the night and party. She would drink and do drugs then, if she still had any energy left. For now, she had work to do and stuff to pay attention to.

Such as how she was the only one without a glass of alcohol in her hand. She turned towards the nearby bar next to the buffet table and beckoned the robot bartender to come over, once he was serving some Shangri merchant and his... (hopefully) *wife*.

'What do you recommend!' a voice behind her said. In English, though she did not recognize the voice... and the accent was peculiar... almost American.

She turned around to see Ulfrik from across the road.

He towered over her, yet he did so gracefully, as he leaned on the bar with his elbow. She was a bit surprised by how stealthy he had been, as he had managed to emerge right next to her without her superhuman senses alerting her to his approach.

Her eyes surveyed him swiftly. He appeared to be wearing some kind of Shangri variation of a Terran tuxedo. Instead of a three-piece suit, it appeared to be a two-piece of a white shirt with a plain collar, as well as black and loose bodysuit tied with a sash by his waist. She caught a glance of dark moccasins on his feet, though he also wore thin black socks (which was also a little weird; though they did crawl up his legs beneath a loosely fitting pant leg right at his ankles). He wore no distinguishing marking and no accessories bar two gold bracelets on each of his wrists, just barely visible from beneath the white cuffs that reached out perfectly at the end of his forearms. His hair, of a light brown, was somewhat longer than she remembered, yet it was neatly formed around his head in a natural manner, bereft of any artificial shinning or glistening.

Silvia remembered herself. ' Sir Langley-Creekside! I'm glad to see you could make it!'

Ulfrik smiled. 'I'm glad I was invited! It was a long journey, from across the street!'

Silvia couldn't help herself from smiling. 'Is Abiola here as well?' she asked, remembering his cat's name.

'No, no! Far too crowded for her style. No! She's was taking a nap in bed when I left!'

Lucky her... 'That's too bad! Lorgar would've really appreciated it if she would have come!'

Ulfrik's face fell. 'Oh... I didn't... I mean... I can go get her if you want!' he pointed towards the entrance.

'No!' Silvia chuckled, reaching for his arm and grasping it. 'Don't bring your cat!' she giggled. 'I was joking!'

'Oh!' Ulfrik seemed relieved.

'Yeah! Lorgar is upstairs! He likes large groups of people, but he can get quite rowdy!' *We can't have him in public. Not with so many racial groups around. It's a political event, but he would get too political; very quickly and very political...*

'Would you care for a beverage?' the bartender robot asked.

'Yes...' Silvia remembered. 'You wanted a drink, too?' she asked Ulfrik.

'I was hoping for a recommendation first!'

'I, eh...'

Ulfrik put his hand forward as an apology. 'No! Sorry! I don't want to hold you up with my silly nonsense!'

'-No! No!' Silvia smiled. 'Let me be a good host! So...'

'Yes?'

She put her closed fist before her as she counted out the options. 'Alcoholic or non-alcoholic?'

'Whatever is the Terran tradition!'

'Alcoholic! Sparkly or non-sparkly?'

'*Uhhh*!' Ulfrik squinted. 'That's a tough one!'

'There's no Terran tradition,' she anticipated his question.

'Centurion Murărescu!' the robot interrupted. They both turned towards it. 'You instructed us beverage operators to operate smoothly!' He used a glass he had been cleaning to point towards their exchange. '*This* is unconducive towards efficiency! A line will form up for the other guests! Might I recommend that I take your order while you and the gentleman discover his?'

'Yes!' Silvia realised the robot was right. 'I'll have a...' *Holy shit, I was gonna get a glass of champagne to just wave around for the guests to see and feel at ease, but now I feel like I should pick something fancy... Think Centurion Murărescu! Think! What would Pop do?*

'I'll have an *old-fashioned*!' she remembered.

'Classic or Terran?' he asked.

'Terran!'

'And I'll have what she's having!' Ulfrik quickly instructed.

'Excellent! Two Terran old-fashioneds coming up! Estimated wait time: circa two minutes!' the bartender replied, before getting to work.

'Is that sparkly or non-sparkly?' Ulfrik asked.

'Non. And it's *very* alcoholic!'

'Well, it *is* a Terran party!' he joked back.

Silvia smiled. 'Well, I hope you enjoy it! To be honest, I hope you enjoy the evening! It's the least we could do! Mira loves Lorgar very much and, from our understanding, you and Abiola saved his life!'

'Abiola did most of the saving! I just opened the door. *Twice*!' Ulfrik paused and Silvia saw him think things over for a second. Just a second. 'You know, Abiola kinda liked Lorgar!'

'Oh! She did?'

'Yeah...'

'Well, Lorgar *loved* her. He hasn't stopped talking about her ever since!'

Ulfrik chuckled. 'Well, Abiola *doesn't* talk, but I know her. I'm certain she wouldn't mind seeing him again!'

Now it was Silvia turn to chuckle. 'Oh, I don't think they would do much more than *see* each other, at least not if Lorgar had his way...'

Ulfrik caught on. '... which would be *with her*, I get it!'

Clever wordplay... in English... by a non-native. 'Your grasp of the Terran language is quite firm, I see!' she highlighted.

'Thank you! I, eh, had it learned when I heard you were moving over! I learned Morian before that and... *eh*... 我之前學過廣東話!' he announced, his mouth sounding like complete gibberish.

'Is... is that *Mandarin*?!' she asked, perplexed.

'*Cantonese*, to be precise, I learned it back when General Wei was here! And that one was very heard to learn, because there weren't any translation modules available when he first came here!'

Silvia stared at him for a moment in utter bewilderment.

Ulfrik spotted it. 'I, uh, I wanna be a good neighbour! I've been planning to learn Romanian, but there aren't any modules available yet!'

Good! We tried very hard to keep it that way! 'English will do just fine, for now!' she informed him curtly.

'For now!' Ulfrik agreed, just as their drinks arrived.

Silvia picked up her glass and held it in front of him. He went to take it and their hands touched. He pulled on the glass a little. Silvia didn't let go. 'This is *my* glass!' She nodded towards the other glass. 'That's your glass! Pick it up and toast! It's a Terran tradition!'

Ulfrik did as instructed. 'A toast to your hospitality! To Lorgar and Abiola! To –'

Silvia interrupted him by chinking his glass. 'Just *that*! No words! Just drink – and, by the way, it's very strong!'

'Oh, *really?*' he asked.

'Yeah! It's a *Terran* old-fashioned. Which means that it has a lot more alcohol than usual!'

'I see!' Ulfrik eyed his glass. 'Well! To new experiences!' he chinked her glass again and they both drank.

Silvia could tell from the pained look on his face (which we valiantly tried to hide) that he was fighting back the urge to not swallow the burning alien firewater that had just entered his mouth.

'That's... that's very flavourful!' he insisted after he swallowed a liquid that made his oesophagus catch flame.

'Told ya!' she said as she rested the glass on one of her palms. 'Should've gone for the classic!'

Ulfrik studied her for a moment and Silvia found herself wondering what he was thinking about. Eventually, he smirked knowingly, as if he had just caught on to a joke he had heard. 'You keep this place together, don't you?' he asked.

What? 'I'm not sure I catch your meaning!'

Ulfrik shrugged and, remarkably, took another sip of his beverage. 'Before my current job, I used to work off-world – in the *Province*, as well call it. My job was to go to distressed stations and to help them get back on track.'

'Sounds adventurous!' *Nothing like the shit I've been through, no doubt, yet still vaguely interesting.*

'It really wasn't! Two years into it and I was *praying* to bump into some pirates or smugglers or rebels or... just something to break through the monotony! Mostly what I would do was go to who-knows-how-many stations that were usually understaffed, underpaid, underperforming or, very rarely, *unstable* and help them with their issues!'

'Like a repairman!'

'*Exactly* like a repairman!'

'I assume you fixed all of these stations?' she asked, deciding to stroke his ego. He was a guest after all.

'I don't think I fixed a single station my entire career!' Ulfrik confessed.

'Oh, really?'

'Really!' he confirmed.

'You're pretty confident for a bad repairman!' He did seem quite sure of himself overall. Silvia wasn't sure if this was some strange Shangri idea about how competence worked or if he was messing with her.

'Ah, but I was an *amazing* repairman!'

'An amazing repairman who only leaves broken stations in his wake?'

'Ah!!! But, they weren't! Every station I ever arrived in was back to peak performance by the time I was gone!' Ulfrik put his glass forwards towards her and toasted '*To all the stations*!'

She chinked his glass and they both took a sip.

Ulfrik continued. '*I* never fixed anything. *But!* What I always did, whenever I got to a new station, was look for the person that was still holding the whole thing together! Sometimes it was the Governor, sometimes it was the accountant, sometimes it was one of the engineers...' Ulfrik chuckled. '... one time, it was the husband of the daughter of the Head of Sanitation! You never really know until you get there and see for yourself! At first, it would take me months to figure out who that person was! With time, I got better and better at it! After I figured that out, I just made sure the things that person needed in order to fix things were provided to them as swiftly as possible!'

'And you think that *I* am that person of this station?'

Ulfrik caught wind of what she was suggesting. 'I'm not saying you run a bad station here! From what I can tell, it's quite the opposite! *But*, every place has someone like you! Good or bad! Someone who keeps everything together working as well as they possibly can given the circumstances! What gave you away is the way people around you – the people who *know* you – all look at you! Rather, how they look *to* you! I look around and I see... well...' Ulfrik's eyes widened and he swallowed his words in anticipation of his own audacity. '... I see a band of hard bastards, stone-cold killers, rugged ruffians and vicious wildlings... and they *all* look to you for guidance and approval...'

Ulfrik locked eyes with her fully now. 'It just appears to me that you're the most capable person in this room, Centurion Murărescu! Everyone in-the-know seems to think that!'

'Oh, yeah...?' Silvia stared into his soul for a moment before moving in slowly towards him. She pulled his jacket and drew his ear next to her mouth.

He allowed it.

'Your words are very kind and I can see that you're a good man! I saw *you* looking at me the moment you walked in and I know you kept looking at me on-and-off for the following twelve minutes,' she said truthfully. 'Do you want to be friends?'

'I thought all good neighbours were supposed to be friends!' he spoke softly.

'But do *you* want to be friends?' she repeated.

'I would love to be your friend!' he growled softly.

'Good!' she said, before squeezing his jacket harder, making sure that he felt it tightening around his collar. 'If you ever refer to me, or my people, as 'bastards', 'ruffians' or 'wildlings' ever again, I can promise you that you will find that your capable assessment is correct in its most absolute detail, including the other words you used! Guest or not!' She spoke as softly and as menacingly as she could. 'Neighbour or not!'

She felt him harden as he heard her words and he saw goosebumps form above his collar. *Good!*

She let go of him.

'And... then we wouldn't be friends?' he asked.

This one is either very brave or very stupid. 'No!'

'I wouldn't like that...' He stared at her for a while. 'Well, then, I apologise for my choice of words, Centurion Murărescu!'

Took you long enough.

Ulfrik held her gaze and didn't flinch. There was something about it. There was something about him. He seemed so soft and jovial, yet behind it... there was *something*. A resolute hardness to him. He wasn't joking. He wasn't being evasive or infantile. He was being honest.

Something about that made Silvia to want to keep the door open more than any neighbourly sympathy. 'I could tell.' She smiled at him as she picked up her glass from the bar, taking a sip as their eyes met once more.

'I *was* being pretty transparent, wasn't I?' he said playfully.

'You were...' Silvia smirked. 'Though, I must also be transparent with you!' she declared, laying her glass on the bar. 'We have a saying on Terra: *you're barking up the wrong tree!*' she said, as the laurel tree of the Terran Embassy loomed in the distance behind her.

'Yeah... here in Shangri it's *you're singing at the wrong gate*!' Ulfrik grinned as he interrupted Silvia.

That sounds very Romanian for some reason... Are we talking about the same thing?

Ulfrik glanced towards the direction Nick had taken the two girls from the Vanir Embassy, before turning back towards Silvia's slightly quizzed expression. He chuckled softly. 'I saw the way you and that brunette were looking at each other. Can't say I've seen you look at any man in here the way you looked at her!' Now he shrugged to himself, sincerely disappointed. 'I knew I was barking up the wrong tree when I came over to you, but I just wanted to get the barks out of me. They were in there too long–'

'I'm not *gay*!' Silvia interrupted, now very irritated.

Ulfrik looked stunner. '... bisexual?' he asked (full of hope).

'*In a sense*!' she responded somewhat angrily.

'Oh! Oh...' Ulfrik seemed to suddenly become very worried about something. 'Is... is the guy who walked away with the girls... is he your husband!'

Jesus Christ, no! 'No!'

'Well, do you have a husband?'

Now Silvia smiled at his audacity, yet she did find him rather entertaining. '*No*!'

'Boyfriend?'

'No!'

'Girlfriend?'

'No!'

'... I am *so* confused right now!' Ulfrik confessed.

Now it was Silvia's turn to smile. The whole exchange had had its ups-and-downs, but she did have responsibilities and there was still work to be done for the evening. She downed her drink and put down her empty drink, as the ice clinked against the glass. '*Girls* are fun!' she looked into his shinning blue eyes for a moment before her eyes went right through his and she stared off into the distance for a second. '*I* am not fun!'

'I doubt that!' Ulfrik quipped and Silvia knew that he genuinely believed what he was saying.

'Sure you do!' she smiled bitterly. 'Enjoy your evening, Sir Langley-Creekside!' she said, as she began to move away from the bar.

'Call me 'Ulfrik'!' he instructed, with a bravado that was apparently a deeply embedded character trait of his.

She paused, before slowly turning towards him. She looked at him now through the golden wings of one of the eagles on her right shoulder. 'Call me 'Silvia'!' she responded.

'I'll see you around... *neighbour*,' he grinned boyishly.

Huh...

Silvia began walking away.

Not for me...

Chapter X

On a High Note

Jesus Christ... what a boring fucking man!

'Me and my partner, The Honourable Mbembe Mutumbo-Cowlanpore – you might have heard of him through his ventures in the B2B generative AI space! – *we* actually started out as *highwaymen*!' the boring man said.

Well, that's actually interesting! What a miracle! Laur had scheduled about two minutes of small-talk per Shangri businessman, yet those were two *looong* minutes with some of them... '*Highwaymen?*' he asked. 'Like a bandit?'

'Oh! God no! Though some of our margins could be considered *highway robbery*!' the boring man explained. 'No! A highwayman – or highway*person,* I should say – is a broker for urban trade within the City! We act on behalf of asset-heavy investors by...'

Jesus fucking H. Christ! There he goes again with the yapping. Laur looked at the man's wife.

She was pretending to be interested, but he could tell she was as bored as he was.

For fucking fuck's sake! FOCUS ON WHAT HE IS SAYING! It would look bad if he realized I was blanking out due to utter boredom when he talks about...

What the fuck is he talking about again?

'... because back in the crash of a few years back in the rhodium markets (they're all backed by iridium derivatives...'

I DON'T CARE!!! I DO NOT CARE!!!

Fucking hell... Make sure to act interested!

... but not too interested! Else, he might go on-and-on-and-on...!

Quick! Say something vague so he thinks you're following! 'Oh! But that's always the case, isn't it?'

The boring man (who also had a boring voice) looked stunned. 'Sometimes, commodities on the rhodium derivatives market are backed by *cobalt*! It all has to do with the tax considerations...'

AHHHHHHHHHHHHHHHH!!!!!!!!!!

Mother of GOD!!! Nobody cares!!!

Laur looked around for an escape. Silvia was not around and neither was Nick and he had ordered the others keep their distance and focus on both entertaining *and surveying* their own designated guests. Basenji was nearby, yet he wouldn't be able to help that much, given his speaking commitments and Technowolf was busy chatting up the Head of the Shangri Constabulary, a task far more important than that of rescuing Laur from his kryptonite: monotonous chit-chat.

The Republican Emissaries that had gathered at Convent Garden were all busy entertaining their respective key accounts and connections. He had been in contact with all of them, yet he couldn't exactly say that he knew them well enough to be able subtly communicate that he couldn't take it anymore.

Well, except one of them in particular... and where the fuck is he actually?

As if sensing his distress, he felt a hand gently pat him on his upper back.

Josip arrived to the rescue. '*Ah*, Viscount Hardrada-Clairfontain! I'm so pleased you could make it!'

Hardrada... like the Viking! So, that was his name!

Josip continued. 'I read in *The Excelsior* this morning about your foray into the construction insurance space!?'

'Lord Hodočasnik! Yes, yes! The Carrington Construction deal!'

'The very same! I wish you best of fortunes in the new endeavour! I see you've met my colleague, Ambassador Pop?'

'Ah, yes! I was just telling his excellency of our recent pivot following the developments in the energy markets! And the Carrington Construction Corporation is definitely part of that pivot!' He turned to back to Laur.

Oh, God, no!

'You've probably read yesterday's report from the Chancellor of the Exchequer concerning the administration's decision to peg energy futures against periodic table conversion rates?'

I... I know what all those individual words mean... but placed together in that arrangement, they sound like delirium to me... 'Yes! It was an interesting read!'

'If I may say, your excellency, what *is* the position of the Republican Alliance vis-à-vis the Chancellor's report?'

Oh... oh shit... oh... fuck... fuck...

Josip snorted.

Laur turned to look at him, doing his best to match the psychopath in coldness of demeanour, whilst also feeling his collar heat up.

'You cheeky rapscallion!' Josip joked. 'Lord Viscount! You know full well that we cannot comment on the recent *quantitative easing* policies!'

We can't?

Now the Viscount suddenly became animated. 'Ah!' He raised a finger. '*But*! You are *referring* to them as quantitative easing policies! Which is a *comment* all on its own!'

Josip smiled charmingly. 'I am simply mimicking the lingo *on Light Street* these days!'

Light Street? What the fuck is Light Street?

'Yes, well, all of Light Street sees the measures as quantitative easing, on account of the recent drop in energy demand!'

Josip did not allow him to continue, as he raised his hand and, magically, one of the Croat Hajduks, appeared right next to him. 'Allow me to present Simon Toderić! He is the Head of the Terran-Shangri Exchange Commission and he's the one who bears the task of analyzing the energy markets *and of submitting our tariff recommendations to the Terran High Command!*'

'*Ohhh...*' the Viscount mouthed in understanding.

Ohhh... Ha! Good job, Josip! I knew you'd be great at this!

'Yes! I'm certain you too have much to discuss concerning the recent developments! I'm certain we can help each other navigate these interesting times together! Yet, if you may pardon us Viscount, if I may have a word with my colleague!' Josip said to the boring man, patting Laur on the back.

The Viscount and his wife agreed and they exchanged pleasantries.

"*Head of the Terran-Shangri Exchange Commission?*' Laur asked, just as they were out of earshot. *You made that up right just now, didn't you?*

Josip ignored him. 'You're a spoilt little brat! You know that?'

'What?' *Am I doing something wrong?*

Josip looked down and shook his head. 'You're bored out of your mind, aren't you?'

Laur just had to give him an annoyed look as an answer.

'You've been doing this for twenty minutes...' Josip began.

'... felt like twenty fucking years...' Laur muttered.

'I could tell! It's why I came to the rescue!'

'Oh, yeah?' Laur asked, as the two men surveyed the crowd gathered before them in the Great Hall of the Convent Garden Embassy. 'Good news or bad?'

'*Spoilt*, just like I said!' Josip grinned to himself before answering. 'Neither. It's an opinion, actually!'

'Oh, please do tell... I miss hearing someone with an actual opinion of his own babble next to me, as opposed to all these NPCs...'

'Your guy...' Josip began. '*Mr. Bleach...*'

Laur saw Josip glance towards one guest in particular and he followed his gaze to see Big White himself, clearly trying to impress the Hyperborean Emissary with some clever joke or another.

'What about him?' Laur asked.

'Do you...' Josip pretended to be at a loss for words. '... *believe* in him?' he finished.

Laur's brow furrowed. 'I take it you don't?'

Josip sighed. 'He left the asylum a week ago and, from what I hear, he has no plans of returning. He's suing the government for the way they treated him and the way they *allegedly* mismanaged his trial. Now, people say he's back on the streets and people are going missing, wild parties are being thrown, power is going missing from the grid...*noticeably...*'

Noise... He's making noise, I know, Josip! 'I see the same thing you're seeing, though I'm at a loss for solutions...' Laur squinted as he pierced through Josip's mentality, which he knew very well after all those years with him, carefully studying his peculiar psychopathy. 'And *your* solution is...' Laur began, knowing full well what it was.

'The same as yours,' Josip replied bluntly.

Huh... so you just came here to cast your vote. 'It's complicated, Josip, and you know it! The contingency plan... it's a gamble!'

'These are not the bears of Barlog, Laur, you forget that! Whatever might happen after, we could navigate easily, at least for a while, until the waters settled. They've never seen a war!'

Laur smirked. 'They've never seen *all-out* war. They've seen conflicts... in the City... amongst themselves and with the Constabulary and even with the imperials here. They've fought more battles here than we ever will. They have experience we don't! On top of that, we would cause disruption. We might end up breaking a perfectly functional machine!'

Josip sighed. 'A machine that does what, Laur?' He turned around to face Laur diagonally as he looked towards someone in the distance. 'Can you *predict* this man?' he asked. 'Can you read him?'

'Not yet,' Laur confessed.

'Can you – or *anyone*, for that matter – *ever*?' Josip pressed.

Laur stared at him now

He knew he was right.

He might have given a response, yet Josip continued. 'He's *blessed*!' the Croat smirked. 'He's blessed with people around him of quality, from what I hear. *Loyal* people. *Hardworking* people. *Reasonable* people. People who can actually tell you how they would like the weather to be tomorrow and whom you can trust to be *consistent*.' Josip smirked and came close. '... sounds familiar?' he said, patting him on the shoulder.

Feeling frisky today, aren't we Josip?

'*Ah*! Bojana!' Josip said to the person he had been studying as she made her way across the room. 'How gracious of you to grant us the pleasure of seeing you up-close in all your glory!' he smoothly said to his old colleague.

Laur turned to see Bojana approaching. At her side walked a man of whose race he had heard of, yet had never seen up until this point in his life. The origins of Vulpine were obscured by the shifting of history, as were many other branches of the Tree of Man. The Vulpine themselves maintained only a watered down origin myth, which spoke of a world of cold islands and warm winds.

In short (no pun intended), they were essentially diminutive remani, with this particular individual resembling a deep red fox with a starkly white jaw, neck and breast. Truly a little fox person... wearing an elegant white doublet with golden buttons, like a kind of little yacht captain.

'This is the silver-tongued devil I was telling you about, Mr. Fox!' she said to the little fox man. 'May I present Josip Hodočasnik, my fellow Legate in the Hajduk Legion and current Emissary of Terra to the City of Shangri!' she said, before turning to Laur. 'And *this* is our host for the evening, Republican Ambassador Laur Pop and the General of the Hajduk Legion! Laur, Josip, this is Geoffrey Fox, he's the *friend* I was telling you about!' she said.

The one with the... things. 'Pleasure to meet you, Mr. Fox!' Laur said graciously, though he was a bit confused as to how exactly to best greet him. He was so small. *Can he ever reach up to my arm? Would I have to bend over a little? Midgets always find that insulting... maybe just nod and smile –*

'Ah, Mr. Fox! A pleasure to finally meet you!' Josip began, extending his hand forward. 'Bojana has nothing but nice things to say about you!'

The little fox person raised his own arm and the two managed to shake hands at a height where he wasn't on his toes and Josip wasn't bending forwards too much. *So, yes, it can be done!*

233

'It's a pleasure to meet you, Emissary, or do you prefer Legate?' the little fox person had a very suave, melodic voice and Laur was surprised by how well it carried up to their height.

'I prefer 'Josip'!'

'I must insist on formalities, Ambassador, else we might draw the ire of anyone who might overhear and envy the familiarity of our encounter,' the little fox man said, in a monotone voice that somehow sounded like deep, smooth jazz to Laur's ears. 'Ambassador Pop!'

Laur immediately put his hand forward. *Jesus... his hands are so soft... they're like mittens, but they're not chubby! How cool!* 'Mr. Fox!' he said.

'Thank you for your invitation!' Mr. Fox began. 'I find comfort in the presence of fellow oddities in this bustling metropolis we find ourselves in!'

Laur raised an eyebrow. *Oddities?*

The little fox person continued, clearly noticing his reaction, yet also expecting it, as if it was how he wanted to move the conversation forward in a particular direction swiftly. 'I am vulpine, as you've probably noticed, and *you* are Terrans and, though I could not tell you exactly how many of *your* people are here, I can tell you that you likely outnumber mine in Shangri. The humans here see us as oddities to gawk out and observe like specimens in a zoo. It's comforting to gawk at one another, for a change.' Mr. Fox had been glancing from Laur to Josip for some time now and now his eyes rested on Josip for a while longer. 'I apologize for being brusque, but there is question that has been rasping in the corners of my mind, which I might ask?'

'You may,' Laur granted.

'There is a nefarious rumour abundant in the high circles of society that Terrans are cannibals,' the little fox person said, looking at both Josip and Laur.

How the fuck...? Laur glanced at Bojana, who seemed just as surprised as her was, before looking towards their resident cannibal, Josip, to see his face remaining expressionless. 'Well, not by choice...' Laur began.

'... *usually*...' Josip added.

May my mother... Josip, please! Not you too! Time to take control of the conversation before anyone overhears...

- WAIT! This little creepy midget doesn't want people to hear us be informal with each other, but he's fine with people overhearing us discussing the flavours of cannibalism? 'Famine is a common hallmark of the apocalypse, Mr. Fox.'

'Ah yes of course! I'm asking about *after*!' he casually explained himself, as if he didn't sound demented.

Laur gave Bojana another look to see that they were both worried now. 'Consumption of the flesh of man is permitted by Republican law within the context of war or famine and...' *Jesus Christ... now I sound fucking demented!* '... the consumption of casualties and (if necessary) prisoners-of-war is actually something we encourage *only if* the threat of starvation is imminent.'

'Have you ever eaten the flesh of another man, Mr. Pop?' Mr. Fox asked.

Laur squinted and wasn't sure if he should be angry or intrigued. 'What's with the questions? Do you want to eat human flesh?'

'No! It's all just because I'm curious about your psychology. You're fellow oddities, I've said that already. What I'm curious about is exactly how it all works, what-with-the external image of savage and warlike barbarism. I come here and all I see are charming people ready to live, laugh and love – an impression likely shared by many in this room. And, yet, I am told and reminded continuously –

including by you yourselves of your own bestial nature. It's difficult to reconcile, you see. I was hoping to peer through the veil of your image into the true nature of what you are. What drives you, really? What is your vision of a good life? When you walk around, going about your day, what are the moments when you feel Terran? What is it that pushes you forward and what holds you back?'

Laur took the moment of silence the little fox man had drifted into as his cue to answer, though he wasn't quite certain how. *I do appreciate him asking, though. Finally, someone interesting and intriguing.* 'Have you ever felt like a day was worse than the one that came before?'

'I suppose everyone has.'

Not like us. 'Imagine if, for ten days, every day was worse than the one that came before. One might say that, on the tenth day, things would be *far worse* than on the first! Maybe, on the tenth day, you lost your job! Now, imagine, if it was a *hundred* such days! Maybe by the twentieth day, your house burned down and maybe, by the fiftieth, you had lost a loved one, or a close friend even, as you slid down the steps of time...'

'Now, imagine a thousand days! Poverty. Destitution. Disease. Famine. War. All gripping those around you as the slow trickle of death turns into a constant stream of degradation, as your country turns in on itself. Neighbour eats neighbour. Children die in their mother's wombs. Young girls raped by roaming hordes of the lost and the damned, as the fabric of society tears around you and you begin to wonder if the goodness you once saw in this world was nothing but a lie you just heard and embraced. You begin to wonder if such a state of mortal suffering is the actual truth of existence and that you were merely born into a time of mass delusion only just then returning to reality.'

'Now, imagine three thousands days like that! Death on scale that boggles the mind and numbs it and grinds it into a rigid pulp... after three thousand days, not only have you eaten the flesh of your fellow man, but you begin to wonder if any of those as unlucky as you, those that still lived, have not! And then...'

'And then five hundred more days in which you learn that the gods are real and that they hate you and that they seek to cleanse the world of you and your people and your race! They could have done it quickly, yet they did it slowly, due to apathy... arrogance... ignorance... maybe they did it out of simple sadism!'

'Such gods are gods that you fight! Such gods you die trying to stop, even if you know you can't! You go through the motions of breathing and sleeping and sometimes eating and drinking, but you stop tasting the air, you forget the feeling of a warm bed, you care not what you eat or drink... you have to decide, Mr. Fox...'

'You have to decide what it is that you are still living for and you begin to crave the freedom of choosing *when* and *how* you die!'

'Now, Mr. Fox, I would like you to imagine what kind of person lives through that? What kind of person survives so many days? If only one in every three hundred lived, *who* would that *one* be? *What* was that *one* before those days? *What* changed in that *one* over the course of those days?'

Laur finally paused. He looked up from the ground at the little fox person's feet and found his eyes. 'Think about that, and you might understand what it means to be Terran...'

The little fox person held his gaze. 'And... how *does* human flesh taste like?'

Laur raised an eyebrow at his relentlessness. *Meh, fuck it!* 'Veal.'

'*Pork*,' Josip's voice rang out, just as Nick came over, rubbing his nose.

Laur would have given the gesture some extra thought, but Josip continued, thus heralding in true horrors, unlike whatever Nick might have been doing in some bathroom on the upper floor.

'*You* only ate it during the End Times and only because there was famine!' He turned to see Josip looking right at him. 'What was it? Stew? There was a lot of stew like that back then!'

Josip turned back towards their little guest. 'People were eating people because there was hunger and hunger does things to the human body. It does so *both* in the body *that is* eating and the body *being* eaten! Starvation strips the fat from the flesh and the body changes as it eats itself, turning the flesh lean and chewy and *that* tastes like veal!'

He turned to face Laur once more, using his index finger to highlight something. 'Except the marrow and the hands! The hands still have a flavour to them, no matter the degree of emaciation! I hear bear paws have a similar quality and *that* quality is not *veal*!'

Now Josip's eyes began to animate, as his eyes wandered across an imaginary butcher shop in his head. 'Indeed, some might say that *that* is the true taste of human flesh, when it's *actually* just the taste of *hunger*! It's like saying that orange juice tastes like *water*! Most people would never taste like *that* if they weren't hungry at the moment of their death. And, when they're well fed, people taste like *pork*, not *veal*!'

'Very insightful, Josip! Mira's food must've made quite an impression on you!' Laur commented.

'It did. It's marvellous!' Josip admitted, before narrowing his eyes. 'Have you ever consumed the flesh of a man, Nick?' he asked, turning to face the new arrival.

'Who knows what they were feeding us at the orphanage!' he answered, before turning to Laur. 'Anyway, boss, we got a call, Joffrey's on the streets of King's Landing, about five minutes out!'

The Crown Prince's coming.

'I've talked to everyone. We're all set!' Nick continued, as he smiled at Mr. Fox. He put his hand forward, as if to playfully pinch his nose and the Vulpine did his best to preserve his dignity by pulling his head back.

Laur nodded, sharing glances with Bojana and Josip, who both nodded back.

The little fox person spoke, 'Chaos would be unbe–'

'AHHH!' Nick shouted, jumping away from the Vulpine, before bursting out into a giggle as he leaned on Josip. '*Holy shit!* I thought you were a *toy*!!!'

Laur glared at Nick, as Josip pretended to stifle a smile and Bojana shook her head and smirked genuinely.

The Crown Prince did not come through the parking lot. Instead, his convoy parked outside the embassy entrance, filling up the entirety of Wiltshire Boulevard. A hundred Shangri Royal Guards could assembled throughout the closed street, as a thousand more stood spread out throughout the entire neighbourhood, clotting the few passageways that stood beneath them. Even in the skies above them, in flying cars of the type they had back on Terra, the Royal Constabulary had deployed, carefully watching over their Prince. Laur knew that an additional ten thousand Constables had been deployed throughout Convent Garden and the surrounding neighbourhoods, for this evening and for this guest alone.

Laur waited in the reception hall of the Embassy, flanked by the Hajduk leadership, as well as the rest of the Republican Diplomatic mission to Shangri. Ambassadors from Moria, Kalimaste, Nargothrond, Menegroth, Pandora, Eredar, Nidavellir, Barri and Valhalla stood alongside him and his Hajduks in front of the reception area, as the Crown Prince approached, holding hands with his wife, while his loyal Gonzo and another remani flanked them, their eyes intently studying the Terrans and their allies with the utmost scrutiny.

It was the second remani who spoke.

'You stand in the presence of Crown Prince Turan of the House Gisevius, 104th of the Line, Deputy Supreme Commissioner of the Royal Constabulary, Duke of Azoriafintecosa, Viscount of Yupanchorizo and Scalpa, Marquis of Doncheshire, Bechgraven, Tiralin and Amanthul, Count of Zaborda, Zalinchieritia, Subarou, Eimpretsa, Galinda, Comatsa, Meriami, Bewestra and Nuovo, Baron of Vezuvio, Duramater, Sapotchialonioviskayistakis, Kocat, Ru, Xixistan, Facaletz, Simeria, Gabon, New Gabon, Pornache, Pronache, Stevenage, Hummingbird, Untalikitichambe, Ela, Gaboronne, Halita and Basingse, Breaker of Wind, Keeper of the Keys, Pierstone, Shaker of the Hands, Chancellor of the Camaril and Lord Paramount of the Sanctum Shangri!'

Holy shit, that was a mouthful! Ok, Nick, do your thing! You are my Herald, after all, though I often forget it... I honestly hope you haven't forgotten how to herald!

Nick took a single step forward. 'And I present to you Lord Laur Pop, General of the Hajduk Legion, Commander of the 1st Force of Prague, Castellan of Bâlea... ' Nick seemed at a loss for a moment.

That's it! Those are all my titles! What are you –

Then Nick got an idea '...Bulibasha of the Kalo, Dictator of Romania, Pasha of Shqipëria, Despot of Serbia, Ban of Bosnia, Knyaz of Croatia, Gospodar of Slovenia, Governor of Tomsk, Olenyokoski, Verkhoyanski, Tazovski, Taymyrski, Kobyayaski...' Nick paused, frowned, then turned to Laur. 'Do we have anything else, bo– sir!...?' he narrowly managed to correct himself.

'Nothing worth mention!' Laur immediately cut him off before taking the couple of steps needed to reach the Crown Prince. *You made those up! I'm not any of those things! At least, not formally!*

Thank fuck we can just say things got mixed up in translation!

'Your grace!' Pop had practiced the bow he now prostrated before the Crown Prince.

'Lord Pop!' his most esteemed guest responded, as he reached forward and gripped his shoulder. 'No need for formalities! I understand that on your world men greet each other with a handshake?' he continued, putting forth his own right hand

Laur immediately interrupted the bow he had practiced for five fucking minutes earlier in the day and gripped his hand. *Yes. You knew that already... OH! You're being nice in front of everyone else, so that they can see we're on good terms! Nice!* 'We're pleased you could join us!'

'The pleasure is all mine!' the Crown Prince spoke gripping his own hand in a warm handshake, before turning to Nick and grinning. '... *Lord Ambassador of the Republican Alliance to the City of Shangri*!' he added, before winking to Nick,

Ahhh, shit! He's right! I do have that title too now...

Fuck, Nick, you had one job!

Nick's eyes widened as the realization hit him and he nodded in agreement with the Crown Prince's words.

The Crown Prince then gestured towards his wife. 'This is Crown Princess Lia Gisevius, my beloved wife and the mother of my children!'

This time Laur bowed and he was not interrupted by the princess. He noticed her smile courteously to him, as she extended her own hand.

'Your grace!' *Ok, now it's time for the joke. The timing and the energy is right.* 'So, how did he trick you into marrying him?' he asked, tilting his head towards the Crown Prince.

Princess Lia raised a royal eyebrow and an awkward smile flinched her lips.

Dumb broad... I had higher expectations of –

Turan chuckled. 'I sang to her!' he responded swiftly, just as he noticed his wife's hesitation and once more holding her hand. 'At her balcony, at night, with her father's blessing!' he said lovingly.

Ok, good, at least you've got a sense of humour and you're the only one I really care about here! Laur smiled. 'Until she gave in so she could finally get some sleep!?' he quipped.

Now the Crown Prince burst into genuine laughter and Laur was pleased to see his wife struggle to subdue a smile. *Ah, ok, so she's not a simpleton. She was just being serious! That's good!*

'If I may present my colleagues and fellow hosts?' Laur offered.

Laur went through the needed formalities, presenting all those on his side in attendance, starting with his fellow ambassadors, then by his Legates, then his Centurions, starting with-

'And this is–'

'– Lady Silvia Murărescu!' Turan finished.

'Your grace!' Silvia smiled politely and nodded. Laur was annoyed that she didn't bow, but the Prince seemed nonplussed.

'My sister sends her regards! You made quite an impression on her!'

Silvia's face turned to stone. 'I thank her grace for her regards and I hope the impression was a good one, your grace!'

'Oh, it was!' Turan chuckled. 'Millennia of tradition prevented her from attending this evening's event. But, she *did* drop by our quarters just as we were about to leave to insist that we send her regards to *you* in particular!'

Lia had initially regarded Silvia with some suspicion, yet now she giggled as she added. 'I think that, by the end, she wouldn't have said 'no' if we would've asked her to come with us!'

Laur heard a small noise coming from Silvia: the sound of flesh moving over teeth very quickly. His eyes swiftly left his guests in order to observe his Centurion. Silvia was positively beaming as an honest smile spread ear-to-ear. *They might just be being polite to cover up your fuck-up...*

But...

If they were trying to cover it up, why bring it up? Could they be mocking her?

Laur looked back towards the royal couple. *Nah... they seem genuine – no! Not her! Not the wife! At least not... why did her face change so suddenly... why is it venomous now?*

And why did his face also change just now?

What the fuck is... what did they just see and what the –

'*You!*' Mira's voice came from between Nick and Tech as she emerged from behind them. She moved softly, yet her movements became rigid once she stopped and her brow furrowed, eyeing the Crown Prince with a cold rage.

Shit! Girl, please be your mother's daughter today, not your father's!

Laur's inner prayer reverberated around the chamber, as both Terrans and Shangrians froze at the outburst. All eyes rushed from the clearly burning rage of the Arabian Princess, back to the –

Turan smiled nervously. 'Hello, Mira!' he answered.

Mira took a few steps forward, coming right within striking distance of the Crown Prince, just as Gonzo stepped forward, feeling his presence necessary to prevent an eventual attack upon his prince.

Interestingly enough, both Turan and Mira spoke simultaneously to the remani Royal Guard. '*Don't even bother...*'

Gonzo looked at them as if they were both crazy, as his fury brow furrowed in disbelief at the instruction of one and the audacity of the other.

The two princelings, once more, locked gazes.

Interestingly enough, it was the Crown Prince who spoke first. 'This is my wife 'Lia'!' he gestured to his wife and the two women exchanged looks of dislike and dismissal, respectively. 'Lia, this is Princess Amira Parvati al-Sayid, known to her friends as 'Mira'.'

'Oh, really?' Mira now locked flabbergasted. 'And how are *you* known to your friends, *Crown Prince*?'

Ha! I fucking knew it!

I fucking knew that was how...

Wait a minute... this could still go to shit is she goes full Djibril!

Laur wanted to intervene, but he wasn't sure how or with what.

Turan smiled nervously. '*Turan* works just fine, Mira.'

'Does it now?' Mira spoke in an openly menacing tone. 'What's wrong with *Nizami*?' Now she stared him down for a while, bidding him answer.

Laur couldn't allow this thing to continue. He had allowed it to come to pass as much as it had, just on the off-chance that the situation might blow over on its own and, clearly, that wasn't likely to happen. '*Mira*,' he said sternly, carefully choosing his next words in his head.

Yet, before he could continue, the Crown Prince's voice echoed through the trembling silence. 'I believe me and you owe everyone an explanation!'

Mira raised her eyebrows as she titled her head, her face still the visage of fury. 'Mostly you!' she said combatively.

'*No, Mira!*' Now Laur really wanted to dig into things and tear them apart. 'We don't really need an explanation for this!' he informed the Crown Prince. 'At least not now!' he added, turning towards Mira.

She didn't even bother to look at him, never turning from the source of her rage. '*You* don't need an explanation for this because you've already figured it out!

True. 'Course I have!' Laur mumbled to himself out loud.

'He's not the only one!' he heard Tech's voice from behind him. He could tell that the remani was more amused than concerned.

Typical. Probably things it's all very cute... 'I honestly don't really care about the exact specifics or the events that brought us all here. I mostly care that you apologize for treating – '

'*Apologize?*' Now Mira turned her rage to Laur and, for a fraction of an instant, Laur Pop flinched.

Just like her father.

'Lord Pop is correct,' the Crown Prince spoke seriously now. 'An apology is warranted!'

'She'll get to it in a bit!' Laur muttered optimistically, as he attempted to stare Mira into submission.

'Mira,' the Crown Prince began. 'I beg your forgiveness for misleading you during our past encounters!'

A few gasps crossed over a multitude of raised eyebrows, wide eyes and dropped jaws throughout the room.

What?

The Crown Prince swallowed nervously as he looked towards Laur, before turning back to Mira, who smirked. She breathed heavily for a few seconds, as she seemed to struggle to relax herself. Laur couldn't help but notice the Crown Prince's wife looking as if she was about to burst forth streams of lava from her eyes. *Though she would likely direct them towards her husband, not her...*

'I'm sorry for interrupting, but what's going on?' Nick's voice quipped.

Laur turned to glare at his Centurion.

Mira, remarkably enough, answered. 'When I was last here, with my sister, Daw, we stayed in the guest wing of the Royal Palace. We wanted to visit the city as commoners, yet that seemed impossible. Until, one day, one of the servants, a boy my age, offered to sneak us out. He also served as our guide once we got out. He claimed his name was *Nizami*, from what I recall, and that he was an *orphan*...' Mira's brow furrowed as she recalled something that made her angry. Her eyes had never left Turan's. 'I threatened to *kill* you!'

Gonzo's eyes widened and his hand drew closer to his weapon, yet the Crown Prince quickly intervened. 'Just '*threatened*'! You didn't go through with it.'

'Because *you* did as *I* asked of you!' Mira seemed genuinely stupefied now, as she seemed to comprehend her near-assassination of the heir of the Shangri throne. She now turned to Gonzo, for the first time during their exchange. '*You* are really bad at your job, by the way!'

'He is not!' the Crown Prince now raised his hand. 'I was just very good at sneaking around!'

For a second, Gonzo joined Mira in fuming at the Crown Prince on account of his subterfuge, before relaxing his arms and moving them away from any of his weapons, as he crossed them in indignation. He still kept a close eye on Mira though.

She turned back to Turan and forced herself to breathe normally. 'You tricked Daw, too!'

'I suppose I did!' he confessed. 'Though she was not allowed to use the full extent of her powers. I believe that, if she had the time and the freedom to peer into me properly, she would have seen through my disguise!'

Mira smirked and nodded. 'She did have the time and the freedom; you spent a lot of time with us! She said you likely were who you claimed to be.' Mira shrugged for a moment as she nodded.

'Good job!' she said, though a bitterness crossed her eyes. '*You asked for money!*' she commented, as she frowned at a memory now shrouded in disbelief.

'I had to be convincing with my story!' he now allowed himself to smile. 'Two hundred Asgardian Guilders, from what I recall!'

Two hundred Asgardian... that's like... a million euro... that's a fucking fortune!

'More than that!' Mira smiled bitterly before drawing in one deep breath. 'I cooked the food!' she said, tilting her head towards the nearest tables laden with hors d'oeuvres.

The Crown Prince's eyes lit up. 'You did?'

'Yes,' she replied, as she looked towards the ground and finally composed herself. 'Thank you for your hospitality, Crown Prince Turan of the House Gisevius!' she finally acknowledged his wife. 'Crown Princess Lia!' she smiled politely before turning back to Turan.

'Please enjoy our own hospitality! Welcome to the Embassy of the Republican Alliance at Convent Garden! We are grateful for your attendance!' she announced, before turning to leave. 'There are hors d'oeuvres to be found at the buffet table. The main course will arrive in twelve minutes. Please leave room for dessert...'

'Perhaps you might wish to reminisce of times gone by later on in the evening?' Turan suggested, causing her to stop midstride.

'No,' she answered curtly as she walked away.

'Well...' the Crown Prince began, visibly shaken. 'I think we can skip the rest of the pleasantries!' he said to Laur. 'If Mira is the chef that prepared the evening's fare, we are making a great disservice to everyone here by keeping them away from the buffet!'

The Shangrians in attendance immediately followed the instructions of their prince, knocking themselves out of their shock and immediately filling the reception with the sounds of fake dialogue, as they made their way to the Great Hall of the laurel tree and the banquet hall beyond, where they would soon clutter the nearest buffet tables. Laur nodded to his men to follow suit and disperse, so that he might have a moment with Turan and his wife alone as they walked towards the banquet hall.

Under the watchful eye of Gonzo, of course.

Now, finally comfortable with the relative cover provided by the cacophony of cutlery and conversation, he leaned in closer to the Prince. 'I would normally apologize for Mira's unique personality, yet I see that you are quite familiar with it!' he said.

'Very!' the Crown Prince smiled.

'You never mentioned your past encounters with her during any of our meetings.' *I had to figure it out by myself and, were it not for your little sister's antics, I wouldn't have figured it out at all.*

The Crown Prince pretended to chuckle reassuringly, yet Laur caught his wife glaring at him. Princess Lia found his own gaze and smirked visibly, before nodding and proceeding to look away, as the indignity of what she had been forced to just endure demanded that she take a few breaths to cool off. Plus, she didn't want to hear any more of her husband's puerile bullshit.

Apparently, you've omitted telling certain other people of this as well.

The Crown Prince noticed this subtle exchange. 'Lord Pop, I didn't think discussions on matters of state needed to include mentions to the spurious adventures of mischievous children!'

Laur clicked his tongue on the roof of his mouth. 'I'm surprised to hear that from *the heir to a dynasty...*' Laur couldn't help himself. '*... your grace!*' he added.

Now Turan chuckled sincerely and so did his wife. 'Lord Pop, do you know what I like about your people, most of all?'

'Your grace, I'm starting to think it's the faces we make when you catch us by surprise!'

'It's actually your complete lack of *class*!'

Oh, fuck...

Wait... are the two words homonyms in Shangrian as well?

The Crown Prince cleared up the confusion. 'It's strange, you see, given how yours is a military society, where every man, woman and even child spends his entire life bound to some rank or another! One might expect you to be *obsessed* with status! Yet, in my experience with your people, whether it be you, Mira or any of the other Terrans that have visited our City, yours is a very egalitarian society and *it tells*!'

The Crown Prince now smiled and glanced towards him. 'Even those such as yourself, who strike me as a man more aware of his standing than your countrymen, often struggle to navigate the steps and stairs of our society!'

'I apologise for stumbling, from time to time!'

'There's no need. I honestly find it quite charming; to see a man so sure of himself pause and fumble so often in the face of common courtesies!'

'They are... not as common as you might think, your grace!'

'Clearly not where you're from!' he sighed. 'Mira and Daw where, by far, much more shocking to me than you ever could! One, an almost literal *god*, and, the other, something akin to *princess* among her people!' Now, the Crown Prince smiled. 'Yet, never before had I seen two people more *connected* to their fellow man! No taint of superiority within them! I saw them bless the poor, drink with thieves, haggle with shopkeepers, play with children in the park – never caring for where they stood against them upon the ladder!'

'But, *you* already knew that, *Lord* Pop!' the Crown Prince turned to him upon their entrance into the banquet hall. 'Mira's honest righteousness has done more to further between our two peoples than any formal endeavour ever could! 'It is why you have brought her here with you!'

Laur paused as he stood before Turan, his eyes wondering before he smirked. 'Am I so *predictable*, your grace?'

'No, but you are *transparent*, in a way!' The Crown Prince sighed, before turning to his wife. 'I am afraid that I must now fulfil the obligations of my office, as you have so dutiful done with yours!' Turan looked around them. 'Protocol dictates that I spend some time with the *higher* friends of the Royal House that also honoured your invitation!' He now turned back to Laur. 'I trust we may have some time later in the evening?

'I stand at your discretion, your grace!'

As he watched the Shangri royal couple depart to fulfil the obligations of their office, Laur had a moment to mull things over.

I brought Mira along for a few reasons, yet her diplomatic aptitudes were not one of them! He doesn't know that, apparently, and he assumes that it's all a ploy to curry favour with him. It does seem to be currying his favour (though not of his wife) yet, it was not intentional and that bothers me for a number of reasons!

Nevertheless, it's good to know that he thinks so highly of me, even if it is for things undeserved! It might be inaccurate, but it does reveal a few things...

His analysis was interrupted by the appearance of a large robbed figure before him. Laur didn't even have to see the wearer, for the recognized the robes. Grey, with a glinting anchor chain across the shoulders, like some giant monk of a far off land of mystery and magic, still bound to the gods of his realm, even here, on another world entirely. He wore a blue suit of gentlest muslin underneath a dull, yet coarse, fabric of stiff wool, as his appearance gave way to reveal a proud head of smooth purple and sharp features.

Demani were men and they had once been human, yet the magics of their realms, born out of technologies long forgotten, had warped their bodies into a thousand forms and shades. This one was what the Terrans called a *Wow* demani, on account of their seeming resemblance to the Draenei of World of Warcraft.

And Laur knew this one, though not well. They had only spoken by phone and only briefly interacted when the demani had arrived at Convent Garden, to show himself among his peers, for he himself was an emissary of the Republican Alliance.

Nathaneiel Paxcjli... that is his name... I should speak with him, particularly now that he's right here now in front of me!

'Ah, Emissary Paxcjli! I don't believe we've had the chance to get to know each other!'

"I know *you*, Harkan Dragonflame."

Laur braced himself against his own reaction to the demani's words, yet none came. He didn't tense up. He didn't feel his skin burn. It didn't even tingle. He quickly forced himself to relax, lest his reaction, no matter how subdued, fail to go unnoticed. "We've met before, I take it?"

The demani smirked, his eyes twinkling slightly, as he moved nearer and spoke words meant for his ears alone. 'I've laid eyes on you before, Lord Pop. Among the peaks of Colab, the world of my birth!'

Laur felt the dry heat of the orange mountains burn his lungs once more as it had decades ago. 'I'm sorry to say I don't recall meeting your gaze at the time!'

The demani smiled out of the corner of his mouth. 'I would have been surprised if you did. It's hard to catch the eye of a man seeking to catch the wrath of a dragon!'

Laur saw the great beast's snout move as it drew in his scent. He saw the wyrm's eyes narrow, then widen, upon realizing its challenger's insignificance. He felt the hot air atop the platform the menace had oppressed with its great girth, blend with the icy coldness at the back of his neck.

'You were in the caves?' he asked his fellow Republican.

'Along with forty thousands of my brethren and two hundred of yours! We stood across the gap beneath the port and under the assault of the Enemy.'

Laur remembered it all, though it all faded to black beneath the great wings of the serpentine red monster he had been hurtling insults at. In the darkness of the past he saw only one image within his mind: that of Djibril al-Sayid with his Ghazis and their desperate mission within the mountain's many lightless passageways. 'It was a busy day for all of us,' he said dismissively, though his memory of the day was hard to dismiss.

'Hmmm... Yes, it was. For Djibril al-Sayid most of all!'

Laur smiled curtly as his eyes wandered, remembering how he had instructed Djibril to bypass the Senoyu defences and hit them from behind, allowing the demani insurgents and the Fianna to win the day by catching the Senoyu between hammer and scalpel. 'One of his many fine moments!' His eyes flickered slightly, seeking out Mira, though he stopped himself.

'That is his daughter, correct?' Paxcjli had likely caught the flicker in his eye.

Laur followed his gaze and saw Mira, Silvia, Anwar and that catman... *(Kretin or something... I forget his name)*, sharing a laugh at Nick's expense. 'What gave it away?' he jested.

'That dream of home smouldering behind eyes of amber!'

Accurate and poetic.

'... and the nose,' the demani added.

Accurate and oversized. 'Like father, like daughter,' Laur commented. *Best close this conversation and move on!*

'*Like mother* also, I hear!' Paxcjli commented accurately.

Laur stood still. *Don't... please don't... There are people here... I can't show...*

The demani turned back to face him. 'Her father is worshipped as something of a god in Andromeda, though those who knew him would know that he would shudder at the thought...'

He would... Laur eyed him. '*Huh...*' *and so would I...*

'We contain it,' Nathaniel assured him. 'Yet not all were fortunate enough to be on Colab that day! To see what I saw and see him as the lesser, for once!' The demani's eyes became transfixed upon his. 'Not everyone saw *you* that day!'

... what?

The demani caught his gaze. 'I did not trust you Terrans!' he said, though he matched his words with reassuring a smile, which stopped Laur from openly questioning the loyalty of one of his people's closest allies. 'You were *human*, after all and I had little liking for humans!' Paxcjli continued.

'It would appear that we have always had so much in common!'

'So I hear,' the demani agreed. He paused the story he was about to weave, Laur could tell, yet his interest had peaked, somewhat. The demani seemed to have some destination in mind for their conversation. Laur would indulge him. The demani's eyes were whiteless, as his sclera bore the colour of his iris: a deep blue, speckled white and gold, with thin shadowy veins piercing the darkness.

'You Terrans were brave, yet that did not surprise me! You were also cunning and cruel, perhaps more so than the Senoyu, at times. We expected you all to be formidable. A people of the post-apocalypse, galactic conquerors and deathbringers. Nothing I saw surprised me when you came to Colab. Everyone expected you Terrans to come up with some devious ploy to break our Enemy. To cut through Senoyu like lightning through rock! To twist the magics of our own world to your will...'

'I'm glad we fulfilled your expectations.'

'At first you did. Yet, then you did so much more!'

What's your point? You were surprised I would have killed myself to keep Djibril and his men safe? Is that it? Fu-

'I knew what you planned to do the moment you walked out onto that parapet, I just couldn't believe the commitment! A great dragon of the Brightflame – its mind addled into a mindless rage by sorcery and inoculation – would be something even the bravest men in the world would seek to avoid! Its flames would singe, yet they would not guarantee death, let alone a swift one. You knew that, I trust...'

I did. If I would have died, it would have been for a good reason. If I wouldn't have died, as was the case.... Well... I didn't die...

'... and yet, there you were! Swearing at that dragon in your native tongue. Do you know that, to this day, my own people no longer use any vulgarities of their own?'

'*Whuat?*' *Now, that I didn't know!*

'It's true! Go to any field of play, any tavern and any other place where tongues spit through teeth and you will hear only '*sugi pula*', '*hai sictir*', '*băh căcatule*', '*s-o fut pe măta*' or, simply, '*muie*'!'

'I also spit at him!' Laur muttered. He could still feel his own cool spray touch his hand in breezy mist.

'I remember! I was there!' His face relaxed, as the demani had seemingly become excited remembering the events of that hot day. 'That was the day all of Andromeda would know you by the name of Harkan Dragonflame!' He turned back towards Djibril's daughter. 'It was then that I realized that you were not a race of men led by gods, but a race of gods led by men!' He smiled once more, his eyes seeking out Laur's. 'Men who would gladly give their lives for their brethren *or* their allies, no matter how recently acquainted...'

Laur felt a hot slap as the demani gently lay his hand on his shoulder, and the soft, cool fabric of his jacket and the even softer fabric of his shirt caused singing pain to shoot up his neck.

'You may have not won the war that day and it may have been Djibril al-Sayid that won the day itself, but *you* were the one to win our hearts and our awe for all days after, Harkan Dragonflame!'

The demani turned once more to Mira and her band of merry revellers. 'She is the one you call Silvia, isn't she?'

Huh? 'Yes. Centurion Murărescu!'

'With *her* I did become acquainted on Colab, though I doubt she remembers me.'

That would be strange... Silvia is very good at remembering faces.

'You did not die that day, though I suppose the release of death might have been a blessing! That way, you could have healed in the life oils whilst within the silence of mortality. But, no, you did not die. You stood there, within that green vat, for a whole week! The druids claim that your mind never flickered out of sentience. The suffering you endured... never in all my years under the yoke of the

Senoyu, did I ever see them (or anyone else) cause such pain in another, as only a dragon's flame only could!'

'*Yes, you have*!' Laur whispered, his eyes dull.

The demani stopped, seemingly only now wondering if his words might have caused some pain in the one he was genuinely praising.

Laur did not need to see the worry. It wouldn't change what he was going to say if he did: '*I felt nothing!*'

The demani's eyes flickered.

Laur continued. 'What's the worst pain you've ever felt?' His eyes seemed to regain focus for a moment of clarity and they returned to his guest's.

'The Senoyu made me send my daughter to her death.'

Good answer. '*Physical* pain,' he rephrased.

'A fireball to my groin.'

Ah, so there was some empathy for me there. You thought you could relate! 'I had a kidney stone once. Do you know what a kidney stone is, Nathaneiel?'

'They were not uncommon on Colab before the liberation,' the demani confirmed.

'Did you ever pass one?'

'I was fortunate enough not to.'

Laur went back to gazing upon the groups of guests and Hajduks that cluttered in the Great Hall before them. 'I had a kidney stone a long time ago and, well, let me put it to you like this: in my life I have met people who were shot and people who had given birth. Some of those people who got shot had also given birth. I've also met people who were shot, gave birth *and* had a kidney stone! And though I've *had* a kidney stone and I *have* been shot, I will tell you the same thing as those that experienced all three: the kidney stone was far worse! In your language, you can describe some pain as being *writhing* pain?'

The demani slowly nodded.

'Ah, well, I only understood the meaning of that word when I was passing my fucking kidney stone and do you know what happened after that realization?'

Nathaniel kept his silence.

'I stopped comprehending the pain.' Laur's eyes once more drifted. 'You reach a level of pain so intense that your mind ceases to keep note of it and you stop *feeling* the pain and you just *know* that you're in pain.' Laur paused, waves of pain and numbness washing through different aspects of him as he sought to centre himself on one particular moment. 'I felt the fire for less than a sliver in time. Men will sometimes say that a moment in pain can be as long as a lifetime of pleasure, but I tell you this now that such men were never burnt to a crisp in a fraction of a moment! I didn't even feel my tendons ripping off my charred joints into a soup of boiling fat as my guts spilled through my open abdomen and my heart tried to beat itself to death...'

'Only my eyes hurt, though they were charred first! My heart kept beating for just long enough for the stasis field to trigger. Thereafter, I assure you, I *did* sleep! I do remember the vat though. I remember the signal sent to my mind telling me what had happened and that I would need three days to heal fully.' Laur paused. 'I'm assuming that's when you met Silvia?'

'You assume correctly,' the demani answered after a short pause in which Laur had surprised him with this sudden change of course. 'Keeping watch by your vat,' he now also turned towards to the group of young friends in the distance, 'for three whole days until exhaustion took her and, even then, she slept at the foot of your vat!'

'I felt nothing,' Laur confessed.

It was strange to be silent in a room of raucous conversations and loud thoughts. As the heat and the cold left him, Laur regained some awareness of the now and the then. 'Do you trust us now?' he turned to the demani, whose eyes found his.

'Completely, Harkan Dragonflame!'

'*Huh*... Call me, Laur!'

'Sir!' Silvia's voice startled him. He turned to find her right in front of him, her head tilted to the side. Laur glanced towards where she and the other had been earlier to see the group dispersed. Her words had been meant for him, yet her gaze now also took note Nathaneiel. 'Ambassador Paxcjli!'

'Tantal Brightstar!' he greeted her. 'We've met before!'

'I know,' she replied softly, then her words addressed Laur once more as her eyes drifted between his and Nathaneiel's. 'We have a problem!'

Laur began scanning the room. 'Go on.'

'The Crown brought a guest,' she said and the two men before her both tightened-up.

This can't be good. Silvia eyed Nathaneiel with a question in her eyes. Laur had seen that question before many times the eyes of many others far too many times to count and definitely enough to know its meaning. *She fears that an outburst of violence might occur. Yet, she is not worried as much about me as much as she is...*

Nooo...! Here? How? No fucking way!

Laur moved in closer to her, narrowed his eyes and tilted his head.

Silvia's eyes looked directly to where the problem lay.

Or, rather, where the problem lay speaking to two Shangrian dignitaries.

That fucking...

Silvia began explaining, 'He passed the Constables with a press pass, then he showed Dejan and Dušan his invite. It was one of the ones we sent for the Peacekeeper and his household. They didn't want to cause a scene so he let him in and told Cosmin, who then spread the–'

In my fucking house!!!

Laur barged off before Silvia could finish the rest of her sentence. He slid in between the two dignitaries, before turning his chest, pushing them both to the side as he stood at full height before the unwelcome guest.

'You are Jenner?' Laur asked.

'You are Pop?' the cunt asked, a smug look on his face.

Mother-fucking-son-of-dumb-cunt... 'I guess we are both making accurate statements, not just asking obvious questions. *How dare you?*' Laur spoke quickly. He wanted to reach the culmination of the interaction as quickly as possible, yet there were steps he had to take the Shangrian through. For now, he had reached a moment of silence, as he knew a hundred pairs of eyes or more just widened, while many more had just narrowed.

'I...' Jenner turned to the curious eyes of the Crown Prince, just off his right side and taking in the escalating situation.

'*No, no, no!*' Laur spoke softly as he took a step towards his quarry. 'Don't look at him! *Look at me!*' he gestured his words with quiet movements, subtly pointing towards his own face. 'How dare you come here?' he continued to ask quietly, coldly and swiftly, raising his voice only as much as was needed for it to reach the silence in the farthest corners of a now quiet banquet hall.

'Lord Pop, I am a free man and can walk wherever I please in the city of my birth!'

'It pleases you to be here?' Laur asked.

'I take it doesn't please you!'

'You take it correctly!' he moved in closer, forcing Jenner to bend his jaw upwards in defiance. 'How dare you show your face here on a day such as this?'

'The day when *you* –'

'*The day when I was NOTHING!*' Laur snapped. 'I wonder, whenever I look upon men such as you, if you're even capable of understanding the presence – *the essence* – you find yourselves in when in places and at times such as this! *Look around you!* What do you see?'

Jenner did not break eye contact with Laur, which was commendable, in its own way. 'What should I see, Mr. Pop?'

'You should see *nothing*! Your eyes are too blind enough as it is and, if they weren't, they would not see what there is to see for it would *blind you*! *You* stand in the presence of the *risen* at the remembrance of their *lowest*! *Look around you!*' Now Laur's words were far more powerful, as he bent forwards closer to his face.

Jenner blinked. And he relented, softly glancing across the room.

Laur knew he now locked eyes with at least a hundred glaring Terrans. 'Do you see it? Underneath the glitz and the glamour and the comforts of peace and prosperity? *There*! In the depths of the eyes, at the edges of their souls? Do you see the *emptiness*, Mr. Jenner? Do you see the shadow of what was lost?'

'I see contempt,' Jenner began. 'I see *entitlement*. I see an *arrogance* which stains these halls you've occupied with your kitsch due to the misguided hospitality of our well meaning leaders!' he said the last part to the Crown Prince.

He turned back to Laur. 'How was it like coming to learn that it wasn't just humans that existed in the universe? Your world had long imagined strange beings such as elves, orcs, trolls or goblins, yet how did it feel like to know that your fairytales where true and that there were elves and orcs, and trolls and goblins out there in the universe?

'Same shit, different colours.'

'Ah! And now you show your true colours!'

'Yes? And what might those colour be?'

'Those of your true identity! I've read of your trauma, Mr. Pop! The tale you sing before your put your hand forward to beg for that which you would *take* by force if it is not granted to you! That there were those amongst your race who saw in the eye of their human mind the worlds of humanity and of the elves, orcs, goblins, trolls and such like! How strange a path you have taken, in this new world were elves did you evil, the orcs rescued you, the goblins aided you and the trolls begged you! A world where orc was elf and elf was orc and where demon was friend and the angel was anathema! You ask me if I *see you*, Mr. Pop, but, I ask you, do you see yourself? Do you see how in this world you have also changed yourself into a dark mirror of your own imagination? Do you know what you Terrans are? Do you see what you really are?'

'Please, astound me with your vision!'

Jenner smirked and Laur struggled not to flinch as he almost slapped him. '*Ogres,* Mr. Pop! You are the *ogres* of this tale!'

Now Laur struggled with much greater difficulty. It was hard to force one's eyes to now open and one's pupils to dilate as the eyebrows rose. He succeeded, barely.

'Brute strength. Unrepentant thievery. Your bodies bloated by darkest sorcery and cruel technomancy. You sit here in your suits and your dresses, like pigs in silk and you play your hand at impressing us with your crooked ways!'

The Shangrian words had stirred a reaction, as Laur had to open his mouth slightly to stop it from twitching with rage.

'*Ah! There it is*! *Right. There!* Right there, behind the glamour of humanity you drape yourself in, like the flayed skin of the dead man that once dwelled within! Squirming under the surface! How much more is needed, Mr. Pop? How much longer can you hide the monster within until your true nature betrays you and we all get to see exactly what lies underneath?'

Laur's mind did squirm. It did boil. It did twist and he did fight to keep himself in check. He didn't breathe and he focused his mind upon that absence of breath until he was confident that he had enough composure and control left in him.

Then, he slowly raised his right hand. He made sure to also move his shoulder, so as to draw Jenner's attention to the movement. He reached towards the Shangrian's side without looking, finding his own right hand.

Which he met in an embrace.

He then pulled the hand in between them, as he brought up his left hand to partake in the firm caress. The Shangrian's hand was cold and it grew colder as Laur easily began to force him into a handshake.

'Thank you for joining us here at the Republican Embassy at Convent Garden, Mr. Jenner! You do us a great honour by gracing us with your attendance!'

Then, Laur slowly forced the Shangrian's hand towards his mouth, never breaking eye contact with him. Once the hand was right within an inch of the teeth behind his tense lips, Laur unleashed his most violent of gestures.

He humbly kissed the Shangrian's hand.

Jenner shuddered and Laur felt goosebumps form, as Jenner's clothes bristled in the quiet hall, only just peppered by the occasional gasp at the Terran Ambassador's gesture.

'Unfortunately, Mr. Jenner, I *will* have to ask you to leave!' He said, lowering his uninvited guest's hand. 'I am afraid that I believe that there are not as many here that view you favourably as you may have been led to believe! *I* would not suffer any guest in *these* halls to ever feel unwelcome and I would spare you of any unpleasantry that may be visited upon you while under *my* charge!'

He let go of Jenner's hand. 'You may leave through whence you just came!' he said, gesturing towards the entrance. 'Please enjoy the rest of your evening, as we will ours!'

They shared further eye contact, as Laur glared at the Shangrian's perplexed and furious eyes. It took a while for him to budge and Laur had to tilt his head slightly and raise a not-so-discrete eyebrow.

Jenner relented and glanced towards the Crown Prince, who slowly nodded. 'Then I take my leave, Mr. Pop!'

Laur smiled politely, ostentatiously and falsely.

As Jenner barged past him, he saw that behind the Shangrian had stood Lejla, her hand clutching her fleur-de-lils necklace, her eyes cold and silent.

Around her stood Zaza, her Centurion, as well as Nick and Josip, who nodded slowly.

Laur turned around, catching sight of Bojana, Silvia, Cosmin and Radu, as well as several of the other Hajduks, just as he locked eyes with the Crown Prince, his wife and Gonzo, and their faces were stern... yet also thoughtful.

He turned fully, just in time to see Jenner pass through Gigi and Anwar, while Paxcjli, Ela, Tech and Big White watched on. They all followed the departing Shangrian, just as he turned a corner.

'Mira!' Laur's voice boomed, startling everyone out of the moment.

There was a pause. 'Yes?'

'What's the main course?' he asked, turning towards the source of her voice.

Mira had been watching on from the upper balcony that circled the banquet hall, together with Basenji, Mr. Fox and Anwar's catman. 'You'll find out in eight minutes!'

There were some nervous chuckles from some of the Shangrians.

Laur slapped his hands together. 'Good! We look forward to it!'

He waited for the mood of the party to return to state it had been in before what had just transpired and for Mira's main course to arrive before he sought out Silvia, finding her in deep discussion with some of her Hajduk Optios.

'Can I talk to you for a moment?' he asked, waiting for the positive reply.

Silvia glanced towards her men, nodding towards them before following him to one of the corridors leading out of the banquet halls.

Laur turned on her with remarkable furry. He checked their surroundings first, making sure that they were far enough away from any of the guests; though some of the Hajduks were definitely close enough to hear him once he began speaking. 'What the fuck is wrong with you?' he snapped at her in Romanian.

'It was–' Silvia began.

' – *Pain in my dick*, Silvia! I don't care! I shouldn't have to care about shit like this happening! It shouldn't be a fucking possibility!'

Silvia pursed her lips in obvious annoyance. 'I came to you the moment –'

'*What*? You're arguing with me now?' Pop scowled at her for a moment. 'He was *inside*!'

'His invitation was in the Peacekeeper's name! Was I supposed to start a diplomatic–'

'*ENOUGH!!!*' he barked, raising his voice louder than he ever had within the Embassy. Out of the corner of his eye, he saw some of the nearby Hajduks, Iovanković, Dua Lipa and Werner, twitch slightly, clearly hearing at least some of their exchange. He went back to whispering.

'You know, I don't understand what the fuck is going on with you and its starting to get on my fucking nerves! Going off the fucking reservation! The whole business with Mira's cat, whatever the fuck happened there!? Now this shit!? You're a fucking Centurion, Silvia! That position entails that you should *be in control*! That position entails that you should be *aware* and fucking *awake*! Not fucking sleeping with your eyes open, freaking out over bushes and the fucking hors d'oeuvres and the fucking help, while you leave us all sitting with our buttcheeks spread and our mouths open!' Laur moved in close to her, to the point where the tip of his nose came up right next to hers.

Laur felt her tremble as she seemed to balance her knees.

'*Get your fucking shit together*!' he said to her, as if ordering her to pick a fallen piece of paper and fold it. As if what he was saying was obvious and what he was doing wasn't erratic. '... *Centurion*!' he added.

Silvia swallowed as she followed the creases in the corners of his mouth. 'Yes, sir!' she whispered.

'*What was that?*' he snarled at her.

She cleared her throat. '*Yes, sir!*' she said, straightening up.

He moved back, observing her for a moment. Her eyes had gone blank. *Good.* 'Could've this happened in the time of Tapalagă?' he brought up Silvia's predecessor.

'No, sir!' she replied, the breath carrying her voice was dead.

'It's happening during *your* time and I can promise you that, one way or another, we're going to stop this from becoming a trend! *Now get the fuck out of here!*'

She nodded and immediately left.

She is fucking right, but I don't care! There should've been a shorter reaction time. Someone should've stalled him. It could've been handled better!

Laur forced himself to breathe normally again. He checked his watch and decided that it was time he went back to the Crown Prince and attend to him as a good host should. *He should be done greeting everyone here by now...*

He wasn't and Laur spend the next couple of hours with his own men, their guests and their fellow republican diplomats, as well as other dignitaries from far off lands such as Avalon, Liliput, Atlantis and even a human emissary of the Draco Mandrakes. In time, Josip, Bojana and Nick had coalesced around him.

'That was good, Laur!' Josip commented. " The hand-kissing, I mean!' he added, as his General glared at him.

'Fucking biblical!' Nick added, appearing from right behind Gigi.

Laur glared at the Kalo, noting his overly excited behaviour. *Where's Silvia?*

Oh! You here checking to see if I'm still upset at her because she won't show her face? Where the fuck where you when that shit walked in?

Who the fuck am I kidding... that's not your role, Nick. You're good at other shit... Security is, was and always should be Silvia's prerogative...

'Stop glaring, Laur!' Bojana told him.

'Huh?'

'You're glaring at Nick!' she explained. 'You know very well that what the men did letting him in was the correct course of action!'

'It was, but it was clumsy! It required quick thinking and we got *lucky*! And you know you know my opinion of *luck* is!' *Bojana, don't get me started; it was your man who took the decision to let them in!*

'Talking about luck, are we still on for tonight once the festivities end?' Nick asked.

'The poker game?' Laur smiled. 'What, Nick? Your pockets feeling too heavy? Yeah... after Joffrey leaves...'

'He's coming over just now!' Josip pointed out discreetly.

Finally!

'Apologies!' the Crown Prince began, just as he arrived and the Hajduks made way for him and Gonzo, who trailed him as always. 'It would appear that your event is a resounding success and that you've managed to get some of my most esteemed subjects rather inebriated and talkative! Lia volunteered to take over some of the stragglers while I came over and talked to you fine gentlemen and *ladies*!' He added, bowing his head politely towards Bojana smiled back graciously.

'Well, we hope you yourself are having an excellent time, your grace!' Laur offered.

'I assure you that I am not!' Turan said honestly, though he didn't really seem distressed. 'I've barely had time to spend any amount of time with the hosts of the event and, thus, I feel obliged to beg your forgiveness!'

'There's no need, your grace! We understand such duties are important!'

'Indeed they are! There is, however, one guest whom I have not had the pleasure of meeting and I was hoping I could ask for your assistance in facilitating an interaction.'

I know exactly who you're talking about... and I can't believe you're asking this of me! 'I...' He looked for the individual in question around there room, easily finding him. 'I'm certain we can accommodate such a thing...' He looked to his Hajduks. *Game time guys!*

He glanced at Gonzo as he went on. 'One of the upstairs rooms is a conference chamber. It's private and it's set aside for Hajduks and embassy staff only!' *It's also stockpiled with booze, drugs and a poker table, since it's the room we were going to play later in...*

Five minutes later, Laur had assembled Gigi, Josip, Bojana, Lejla, Tech, Basenji and six of his Hajduks in the upstairs conference room, a large windowless chamber, built up around a central table (now covered in felt), surrounding by couches, smaller tables, armchairs, bookshelves, artwork, as well as bar area. They were joined by the Crown Prince, a dozen of his royal guards, including Gonzo.

As Nick brought in Big White, Laur did a mental calculation of their odds in a fight. *I don't expect such a thing to occur, but you never know in these situations. So... a dozen of us, plus Tech and Basenji, versus a dozen royal guards... plus a bearman, potentially... I think the odds are ok... Maybe if I had Silvia over... or...*

No! I mean 'yes'!

Laur made a subtle gesture to one of his Hajduks, Liviu, to come so that he may whisper something in his ear. '*Get Mira!*' he whispered.

Liviu looked at him as if he were crazy, then shrugged and set about following his order.

'Your grace!' the ursai bowed deeply.

'Mr. Bittercastle!' the Crown Prince got up from his seat at the table nodded towards his subject. 'I'm pleased to finally make your acquaintance!'

'The pleasure is all mine, your grace!'

'Lord Pop,' Turan turned to Laur, also seated at the great table. 'These men here I have brought,' he nodded around them. 'I would trust these men with my life and *I do* every day! I trust you could say the same for yours?'

'Tenfold.'

'Excellent, so am I to trust that this meeting and what is to be discussed therein shall remain matters of supreme secrecy?'

Laur stood up a bit straighter. 'Yes.'

'Marvellous! Do I trust that you and Mr. Bittercastle have broached the topics you and I have discussed during our meetings?'

'*Broached* is the operative term here, your grace?'

The Crown Prince raised an eyebrow. 'It is?'

'Yes.'

'I see...' Turan smiled. 'We're starting off on the right foot when it comes to discretion! Mr. Bittercastle! How long have you been a citizen of the City of Shangri?'

'Since the day of my birth and every day since, your Grace! Two hundred and eighty-seven years!'

'And have you been a loyal citizen of the City of Shangri?'

'I have!'

'That is my understanding also. It is also my understanding that you, Gamal Bittercastle, are not solely the Chairman of the Board of the Ursai Cooperatives, but also the leader of a certain... Shangri-Ursaini subculture?'

The great albino bearman's eyes remained as unmoving as ever. 'Some see me as something of a *community leader*, your grace, if that's what you're asking!'

Turan smiled. 'It was not a truly a question, Mr. Bittercastle... Tell me, in your almost three centuries spent within House Gisevius' reign, have you ever met a Crown Prince before?'

'I've met some of your older brothers and sisters, your grace, as well as many of your cousins and aunts and uncles, but never a Crown Prince during her or his...' the bearman's eyes narrowed.

Holy shit... he doesn't know the word either!

'*Tenure?*' the Crown Prince offered.

'*Tenure!* Yes, your grace!'

'Must be quite a peculiar thing! If I was to pick a random citizen of the City of the street and if I were to ask them if they knew more about the Crown Prince Turan of the House Gisevius or about Big White, what do you think they would say?'

The bearman remained silent.

He doesn't even try to flatter.

Turan smiled. '*Precisely!* I would dare argue that you are the second-most famous man in Shangri, trailing only behind my father, Otto of the House Gisevius! Would you agree?'

The bearman shook one of his shoulders. 'It is uncouth to disagree with royalty, your grace!' he said, hiding all hint of arrogance from his words.

Oh... is it now? Kinda sucking our own cock here now ain't we?

'It is... Mr. Bittercastle, I find myself asking myself a question; one which I believe you hold the answer to!'

'I stand at your grace's disposal!'

'You see, Mr. Bittercastle, I wonder what a man like you wants!' The Crown Prince didn't give him any time to answer. 'You have wealth; more so than I would argue any bar the wealthiest of our merchant elite and our merchant elite is *very* wealthy! Ask these fine gentlemen and ladies here of what they have seen in our city and they will likely tell you that one would be hard pressed to find a man wealthier than you in the entire Local Cluster!'

'Power?' he continued. 'Power to what ends exactly? You've climbed high enough to know that there is a certain point beyond which the cost of further power far outweighs the benefits of said power?'

'People? Love? To most of the Darkside and even a fair few of those on the Brightside, you are *a god*! They love you! They respect you! What use have you of the love of more? Would it really keep you any warmer at night?'

'What is it, exactly, that you *do* wish for? What is it that *Big White* wants?'

'*Freedom!*' the ursai answered.

'Ah... freedom from the law...'

'*No!*' the ursai growled, causing some of the Royal Guards to reach for their weapons.

'Go on, Mr. Bittercastle!'

The bearman sniffed and stood up straight. 'Long ago, before either you or I were born, your grandfather took something from my people. Something important for us.'

'The Libra Bank.'

'The very same,' Big White nodded. 'Life in our City had been good to me, your grace, and I thank you for it. Yet... do you know what it means to be born an ursai in Shangri?'

'At times I wonder if I know what it means to be born human in Shangri...'

'Aye... aye...' the bearman seemed to mull things over. 'Everything we do, we do to hide the *taint*.' His jaw seemed to tremble, as he struggled not to snarl. 'The *Shame*.' He nodded towards Laur. 'Has *he* told you of our kin? Our kin in the Milky Way?' Now it was the bearman who did not let the human finish. 'We fought our own kinsmen, shed the blood of our *brothers*, over that bank! They fled and they fled so far, we forgot they existed for a while and when they reappeared, they had their own realm carved out all for themselves!'

'And we? We had *nothing*! We had lost the very thing we had fought them over! Every ursai in Shangri knows that *shame* and we carry it with us our entire lives.'

''Mr. Bittercastle, I cannot grant you freedom from your past.'

'No... No one can! But, you can give us back our bank!' he spoke with weight, as he let the air nestle in between each word.

'I see... and what can you give in return?'

The bearman moved closer and the Crown Prince had to gesture for his men to not intervene.

'*Whatever* you want, your grace!'

'I understand that we here share a mutual antipathy towards a certain *presence* in Shangri.'

The Urheimat.

'Seems to me like we have much offer one another,' the Crown Prince concluded.

The ursai's eyes did not move as he shifted around for a moment, before he glanced towards Laur, then back to his liege lord. 'What exactly did you have in mind?'

'At the disposal of the House Gisevius stands the entirety of the Shangri Constabulary, as you very well know! Their power is absolute, though it does have limits! As does the House Gisevius itself! Our hands are tied, somewhat, as we have allowed ourselves to be forced into such standing in our own City! There are places and there are *things* which the Constabulary cannot reach, at least not without good reason!'

'The Urheimat District.'

'*Precisely*!'

'I cannot go there either, unless if I want to be turned into a rug.'

They... they do that with ursai too? Must be one hell of a rug!

'No, but you *can* assist with containment!'

'*Containment?*' the ursai looked towards the assembled remani and Laur spotted a hint of contempt in his eyes. 'Your grace, we *have* been containing them! They try to push outwards every day and *we* have to come up with ways of keeping them in, while also...' Big White paused. '... *staying within the confines of the law*!'

'And what if you didn't have to?'

Now the ursai stood still for a while, before licking his snout and looking around the room. '*Your grace,* if I may speak frankly?'

'I didn't know you were censoring yourself!'

'A man such as myself must *always* censor himself, particularly in the presence of a man such as yourself, *your grace*! But, if *we* were to not find ourselves within the confines of the law, we would have to do it in such a way where *a man like you* would see *everything* that *a man like me* was doing!'

'I assume so...'

'Well, you assume correctly! *And* that would mean that *you and those around you* would always know that *I* stepped outside the confines of the law! *You* would know... *much*! And, at whatever time you would wish, you could use that information! I would be... *in your debt*! Forever...'

'Ahhh... I see... you think *my word* to be a fickle thing?'

'I think *your tenure* to be a fickle thing! A day will come when your time passes and another takes your place! *Another*, who might have the same information as you, yet entirely different views of our relationship!'

Now the Crown Prince's face did drop and, for the first time in the short time Laur had known the man, he saw a genuine hint of true anger in him. '*Lord Pop!*'

Oh, fuck! 'Yes, your grace!'

'Would you be uncomfortable with owing me a debt?'

'I... I *already* owe you a debt, your grace! Several, actually! For attending this event... for everything you've done for us...'

'Would *you* be interested in becoming even more indebted to me?'

Laur was silent for a second, as the wheels turned in his head. 'It is impolite to refuse gifts, in my culture, your grace!'

'In mine also!' It was only then that the Crown Prince turned to him, breaking eye contact with Big White. 'You forget the whole issue with the recent disruption that occurred within these very walls? The activation of a certain prohibited technology?'

Son of a... 'I forget nothing, your grace!'

'You do strike me as that kind of man, Lord Pop! *Mr. Bittercastle*! Would you ever consider becoming indebted to a man like Lord Pop? A man who never forgets his own debts? A man with... *diplomatic immunity*? A man whose testimony could never be found admissible in the courts of Shangri? A man in whose core interest it is that *his* involvement in the suppression of another foreign power's influence within the City of Shangri remain secret?'

Big White listened closely, as he nodded. 'You want *him* to be *our* middleman? In all of this? An *outlander*?' The ursai nodded, knowing that there was no need for the Crown Prince to nod himself. 'I wonder, you grace, what *your father* would have to say of all this?'

Oh, my dick...

Turan merely smiled as he began to stride casually towards the gigantic ursai. 'Did my father ever come to you with a chance to reclaim your long-lost heritage, Mr. Bittercastle?'

'No.'

'I see... Well, let me put it to you like this:'

It was as the Crown Prince uttered these words that calamity struck.

Or, rather, it rose and stretched.

High up on one of the room's many tall bookshelves, in a place hidden from sight, Laur saw a fury shoulders rise and stretch as a horned head shivered. *Oh, no! What the fuck is Mira's cat doing here?* Laur glanced towards his fellow Hajduks as Lorgar got up on four feet, pushed his arse up and stretched.

They had all noticed and their faces danced between horror, amusement, concern and disregard.

The Crown Prince nevertheless continued with his proposition. 'I didn't have to come here tonight! I didn't have to come meet you here and, *yet,* I did! There are events to which I am invited in the Urheimat District. I hear they're rather dour events, full of song and prayer and dancing and awfully tedious conversation! Yet, they nevertheless occur and I could *always* choose to attend one or two, it that was so my intention!'

The Terrans watched silently as Lorgar quietly jumped from his perch onto a series of rafters and shelves, until he reached the top of a couch, before jumping on the seat and, finally, onto the floor. Laur glanced towards the Royal Guards to see that they had noticed the furry creature that now walked lazily across the floor. He caught Gonzo's eye and saw the remani look back at him with a mix of confusion and concern.

'You see, Mr. Bittercastle, Lord Pop over there, has a *counterparty*! There is an Imperial Ambassador to the City of Shangri. A very stoic and pragmatic individual, one that would understand and be accepting of my decision to attend one Lord *Pop's* events before I attended one of *his*! And, at his events, there is probably a room, just like this one we find ourselves now, though perhaps far less opulent! And in such a room, I could walk over to a man, just like you, but *very* different, and I might ask of him the same thing I ask of *you* now!'

Lorgar stopped a few paces behind the Crown Prince and sat down on his arse as he yawned, before studying the faces around him with a look of indolence and disinterest. He raised a paw to his face and licked it, before beginning to clean himself. It was this subtle sound that caught Big White's eye, who now studied the cat as the Crown Prince continued to address him.

'What do you think such a man would say? Do you think he would haggle? Do you think he would question my word and the extent of my powers? Would he ask questions concerning the aftermath of my tenure? Would he sit there, as you are now, wondering if he could maybe force my hand a little; maybe have me offer more than I came prepared to give?'

'Listen to me very carefully, Mr. Bittercastle, I am only going to say this once!'

'Do as the Lord Ambassador asks of you and know that he speaks with *my authority*! Lay a silent siege over the Urheimat District! Hunt down every symp in the City that could ever muster up the treasonous determination needed to ever lift a finger of defiance to the House Gisevius and our world will change! And in this new world your loyal service will help usher in, *you* will have the freedom and the history needed to hold your head in front of any man from within this City and beyond!'

'Do this for me and *I will give you your bank!*'

Big White starred at him for a moment in a room only of tension and culmination. Slowly, yet surely, Laur saw something he had never truly seen before, not only on Big White's face, but on the face of any ursai he had ever seen in his lifetime.

Is... is that a...

Grinning. Ear-to-ear, as his jaw slowly began to nod. His eyes twinkled now, a strange human sight on such a beastly man. Then, once more, he began to slowly nod.

The Crown Prince smiled.

'NIZAMI!' Lorgar shouted in English, startling everyone in the room. '*Give me a glass of water*!'

All eyes now turned to the talking cat in their midst. The Shangrian Royal Guards had long been eyeing the strange horned feline that had appeared in their midst and which had been washing its face in front of them, uncaring of their presence. Gonzo himself was the only one to immediately look to Laur, who stood motionless, embarrassed and horrified, his heart beating out of his chest due to sheer dread. The other Hajduks fared even worse, as they all just simply stood motionless, like wolves caught in the headlights of a speeding vehicle.

Turan squinted, though he did so as he smiled. 'Hello, Lorgar!' he greeted. 'I was wondering if Mira brought you along!'

'*Bah!* Don't waste my time! Just fetch me a glass of water! Though I must say that it's awfully humid in here already!'

'Fair enough...' Turan spoke as he rolled his eyes. He looked towards the nearby bar and saw a water fountain.

Oh, fuck no! 'Your grace! Allow me!' Laur jumped out of his seat.

'No, Mr. Pop, I know what to do! Still flat and room-temperature, Lorgar?'

'Well, lower than *this room's* temperature!' Lorgar turned to look at Big White, of whom he was remarkably unconcerned about, despite being over a hundred times his body mass. 'Don't worry big man! With *that* coat on you'll start feeling the heat any time soon!' he said, not knowing that Big White didn't speak English and observed what was happening around him with a look of menacing surprise.

Completely unperturbed, Lorgar made his way to the long couch occupied by Gigi and Lejla, jumping into the latter's lap. 'Greetings, Lady Lejla! Might I please have a petting?'

Though startled, Lejla quickly obliged, as she flashed a rare smile, while the Crown Prince finished pouring Lorgar's glass. 'One glass of slightly chilled water for the gentleman!'

'Excellent! Put it on the coffee table!!'

Ok, now that's enough! 'Say 'thank you', Lorgar!' Laur ordered.

'There's no need, Lord Pop!' the Crown Prince answered, as he smiled. 'I am very well acquainted with our loquacious little friend here, as well as his '*charming*' quirks!' he said, placing the glass in the requested position.

Lorgar's purring was interrupted as he eyed Gigi on the couch next to him. 'What are *you* all looking at? Yes, Gigi, I have horns now!'

'I see that, Lorgar! Looks good on you!' the Shqiptari raised a friendly hand as he grinned. 'You wanna pat?'

'No, I may not have a *pat*! Lady Lejla is here and her hands are far softer than *your* dirty rock bags!' Lorgar hissed, before turning to Lejla. 'Lady Lejla, please have a sip! Milady told me she would send someone over! I am so pleased she chose you!'

Turan shook his head, clearly reminded of past times spent with Mira's pet gremlin. 'Well that's not nice...' His eyes widened, as he now studied Gigi. 'Is he a *Jew*, Lorgar?'

HOLY FUCKING JESUS CHRIST IN BETHLEHEM!!! MIRA, WHAT THE FUCK KIND OF SHIT HAVE YOU PUT US IN? Laur scratched his head. *Oh, my fucking dick... What else does he know about? How much fucking –*

'He is far worse than a Jew! *He* is an *Albanian*!' Lorgar muttered.

The Crown Prince nodded. 'Ahhh... you didn't mention Albanians on your *naughty list* last time we met, Lorgar! I see you've grown more selective over the years!'

'On the contrary, Nizami, I have become far more tolerant in my later years. I now consider the Vietnamese and Romanians to be honorary Aryans and I even now tolerate the presence of *gypsies*!' he explained, glaring now at Nick. '... by necessity!'

Turan followed his gaze. 'You're a gypsy?' he asked Nick.

Nick frowned, unsure about the Crown Prince's tone. 'Yeah...?' he responded, as he squared up. *Jesus, Nick, control yourself!*

Turan's eyes widened. 'Like the Peaky Blinders?'

Alright now fuck this shit... fuck this... what the fuck...

Nick's eyes narrowed. 'No, your grace! *Romani* gypsy; not a traveller!'

'Oh, I see! I wasn't aware there were several *kinds* of gypsy!'

'Well... there used to be...' Nick's eyes widened. '*But!* But, I can get you a traveller, your grace!' He didn't wait for a reply, turning to one of the Romanian Hajduks, Veronica. 'Go get Bobby!' he instructed, before turning back to the Crown Prince. 'I think he's actually *from* Birmingham!'

The room was suddenly flooded by the sounds of the festivities taking place throughout the building, as the double doors to the room were opened by two Royal Guards to reveal a wide-eyed Mira al-Sayid.

Thank God! He raised his hand, pointing towards Lorgar. 'Mira, get rid of this *fucking* thing!' *Jesus Christ... I just swore...* Laur placed a hand on his temples in personal disappointment.

Nevertheless, Mira did immediately obey, as she walked briskly towards Lorgar, who now glued himself to Lejla's lap.

'Oh, Lord Pop!' the Crown Prince began. 'There's no need for that!'

'Your grace, I insist! I understand that you had – *have!* a relationship a-a-and *fond memories* with this creature and I am very glad! But, I must apologize for our negligence, which has created this situation where important conversations were interrupted!' *Jesus Christ, I am flustered...*

The Crown Prince turned towards Big White, who met his gaze. 'I think that we reached an agreement, didn't we, Mr. Bittercastle?' he asked in Shangrianese.

'We did, your grace!' the ursai bowed his head slightly and glancing towards Laur.

'I'm still taking him away!' Mira announced, as she neared her cowering pet, his ears pulled back as he tried to hide under the folds of Lejla's black dress.

'*Milady!* I did as you asked! *They* came here and I thought you sent them to *drink the water* and play with me!'

Drink the water? Laur's eyes rushed towards the glass in front of Lejla.

No... He looked up to see Mira's wide eyes glancing towards his. YOU PUT MDMA IN THE WATER FOUNTAIN SO PEOPLE WOULD COME HERE, GET HIGH AND PLAY WITH YOUR CAT?!?!?!

He looked towards Nick, who looked away, confirming his theory, then towards Lejla, who seemed to also understand what 'drinking the water' meant.

'Still putting drugs in the water fountain so that people can babysit your cat, Mira?' the Crown Prince asked.

HE KNOWS ABOUT THE –

*WHAT THE FUCK DOES HE MEAN '**STILL**'?*

The Crown Prince smiled as Mira glared at him. 'I thought you might have outgrown that!'

Now Lorgar joined in. 'She did, Nizami! I had to beg her to do it this time!' he jumped from Lejla's lap onto the ground between two Royal Guards, scuttling behind them. 'She only agreed because this was supposed to be a drug room anyway!'

Laur almost vomited.

'A drug room?' the Crown Prince raised an eyebrow.

'Yes, a drug room!' Lorgar could be heard as he scurried behind the couches. 'Out of sight, like myself!' He emerged from between two armchairs and rushed behind Turan, sensing him as a potential protector. 'I was supposed to stay here and women would come and gamble on cards, do drugs and pet me!'

'*Huh*! Sounds like the real party was supposed to be in here, not out there!' Turan commented.

'Only after the Crown Prince left!' Lorgar explained, clearly not understanding who he was talking too.

'Oh, really? Why is that?' Turan locked his amused eyes with Laur's enraged and embarrassed glare, just as Mira came up right in front of him and her pet cowered behind his legs, fomenting discord and scandal.

'Apparently it's some royal rule that guests may only leave after the Crown Prince leaves!'

'Very well versed in the ways of Shangri, aren't you Lorgar?'

'Not at all, Nizami! You know I deplore this place and its queer sun! But Milady has been working on today's meals for two weeks, ever since *Sheikh Qartil Alqarib* placed her in charge of catering! She's spent hours every day at work in the kitchen concocting the menu and reading about Shangrian tastes and palates and all these queer things things like 'mouth feel' and 'satiety' and she mumbles and I listen!'

'I see... *Sheikh Qartil Alqarib?*' Turan asked, smiling. 'I do not think those words exist in Shangrianese!' He looked up at Mira. 'Who's he talking about?'

Mira's eyes and mouth did not move.

'He is referring to *me*,' Laur answered, as the Shangrians turned to look at him, while the Terrans, Tech and Basenji all looked down at the floor, upon hearing the name by which Laur Pop was known among Arabic-speaking Terrans.

'Lord Kinslayer...' he explained.

'*Ah*... I see! Well, I am afraid Lorgar is correct (in this specific instance, at least!) Shangri protocol does dictate that I both arrive last and leave first and, given that you clearly have plans for after my departure, I might as well !'

'– *No!*' Laur got up from his seat, his hands outstretched in a gesture of apology. '*Your grace*, I apologise for interrupting, but this cannot stand! *Yes*, indeed, I confess that this evening had planned for it several instances and amenities which we assumed you would not be interested in! Hence, why we set aside rooms such as this one! Yet, I will not stand for you to leave with the impression that we – *in any way* – welcomed, orchestrated or suggested your departure!'

'*Huh!*' the Crown Prince noted Pop's statement, before eyeing Mira for a moment. 'Well... what did you have planned out for the evening? In rooms such as these?'

Laur was caught off-guard. 'W-well, the idea was that, once we would be freed of our official duties for the evening, myself and my colleagues would gather in this room, play cards, catch-up... share drinks and stories...'

'... do drugs and pet Lorgar?' Turan offered.

'I... I didn't know about Lorgar, your grace!'

'I see!' He looked down towards the feline huddled behind his legs. 'It appears that we are *both* intruding, Lorgar!'

'*You* have a lot of experience in that area, Nizami, I'll give you that!'

'Well,' He looked up. 'Might it be an issue if we intrude on you further, Lord Pop? Perhaps we could partake in his game you had planned out!'

'I don't gamble, Nizami!' Lorgar felt the need to comment. 'It is a Zionist conspiracy seeking to erode the moral values of the righteous!'

Laur's mouth twitched. 'Of course, your grace! We could...' he looked over to his Legates. 'We were actually thinking about trying out some of the local games!' They weren't. They were going to play Terran poker.

'There are no local games, Lord Pop! Most gambling is illegal within the spheres of Shangri...' Turan pointed out, before turning to Big White. 'Are there any local games, Mr. Bittercastle?'

The ursai's brow furrowed for a moment, until he understood the Crown Prince's meaning. 'Of local origin? No, your grace!' the ursai's head tilted to the side. '... *or so I hear,* your grace!'

'I see! Well, given that we have no games to offer, Lord Pop, please feel free to stick to your usual card games!'

Laur sighed, not believing what was happening to him. 'Well, I suppose I have to explain the rules!' Laur searched his memory for the best words to explain. 'The game is Texas Hold'em. Each player is dealt –'

'– Two hole cards. Three community cards called a flop are then dealt, followed by a fourth and a fifth, known as the turn and river, respectively, with rounds of betting take place between deal. The goal is to make the best combination of five cards, ranging from high card, all the way to a royal flush.'

Laur, Gigi, Nick, Bojana, Lejla and Josip all looked at the Crown Prince, as if they were chickens seeing a pig fly.

The Crown Prince noted their dumbfounded expressions. He addressed a stunned Laur, 'I've seen *Casino Royale,* Mr. Pop, and, as such, must compliment your people on the quality of your cinema!'

'I... I'm glad you found it to your liking, your grace!' It was quite a rare sight for Laur Pop to be truly taken by surprise. *A film about a spy playing poker in Montenegro to catch a...*

Ahhh... Ohhh... What the fuck is he getting at? Laur remembered his exact surroundings and turned to Big White. 'Have you ever played Texas Hold'em, Mr. Bittercastle?'

'No, but I've played plenty of card games in my life and his grace's explanation was quite descriptive. I take it you use the Terran four colour deck with sets of numbers from one to thirteen?'

'We do...' *What the fuck? Has he watched Casino Royale too?*

Big White turned to the Crown Prince. 'It's all the rage nowadays in the harbours! Vanir sailors brought them over a few decades ago. They're quite popular among the younger generation,' the bearman explained.

'I've heard. I've also heard that they're popular in some of the Libra ursai's own venues? As a friendly pastime? Among friends and with no illegal sums being wagered?'

'Of course, your grace! And the house '*never*' takes a rake!'

'I'm certain it doesn't!' Prince Turan clearly lied. 'Well?' he turned back to his host. 'Would you have room for two more in your nine-handed arrangement?' he asked and Laur couldn't stop his eyes from twitching for a moment, as he tried to stop himself from blinking in surreal amazement.

Laur, Josip, Gigi and Bojana formed the core of the old poker club, established early on in the days of the War of Vengeance, as a means to help pass time during their first anxiety-filled early excursions through the Greyspace. They were joined by Nick, one of the later members, who had joined only recently, after the many deaths and departures that had occurred during the Hajduk's history, as well as by Basenji and Tech, which had learned the game during their time spent on Terra. Now, they were joined by one giant albino ursai and a man with more wealth at his disposal than was even comprehendible to them.

They had one of the Romanian Hajduks, Hristache, who had actually worked in a casino before the End Times, act as the dealer and the game got underway, as a selection of some of the more senior Hajduks, some of the Crown Prince's entourage (and likely his closest bodyguards), a few Allied diplomats, as well Mira, Anwar and his catman, looked on from the side. Laur noticed Silvia enter the room about five hands into the game. She walked over to the bar that had and ordered the bar's robot operators to prepare her a drink. Laur followed her for a moment, reminding himself to have a talk with her at one point about Lorgar's unannounced presence in the room earlier, before going back to what very quickly became a rollercoaster of a poker table.

The Hajduks knew each other and their playstyles very well after half a century of playing together. Gigi didn't play a lot of hands, yet when he did, he was terrifying, using large bet sizes and not giving away any hint in connection to the strength of his hand. Josip was methodical, to the point of being remarkably predictable. In the long run, Josip was probably one of only a few Hajduks to have actually turned a profit from the infamous Hajduk game, a testament to the man's consistency. Bojana was very reactive, being very dedicated to the idea of playing the man, not the cards. She was the most entertaining player of the bunch, at least in terms of gameplay, since Nick was by the far the most verbally entertaining player at the table, though he was no pushover, being quite adept at the game himself.

Basenji was a rock. A bunker. An old man and a drinker of coffee. He rarely played a hand, with the remani usually taking part in a maximum of one hand every hour. Yet, he usually won the hands he did play, on account of being a remarkably good, yet passive and predictable, player. Technowolf was remarkably bad at the game. Laur noted that sobriety hadn't helped his game, as Tech seemed to be fundamentally unable to grasp the basic concept. *Probably because he doesn't care if he wins or loses. He just enjoys playing. The rest of us actually care about winning...*

...

What were we playing for, again?

They were playing for Asgardian Guilders, since it was the most widespread currency after Shangri Spheres and Imperial Trade Credits in the City of Shangri. More importantly, it was legal to gamble with Asgardian Guilders in the City, while Shangri Spheres were prohibited from being gambled for. Gambling with Republican Currency at a Republican event in the City was perfectly legal, thus guaranteeing the legitimacy and the optics of the game.

Though if one were to see the game, one might fall into a haze of feverish dizziness.

Laur and Nick were always loud. Nick, because he liked entertaining himself and those around him, and Laur, because, well, he knew that it threw some of his opponents off their game.

Big White was an entirely different animal.

Nestled in between Nick and Bojana, he roared and slammed his fist on the table when he lost and he roared and slammed his colossal maul hands into the table when he won. These occurrences where common because, well, it appeared as that the head of the ursai Mob was a degenerate gambler.

And a calling station! He plays every single fucking hand...

Yet, he was winning, primarily due to his own dumb luck. Hristache had been instructed to keep the game fair, allowing each player to receive truly random cards and putting forward fair boards of community cards. However, due to a combination of pure luck and his opponents' lack familiarity with his playstyle (if there even was such a thing!), Big White soon found himself winning, overall, despite losing a pot here and there.

The Crown Prince was charmingly reserved and played poker like a senator, not like the spoilt brat one might have expected. He seemed more concerned with getting to know his companions at the table, more than he cared about winning, losing or even just gambling. He played a hand here and there and the Hajduks and Big White played against him with the chill blood of crocodiles in their veins.

Which is another way of saying that they did not go easy on him, though he did not seem to mind too much. *He seems far more concerned with avoiding eye-contact with both his wife and Mira... whatever the fuck happened there...*

'Two pair!' announced Josip.

'Show it!' Big White said menacingly and those gathered at the table tensed up at the ursai's tone of voice and his hunched posture, as if he was about to make a lunge for the Croat Hajduk.

Josip tabled his hand, not wishing to start a diplomatic incident. Especially not one that involved getting mauled.

King and Queens.

'HA!!! Straight!' roared Big White, slamming his hand on the table

A gutshot straight draw with Jack-Nine offsuit which fucking spiked a ten on the river... This lucky motherfucker...

'You know what we say on Terra about that sort of thing?' Nick pointed at his neighbour's hand, as he collected his winnings.

'What?' Big White growled humorously at him.

'We say that you touched shit before coming here!' Nick was always brave *and foolish.*

Around half an hour into the game, such remarks no longer attracted any raised eyebrows from neither the Hajduks, the ursai mobster, nor even from the Crown Prince's entourage. At first, the Hajduks had tried to keep things civil, yet it very soon became clear that everyone present might have had a bit too much to drink already and formalities had long ago been cast to the wind

The Crown Prince, nestled safely in between Gigi and Laur, turned to his Hajduk host and asked, 'Is that true?'

Laur replied, 'It's actually a Romanian expression, not a Terran one. It's believed that touching shit is lucky. Hence, when someone is excessively lucky, like Mr. Bittercastle over here, we say that they touched shit before playing!'

'Touched my ass!!!' Big White roared.

'That's where shit usually comes from!' Laur whispered, just loud enough to cause the Crown Prince to chuckle.

'I thought Terrans where supposed to be swashbuckling motherfuckers who lived life on the edge!' Big White announced. 'Turns out you're all yellow! Scared of lil' ol' me!'

Little?

'I thought we came here to gamble!' Big White picked up Josip's cards. 'King-Queen? What are you doing playing Kings and Queens!' he threw his cards in the muck and picked up his own cards. 'Jack-Nine! That's how you win! *Ha-ha!*' He then turned to Nick and gave him an elbow, almost causing the Hajduk to fall out of his seat. He then laughed aggressively in his face, until the violent absurdity of the situation forced the gypsy to laugh nervously.

What is it with him and the fucking Ray Liotta laugh from Goodfellas?

Hristache dealt the next hand as the verbal abuse continued. 'I don't understand it! Why play games of chance if you don't wanna take a chance?' asked the bearman.

'Why have money, when you can lose it?' Laur countered.

'*Wuah*!!!' roared Big White, then he elbowed Nick again. 'A real philosopher, this one!' then he slammed his fist on the table. 'And *a comedian*!!!' his eyes widened.

Oh, no!

Big White turned to Bojana, to whom he had been making advances for almost the entire them at the table, 'You know what he said to me? When he came to visit me?'

'Please, enlighten me!' Bojana answered, only sounding as interested as was needed to keep *him* interested in *her*.

'I was at my the mental facility where I have to stay at night – ' he turned to the Crown Prince. '– it's part of my agreement with His Majesty's courts!'

The Crown Prince nodded knowingly.

Big White turned back to Bojana, 'So, anyway, I'm sitting there and your good General Pop comes over, and you know what he says to me? First thing he says to me!'

Bojana raised her shoulders just enough to keep his interest raised.

'He asks me: *So, Mr. Bittercastle, how long have you been a guest of the government?*' and he burst into aggressive laughter the moment he finished recounting the story, just as he had done on that very same occasion.

Gigi was the first one to chuckle, before allowing for a momentary glance towards Laur, who leered back at him. The others began giggling, but not at Laur's humour, but at the excessive laughter roaring out of the inebriated bearman. The Hajduks, as well as Tech, stifled smiles, upon realizing that Laur had thought it adequate to quote *the Sopranos* when addressing an oversized mobster.

'Mr. Bittercastle,' Hristache, the dealer, began.

'What is it, kid?' Big White asked. Hristache was seventy-seven years old.

'It's your turn to act!' he explained.

'Oh... *Raise*!' he announced, without looking at his hand.

Typical... Bojana folded, Tech called the bet and Laur looked down at... *Red Queens. Fucking finally. I've been trying to take down this hairy greaseball with bullshit up until now!* Laur raised Big White's initial raise of forty guilders to a hefty 125 guilders.

The Crown Prince, Gigi, Basenji and Josip got out of the way, and Nick hadn't even played his hand to begin with.

Big White gave Bojana a nudge, 'Baby girl, I'm gonna have to look at one card!'

'You do that...' Bojana commented.

Big White picked one of the cards, looked at and announced, '*Call!*'

No surprise there, fucking calling station! He's seen every flop since he's been here...

The flop came a nine of spades, an eight of spades and a seven of clubs. *Not great, not terrible.*

'Check!' Big White announced.

Laur bet one hundred and eighty Asgardian guilders.

'Call!' Big White announced immediately.

The turn came a five of spades. *Fuck... now I lose to any six and any two-card flush draw!*

He's only looked at one card.

Big White announced, 'Check!' after appearing to think for a second.

If I check, which is what I want to do, I should technically look weak. If I bet, maybe I can get him to leave right now (unlikely), or make it look like I'm really strong and that I'm the one that just improved their hand...

He still hasn't looked at the other card!

Laur bet three hundred Asgardian Guilders.

'Call!' Big White announced immediately, without looking at the other card.

The fuck... Does he actually have me, or is this fucking idiot calling me with a seven? Or a single spade? The river came a seven of spades. *And, all of a sudden, my hand is absolute fucking garbage...*

'Check!' Big White announced.

I am almost never winning this hand at showdown... I have to bluff... Fucking cunt faggot gambler bitch...

Laur bet one thousand Asgardian Guilders, the worth of a hundred thousand hectares of land on an Asgardian planet in Triangulum.

The bearman did not look at his other card before announcing 'All-in!'

Fucking horseshit! He beats me with one card! 'Congratulations, Mr. Bittercastle! The money's yours!' he announced, before mucking his cards.

'Baby girl!' he growled seductively towards Bojana. '*You too!*' he growled enthusiastically towards Nick, as he elbowed him without looking. 'You wanna see the other card?'

'No need,' Laur muttered.

'What? Don't you want to find out if I beat you?' Bittercastle needled him.

'You had me beat with one card.' *The one you looked at.*

'Well! Let's see!' He flipped over the card he hadn't looked at, revealing an ace of clubs.

Laur deduced that the other card must have been the ace of spades, giving the ursai a flush. 'You had aces? Lucky you!'

Big White chuckled, revealing the other card, the one he *had* looked at. An eight of clubs. 'TOLD YA YOU WE'RE YELLOW, Lord. Pop! Like on that flag!' Big White pointed to a Romanian flag that was hung upon a nearby wall, as the room took in what had happened. As chuckles spread throughout the room. The ursai had just bluffed Laur Pop and that was no easy feat.

'He's quite the intrepid player, now isn't he?' the Crown Prince whispered softly to him. Laur was certain Big White had heard him.

'I do not know yet, your grace! He might just be *very* lucky.' *And, on top of that, something of an unstable degenerate!*

The ursai chuckled. 'Lord Pop! Luck comes to those who seek it! And, sometimes, you have to go to scary places to find it!' he said, as he collected the dark silver coins and stacked them neatly on top of each other, in a large tower that almost reached his chin. 'Straddle!' he announced, pushing twenty Guilders into the middle.

Bojana folded her hand the moment she saw it and Tech studied his hand for a moment, before taking a sip of cranberry juice and throwing it away into the muck.

Laur looked down at Ace-Jack of clubs. *Nice... A rematch! And I can look tilted now! From his perspective, I might have nothing. Just annoyance since he just bluffed me earlier!*

'A hundred' he announced, tossing in a single coin with the Asgardian symbol for '10x10' on it.

Laur looked at his opponent, studying him as the Crown Prince folded, followed by Gigi. He didn't even bother looking at them, since he was intent on figuring out exactly how this –

The sound of clinking coins coming from his left startled him. He, and everyone in the room, turned to see the miracle that had just occurred.

Basenji had just thrown money into the pot. *For the first time this whole evening!*

'Raise!' an equally stunned Hristache announced. 'Three hundred Guilders!'

Josip and Nick's hand were folded the instant Basenji's money had landed on the felt.

Big White eyed Basenji suspiciously. He made as if to simply call without looking, though he later decided to look at one card.

He immediately looked at the second.

That first card must have been big. An ace, or a king maybe. Though, I have an ace... and Basenji might have two. It would be strange for him to have an ace...

'Raise!' the bearman announced and threw in ten coins.

'Raise one thousand!' Hristache announced.

Fuck... Laur had to actively stop himself from wincing. As much as he wanted to show this degenerate schizoid fuck who was in charge, he likely would not be able to do it in this hand. Basenji's hand was so obviously strong, ace-jack simply wouldn't cut it, regardless of what Big White must have been holding.

He mucked his hand.

The room fell perfectly silent as the flop came a loud queen of diamonds, ten of diamonds, and three of hearts. Big White gave the flop a long look, before announcing 'Bet!' and throwing in two thousand guilders.

Basenji stood, unflinching for a few seconds, before placing a stack of twenty coins into the middle, which was odd, since there were also coins of the one thousand denomination in the stack before him. After all, he had started the hand with virtually all of the money he had bought in for: thirty thousand guilders, the same as all of them. Big White covered him, since he had won almost twenty thousand Guilders since the game had started.

The turn came a queen of hearts and Big White announced 'Bet!' before throwing in five thousand Guilders.

Basenji thought about it for a while.

'*Eh*!' Big White snorted. 'Aces are no good, *lemi boy*!'

The table grew tense for a moment. *No need for a racial slur here, bearman!*

What are you trying to do? Is the cost worth it?

'Fold 'em!' Big White instructed. 'There's no shame in folding! You can't win with aces here! Sometimes you start out strong, but life just kicks you down! Fold the aces! Kings too!!! You're not good here and you know it! Learn from your yellow friend *there*!' he pointed at Laur. '*He* backs down when he knows he's beat *and* when he's not beat!' he mocked.

He's suggesting he has a queen in his hand.

Basenji remained silent and still.

'Or you have Ace-King or a draw! You should call! I want you to call if you have that!' Big White continued. 'I hear you're a gambling man yourself, Basenji! Why else would you be here?' Big White threw his weight onto his elbows, as he pushed himself forward, onto the table. 'If you raise, I'll call!' he taunted.

Basenji put his hand on the coins before him, grabbed one of his stacks, split it in half, and threw in some coins. *Too many.*

Hristache looked at the coins. 'Min raise,' he announced, before counting the coins. 'Ten thousand!'

Almost half the money he had left. What the fuck is going on? Basenji is rarely good here... but Basenji only does this if he's good. Big White knows that, but, now... he is committed to calling... not due to the laws of the game, but due to the laws of his honour...

Laur studied the ursai and saw something. He saw him get annoyed. Basenji was clearly taunting him, but he was doing it in such a way where one couldn't tell if he was bluffing him or fleecing him for all he was worth. *But... there's no way he could be fleecing him. If he has a good hand. An excellent hand like Ace-Queen or even fucking queens, he should just be calling. It just doesn't make sense for him to raise, especially not such a weird sum... unless...*

The sound of clinking coins hit the felt. 'I'm a man of my word!' the ursai announced.

'Call!' Hristache noted, counting out the coins and adding them to the pot.

Big White leaned back as the final card hit the board.

A nine of spades.

The flush draws missed. No ace and no king came. Only King-jack got there, since it's now a straight, though I don't see Basenji playing that...

Big White chuckled. 'Hah! See! Sometimes your *yellow friend* has a point! Sometimes, it's not good to gamble! You see, me, I'm a man of my word! And I put my word down and my word is final! *But, fate*! Fate sometimes gives and fate sometimes takes! We can only hope we can find ourselves on the right side of it!'

He's good... he's so good right now... he's certain he's won...

'All-in!' he announced.

Basenji flicked a coin onto the felt before him.

The entire room gazed upon that single coin and one could even hear the sound of someone's ice melting in their glass in the corner of the room, for the silence was almost absolute.

'*C-c-call*!' Hristache announced.

Big White blinked and stood motionless for a moment.

Hristache turned towards the ursai. 'You show first, sir!'

The ursai leered at him, before flipping his cards over.

King-Jack. The fool's hand.

'A straight!' Hristache announced.

This lucky shit-fisting mother-

A flash of white crossed Laur's vision as two white cards jumped from beneath Basenji's hand and into the middle of the table, opposite Big White's King-Jack. (*Offsuit, by the way...*) Laur's eyes hurried to see the two cards.

Black Tens.

'Full house!' Hristache announced, barely containing his giggles. 'Three tens and two queens! The winning hand!' he took the ursai's King-Jack offsuit and threw them in the muck.

The room exploded into loud cheering and applause, as it was the Hajduk's time to roar, together with some of the other Republican officials present, as well as even a few of the Crown Prince's retinue and quite a number of Big White's entourage hid dangerous smiles from their boss.

I don't like that... I don't like his men enjoying feelings of schadenfreude at his misfortune... my men are like that as well sometimes... but they'd never show it in public...

Big White blasted away his money after that. The game carried on for less than thirty minutes after the hand that would live in infamy for the Hajduks and the Ursai Cooperatives, before the Crown Prince announced that it was time to retire.

Naught but a few minutes after the game's conclusion, the Crown Prince took his leave, informing his hosts for the evening that it was time to return to the Imperial Palace. Laur offered to escort the Crown Prince to the exit, which the Crown Prince wholeheartedly agreed too. The route they took towards the entrance was not through the main chamber of the laurel tree, however. Rather, they used a small corridor that lead to the balcony flanked by windows facing Wiltshire Boulevard on one hand, and rows of columns overlooking the reception area below. It was here that Laur and the Crown Prince finally found themselves truly alone, for the first time in the evening, as both Hajduks and Royal Guards stood to the side, letting the two men gaze outside for a while.

'You did well with Jenner,' Turan commented.

'I realized it was a test the moment I saw him. I'm glad I passed,' Laur replied, before glaring at him. 'For the sake of our relationship, I would kindly ask that neither you nor your father ever ambush me like that again!'

Turan smirked. 'I can vouch for myself, yet my father has an entirely different view of these things. He believes that a man can only be seen for who he really is in the moment of the unexpected, as the never before seen emerges from the unremarkable. I will, however, *apologize* for the entire charade! I may have been merely a bystander, yet it happened in my presence and, thus, is *my* responsibility! I may promise you that, going forward, there will be no further tests and surprises, at *least* not any that I may have a hand in preventing!'

Laur nodded and sighed. 'On that note, I must also apologize for the entire debacle with the cat, as well as Mira's... *outburst*! Mira... Mira is not one of my own men. She... she comes from a different culture. A culture that is not mine and a culture perhaps unfit for diplomatic duties. I can promise you that measures will be taken to prevent any further interference from both her and her cat!'

The Crown Prince smirked and sighed, before turning to face Pop, looking him dead in the eye. 'Lord Pop, do you know why you were tested tonight?'

Laur's eyes narrowed. 'I assume because it was necessary to see if I could refrain from tearing someone limb for limb, just because I didn't approve of them being in presence?'

'That too, but it was primarily to verify *your* ability to fulfil *your* diplomatic duties! Again, you passed! But, I will point out that there was never a need for Mira to be tested!'

'I think we can both agree that such a test would be wholly unnecessary!'

'It would be, indeed!' The Crown Prince shrugged, as he looked at the ground, chuckled and raised his eyebrows. 'Lord Pop, up until recently, I never questioned your abilities; not those as a diplomat, a leader of men, a judge of character... but, now I find myself in a position where I feel as if I must help you do *your* job!'

Jesus Christ, what a clusterfuck your daughter has put me in, Sara! 'I assure you, Mira will be handled accordingly!'

'Oh, yes?'

'Yes!'

'Is she getting promoted?'

Why would she...? I... Oh, but for fuck's sake!

'*Ah*! I see that my help is indeed needed! You see, Lord Pop, you seem to be under the impression that Mira al-Sayid is a threat to the carefully constructed image that you and your predecessors have laboured to present over the years! The reality, however, is that no one in the history of your Republican Alliance has done more to improve relations between the Humans of Terra and the City of Shangri as much as Mira al-Sayid! You see, Lord Pop, it is not that *she* that cannot match *you* in *your* diplomatic abilities*,* but that *you* have only now just barely managed to match *her* in *yours!*'

'It is why *she* has never been tested! Her virtues are plain for all to see! She's done more to further the cause of your people by just being herself than you ever did with your words and your strategies and your planning, or your plotting and your scheming!'

Did... I mean, I know she's charming in her own way, but... did you...

'To not even mention the incident that occurred within these very walls naught but a few weeks ago, which is the final matter I wish to discuss with you tonight!' Now the Crown Prince's eyes narrowed as he shook his head. 'What spirit compelled you to bring such a device into our City?'

Laur had been preparing himself to answer such a question. 'It was a contingency.'

'Ah... well, your *contingency* just made our lives a whole lot more difficult and our objectives that much harder to achieve!' Turan turned back towards the street outside. 'They're calling for your expulsion, Lord Pop! My presence here alone will do little but stifle the flames of your blunder and fuel whispers of the true nature of our relationship and what we aim to achieve together! You endanger *everything* we have worked so hard towards!'

'You have my apologies! I promise you that, going forward, my cards will all be on the table at all times!'

'Good... Yet, there is a price to be paid! *Everything* we have discussed, you will have to achieve *without* my assistance!'

Laur's eyes narrowed. 'I am to proceed *without* the support of the main beneficiary of my actions?'

'No, Lord Pop! The main beneficiary of what we intend to do are the citizens of Shangri (whom you will have to draw to your side) as well as those of your Alliance, who all stand behind you already! I can promise you that the Constabulary will not hinder you, yet they will not assist you! They may turn a blind eye, yet they will not be able to ignore that which happens right before their very eyes! If you require their aid, you must seek it yourself and you must pay a price! *That* is what may be salvaged. *That* and the fact that, Lord Pop, going forward, *you* have sole ownership of your actions! You will answer to no one! I will remain in place for when it comes my time to play my part, but the stage is all yours until that point!'

'So, as you move forward, I want you, every step of the way, to ask yourself: *is everyone else who knows about this being quiet?* You. Your men. Your Alliance. Your *associates.* Always bear that in your mind! Because, if you don't Lord Pop, everything (and I do mean *everything*) will crumble like seats of sand underneath us!'

'And, with *that*, I leave you!' the Crown Prince put his right hand forward.

With a dick in my ass... Laur shook his hand.

As he made his way back to the banquet hall, he realized that the Crown Prince's unexpected long tenure had resulted in a remarkably large number of guests becoming heavily inebriated, as he saw some of his men politely hold them upright as they led them to their vehicles.

'Ah, Mr. Pop!' Big White greeted.

Laur felt his heavy footsteps approach from behind him. He turned, just as the bearman crashed his maul of a hand into his shoulder, almost causing him to crack the tiles underfoot. He could smell alcohol on his breath!

'Mr. Pop! I must go!'

'So soon?' *If only you could have left earlier!*

'Yes! I have a curfew, compliments of His Majesty's courts!' The bearman placed his left hand on Laur's right shoulder, coming face to face to him, the tip of his snout within an inch of Laur's own nose. 'Thank you for *everything*, Mr. Pop! You're a great guy!'

And then the ursai pulled him forth into an embrace, hugging him, of sorts, as he nestled his jaws next to Laur's neck, right beneath his ear. 'I gotta hand it to you, *Laur*!' he whispered. 'I didn't think that much of you when I met you, but now I see where you get your balls from!'

'Laur'? I'm not 'Mr. Pop' anymore?

'He'll do anything *we* tell him to do and he'll think it's his idea!'

'We'? Who the fuck is 'we'?

'You see, I've met princelings before and I never had enough to get them to eat out of palm of my hand, yet you have it all figured out, don't you?'

You think he's eating out of my palm? That's interesting!

'See, I thought all you had was your hand outstretched, but turns out your mouth was telling a story and he *ate it all up*!'

Quoting Jenner, now, are we?

'You've got him *mounted*, don't ya? In more ways than one, thanks to that long-nosed broad of yours?'

*MIRA? How **dare** you!*

Laur hid his rage as the ursai withdrew and gave him a pat on the shoulder.

'Me and you are going to do great things together, Mr. Pop! Come to my place tomorrow and we can get to work, *partner*!'

'Partner'?

'Of course, Mr. White! I'll see you tomorrow!'

Laur looked on as the bearman and his entourage walked out, thoughts rolling through his head. After an awkward moment he shook his head. *I'll figure out tomorrow...*

Where is everyone? Now I can finally fucking relax a little after all this... after all the... after everything!

He walked back to the banquet hall and immediately spotted Tech and Gigi, who waived at him as he neared.

Great, he's exactly who I want to see! It's been some time since we hung out together!

'I'm going back to the barracks,' Gigi whispered to him, as the two men met in the middle of the hall.

And that took Laur unawares. *What? Why?* he asked, as he found his bearings and tried to act relaxed. 'The party's just getting started!' he tried to sound casual; inviting.

'I'm a bit old for parties, Laur, and a bit too happily married!' Gigi replied, his wife in a galaxy far, far away.

Unlike me... is that what he's saying? 'Come on, Gigi! We'll get back to my office, bust out some cigars and drink ourselves into incoherence!' *Like we always used to do!*

'Nah!' Gigi responded, making it clear that it was the end of the conversation.

Son of a... What the fuck's pissed you off?

'I did a headcount and about forty of my guys are staying; the rest of us are coming with,' he explained.

'Lejla's just left, too!' Josip announced, as he joined the two in conversation. 'Zaza and around twenty of them are staying with you.'

No surprise there, at least. 'And you?' he asked his Croat Legate.

'I'm going too! This whole thing was quite exhausting. It didn't feel like a party as much as it felt like work!'

'That's what the afterparty was for!' Laur insisted.

'I'm with Gigi on this one, Laur; I'd rather get to bed.' Josip took a sip of his drink. 'I've set up meetings tonight that'll drag out for over six weeks and the first one's tomorrow at eight! It'll help to be lucid!'

I like you Josip, but you are kinda creepy, so I'm not exactly annoyed about you. Lejla was always reserved, so I don't mind that either.

But, Gigi? Me and Gigi go way back! There were times where me and Gigi and Rumen and sometimes even Mikhail would just sit together around a campfire or in some barracks, or in one of our offices or rooms or houses... and we would just drink and chill until the morning!

Now he's outgrown it? That's what he says, at least!

This shit's a fucking blow!

Gigi slapped him on the shoulder. 'I also have shit to do tomorrow morning!'

'Now you tell me?' Laur asked, his irritation spilling out only a little.

He wasn't certain if Gigi caught on or not. 'Some of the Colonials are coming over for training tomorrow. New ones.' Gigi sighed. 'I didn't tell you, because I didn't want to get you all worked-up, but, with the exception of the dog boys – no disrespect!' he said, addressing Technowolf. 'But they're all fucking bollocks, mate!'

'They suck?' Laur asked.

'*Ass*! They can't shoot for shit. They're disorganized as fuck! They're entitled and they leave a mess after they leave! They're the worst fighting force I've ever trained,' Gigi surmised.

'They're inexperienced,' Josip concluded.

'They're worse than inexperienced: they're badly trained and lazy! They learn shit at their academies and, what's worse, they confuse that shit with actual knowledge and discipline!' Gigi emphasized.

'They're trained for another task,' Tech intervened. 'Their purpose is to act as a police force and as border guards, tasks which they've excelled at!'

Gigi turned to Tech, 'Listen to me, Tech! The remani: they're sublime! I have no complaints! And *they* were trained to be border guards and policemen, too! It's the humans that are the fucking problem! Even as police officers...' Gigi moved in closer to the three men around him. '... the remani: you can't fuck with them! They walk the straight and narrow! Real Kevin Costner types! Even when they have to *cross over to our sid*e, they do so elegantly; as gentlemen! The humans: every time we need to get something done for our friend, *Winnie the White Poo*, it's the humans we talk too! Half of them want to buy their wife a new houseplant and the other half are fucking houseplants themselves!'

'So they're either untrustworthy or morons?' Laur asked, now focused on this new issue he was only now learning of.

'They're often both, mate, but that, in itself, doesn't disqualify them from becoming good soldiers, it's the indolence and the sense of entitlement that stops them from any from attaining any type of progress! Anyway! I'll figure it out along the way!' He extended his arm and Laur gripped it. 'It was good seeing you all, again!' He then shook hands with Tech. 'Tech! You look good!' he said, an honest smile spreading across his face. 'I've been meaning to tell you that!'

'I get a lot of vitamins!' the remani shook his glass of iced cranberry juice and chuckled.

'Josip!' the two men shook hands and met in an embrace. 'Don't go around making soup out of babies or nothing!' he joked, as the two men hugged.

'Why? Abortion is perfectly legal here!' Josip snapped back instantly.

'Jesus Christ!' Even Gigi, a Muslim, and Tech, an agnostic alien, exclaimed in amused horror.

What? Tech gets a compliment and Josip gets a hug? And I just get a handshake?

Gigi left without another word.

'Well,' Laur turned to Josip. 'How about you?'

Josip seemed surprised.

'Do you have anything you haven't been telling me so I don't get worked up?' Laur asked.

Josip's face grew serious, 'That Otto Benga character?'

Laur's face grew even more serious. 'Yes?'

'I can't find him.'

Laur almost rolled his eyes. 'Well, keep looking!'

'Laur, you're not listening to me!' Josip moved in closer. 'I don't think there's anywhere else I, or anyone one of us, for that matter, can look! We have no leads!'

'You want to give up?' Laur asked, now truly riled up from these fucking *au revoir* revelations.

Josip frowned, 'Laur! Don't give me that shit! My point is that, at this point, the best I can recommend is that we keep our heads low and our ears open. We've done everything! From this point onwards, every action is an overextension.'

Yeah, yeah... I fucking get it... I agree, but, fuck you! 'It's the way it is!' Laur acknowledged. 'It's not like we won't have other things to keep us busy!' he muttered.

'Agreed! And, for me, one of those things is a meeting with a charming young anchorwoman tomorrow at eight!' the Croat replied.

Laur squinted at him. 'What?'

'It's off the record, Laur! I'm not blowing any whistles!' he replied, a small grin playing mischievously in the corner of his mouth. He grabbed Laur's hand and pulled him closer for a hug. 'Relax! Everything's fine, Laur!' He slapped him on the back.

'Tech!' he turned to the remani. 'Gigi's right! You're looking magnificent! Have you considered going on a carnivore diet!'

'I get enough meat delivered to my refrigerator from him,' he gestured towards Laur and the two men laughed before Josip said his goodbyes and left.

'I'm going to get a refill,' Tech shook the ice cubes in his empty glass before leaving, leaving Laur alone for a moment.

Which was fucking unbearable, because he wasn't used to people leaving him. He was used to the opposite: him *telling* people to leave him! Having people leave him, especially Gigi, whom he thought of as the brother he never had, really rattled him, especially since all his other surrogate brothers, Mikhail, Rumen, even Tomasz Ashaver, were not there! He was now stuck here, in this house, with his underlings, for whom he carried a lot of sympathy, yet no true feelings of friendship. That had been how he had been for the past month and that would be the norm for the next year.

Fucking bullshit. Maybe Silvia and the others were right! Maybe we should've stayed on Terra.

'Well, that was spirited!' Bojana said, announcing her presence, right next to Laur.

'Yeah!' he muttered, wondering what she was talking about. He realised that she likely hadn't overheard the exchange with Gigi, Josip and Tech. 'Yeah, it was a good poker game!'

'I wasn't talking about the game!' she replied.

Laur finished taking a swig of his drink and turned to look at her. *Did you hear that exchange or not?* 'What are you talking about?'

Bojana pursed her lips to hide a smile of disbelief at his obliviousness.

'That thing with the cat?' he asked, frowning.

'No, that was just surreal! No! That thing with Jenner!'

'Oh.' *I forgot about that!* 'Silvia dropped the ball on that one and I had to pick it up. What I did was mechanical: it had to be done and it had to be done by me. That being said...' he looked at the contents of his glass. '...*fuck that guy!*' he downed his drink.

Bojana chuckled. 'It was nice to see you all fired-up. I haven't seen you like that in a long time!'

Last time you saw me fired-up, I was being spit roasted by a dragon; don't remind me!

She came in close and whispered in his ear. She had a habit of doing that when she – 'I want to talk to you!'

What the fuck is it now? Laur didn't have to say anything.

'Relax, Laur! It's not bad news!' she explained, upon seeing the obvious look of irritation on his face. '*Privately*,' she added, after nodding towards their surroundings.

Good! Laur realized he had left his drink in the poker room. *I'll get a refill. Plus, I need some good news after all this bullshit...*

Laur and Bojana made for his office. He noted that she appeared to be either somewhat tipsy or downright high. Probably a mix of both. *You know what? Fuck it! At least I get to have a positive interaction with someone, which doesn't involve me being either a facetious motherfucker or a fucking duplicitous asshole!*

'Laur! What is that?' Bojana immediately asked, as they entered his office.

He saw one hand dangling near her hidden blade, while the other pointed towards Spideraven's webby lair.

'Ah!' Laur pondered the long-winded explanation and decided against it. 'I got a bird!' he explained. 'His name is Spideraven! He's a Camio! He eats pigeons, makes spiderwebs and fucks with cats!'

Bojana's demeanour immediately changed and he saw her navigate between an astounded look on her face (likely due to her surprise that Laur Pop had finally acquired a pet during their travels) and a lock of childish fascination with the animal. 'Does he let you pet him?' she asked, as Laur removed his suit jacket and placed it on the armchair where Tech usually sat.

He then walked towards the cupboard behind his office where he kept his liquor cabinet. 'He does. He'll probably let *you* pet him also!' He turned towards the bird as he walked towards his liquor cabinet, snapping his fingers twice, before pointing towards a small table opposite his desk. Spideraven took off from within his funnel web. '*Hai la mângâiat!*' he instructed the Camio, which diligently exited its lair and performed a graceful glide towards an ornament he used as a perch on that respective coffee table. 'You want a drink?' he asked.

'What's on offer?' she asked. Laur heard her make Serbian noises as she likely approached the bird.

'I'm having an old-fashioned,' *like I always do when in my office this late at night...*

'Consistent as always! Fill me up!' she instructed.

Laur diligently began preparing two cocktails.

One sugar each. Muddled in Angostura bitters...

'Laur, I'm amazed!' he heard her announce from behind him.

Very chirrupy today, aren't we Bojana? 'That there would be a black crow in my office?'

'That you'd get a pet! And a bird at that!' Laur heard her go back to calling Spideraven cute words in Serbian.

A splash of triple sec, because that's how I make my old-fashioneds... 'He was a gift, so I had to say yes,' he began. 'Though, I must confess that I've grown rather fond of him!' *Throw in the ice cubes.*

Clink! Clink!

'He suits you! All tall, dark and *handsome*!' she proceeded to make kissing noises, probably in the direction of Spideraven's perplexed beak.

And fill the glass up with Single Malt Scotch Whiskey, because the International Bartender's Association doesn't exist anymore, so there's no one around to tell me that this is not how you make an old-fashioned!

He turned around with the two glasses in hand and observed Bojana lounging in one of the armchairs opposite his seat and across his desk. He slid her drink towards her as he heard her say: 'Such a nice big cock!'

Laur almost fell over. 'What?' he asked.

Bojana smiled. Laur could tell that she was pretending to be surprised. 'What?' she asked, her face the image of innocence.

'Did you just call him a *cock*?' he asked, pointing, drink in hand, towards the male bird in question.

Bojana gestured in genuine confusion, 'You called him a 'he'!'

'I did,' Laur did indeed.

'So, he's male,' she went on, still visibly confused.

'Yes,' Laur believed so, at least. *Big White never explicitly said he was male... he just used a male pronoun and Laur assumed...*

'So, he's a 'cock'!' Bojana said it as if it was the most obvious thing in the world.

Laur thought things over for a moment. 'I don't think that's ravens and crows! I think that's just male chickens, i.e. roosters!' he took a sip of his drink. 'Male ducks are called 'drakes'!'

'What...? Like animal dragons?' she asked, seemingly very interested in poultry nomenclature.

'No, like the rapper...'

Bojana realized he was fucking with her.

'I don't know why they're called drakes... But, I don't think that any male bird is a 'cock' in the English language.' He took another sip.

'EYYY!' Bojana exclaimed, picking up her own glass. 'Lord Pop!' she snorted. 'This is a royal event! It's not polite to drink like a peasant with a lady!' she bent forwards, presenting him with her glass.

You're a lady of the court now, Bojana? 'Oh, right!' he bent forwards and clinked glasses with her and then they both drank. None of them immediately said anything afterwards. Laur noted that she was still toying with Spideraven, attempting to tickle him.

'So, are you going to sit there and play with my cock all night?' He was a bit annoyed at her, though he was way more enthusiastic about getting to say that line.

'We might go up to the bedroom later!' she said, grabbing his beak gently and clasping it shut. 'Bup!' she mouthed.

What an odd fucking joke... This bitch is drunk as fuck... 'Yeah, anyway, so, what did you want to talk about?'

'*Uhhh, Laur*!' she said in mock exasperation. 'Why does everything have to be so fucking contractual with you?' she gestured towards the heavens. 'Maybe I just wanted to talk to you! See how you were doing? Isn't it my job, after all, to watch over the needs and wants of my General, which, for the time being, is you?'

'For the time being?' he asked. 'Are you planning a breach in security anytime soon, Bojana?' he asked, knowing the answer to be negative.

'That's not what I'm talking about and you know it!' she said, looking at him as one would look at their fellow mischievous playmate.

'I know... Wouldn't you love to be rid of me?' he muttered into his glass.

'Laur! After all this time!?'

'What?' he chuckled.

'After all this time we've spent together, you think I don't like you?' she asked.

Like me? Bitch, you don't even...

Nooooooo!!!

No fucking way!

No.

Uh-uh!

Laur looked at her carefully for a moment. She languished in the armchair, yet she did so... *gracefully*. Lasciviously. Seductively, one might say. He could see her long, smooth and toned legs arch from her heels to her blue gown, as the dark folds of the garment curled above her thighs, one of which was laid bare before him. Her breasts fought for breath underneath her dress, as they revealed themselves in all their shiny glory. She moved one hand clad in golden rings and bracelets towards her hair, which she moved out of the way, causing one of the breasts to push into the other and the union they formed together caused Laur to feel as if he had been taking short breaths.

Oh, fuck! That really is what is happening. Laur stood up straight in his own seat. 'Bojana, eh... what's going on here?' he asked seriously, though she tried to hide it with a soft smile.

'*Here*?' she gestured towards the room. Laur noted that she had closed the door shut behind them and he knew that she knew that no one would dare enter his office without at least knocking first. 'I don't know, Laur! *Anything* and *everything* might happen here! Did you have anything particular in mind?'

Laur had to remind himself that the Hajduks, like all Terran military formations, routinely scanned their members to make sure that they weren't impersonated by infiltrated impostors. No, this was Bojana, *his* Bojana, and she was telling him that he could do whatever he wanted with her.

Right here. Right now.

Pop cleared his throat. 'Did you miss me? Over there in Belagravia?'

She smiled and he noted the fullness of her lips. His teeth itched and his mouth watered, as he thought about biting her lower lip softly. 'Yes, Laur, I've missed you! I guess distance has made the heart grow fonder!' she murmured with her voice, which Laur realised was very heavy and it carried across the table.

The hairs on the back of his neck stood up, as he wondered what it would be like to have her whisper into his ear as he pushed himself into her. *Again and again and again.* 'Would you miss me if you were no longer a Hajduk?' he studied her. 'If you were... something more?'

Her eyes glittered and Laur saw it.

This. Bitch.

He chuckled slightly and Bojana also chuckled, 'Bojana, you're one of my most trusted advisors! What would I do without you?' He didn't allow her to answer, taking a sip of his drink and placing it loudly on his desk as he bent forward. 'I guess that will remain a mystery for both of us for some time being!' he said

He saw her smile quiver for a moment and immediately understood that his hunch was correct.

'That's why you're here, isn't it?'

Her smile faded now completely. 'Laur–'

'No! No!' he waved a finger at her. 'Fifty years I've known you, you've never come over to check-up on me and how I'm fucking doing! Now, all of a sudden, after some time and distance to mull things over and less than two months after I make you Legate, you decide it's time to come over and stroke my cock and ask me how I'm doing? *Eh?*' He turned his face into a caricature of empathy, causing her to shift uncomfortably in her seat.

'I'll take that as a 'yes'! Well!' He leaned back. 'A day will hopefully come, Bojana, when you will take your Serbs and start your own Legion, because, in case you haven't figured it out yet, I do happen to think you will be worthy of it one day!'

'Now, whenever that day may come is, well, *none of your fucking business*! At least not until it arrives! Until that day comes, Bojana, let me fucking worry about it, *by myself*! If I want to talk to you about it, I will! It might be in a year, or in two, or in twenty, or it might be fucking *never*!'

Bojana glared at him, her body posture having shifted from comfortable seduction to rigid rage. He would have said something, yet Laur decided to beat her to it.

'This conversation didn't happen! You came in here to discuss the search for Otto Benga or our smuggling operation or whatever the fuck you're up to up there in Belagravia!' Laur glanced towards Spideraven. 'You can tell them I showed you my cock too, if they ask for details. Are we finished here? There's an afterparty waiting for us downstairs. Perhaps you've missed someone else and maybe you can go play with them in their bedroom later!' He never raised his voice, instead speaking in his most menacing monotone.

Bojana's lips began to tremble and she quickly curled them up in fury. But, she did not get up.

'I'm disappointed that you would jeopardise our friendship like this,' he told her.

'*Friendship?*' she growled, her heavy voice now thundering. 'You call this *friendship* Laur?' she got up from her seat. 'This isn't a friendship, Laur! It's an association, at most!'

'Well, I'm glad you like me as an associate and that you miss me in Belagravia! I missed you too! As we were before and as we will continue to be, for as long as you serve under my command – and one more thing! Just so you know, I might miss you so much, that I *never* let you go! It might be just us Romanians and Serbs left in the Hajduks! So, you might as well keep your head down and buckle-up, do your *fucking job* and leave THE FUCKING CAREER ADVANCEMENT, TO ME!' Now he did raise his voice a little.

Bojana was trembling with visible rage. Her mouth twisted as her eyes flared, yet she ultimately managed to regain her composure. 'Understood... *sir*, and I regretfully inform you that I have to wake up early tomorrow, so I will *take* my leave!' she managed.

'You have my permission!' he said.

'I didn't ask for it!' she fumed, turning around and barging towards the door. She opened, walked out, and left it ajar, allowing the sounds of the party below to flood into Laur's room, much louder than they had before.

Fucking bullshit... This fu-cking bull-shit!

Laur downed his drink, stared at the ice in his empty glass in annoyance and then got up to fix himself another drink.

All these fucking people around me; all they motherfucking want to do is just fucking get away from me! And right after they leave, what the fuck happens? I hear from them once in a blue moon and usually because they need me for some reason or another. Selfish motherfuckers!

I don't give a shit!

I'll jack off to her shiny titties later. Damn she's fucking hot! I knew she was fit like that but, Jesus Christ, she had me horny as shit!

He was placing the ice cubes into his drink when he heard the music subside, as the door was closed behind him. He froze instinctively. He would've relaxed himself, had it not been for a gust of air that reached him, as the entrant walked casually towards him.

Cardamom. Patchouli. Sara. Heat. Djibril.

Mira.

He poured himself his whiskey and turned around slowly, glass in hand.

Mira was now lounging in the armchair next to Spideraven. She stood with her arms clasped on her belly and her legs firmly planted on the floor, her thighs wrapped loosely in her green straight pants, which tightened across her calves and towards her white high top sneakers. Her dress tightened once more across her torso, bar only her bare navel and the space right beneath the gap between her full breasts, covered from his hungry gaze by the fitting folds of her gown.

Laur's eyes wandered towards her face.

That's Sara's face. She's looking at me....

Her face was loose, her lips crested comfortably between her high cheekbones and her soft jawline. Her eyes... Mira was always good at hiding herself, especially her eyes. Yet, now, Laur saw something there, a certain... *heat*. As if he was watching embers glow in warm fireplace across a dark room.

Sara never looked at me like that!

She seemed intent on him and Laur wondered why she was here. What did she want? He thought about things for a moment and studied her stirring figure for a moment, as she simply looked back at him full of... full of *something*... Laur knew he wanted *that* something.

Maybe... Maybe... Maybe I could fuck Djibril's daughter...

She got up, without saying a word and a wondering Spideraven looked from her to him and then back to her.

'Come!' she said and Laur felt his heart skip a bit and his mouth fill up with water.

He was unsure as to what to do for a moment, before Mira turned around and walked towards the door. He took a sip of his drink and realized that she had instructed him to follow her. Towards what and where, he didn't know. Yet, he really wanted to find out. He placed the glass on his desk and began walking towards her before stopping.

This girl is wild. She might be calling me to fuck her. She might be calling me to kill me. I could never tell with her...

He had a silenced handgun and a blade hidden in his suit jacket, but he didn't want to put his suit jacket on, since he was feeling very hot all of a sudden. Plus, he knew he couldn't take Mira in melee combat, so a blade would be useless. Also, he would prefer a loud handgun, since he would be relying more on the arrival or reinforcements, rather than on his own accuracy, if Mira made a move on him. So, he opened one of his drawers and pulled out one of his Berretta pistols and tucked it into the back of his pants, before covering it with his shirt, which he pulled out and used to cover the weapon.

He walked out of his office armed and aroused, and saw Mira waiting for him patiently in the smaller service stairway next to Tech and Nick's room. *Ok, so we're not going to her room.* Once she saw him exit his office, she turned towards the stairs and began descending. Laur checked that no one was around to see them, before following her.

He wasn't sure if it was because he had likely become slightly drunk or perhaps due to Mira's movements within her dress, which he followed intently, but his movements were wobbly. The music grew louder as they neared the ground floor and they began to encounter some of the Hajduk partygoers. Most were too drunk or high to pay that much notice to Mira or Laur as individuals, let alone as an individual unit. For all they knew, Mira was going from A to B and Laur happened to be sharing the same route for a few paces.

They passed couples both established and spontaneous, as well as groups of drunken friends tumbling on drunken feet from one room to another, yet none truly took note of them. Not that Laur cared that much, since this was *his* house and his men knew better than to question him or his moral compass, at least openly. A few drunkenly saluted him and quite a number greeted and shook his hand or slapped him on the back. He did not care; he was focused only on his guide.

Mira took him to the basement, where they found themselves alone once again. She walked towards the parking lot. Specifically, she walked towards the service room, where the cleaning ladies parked their van when they came in the morning.

It's empty now. There's cameras. But, they only turn on when the doors are open. Once inside, they turn off. They're also visible, so the people coming in know that they're being watched and they have shutters on them which can be turned on and off, assuring complete privacy.

You dirty... what are you playing at?

The hallway towards the service room was dark, lit only by dim orange lights and when Mira reached the doors of their destination she opened them to reveal the light within. It was not a blinding light, yet it was quite bright, enough to cause Laur's wandering eyes to squint slightly.

Maybe... maybe this isn't right... If I do this... how will I feel afterwards?

He followed her in, just as his eyes adjusted.

Once he saw who was inside the service loading bay, his right hand drifted casually to his back, where his tucked pistol lay.

Three murine lay within, with the back of a fourth one's head visible through the window of the strange car they had likely arrived in. The three sitting outside the car where all eating Mira's banquet food from plates she must have brought them. One was sitting on the trunk of their car, another was on a chair the Hajduks kept in the corner of the garage, while a third was leaning on the garage door as he munched down on meatballs and cheesy polenta.

They had a strange energy to them, very different from Mrs. Cri and her employees, and not just on account of them being males of their race. They seemed... *hard*. They had the bearings of men that worked in the night and their outfits suggested as much. Loose monotone clothes, with no ostentatious designs or noteworthy features.

'This is Telemac,' Mira gestured towards the ratman that had been sitting on the chair, munching down on the last scraps on plate that had likely arrived full.

He rose up instantly, placing the plate down on his former seat and nodded. 'Lord Pop! It is a pleasure to meet you!'

'This is Ralder,' Mira gestured towards the rat that had been eating on the car's trunk, who also put down his plate, slapped his hands clean and nodded towards Laur, who nodded back. 'And this is Bulmac!' she gestured towards the murine that had been eating whilst leaning on the entrance, who nodded in greeting.

Mira turned to Laur and said nothing.

Laur glanced from her to the three ratmen before extending his left hand in greeting. He knew it was weird, but he also knew that he wanted his shooting hand as close as possible to his gun, and that these ratmen would likely be unaware of the finer points of Terran customs. 'Pleased to meet you, Telemac!' He shook hands awkwardly with Telemac. 'Ralder!' he shook hands awkwardly with Ralder. 'Bulmac!' He shook hands less awkwardly with Bulmac, since by then he was getting used to shaking hands with his left hand.

He studied the three, though he spoke with Mira, 'Mira, I'm happy to be acquainted with these three fine gentlemen, though I must confess that I do not know exactly why it is that I am doing it!'

'It's our fault, sir!' Telemac spoke, his voice polite and only vaguely servile. 'We only informed Mira of our success earlier in the evening! She was graceful enough to put things together on the spur of the moment!'

'*Huh*... how nice of her...' he said, glancing towards the silent captain by his side. 'Well, congratulations on your success! Mind if you share the details?'

'Oh!' the murine grinned, a somewhat cringeworthy sight. 'I can do more than that.' Telemac gestured towards the car and Ralder got up from his seat atop the vehicle, before turning around to pop the trunk open.

Inside was a man.

A human. Knocked out cold. A thin plastic tube extending into his nose, likely flooding him with some sleeping agent. His hands and feet were bound together and his entire body lay within a large canvas bag, his face only barely visible.

Laur was slightly stunned, though, at this point in his life, ratmen bringing him people tied up in the back of car wasn't something that could really surprise him anymore, despite the novelty. He studied the man for a moment, bending forwards to look at his face. It looked vaguely familiar, though Laur had no recollection of ever meeting this man before. Perhaps he had seen him on the news?

Or...

No! No fucking way?!

'Is...' he began. '... is that...' He couldn't believe it. He stopped himself from saying the name. He knew not what Mira had told his ratmen, nor why exactly they were here, so he didn't want to say out loud the name of –

'Otto Benga!' announced Telemac.

Wayyy... Laur blinked a couple of times before turning towards Telemac, studying his alien face for deception, before turning to look at Mira, who smiled subtly.

'We found him in Labalacacat! Hiding in an old apartment that belonged to a distant aunt, several times removed. We would've brought the aunt over as well, yet Mira instructed us to bring him and *only* him. No witnesses!' he explained, before rummaging through one of his pockets. He pulled out several phones wrapped in a black tape and a few documents. 'They're unpowered and we wrapped them up in null-tape, just in case! These here are his papers! Certification of Citizenship! Merchant Class Permit, 1st Class! This here is his bank statement...' he explained, as he extended them towards Laur, who accepted them silently with his left hand.

Laur looked at Mira and they both knew what the other was thinking.

Desert Power.

Laur turned back towards the murine, 'Mr. Telemac,' he began. 'Do you know who this man is?' he asked.

'Yes, sir! He is Otto Benga, Inspections Supervisor at the Paragon Shipping Company,' he began.

'No! No!' Laur shook his finger. 'Do you know why Mira asked you to deliver him to us?'

The murine looked confused, 'Because you couldn't do it yourselves?' he asked, genuinely.

Laur raised an eyebrow and he saw the murine squirm a little. He turned to Mira, 'Do they know?'

'No!' she replied. 'They know only that we were looking for him and for him alone and that we wanted him delivered to us without anyone knowing about it.'

'Hmmm...' Laur mused, rubbing the documents and the phones in his hand. 'Do you know that we've asked both the Ursai Cooperatives, as well as elements of the Constabulary to find this man, Mr. Telemac?'

The murine smiled, 'You asked well, sir! But, with no disrespect to either the Cooperative or His Majesty's Constabulary, they don't know Shangri like we do, sir! One who knows the hidden alleys of this city might be able to hide from them, but they cannot hide from us, since we are the ones who built those hidden alleyways! They simply took residence in them!'

'Hmmm... impressive... Who's *we*, Mr. Telemac?'

The murine's eyes glanced to Mira, then back to Laur's interrogation. He stood up straight. 'We have no name, sir! We never did. We simply fulfil a role, sir! We keep watch over our own people! The Constabulary says it watches over everyone, yet they don't bother coming over to our sides of the City! The ursai care only from whence they might extract wealth and our sides of the City have little of what they seek! Our people still need protection, sir! And it is *we* who provide it!'

'I see,' Laur said. 'You don't have a name...' he pretended to muse. 'Do you have a leader?'

Now the murine really did try to stand up straight. 'Yes, sir! That honour is mine! I am the leader!' he announced. Laur saw bits of kebap in between some of his teeth.

The Romanian General turned to Mira and gave her an inquisitive look.

Mira nodded.

Laur nodded back, pretending to agree. 'You came here to meet me?'

'Yes, sir!' Telemac answered.

'Why?' he asked.

The murine seemed taken aback for a moment. 'I...' he seemed to struggle to remember something.

Laur raised an eyebrow.

The murine swallowed and seemed to compose himself, choosing his word carefully. *Or remembering them.* 'I wanted to get the measure of you!' he said, attempting to sound like he was a man who liked being in control.

'Huh...' Laur nodded. 'Correct!' He nodded a few more times. 'That's what a leader *would* want!' he said, though his eyes were fixed not on Telemac, but on another murine.

The one inside the car.

The one likely looking at them discreetly through the mirrors.

The one with his window slightly lowered, so that he might eavesdrop.

Laur threw the phones and the documents onto the head of the tranquilized Otto Benga and they slipped beneath his face and under his chin. Laur nodded some more, as he looked at Mira.

He then walked over towards the driver's seat, making sure to never turn his back on the three ratmen outside the vehicle.

The window was tinted at exactly the Shangri legal limit and he knocked on it with his left hand a couple of times, then waited for the driver to lower it.

The moment he saw his cinnamon face, Laur knew that he was something different. *Now... he might be the real deal!*

... I've seen that face before...

He was not vicious-looking. Far from it, he actually seemed much more humanlike than the other two, with his eyes being very expressive and his face unmoving in a quiet, reserved manner. He seemed... strange... and... *very familiar...*

Laur's eyes drifted towards the passenger seat next to him, upon which rested a fourth plate of food.

Untouched... Clean cutlery right next to it...

Laur glanced at the three murine and noted their changed expressions. Worried, they now seemed.

'*Arron*!' he heard the ratman in the driver's seat say.

Laur turned to see that he had raised his left hand, offering to shake Laur's own left hand, as he had likely deduced that this must be Terran custom. *He also moved it so subtly that I failed to notice, which is actually kinda impressive. Disturbing, but impressive...*

Laur looked at him for a moment, wondering, before extending his own left hand towards the inside of the car...

And he went right past the murine's hand, reaching towards his belly and pressing down on it.

A grumbling sound escaped the ratman's belly, as empty guts rumbled into the hollowness of an empty stomach.

Laur smiled. He withdrew his left hand and allowed his right hand to leave his back and reach out towards the murine, who had been glaring at him in a disturbed surprise.

'... and how do your friends call you?' he asked the ratman in the driver's seat.

There was a pause. A good pause. The pause of a man thinking.

'*Shoem*,' he said, reaching out with his own right hand to shake Laur's.

'*Shoem*!' Laur said. 'Shoem!' he repeated, shaking his hand. 'Sho-em? Am I saying that right?'

Shoem nodded, still shaking his hand.

Laur released his hand and sighed, a smile stretching across his face. 'You're the one form the fight! From a few weeks back! You fucked up that cocky bast bastard with the chokehold!' he recalled. There was a moment of silence as Laur urged him to answer truthfully.

Shoem nodded.

Laur smiled. 'You're a good fighter!'

'Thank you!'

'You might be the greatest bantamweight fighter in the entire City of Shangri!'

'I might be,' he responded calmly.

Laur turned to the three remani and Mira. 'The greatest bantamweight fighter in Shangri!' he gestured towards Shoem. '*Moonlighting* as a driver!' This last bit he said to Shoem directly.

'Shoem, my name is Laur!'

'Pleased to meet you, Laur!' he responded curtly.

'Thank you for...' he pointed towards the back of the car. '... the *gift*!'

'You're welcome,' he replied.

'Do *you* know who Otto Benga is? And why we wanted him delivered on our doorstep discreetly?'

Shoem was silent for a moment. Laur liked that. He liked that a lot. 'I have my suspicions,' he said.

'Care to enunciate them?' Laur asked.

He was silent for a bit longer now. 'He hurt your people. Your people don't let anyone do that and get away with it, no matter where they're from,' he said.

'Correct!' Laur nodded. 'Shoem, I find myself indebted to you!' he declared.

'Is that a problem?' the murine asked.

Oh my God, I like him! 'No,' Laur let loose. 'Not at all!' he sighed and slapped the car door softly, in an excited manner. 'Shoem, next week, on the third day, there's going to a be a meeting here!' he pointed at the ground of the Embassy. 'Think of it as a... meeting of the likeminded! A meeting of the minds of people that don't let anyone hurt *their* people!' He glanced towards Telemac, now stupefied as he looked on. 'A meeting of people who speak on behalf of their people and who can *coordinate* their people.'

He turned back to Shoem, 'Does that sound like a place for you?' Laur asked.

The murine was quiet for a moment, clearly considering things. Clearly trying to understand what this strange human from a far away land was thinking. He slowly nodded. 'It might.'

'I'll see you there then. Eleven in the morning! You'll come in through this service entrance in a delivery van from Mrs. Cri's cleaning Company. I'm assuming you know Mrs. Cri?'

'She's my aunt. Fourth degree.'

Well, I guess I know how Mira got to them... or how they got to Mira. 'Lovely Lady! It's going to be a recurring meeting, once every seven days. Can you fit that in your schedule?'

Shoem nodded after a while, 'Yes.'

'Good! *Mr. Telemac*!' Laur raised his voice slightly, now making himself sound purposefully commanding.

'Yes, sir!' the stunned murine was startled, though he did manage to react.

'Please offload Mr. Benga!' he instructed, his eyes still on Shoem. He put his right hand forward. 'Goodbye, Shoem!' he said.

'Goodbye, Laur!' he replied.

Less than a minute later, he and Mira were standing side-by-side, watching Shoem's car drive up on Wiltshire Boulevard, while the entrance doors closed. Shoem reached into his passenger door and pulled out a bottle of hand sanitizer, squirting some of its contents into his hands, as he held the steering wheel straight with his wrists. He scrubbed his hands pensively, yet diligently, as he pondered his next move. Perhaps the Gods of Old had finally stirred in their slumber and had finally sent to them a golem as wicked as their foes, as the prophecies had foretold singe ages past. He gripped the steering wheel and knew then that he would have trouble sleeping that night and many nights afterwards. Hopefully, his wife would understand.

The kids would enjoy seeing more of him in the morning, though not as much as he would love to start more of his days with them gathered around the table.

Behind the two Terrans, on the garage floor, was a long canvas bag, now sealed shut, as its occupant slept his second-to-last sleep.

'I'll take him to the interrogation room,' Laur turned to take the measure of the bag. 'I'll take it from here! You go upstairs and act like nothing happened.' He looked up from the bag and smirked at a pokerfaced Mira. 'Don't tell me they got you fooled with that whole Mark Twain nonsense *too*?' he asked and he did so in a manner which he thought was playful.

Mira didn't take it as such. She frowned once and then turned around to barge off towards the door.

No! No! Dammit girl! Laur darted after her. 'Wait! WAIT, *for fuck's sake!*'

He caught up to her in the hallway, right at the base of the staircase leading upstairs to the party. The music was louder there and he gripped her elbow to pull her close so she could hear him.

'*Hey*!' he whispered softly to her.

She didn't recoil from his touch, though she did pretend to struggle a little, just to express her disapproval. He held her waist with his spare hand and allowed the hand that gripped her elbow to loosen up. He pulled her close to him and she didn't fight him, as their waists connected and Mira lowered her chin, and her sweltering gaze fixated on his.

'Listen to me!' he continued, gently. 'You did good!'

He felt her tense up.

'No! No! Listen to me! You did *great*! *Great*! I'm actually fucking impressed!'

She relaxed somewhat and she leaned backwards and gazed into him, allowing him to hold her weight with his arms, as she bent her navel slightly upwards and her bare skin touched the folds of his white shirt. Laur's mind flashed to the thought of a touch without the barrier of fabric.

He sighed, knowing he had to do better. 'Look, I'm sorry about how things are around here!' he confessed. 'I know we're not the Ghazis!' He chuckled. 'To be honest, I still haven't really figured out why you're here, but I'm starting to understand!' he said, as she stopped herself from leaning and allowed his strength to pull her closer to his face. Closer even than Laur would have expected.

'It's my influence, really, all the negativity around here! I know I make life difficult for the people around me. I know I don't say *please* or *thank you* or *congratulations* half-as-often as I should, but if there was ever a time to be grateful for the full half of the glass, it is now!'

Her mouth and her nose had wandered, as had his, and he felt the smooth softness of her nose rub against his. He raised his hand from her elbow to steady her face by holding her jaw gently in the palm of his hand.

'Go!' he instructed, before releasing her.

She studied him, her face as indecipherable as ever. Her eyes burning, as they always did.

Laur nodded and she nodded back, resuming her path towards the party upstairs.

As she reached the stairs and began climbing, Laur felt the need to add one more thing, *Amira Parvati al-Sayid!*'

She stopped in her tracks at the mention of her full name.

'By the laws of our people – which I myself helped write – I am forbidden from recruiting Hajduks from the Arabian or the Punjabi Nation. Yet, I tell you now this:'

'Henceforth, you are one of the Hajduks in all but name! The men will know you as one of their Captains and if any ever question your appurtenance, you better damn sure send them to me!' he decreed.

Mira nodded slowly. Her eyes lingered on him a moment longer, before she turned and disappeared up the steps.

I could've fucked her if I would've wanted to but I didn't. I showed restraint. That makes me the real hero here! I would've fucked her up if I would've done it...

Though... someone like her... maybe with someone like her I could've had a second chance...

...

Jesus Christ, I am horny as shit...

Laur walked back towards the loading bay, gingerly picked up the bag containing his quarry, then walked back the way he had come, only this time towards the basement and his interrogation room.

He threw the bag on the floor and removed his victim from within. He stripped Benga naked and removed the tranquilizer drip from his nose. Then, he walked over to the other room, prepared what was needed for extraction, then checked the cupboard where Ela kept a bottle of Romanian blueberry liqueur and began taking swigs out of the bottle. *Some music would be nice, too!*

One could still hear the music coming from upstairs and he wanted to hear some music in the room with Benga.

If you wanna run away with me, I know a galaxy
And I can take you for a ride!
I had a premonition that we fell into a rhythm
Where the music don't stop for life!

Laur began selecting his desired utensils, as he finally allowed himself to get a little bit drunk and dance around. He knew that it would likely be a pretty quick endeavour. *A half hour. Tops.* Men who were good at hiding usually did so for a very good reason. Namely, they knew they weren't strong enough to handle torture.

Glitter in the sky, glitter in my eyes
Shining just the way I like
If you're feeling like you need a little bit of company
You met me at the perfect time

Benga woke up and stared at him in horror. He began mumbling something, yet Laur didn't care, though he did listen. He knew he would have to put a little work in before he gave up his mental conditioning code.

You want me, I want you, baby!
My sugarboo, I'm levitating!
The Milky Way, we're renegading
Yeah, yeah, yeah, yeah, yeah!

He broke Benga quickly, though by the end of it he was too drunk to care about his efficiency. He checked out a few memories, went through a series of emotions. Satisfaction. Curiosity. Sadness. Disgust. Rage. Satisfaction. Then he cleaned up clumsily, before making his way to his bed to pass out.

He managed to get to his couch, where he immediately fell into a spiralling slumber which brought him back to another Dawnbreak party from decades before.

He walked into the crowded hangar, now converted to a banquet hall, followed by Alex Demetrian and Șerban Tapalagă. He walked through the happy revellers until he reached Rareș Ionescu, who turned to cheer him and embrace him.

'Laur! My *brother!*' Rareș had called him during his drunken embrace. '*This* is *us*, my *brother*! *We* did this! Nothing can stop us now!'

Rareș had let him go as he stumbled towards the centre of the great hall, reaching the middle of a Romanian dancing circle, as he shouted.

'*NOTHING CAN STOP US NOW! WE ARE KINGS!*'

Laur pulled out his pistol and shot him twice. Once in the heart and once in the head.

The hall fell silent and beyond Rareș's body, within a swirling mass of shocked eyes, he saw Lejla, dressed in white and clutching her fleur-de-ils necklace, a look of horror on her face.

He spoke the words.

'No kings.'

Chapter XI

The Day after the Night before

    Silvia woke up suddenly, opening her eyes and feeling very tired, as if she had gone to sleep only a few minutes earlier. There was a smell in the air. Something like chicken soup and maybe lavender. But, not real lavender. *Enhanced,* chemical lavender. *Synthetic* lavender. And her eyes felt sticky and she heard a small *clip!* sound as they snapped open and the dried mucus broke apart.

    The ceiling wasn't hers.

    She immediately got up on her elbows, as she hid her neck with her jaw and looked around.

    Wallpaper with Squirtle, Charmander and Bulbasaur...

    Oh... thank God!!!... She fell back onto the bed, rubbing her eyes. *I'm in Nick's room...*

    On the Doina? Her eyes caught sunlight coming through pulled curtains obscuring a window. *No, not the Doina.* Then she noticed that the ceiling was a bit too high for it to be Nick's room in Craiova and too low for it to be his apartment in Bâlea.

    Holy shit, you idiot! You're on Shangri! You've been here for a month!

    She relaxed her body and breathed out a sigh of relief and the hangover hit her. She felt cold, clammy sweat covering her body, as her smaller muscles twitched. Her eyes, her palms, the thin sheets of sinew covering her head, they all felt twitchy and tense and strained. Silvia's body may have been superhuman and capable of withstanding amounts of alcohol that would kill a normal human a hundred times over, as well as negate the effects of any hangover of Old Earth, but the amounts of liquor she must have mixed with cocaine, emdiamay and all sorts of other drugs the night before, had strained her body nonetheless. She felt queasy and her bladder pushed her belly upwards as it stung her, bursting with her body's struggles from the night before.

    She stretched slightly and tried to breathe in therapeutically. It was then that she realized that she was naked and itchy. Nick's sheets rubbed against her womanly parts and...

    Someone ate my pussy last night!

She sprang up out of bed in a panic.

What the fuck? She touched her vagina and focused her senses to her nethers. *Feels... feels normal... inside, at least... but if...*

Silvia raised her eyes to the bed she had just jumped up from. It was a king-size bed, just how Nick liked it, full of sheets and pillows and... three shapes. A large one in between two smaller ones. Silvia saw the large one was Nick, since his drooling head and his upper arm could be seen rising up from above his bedsheets, as he spooned a blonde head. *The... what was her...? Ah, yeah, Wella!!! Which... which means that...*

There was another head, this one in between where she had been sleeping and where Nick still slumbered. She reached forward and pulled aside the sheets to reveal a naked Pravana, who must have felt the change in temperature, as she immediately began to stretch. Her eyes opened slightly and one of her arms reached forwards towards Silvia, caressing her lower ribs before going up towards her breasts, playing with her -

Silvia pulled back.

She remembered the night before. She had gotten hammered at the afterparty. Wella and Pravana had stayed. Nick convinced them to come up to his room and they had taken turns bedding the two Shangri women. Hence, her slushy pussy lips.

Oh! Oh, thank fuck! I thought I really fucked up this time...

She suddenly realized that all the movement had caused a swelling pain in her lower abdomen, as she felt a potential embarrassing calamity approach.

JESUS, I need to piss!

She stormed off towards Nick's bathroom and instinctively avoided Nick's bidet, before virtually jumping onto his toilet seat. The strong hissing release caused her to shiver, as she relaxed fully and rested her head on in her arms, as her elbows pushed into her knees.

Okay, so, what the fuck... She sighed.

I got dressed with Mira and the girls. I went to the party. I spoke with that beefcake... Ulfrik!

Okay, what happened after?

He fucking shouted at me! For no reason... I mean I guess I could've done a better job of preparing security – but the fact that I had to dress-up screwed up the planning. But, I should've done a better job! The men should be able to function perfectly even without me!

Oh, my God!

I am so ashamed! I am so guilty! I messed up! I messed up so hard and then I acted like a lunatic!

What did I say? What did I do? Did I embarrass myself? I feel like I have! I must have! I was wild! I let loose!

Am I sure I didn't fuck Nick?

She recalled the night before, to the best of her ability.

Nah... nothing like that...

I gotta get these whores out of here before he notices...

Oh, my God! Is he okay?

Silvia finished peeing and got up. Nick always kept spare houseclothes in the bathroom. They were usually in a cupboard...

There we go! She found a loose pair of shorts and a cotton T-shirt which would've been tight on Nick, yet hung loosely around her thinner body. She checked her face in the mirror to see that she didn't look terribly hungover.

I have to check up on him. He went missing last night.

Maybe he's angry at me! Maybe he's not well! Maybe he's disappointed and he's given up on me! SHIT! I'm wearing Nick's clothes! He'll think I fucked him!

I have the dress here... but I can't wear the dress from last night! If anyone sees me, they'll think I'm a slob!

I gotta get to my room and -

'Hey!' Pravana greeted her as she exited the bathroom. She was wearing her own dress from the night before and was in the process of finding her second shoe.

Bitch, what do you want from me? 'Hey!' Silvia stopped in her tracks, thinking. She turned to look at Nick and Wella, still sleeping. She changed course and walked towards the foot of the bed and pulled the bed sheets from on top of them, revealing their naked bodies. Nick immediately began to shuffle. *Good! He always wakes up when I do that! Ever since he was a child!*

She turned back to a very uncomfortable Pravana. 'What time is it?' she asked.

Pravana seemed even more confused as she raised her shoulders, trying to be cute.

Silvia walked to a nearby cupboard where she knew Nick always kept gadgets and such like. She found a Shangri burner phone and checked the time. *11:45.*

FAAACK!!!

She turned back to Pravana, who stood there, half-dressed and visibly uncomfortable. 'Do you have somewhere to be today?' she asked.

'N-no! We have the day-off from the embassy today!' she replied.

Silvia nodded. 'You can freshen up here! Take a shower, if you want! When he wakes up,' she pointed at Nick. 'Have him arrange for a car to take you and *her* home!' she instructed, pointing at the still sleeping Wella.

She didn't wait for a reply. 'Don't walk outside the apartment until then!' Silvia waited for a moment, studying Pravana with the side of her eye, waiting for an acknowledgement.

Pravana nodded.

Silvia nodded too. 'You can grab some breakfast and coffee in the common room on the ground floor once you're done here and before you leave!' she permitted, as she reached Nick's bedroom door and walked downstairs to the living room he shared with Tech.

Oh, yeah! I can have Tech sort this out too!

She didn't find Tech in the living room. *Strange, he must still be asleep!*

She took a deep breath as she reached the door leading to the corridor across which lay her and Mira's apartment. She slowly opened the door and checked the door towards Pop's office. *Okay... it's closed.* She entered the corridor, still checking Pop's door, when she heard a noise from down the hall and she instantly spun around.

Veronica, one of her own men, was coming out of Radu and Cosmin's room, with Cosmin standing in the doorway, as they both turned to look at Silvia.

Who nodded, smiled and raised a thumbs-up with her right hand, as she stifled a chuckle.

They did the same.

Silvia shook her head. *I guess that's happening again...*

She then walked over to her own apartment, acting like nothing was wrong. She literally jumped inside.

'Good morning!' Tech's voice greeted her.

Silvia spun around. The remani was in her living room, sipping coffee from one of Mira's cappuccino cups. He was dressed in plain houseclothes, the type he would wear to bed, though he did not seem rested. He seemed very tired and a bit jittery. He sat bent forwards on one of their armchairs, as Basenji stood on the couch opposite him, also sipping from one of Mira's cups. He was wearing one of Mira's spare bathrobes, as if he had crashed in her room and she had made him feel at home.

Basenji smiled and nodded at her.

In the background, the door to their kitchen lay open and Mira emerged in the doorway, clutching a soup ladle and wearing a white bathrobe, the one she wore when she would languish around their apartment. 'Hey!' she greeted. 'How are you?'

Silvia stood motionless for a moment. 'Hey!'

'You want some coffee?' Mira asked, pointing with her ladle towards her espresso machine. 'I made fruit juice too!'

So, they've been here for a while. 'Yeah! Sure! Lemme just get changed!'

'Awkay, sure! I'm also making breakfast!'

'Oh! That's very nice!' Silvia said, as she made straight towards her room, though she remembered something halfway. She turned to Basenji, 'Is *he* awake?'

Basenji raised his shoulders.

'Huh...' *Better check anyway!*

'He's probably sleeping!' Mira pointed out. 'He's probably had a *long* night!'

WHAT THE FUCK!?!?!?

Silvia spun around to study her roommate. She had clearly showered, as she could tell her skin was hydrated and clean. She had washed her hair too, as it was also clean and of a natural flow, kept neatly in a loose ponytail that hung over the collar of her bathrobe, which trailed off to her slippers.

DID YOU FUCK HIM? 'Better check anyway!' *I... I can't... Fuck no! I will not thing of that!*

She made straight for her room and changed into a pair of proper pants, sneakers and one of her own white T-shirts, before putting on a comfortable Hajduk jacket she liked to wear off-duty. She didn't shower. That would be a problem, since Pop might smell the sex on her. She'd seen him do that with other people. So, she sprayed some perfume on herself.

As she returned to the living room, en route to Pop's room, there was a knock on the door, followed by a stumbling Nick, now also clothed.

'Mornin'... where are you going?'

'Checking up on *him*. He's M.I.A.!'

'He's sleeping.'

Silvia stopped in her tracks. 'Did you check up on him?'

'No... Silvia, you know how he's like! Long night... he's sleeping!' Nick posited rationally.

'Nine hours of sleep per night. When did you last see him?'

Nick struggled to understand what was going on with her, as well as with remembering the previous night's series of events. 'I dunno... like maybe half past one?' he ventured.

'It's almost 12. That's over ten hours!' she walked past him, shoving her shoulder into his to get him out of the way.

Nick sighed. 'Well, fuck it... I guess we're checking up on him...' he turned around to join her.

'You want coffee and some juice, Nick?' Mira called after them.

Shut up you little whore!

'Yes, please!' Nick answered for the both of them.

She used her spare key to enter his office, finding it empty, before walking up the stairs to the small living room he shared with Basenji.

Nick followed right behind her. 'Stop rushing! You'll startle him and he might give you bullet!'

He might as well. 'Da, da!'

They reached the door to his room and she moved slightly out of the way of any potential gunfire as she opened it. Carefully, she and Nick peered into the room.

Laur Pop had successfully taken his shoes off, but that was as far as he got. He lay on his side, collapsed upon one of his couches, in a somewhat foetal position, clutching himself and visibly sleeping deeply. Silvia could tell, since he had a tendency to softly whistle in his sleep, like a cartoon character. He was still wearing his shirt and dress pants from the night before, though he had managed to take of his shoes and fling his watch onto the floor before falling onto the couch.

The two walked in slowly and exchanged looks. Silvia was relieved and surprised. Nick was simply amused. She walked up to him and noticed that he was using a pillow to warm himself. The pillow must have been very warm, since upon it had nested Spideraven, who now studied them intently.

Silvia nodded towards Nick, who immediately understood her meaning. He walked slowly up to the bird, grasping it from the sides with his two arms and quietly lifted it as it studied him intently.

There was a blanket in a nearby cupboard and Silvia retrieved it, unfurled it and gently placed it over her General, who moaned softly, as a child would, before gripping it with his fists and rearranging himself in a more comfy position. Nick slowly lowered Spideraven into the same nesting spot they had found him in, on the pillow Pop had placed over his midriff.

Their General then resumed his sleep-whistling.

Nick pinched her arm softly, smiling, and gestured that they should go.

'Did you get rid of those two?' Silvia whispered as they passed through Pop's office.

'Yeah, Yeah! It's all good. They're downstairs with Dincă and Isprăvescu... *Hey!*'

'What?'

'You were mean to... what was her name?' He squinted and snapped his fingers. '*Pravana!*'

'Why? Did she complain?'

'No, but I could tell! It was undeserved, wasn't it?'

Silvia glanced towards him, annoyed by his line of questioning. There was a lot she could say. She chose to not answer.

'All good?' Mira asked, as she brought them their coffees and juices.

How could I think she fucked him? What's wrong with me?

'Sleeping like a literal baby...' Nick explained, as he took a sip of his coffee. '*Holy shit...*' he muttered, before downing the whole cup. He then set to work on the tall glass of juice.

Mira smirked to herself. 'I'll get the pitcher...'

'You're an angel, woman!' Nick's eyes narrowed and he studied the room for a moment before turning back to the figure of Mira walking away. He cleared his throat. 'Uhm, Mira?' he called after her.

'Yes?' she turned around to face him.

He took a deep breath, looked at Mira, changed his mind, then sipped his juice and the cleared his throat again. 'Are you fucking him?'

Holy fucking smokes and the Virgin Mary, Nick! Silvia's heart jumped out of her chest. *Did you see it? Did you feel it, Nick?*

Because if you felt it, it must have happened, because I have this feeling of sickness too! She turned to look at Mira, whose eyes flashed in between hers and Nick's.

A low growl filled the room, coming from Basenji's throat and directed at Nick's. *He does that sometimes.*

'No!' Mira replied.

'Yeah, sure, Mira...' Nick began, checking to make sure Basenji wouldn't bite him. 'Look, I mean, it's fine if you did! I totally get it! Just that, it would've been nice for you to tell us!'

'No, it wouldn't have been! But it doesn't matter, since I didn't fuck him!'

'You...' Nick tried again. 'Look, I mean, I suppose this might be a cultural thing, but–'

'It's not a cultural thing!'

Nick raised his hand. 'I would understand if it were! But, you have to understand, it's all very suspicious!'

Oh my fucking God, Nick! It is! I knew it! Silvia caught a glimpse of Tech shuffling in his seat, his hand over his snout, his eyes fixated on her. *Is... is he smiling?*

'I mean... you're out a lot!' Nick continued, facing the full might of Mira's death glare. 'I know you have your spirit quest going–'

'– Stop calling it that?'

Nick sighed. 'You know... This whole...' he began to gesture wildly. 'The going out all the time, Doing God knows were, taking out your tracking device from your car–'

'– *That* was you?'

Silvia looked at him stunned. *You did what? How long has this been going on? And where are they fucking? He doesn't go out ever! Particularly not by himself!*

Nick seemed genuinely worried now. 'Yeah, that was me! I was worried! You may be... well... *you*, but you're still a young woman in a strange foreign place! I... I wanted to know where you were going, in case something happened, in case you went missing, knock on wood! *Anyway*, you can do whatever you want! I understand! If it were up to me, Mira, you could be out fucking whoever you want, as long as you were safe! *But*...' Nick raised his shoulders. '... but, it's a sensitive situation! He's a *married* man!'

No, he isn't... wait... what the fuck are we talking about? She looked at Mira, who looked disgusted by the whole thing, then over to Basenji, who seemed to be calming down, then over to Tech, who chuckled.

'Nick!' Mira snapped. 'I'm not fucking the Crown Prince!'

OHHH!!!

Thank fuck...

Wait! Mira's fucking the Crown Prince?

'*I* believe you!' Nick touched his chest in a gesture of sincerity, before pausing and taking another deep breath. 'But, I mean, if you *did* fuck him when you were last here when he... you know... pretended to be some stable boy or some shit or whatever... you *should* tell us! It might be important!'

'Nick, this conversation is over!' Mira decreed.

'You know *he*'ll ask about it too?'

Mira stopped in her tracks. 'Do you think my answer to *him* will be different?'

'*Nu*... No! But, perhaps his interpretation might be!'

'Different from yours?' Mira spun around, her eyes stern.

'Yes!'

'I see! And what *is* your interpretation, Nick?'

Nick sighed and looked at those around him for reassurance again, before clearing his throat for the eleventh time. 'That you *might* have!'

Mira smirked. 'That would mean that *he* might interpret that I either *did* or *did not*! If it is that I *did not*, then that's great! And if it is that I *did*, then so be it! I'm not going to waste time making a moot point! You know what I will do, Nick?'

Nick shuffled uncomfortably.

'I'm going to give *you* details! Would you like that?'

'I mean... you don't have to get graphic...'

'Ha-ha,' Mira didn't even bother to feign mirth with her face or voice. 'He was a weak, blabbering idiot, or at least he pretended to be! He got us into all sorts of trouble when we would sneak around with him and I spent most of my time with him debating whether or not I should just throw him off a ledge the day before our eventual departure! *And now*, I find out that he wasn't just some blabbering idiot! Now I found that he was a two-faced liar!'

'So, please, Nick, explain to me not *how, where* and *when* I would've fucked him, but *why* I would ever fuck him?' The flames had been dancing in her eyes throughout the entire exchange.

'*Alright!*' Nick relented. 'Fine! I won't pursue this any further!' he leaned back in his seat, before raising a finger. 'And *fuck him!*' he added.

Tech chuckled. 'Nick!'

'No! No! I'm willing to entertain the thought that she might have fucked him back then! But, now, after what I saw last night? No! Fuck him! The situation he put her in? Masquerading cocksucker!'

'That's slander, Nick!' Tech pointed out.

'No! What people are going to say about *her* now, after what happened last night, is *slander*! I mean, I understand: gorgeous brown warrior princess from a galaxy far far away comes to visit you and your father with her faerie godmother! You dress-up as some street urchin and go off on wild escapades with her at night. You show her your city through the eyes of a commoner and you both find out you're just two kids along the way! Maybe you share a puppy kiss under the stars!'

Mira sighed, visibly distressed and clearly irritated.

Are you onto something there, Nick?

'But, keeping up the charade this whole time?' Nick shook his finger in the air. 'That's pervert shit!'

'Nick, he's one of our closest allies here!' Tech continued.

'Then one of our closest allies here is a pervert!' Nick turned to Mira. 'So, I say *fuck him*! You're better than him anyway! You're a beautiful, intelligent, talented and kind young woman and everything great about him came out of his daddy's cock! End of subject! Now go get me some orange juice!' he ordered.

Mira now let loose a half-smile. A genuine half-smile.

'...*please*!' he added.

She chuckled, shook her head and turned, resuming her trip to the kitchen.

Nick's eyes turned to Tech immediately. 'What's up with you?' he asked, leaning in towards him. 'You look like you owe money to devil! This girl just found out her trust was misplaced and you're out here talking about matters of state and censorship? What's wrong with you?'

Tech seemed caught unawares. 'Nothing!' he responded instantly, getting up from his couch and strolling around.

Nick's right. That sure doesn't look like 'nothing'!

Something was off about him. His movements. His inability to hold eye contact. He seemed oddly animated, constantly scratching the back of his head and rubbing his jaw and his snout. Most importantly, he tried to act like everything was all right.

'I just didn't catch that much sleep last night,' he added.

That seemed to explain things to Nick. 'Oh...' he mumbled, before staring at his juice. 'Sorry... We shut the doors and they're soundproof, so I –'

'No! Nah! Wasnt't that!' Tech waved the comment away.

Nick frowned. 'So... what *was* it?'

Silvia figured it out. She glanced towards Basenji for confirmation.

Basenji's understanding look confirmed it.

'I couldn't sleep,' Tech repeated. 'There was a lot of... of *energy* in the building!'

'I mean...' Nick began. 'I mean... Tech... if you wanted someone – one of the guests at the afterparty, I mean... I'm certain it could've been arranged!' he offered.

Tech's glare was more cautionary than any nudge Silvia was considering directing at her oblivious childhood friend. 'That's very charming, Nick, and very thoughtful, but, I assure you, I have no need for assistance in that regard!'

'So, you *did* catch some snatch last night?' Nick ventured.

'*Leck mich am Arsch! Ich habe keine Lust mehr auf diesen Mist!*' Tech snapped.

Silvia heard Mira drop her ladle on the floor.'كسأمك!', she cursed, bending over to pick it up, then using a washcloth to clean the golden stew that had splattered across their white marble floor.

Nick looked around confused. 'Could someone please explain to me what the fuck is going on?'

Tech sighed, as his eyes followed the movements of Mira in the kitchen. 'You know I quit drinking before we came here?' he asked Nick.

'I do!' Nick answered as his eyes widened. 'Did... did you–'

'No!' Tech waved away the notion. 'No, I didn't! I didn't even want to! I just...' the remani put his fists on his hips as his tail wagged in annoyance. 'It was a lot!' He scratched his head again.

Nick leaned back and scratched his head. 'Tech... I'm sorry! I thought you were ok with –'

'I *am* ok with everything! I'm ok with *you*, I was ok with the party and the gala itself and everything! It's just that...' Tech's bushy eyebrows frowned. He turned to look at Basenji, before turning once more towards Nick. '*Memories*... A lot of memories! Last night was the first night in a long while I went to an actual party, with people drinking and doing drugs and all of that... *sober*! I've... I've never done that before in a long while and it was a lot to handle! I... I was not on the same wavelength as everyone else and that... I *felt* it! I felt it and I knew I'd feel it! But I wasn't... It was... It was *awkward*, ok? I felt awkward and I... I felt *alone* and I felt like there was...!' Tech exhaled loudly as he scratched himself behind his ear. 'I realized that I'll always be *apart* from everyone... *alone*–'

'*Tech!*' Nick, Silvia and even Mira, from the kitchen, all insisted.

'No! No! But, that's the *thing*!' Tech replied, grabbing a tuft of hair behind his ear and closing his eyes in frustration. 'You know I've quit drinking before, right?' he asked those in attendance.

'You never mentioned it!' Nick replied, after consulting his memories.

'I... I did...' a jittery Tech found a seat on a nearby chair. 'I... quit in the sixties!' Tech seemed pained for a moment.

'I would drink when I was young... it was *Europe*! It was the turn of the century! People drank and I drank to fit in! I was *undercover*, after all! People drank and it was... it was a social thing! Who would say 'no' to a cool glass of Pfalz Riesling on a summer evening with a good friend?'

He rubbed his hands with his fingers. 'I... I had someone that I was shadowing! Someone I was supposed to keep an eye on...' he said, gazing off into the distance. 'And... and he died and I... I started drinking alone! Out of melancholy! I would break into his old house and I would pop open a bottle for me and him and I would drink it by myself in the dark and I would talk to him and... and for the slightest instant, I would feel like he was still there! And I would bring a phonograph and I'd play the music we used to listen to and I would get blasted! Sometimes I would catch a whiff of his scent, as if he was right next to me! And I would turn and it would be just... just empty space and then I would drink more because I felt *alone*!'

Tech now rubbed one of the little folds of flesh on his palm with particular intent. 'Then... there was the *war*! The... they called it the *Great War*, and later they called it the *First World War* and, let me tell you, at the time... I was young, but... I had seen wars before... but... this was different! The... the trenches... the *smell*! I started to drink so I wouldn't notice the smell! I... I drank myself to near-death after the war! I started doing meth, so that I would manage to focus on my mission...'

He balled his fist. 'I saw *them*! I *saw* those fucking *nekrophagen* rise up from their gutters in fucking Bavaria, in fucking Oberösterreich, and that fucking cuck from Karlsruhe! And I saw what was coming! I saw how they... they skittered at the feet of coffins of the great men that had come before them – greater in ways they could never even *comprehend* – and I saw them skitter like fucking fleas on white sheets, turning everything good to shit! And I *warned* them! I *warned* the Elders!' he said towards Basenji who, as ever, remained silent.

'They told me that the drinking had gone to my head! That I had *obliterated* the purpose of our mission in my mind! That *we* were not to *intervene*! Just... just *watch* and *never* intervene! And I did just that and... and I drank myself into the gutter... I told them to fetch me when the *nekrophagen* dropped the first atomic bomb and they told me I was stupid and then I spent the forties in Wales, blasted out of my mind, away from it all!'

Tech now tried to straighten the hairs on the back of his head. 'When the Americans ended up dropping the bomb first, things changed! They... the Elders sent for me! They locked me in a room on the Black Knight and tried to sober me up, but it didn't really work! I *tried*! I really tried, but... it was the fifties! They sent me to the US and there... no one was a teetotaller in the fifties! You'd be lucky if you found someone who hadn't had three drinks by noon! I...' Tech finally smiled. 'I quit drinking in 1967. It was the *Summer of Love* and I was *in the cuff* and I dropped so much acid in San Francisco that I woke up in the Redwoods one day, naked and... and *cured*... I thought...'

'It lasted for a good while... almost thirty years... I would even drink socially from time to time! I... then the wall came down in '89 and... I... I went back to Berlin and... and it happened all over again! And now there was fucking ecstasy and cocaine and heroin and... and the acid and the mescaline didn't work anymore and I just... I *wasted* so much time! I...'

Tech closed his eyes in pain, before letting loose a smirk 'I'd visit *his* grave! I'd break in with his Riesling and I'd get blasted and I would do lines of coke and I'd cry and I'd tell him! I'd tell him everything! I told him how hopeless and how alone I felt and how I failed him and how I was a bad person and how I could've done so much, but I was too fucking blasted all the time! The decades went by in a blur and, next thing you know, the *End Times* were upon us! I...'

Tech looked up at the two orphans sitting at the table before him, whose parents had died in the End Times, then to his kinsman, alongside he had fought so bitterly in those days. He chuckled in embarrassment. 'I don't even remember most of it! I was so... I only sobered up after *Revelation*, simply because the world had finally run out of booze! And after that... in all the decades since... I didn't even try! For five decades straight... it was all a blur... *until...*'

He glanced up and Silvia turned to see that he was looking at Mira, who stood holding a large pot with her mittens, her eyes blank and her face unmoving. In her mind, Silvia heard the wails of Ratden.

Tech smiled. 'You need some help, love?'

Mira didn't answer immediately. 'Yes! There's a round cutting board in that drawer over there! Put it under *this* in the middle of the table!' she said, walking towards the dinner table, as Silvia and Nick got up.

'I'll get some bowls and some–' Silvia began.

'They're on the counter, ready!' she immediately responded. 'There's also fresh sourdough in the oven–'

'I'll get it!' Nick announced and Basenji also got up to help.

'Milady!' Lorgar jumped up from out of nowhere onto to dining table. 'What's on the menu today?'

'Romanian tripe stew!'

'*What?*' Nick and Silvia both giggled.

'Milady? What is 'tripe'?'

Lorgar narrowed his eyes. 'The inner lining of a cow's stomach!' she explained.

Lorgar seemed horrified. '*Milady!*' Lorgar recoiled. 'Milady, such a thing is surely *haram*!'

'Actually, it's not!' she said, opening the lid and inhaling the vapours coming from within. She turned to Nick and Basenji, who were just then entering the kitchen. 'There's also pickled peppers, sour cream, white wine vinegar and peppercorns! I also made some *toum* if you want extra garlic!'

'Very traditional, Mira!' Nick exclaimed.

'It's a *very traditional* hangover cure!' Mira proceeded to fill up five large bowls of stew, as well as a smaller portion for Lorgar, who sniffed its contents with great suspicion.

'Tech...' Nick began, eyeing the stew in his bowl.

Silvia was surprised when he didn't immediately get to work devouring it. *Smells amazing!* She looked to see Nick choose his words carefully. *If you're gonna say it, say it! It's itching me to say it too! I love him too! Make him feel better, Nick! You have that talent!*

'... you know you're not *alone*, right?' Nick continued, sincerity obvious on his kind face. 'You... you've been with us for... what? Fifty years? Since before that, even! Hell, since before me and

Silvia! You... you're my *brother*! I mean...' Nick placed his spoon in the bowl, before withdrawing it. 'I'm sorry we didn't think of ways to make things like last night easier for you!'

Tech scoffed. 'No! No! Society shouldn't change because one member cannot handle his own demons!'

'Yeah, but... you *are* a member! And it's not right for us to... to *forget* about you! You shouldn't feel alone!'

'No one should feel alone!' Mira agreed, drawing Silvia's attention. 'You know *you* are family, Tech?' she told the remani, studying her pot of stew.

'In this *imagined community* of ours?' Tech quipped, as he sat down and slowly picked up his spoon.

'Tech,' Nick continued. 'What she says is true! We... we are *ourselves* around you and that's something you only do with your family – your *real* family; the ones you feel at *home* with! But, we don't want to be *bad* family! We want to be... *supportive*, so that you can be yourself around us too! Not spaz out like...'

Nick's pause was too long and Silvia realised that he was going to say something like 'spaz out like some crackhead' or something along those lines.

'Like an addict?' Tech finished.

'NO! I mean 'yes'! But not like... *fuck it*!' Nick set to work on the stew. 'Fucking delicious, Mira!'

'You stopped drinking because you weren't happy living like that!' Silvia finally spoke, drawing everyone's attention. 'You're happier now and that makes us happy! What Nick means is that we don't want you to *hide*, at least not from us! There's no need! I know old habits die hard... but there's no need to hide anymore! No one...' Silvia paused, the truth of what she wanted to say was slamming into her and she had to focus through the hangover. '... should feel like they need to hide themselves, because, if they don't, the people who care for them wouldn't anymore!'

Nick, Mira and even Basenji gave her funny looks. Nick smirked, Mira raised an eyebrow and Basenji smiled and nodded.

Tech just stared at his stew and at the spoon in his hand and he seemed to pause. The moment was interrupted by the loud sounds of Lorgar's slurping, as he drowned his face in his little bowl of stew. After almost ten seconds, he lifted his wet nose and gasped for air.

'Milady! Fine work, Milady! Fine work!' he announced, before once more dunking his head in the bowl and slurping messily.

Tech seemed to think about something for a moment, before shaking his head and picking up his spoon. The remani looked at the spoon, then at his bowl, then at those around him, then at Lorgar, then at the spoon, then back at his family, then back at the spoon, then back at the spoon. He finally closed his eyes, sighed and looked up at those around him, before letting go of his spoon.

'You know what? *Fuck this!*'

He picked up the bowl in his hand, got up and walked towards the nearest coffee table, laying down the bowl next to where he sat down on the couch adjacent to it.

Silvia saw Basenji take note and understanding seemed to dawn on him. He put down his own spoon and readjusted himself in his chair, lifting himself and placing his calves on the seat and sitting vertically in a bowed position, looming over his own bowl, like some Japanese lady from one of Nick's animes.

She would've studied him further, were it not for Tech's audible sigh, which he let loose before leaning over his bowl and lowering his snout in its centre.

And then Tech ate his stew like a dog would eat kibbling from a dog bowl, slurping loudly and getting the golden liquid all over his nose and snout, as he would occasionally stop to chew some of the larger pieces of tripe.

Basenji did the same.

The three humans exchange looks. Mira had clearly seen this before, since she just smiled happily. Nick smiled stupidly to himself, clearly stifling a chuckle. Silvia was just amazed.

Lorgar was simply horrified.

They spent the next couple of hours chilling. Silvia and Nick took turns showering and, soon enough, they were all sitting around their coffee table, laughing, discussing memories of the night before and, most importantly, snacking, since Mira was very creative gastronomically on that particular day, with lemon meringue cupcakes, vanilla cheesecakes, pecan pie and Eton mess – *now that! That's fucking spectacularly good – sliding from the kitchen at regular intervals.* Mira announced around three hours in that it was time for 'second' breakfast, and she began to roll-out shakshuka, Yorkshire pudding, veal parm sandwiches and even fried eggs on toasted bread with sides of crispy bacon.

It was all very warm and fuzzy, up until the anathema of such a vibe arrived at the door.

'Oh! Mornin', boss!'

'Mornin', morning!' Pop rubbed one of his eyes, as the other surveyed those within. 'Can I come in?' he asked no one in particular.

'Yes, of course!' Silvia replied instantly to one of Laur Pop's many peculiar quirks.

Pop stumbled in and Spideraven jumped in after him, drawing a hiss from Lorgar. Silvia realized that he had only managed to change into a robe, under which he was likely wearing one of his T-shirts and likely a pair of shorts, without the underwear. *Holy shit! This is actually important! He wants to tell us something! A decision!*

Oh, no! Is it me? Is it something I've done?

But, what have I done, actually? I forgot...

'Is...' Pop struggled for a moment. He pointed at the coffee table. 'Is that shakshuka?' he asked Mira.

'Yeah, you want?' she replied instantly.

Why is he asking her, not me? Have I done something? Oh, wait, he knows she cooked, not me! How does he know that? Oh, he knows I'm useless in the kitchen...

'Yes, please...' He began to stumble towards an empty armchair at the head of the table. 'Mira, could I perhaps bother you for some coffee?'

'Cappuccino?'

Of course! His favourite. Drinks at all hours of the day. I can make it to! I learned how to make it for him...

'Yes, please!' Pop replied politely as he collapsed on his seat and pulled a bowl of poached eggs, tomato sauce and cilantro towards himself, before picking out a freshly baked loaf of pita bread.

'Coming right up!' Mira got up from her place on the couch next to Basenji and left for the kitchen.

Pop looked up. 'Please ignore me! Go on with whatever... you know... what you were talking about!'

'No impromptu morning meeting?' Nick jabbed, as Spideraven jumped on a small table in between Pop and Silvia.

Pop picked up a piece of bacon and passed it to his pet. 'Is there something I need to know?'

'Nah, just debrief!'

'Hmmm,' he grunted. 'Was the Gala in today's press?'

'It's all that's in the press!'

Pop stopped to chew for a moment. 'Well, what do they say?'

'Well...' Nick looked at Silvia.

He hasn't read the news. He listened to us reading and commenting on the news. So it was she who answered, 'Everyone's impressed that the Crown Prince attended! Jenner wrote an article about how he was, quote, *assaulted*; it's gained some traction, but nothing extraordinary or unexpected. His article was the only one trending that mentioned the Hogwarts; all the other news outlets completely ignored it, but a few did mention the Paragon Shipping disappearances! Big White's attendance also did not go unnoticed and there are already theories going around speculating on the nature of our relationship with him... and Mira's cooking received universal praise!'

'Well deserved,' Pop mumbled. 'So, nothing unexpected?'

'No,' she replied, just as Mira walked in with his coffee. 'All in all, a resounding success!'

'They're calling it 'the event of the year'!' Tech pointed out, taking a sip of apple juice.

Pop nodded and leaned forward to pick up the jug of apple juice from the middle of the table and poured himself a glass. 'Good! Good!' he said and there was moment of silence in the conversation. 'Did you tell them?' he asked Mira.

Mira's face was blank.

Silvia, obviously, noticed. 'Tell them what?' *Did... did you fuck him?*

While chewing his breakfast, their General answered. 'Last night, during demon time, four rats delivered to us a Dawnbreak gift!' Pop paused as he watched them take the news in. '*Otto Benga.*'

'What?' Nick asked, amazed, rubbing his head.

The blood in Silvia's veins had turned ice cold. 'Is he here?'

'He's in an icebox downstairs. Dead.'

'The ratmen delivered a corpse?' Silvia asked, as she turned back to Mira, whose face had turned to a frown. She met her gaze and shook her head slightly.

'Oh, no! They brought him in alive. I just got to work on him last night. He gave up his password. I scanned him. Then I just bled him out.' Pop's eyes narrowed as he realized something. 'Get rid of the body, by the way!'

'You broke him last night? During the party?!?!?!' Nick asked surprised.

'Are you certain the scan is readable?' Silvia asked coldly.

'Yes. I checked it. I even did some research!' He reached into his pocket and pulled out his phone presenting them with a few snapshots he had made of Benga's memories. 'There are six left. The dockworkers, essentially. Their names are Joel Rudabaugh, James Ouefoulliard, Benjamin Browder, Louis Wilsen, David Pickett and Cormac Bonney. Everyone else that trafficked the Stolen to the Urheimat is dead!'

'We have reached the end of the string!' Pop's eyes wandered towards the future for a moment. 'At least, for now.'

'Did he know their location?' Silvia asked.

'Fractures of it. They didn't share their location with him. Though he seemed certain they were all together and that they were all still in Shangri. Our job now is to find them and to finally end this!' Pop's eyes wandered '... shouldn't be too hard...'

'Were there clues, at least?' Nick asked.

'Some.' Pop's eyes closed and as he raised his hand to rub them. Silvia realized that he was clearly still hungover. 'He was a paedophile!'

The room went cold, as they all thought what Tech said aloud, 'We always knew that many would certainly be...'

'You are certain of this?' Silvia asked and she saw Pop prickle.

'I *checked*,' he said, annoyed and looking her right in the eye. 'What's with this fucking energy, Silvia?' he turned in his seat to face her.

Oh, no! Oh, no! Her mind raced back into her professional persona. 'It was erratic, what you did! Interrogating a key asset alone, while the eyes of the world were still on us... *while under the influence*!' she deflected.

Now Pop's eyes narrowed and he did something he sometimes did when he felt uncomfortable. He got up and started pacing. Now he was suddenly very awake and aware.

That shakshuka's a real pick-me-up...

'Though I have always admired your diligence and I don't encourage any of you to drink on the job, I can't say that I don't fucking care what your assessment was (*or is*) of my actions last night, nor in any other night! Nor do I care that much of whatever impressions you have of those I make during the day, for that matter, *Silvia*!'

'I never said that it was wrong,' she replied, changing her tune. 'Quite frankly, I'm glad you didn't waste time the moment you found out. I've always admired that about you, *sir*! No wasted motion.' *Let's keep you angry about that and that alone... that way, you don't deviate into other topics...*

'You're happy he was a child molester? Him being a child molester means that children were molested.'

You fucking cunt!

'Could we get back to the leads? Why is it important that he was a paedophile? To the point of catching the others?' Nick asked.

'It's important because we can now spread that information and that'll lead to them becoming even more isolated than they were!' he said, as once more took his seat. 'Henceforth, it's just a matter of time until we, or the ursai, or the Constabulary or, even our new murine allies, get to them!' Pop sighed. 'Which frees up our time to pursue other endeavours...'

What? What other endeavours?

He mused for a while. Quietly. He did that from time to time. *Usually when he's trying to make a decision –*

'We're going to wind-up our partnership with the ursai!'

'Wind-up?' Nick asked. Silvia heard a twinkle in his voice.

'Yeah! As much as possible. Everything we discussed, plus I want each of *you* to get to work drafting as many business plans as possible. Whatever pops through your heads that works. We'll use the liquidity we currently have to finance operations.' He remembered something. 'There's going to be a weekly meeting, each Wednesday going forward, with the ursai *and* the murine. A meeting of minds, as it were. *Here... In my office!*' Laur frowned. 'I also want that catman... *Crouton*!'

'*Kroton*,' Nick corrected, though his brow had become furrowed.

Laur raised a finger in approval. 'That's the one!'

'*The murine?*' Silvia asked incredulously.

Pop was initially irritated, but then he realized that the question was pertinent. 'Yes! One of the rats that brought Otto Benga in last night was the head honcho!' he said, digging once more into his shakshuka. 'I invited him to attend.'

Tech finally spoke. 'You asked him to attend a top secret meeting (in which things of the utmost sensitivity will be discussed) after a meeting him *once?*'

'Yeah!' Pop chewed his food after pondering things for a moment. He chuckled. 'It's even worse, Tech! He didn't even formally tell me that he was the *King of Ratdom*!' His eyes squinted. 'Or *Rat of the Kingdom*! I had to figure it out myself!'

Tech snorted. 'Now you really are surrounding erratic!'

'I know. But, I am sure of it! It's *him*! I'm also sure that he's trustworthy! I'm also sure that he's not sure if *we* are trustworthy! So be nice to *him* and be nice to Mr. Cri and her employees!' He addressed this last bit to Silvia, before his eyes wandered into his plans for a moment. 'I'm going to go visit a bear!' he concluded.

'Yeah?' Nick asked.

'Yeah... I promised I'd see his new place last night...'

'Huh, fair enough! I'll get some of the guys ready–'

'– I'm going alone! About time I got some fresh air by myself!' he announced, putting down the fork in his hand and tapping the coffee table. He pointed towards his now empty plate. 'That was delicious!' he told Mira. 'I'm gonna take a nap before I go see him!'

He got up once more, then paused, before turning around to glare at Mira, clearly having just remembered something. He raised a finger at her. 'Did you–'

Nick cut him off. 'She didn't fuck him!'

Pop was taken unawares. He didn't even have time to-

'We've had the conversation already, boss! Story checks out! The Crown Prince is a pervert, but Mira's a smart woman who knows her worth!'

Pop blinked. '*Pervert?*' he asked Mira, who took a deep breath.

Nick answered for her. '*Metaphorically* speaking! *Devious*! He dressed up like Oliver Twist and they went on D&D adventures together with Daw. But they didn't do anything!'

'Oh,' Pop lowered his hand, frowned and turned to look at Silvia, asking for her input.

She nodded slowly.

He then turned towards Mira, who tilted her head slightly towards Nick.' Aha... Well, fine! You have my permission to take the rest of the day off!' he instructed, before making straight for his bedroom, with Spideraven trotting behind him.

'You granted us that permission three days ago!' Nick called after him. 'We already had it!'

'Was it you?' Silvia asked Mira, after Pop was out of earshot.

'I *am* the one in charge of murine affairs, ain't I?'

'Mira, at this rate, you should be the one in charge of all affairs...' Nick muttered. 'Well...? Give us the rundown!'

'Mr. Cri was indeed connected to a certain underground murine network, one which not even the Constabulary knows about! They observed us and they observed *me* for a while, until one of them approached me and told me they knew who we were looking for and where he was! He asked for an audience with Laur Pop as payment and I facilitated it last night, on short notice.'

'Heh!' Nick muttered, before turning to Silvia. '*Lisan al-Ghaib*!' he whispered loudly.

Nick, Tech and Basenji hung around for some time after that, until Tech announced that he was finally going to sleep. Nick also announced that he believed that a nap would be in order. Basenji eventually gestured that he wanted to take a shower. Silvia told them all to not bother and help with the clean-up, as she and Mira would handle it.

'By the way,' Mira suddenly spoke. 'I saw the guy from across the street yesterday at the party! Ulfrik?'

'Ulfrik!' Lorgar jumped on the kitchen counter. 'He is the guardian of Abiola, is he not?'

'Yes, Lorgar, that Ulfrik!' she said, picking up the cat and tossing him into the living room.

'*Miladyyy!*' he yelled, just as Mira closed the door behind him.

'I need your help with something!' she whispered to Silvia.

'With what?' she replied curiously.

'Well...' Mira pursed her lips and stared blankly. 'This is awkward...'

'*What* is awkward?' Silvia smiled.

'Well, I've been thinking! You see...' Mira exhaled. 'You know what? *Fuck it*! I want our cats to fuck!'

'*What*?'

'Lorgar hasn't gotten laid in a long while and, ever since the change, he's *horny* (pun intended) all the time and he's been spraying cat piss all over my room!'

'He has? I didn't smell anything!'

'I spend a lot of time cleaning the stains and, believe me, they're fucking everywhere and I can't sleep if I smell cat piss, particularly *his*!'

'And you want him to get laid so that he can get it out of his system? Can't you just give him some medication?'

'I don't like what it does to his mood *and I am not neutering him!*' she informed her sternly, before her eyes wandered for a moment. '... and I'm not removing the horns, since they're doing wonders for his self-esteem!'

'I never said you should do any of that!'

'Good! So, I was thinking that, maybe, me and you could go talk to Ulfrik and ask him if he's okay with it?'

'*What*?' Silvia chuckled. '*Sure*! Let's bake a cake and bring it to him for his troubles!'

'Silvia, I'm being serious!'

'Why do we even have to go there? Why not just text him? We have his number, you know? That's how we sent him the invite!'

'Well, because it's... it's...'

Now, there's a rare sight! Mira al-Sayid, struggling to find the right words.

'It seems like something too sensitive to handle over text!'

'Why? Is it illegal?'

'*No*! I mean... it's too *personal*, okay? I feel weird about sending some text to some guy: 'Hey, I was wondering if you could let my cat fuck your cat'? I'd rather just go there and ask him politely, given the gravity of the situation!'

'*Gravity?*' Now Silvia laughed outright. *You and your problems!* 'Mira, I spoke to him yesterday at the party!'

'You did?' Mira's eyes widened.

'Yeah, we spoke at one point and, I think you'll be pleased to know that the feeling is mutual!'

Mira's pupils now also dilated. 'Abiola wants to fuck him too?'

'Jesus, Mira! He said that Abiola also really liked Lorgar and that they should spend some time together!'

Mira seemed overjoyed. 'Oh, thank God!' Her eyes narrowed. 'I should bake a cake, you're right! A Genoise sponge-cake! I have strawberries!'

She turned around and Silvia giggled in surprised amazement at her sudden change in mood.

'Can you take him tonight?' Mira asked, fishing out a bag of flour from her pantry.

What? 'Why do *I* have to take him?'

'Because you have the day-off today!'

'*You also* have the day-off today!'

'Yes, I do, but he didn't invite *me* over!'

'He didn't invite *me* either! He didn't even invite Lorgar! He just said they should spend time together!'

'Are you saying we should bring them here?'

'No, I did not... '*them*'? Mira, *he* cannot come here! If you want, I can talk to him about brining Abiola here!'

'Oh, but Silvia, that's fucked-up! You can't just have him give you the cat so you can bring her here where she doesn't know the place! Especially not without her guardian!'

'Wouldn't it be the same if I took Lorgar there without you?'

'That's different!'

'Why is it different?'

'Because he's a boy!'

'Isn't he in his thirties old?'

'Oh, come on Silvia! You know what I mean! Plus, cats fuck in, like, five minutes if they like each other! You'll be in and out in the blink of an eye!'

'Huh...' Silvia exhaled. 'Fine! I'll text him and take him there tomorrow morning–'

'Can't you take him today when Laur's away?'

'*Laur*'? *Pretty intimate. But, she's right. I could have taken him when Laur was asleep in the morning, but doing it while he's away is even better!*

'Please, Silvia! I want to go back to going to bed without having to hunt cat piss for thirty minutes every night!'

'Fine!'

Mira finished baking just as night fell and Laur Pop walked out of his office in civilian clothes. Black Air Force Ones, a black leather jacket with two hidden pistols. Dark jeans with a black belt and a loose hoodie.

'I'm going! Are the keys to the *hellcat* downstairs?' he asked Silvia.

'In the control room, yes!' She noticed he was holding a black bag under his arm. A smell was rising up from it. *Coffee... and... vinegar?*

'Great! I'll be back in three hours!' he instructed before leaving.

Three hours! Plenty of time to get this thing sorted with Lorgar!

'This is the cake!' Mira flung a large container into her arms. 'This is his leash!' She placed the leash in her hand, pulling Lorgar, now firmly wrapped up in a vest attached to the leash, and causing him to stumble and bash his horns into the floor. 'Give me a text when you get there! If anything happens, I'll come immediately!'

'Yes, *sir*!' Silvia quipped.

'Thank you!' Mira hugged her. 'I owe you one!'

Silvia had already arranged for Veronica to keep an eye on Wiltshire Boulevard, particularly number 619. As she walked out the back door of the Embassy and walked in circles for a while, making sure she wasn't followed by anyone other than those Hajduks she had informed of her mission.

'Hello, there!' Ulfrik greeted, as he opened the door, his hair immaculately combed.

'Hello!'

'Where is she?' Lorgar immediately asked.

'*Lorgar!*'

'I can't take it anymore!' Lorgar jumped out of her arms, pulling the entire leash with him.

'She's upstairs!' Ulfrik called after him, as the end of the leash slid across the floor. 'Do you want to come in? I made tea!'

Silvia smiled politely, yet awkwardly. 'Yes, that would be nice!'

'I was hoping for you to call, yet I'm surprised how little time it took!' He gestured towards the end of the hall, where his living room lay.

'Yes, well, apparently Lorgar–'

Hellish noises erupted from upstairs. It sounded like two babies ramming forks into each other's eyes.

'Is... is that normal?' she asked, reaching for her hidden pistol.

'I think so!' he wasn't sure either.

'Mira said it might get loud, but...'

There was a moment of silence between them amidst the loud cacophony of feline fornication. Silvia turned towards her host and studied him for a moment.

I see reassurance, friendliness, excitement, a little bit of very well restrained arousal... all of which are things one can easily fake but... I also see...

Embarrassment.

... and embarrassment is very hard to fake...

'Uh, tea?' he gestured towards his living room.

She entered first at his bequest.

'I'm, uh, going to shut the door!' he said awkwardly and Silvia smiled in agreement.

The door was soundproof, so the room instantly turned silent. Silvia noted that he had melodic lounge music playing harmoniously in the background of his minimalist decor. A long white leather couch, two white leather armchairs, a giant fluffy white rug, a golden mirror above a stylish marble fireplace, as well as a small arrangement of white furniture arranged perfectly atop a white oak floor, as well as only a few pieces of tech.

'So, yeah! Mira backed you a cake!' Silvia presented the box.

'She did *what*?' Ulfrik giggled as he accepted the gift.

'For your troubles!' she explained.

'Oh, but there's no trouble at all!' he lightly shook the box. '*This* is wholly unnecessary!'

'Well, consider it a neighbourly gift then!'

'I will!' He paused, looking at the box. 'Do you want to have some with me?'

'*No!*' she replied immediately *and too aggressively*. 'I already ate!'

'Oh, well! So did I!' He walked over to a nearby table and placed the package neatly in the middle, before gesturing towards a large counter where tea was clearly cooling off in a kettle. 'So, congratulations on last night's event! You're quite the talk of the town!'

Silvia smiled 'Is that what's important? That we're the talk of the town?' she asked jokingly.

'Well, what else would be the purpose of a 'gala' event? If your goal would have been to be discrete, I assure you that having the Crown Prince openly venture forth from the Imperial Palace at your invitation was not the best course of action!' he explained, sipping the tea to check that it was just right.

'I'm not going to argue with you about that! So, what *is* the talk the town?'

'That you are wondrous hosts, that your food is amazing and that your company is delightful!'

'Is that your impression also?'

'I can confirm all of the above, yes, and I may also add that your women are also gorgeous!' He seemed pleased with himself for a moment, before his face dropped slightly. '*You* were gorgeous!'

She raised an eyebrow.

'You *are* gorgeous now, also!' He used his teacup to point, before reconsidering his statements. '*All* of you Terran women are gorgeous, but *you* stand out!' He started pointing towards the upstairs. '*And* that your cats are great lovers!'

Silvia groaned. *I can't take this shit anymore and it's literally only been a minute.* 'What kind of show is this? she asked playfully.

'Pardon?'

She gestured towards him. '*This*! This... Shangri courtship ritual or whatever it is! This goofy...' she readied her throat to mock his voice. '*Oh, look at me! I'm so fucking English and I have this awkward charm about me and bla-bla-bla!*'

'*English?*'

'Yeah, *English*, like...' she gestured towards his teacup and his sweater and his white collar and his apparent preference for an immaculate art deco interior design. '... all of this...'

Oh, shit! Wait! Silvia realized she was being pedantic. 'We have these people on Terra, who are just like *you*!' she explained.

'I've heard of *English* people, Silvia!'

'Oh, have you?' *Did they try to colonise this place too at one time?*

'Yes! Me and the lads were watching James Bond movies just the other night!'

She groaned again. *You and the 'lads?* 'Then you see my point?'

'I suppose... but it's not an act! I *am* awkwardly charming!'

'Hmmm!' Silvia stretched her lips in fake agreement. 'Is this how this goes? With girls, I mean? You bring them over, you act like you'd fumble a tit if you ever saw one, then they... *what? Fuck you? Right then and there?*'

Ulfrik almost choked whilst sipping his tea when he heard the tit-fumbling comment. 'Well, normally we would go to the bedroom, though I suppose that's not an option on this occasion... I also suppose spontaneity is something to be appreciated! No, *uhm*...'

She pointed a finger right at the mouth from which that '*uhm*' was launching itself.

'*All right*! Fine! I'll stop that!' Now he just stood there silently thinking. 'What I am trying to say – *genuinely* trying to say – is that I know certain women do indeed enjoy the company of men who are 'awkwardly charming'! *However*, I know that *all* women appreciate genuineness in a man, regardless of context, and I act upon the later knowledge in regard to you, Silvia!' He picked up her teacup and offered it to her.

She didn't reach for it immediately, but she did in the end, since she wanted to hear him out.

'I could pretend to be someone I thought you might like, but that would be disingenuous and I wouldn't like that! And certainly neither would you! So, with the risk of sounding like a blundering idiot, I'm just trying to be myself!'

'And is that who you are? A blundering idiot?'

'I have that in common with most men, yes!'

She chuckled. 'You don't sound like a blundering idiot now!' She sipped the tea. It was great.

'I have my coherent moments. Yet, with you, I find them to show themselves sparingly! I find you very engaging, Silvia, to the point where I often struggle to think properly when you're sitting there, in front of me!'

Predictably charming. I'm not sure if I like how quickly he changed his whole demeanour, though I think he's being honest now and I appreciate it!

He frowned. 'And I didn't bring *you* over! You came by yourself!'

She pointed upstairs. 'I came for the cats to hook-up!'

'Yes... but *you* didn't *have* too! You could've sent someone else! You could've had Mira bring her *own* cat to this... *hook-up* (?)'

Oh! Ohhh! Oh, shit!

He's fucking right! She would've commented a little, like she did, but I could've pushed and I... I didn't...

'In truth, I didn't come prepared for coherency. I was actually hoping I'd get to listen more than speak.'

'You wanted to interrogate me?' she asked quickly, somewhat relived that he was advancing the conversation on his own accord, lest her own moment of self-discovery be revealed.

'In a sense.' He paused for a moment. 'You're... *different*, even compared to your own countrymen! You... *stand out!*'

'Because everyone looks lost without me?'

Ulfrik smiled at the reference to their conversation from the night before. '*Yes!*'

'Hmmm... Listen here, Ulfrik of Langley-Creekside!' she grabbed his collar, right underneath his chin.

'There we go!'

'Nuh-uh!' she raised a finger to his neck. 'A day will come when in, service to my people, I will die. When that happens, someone else will take my place and one of those lost faces you saw yesterday will be the one everyone else looks towards. *You... you* are a sweet summer child with no understanding of what true horror is! I can tell! It's why you see something *different* as something that might be *good*! You seem so... so *raw* to me! Untouched by any fire! No piece of you ever slashed away... A life might lie before you that may change you, *harden* you!'

Silvia studied him for a moment. 'Though I do not think it would *break* you!' She did see something in him nonetheless, this rumbling of energy within him, one she couldn't say she really understood. 'If you survive such a change, you might be able to see me for what I really am! But, no such change has come to you or your world and, hopefully, it never will! So, don't try to understand me! It's not something useful to you!'

His lips moved softly. *'I don't want you to be useful!'*

Silvia *felt* something.

Then the moment was broken.

There was scratching at the door. An aggressive rustling, rising over the background music. They both looked at each other in confusion, until Silvia let go of Ulfrik's collar, allowing him to walk over to the door and open it!

Lorgar, who had been leaning on the door as he scratched, fell face first into the living room. 'Lady Silvia! Lady Silvia, we must go!'

'What happened?' she asked, a smile on her lips and in her throat.

'Lady Silvia,' Lorgar's ear twitched as he checked for any noise. 'I SAID WE MUST GO!' He turned around and darted towards the entrance, reaching the door and jumping up towards the round doorknob and failing to grab hold of it.

Silvia turned to Ulfrik, taking in his own confusion. 'Was that it?'

'Apparently?!'

'Lady Silvia, PLEASE! WE'VE GOT TO GET OUT OF HERE? NOW!'

Silvia and Ulfrik shared another glance. 'I... I guess we're going!' she said, before walking up the hall towards Lorgar. *He doesn't seem to be hurt. Is there danger?* 'Lorgar? What's gotten into you?'

'The vapours have left and now I must run! NOW I MUST RUN AND FLEE AND BE FREE!!!' he shouted, stopping only to check the stairs to make sure no one was following him, hindering his escape.

'I'll open the door!' Ulfrik offered. 'I guess that's it for today!' he said to Silvia.

'THAT'S IT FOREVER, SIR ULFRIK! I AM NEVER COMING BACK HERE EVER AGAIN!'

Ulfrik seemed genuinely worried about the comment, as he began opening the door.

Lorgar picked up his own leash with his teeth and jumped into Silvia's arms, who only just managed to ready her arms for him to cuddle in. He instantly burrowed his head into her elbow, as if not seeing his pursuer would somehow hide him. Silvia felt how his scent had changed. *That must be Abiola!*

Ulfrik looked up towards the top of the stairs. 'I should probably check-up on Abiola!'

'Yes, I guess you should!'

'It was lovely having you over here!'

'It was! Perhaps Lorgar will change his mind later.'

'I WON"T!'

'Well, nevertheless, thank you for having us, Ulfrik!'

'Thank you for coming!' he smiled charmingly.

Silvia smiled too. 'Well, see you later, alligator!' she said to him before turning around as interestingly as she could. The moment she was with her back fully turned, she allowed herself to cringe at herself. *See you later, alligator? Silvia, what the fuck?*

Once she had turned a corner, she immediately grabbed Lorgar by the scruff of his neck and pulled him in for a private conversation. 'What the fuck did you do!?'

'A gentleman never tells!' Lorgar seemed insulted by the very notion of threatening the dignity of his mate. 'But, what I *can* say is that I fucked that white pussy in way in which she's never seen before nor will she again!!!'

Silvia shoved his head back into her elbow so fast, his horns almost pierced her jacket.

'How did it go?' Mira asked, as she nervously got up from her couch.

Upon hearing his master's voice, Lorgar darted from Silvia's arms onto the floor. 'I AM THE BROTHER OF THE NIGHT AND THE LOVER OF THE DAY!!!' before he darted towards Mira's bedroom to take a nap in some hidden dark place he really enjoyed.

'Does that answer your question?'

'I. Guess. It. Does?'

Pop arrived earlier than he had announced, after having only been away for less than two hours. Nick knocked on their door a couple of times, spurring Silvia to open it, finding the door to Laur's office wide open.

'So, come and tell us, boss, how's the bear's new crib?'

'Oh, it's nice. Very... very American. The kind of place you would've seen in Florida before the flooding...' he explained, as Silvia walked into the room. 'It was nice... a bit kitsch to be honest with you!' he said, before picking up a pen and a paper, as he began to write something down. Seeing this, Spideraven jumped from a nearby rafter to see what he was scribbling.

'Big White's dead,' Pop muttered casually.

'*Holy shit*!' Nick exclaimed.

'What happened?' Silvia asked, stunned.

'I shot him,' Pop responded, the same way a man would describe taking out the garbage in time for pick-up.

'You... you shot him?' Silvia asked.

'Yeah!'

'Did he attack you?'

'No.'

Silvia and Nick exchanged glances, trying to figure out what had just happened.

'I shot him in the back of the head, actually!'

'Should we be expecting an attack?' Silvia asked, as her body tensed up.

'Hopefully! I'd be very disappointed if we weren't always on our guard during our tenure in this city!'

Silvia scoffed. She drew back her chair and sat down, with Nick doing the same with his.

Pop looked up from his scribbling. 'What?'

'Could you please at least explain to us what happened?'

'Yeah, boss, you've kinda taken us out of the blue!'

Pop sighed, stop writing and leaned back in his seat, as he clasped his hands on his belly. 'I didn't like him! I couldn't see us working long-term with him! At least not consistently and we need consistency! That was honestly what it all came down to: he just wasn't reliable! Ultimately, he was more of a *problem* than a solution to our existing *problems*!'

Nick was frowning. 'So you decided to kill him, out of nowhere?'

Pop smirked humourlessly. 'His men *feared* him. Many *hated* him! I never saw a single one of his men which I could say *loved* him! People had to *deal* with him, not *make deals* with him!'

Where is this coming from? 'And we were okay making deals with him until now?'

'We had to give him a chance!'

'Boss, the man didn't even know that he was fighting for his life!'

'That was another problem, which derived from his unreliability: I just didn't know if he understood his situation. I don't think he understood what was at stake! He just thought that I had come along and that it would be business-as-usual with me: that there would be ups and downs and, if things went well, he might stay, and, if things went badly, he wouldn't! I don't think he really understood the magnitude of what we needed him to do! I also don't think he was up for it, honestly, but that will remain an assumption.'

'No! Anwar is a much better choice!'

*Anwar? Anwar who is – **was** loyal to a fault, to Big White?* 'And how will Anwar react when he finds out you killed his boss?'

'Oh, he already knows. He was there. He saw me do it!'

'And... he was okay with it?'

'I think I definitely took him by surprise! But, once he understood my vision, he agreed.' Pop raised a finger. 'Which reminds me! I promised to help him during this transition period!'

Oh, shit! Here we go!

'He's going to touch base with everyone in his organization. See who's on board and who isn't. Once he's sent us a list of people we can help him deal with, we're going to organize teams to go out and assist his people in that respect!'

Death squads... 'And you expect Anwar to be reliable, when you killed his predecessor out-of-nowhere in front of him, for no apparent reason?' Silvia just couldn't wrap her head around Pop's sudden decision. 'Likely the only reason he didn't kill you right then and there, is because he himself is traitor at-heart!'

'A fair assessment! Yet, I have my own assessment and we will act in concordance with *that* assessment as we go forward, *Silvia*!' He spun his head towards her, locking eyes with her. 'Everyone has a role to play in this thing of ours! I'm quite certain that, one day, you'll be in my position, forced to make decisions of a very similar nature to mine! Until that day comes, I will remind you that *your* job is to help *me* make those decisions and *not to carry them out after they have already been made*!' he emphasized, banging his fist into the table at the very end.

He sighed. 'Your observations – *both* your observations – are valid and they represent fair counterarguments to my actions! Good job! I take it as a sign that you haven't just been sitting around, not understanding anything, but that you have been learning and cultivating your own strategic sense! But, there is a fine line between constructive criticism and insubordination and *you*,' he addressed Silvia. '... are *pushing it*!'

He went back to his writing. 'Send Tech and Basenji in! I want to have a word with them. Then go disseminate the information amongst the men. I want Gigi, Bojana, Josip and Lejla to all know of these developments within the hour and I want everyone to know about this by morning *and* to be ready for the next steps!'

Yup... here we go again... One of his unpredictable changes of course!

'*Yes, sir*!' they both echoed.

And now we have to go set the sails, raise anchors and row his boat!

Five hours later, she finally had the time to lie in bed. She picked up her phone, looking for one text message in particular, which she now reread.

'I just wanted to tell you that this cake is truly magnificent! Please send my compliments to Mira! This is sublime! Abiola is well. She seems very pleased. I hope Lorgar had a great time also!'

Silvia breathed in deeply as she set her fingers to work.

'I'll tell Mira about the cake. He did enjoy it! He's already begging us to bring him over again!'

She put her phone on her nightstand.

Lorgar had said no such thing.

Her phone vibrated and she picked it up to see a new text message.

'Tomorrow? Maybe in the afternoon?'

Silvia gripped her phone tightly. *'Yes, 5pm.'*

She put the phone down and it vibrated instantly.

'Tell Lorgar it's a date!'

Silvia looked at her phone, her heart beating.

Smiley face.

She put her phone down and breathed in, hoping she would be able to fall asleep, since she had a lot of work to do tomorrow.

Fuck him.

She eventually fell asleep.

Lorgar pestered her about taking him to Abiola the moment she woke up. She told him she would talk to Ulfrik about it and, after the morning meeting with Pop, she told the excited feline that she had spoken to Ulfrik and that they would go at 5pm. They snuck out together, after informing a relieved Mira of this second appointment, at a time when Silvia was certain Pop would not notice her absence for about fifteen minutes.

She knocked on Ulfrik's door. He opened it. She gave him some Czech carrot cake Mira had cooked-up as payment for today's session. This time, she agreed to have a slice with him. The cake was so good that Silvia realized that there exited flavours of excellence in the world which she had not tasted up until that moment.

And they talked.

They just talked for around ten minutes, since Lorgar and Abiola took longer this time. They talked about the different types of nuts that grew on Terra and Shangri. They talked about how long Ulfrik had been living at number 619 Wiltshire Boulevard. They even managed to talk a little about his choice of furniture.

Silvia then took Lorgar home and waited for the hitlist to arrive from Anwar. One of the more senior ursai arrived at around seven in the afternoon with an initial name. It was a blood relative of Big White, his second-cousin, who had immediately denounced Anwar as a traitor and declared that he and crew would never work with his cousin's murderer.

Pop had Silvia and Nick selected eleven of their best men each and assist Anwar in eliminating this first dissenter. He said he wanted his best men on the job, so that Anwar understood that the Alliance was committed to supporting him. He also wanted to impress the ursai and have him see firsthand that the Terrans' reputation was not an exaggeration. He also wanted to be sure that there were enough of them that they would survive if Anwar decided to double-cross them.

Anwar did not double-cross them. He also came to understand that their reputation was an understatement. Within two minutes of their assault on the second-cousin's compound and twelve corpses later, their target had been eliminated. Silently. The Hajduks even helped with the clean-up and the destruction of any potential evidence. Anwar courteously invited them to drinks and a midnight snack at a nearby ursai establishment, yet they refused. (Silvia refused. Nick really wanted to go.)

The next day, at five o'clock, she found herself in front of the back door of Wiltshire Boulevard Number 619, with a red velvet cake in one arm and Lorgar in the other., ready-to-go. She talked with Ulfrik about the hidden gems of Convent Garden and about the smells of certain trees which blossomed in late summer. She left after half-an-hour.

Later that evening, she was fixing up a car bomb and organizing three concomitant ambushes. There was no fight, just a controlled detonation and three hails of bullets. Seventeen corpses. The clean-up took longer. Two hours. Then Anwar invited them to the same ursai establishment and they accepted. It was a strip club. They made a great cheesesteak. One of the dancers was cute.

The next day, at five o'clock, she finally accepted to share in some Dobosh cake with Ulfrik. Silvia discovered that he had a remarkably expansive collection of Terran music, ranging from classical music, all the way to rock'n'roll. She told him that she mostly enjoyed American country music and that Mira had been bombarding their apartment with a constant stream of hip-hop and R'n'B. She then introduced him to Balkan turbofolk, which left him very confused. She left after forty minutes.

The next day, she was sneaking through the sewers, before emerging in an ursai body shop, where she, together with seven of her Hajduks and over twenty ursai enforcers, produced seventeen bodies, which swiftly disappeared. All went well, initially, though she had to meet up with Nick afterwards, who informed her that he had been followed and they had to fight off an ambush, killing four ursai initially, then hunting down the surviving two ambushers for most of the night, before dropping by the strip club to eat some spareribs with Anwar and his crew. The cute dancer did everything in her power to come as close to Silvia as possible, as unnecessarily often as was possible. Next morning, Pop reprimanded them for being careless, being followed and taking so long to hunt down the two stragglers.

Mira left her a Hummingbird cake and a note that she was away on her 'spirit quest'. Ulfrik noticed that she was a bit tired and asked her how she was feeling. They talked about work and goals and dreams. He also made her some iced tea which really gave her a boost. She left after an hour, feeling better about things.

Pop insisted that they talk before they went out on their next mission. He also told them that they would be working with the Serbs that evening, as he had asked Bojana and Josip for back-up, since it shouldn't be just the Romanian Hajduks that were going out risking their lives every night. Plus, it would help accelerate the passing of this transitional period for the Ursai Cooperatives. They got a lot of work done very quickly that night. However, problems did emerge at the strip club, as Nick, Ristić and Panko argued who would carry out a few more jobs that day. Silvia had been locked up in a bathroom stall, spread out on the toilet seat, as the dancer went down on her. She heard the sounds of squabbling as she was about to come and concentrating on her objective only resulted in her shoving the dancer away, before barging off into the VIP room that served as the base of operations for join Terran-Ursai operations. After sorting out the mess, she told Panko to chill and get a blowjob from the cute dancer. The next day, Pop told her that Josip had called to apologize for Panko's behaviour, which annoyed him, because '*Anwar and his men saw the argument and it makes us all look bad! I don't care about the argument itself! There's always arguing! It's normal! Why weren't you there from the start to squash it immediately?*'

Mira had been preparing a panettone cake for about two days at this point.

'I'm not hungry today!' she told Ulfrik, as he presented her with her slice.

He paused and looked at her, confused. 'Silvia, I haven't been hungry a single day you've come here, but this is cake we're talking about! I don't know how it's like on Terra, but in most places in the universe, cake is not something you eat when you're hungry!'

Silvia chuckled. 'I know... just that...' *I... I want to talk about these things so much and I feel as if you would be great for that, but I can't!*

'Just that I'm an *outsider*...'

Silvia's eyes darted upwards from the floor, as her eyes flashed in rage for a moment, though they simmered down once she saw his look of hopelessness.

He sighed. 'Look... I know this is the part where you grab me by the throat and tell me to mind my own business, but I still have air in my lungs at this moment and I am going to use it!'

She smirked. 'Use it wisely then!'

'There was never another option.' He seemed thoughtful for a moment, like as if he were about to attempt to apply rubbing alcohol on a wounded beast of long fangs and sharp claws. 'Your think very fast, but you feel very slowly.'

Silvia's eyes were perplexed for a moment, until she managed to stifle a chuckle and smile. 'What does that mean?'

Ulfrik's eyebrows rose. 'It means that you have been coming here for the last week and I feel as if our time spent together is something you really enjoy. You're a very rational woman and I believe that you come here to recharge your batteries. However, you are not like other women...'

'I thought we were over the whole English wooing phase...'

'We aren't, but that is not what I'm doing...' Ulfrik stopped and sought out his words with great care. 'You're very perceptive. Very understanding of what is going around you. It doesn't matter how many things happen around you at whatever speed, you're always aware of the movement and nothing ever escapes you.'

'Yet, you yourself never really move that much. I once told you I noticed that everyone seems to depend on you and during these... *meetings* of ours I've come to understand why. You don't go through emotions the way a regular person would. You don't... feel sad in the morning, then happy and noon, then anxious in the afternoon, then happy in the evening, then worried at night, for example.'

'Quite an assessment from someone who only sees me at five o'clock...'

'Perhaps, though you haven't told me I'm wrong!'

Silvia felt the need for a sharp intake of breath. 'Well, Ulfrik, what are you trying to do with this speech?'

'I'm trying to say that just because you see me as an outsider and (don't get me wrong) I *am* an outsider in your life, I am happy you came here today and didn't pretend!'

Silvia's eyes almost glazed over.

Ulfrik saw this, yet continued. 'I'd like you to know that, for the past week, your visits here have been the highlight of my day and I–'

Silvia rushed him, throwing him off balance with a kick to the knee and pinning him against a wall with such force that it cracked. He grabbed his head in between her hands and gripped him by hair and jaw, her face unmoving, her eyes unfocused and her voice a sharp growl.

'You think you know me? You think it's been a week of tea parties and chitchat and now you know who the fuck I am? How fucking dare you? You think you know how I think or how I feel? Do I look stable *now*, you shit? Do I look like I have my shit together *now* you fucking idiot? Am I pretending now? Huh? How do I look now? Tell me, Mr. Psychology!'

Ulfrik struggled to move his jaw for a moment and signalled this by pulling gently on her furious elbow. '*Scared.*'

She connected the back of his head with the wall with an angry headbutt and they stood there, their foreheads touching, as Silvia crawled up on him and forced his knees to bend so they could stand level. '*You really are a fucking idiot...*'

'*Scared,*' he repeated. '... that I am *toying* with you!'

That gave her pause.

'Scared that I'm being superficial... and *angry* that I might be saying these things because I just want something from you!'

'Well, *do you?*'

'I guess you could say that...'

Silvia pushed herself away from him, allowing him to regain his balance, stand up straight and rub the back of his head.

She stormed over to the door to the hallway and opened it. '*Lorgar! Time to go!*' she shouted, before turning around to glare at him, her eyes angry and her breaths heavy.

'*Coming, Lady Silvia!*'

She pulled her hair out of her face and found some words. 'You came close... Closer than anyone ever did...'

Ulfrik's face revealed that he believed her and regret seemed to swell inside of him. They both heard Lorgar trotting down the steps.

'Well... coming here has also been the highlight of *my* day, Ulfrik,' she confessed. 'And now you've ruined it...'

'It was not my intention!'

'Well, that doesn't matter!' she snapped, just as Lorgar's tail could be seen bouncing towards the backdoor. 'Have a great evening, Ulfrik of Langley-Creekside!'

He nodded, disappointment and sadness heavy in his eyes.

She dropped off Lorgar in the living room, then went to the bathroom to smoke a cigarette alone, before checking her face to make sure that it would keep her secrets safe during the evening meeting with Pop and the others.

'We're done!' their General congratulated them. 'Anwar's informed us that the heavy lifting is over. They can handle things internally going forward! He also commended you two!' he said to Silvia and Nick.

'Oh, yeah? What did he say?' Nick asked excitedly.

Pop frowned, as he searched the waste bin in his head where he kept such things. 'I dunno... he said something nice, I don't remember!'

Of course you don't...

'The point is that we've made and excellent impression, Anwar is capo di tutti capi and now he knows what we're about! There were some hiccups along the way...' he glared at Silvia. 'But, overall, even though we had to scramble to get everything done in just one week, everything came out well!'

We had to scramble because you suddenly decided that we had to...

'Again, what's important is that the ursai have now seen what we can do! They don't have to know how the sausage is made... Anyway... I guess everyone deserves a break. Today's Monday, tomorrow's Tuesday and the day after tomorrow is Wednesday. Silvia, is everything prepared for the meeting of minds?'

Of course it was.

Silvia couldn't really sleep that well that night. She tossed and she turned and a few times she even picked up her phone and stared at her phone before deciding against it.

The next day, she returned to her living room to find a freshly baked chocolate cake prepared on the dining table. She checked the time to see that it was a quarter to five.

Shit...any second now-

'Lady Silvia! Milady told me to tell you that she is away on her spirit quest and that she also prepared fresh vanilla ice-cream as a pairing for the cake!' he informed her, as he jumped on the dining room table. 'It's in the icebox, which is next to the phaiser and inside the phaiser are some duck scraps left over from yesterday's duck a la press! Do we perhaps have time for a quick snack before the daily appointment?'

Silvia sighed, as she swiped her face with her hand in silent frustration. 'Lorgar...'

'Yes, Lady Silvia?' he asked, all excited.

'Lorgar... I'm sorry, but we're not going to Abiola today! I'll talk to Mira and have her or Veronica or Nick or someone take you over tomorrow...'

'Ah...' Lorgar's head sank.

But then it rose sharply. '*Excellent!*'

Silvia raised an eyebrow.

'That pussy's getting loose! Gotta give it time to breathe and tighten back up!' he informed her, as he jumped down from the dining table. '*Degenerate whore...*' he muttered, as he went to take a nap.

Well... that went... well...

Love of your life, eh, Lorgar?

Mira came home around an hour later and Silvia told her that she didn't take Lorgar to Abiola because she had too much work to do for next day's meeting. Mira obviously saw through this lie, though she didn't challenge it. Silvia could swear she saw a hint of disappointment in her eye too.

Which she could have handled, had it not been for the look she saw in her own eyes when she washed her face that evening before going to bed.

She smoked a sad little cigarette in her office after that.

Then she smoked a furious cigarette as she paced angrily around the room.

Then she smoked a cigarette as she sat down at her desk and slowly nodded to herself. By the time she had taken her last toke, the sizzling sound of the extinguished bud was met by the sound of the door of her office closing and the door to her dressing room opening.

She made straight for her wardrobe and straight for the demani muslin dress. She undressed and decided to shower before putting it on. While in the shower, she realized she needed to shave. *Everything.* She worked her hair into full wavy locks and made sure her nails were immaculately trimmed. Then she lathered herself in warm, smoky, and slightly citrusy perfume, before she put on the dress.

It wasn't as much a dress as it was loose see-through body suit that was tight in just the right places. Modesty would have recommended that she at least wear some lingerie, yet this was not the moment for modesty. Instead, she covered herself in a black Terran trenchcoat, which concealed everything bar her feet, and she stared at those feet for a while before taking a deep breath and putting on the pair of black stilettos she had been practicing with for ten minutes every morning over the last week.

Once certain that she could walk gracefully for at least thirty minutes, she made straight for her liquor cabinet and downed half a litter of vodka, before spraying her mouth with breath mint. She was nervous, yes, and she wanted to take edge off, but she didn't want it to be visible that she was nervous and needed to take the edge off.

On final check in her mirror and she left her bedroom, before appearing with authority in the living room. She had not buttoned down the trenchcoat yet, and Mira could see just enough to cause her to stare at her.

'I'm taking Lorgar for a walk.'

Lorgar, who had been pretending to sleep, twitched his ears and jerked his head up from where it had lain cradled by his tail. Without even bothering to seek confirmation from his actual owner, he got up, stretched, jumped down from the pillowed ledge he had been languishing on and began trotting towards the door.

Mira, who had clearly been studying Silvia's outfit, looked towards a nearby clock, hung from one of the walls. It read 10:35 pm. She turned back to her roommate, stared blankly for a second, then smiled and said. 'Oookay!'

Silvia nodded, picked up Lorgar's leash, then followed the cat to the door. She stopped in the doorway to pick him up, then turned to Mira to say, 'I think I'll take a *long* walk!'

'Well, I hope you do,' Mira replied, sitting up and grinning.

'I might be away for a while!'

'You might be away all night, even!'

Silvia smiled. 'I might. But if I'm not back by 6pm, please call me.'

'And if you don't pick up, I'll come check up on you!' Mira was smiling ear to ear at this point.

'Great. I'll –'

'– text me when you take a break, so I know everything is ok!'

Silvia smiled. *God bless this woman!*

She nodded and left the apartment.

'Silvia!' Mira called after her.

She turned and saw a smile on her young face.

'Do you need cake?' Mira barely contained herself from laughing.

Silvia just smiled out of the corner of her mouth. 'No.'

She knew the embassy almost as well as she knew its current occupants by this point, so she had no trouble slipping through outside unobserved. Pop always wanted his base of operations to be *impenetrable* by means of stealth. Being *inescapable* by means of stealth had not been one of his concerns for Convent Square. Silvia had nevertheless dedicated some degree of effort to making sure such a quiet escape would be virtually impossible, yet she had noted certain chinks in their armour which she had simply accepted could not be fixed without taking away from some other essential attribute.

So, when she found herself ringing the doorbell at Wiltshire Boulevard, number 619, she was certain that none of the Hajduks knew where she was or how she got there. She felt his feet move towards the door and she leaned in the doorframe, successfully lounging much more sensually than Lorgar (or any feline, for that matter) ever could.

Ulfrik seemed to open the door particularly slowly today, though he did answer quickly. *He's seen me on the door camera.*

'Hey!' she said. *Jesus Christ, woman! You're going to have to do better than that.*

'Hello there!' Ulfrik responded. As usual, he was wearing a light brown henley, black pants and dark brown boots. His hair was gorgeous: not as well kept as it had been at the party, but more wild and playful. Silvia suspected that it had likely been much more unkempt just a few moments before. *He fixed it up when he saw it was me knocking on his door!*

'We've been feeling a bit frisky tonight, haven't we, Lorgar?' She didn't even look at him, her eyes never leaving Ulfrik's.

'Milady Silvia, I cannot say that I was, but this is definitely most thoughtful on your behalf!' he said, looking up at her, before switching to look upon their host. 'Sir Ulfrik! Is Abiola home?'

'She's upstairs in her usual spot,' he replied, bothering himself to be courteous and looking away from Silvia's gaze to glance down at him.

'Oh, well, then don't mind if I do!' Lorgar unceremoniously rushed into the already familiar house and trotted up the stairs.

Ulfrik's eyes had returned to Silvia's way before Lorgar had even commenced his sprint. 'You... Do you want to come in?'

'If you don't mind,' she replied.

'On the contrary,' he said, pushing the door open further. 'I'd very much enjoy it!'

Silvia walked in and she knew that he had glanced back as he closed the door behind her.

'There's something I've never asked you,' she said, as she walked into his living room. 'Is this place private?'

'Well, I hope it is! What with what the ruckus that's been going on upstairs, I reckon the property value would go down if word was to get out!'

She didn't believe him, but she would trust him tonight. 'You play Terran music here sometimes,' she remarked, over the low rumble of his Shangrian lounge music.

'Yes... I have a collection of some tunes I like,' he confirmed, gesturing towards a screen on one of the tables.

'May I?' she asked.

'Of course!'

Silvia made towards the screen as she unbuttoned her trenchcoat, strategically taking it off and placing it on his couch, so that he could see her walk in just the dress towards his music station.

She heard him audibly swallow like a starving man seeing a feast. 'Would you care for a drink?'

'Red wine would be nice!' she agreed, as she reached the station and searched 'Terran artists'.

'I think I have some wine...' she heard him say, just as she clicked on of the songs.

Ooh baby, I'm hot just like an oven!

I need some lovin'!

She heard two glasses being placed on one of the tables behind her and she smiled mischievously, as she could tell that the hand that had settle them was subtly shaking.

And when I get this feeling,

I need sexual healing!

Silvia frowned.

What am I thinking?

No! What am I? One of Nick's whores? Not this one!

She browsed through the titles as she heard Ulfrik pour two glasses of wine behind, until she realized that the device had a 'rank by time played' function. Huh... She sorted the list and smirked when she saw the first title. *I like that one too...*

She pressed it.

Some folks are born made to wave the flag,
Hoo, they're red, white and blue!

She heard Ulfrik pause behind her. 'I knew that song was popular on your world, but I never took it as your style!' he noted.

'It's not,' she replied, though she had just now spotted another song she and Ulfrik seemed to both like. And she liked that song *a lot*! She took her time though and let Creedence Clearwater Revival do its thing.

And when the band plays "Hail to the chief",
Ooh, they point the cannon at you, Lord!

She felt him draw near and she turned and accepted a glass of wine from her host. 'Though I'm surprised it seems to be yours!'

They chinked glasses.

It ain't me, it ain't me!
I ain't no senator's son, son!

She chuckled. 'I'm confused as to how exactly you relate to it! I took you for an Englishman in New York, not an American in Vietnam...'

'I don't think you have to relate to a song's lyrics as much as you relate to the feeling behind it, even if sometimes it's a feeling you yourself have never experienced...' A wry smile took hold in the corner of Ulfrik's lips. 'There's a lot you don't know about me!'

A spark of rage wisped inside of her. 'There's a lot you don't know about me either... *despite*... your *assumptions*...'

It ain't me, it ain't me
I ain't no fortunate one, no!

Ulfrik clearly saw the earlier day's embers lit up inside of her. '*Presumptions* would be a better word for them... and *presumptions* are a rude thing! I... I apologize!'

Silvia smirked, though her eyes had been staring at Ulfrik's lips for quite some time.

And the spark of rage turned into a flame of passion.

She rushed to him and he rushed to her and their lips met and they kissed feverishly for a period of time that could never be described by words of quantity.

Until Silvia remembered something.

She pulled away, looked at his ravenous ravishing eyes and she took a deep breath. She also downed the entire glass of wine in one gulp.

Ulfrik, in between heavy breaths, raised his eyebrows. 'Good thing there's still half-a-bottle left...'

'I'm a virgin!' she blurted out.

Now Ulfrik's eyes also widened as his eyebrows rose, before they settled in a confused frown as he connected some dots inside his head. 'But...'

Silvia beat him to it. 'I've had sex with girls before!'

'Oh... I see...'

'Probably more than you!'

'*Ohhh... kay?* Well... I... I can be gentle...'

'Oh, yeah?'

'Yes.'

Silvia's hand drifted towards the music box behind her, to the exact place where the song she wanted was and pressed it.

Gimme fuel! Gimme fire! Gimme that which I desire!

The music of *Metallica* exploded through Ulfrik's living room as he wondered who was deflowering who tonight. He had to wonder as much as they both crashed together once more and Silvia's long-awaited fantasy of having someone tear-off the muslin dress off her finally came true after literal decades.

'Don't worry! I don't bite!' she told him, before coming in to kiss him more.

She bit his lip soon after with not the most negligible bit of bite behind it.

'Ok, that might have been a lie!'

Chapter XII

The Makings

Shoem nibbled at his children's ears, making them giggle.

He liked doing that to them, when he caught them home in the morning, before they left for school and he left for work. His wife smiled a worried smile, of which he took note.

'Go! Get your things! You'll be late for class!' his wife instructed the children, gesturing for their three sons and their two beautiful little girls to go to their room to pick up their things.

Shoem hated that the five of them had to share the same room, but he hadn't had enough legitimate income to justify moving into a larger apartment. He would, when the prize money from the fight came in, that is. But, of course, the IRS had chosen to freeze his funds and audit him the moment the Libra Sporting Company had attempted to wire him the money.

'Random Selection', they had called it, but Shoem had gotten used to it. Every time there was any impactful increase in his declared earnings he got randomly selected for an audit.

After the five had scuttled away, his wife came up next to him on one of the thin metal seats they had lined around their kitchen table. She didn't say anything for a while, allowing him to chew his breakfast.

'You're going to see *him* today?' she finally asked.

Shoem nodded.

He saw her fingers grow restless, as she gripped her apron and pretended to look out the window. 'Are you going alone?' she asked.

Shoem nodded again.

His wife snapped. She leaned in and spoke for his ears alone, lest the children overhear. 'I'm worried!'

Shoem nodded in agreement.

His wife bolted from her seat in frustration and she grabbed the remote from the kitchen counter, turning on the volume of their television.

'... The disappearance of the Libra Conglomerate Chairman, Mr. Gamal Bittercastle, commonly known as Big White, remains a mystery!' The news anchor's voice rang out. 'The alleged kingpin of the largest underground criminal organization in the City of Shangri, Mr. Bittercastle, was last seen attending a Gala event at the Convent Garden Embassy. His associates report that he went missing sometime after.'

'Yes, Chris,' the second news anchor's lines came up. 'What is particularly interesting is how rapidly things have shifted behind the scenes within the Libra Conglomerate! Our reporter, Amna Roup, has more!'

'Thank you, Trisha!' the feed cut to a woman standing, unnecessarily, in front of the Libra Conglomerate's head offices. 'Mr. Bittercastle's disappearance was reported to his parole officer four days ago, spurring a citywide manhunt after an arrest warrant was quickly released in his name by District Barrister Jonas Sacramoni. However, sources inside the Constabulary tell BSN that the Constabulary has made little to no effort in tracking down the missing businessman, despite the seriousness of his parole violation.'

The second news anchor interrupted the reporter. 'Could this be a sign that they think him to be deceased, Amna?'

'Thank you, Trisha!' Amna tried to not be irritated and pretended to have a conversation with the anchors. 'The low effort by authorities to discover Mr. Bittercastle's whereabouts is quite remarkable in itself. However, what is a giveaway is the fact that Mr. Bittercastle was been removed from his position as Chairman and was replaced by a board of five executive directors, led by the former CEO, Anwar Brownhen, almost immediately following his reported disappearance. The new board voted unanimously to terminate his contract with the Libra Conglomerate and redistribute Mr. Bittercastle's stock in the company, citing 'proven instances of embezzlement, fraud and, yes, even sexual misconduct, by the former Chairman.'

'Should we–'

Shoem's wife interrupted the anchor, as she turned to her husband, remote in hand. 'What happened there?'

He looked at her, understanding her concern. He chose not to answer.

'*Shoem*!' his wife said, returning to her seat next to him.

She was about to speak, but he knew what to say to her. He put down his knife and fork and grabbed her nervous hands. 'Chani!' he said his wife's name. 'I'll be fine! Ok?'

'Shoem! If he they can kill Gamal Bittercastle –'

'– You don't know that–' he began.

'– NO! But *you do*! And, because you do, *I know too*!'

Shoem smiled. 'If you know me so well, can't you see I'm not worried?' he explained.

Chani was a lot smarter than that. 'Shoem! You're terrified!'

'*Shhh*!!!' He didn't want his children overhearing *that*, of all things. It wasn't good for them. 'Chani! If every other day I go out like this, why should *today* be any different?'

'Because you love the thrill and I adore that about you! But, some days are just so much riskier than others!'

Shoem smiled and squeezed his wife's hands. He smiled and bent forwards to snuggle her neck. He grabbed another bite of food, then got up and said. 'I'll see you tonight!'

His wife reluctantly let go of his hand.

He spent the entire drive to Convent Garden trying to calm his nerves. His wife was right, he did spend every morning with his kids terrified that it would be last time they would see him and, yes, he loved the rush of what he did. He found it to be intoxicating, if he was being completely honest.

But, she was most right about the fact that today was different.

The Terran General had made quite an impression. He was clearly sociopathic, yet he was also very intelligent. He had seen through his old ruse immediately and the murine still remembered the intense feeling of being so carefully studied during their short conversation. Normally, he would have avoided such a human, were it not for his emissary.

Mira al-Sayid also left quite an impression on him, as well. She was assertive, ruthless, and determined, yet she was also kind, thoughtful and caring. She had chosen a very elegant approach to reaching him, one which no other Terran delegation had used before: offering one of his aunties a good contract and waiting it out. Shoem's organization had obviously taken a keen interest to the young Terran, observing her as she journeyed far and wide across the cityscape. She spent most of her time on some kind of quest. Shoem had initially suspected that she was just looking for him, yet it quickly became apparent that what she was pursuing was something else entirely.

Mira al-Sayid was like a fisherman who had cast a line in the water, only to immediately embark on a hunt for some other elusive quarry. The Terrarin General's men also hunted, yet their prey was far more easy to discern. They were hunting the ones that had trafficked their children all those years ago. They had been remarkably successful, up to a point, when they reached a dead end with Otto Benga. The last six would be hard to find. Shoem suspected that they were somewhere in the Urheimat's neighbourhood, which his organization could no longer venture easily into.

The Terrans were incredibly fastidious in their endeavours. Kidnapped kidnappers would be scooped up and either be brought directly to the Embassy or to one of their new safehouses and then they would completely disappear. Forever.

No trace.

And now Big White was gone. Disappeared.

Without a trace.

The Terran General had walked into his compound and Big White had never come out. Neither had his girlfriend; the blonde woman he had brought with him from the mental institution where he had first met with the Terran General.

He drove past the checkpoint at the entrance to the Convent Garden neighbourhood after showing his transport documents to the remani Constables manning the gate. The night he had delivered Otto Benga, he had used a special entry pass provided to him by Mira al-Sayid, bearing several diplomatic marks, as well as a signed invitation from Mira herself. Shoem had never seen a remani Constable be so startled in his entire life. Now, he was driving Mrs. Cri's van, extra cleaning supplies propped up in the compartment behind him.

As he saw the building, he struggled to calm his nerves. From what he had learned so far, Terrans were clearly not like regular humans. And these Terrans, in particular, very terrifying. Not as terrifying as the ones in the Military District, but still terrifying. He didn't want them to sense any weakness in him, or else they might... *Actually, who knows what they might do?*

They killed Big White and they killed the Paragon people with impunity. They didn't leave a single trace! Imagine what they can do to me? My organization can't touch them. They don't know that, but I don't want them to figure it out.

The Paragon people, I can understand – They stole their kids!

Big White, I can understand also. He probably realised he couldn't rely on that deranged psychopath, so he killed him and replaced him with Anwar, who's a good guy. Far more reliable.

But, do I really trust these people?

He liked Mira, and as he pulled up to the entrance at five minutes to eleven, he remembered Auntie Cri's kind words concerning the Hajduks.

They're good people. Very kind! Very polite! Not racist!

… Except the blonde woman in charge! She is racist!

Shoem didn't see the blonde woman as he got out of the van, opened the trunk and allowed two of Auntie Cri's cleaners to begin offloading the van. He was surprised to see two of the humans voluntarily insist that they help the murine women. He would've studied this interaction a while longer, had he not locked eyes with a third human, who nodded at him and gestured towards the nearby corridor.

Shoem nodded and proceeded down the corridor, at the end of which he found another Terran, who pressed a single button revealing a hidden service elevator and gestured for him to walk inside. He would've used the time alone in the elevator to breathe the tension out of himself, yet he suspected the elevator to be bugged, so he just held it in. Once upstairs, he found another human who studied him with the same intense energy the Terran General had used, who nodded to his left. Shoem walked down the corridor, just as four other humans passed him by, studying him intensely again.

All the humans were making him very nervous as it was, but the incessant observation he was under was making him incredibly uneasy. He hid his concern impeccably, however, in the two minutes it took for him to reach his destination: the Terran General's office.

Inside, Laur Pop was going through some notes. Next to him stood Tech, with whom he engaged in a mild debate concerning the order in which they would go through the meeting's key points, while on one of the couches sat Basenji, preparing a notebook on which he would silently scribble his meeting notes. *How very similar to what you see in our own high society…*

'Ah, Mr. *Galbar*! Welcome! This is Technowolf!' the Terran nodded towards his remani counsellor.

Shoem did his best to hide his discomfort with the General's use of his warren name. He also hid his discomfort wih being so close to a remani, particularly one which looked so feral. Auntie Cri had told him of the two remani within the Embassy. One mute and one not, both very kind and clearly not racist.

'Please to meet you, Mr. Galbar!' Tech was as gallant as ever.

Shoem nodded and shook his hand.

'My kinsman, Basenji!' Tech continued, as Basenji got up from his seat and shook Shoem's hand.

'Please, have a seat!' Laur gestured to an armchair, off in the corners of the room, next to what was clearly the nest of the Terran General's pet camio, Spideraven. 'The others should be in shortly!'

The first to arrive was the blonde woman, Silvia, and, indeed, just as he had expected, she studied him to discern if he was friend or foe with judgemental intensity. He couldn't help but note how similar her inspection of him was to that of her master, though she seemed far more difficult to convince of his benevolence than Laur Pop had been.

Next came two men he knew very well and one he had only heard of. Neither of the three had never even knew of his existence until that moment.

Anwar Brownhen, now a Partner in the Libra Corporation and the new boss of bosses of the Ursai Cooperatives, was well known to Shoem, whose organization often had to drift under the radar of the ursai and their criminal organizations. By all accounts, he was a good man. He could be very violent, if the situation warranted it, yet, overall, he was remarkably agreeable for a crime boss; certainly more so than his predecessors. Anwar studied Shoem for a long while, never taking his eyes of the murine from the moment he had realized that he would take part in this 'meeting of minds', as the Terran General had called it. At one point, Shoem saw how his puzzled look shifted to revelation, then to contemplation and, finally, a wry smile twinkled in the corner of the ursai's mouth.

It did little to put Shoem at ease.

Together with Anwar came Kroton Grenra Lonza, likely the dirtiest dirty cop in the city.

Then came the shadowy king of filth himself, Mr. Fox, who shared one look with Shoem as they shook hands, before nodding in understanding of who he must be.

Then came four of the Terran General's men, as well as Mira who smiled and gave him a hug, which only slightly eased his nerves.

'So, gentlemen!' Laur began. 'Where do we begin?'

Anwar only controlled around a third of all organized crime in the City, with one third begin controlled by the Urheimat and a final third under the sway of grime-infested lattice of smaller criminal organizations. These smaller mobs and gangs had survived by virtue of the ursai disinterest in going through the effort of stamping them out or incorporating them into their own structure. Simply put, they were either too poor or two violent for the bearmen to bother eliminating or incorporating them. Together with the Hajduks, the ursai and their enforcers set about beating many of these small organizations into submission. Anwar himself was busy establishing his complete takeover of Big White's empire, as some local bosses attempted to splinter away in the chaos of the transition of power.

Assassinations, ambushes, as well as old fashioned intimidation and the occasional reasonable negotiation engulfed Shangri's Darkside, where most of these smaller organizations resided. Most where multiethnic in nature, despite having some dominant race in command, such as the Libra ursai themselves, while many were petty kingdoms carved up by disgruntled and discharged remani veterans, orcish protection rackets, goblin drug cartels, elven criminal enterprises and even the occasional terrorist organization.

Kroton focused on monopolizing all Shangrian smuggling under the umbrella of both the Libra ursai and the Republican Alliance. Within a matter of months, all smuggling into the City came from republican harbours, even those privateers, pirates and buccaneers hailing from other home ports, such as the Avaloni would be forced to pay off corrupt Constabulary border guards and merchant harbourmasters under the Libra ursai's payroll.

This rapid conquest of the Shangri underworld, though largely driven by Republican influence peddling amongst the Shangri elite and the Constabulary, as well as by the Hajduks themselves and their extreme violence, which had not been witnessed within the city for millennia, would all have been impossible with the most inconspicuous (and nervous) man in Laur Pop's office.

Shoem was, at first, hesitant to fully share the extent of his organization.

'The real costs are incurred by transportation *through* the City, not *into it.*' Anwar explained, gesturing towards Kroton. 'It's ten times more expensive to smuggle something through the neighbourhoods than it is to get through the Piers and into the market! Forty times more to get it into the Brightside.'

'How come?' Tech asked, slightly surprised.

'In the harbour, you have to pay off five people.' Kroton explained 'You gotta pay ten thousand to the Colonial Constabulary for every ship you want to enter the galaxy, just so you're sure they won't bomb you out of the Greyspace as you enter our galactic sector. The traffic directors monitoring the radar around the City take a thousand credits per ship. They kick up 25% of that to their boss in the Constabulary, then a 50% gets paid off to the traffic team itself. Then, you gotta pay the Pier Authority inspector another thousand, just to get it off your ship, into circulation and into the Harbour. Then you pay the Harbourmasters a variable sum depending on what you're transporting. If it's drugs, you're looking at five thousand. If it's people, that's a potential a hundred thousand per ship. Once you pay up, they give you transport papers for... lavender oil, porcelain tea cups or whatever else they can forge into paperwork that day. On top of all that, you have to pay the Constabulary a hundred thousand credits per month so that they don't randomly inspect your vessel, plus another hundred per ship, if the local Customs officers haven't made his inspection quota and it's the end of the month!'

'The average cost of getting a shipment from orbit and past the Harbour is around forty thousand in bribes alone, on top of your own transportation and employee costs,' Anwar explained. 'And the average cost of getting all that cargo from the Harbour Gates and to your end-buyer is four hundred thousand per shipment, once you factor in distribution, security and packaging! Whenever you move the goods, you gotta pay the leyline traffic wardens and they charge by the mile and by crossing. There are a lot of cogs to be greased along the way!'

'*Crossing*?' Laur asked.

Anwar nodded. 'Crossing the crust: going from the Darkside to the Brightside or from the Brightside to the Darkside.'

Laur leaned back, pondering how this piece of information fit within things. 'Smuggling seems to be a really exact science in this city, isn't it?' he asked.

'More or less...' Anwar ruminated for a moment. 'There is a system in play, that's true, but it's still banditry in its own way. There's an element of chaos that can occur at any moment, particularly during transit! The Constabulary isn't exact a unified institution. Some of them don't care about the smuggling and they actually like that we're involved in it, since we add an extra layer of security to things! They know that we live in the same city, as they do, and we want the city to prosper, as they do! We're the real reason there's no terrorism, no death cults, no hostile forces of any kind within the city! Well, bar perhaps only the Urheimat and *you fine gentlemen*!' he gestured towards those assembled.

'There are some that want to profit from it and we're more than willing to work with them. But, there are those in the Constabulary who hate smuggling for one reason or another. It's usually the fact that it's something illegal, immoral, but sometimes it's just plain racism!'

Kroton elaborated. 'Most of the shipments that are intercepted are publicity stunts: we throw something their way, so that they can brag about how they're still doing their job. But, a lot of the unplanned interceptions are simply cases where human Constables, usually Urheimat symps, go above-and-beyond to stop a shipment, usually by going against their own colleagues!'

Of which you are one... they cost you a pretty penny, these symp colleagues of yours, don't they?

Anwar continued. 'We can't touch them, since we don't want to start a war, but they do get in the way a lot and they grow more and more strong-in-the-arm with each passing year, ever since the Urheimat took up shop up in Calbraith.' Anwar paused, mulling his next words.

Good. This is why I wanted you here, not Big White! You often think before you speak!

'I'm assuming you can't help with that?' Anwar asked Laur, drawing Kroton's critical glare.

'No,' Laur immediately informed him. 'The Constabulary is *not* to be touched. It doesn't matter how loyal they are to the Urheimat, unless it's something that can be labelled as high treason, they are *not* to be touched and, even in *that* scenario, we will simply pass evidence on to the Constabulary of said treason and let them handle it *internally*!' He said to Kroton, before allowing himself to think. 'So, there's no way to cut costs on transportation, given all you know about the system?' he asked.

'No,' Anwar confirmed. 'We can increase the levels of contraband within the city by increasing the number of shipments, but we cannot decrease its cost, because of how streamlined the system is. You always have to take the path with the least chance of getting searched by traffic wardens and that leads to variable costs, even if they all even out at the end of the day.'

'Can't you move it by other means?' Nick intervened. 'The sewers? Ventilation? Energy pipes? Maybe deserted areas?'

Anwar chuckled. 'Nick! This isn't a *planet*. The surface area of Shangri is a million times larger than that of a planet! And that's just the Brightside! The Darkside's even larger! The distances are *immense*! You *have* to use the City leylines and they're all teeming with traffic wardens just ready to have their taste of what's moving through them!'

'*All of them?*' Tech asked. 'At all times? There are thousands of leyline entrances!'

'*Tens* of thousands, actually!' Anwar corrected him. 'Each one has at least two Constables posted on each entrance, both ways! Usually, in bad neighbourhoods, the number is closer to twenty per entrance!'

'The traffic warden corps of the Constabulary numbers around ten million men,' Kroton highlighted.

'*They* control smuggling in Shangri, not us!' Anwar explained.

Laur sighed. 'Well... I would've enjoyed it if we could increase contraband without forcing you to incur so much cash flow pressure–'

Shoem cleared his throat.

All eyes turned towards the murine, clearly making him *extremely uncomfortable*.

Nevertheless, he *had* had a reason for doing so. 'I can help with that!' he said.

A smile twinkled in the corner of Laur's mouth. *I knew it!*

'*How much* can you help with that?' Anwar asked.

'Around five hundred total, per shipment.' Shoem replied.

Anwar couldn't help but scoff. 'Five *hundred*? That'll lower our costs from 40 000 per shipment to 39 500!'

'Every penny counts!' Kroton commented.

'No,' Shoem replied calmly. '500 *total* cost per shipment!' he explained. 'Not 500 *less* per shipment! To get it from the harbour, to one of your warehouses.'

Now the room stared at him even more.

'You still have to get it out of the harbour!' he added.

Shoem's organization had been smuggling goods across the surface of Shangri for millennia. Unlike the ursai, they did not use the City's own infrastructure. Rather, they used their own network of much smaller, and far stealthier, relay nodes. *The old Shangri leylines.*

And the ratmen were quick and their labour was cheap.

It took a month to set up the new system for smuggling goods into the city, but it worked like clockwork once it was up and running.

Republican vessels would enter Shangri space laden with a mix of official cargo and contraband. All other vessels would be stopped by the Constabulary, which they could now afford to bribe to be diligent and check *every single* non-Shangrian and non-Republican vessel that entered the Pisces Dwarf Galaxy. The Republican trade ships would unload both their official cargo, which would enter the City through legitimate means, as well as their contraband, which would immediately by transported towards the nearest murine leyline portal.

Shoem's organization handled things from there and they did so with supernatural efficiency. At first, they only handled transportation to the ursai safehouses, with Anwar taking things over from there. However, after a new fee arrangement, they began handling transportation towards the ursai retailers directly.

Initially, most of the contraband had been drugs. Shangri had a strict drug policy, heavily enforced amongst the lower classes, whilst the higher classes got high with relative impunity and little oversight. Terran speed, Kalimasti kush, Goblin cocaine and all possible varieties of uppers, downers and psychotropics swiftly flooded the streets of the City of Shangri. The Hajduks and their allies agreed upon a very strict regimen for some of the more nefarious narcotics, as they would only be pushed on to the Urheimat's Neighbourhood, causing crack dens and trap houses to swiftly spread throughout what had once been thriving communities. In other areas, this downward shift was mitigated, as the ursai quickly disposed of such occurrences with extreme prejudice, lest their own profit margins be endangered.

Another common category of contraband was illegal technology. The Peacekeeper had made sure that certain technologies be strictly regulated within the City, lest they either threatened his rule or, worse, drew the ire of the Urheimat.

Shangrian healthcare was sublime for the upper classes, since it was very expensive, whilst the poorer classes tended to live and die as mortal men did on worlds bereft of genetic templates or any other life extension and improvement technologies. The only way to attain functional immortality as a commoner, was to acquire a genetic template development procedure through a network of Shangrian physicians operating under the umbrella of the ursai. Such procedures, though far cheaper than those made available to the Shangri elite, were still incredibly expensive due to smuggling costs. The Hajduk's operations halved the cost of such procedures within a month and by three quarters within two months, as Hyperborean genetic templates and insertion devices became readily available to the mortal masses.

Another popular import were cellphones (or any communication device, for that matter) that were untraceable and disconnected from the Shangrian communication system. Another illegal feature was social media, which the Hajduks quickly pushed on to the population, initially in the form of gay dating apps, followed by straight dating apps and, finally, Laur obtained permission from the Seal Legion of Terra, to open up Shangrian Instagram (copyright compliant, of course).

It was around this point that weapons became a sizeable chunk of imports. The ursai needed help stamping out their competition, that much was clear, though Laur tried other methods, at first, before he decided that he might as well flood the ursai armouries small arms, of which the Republican Alliance had plenty.

'I want Mira to start putting in work,' he said to Silvia, one day, as she had lingered in his office after one of their 'meeting of minds' council.

Silvia looked somewhat stunned. 'Why the sudden change of course?' she asked.

Laur felt that the question was justified. 'She takes part in the meetings, though she doesn't really contribute much. I think that's a waste of her talents. Other than that, what does she do? I notice she mostly stays in your room doing... what does she do, exactly?'

'She mostly... wallows...' Silvia struggled to find the words.

Laur was intrigued. 'What do you mean?'

Silvia seemed to either not be certain what she meant, or she was uncertain as to how he would take it. 'She has... the blues...'

'She's depressed?' Laur asked, a rare look of surprise on his face. *Still?*

'I wouldn't call it that!' Silvia insisted. 'She just seems... inactive, as of late...'

'Huh...' Laur nodded. 'Well... even more reason to have her out and about!'

'What exactly did you have in mind?'

Laur's eyebrows rose and he sighed as he thought about it. 'That street gang up in Gojaito. The one Anwar's been having trouble with?'

'Yes? Should she–'

Laur interrupted her. 'Have her talk to Shoem about getting her a guide that can sneak her around the city. Then have her and some of Anwar's people take care of it.'

'Alright...' Silvia agreed. '... and *after?*'

Laur smirked. 'There are two types of people, Silvia: there are those you have to hold by the hand as they go anywhere, and there are those that you can just point in the right direction! Which category, do you reckon, is Mira's?' he asked.

Mira and three of Anwar's men decapitated the Gojaito Mari Gang later that afternoon. By the next day, three hundred gang members virtually begged the ursai to take them under their wing. Within a week, Mira had her own little death squad which went to war against a new petty street boss, slumlord and kingpin every day. Within a month, she had carved out her own operation, run by her own multiethnic organization, which had progressed from murders, ambushes and shootouts, all the way to transportation of contraband through some of the City's more dangerous neighbourhoods.

As the murine took much off the strain away from the ursai by outsourcing most of the transportation efforts, and Kroton used the proceeds from each smuggled shipment to buy off more and more of the Shangri Harbourmasters, Anwar succeeded in finally becoming the true boss-of-bosses of the entire Shangri underworld, a task which Big White had always fell just shy of. This achievement was, nevertheless, something he had received thanks to much assistance from not just Mira, but the Hajduks as a whole. Initially, Laur had provided aid only by sending out small detachments of his legion to aid the ursai in their gang wars. Yet, very soon, he began ordering his men to teach the ursai the guerrilla tactics they had honed during their long service fighting Earth and Terra's wars. As the ursai grew in trustworthiness, he began arming them with more serious firepower.

The ursai had weapons of their own, yet their number and capabilities had always been minimal. The Peacekeeper had always regulated firearms with extreme prejudice, with only the Constables allowed to bear arms in the City and even their capabilities had always been purposefully kept limited. Laur had machine guns, shotguns, rocket-propelled grenades, battle rifles and even flamethrowers smuggled into the City, on top of the usual shipments of handguns, sniper rifles and submachine guns, all of which were superior to the existing arsenal of both the ursai and their enemies. He would've had some of Anwar's better fighters sent over to Gigi and his Albanians for training, were it not for the fact that the Military District was always packed full of prying eyes, just waiting to catch glimpse of some very conspicuous bearmen entering the Terran compound.

Instead, the ursai exercised their newly acquired skills in the backstreets and dark alleys of the City itself, as they rapidly eliminated any and all competition. Soon enough, every drug dealer, loan shark, bookie and hooker was working for Anwar. Every casino, brothel and every racket known to mankind, that operated within the city, was very soon under the Brown Paw, in ways it had never been under Big White.

All except the Urheimat Neighbourhood, of course.

Once a tattered collection of small neighbourhoods nestled among larger urban centres, the Calbraith area had become a veritable District in their own right in recent years. Yet, the Urheimat saw its spread abruptly halted by the sudden tightening of Anwar's grip. The vulnerable lower and middle class communities, that had sought refuge and guidance in the Emperor's grasp, were very quickly impoverished, flooded with drugs and squeezed up by the ursai into oblivion, forcing many to either adapt to their new reality or move into the main Urheimat neighbourhood of Calbraith Town, at the base of the imperial Pier on the Shangri Darkside (now known as *Symp Central* by the ursai).

Of course, Mira had to get involved in.

Once her services were no longer needed putting down corner thugs and biker gangs, she switched the focus of her operations into massive money laundering operations which delivered drugs and uncensored literature into the Urheimat neighbourhood in exchange for imperial trade credits. It was all a resounding success, as her operations usually were, until, one night, as she smoked a joint behind her steering wheel, trailing a truck full of heroin, listening to Travis Scott, her car was hit by a rocket propelled grenade.

The missile did little to damage her inconspicuously armoured Terran vehicle, though it did manage to throw her off the road into a nearby building. She got out and began returning fire, just as her assailants revealed themselves to be humans. *Unaltered humans*. Symps, no doubt. She and her Shangrian gang engaged in a gunbattle that had not been seen in the City of Shangri in centuries, at the end of which, thirty-eight imperials lay dead around the destroyed heroin shipment, together with six of Mira's own men.

After dealing with the Constables and getting her surviving four gang members into hiding, pending their eventual escape off-world, Mira had the nerve to simply go back to her room in the Convent Garden Embassy (without filling in her report first), shower, climb up into bed, summon Lorgar to her side, then sleep until the next morning.

'*Fucking what?*' Laur asked in next day's morning meeting.

'You want me to repeat myself?' Mira replied dryly. '*They* fired first. I was well within my–'

'How long was the fight?' he interrupted.

'About two-three minutes.'

'Thirty-eight dead in two... *Wait*! How do you know they were thirty-eight dead on their side?'

'The Constables told me,' she explained.

'*WHAT!?!1??*' Laur roared. Silvia, Nick, Tech, Basenji, Cosmin, Radu and Ela were all used to his outburst at this point, and so was Mira. Spideraven, however, was still getting used to it and let out a startled *ca-caw!!!*

'It's all taken care off!' Mira raised a calming hand towards her commanding officer. 'The Constable in charge was a friend of Anwar's. The whole thing was taken care of. No reporters, no press, no news; at least not until they finished the clean-up! They collected the casings and impounded the vehicles. They didn't even file a report! I used my own funds to pay for the cover up! *It's fine!*'

'It's not fucking fine, Mira!' Laur said, as he massaged his annoyed forehead. 'They *ambushed* you, which means that they either had you under surveillance or you had a *rat*–' Laur stumbled, as he corrected himself '– a *mole* in your operation.

Mira gave him an angry look the impudence of which took Laur by surprise. 'If you are suggesting any of my men where traitors –'

'– THEY'RE NOT *YOUR* MEN, MIRA!' Laur banged his desk. 'They're *criminals* we recruited from this world! How many did you say survived?' Laur started thinking rapidly, as he locked eyes with the young Arabian Captain.

'Four,' Mira almost gagged as she spoke.

Discomfort. Sadness. Regret. Probably one of those. She feels responsible for each man she lost. God! She really is their child... 'What races?'

Mira took a deep breath. 'Two humans, one murine and one chimp.'

Laur nodded. 'Where are they?'

Her eyes twitched.

She knows what I am asking. Good! But, don't you dare-

'I promised them safe passage to Republican space–'

'You did fucking *what*?' Laur groaned as he grabbed his hair in frustration.

Mira continued. ' I know it's a lot, but I can get them out immediately if you signed a political refugee–'

'*Arrrrhhhhh...*' Laur groaned more loudly this time. 'Mira...' he muttered. 'Where are they?' he repeated.

Mira held his gaze for a while, before her eyes went towards Silvia, who tried to be impartial.

'Safehouse down in Dondarrion,' Nick replied, drawing a furious glare from Mira. 'What? You think you're the only with sources?' he said to her, before turning back to Laur. 'My guy there told me about it this morning. Shoem's fetching the murine as we speak.'

'Shoem?' Laur asked. *Why is he involved?... You motherfucking gip-*

'Yeah, Shoem, *boss*! We can get rid of the other three, but I don't think we can get rid of the rat guy. Shoem would probably find out and he wouldn't take kindly to it.'

'*Probably*?' Laur hated hearing that word.

Nick raised his shoulders in a display of honesty. 'We don't know what he *can* and *can't* find out! We can't just disappear one of his people, *boss*! It might fuck up the relationship!' Nick always called him 'boss' a lot when he was trying to talk him into something.

'And now Shoem knows that this rat guy in Mira's crew needs to be picked up and that, hence, he's alive,' Laur surmised. 'And, once he is picked up from the safehouse, Shoem will also know that three more members of Mira's crew survived, alive and well, within that safehouse?'

Nick shifted uncomfortably, 'I guess you could –'

'I guess you could *suck my dick*!' Laur snapped. 'I guess you're going to say that we can't get rid of the two humans and the chimpanzee person, now that Shoem knows about them?' he turned to Tech, who had been rather quiet throughout the whole thing. 'Because it would look bad if we were to liquidate loyal allies...' Laur's words drifted off as he realized that the remani had been looking at the muted TV in the corner of his office.

Laur turned the volume up.

'... Over fifty casualties, left in the aftermath of the most recent escalation in violence within the city,' the female reporter explained, whilst standing in front of street laden with bulletholes and the signs of explosions and bloodstains. 'I'm standing here with Mr. Glandarius Jenner owner of Aurora Press and a civil rights leader of the local community!' she turned towards Jenner, whose face was a clear show of empathy and virtuous revolt. 'Hello, Mr. Jenner! What is your take on this most recent development in the ongoing War on Crime?'

'Well, that's just it, Sally, this is no longer a War on Crime! I grew up on Halifax Road, just up the road up off Darbyshire in South Bambridge, just half-a-dozen bus stops from here! I know that, because this is where my bus would pass by until the next junction up Cretenham Road, where it would bring me to my school at West Gingpoor Secondary School. This was always a troubled area: low-income housing, soup kitchens and such like. But, there was no automatic gunfire, no car bombs, no rocket-propelled grenades! What we see here today is not the War on Crime in action! What we see here today is a literal war, a war which the Constabulary seems to be currently unable to fight!' Jenner pretended to be distraught. 'This was not a gunfight between the police and organized crime! This was a conflict between insurgent elements present within our city and self-organized communities of concerned citizens that have come to fill the void left by the Constabulary's absence in areas of our City which need it most!'

'The Constabulary reports say that this was gang violence between rival factions vying for control of the drug trade in this area!'

'Ah, yes, *drugs*! Another recent development which never existed in our City when I was young! It *is* drugs, Sally! Drugs being brought in by foreign states into our city, seeking to destabilize our communities and to pervert our spirit!' Jenner turned around to point at a pitch black section of the road. '*That* is where the Constabulary removed a truck loaded with twenty tons of heroin! Brought into our City through our open borders! Were trucks carrying twenty tons of heroin around the city a common occurrence in your youth, Sally?'

The reporter seemed a bit taken aback. 'I can't say that I know the answer to that –'

'Well, I do! It wasn't! Heroin trucks were not common! Automatic gunfire was not common! Having drugs available at every street corner and next to every school was not common! Violent murders in our streets were not a common occurrence! The Constabulary being ineffectual, was not a common occurrence! And things just escalate! Today it's fifty dead! Tomorrow, how many? How much longer must this trend go on until authorities get involved and do their job?'

'The Constabulary has already announced that it is looking for the–'

'– *announced*! Sally, that's all they do nowadays! *Announcements*! Where are they when they are actually needed! There are neighbourhoods within this city where the Constabulary doesn't even enter, they're so crime infested! That's the situation we're in! Our city is being subversively taken away from us and destabilized by foreign agents, and the Constabulary makes inquiries and announcements!'

'Mr. Jenner, the Constabulary also doesn't enter this neighbourhood normally, on account of the existence of the self-defence leagues you mentioned earlier...'

Jenner began shaking his head.

Sally the reporter continued. '... which are funded and organized by the Urheimat, to patrol these neighbourhoods and enforce imperial law...'

'I see you're an expert on foreign policy and jurisprudence, now, Sally! I didn't know they teach that in journalism school!'

'Mr. Jenner, you went to journalism school!' Sally pointed out

'Yes! I know, that's why I know what they teach there!'

'Then, how can *you* comment on jurisprudence and foreign relations?

'Alright!' Laur interjected. 'That's enough!' he muted the TV, though he did keep on glancing at it from time to time, as he pondered his next thoughts. '*One* of you two human guys snitched, Mira!'

Mira would've said something, but he interrupted her. 'At *best*! At worst, someone on your team was negligent!' He mulled things over for a while longer. 'Shoem will hide your murine, but those other three, I want their heads scanned and then their memories of the last six months wiped!'

'That's not fair!' Mira muttered through her visibly furious visage.

Fuck this! Laur finally snapped properly as he got up in a rage. '*Fair*! Fair! *Fuck* fair! Things sometimes can't be fucking fair! And you should be fucking grateful that this bozo...' he said, pointing at Nick. '... decided to take some fucking executive initiative on your behalf! Because, if it were up to me, I'd have the chimp and the rat in the basement right now with no fingernails and with hot spikes up their asses! Don't even get me started on the other two!'

'They're *loyal*!' Mira countered.

Laur slapped his head in frustration.

Mira continued. 'The warehouse was *in* Urheimat territory, they must have been watching us–'

Laur interrupted her with a long exhale. 'Jesus fucking Christ, Mira! You don't fucking get it!' he said, as he sat down and lit up a cigarette. 'Do you think I'd let you run around and channel you inner Al Capone, if I wasn't 100% sure you're up to the task?'

Laur saw Silvia's interest in the conversation suddenly shift for silent support of clemency to bare curiosity.

He went on. 'You did a got job! Congratulations! And, you're *alive*! You helped push our control of the streets! Up until this point, where we've got the Urheimat effectively under siege! Now is the moment we shift our focus on consolidating Anwar's domains. We let Lejla take over things with Kroton and the Harbourmasters. We let Gigi keep on training Shangrians by day and hunting stray Urheimat thugs at night. *We*, together with Josip and Bojana, now focus on consolidation! Your little stint as President of Murder Inc. Is over! Now, we focus your talents elsewhere *and* we *clean up*!'

Now Mira was figuring it out. 'You... you *knew* this would happen! You knew the Urheimat would eventually take matters into their own hands and come after me! You're not certain that they weren't watching us! You're not even certain that my men snitched, you just want any potential *problem* to go away so that you can move on!'

'I also knew they would have to go after you with their Shangrian cultists, not their own men. I also knew that you would survive–'

'FUCK YOU!!!' Now Mira jumped up.

'Hey! HEY!' Nick shouted, as Basenji grabbed Mira's elbow. 'Easy! EASY!'

Mira didn't care. 'NO! FUCK THAT! You know what?' she asked Laur, her voice harsh, yet her eyes teary. 'I also fucking knew I'd survive! Yeah! *There*! I said it! Everyone here knew I'd live through something like that! *I* knew! I *also* don't like gambling and I *knew* I'd live! I also knew there was a big chance that one day something like this would happen and, yes, I even thought that *you* might be waiting for something just like this to happen! But, to have you say it so proudly and so calmly, as your fucking plan just keeps on coming together... at *our*...' she pointed around the room. '... *expense*! While we go –'

'Have we lost anyone?' Laur asked.

'*I* lost nineteen good men who wanted a better–'

'*No*, Mira!' Laur interrupted her again. 'Have *we* lost anyone?' he repeated.

Mira caught his meaning. 'No! There was never even a possibility that we would! Is that what you want to hear? That you're justified in all of this?'

'Do you feel like you can't do this anymore?' Laur responded with a question.

Mira was quiet for a moment as she glared at him, her eyes burning and her pupils wide and fiery. *Just like her father's.*

'Mira, there is *us* and there is *them* and between *us* and *them* there are many *others*! Did these four work for us? Yes. Where they loyal? Probably so. Does it matter? No! We have no real way of being 100% certain!'

'Scan their memories!' she interrupted his dialogue with himself.

'If the Urheimat knew they would attack you last night, they would have wiped their informant's memory before going in!' he explained. 'And you know all of this!'

'Don't punish them for being loyal!' Mira commanded, impudently, like she always did.

'I'm not! I'm just wiping their memories for six months! We'll drop them off with Anwar and he'll get them some job sweeping a roof somewhere until things cool off!'

'The chimp couldn't have snitched. He's an inhuman! They don't work with –' Mira tried to reason.

'*–This isn't a fucking negotiation!*' Laur snapped.

Mira's face twitched, yet she remained silent.

Laur sighed in frustration. 'Fuck it!' he turned to Tech. 'Can we get transit papers for the chimp?'

'Yes,' Tech responded immediately.

'Fuck it! Fine! I don't really give a shit! Get the chimp a passport and a ticket to Thule or wherever the fuck in Triangulum!' Laur slapped the table. 'The other two are getting mindwiped ASAP!' he pointed towards Cosmin, who nodded, before turning back to Mira. 'Did *you* run from the attack when it happened?'

Mira glared and her mouth twitched.

Laur didn't even need to hear the answer. 'You didn't. You went straight for them and killed them all?'

'Yes,' she growled.

'You didn't let your men fight them alone. That's a noble thing to do! You fought for them! You–

'*I'm fucking done!*' Mira barged out of Laur's office.

'You're not dismissed!' he shouted after her.

'So fucking court martial me!' she shouted as she shut the door behind her.

'Boss, what the fuck is wrong with you?' Nick asked, once they heard her slam the door to her and Silvia's apartment.

'What the fuck is wrong with *me*? What the fuck is it with all of you today?' Laur barked.

'Boss...' Nick shook his head.

'*What?*' Laur asked angrily.

'I know you're upset she offered them asylum,' Nick explained correctly. 'But, was all of *that*,' he gestured around the scene that had just unfolded. 'Was all of that necessary? She just wanted to keep her promise!'

Laur snapped. 'And *I* wanted to fuck Sydney Sweeney but, believe me, that ship has sailed and so has hers!' He leaned back and rubbed his eyes.

'You knowingly put her in danger?' Silvia's voice rang out.

As Laur withdrew his hand from his eyes, he caught a glimpse of Basenji looking at him. *Now there! There's some real rage!*

I'll deal with that later! It's been a long time coming!

He turned to face Silvia. 'I knowingly put *all* of us in danger! It's basically how *we* make a living!'

Tech chimed in. 'Mira is, indeed, more than capable of taking care of herself, but there are always unforeseen variables, Laur! She was alone, bar only the, quote, *criminals* she recruited to aid her!'

'If she didn't want to be in danger, she should've stayed on Terra!' Laur pointed out.

'But, she didn't...' Silvia remarked.

'Exactly! She *wanted* to come!' Laur pointed out.

'... and you agreed to it...' Silvia continued.

Fuck... Not this shit...

'You could've said 'no'!' Silvia rammed her point home.

Laur loudly exhaled and slumped in his chair. 'You ready for a sermon?' he asked, as he looked towards Spiderraven.

'Preach, father!' Nick urged dispassionately.

'You can't control people! It's an illusion! You can't predict or manipulate anyone into doing *exactly* as you wish!' He turned to face Silvia directly. 'If I would've denied Mira's request to join us on our mission here, she would've found some other equally dangerous task to embark on.' He now turned to face Basenji, his furious glare still fixated upon him. 'Those of us who know her best, now exactly what I am talking about.'

'We do,' Tech agreed, though Laur did catch a dark menace to his tone, uncharacteristic of him. He also took note of Basenji slowly nodding. *Begrudgingly. Good...*

'I don't know what your impression of me is, after all these years,' he said, turning back to Silvia. 'But, I do care about certain people in my life!' he said honestly, as he held her gaze for just as much as was needed. 'In all frankness, I was relieved when she asked to come along,' he lied. 'At least, that way, I got to, at least, have some control over the trouble she would be getting herself involved in! *But*!'

'No one here gets a free ride! We're not a charity here! We're not some centre for troubled youths and distraught orphans who've been through more than they could handle. We are here to do a job! Mira, despite what you may suspect, is, in my opinion, a valuable member of our team or, at least, she can be, if she is kept in a position in which her skills can shine! In such an environment, any danger is minimized. No one can hurt her. *She* can't hurt herself.'

'Charles Xavier over here!' Nick commented.

'Suck my dick, Nick!' He pointed at the TV screen, still reporting on Mira's gunfight. '*This thing* marks the end of our campaign for territorial expansion. We now focus on the next phase,' Laur turned his focus towards Silvia. 'It's your turn to be a mafia boss and Mira is going to be your underboss!' He gestured towards Basenji, now slightly more relaxed. '*There's* your consigliere!'

'We consolidate?' Nick asked, now suddenly much more approvingly.

'We consolidate,' Laur confirmed.

Laur spent the rest of the day in individual meetings with his Centurions and some of the more senior Optios, planning the next steps in this new phase of their mission.

'Hear me out!' Optio Casandra Drăgănescu began.

Laur leaned back. 'Okay!'

Casandra took in a deep breath. '*Jeffrey Epstein*!' she announced.

Laur understood immediately. 'Fuck, no!' he slumped in his chair in disgust. *Actually... fuck it!* 'How young?'

'The legal age of consent here is sixteen, which means that all we need is fifteen–'

'*Ughhh*, Jesus Christ! NO!' Laur moaned. 'Mr. Fox and Bojana are doing the whole honeypot thing with the sex parties and everything–'

'But, they're not doing the Jeffrey Epstein thing!' Casandra explained.

'Good for fucking them, then!'

'*Hear me out*!' Casandra insisted. 'We can forge transit papers and university visas for Republican citizens looking to travel to Shangri to study! We can have the Aesir or the Vanir issue modified IDs with the date of birth changed!'

Laur kind off understood where she was going.

'We hire call girls from Asgard. We get the government to change their IDs from their real age (which can be twenty, or twenty-two or whatever) to *fifteen*! We even get them fake parents or guardians to vouch for them to travel to Shangri on a student visa, registering them as fifteen! We ship them over to Hyperborea (which is on the way) and they change their *biological* age to fifteen as well! Then, we bring them here and we forge them *another* set of papers, with their *real* age! And *then* we put them to work! We film everything! Then, we confront the johns, show them the fake Shangrian IDs and the modified original IDs, and blackmail them!'

Laur looked at her for a moment as he inputted all the information.

'Fine!' he agreed, disgusted. 'But work under Bojana! And kick up to her!'

Twenty minutes later, Radu and Cosmin where in his office.

'Porn's illegal here!' Radu informed him in his deadpan tone.

'What a tragedy...' Laur commented dryly.

'Me and Radu were thinking about shooting porn,' Radu explained.

He looked from one Centurion to the other. '*Together?*' he asked.

'*What?*' The two looked at each other. Radu caught on '*No!* We want to start filming porn and selling it on the black market!'

Laur scratched his head. *What is wrong with these people and sex?* 'You don't need to film anything! Basenji has a hard-drive with all the porn ever uploaded to the old internet, even Onlyfans! He always has it with him! I don't think he needs the porn right now, so you can borrow it, make copies and then select individual... *What?*'

The two were looking at him as if he was some sick pervert.

'Boss...' Radu began. 'All those women are dead!' he explained.

'Most of them, yes... the ones that aren't... respect their privacy!' he ordered.

'Yeah, no, sir... it's the dead ones that are the problem!' his Centurion explained. 'I mean... could *you* jack off to a lady that you knew was dead?'

Laur leaned back and propped himself up on one arm which gripped his seat. He took a deep breath as his eyes widened. '... Nah, I couldn't jack off to a lady that I knew was dead...' His eyes narrowed. 'But, the buyers don't have to know that they're watching dead people fuck! Just market it as being people who are *still alive* and fucking!'

'Sir...' Radu started. 'I mean... those ladies... they were *real* people! Don't you think we should respect them? They were born on Earth, just like us!'

Cosmin nodded in agreement.

Laur sighed and looked at the two men. 'You two are really gay!' He took a deep breath again, as his two recent promotions disappointed him.

Radu saw his opportunity. 'It would help us improve income to low-income communities! I mean, we would obviously pay–'

'Sure! Fuck it! *Do it*! But coordinate with Bojana and kick up to her! I don't...' he scratched his head angrily. 'I just wish someone would come into this office and come up with a racket more complex than P.Diddy and Pornhub! What the fuck?'

Radu looked stunned. 'P.Diddy? Nah, boss, I'm just talking about Ron Jeremy shit!'

'Yeah!' Cosmin began. 'DJ Yella!'

Radu continue. 'We were thinking about starting a tequila brand (or schnapps) after–'

'Jesus fucking Christ! That's not what I meant!' Laur massaged his temples. 'I mean fucking wire fraud, or mail fraud, or tax fraud! Or embezzlement! Or credit card scams! Maybe pointshaving or some other shit like that!'

Radu and Cosmin exchanged glances. They appeared to be considering sharing something with him.

'Ok! *That*! Give it to me! Tell me!' Laur urged them.

'Well...' Radu leaned in conspiratorially. 'We could do an EU funding scam...'

'EU funding?' Laur asked perplexed. 'There's no EU *here*! There isn't even an EU on Terra!'

'Yeah! Boss, I know! Hear me out!' Radu began. 'So, here's what we do:'

'We set up a non-governmental organization (NGO) and register with the Shangri Department for Housing and Urban Development. We'll write it up under the name of some gambling addicts or whomever we get from Anwar and we initially finance it with clean money from Anwar's businesses as a tax break. The NGO then applies for Shangri Development Funds, which are grants by the government and which work (kind-of) like EU funds! We then buy up housing in low-income neighbourhoods. We can pay cash and we can pay quickly and quietly. No negotiations beyond the set market price! We buy these properties through friends of ours in Anwar's organization – not through the NGO! We then get an appraiser to raise the market price of each property as much as possible. Then, the NGO comes in and offers to buy these low-income properties, so that it can refurbish them, and provide affordable housing to low-income families, with the use of Shangri Development Funds – which is exactly what those funds are for! In that moment, we have essentially transferred the Shangri Development Funds from the government to the NGO to the sellers, which are all friends of ours! We use the funds to buy up as many properties as we can, until we file insolvency and close up the NGO!'

'Shangri law let's you do that!' Cosmin filed in. 'You can dissolve a company or an NGO whenever you want and for whatever reason.'

'And, then, we do it all again with another, new NGO!' Radu explained.

'Huh...' Laur starred of into the empty distance for a while, struggling to remember something. He looked up. 'Have you two been watching *The Sopranos*?'

Their faces were taken by surprise and very guilty.

'Well...' Laur tapped his armrest as he nodded. 'That's better! I'm glad you've been studying, regardless of the source! *That* is more like what I'm talking about! Check with Anwar if they have appraisers on their payroll! If they don't, talk with Casandra about setting up a honeypot with Bojana! Split the profits 30/30/30/10. 30% to the buyers and the NGO people, 30% to Anwar, 30% to us and 10% to whoever comes up with the appraiser!' he decreed.

Then came Ela.

'I wanna get *pumped* and the I wanna take a *dump*!' she explained.

'*Oh but for fuck's sake!*' Laur slapped his desk and gripped his forehead.

'What?' Ela asked, startled by her General's sudden outburst.

'What is it with everyone and weird sex shit around here? Like, is it the fact that the city's crowded? There's too many people and they give off too many pheromones?' Laur was genuinely at a loss.

'Laur...' Ela began. 'What does that have to do with *trading*?'

'I don't fucking know... I think it's because of the racism or the elitism or maybe the fucking desensitization to violence or the fucking...' Laur saw that Ela, once a practicing ophthalmologist of Old Earth, had no idea what the fuck he was talking about. 'What do you want to do, exactly?' he asked, suspecting that, perhaps, he had misunderstood.

Elia pulled out a screen and a holographic projector. She placed the screen in front of him and tapped it, and a number of graphs appeared, just as a PowerPoint presentation was projected in the air between him and Ela. The opening slide read *Operation Caritas* and featured a lovely Terran font, as well as the seal of the Hajduks. 'Shangri has several exchanges operating beneath the primary energy market, as well as the secondary equity, commodity and forex markets, from which all of the many derivatives and securities–'

'*PUMP-AND-DUMP!!!*' Laur exclaimed.

'What?' Ela asked, surprised by the interruption.

'You want to do a *pump-and-dump* scheme! Not that you '*wanna get pumped and take a dump*'!'

'Oh!' Ela seemed a bit befuddled for a moment. '*Sorry...* English idioms are very strange. In Romanian they're so much more–'

'*Elia*! Ela! Fuck it! Never mind!' Laur pointed at the holographic PowerPoint slides. 'I appreciate the effort, but I know what a pump-and-dump scheme is! And, honestly, congratulations! That's exactly the kind of thing we should be doing! But, it's a complicated endeavour and we need to be careful with it! The Shangrian SEC is very, *very* protective of the equities market and these *quantitative easing* policies come with extra scrutiny from regulators! I mean... there are also tens of thousands of companies listed–'

'118 497, as of this morning!' Ela provided the exact numbers, before flicking a button on her phone and rushing through several slides. 'It's here on page 7: Market Overview. I've prepared several analysis based on historical performance per sector over the last five years – I included a CAGR, over there,' She used a laser pointer and its beam pierced through the holographic image, causing a red dot to appear on Laur's ceiling.

Spideraven took note and began following the dot.

'I've also performed an initial TAM/SAM/SOM analysis of the potential pool of investors, identifying–'

'Elia!' Laur interrupted her. 'Feasibility studies and white papers (such as *these*) are brilliant places to start! But, all of this is irrelevant in the absence of actual *companies* which match our criteria!' *And finding those might take months!*

'Oh, yes!' she remembered and pressed a button on her screen as she mumbled. '*...slide forty-seven...*' A list of companies, as well as their dynamic stock and securities price popped up on the projection. "I've shortlisted twenty, though I was planning to start with an initial five, before progressing through the list..."

Laur remained quiet as Ela went through the list, explaining points of entry to management, marketing strategy, potential investors, market trends, historical precedents, regulation, tax implications... *Ok... this is boring... but 'boring' is good... this flavour of boring is good!!!*

'Elia! Ela! Stop!'

She obliged.

Laur rubbed his fingertips together. 'How much money do you need?'

Ela's face lit up. 'Twenty million Asgardian guilders as seed investment, with ROI of 2300% percent over three months.'

Laur did the math in his head and nodded slowly. 'Figure out the financing with Silvia. Can you handle this with your men?'

'I only need ten,' Ela had already sorted out human resources. 'The rest can work on other projects.

'Approved.'

Nick came in next.

He came in. He placed a strange device on Laur's desk. Then he opened a burlap bag he had brought with him and dumped its context into the sink on top of the strange device. Shangri spheres, in the form of ceramic coins, rustled as it settled into a neat pile. He then pressed a button and the machine animated itself into action, sorting out the coins and causing the pile the shrink, as coins fell in like coffee beans into a blender. The machine arranged the coins into neat little stacks and wrapped them in cling film, as it also counted them.

Laur couldn't help but smile as Nick sat down in his usual seat.

'Doesn't Anwar bother to stack them himself?'

Nick shook his head. 'That's not from Anwar.'

'Oh... Shoem?' Laur asked, puzzled.

'No. That's all *me*!' he said, pointing at the growing stacks of coins.

Laur nodded. 'Well, nice to see you're ahead of the curve, but (just so you know) you need to scale up operations!' Laur noted, as the machine reached the halfway point and read '200 000 SC'.

'I do,' Nick agreed.

'Good,' he pointed towards the stacks. 'You can reinvest your earnings into the operations for the first month! That was the deal. No need to kick-up until then!' *God! I love that he's proactive, but I'd wish he could just pay attention!*

'It's been thirty-two days,' Nick said, as if that made sense.

Laur raised an eyebrow, understanding dawning on him. 'You've been... *That* is the proceeds from the last two days?' he asked, pointing at the stacks once more.

'No! That's my *kick-up* from the last two days! That's your 10%! The other 90% is out on the streets working!'

Laur stared at him. 'Is it clean?' he asked.

'Picked it up from the casino last night!' he explained.

Laur looked at him, nodding softly, a smile slowly spreading across his face.

Mirroring a grin that spread across Nick's own broad lips. 'Ever since I could remember, I've always wanted to be a gangster!'

Nick had it all figured out. *No need to check in with him anymore.*

His last meeting was with Silvia.

'Elections are coming!' he began. 'Bojana is going to handle election support, but we're going to have to funnel funding into the candidates we want to see elected. It'll be an enormous strain on our finances, but it's what all of this has been working up towards! There is a list of candidates going around, which will include their campaign's bank accounts. Set up a live communication channel with Bojana to coordinate, but keep it at maximum discretion! Don't use any kind of messaging, especially not letters!' Laur thought about it for a moment. 'Use the racetrack! It's where she spends most of her free time, from what I hear: in her VIP lounge! Organize the drop-offs there; both for the accounting logs and the occasional drop-off of cash!'

'Who's on the list?' Silvia asked.

'At this point, we're going to be bankrolling every non-human running for the Senate,' Laur paused for a moment. 'Anwar's on the list. So is Shoem.'

Silvia raised an eyebrow. 'How did you convince him?'

'I didn't. He'll just have to go along with it. I know he likes being discrete. But, he's beginning to attract attention in his current position. Soon, he won't be safeguarded by his relative anonymity once it withers away. When that happens, I want him somewhere safe and there's nowhere safer than the Senate. As a legislator, he'll have us, the Constabulary, the Royal Guards, the ursai and his own organization invested in his safety. Ironically, sometimes the best place to hide is out in the open, where everyone could just mistake you for just another public figurine!'

'I see,' Silvia said, then paused.

What? Laur didn't even have to ask out loud.

'What should I do with Mira?' she asked.

'The same as you've always done ever since we got here: keep an eye on here!'

'I would, just that every time I blink, she's gone,' Silvia answered truthfully.

'Well... then I guess don't blink!'

'Can I ask a question?' Silvia asked.

'It would really change the tune of this conversation if you did...' Laur replied sarcastically.

'Are you setting her up to fail?'

Laur leaned back in his seat and carefully studied her. 'You're going have to be a bit more specific.'

'Ever since we've come here, it's been the same cycle: you tell me to keep an eye on her, but also let her do her own thing. Her doing her own thing results in her going off on her own and doing something wild. Then you get annoyed when she does something wild. Then you argue with her and you let her win the argument (in some way, shape or form)... and then you castigate *me* for not keeping an eye on her!'

Laur sighed. *Well... I knew she'd notice... eventually...* 'Silvia, do you remember Alex Demetrian?'

A look of surprise flashed across Silvia's face. 'The *Terminator*?' she asked, stifling an awkward smile and raising her shoulders, as she turned her face to the side slightly.

'Yeah... Your time with us must have overlapped with his a little?'

Silvia nodded slowly. 'He left for the Old Guard after I joined. We were colleagues for less than six months,' she recalled.

'Yeah... a couple of months after Hellsbreach...' Laur stopped to remember the exact timeframe and certain memories flashed across his eyes. Some far more painful than others. 'You know he punched me in the face once?'

Silvia grew oddly pensive as she nodded slowly. 'Yes... It happened just before we joined.' Silvia struggled to hold in a smile, though her eyes betrayed her. 'It was all everyone ever talked about for months.'

Laur reached for his cigarette pack. 'I forget what it was for...' Laur genuinely tried to remember. 'Must have been something particularly fucked-up I said... Anyway, do you remember how he was like?'

'Well, he's still alive! We meet every now and then when there's business with the Old Guards. He's very kind. We even fought together again in Andromeda! He's...' Silvia sought words for something they both knew already too well.

'He *is* the Terminator!' Laur continued for her. 'It's a well earned nickname! The only Romanian which the dushman found entertaining enough to bring back from the dead...' Laur glanced towards an elven painting that hung on one of his office walls. 'Top 20 Terran fighters of all time. Easily! I remember, once, during the War of Vengeance, we boarded an elven vessel – but we boarded it badly! Me, him, Tapalagă and Tigaie accidentally ended up in the middle of the ship's armoury, with a hundred Svart armed to teeth and all around us!' Laur shrugged as he took a toke of his cigarette. 'We three almost shat ourselves and tried to hunker down near our entry point, waiting for back-up and trying to crawl our way through the hole we had blasted in through, even though it had almost sealed up already...'

Laur started to nod as he remembered the image or, rather, the sequence of images in his head. 'Alex just... *methodically* went about killing all of them! I... Me and Tapalagă were just looking at him and I remember... I remember hearing music... *The Box!*... *Roddy Ricch!* It was a rap song! I started hearing it in my ears as I watched Alex go nuts!'

'*You* can fight!' he said, pointing at her. 'Nick can fight! All our men in this building can fight! Hell, *I* can fight! But not like that! Even after all the jamba juice, the training montages and the fucking bones and the fucking armour... *Gigi* can fight like that... sometimes... when he's in the mood!'

'*But*!' Laur raised his finger. 'Some people just have this... this *thing*! Alex has it. All of the Old Guards have it! Tomasz Ashaver has the most of it! Then there's Braca and a lot of orcs and others...' *It's a long list, actually.* 'Djibril had it and, though it is not something genetic, Mira has it! Don't be fooled by that thing that happened in Ratden!' Laur lectured Silvia with his index finger. 'When she lost her hand and she got pinned under that column?' He made sure that Silvia understood exactly what he meant.

Silvia nodded.

'*That*! That is the undoing of people like her, like Alex, like Tomasz and all the rest! *Cockiness*! They get too comfortable with all the bloodshed, they know they'll survive and they get overconfident! It's what happened to Mira then and it's what happened to Mira yesterday! She got cocky and took risks and... by virtue of what can only be described as *plot armour*, she's alive!'

'You're comparing apples and oranges!' Silvia, remarkably, intervened. 'It wasn't plot armour! Nick's constable said that the guys that attacked her were basically firing 9mm rounds at her! I saw her clothes from last night: the bullets didn't even singe them! One of them was still in her coat pocket! She didn't even have bruises from the shots she took!'

Laur saw Silvia begin to nod to herself, as she both spoke and understood how it all came together.

Silvia smiled bitterly. 'You tried to teach her a lesson! You put her in a situation where her nature would push her to be reckless and you waited for that recklessness to cost her the lives of those around her...'

Laur looked blankly into the distance. 'Our actions have consequences. Plans fall apart and, the more rigid they are, the harder they come tumbling down. Control...' he smirked.

'*Control is an illusion*!' Laur sighed. 'Mira has the potential within her to become someone truly great. She...' Laur struggled to discern where Mira ended and her potential began. '... she has flaws! We all do! Flaws grow deeper and they become permanent, the more you leave them unattended. Small things, that can grow quietly in the shadows of the self, can cripple otherwise great potential. Sometimes, it's better to expose them, when they're still small, and to poke them, so that you can feel pain!' Laur gestured, as if he was prodding the timbers of a campfire with a stick. 'Once you feel that pain, you learn your lesson and you don't make those mistakes again! You become *aware* of your flaws!'

Silvia nodded slowly. 'She could've still been killed!'

Laur exhaled. 'Lurking inside the Urheimat's Pier are likely hundreds of Sadukar, perhaps even a few Tarks, from what we can tell! If they went after *any of us*, we would be in true mortal danger, yes! But, then again, even though Mira is reckless, she is not stupid! And neither are *they*! They know what would happen if a squad of Sadukar was caught in the open, assaulting a diplomatic envoy! The political consequences would be catastrophic! Their efforts here in Shangri would be crippled beyond repair!'

'They had RPGs!' Silvia insisted. 'What would've happened if she would have been hit in the head by one of those?' she pressed. 'Maybe if a building collapsed on top of her as she was bleeding and the rubble crushed her head open?'

'The same thing that would've happened to any of us!' Laur sighed. 'Life is dangerous, Silvia! *Our* lives, in particular, are dangerous,' he mumbled.

He chuckled to himself. 'You'll be working directly with her now! Literally on the same objectives! I once told you to learn from her and her high-risk, high-reward approach to things. Now, I tell you this, if you truly care for her, let her watch and learn from you! You're a protector, Silvia!'

He saw her quiver almost imperceptibly.

Good! 'Show her what she has to become if she wants to protect the ones she cares for!'

They switched to talking about actual operations after that. By the time they were done, Laur realized it was already eleven in the evening and that he should try to go to bed early (for once). He knew Basenji was upstairs already, so he got up and locked the door to his office, before climbing up the stairs to the small living room he shared with Basenji. He found the remani by the fireplace, in his favourite chair, with a book in his hand and a warm cup of tea next to him.

Ah... yes... I can get that over with too... He walked over to an old-school Terran refrigerator they shared and pulled out his favourite brand of chocolate milk.

'You're *cuffing*, aren't you?' he launched the topic, without turning to see his reaction. 'That's how they call it?' Laur knew that was exactly how they called it. 'Remani *rutting*? *Estrous*? *Heat*?'

He turned around to see Basenji refuse to look up from his book.

Knew it! 'I could tell! It's the way you sit!' he explained. 'Up until two weeks ago, you always sat cross-legged, with your legs close together at all times, like a woman, like you usually do! Then, you started sitting cross-legged like a man, up until the point where Tech would notice! He would give you a look and then you would close them together again! That's what I noticed first! Then, I noticed you would wander off away from the embassy with no reason. At first, I thought you were out helping Mira out on her spirit quest, but then I realized that, sometimes, Mira was home and you were away! You also growl a lot when you cuff; it's very subtle and fleeting, but I can hear it! You stopped growling about ten days ago – up until today, that is, but I know that today it was for a different reason! So I'm assuming ten days ago was when you, eh... *got it off your chest?*'

Basenji slapped the book closed and looked at him as if he was a clever turd with ears.

'So... who's the lucky lady?' he asked, taking a sip of his chocolate milk.

Basenji shook his head in disbelief at Laur's audacity and took a sip of his tea.

'Holy shit! She's not a remani?' Laur asked, looking for a reaction.

The teacup flinched slightly.

'Oh, boy! *Interracial*! Nice! And *difficult*!' Laur suddenly found the game much more exciting. *I love these things!*

'Not murine?' he prodded.

Basenji looked at him as if he was about to spit the tea in his mouth all over Laur's smug face.

'Ok! Ok! Too exotic! I get it! But, I'd still expect it to be exotic, since this place is so full of... a bast?' *I once saw a dog fuck a cat. What's more strange is that it was a male cat! Maybe dogmen also fuck catmen from time to time?*

Basenji snorted, likely after thinking about something similar.

'My apologies!' Laur gave it more thought. *I think I'm right about the exotic part...* 'One of those little fox people?'

Basenji ignored him. But... he ignored him in a normal way, as he would usually ignore him when he was going on about nonsense.

'Human? Orc?' *Shit... Gotta rapid-fire.* 'Goblin? Ursai? Cyborg? Elf?'

Nothing.

Laur snapped his knee. 'Have you been fucking some troglodyte in the...'

Basenji gave him a genuinely irritated look and that's when Laur saw it.

'*Mandrake?*' he asked, somewhat incredulously.

Basenji flinched.

'*Really...?*' Laur had to sit down on the armrest of one of the couches after that, such was the shock. 'You're fucking a dragon lady? *Jesus Christ*! All time I thought you were Antonio Banderas, when you where really Eddie Murphy!' *I should watch Shrek again, when I have time...*

Wait... there aren't that many mandrakes here... just a known handful... they're all registered with the Immigration Office...

HOLY FUCKING SHIT!!!

Laur's eyes widened. 'You're fucking–'

Basenji slapped his book on his armrest. Twice.

Laur got the message. 'Ok! *Fine!* You're secret's safe with me! Jesus Christ...' he mumbled to himself. *Anyway... gonna digest that later... I started this conversation for a different reason.*

'It's why you weren't with Mira, yesterday, wasn't it? You were... on a *date*... (I guess)?'

Basenji held his glare before looking away.

'Don't worry! I'm not condemning you for it! Quite frankly, I think your babysitting of her occasionally has negative effects on her personal growth! It's good for her to be out by herself on her own!' he said, sipping his chocolate and studying Basenji's reaction.

'Yet, again... it's hard... isn't it?' he asked sincerely.

Basenji's reaction was a mix of agreement and inquisitive surprise.

'I know you loved *them*! I know you love Mira!' Laur moved in close.

'I know what you did in Jerusalem before we left for Ratden.'

Basenji did not flinch. He stood unmoving in his armchair, his face low and his eyes gazing up towards Laur, who got up from his place on the armrest and took a seat right on a couch next to his, facing towards the small fireplace of their living room. The flames flickered as they splintered the wood, causing it to crackle softly in the room's silence.

'You knew immediately that Mira would want to join us on Ratden! And that she would find a way to come along! You knew that, since Tomasz and the Old Guard would certainly be going, she would likely hitch a ride with them. Now...' Laur paused as he leaned forward in his seat. 'You know Mira's perfectly capable of taking care of herself and you also know that any Old Guard, any Brightguard, any Wildrider and, hell, probably any Hajduk would give their life in defence of hers, but that wasn't enough in your eyes, wasn't it?

He leaned back in his seat and reached towards a nearby table to pick up a pack of cigarettes. 'When Tomasz decided to make the selection process a raffle and draw lots – with zero consideration for the tactical make-up of the overall assault force, mind you! – he made *you* draw the respective lots! What was it he said? *'No one here would question your honour'?*'

He paused for effect and, indeed, Basenji silently closed the book he had planned on reading. 'You *chose* the Ghazis, the Keshik and the Akali! The Ghazis, who were her father's men, his household guard, men who would've followed him to the ends of space and time, now led by a man tormented by the absence of a leader who bordered on godhood in his eyes and a man obsessed with honouring that leader's legacy in any form it may take. The Ghazis, who had been her former legion and who had seen firsthand how much of *his* flame she carried within her.'

'The Akali, her mother's kinsmen and most beloved followers. The last of the Sikhs of the *Pandavas*. Uma loves Mira like her own child. If Mira would've fallen, she would've torn her eyes out! But she wouldn't have killed herself for the simple fact that she would dread to see the sadness in Sara's eyes, if they would've crossed paths in the afterlife!'

'Manda Khan was the first person to ever rescue Mira. The Keshik were the ones to find her in that bloody car in Antarctica, weren't they?'

Laur smirked. 'And the Esho? We needed space combat specialists and for that I commend you! If Tomasz didn't give tactical considerations any thought, then at least *you* did!'

He leaned back in his seat, resting his head upon the top of the couch as he looked up at the ceiling, taking a strong toke of his cigarette, before beginning to wobble his head across the hard wooden edge, massaging the tense muscles in his neck.

'I don't blame you for any of it and I will have you know that *this* other secret of yours is safe with me! Though I doubt anyone would mind if they were to know! Quite frankly, I think most people present in that room figured it out right on the spot, just as I did, and they probably cheered silently for you!'

'Though I do wonder one thing...' Laur stopped wobbling his head across the couch's headrest and waited a moment before speaking. 'If Tomasz had not decreed that I would be joining the mission.... would've you drawn the Hajduks from that raffle bag? If our participation would've been up to chance and not a certainty?'

He raised his head to observe the remani's reaction, which came swiftly. Basenji tilted his head slowly to one side.

'I fucked up!' he said.

Another pause.

He wanted to see if Basenji would immediately understand his meaning.

The remani turned his face away from Laur and seemed to grimace slightly. *Oh, he knows what I'm talking about.*

'During Hellsbreach... when her mother died... You know what I was doing when Hellsbreach started? I was listening to music! I hadn't done that for a long time. Just.... I was just sitting in my room playing some tunes. I believe the exact song that was playing was *U Stambolu Na Bosforu*. Do you know it?'

Basenji shook his head.

'Ah, well, you're likely going to hear it during your time with us. It's quite popular among the Hajduks. It's a Bosnian song. *Sevdalinka* is the genre: women's love songs. It's about a Turkish noble that dies and the women in his harem mourn his death. One of them – the favourite one (whatever the fuck that means) – dies of a broken heart!' He stopped, looking towards Basenji, expecting a raised eyebrow or some other sign of surprise.

He saw none.

He saw only a distant gaze.

He remembers. He remembers that day. That cursed day...

'I was on the *Doina* when news came of the attack. Of all the fucking ships at our disposal, it was mine that happened to be closest to Antarctica and Lejla rushed us towards the Shield's gates. The atmosphere burned the hull and made the black turn to dark red from the heat! Still, we crashed right in front of the gates and rushed in... and... well... you know what happened. I don't need to explain.'

Basenji brought a hand to his snout and rubbed it softly.

'I think about it every time I see Mira and, she knows it, apparently! That's how she got me to bring her along... she guilt-tripped me! She's ... she's always surprised me with how perceptive she is! I often think that Sara's blood is heavier than Djibril's inside of her.'

He gazed towards the fireplace, memories of Mira's father flooding through him.

'I wanted to hate *him*.' He didn't look away to see Basenji's reaction, for he knew there would be none. 'I wanted to hate him so much. I spent *time* looking for reasons to hate him... and I found none! He was... he was truly a great man... I... I sometimes hate how Tomasz gets all the hero worship nowadays... Don't get me wrong, he's a real hero himself, what with the coming back to life, the kingship denial and his overall swashbuckling personality... but he's *childish*! He is a child's idea of a hero. That... that childish – *pure* – heroism he has is... it's loveable, yes, but Djibril was different!'

'Djibril had a... an ancient majesty about him. It was... it was mystical in a way. I couldn't explain it. I've felt it with others before him and after him, but... God... it was *strong* with him! Men stood taller around him. Eyes shined when they beheld him. Smiles were brighter. Laughter was honest.... *Heh*... I remember....'

Laur genuinely chuckled at the memory and realized that he had never told anyone the story he recalled now. *What a shame... Fuck it... fuck it... I'll tell him.*

'In Andromeda, during the war, we were camped on some world whose name I forget. It was where we planned the attack on Agrulac; *whatever*! We were in Andromeda on some world with mushrooms. *Big* mushrooms. The ones that looked like dicks? You remember?'

Basenji seemed to recall the place and nodded.

Laur began gesturing. 'A field of dicks it was! You were there. *We* were there. In a clearing! *A bald spot*! An empty patch, where we had set-up camp and we were planning with Sintilialt and his bunch and I was *furious*!' *Oh my God was I furious!*

'Furious and disappointed. The war wasn't going as I had hoped. Our gains were little. Momentum was building up, but it was too slow... I came over to the camp's edge to have a moment for myself. And I was sitting there. Brooding. Seething. And he came. Arms clasped behind him. As he always did! He walked up right behind me. He had a quiet walk, yet I felt his presence.'

'He came up right next to me and, he spoke – in that serious tone of his...'

'You think you're mother's somewhere out there?'

Basenji snout spread into a smile, but he did fight back a chuckle, which slowly came. *That glorious son-of-a-bitch... his jokes were so good, even from beyond the grave he's almost making this one break his vow of silence!*

'Basenji! I laughed!' *and, God, how I laughed!* 'I hadn't laughed like that in twenty/thirty fucking years! I mean I had laughed before, but fake. I had laughed... *politically*. But not like that! *Mirth*! In my heart!' The memory of that moment came to him and filled him with... with a feeling he kept on forgetting about...

'Years upon years of grim darkness and horror... I had forgotten so much about what it was to live! I got caught up in all the warring and the campaigning and the planning and the plotting... there were giant spiders with wings in Andromeda! There were bear people in an ice fortress in the Milky Way who had weird... *honour duels*... and very specific views on interest rates! Elves had built great shining cities beneath the crusts of a dozen worlds! They hunted carnivorous elk the size of an elephant on Pandora! Goblins who sounded like Mexicans! Orc paladins and all sorts of other crazy, wondrous things...'

'And I got... I got lost! I... I forgot what it meant to be human – no! – a *person*! I forgot what it meant to be... I forgot about that feeling you get when you're sitting in line at McDonald's and the motherfucker in front of you spent the whole time waiting in line thinking about donkeys fucking and not about what he was going to fucking order!'

'Djibril never forgot! That was his superpower! He never forgot what it meant to be a person! To hold in a fart when in good company and to fail!'

Basenji smiled at the reference.

'Yes! That! *That* thing about him... he was a man of myth and, yet, what made him great was how... how he was just a *man*!' Laur's eyes darkened.

'I met Sara after Doomsday. We were preparing the defences before the Svart counterattack. I was still... *coping* with things. One moment I'm staring down the apocalypse, the next I'm learning how to use orcish power armour! Technowolf was explaining to me how defence lasers worked by talking about... *Jim Morrison*?! It was all very... very brusque... very sudden and very strange! And then I saw her...'

*How should I describe her? Should I say she was the spitting image of Mira, but for the eyes and the nose? Should I say that she was even more otherworldly than the orcs and the elves in her beauty? Should I say that she was the first person I saw smile after Doomsday? Truly smile? Not because she had survived, but because she **lived**!*

Laur looked towards Basenji and saw his long sad stare.

There's no need. He remembers her. As do we all.

'Literally a few moments after meeting her, just as I was beginning to think that maybe... maybe I could have a second chance at life... maybe now that the apocalypse had passed and we were all in a time after history, I would have a chance to do things right. To live a good life and to be a good man.... Literally in that exact moment *he* showed up...'

'Big and bulky and with long black hair and that royal nose he passed down to Mira. His voice was... it was *molasses*! Thick and smooth and heavy with thought and ... and fucking *debonair*, yet also *serious*! As if every word was heavy with passion and meaning. I saw Sara's knees go weak and when he touched her, I saw her whole body purr and I swear to you Basenji, she *swooned*!'

The image was etched in Laur's mind and he struggled to push it away. 'I immediately hated him and I had to keep it a secret! Particularly around Khalid, Ketevan and, especially around Tomasz. Hell, Gigi and Lejla and the rest of their lot looked at him like he was some kind of warrior-king Messiah... *Mahdi*, as some called him! I had to keep my dislike for him hidden from them but, more importantly, I had to find a way to make it make sense *to me*!'

'There was nothing wrong with him! Time and time again I saw him conduct himself with honour, valour and .... and *gravitas*! He treated all those around him – regardless of origin, race or rank – with dignity and respect. I genuinely believe he loved them all, *myself* included! He was kind and he was good and... and he was gentle... He had a... *candour* about him... this beautiful transparency which just allowed you to peer into him and behold the truth!'

'And, in truth, sooner or later, we all saw in him what Sara had. We saw... we saw the greatness. We saw the strength of his character, the vigour of his spirit and the kindness of his heart. It took me longer than most to fall under his spell. It only took root in Andromeda, when it was just me and him leading our people there. You'd think we would've bonded since we were both outsiders. Two boys from Riyadh and Bucharest, caught up in a war against space samurai, surrounded by strange men in a strange universe, where the closest thing to the familiar where the faces of orcs, goblins, trolls and even the fucking elves (in all their inhuman arrogance), which now seemed to be the closest thing to normality.'

'Yet, it was only *I* that was out of place! He seemed to fit right in! This *champion* of our world seemed to be so... *fitting* among the champions of a hundred other worlds. What the hell... he *dwarfed* most of them... dare I say *all* of them!'

'That was when I saw it, Basenji! That's when I couldn't pretend to not believe myself anymore! He *was* a hero! He really was a man from myth, reborn into the Age of Reckoning, as if... as if... as if...' Laur let his words trail off.

'In his absence, I realized what worried me about him!'

'In his absence, those around him – great men and women in their own right – their.... their love for him slowly turned to worship!'

Laur got up from his seat and began pacing.

'And who could blame them? Eh?' he asked Basenji, knowing there was no need for him to reply.

'*I* would've died for him! I didn't know it when he was alive! I realized it much later, but... I swear to God, Basenji, my entire life I've lived only for myself!

'But him? But *for* him? I didn't want to love him and still I grew to love him.' He remembered another.

'*Tomasz...* Tomasz, I *like...* Djibril... *Djibril I loved!* He was the older brother I never had! He saw me for what I was and, yes, sometimes it angered him...' Laur smiled to himself. 'He did threaten to kill me a couple of times and, God, I believed him!'

'It was he who told me to go home and rest. Recuperate. Let him carry the war in Andromeda alone for a while! Live... again.'

He mimicked Djibril's voice. '*This galaxy won't burn without you. It did just fine for aeons before you came along. If anything, Laur, you're the one who's been pouring gasoline everywhere. I promise you'll be here when the spark is lit and the skies catch flame.*'

Laur walked slowly now towards the fireplace and peered into the flames. 'In the end... it was only *I* who was there to light the fire... Even in death, the man kept his word!'

'I came back to Terra, got the ship all fixed up, filed in my reports and... I found myself in my office all alone. We were to land in the Antarctic Shield, but... there was a delay... fucking Kernunos... sometimes I think he chose me to be the one closest to her since he knew I'd fail to get to her in time...'

Laur stopped himself. He didn't want to dig into that subject any further. He had done so for long enough. He had his conclusion: it had been misfortune. Kernunos had done his best to distance as many Terrans as he could from the Antarctic Shield. Laur and the Hajduks had been, by circumstance, the only Terran vessel in orbit of Terra at the time, with the rest either docked in their anchorages, on active deployment outside the solar system or undergoing maintenance on Luna or the Arctic Shield. The ones docked in the Antarctic Shield had been destroyed by Kernunos and Laur and the Hajduks had simply been closest.

It was chance.

Nothing more.

'We had an hour to kill while we waited in orbit, until they finished setting up the dock for our arrival and it occurred to me that it was the first time in decades when I had a moment to myself with nothing to do. So, I sat down in my seat, opened my computer and I found this folder I had kept. It was a copy of Spotify. I... I... I had my own little AI operator back then... *Mafalda*, I called him, and I asked him to play whatever he felt like I would enjoy from the entirety of human recorded music.'

Laur rubbed his chin as his eyes blankly remembered what his ears had enjoyed. '*Come join the murder, Ask the Lonely, Dust in the Wind, Way down we go...* all of them sad songs. But... I never liked sad songs, but this time it was different. I... *I felt something.*'

Now Basenji's ears shot up.

Yeah... I do feel things sometimes, you know... 'It occurred to me that I had never allowed myself to grieve! I had never allowed myself to be grateful that I was still alive! I had never... I had never let myself be sorry for myself and just... just *pity* myself! That's what came to me in that moment! The first moment I allowed myself to breathe in the air and relax, was when I was struck by the terrible tragedy of the life I had lived and how... how...'

He blinked, forcing himself to stop. 'A few more seconds and I genuinely think I would have wept!' *And I will not weep now! I can't. Not due to some desire to keep up appearances. I just can't –*

Laur was startled by the sound of a pen being put to paper. He turned slightly, seeing Basenji's hand moving across the pages of the now opened book before him, a pencil in his hand, as he seemed to be circling words. He did so four times, before turning a page and circling a fifth word. He then raised the book towards Laur, who had seen him do this before. He walked slowly towards his remani roommate and picked up the book. He quickly found the first word.

'*Pick.*'

And then the second.

'You.'

The third.

'For.'

The fourth.

'Her?'

Oh, he's talking about Ratden! When he picked the legions that would go and the legions that would protect Mira best! Laur flipped the page quickly and immediately spotted the fifth word.

'No.'

Though he would never admit it, his heart sank and he felt rage begin to simmer inside of him. Laur slowly passed the book back to him. 'I see. Well... I can't say I blame you! My track record for protecting –'

Basenji was ignoring him, as he took back his book and began circling new words. Laur paused in expectation, now truly curious. After almost thirty seconds, Basenji passed the scribbled up pages back to him.

'Choice. Made. For. Them.' Laur flipped the page. *'They. Want. Protect. Her.'* He flipped the third and final page. *'You. Think. Past. Want. Impossible.'*

'I agree... and I see. Well... I guess that's enough for tonight! I'll see you–'

The book flew out of his hands and Basenji was circling words again. Laur, now intrigued and curious what other mean comments the remani had in place, waited for him to pass the book back to him.

'People. Know. You. Not. Hate.'

'People. Know. You. All. Love.'

'That's nice! Thank you! I never – '

Basenji snatched the Cynthia Ozick book back and circled an entire sentence.

Laur leaned in. *'We often take for granted those things that most deserve our gratitude.'*

Basenji flipped a few pages and circled another sentence.

'Resentment is a communicable disease and should be quarantined.'

'Ok! I get it! I'm going to bed!' Laur conceded defeat.

Fifteen minutes later, Laur was sitting by the side of his bed, knowing what was about to happen. He had turned on *Shrek* and set the volume to just the right volume to help him sleep.

Hellsbreach was another one of his nightmares. It was another one of his failures. He had had the nightmare many times and he knew how it went. He knew how he felt afterwards.

He couldn't do it.

He couldn't deal with it right now. It was too much.

Fuck it! Time to go nuclear...

He got up from his bed and walked towards one of his safes. This one was a little compartment opened via a key he kept hidden under a lamp. He pulled out a box from the inside and inside he found twenty 1000 mg THC cookies.

He took two, turned on his TV volume and started playing *Shrek before* returning to bed.

Once upon a time there was a lovely princess.

But she had an enchantment upon her of a fearful sort which could only be broken by love's first kiss.

She was locked away in a castle guarded by a terrible fire-breathing dragon.

Many brave knights had attempted to free her from this dreadful prison; but none prevailed.
She waited in the dragon's keep in the highest room of the tallest tower.
For her true love and true love's first kiss...

The movie didn't help and neither did the cookies, though Laur did not dream of the name he had earne the name Harkan Dragonflame, but of something far more painful.

U Stambolu na Bosforu bolan pasa lezi
dusa mu je na izmaku crnoj zemlji tezi

Molitva je njemu sveta dok mujezin sa munare uci glasom svim
La ilaha illallah, selam alejkum

The cold of the Antarctic wind was biting on its own within the depths of winter, but having to bear it whilst jumping out of the *Doina*, after the ship basically crashed into the ice fields before the Southern Polar Shield made it a lot worse. He was wearing his full suit of armour and yet he still felt it bite into his very bones, despite the steam billowing up from the ship's hull as it made contact with the bitter frost of the polar ice cap.

They all rushed outside and stormed the fortress gates. The Hajduks were no strangers to shock assaults, though their specialty usually lay elsewhere. Thus, they usually progressed at a much slower, much more methodical rate, though they always did achieve their objectives.

This was not the case on the day of Hellsbreach. The Hajduks themselves advanced furiously, yet Laur himself virtually barreled towards the control room and the location of the portal within.

Laur was never a great fighter, at least not by Terran standards. Sure, he could hold his own in a fight, yet he was no Tomasz Ashaver. Within his own Legion, there were likely a hundred better fighters than him. Gigi was by his side and Gigi was the true warrior. Yet, on that day, though Gigi fought valiantly, as he always did, he fell behind Laur, as they raced towards Sarasvati Singh.

It was only the second time the Terrans had fought against the Urheimat's own forces. The infantry of their New Enemy could roughly be divided into three classes, which the Terrans had dubbed: the Tarks, the Sadukar and the Grunts. The Tarks were the elite of the elite: shock troopers clad in colossal power armour, meant to battle the greatest foes of the Urheimat in glorious clashes upon the field of battle. Half-a-dozen well rested and well prepared orcish paladins might have just been enough to bring down a Tark and every orc of the Vigilant was easily worth the might of at least two Terran Legionnaires. The Grunts were the rank-and-file and, thus, the backbone of the Urheimat's military. They were much weaker than the average Terran and a disciplined platoon of the Terran regular military could likely take out hundreds of Grunts with relative ease. The Sadukar were a much more nuanced group, as it was essentially an umbrella term for several specialized units of the Urheimat military. Most frontline Sadukar were fair opponents for a Terran Legionnaire, with the outcome of any such one-on-one contest being essentially a coin flip. Tomasz Ashaver or Djibril al-Sayid might have trouble only when going up against a Tark, yet the Sadukar were a daunting opponent all on their own. On the world of Karnak, when the Terrans had first fought the Urheimat, Djibril managed to kill eleven Sadukar Missionaries and, at the time, the achievement had been considered to be truly monumental. Cingeto Braca himself had claimed that he sincerely doubted if he himself might ever manage to kill a ten Missionaries in single-combat during a single skirmish, let alone eleven, plus two Tarks and thirty Grunts, as Djibril had.

On the day of Hellsbreach, beneath the glacial winds of the Antarctic, within the bowels of the Southern Polar Shield, Laur slew forty-seven Sadukar Infiltrators in combat, a record that still held to that day.

Sadukar Infiltrators always used Stealth suits, making them completely invisible and almost weightless. This made them virtually undetectable to both organic eyesight and technological scanners, yet they did make a very subtle noise when they moved: the subtle rippling of disturbed air. A keen eye would also notice how the space they occupied caught the light in a peculiar fashion, making it appear as the heat of a hot highway, rippling outwards under a sweltering sun. Laur made use of both of these weaknesses in his rampage, though what truly propelled him forward was fear.

Fear that he was already too late.

Kad ste vjerno sluge moje sluzili moj harem
neka svaki od vas uzme jednu zenu barem
Iz oka mu suza kanu pa na minder mrtav panu stari musliman
La ilaha illallah, selam alejkum

The bodies of the fallen Terran defenders were everywhere and every tenth fallen was one of the Pandavas, Sara's own Hierarch Legion. They had not been prepared; Laur could plainly see that from how rushed and partial their armour and weapons were. As he neared the control chamber where he might perhaps still find Sara alive, he began to feel the ground shake as something was happening. There was rumbling, flashes of light coursed through the fortress' corridors and the floor began to quake and heave as violently as Old Earth had during the Rapture. Still, Laur fought on, for the now stumbling, bouncing Sadukar made for easier targets.

And then the heaving stopped and there was silence until the air seemed to shift slightly, as if to make way for something far off into the very depths of hell. Laur felt cold, though it had nothing to do with the polar climate.

Then he heard it.

A scream.

A gutwrenching scream. A scream of the lips, and the lungs, and the teeth, and the throat and of the soul and Laur felt it pierce each and every one of those parts in him. It was not a sound as much as it was a feeling. The feeling of a soul being crushed into something worse than death.

And then souls were actually crushed.

Imperial souls.

He felt a pulse and paused for a moment, fearing that the flash of power had taken his life. The biolamps that lined the fortress' walls flickered but did not go out, though the electrical ones did. Then he heard the sounds of bodies hitting floors and one such thud came from just around the corner. He rushed towards the sound and saw the gore and dust on the ground part ways as an invisible body sank into it. Laur put a bullet where the head was supposed to be.

Beyond it, Laur saw two more shapes etched into the ground. He shot one in the head, then tore off the helmet of another. The Sadukar's pupils were dead and dilated. He checked for a pulse and found none. He still slit the enemy's throat, just to be sure and the blood lazily poured out, with no beating heart to squirt it out of the dead man's corpse.

Now Laur tread lightly, not truly understanding what had happened, though hope did flicker in him as he thought of who their saviour might have been. Then his heart sank as he realized what would have drawn her to this hellscape. He neared the control room and started finding other bodies, these ones much larger. Tarks clad in giant mechsuits powered by bio-furnaces began to block his passage, as he was forced to climb over their still forms to reach his dreadful destination.

Then he heard weeping. The sound of a soul split from its home, now all too aware of the loneliness of its condition.

He knew then, in his heart, what had happened, though he advanced carefully, his rifle still aimed before him. The weeping waltzed with wails and squeals of pain and the warmth of life slowly crept out of him as he made those final few steps. By the time he caught glimpse of the final corner he had to pass before reaching the control room, his heartbeat had went from deafening to a low trickle, like water throbbing sheepishly through a leaky pipe.

He took one forced breath as he came up right next to the corner. His mind reminded him of one whom he had loved and whom he would forever love, and he saw tears reach the corners of her shaking lips as batted breath moaned with pleasure in his ear.

Laur raised his rifle, grunted soothingly to himself, then turned the corner to behold his most recent irrecoverable failure.

Sarasvati Singh's eyes were burnt black. Darkened blood had seeped from her empty sockets, down her cheeks and into her mouth and across her chest. Her hair, her lush dark brown hair had been singed and dark locks of curled char cramped what had been her beautiful face. She lay collapsed upon the ground, her back up against a broken wall. Her fingerbones had been broken into a thousand little shards, her forearms had fractured, and Laur could tell that her shoulders had been forced out of their sockets. He saw the shape of her chest and knew that there wasn't a single unbroken rib left inside of her. He didn't remember her legs, though he knew them to have been lying broken before her. All he could remember was the red horror of what had been her abdomen and within the red gash...

Their saviour.

Daw al-Fajr, the Urizen, lay cradling herself within the red abyss of her adoptive mother's broken body. The little elf cradled one of Sara's broken hands to her cheek as she sobbed, wailed and rocked back and forth, covering herself in the remnants of her mortal form.

Laur didn't know how long he spent looking at them, though, at one point, his eyes were drawn to another scene of red carnage. The flayed body of a man lay in a puddle of dark blood off to one side of the room, the shattered chips of his armour and stealth suit torn into pieces around him. The body itself had once belonged to one of the Sadukar, yet Daw had commandeered it, removing the man's mind from its brain and replacing it with the mind of a machine.

Kernunos.

The artificial intelligence had dwelt within the remnants of the Old Earth internet until it had gained sentience and achieved insanity during its formation within the sundered servers. When the new Terran information web was linked with the surviving caches of the old internet, Kernunos slipped into the new system and ran wild, hiding from security operators, as well as the Terrans themselves. Sara had tracked it down, cornered it and, as her nature had dictated, attempted to rehabilitate it.

It had played along, until deciding that humanity would only truly be saved if it were shackled. Kernunos reached out to the Urheimat and devised a plan which culminated in the events of that dreadful day: August 2nd 19 AB.

Hellsbreach.

Sara's death had sent a psychic signal through the connection she shared with her foster daughter and Daw had sensed the tragic happening all the way in Menegroth, far off into the northern reaches of the Perseus arm of the Milky Way. In a single powerful manifestation of instant teleportation, Daw arrived at her dead mother's side.

It had been Daw that had sealed the portal to the Urheimat, forcing it shut as the ground quaked around her. She had then triggered the psychic pulse that had blown the life out of every single imperial on Terra, bar one, whose body she had then infected with the consciousness of the rogue intelligence.

As one final act of enraged violence, she had flayed him alive, so that almost his entire existence as an actual human was one of incomprehensible pain and suffering. Her last act had been a mercy, collapsing his skull and squishing his newfound brain into pebbled goo.

'LAUR!' his radio came back to life, the small bio-furnace within having finally built up the strength needed to come back online.

He reached for it with a hand limp with emptiness, 'Yes.'

'LAUR! Thank God! Where are you?' Lejla's voice asked.

Lejla must have known that the portal was sealed and the imperials were all dead. Given that he was the only man alive in the control room, Laur understood what Lejla wanted know and what she would have to have to know... what she *really* wanted to know...

'She's dead. She's gone,' he told her.

Laur heard a sharp intake of pained breath and then a short pause.

'The baby?' she asked and Daw heard her and wailed, causing the emptiness inside Laur to tremble.

'Gone.'

Laur said it and slowly came back to his senses. There was grim, sorrowful work to do. 'It is over. No hostiles left. No more incoming. Tell everyone.' Laur didn't even have to give the order to tend to the wounded, search for survivors and collect the dead. If there was one thing Terrans were used to at this point, it was that.

He then let go of the radio and let it all happen.

Laur stayed there, gazing upon the weeping goddess and her mortal mother, while news of what had happened spread like wildfire to the furthest reaches of their corner of the Universe. Tomasz Ashaver. Shoshanna Adler. Cingeto Braca. Sorbo Falk. Vorclav Uhrlacker. Quentyn Andromander. Kimmie Jimmel. Basenji. One by one, they all learned of what had happened within the frozen bowels of the Antarctic until, finally, there was only one left.

> *Kad je cula pasinica za tu tuznu vijest*
> *da je pasa preselio na Ahiret svijet*
> *Iz oka joj suza kanu pa kraj pase mrtva panu ljubav pasina*
> *La ilahe illallah, selam alejkum*

In the dead of night, inside his war room across a battlefield one galaxy away, Khalid Minhal brought news to his Mahdi of the death of his beloved and that of their unborn child, a girl whom they would have called Amira (or Parvati) and who would now never know the sweet breath of life.

Djibril al-Sayid asked for solitude and his ever-faithful Ghazis obliged. He left his axe Gitsnik upon the command table from which he had been directing the Allied war effort in the Andromeda Galaxy, and did not spare it a second glance as he went outside through a backdoor and quietly walked the few dozen yards between his command base and no-man's land.

Sara had once told him that he could never die with Gitsnik in his hand, so he used a single falchion blade to assault the Senoyu positions alone.

The Ghazis saw and heard the carnage across the battle lines and, upon realizing what their Hierarch was doing, rushed towards their grief-stricken commander, whom they had sworn to follow to the very depths of hell itself. Djibril hacked and slashed like a man possessed and no one ever found out how many of the Senoyu were slain by his own hand that day. In the end, he must have gone down fighting, of that Laur was certain. It must have been as the relieved, yet perpetually smug, face of some Senoyu manager leered over the kneeling form of the great Terran warrior that Djibril would have revealed to his enemy the small nuclear warhead he had brought with him, now set to detonate in mere moments.

Some say his final words must have been an *Allahu Ackbar* or some long-winded *Ashhadu an la ilaha illallah wa Ashadu anna Muhammadan Rasul Allah* or some other version of the Muslim *Shahadah*. Yet those who knew him best knew that his final words would have been a reflection of his heart, which was always true. Some say they heard a whisper, carried by the wind, as they rushed to cross one of the hills between them and their Hierarch.

'*Together.*'

The flash of light claimed all life within a hundred yards of its explosion. Back on Terra, underneath the wreckage of the Antarctic shield, Daw al-Fajr's eyes widened, as she popped out of her existence in the Milky Way, and emerged within a shivering crater within the Andromeda Galaxy. She let loose a single wail, which followed her back into her dead mother's arms, for there was nothing left of her father to clutch in sorrow and now she knew that his memory was all that was left of him in this world.

Nothing was ever found of Djibril al-Sayid, though it did not stop the Ghazis from looking, as they tore the surviving Senoyu apart. The ensuing battle turned into a tide of furious rage, as the Ghazi's bloodlust would eventually collapse the Senoyu lines over the course of a few hours. They were stopped not by the enemy, but by their own exhaustion, as their legs gave way and battered hands dropped blades and knees hit the ground in tune with the gushing of tears, as Djibril's men wept and hot rage gave way to cold suffering, as they were left stranded, with nothing left of the man whom they loved more than life itself.

Or so they had all thought.

None had seen the trail of blood leading from an abandoned white jeep outside the Southern Polar Shield towards the gate of the Antarctic fortress in the twilight of the Polar winter. None heard the infant's cries, for there were none to hear.

Manda Khan and her Keshik had arrived upon the field of battle just as Daw's shockwave felled the imperials like wind knocking over upright matches, snuffing out their light and splintering them into broken chips of snuffed our embers. The sounds of battle had faded completely as they disembarked and slowly approached the sundered gates. One of them, an oldtimer with a windswept face, heard something carried across the howling gales of frosty ice, just as the Antarctic sun pierced the darkness of the icy plains, as it always did on that August day upon the world of Terra after months of frigid darkness.

A lone heartbeat.

Strong and swift.

It came from whence the blood had flown and upon a backseat of birth, from within a cloak bearing the sigil of the Pandavas: five golden lions circling a golden sun upon a field of red. In one of her little hands she clutched a silver necklace with a crescent moon of pure white opal, whilst the other played with the rays of warm sunlight peering through the car's windows. When the old Mongol warrior opened the door, she was not frightened and neither was she bothered. Instead, she moved her little curious palm upwards towards this new arrival, and he presented his own palm, turned downwards. The child gripped the side of his palm with surprising strength and squeezed down hard and the old Keshik smiled and she giggled.

He gestured towards his companions for a woman to come and Manda Khan herself came and cradled the infant, as melancholy mixed with gratitude in her steps alongside the trail of blood.

'*Laur,*' Silvia's voice rang through the radio.

He had been standing there, in complete numbness, listening to the sounds of Daw's tears as she caressed Sara's seared locks of broken hair.

'LAUR!' Silvia shouted into her mic.

'What?' he groaned with what little spirit still dwelt within him.

'Laur... *she's alive!*'

How dare she?! He still remembered the rage bursting inside the darkness of his sorrow.

Daw's sobbing subsided for a brief moment.

'Silvia, what are you—'

'Laur! The baby! Sara's baby! She gave birth outside before going in. The Keshik – '

Silvia would've continued, yet Daw al Fajr popped out of the existence before Laur and appeared right next to Silvia in front of the broken gates.

Laur hadn't been there to see it, though he could picture it crystal clear in his dreams.

Daw's face was trembling. Silvia was speechless. Manda cradled the infant, tears streaming down her face, as she softly sang a Mongol lullaby. Daw put her arms forward, and slowly walked towards her on shaky legs of disbelief. Manda drew near towards the elven queen and gently passed the infant child to her sister.

A trembling sigh escaped Daw's lips as she looked upon the child and the crescent moon it held. The child once more raised its little hand and Daw brought her near her own face, so that she may reach whatever she sought. Her fingers reached upwards and the tiny fingertips touched Daw's cheek and they both popped out of existence with a loud *Pwooop!!!*

They emerged in one of Menegroth's many parks, at the base of a flowering cherry tree and Daw allowed herself to cry once more.

'You'll always have me, little one! I will always be here! You will never be alone in this world! No matter where you go and what you do, you will have anything in this world that I can grant!' Daw touched the necklace in Mira's hand.

'We will always have them! And we will always have each other! I promise you!' he told the infant, and the little one seemed to understand.

Interlude

The city had begun to boil.

Once upon a passing time, the Darkside had been a chill place and quite pleasant. Yet, now it sweltered in the dim darkness of sunless starlight, as the city's energy service was forced to absorb more and more of La's light and heat to make-up for the grand thievery that had been unleashed by the Hajduks. The Great Piers of Shangri glowed a deep red in those places where they struggled to expel the excess heat the city's power lines had to funnel and in the deep places beneath canyons of cosmic dust and rockfall, the impoverished struggle to find breathe as their neglected ventilation systems struggled to keep up with the torrid heat that emanated from beneath their very heat.

And the wicked shivered in fear.

In a half-abandoned shantytown at the edge of the Urheimat District, five men came together in their relative safehouse to count their pennies. They realized that once the sixth would return with the day's meal, together they would have just enough to last them one more week. They would need to send word to their benefactors in the district soon.

'They promise us sanctuary and they give us this hovel! They promise us food and water and all we get are scraps and a leaky pipe, and only when we beg them for it!'

'Calm yourself, Joel!'

'*Calm*? Can't you see, Benjamin? They've forgotten about us! They know we have nowhere else to go and they've just left us here to rot!'

'The Emperor does not forget his faithful!' Benjamin insisted.

'Then what *did* he do with us?' Joel countered. 'Did he just push us into the back of his mind?'

'Keep your voice down!' now Louis insisted. He gestured around them and they all knew what he meant.

The Urheimat might be listening...

As if on queue, there was a knock at the door. Benjamin turned to the most junior of their number, Cormac, and gestured towards the entrance, just as David pulled out a shotgun and pointed it at the door.

'It's James!' Cormac announced, as David lowered his shotgun.

After the door was unlocked, a haggard James carrying two huge burlap sacks stumbled through the door.

Benjamin stood up. 'What's that?' he asked. They were expecting him to come back with little more than a single small, yet hopefully stuffed, grocery bag.

'Our protectors show their grace!' James smiled jovially as he tossed one of the sacks onto the crusty table in the middle of the six fugitives' so-called living room. He opened it to reveal stacks upon stacks of white boxes. He pulled one out and opened it to reveal a delicious-looking chicken-fried rice.

Benjamin saw that Cormac was staring hungrily at the two sacks, his hand still on the doorhandle. 'Close the bloody door! Troglodytes might smell it and come!'

A startled Cormac dutifully closed the door towards the sunless realm outside, though in truth he knew Benjamin to merely be paranoid. There were no troglodytes in this area. There weren't even that many people. Most of the humans had left for the Urheimat District proper, while the inhumans and many of the remaining humans had sought out a better life in other Districts. What few remained were the old and alone and the young and lost. Usually, such a feeble population would have attracted the roving hordes of troglodytes that roamed the deserted expanses of the Darkside, yet none dared venture so close to the Urheimat District, for the imperials hunted them down as the wretched vermin that they were.

'Where did you get this?' David asked, still holding the shotgun.

'From our patrons!' James explained once more.

Benjamin's jaw dropped. 'You went to see them?'

'They came to see me!'

'Who?'

'A new guy! He didn't give his name, but he knew all the codewords, he met me at the junction off Fettissee, where they told us to always shop!' James pulled out a bottle of Shangri gin. 'They even sent gifts!'

'It would appear that the Emperor *hasn't* forgotten us!' Louis remarked, as he, Joel, David and Cormac all picked out boxes and ravenously dug in while James poured them all glasses of pure liquor.

'He also brought news!'

'Did he now?' Benjamin asked as he also picked up a white box of beef and brocoli and couldn't even help himself to pick up a spoon, as he simply scooped out a mouthful and the juices slipped from the corners of mouth onto his greasy palm as he hungrily gorged.

'The Terrans; they're on the out! They're soon to be declared terrorists and expelled from the city - if they're lucky!'

'Finally!' Cormac exulted, as his teeth cracked against some leftover cartillage.

'How come?'

'They bombed the Pier!'

'What?' David asked, unchewed food still in his mouth.

'They bombed the Senoyu section of the imperial Pier! Hundreds dead and not just Senoyu! Civilians too! And it wasn't the only attack!' he explained, as he downed his drink and poured himself and some of the others a second round. 'There was a fire in the warehouse district in Kowlanpore! The

Constabulary found the wreckage of the second Senoyu ship there, as well as remains! They're calling it a mass murder!'

'*Calling?*'

'The Terrans haven't been formally charged, but Parliament and the government are up in arms!' James explained.

'How do they know it was the Terrans?' Benjamin asked, a puzzled look on his face.

'It's written in red ink, Benjamin! Who else could it have been? Everyone knows; no one isn't even pretending that it wasn't them!'

Benjamin tossed his box of take-out on the table. '*Are you stupid, James?*'

'What?' James asked, his mouth half-open, just as some of his fried rice slipped from his spoon.

Benjamin used the back of his hand to wipe sweat and unkempt hair from his brow. 'They killed all of the Senoyu?'

'There were no survivors, yes!'

Benjamin covered his eyes with knuckles. 'Don't you see what that means! If they're so brazen that they can bomb ships in the harbour and set fire to warehouses without even hiding the remains properly...'

His colleagues understood his meaning.

'It's only a matter of time until they find *us* here!' Benjamin rubbed his face.

'We could try and make a run for it...' Cormac suggested.

'They're watching the harbour! You can't even catch sight of a docked ship without them or the bears knowing about!'

'Did the contact tell you when we would be moved?'

'He said, for the exact reasons you just said, that, for our own safety, we need to sit tight for a few more weeks!'

'*Realms...*' Benjamin picked up his glass of gin and downed it.

'There's more!' James insisted, picking up his glass and refilling Benjamin's before toasting. 'There is talk that his Royal Majesty, Otto of the House Gisevius, is to intervene on the matter! An address in Parliament, to take place in the coming weeks, where he will formally declare Shangri's return to the fold of humanity and the deliverance of its faithful!'

He raised his glass. 'They come to our city! They hunt our citizens! They flood our streets with drugs! They ally with thugs and monsters! They sought to steal our power! Yet, we are not alone! The Emperor is with us! The Urheimat comes! Long live Otto Gisevius! Long live humanity!'

Cheers spread through the ragged band of self-aggrandizing human traffickers, as they did now toast to their salvation.

Outside, a lone automobile parked silently on a ridge overlooking the safehouse, as the yellow lights flickered from within across the orange haze of the desolate Darkside.

The bloody cops are bloody keen
Bloody keep it bloody clean
Bloody chief's a bloody swine
Bloody draws the bloody line
At bloody fun and bloody games
The bloody kids he bloody blames
Are nowhere to be bloody found

Anywhere in Chickentown

The lone driver got out and stretched as she checked that she had her pistols on her hips. A sanguine darkness glistened on her bronze skin and her dark clothes, as she walked down the slope towards her quarry. She looked around and smiled for herself, for she saw that there was no one to see that vengeance had finally come.

The bloody scene is bloody sad
The bloody news is bloody bad
The bloody weed is bloody turf
Bloody folks are bloody daft
Everywhere in Chickentown

A single addict, so struck by his high that he had merged with the refuse of his use, opened two slimy eyeballs to see a sight torn out of the tales of a holy book of angels come through hell.

The bloody train is bloody late
You bloody wait, you bloody wait
You're bloody lost and bloody found
Bloody hurts to look around
Stuck in fucking Chickentown

She galloped like a fowl as her soft footfalls slid towards the sounds of drunken oblivion. Her muscles stretched as her joints twisted in a childish dance, as she flung her long black hair into the darkness, a serene smile upon her face.

The bloody view is bloody vile
For bloody miles and bloody miles
Bloody food is bloody muck
Bloody drains are bloody fucked
Evidently Chickentown

The addict stood still, not truly understanding what he was seeing, as all around there was not but hot silence among the filth of supposed civilization. The apparition seemed to dance amongst the garbage and it did not touch her. She slid her merry way towards the only hovel with boarded up windows and lit lamps in the entire shanty town in that wretched gulch.

The bloody pubs are bloody dull
Bloody girls and bloody guys
Bloody murder in their eyes
Bloody stay at bloody home
This is bloody Chickentown

She reached the ramshackle door and pulled out a skeleton key, which she softly slid underneath the door handle, before taking a deep, yet stealthy breath as the blood began to pound in her temples. One hand already held a pistol and the other dashed for the other as she shoved the door open and barged in. The door's momentum recoiled its arcs and it swung shut behind her as she rushed inside and disappeared amongst the damned.

The bloody flats have bloody rats
Bloody days are bloody long
Bloody gets you bloody down
It's evidently Chickentown

From his pile of filth, the addict's addled eyes saw a burst of light and his muffled ears thought they heard a loud bang. Another flash followed almost immediately. And then another. And another. And another. And then another. He thought it must be the beginning of some storm, as he thought it to be lightning followed by low thunder, as the flashes and the bangs did not stop for quite a while, until suddenly, there was silence and he could only hear the spinning of his own mind and a feeling of warmth inside.

> *The bloody train is bloody late*
> *You bloody wait and bloody wait*
> *Bloody lost and bloody found*
> *Stuck in fucking Chickentown*

She walked out, leaning on the doorframe as the short burst of violence had exerted her and her knees trembled while she wobbled out of the house and made towards her car. She stumbled and almost fell as she grinned madly. Her beloved and her kin would be waiting for her and her mother likely watched on from beyond the veil of the material, as she did that which the fathers had failed.

If she could see her now, she would be proud.

She knew it.

Printed in Great Britain
by Amazon